J. J. Cowan has been a business journalist for more than thirty years, writing on shipping, healthcare, manufacturing and defence. Since 1995 he has covered the communications industry worldwide.

He holds an MA in Politics and International Relations from Aberdeen University, Scotland.

To Vicki

J. J. Cowan

THE TIN SOLDIERS

AUSTIN MACAULEY PUBLISHERS™

LONDON • CAMBRIDGE • NEW YORK • SHARJAH

A CIP catalogue record for this title is available from the British Library.

ISBN 9781787109667 (Paperback)
ISBN 9781787109674 (E-Book)

www.austinmacauley.com

First Published (2017)
Austin Macauley Publishers Ltd.
25 Canada Square
Canary Wharf
London
E14 5LQ

The author wishes to thank Vicki, whose patience and encouragement know no limits. Thank you always and all ways. Rory, Claire and Guy, for their love and support – this is what I was doing all that time. Dave den Hollander, over to you, dear friend. Mark Keville for reading when there were other things to do. Martin Gresswell for inspiration, military and intelligence insight plus a love of Africa. Dorné and Neville for boundless belief, despite all evidence to the contrary. David and Gilly who have always been there for me. Richard Elliott for enthusiasm for my mad plans. Bady M Baldé for explaining some realities of tin and tantalum mining. Maciej Szelezin for anchoring my IT flights of fancy. Philip and Julia Leonard for keeping me to the path through Africa. Justin Young and Tim Colquhoun for generously sharing their knowledge of arms and armaments. And the many friends who nudged me onwards.

My thanks are due to you all, the mistakes are my own. Although this is a work of fiction, I have tried to bring to life the conditions endured by some in Congo's Kivu provinces and neighbouring countries. The characters and organisations in this book are, however, the product of my imagination and any similarity to organisations or to persons living or dead is coincidental and unintentional.

Book 1

Still falls the Rain –
Dark as the world of man, black as our loss
Blind as the nineteen hundred and forty nails
Upon the Cross.

Still falls the Rain
With a sound like the pulse of the heart that is changed to the hammer-beat
In the Potter's Field, and the sound of the impious feet

On the Tomb:
Still falls the Rain

In the Field of Blood where the small hopes breed and the human brain
Nurtures its greed, that worm with the brow of Cain.

Edith Sitwell, 1887 - 1964

Chapter 1
North Kivu Province, Democratic Republic of Congo, Central Africa
Two Years Ago

Barking dogs woke them, the sound of distant gunfire had been muffled earlier by folds in the mountains. Even the youngest knew the sounds of war but this was different, something nearer stirred the family. It took him a second then Raphael recognised the screech as corrugated iron sheets twisted from their mountings, falling hard on the baked earth before the sound was chased away by a rip of automatic gunfire. This time they were unmistakably close.

Above it all rose an isolated scream, no more than a hundred metres away it terrorised them all. It started as a cry of horror, then climbed unbroken and swelled into agony. For an instant it halted the whole family, before galvanizing them into action. There was a pause for a breath, then another scream that Raphael thought might never end, until its source was silenced. All the time the night was punctuated by more gunfire.

Raphael had risen from his bed now, dizzy with half-shaken sleep, dressed only in his shorts and wrapped in a blanket. As he struggled to find his bearings in the darkness, he heard the steel of another tin roof being torn away and falling hard. Baba cursed, told everyone to stand still and listen. Men could be heard shouting now and there was something indistinct in the background that he could not place. There it was again, the sound of a rushing stream. His father spoke again, ordering the children to stay in the house with their mother. Then Raphael knew it too; the other noise was a roaring fire getting louder, drawing closer.

He could hear a tremor in his father's voice as he gave them instructions for their safety. The attack that the village had long feared was now upon them. All around them men and women were shouting, but he could only guess that the threat lay where the village reached the forest. He could hear new cries of terror or pain, there was no knowing which, but fear had come as fast as any wind-driven fire.

There were few metal roofs in the village, but one was their granary and food store, and Raphael knew now why his father was so scared. Without mihogo and

15

beans, there would be too little food until the next crop, and no money for supplies. If their stores were burned, the village would be destroyed as so many others before, its people fleeing into the forest to escape the fighting and seeking shelter from the sun and rain. They had heard of villagers struggling to survive in the forest, searching for water, foraging for food and hunting whatever they could find; but they were farmers, and in the forest they would be at the mercy of the spirits.

No one could stay in the village if the harvest was burned – the Hutu militia knew it. If these were rebel troops pulling back towards the mountains in the north, they would leave nothing in their wake, hoping to starve the Congolese forces that followed them and, as always, the villagers would be the first to die. Boys of thirteen in Nord Kivu knew about scorched earth tactics. Raphael had heard the elders' tales of looting, murder and rape across North and South Kivu and even in Goma's refugee camps. Why did grown-ups assume children could not understand their talk?

He and his father had once ridden in a truck as far as Bukavu near the Rwandan border, on the way they had seen deserted villages and met blind men and amputees begging in the big market. Fear of the rebels and their own army had been the backdrop to their lives, but the conflict had always stayed away from their village. Tonight that good fortune had ended.

His father took down the long crop-cutting panga and stumbled out of the door into the blackness. The three younger children were crying and his mother was hysterically calling him back for fear of the FDLR rebels. Father must have heard her cries but said nothing as he disappeared into the darkness. The soldiers would not hesitate to shoot him if he stood in their way, perhaps he was gambling that he might yet save some food or put out the fire. Raphael slipped on a T-shirt and raced out of the door before Mama could stop him. As the eldest child, it was his job to help each day in the fields. He was strong and quick and he might be able to rescue some food. With his mother's cries reaching desperation as the younger children clung to her, Raphael ignored everything and sprinted towards their store.

The patchy cloud meant there was little moonlight, and with no electricity here the only light should have been from hurricane lamps. Yet a bright orange glow illuminated the trees and roofs along one side of the village. Fire had taken hold of the raised granary huts, the clay walls were already blackened and smoke was pouring from the roof, the poles that strengthened the walls were burning fiercely and the wooden doors had burst open spilling their vital harvest across the ground. One section of metal roofing lay in the fire and already it glowed red with heat while smoke billowed from beneath the other end. People's homes and stores were alight and he could see flames dancing inside while outside the elderly and young looked on helplessly. One doorway framed a flaring yellow picture as another home and belongings blazed brightly, and a few people stood oddly motionless, staring uncomprehending at the tragedy that was engulfing them. A man and woman rushed past with a plastic bucket and a washing bowl, spilling water as they ran, vainly trying to extinguish the fires that had now caught hold of the dry grass roofs. The flames were far above their reach as they hurled water upwards and ran back for more.

It was another sight, however, that brought Raphael up short. There were armed men everywhere, young men – much younger than his father – men he had never seen before. They carried big guns and some held burning brands made of branches and rags as they ran swiftly from house to house setting the thatched roofs on fire, even as the occupants awoke and tumbled out into the darkness. Twenty paces away he saw a villager emerge from his hut carrying his blanket only to collapse as he was cut through at waist height by a long burst of gunfire that came from somewhere out of sight. The man had doubled over even as the impact threw him backwards to the ground and the blanket in his arms fell across his body. In death Raphael's neighbour looked as though he was sleeping outside.

To his left a group of three or four men – in the darkness he couldn't be sure how many – had surrounded a young woman. He recognised two others, her mother and grandmother, who were being pushed backwards by other men closer to the fire. They were laughing at the cries of fear, pushing and pulling them as they herded the terrified women away. He paused only long enough to see the young woman fall, at which point a young soldier darted forward and dragged at her dress as she fought to keep it around her.

Years ago he and his friends had cornered a bush pig in the forest; it had turned and charged at the boys, opening a friend's thigh with a sharp lower tusk. They had stopped it on the points of their fire-sharpened sticks, piercing its red coat in the chest and neck, and the noise it made then was the sound he heard now from a nearby house.

As he looked, Raphael saw movement in the doorway and a woman appeared – but in the flickering light he could not make out who it was. She moved slowly, flapping her hands awkwardly and then he saw that her hair was alight. She was elderly and turned towards him, crying out something – but his legs would not carry him towards her. He could only watch, shocked still and silent, as she took two steps in his direction and began to lift both arms as if beckoning him, before she crumpled like a falling mat. He could see her more clearly now, the silhouetting flames that he had thought were in the house behind were flames that still licked the back of her robe. If she made any further sound as she lay, Raphael did not hear it.

He was unable to see his father and was about to turn back to the house when he spotted him on the far side of the granary. This time Raphael's legs obeyed and he moved closer. Three soldiers were surrounding Baba and his friend, Kigeli. Both the villagers were being made to kneel at gunpoint before the militiamen, with their hands clasped over their heads. There was brighter light from the fires here and Raphael saw that the soldiers were dressed in a mixture of uniforms and ordinary clothes; one wore an army shirt and pale blue jeans, another was in a black vest and camouflage trousers. Even from this distance he could see they were laughing. The shortest of the soldiers took a long drag on a fat cigarette and laughed as another kicked Kigeli in the back, making him fall face forwards on the ground. With his hands still raised, Kigeli's face must have borne the impact.

Raphael may have been shouting as he ran because his father looked up, called out to him and began to stand. As he did so, one of the soldiers raised his rifle to shoot but another stepped forward, lifting his own gun high above his shoulder. He brought the heavy shoulder stock crashing down on the back of Baba's neck. It must have been a glancing blow for his father only went down on one knee, stunned but still conscious as Raphael stopped twenty paces away.

His father was tall, a physically strong man used to work in the fields. He raised his head and shook it; Raphael couldn't tell if it was to clear his mind after the blow he had received or to stop Raphael coming any closer. Baba's mouth moved but above the shouts and the roar of the flames, Raphael could not hear a word. The boy could see his Father mouthing 'Kwenda, kwenda' urging him to go. Perhaps if Baba had stayed kneeling before the soldiers, it might have been different. Maybe he just cared more for his eldest than for the consequences; he began to stand once more. Stronger than the soldiers, he was taller and even in the half-darkness Raphael could tell that they feared him. They stepped away, all three shouting at him to lie down. He made no effort to comply and now Raphael could clearly hear his father's deep voice baying at him. "Run, Raph. Take Mama!"

This could only have lasted fractions of a second but forever afterwards Raphael could picture his father struggling to get to his feet, he would never know his intention as the soldiers stepped backwards levelling their rifles. What they hated or feared was a man who would not lie down and fear them as he should.

When the soldiers fired, he heard every shot that cracked around like breaking branches. Raphael flinched at the gunshots then watched in horror as dark patches sprang up on his father's yellow T-shirt where none had shown before. The wind rush from a single bullet narrowly passed Raphael's right ear. For an instant his father was still upright and his eyes open, then more shots struck him in the back and he toppled towards his son.

Raphael's immobility made him almost invisible in the gloom and perhaps that saved him. The light was poor, the rebels were nervous, but they had just killed a captive and now they gave vent to their relief in bursts of gunfire into his father's body. One soldier stepped forward and raised a panga – Raphael even found time to wonder if it was his father's – before bringing it down on Kigeli's back. No sound reached the boy as the villager slumped forward and lay prostrate at their feet. He posed no threat at all to the militia but in an instant they had switched from taunting to killing and now were intent on destruction. The knife blow had been a clumsy one, catching Kigeli across his left shoulder and upper arm. He started to raise himself with his good arm. This time, as the knifeman stepped in, he had a better angle from which to strike. There was no mistake, the long and heavy machete was well aimed and it sank deep into Kigeli's neck. His legs moved slowly as though he was trying to get up but after a few seconds he lay still.

As Kigeli died, Raphael suddenly came to his senses and seemed to see everything with new clarity. A circle of light was thrown out by the burning stores and standing motionless at its edge he had gone unnoticed amid the butchery, but with nothing else to distract them as Raphael moved they became aware of his presence and the rifles came up towards him. Had he run straight home Raphael would have been killed by the hailstorm of bullets, but instinct told him to dive to his left and the bullets raced away into the darkness where he had just stood. His leap had taken him behind another building; although not enough to offer protection it obscured him from their view for the time it took them to cover the intervening twenty paces.

It was all that Raphael needed. A fast runner, and knowing the village layout where they did not, he sprinted home by a different route. As he reached his house, he could hear soldiers calling to one another in the darkness behind him. If they were coming this way, they would find him soon. Perhaps there were other victims to distract them or they were unable to see him, whatever the reason Raphael was able to race into his house unchallenged, and it was empty.

He stood in the doorway, not knowing what to do. Where had his family gone? They would surely have fled in the opposite direction, away from the fighting and fires. Some blankets were missing and a few possessions were disturbed but otherwise they must have run without collecting many belongings. His mother was fleeing from the danger with three small children. A rushing sense of isolation overwhelmed him, there were tears in his eyes but he could not tell if they were for his father or the rest of his family. His father was dead, his mother, brother and sisters had fled without him, and now he could hear the calls of approaching fighters.

Raphael looked to left and right, but he could see only grey-black outlines of their home. He ran around the back of the house and almost immediately tripped as he fell headfirst across something, someone, huddled on the bare earth. He'd struck his shin which had caused a muffled cry, then as he fell he thought his feet felt a blanket.

"Who is it?" he hissed, terrified that he would attract the militia's attention.

"Raphael," said a small voice, "is that you?"

"Keisha, thank God. Where are Mama and the twins?"

"I don't know," said Keisha and she began to cry, loudly.

"Hush, the soldiers will hear us. They are coming, we can't stay here."

"I'm waiting for Mama and Baba."

"Keisha, you can't, Mama is gone and we must run after her. She will be worried for us," said Raphael, with more certainty than he felt.

"But what about Baba?" asked Keisha. "Where is he?"

"He... he's..." Raphael could not give voice to the words, and he dared not tell her now just as they needed to escape. "He told me to go ahead, and that means you, too," he found himself saying. It was almost true and Raphael had a strong feeling that he must not lie to her, even though he could not tell her the ghastly truth.

It proved enough for Keisha who drew herself up and stepped out of the blanket. "You hurt my head," was all she said.

"I'm sorry, I didn't see you in the darkness. We must go, quietly. Bring that with you," he whispered, pointing to the blanket. "We might have to sleep outside tonight until we find them." Despite his urgings, Keisha folded her blanket with great thoroughness and took hold of his hand. In the near darkness they began to run.

******

It was easier to begin with. Bigger gaps had opened in the clouds, and by the moonlight Raphael could just make out the paths, although from time to time a branch or leaves would catch them unaware and spring back into their faces.

He had no idea if the soldiers were still following them or had stayed at the village to burn and kill. The children were driven by the twin fears of the rebels behind them and of losing Mama ahead of them.

He knew many of the forest paths close to the village, but as they ran on the canopy of trees grew thicker creating prolonged periods of darkness. And being forced to flee ever further from his familiar routes, he was finding it hard to choose his way. They stood in silence for a while listening for tell-tale sounds of pursuit, but there were none. It was only now that Raphael realised he had not heard shooting for a while; perhaps no one was following them.

He had to remember that Keisha was younger than him so they stopped running but never relaxed their vigilance. They were used to going barefoot, but he thought that if the path grew much rockier or disappeared altogether the rough ground would cause them problems. Raphael knew that to get to the next village they needed to cross a steep ridge and then descend to the big river, although he was unsure how far it was.

The path began to rise more steeply giving Raphael some reassurance that he had gone in the direction of the ridge. In the near-darkness they scrambled up muddy slopes far from the village where the trees thinned, the holes in the forest roof widened overhead allowing more moonlight to shine through. They felt crushingly alone though; he had reminded her they must not be seen or heard by

20

any of the men. So Keisha was brave, only betraying her anxiety by the way she bit her bottom lip and the strength with which she held his hand wherever the path allowed. Carefully, they moved forward again by the light of the moon. Sometimes the way became so steep or slippery that he had to pull her up and together they would look for the best route through the growing number of rocks and boulders on the hillsides.

They had been walking for hours when Keisha sat down and refused to get up again. "I'm tired, Raph," she said, "and I'm hungry. And thirsty."

It was still not light but the moon showed a rocky outcrop just above them where the trees were small and sparse. Its overhang cast a big shadow and on reaching it Raphael peered inside to check there were no animals lurking there. He wasn't sure what he had expected to find but they had the place to themselves. She sat down on the dirt patch in front of the rock and asked yet again where Mama and Baba were.

"I don't know, Keish," he said. He wasn't being truthful about their father, but he needed her to be strong and instinctively he knew that she would crumple if she found out now that her adored father was dead. He needed her to keep walking if they were to find Mama and the twins, and since they had not caught up with them despite their speed Raphael was now secretly very worried about how to find them. Nor had he any idea how to break the dreadful news to her.

If others had fled into the forest, surely some of them would have been slow moving. He began to think they must have taken a different path, in itself that was not surprising. They had been running and walking for a long time and there were so many paths. Normally, he would have turned around long before and headed back to the village using the slope and the sun for guidance. But he feared that the soldiers might leave the village this way. If he turned around, they could walk straight into the armed men in the depths of the forest without ever hearing them coming, and he'd already seen what that meant. They could not stay where they were without food, water or proper shelter. All that was left to them was to try and find another village for safety, food and drink and to resume their search from there.

"We can rest here for a bit, but we must move again when it gets light or we may not find the next village." Keisha was now lying down and had pulled the blanket closer around herself. She said nothing and it was only then that he realised she was asleep. So Raphael sat down close beside her, leaned back against the rock and pulled one side of the blanket over his legs against the cold night air. There was no wind or rain, he would see any approaching lights and reckoned he could hear anyone on the path. Raphael kept watch for a while but eventually he, too, drifted into a shallow and fitful sleep punctured by dreams of rushing rivers that turned into burning fires, and of his father teaching him to use the panga.

Raphael woke with a start, unsure how long he had slept. The happy picture of his father was clear and fresh in his mind but it was instantly displaced by the image of his father dying. He felt tears starting in his eyes but at that moment he was mercifully distracted as Keisha moved closer to him for warmth and took even more of the blanket as she slept. The moon seemed higher and much paler, and Raphael realised that in the east above the path they had taken the sky was much lighter now. Dawn would soon follow and so long as there was no rain they would be warmer, but his mouth and throat already felt very dry and they would need water as soon as possible.

He did not disturb her, but watched and listened for danger from the path they had already trod. As the sun rose and its rays began to warm the air around them, he stood up, stretched and looked about their resting place. He could hear birdsong and there were droppings nearby on the ground that he did not recognise, but these were small and whatever had left them was probably no threat. There were no other signs of animal life and crucially no water.

When the sun had clambered its way over the horizon and warmed from orange to yellow, he stooped to wake Keisha. She stirred only slowly, and Raphael had time to look down the valley as mist rose from the ground and picked out the folds of forested land growing ever paler into the distance. He could not understand why the world still looked so beautiful and calm when everything of beauty and gentleness had been stolen from them last night. It didn't seem right or fair that today brought a fine, bright morning like any other when his father now lay dead and unburied in their village. Everyone and everything he loved had been taken or scattered, apart from Keisha. He turned back and saw she was sitting up now and looking at him as he hurriedly wiped the tears from his eyes with the back of his hand.

She didn't appear to have noticed his distress. "Is there anything to drink?" she asked.

"I'm sorry," was all he could say.

Instead of complaining, she stood up, folded her blanket and said, "We'd better go, Raphael, or we might miss Mama."

He could not tell her with any confidence in which direction they should head, he could not offer her any food or drink. And for now, he was happy that she was taking the responsibility out of his hands, taking her bearings from the path they had followed last night. Stepping across the mud and patchy grass and through the rocks they continued on their previous course.

The children descended from the ridge without seeing any signs of life. There was no smoke visible from village fires to guide them. They were heading for the lowest part of the valley to the west, in search of the river he was sure lay in that direction and in the hope that they might find a village somewhere close to it. The day was peaceful, there were bird calls but no sounds of fighting, and here in the mountain forests the air was cooler. Under the tree canopy they occasionally saw pairs of tiny warblers flitting about in search of food for their young, calling to one another with their distinctive trills. Above their heads the children could hear monkeys but these were hard to see in the shadows, even when they strained their eyes against patches of bright sky and renewing clouds.

Almost an hour later the path that they were on gave Raphael the first clue, it widened and the grass petered out where the tree cover was thicker. They had been walking a path for a while with Raphael wondering what animals had created the route they were following. Beneath their feet lay packed earth once more. Further down the ridge he guessed it might become muddy again but here it drained well and the ground was hard enough not to show clear footprints. As they rounded a bend, they startled a couple of monkeys that scampered noisily away down the path and swung nimbly up into the trees. The water that the monkeys had been drinking dripped down the rock wall into a tiny pool before over spilling the path and continuing its journey to the valley floor.

The children raced one another to the water with energy that neither thought they had and scooped it frantically into their mouths. The comfort it brought to their dry throats was immediate, and the joy of washing their faces lifted their spirits. They sat by the tiny trickle of water cupping their hands to catch it where it fell from the rock. The pair waited for their hands to fill and poured it over their heads until they were refreshed, before throwing it at one another and laughing aloud. Raphael was being flicked with water by Keisha and both were laughing until first one and then the other grew serious as their relief gave way to remembrance of why they were here.

The mood had changed instantly and wordlessly they were sombre again. They each took one last long drink. Keisha checked her braids and they set off again, this time with Raphael in the lead.

Hours went by and still there was no sign of a village. When they came to clearings created by landslides or to rock outcrops, they would stop and scan the horizon for the smoke of cooking fires, but there was none to be seen. The game tracks were fewer and thinner, and their spirits sank a little as their descent meant they were swallowed by the forest once more. They were untroubled by the smell of decaying leaves, the constant dripping, unexplained animal cries and almost impenetrable undergrowth, but they shared a deep fear of the forest spirits. Raphael knew it would also be harder for them to see or hear approaching soldiers.

As they ventured lower, thick stands of bamboo sprang up to block their path, stands so deep that the children were forced into lengthy detours. The sandy coloured stems grew so thickly that most animals were unable to penetrate the vivid vegetation, but they knew snakes often lay in the bamboo leaf litter. Bright green leaves danced in their faces, mocking their inability to pass, and broken bamboo stems at the edge fell down across their route catching and cutting them with their sharp edges. It was much more humid here and both were tired, hungry and walking more slowly. Keisha kept looking for patches of earth to avoid treading on the long thorns that lurked in the leaves beneath them. Mostly she followed Raphael's barefoot steps, occasionally being given a piggyback to cross the most difficult ground. But the treetops were spread far enough apart that they could make out the position of the sun to give them some sense of direction. Sometimes they were able to follow game tracks and their progress quickened, but as quickly as the tracks appeared they vanished again or turned away from the children's westerly objective. Raphael knew it was risky but where the forest allowed they would keep to this course along open game tracks, all the while listening as carefully as they could for the rebels.

Hunger was their biggest problem. They were well used to managing on a meal a day but neither had eaten since the previous evening and it was now midday, they had slept briefly in the open and been moving quickly for hours. The growing worry about where to find food was draining Raphael's morale and hunger was sapping their strength. Keisha had done well to walk through much of the night and the sleep had certainly revived her, but he was fearful that they would not find the river or a village. Without help Raphael wondered how much longer they could keep going. He also had a gnawing doubt that they were simply getting further and further from their family but turning back to a devastated village did not seem an option, particularly if the FDLR were still in the area.

From time to time they heard larger animals in the forest, or maybe they were just animals that made a large noise as they moved about the jungle floor – the children never actually saw what caused the sounds. Raphael told Keisha that the animals were more scared of them, although privately he doubted it. When they stopped to rest, a lizard of the brightest green crept down a tree in front of them, untroubled by their presence. With the sun at its highest their thirst was stronger than before and it was getting harder to start again after each rest.

As they moved westwards and descended the ridge so the ground grew damper beneath their feet, the humidity increased and it grew darker again under the tree canopy.

Raphael's stomach had been growling on and off for hours and hunger now vied for his attention with fear that they were lost. "We need to keep going, and try to find out where we are." As soon as he had spoken, he cursed himself.

"I thought you said you knew the way to the river." She stared at him in puzzlement.

"I do, sort of. It's down there."

"What do you mean, you 'sort of' know the way?"

"I know that water runs downhill," he said. "And I know that if we keep going downhill we'll end up at the river." He tried to sound certain. "Now let's keep walking."

Keisha looked puzzled. "But if water runs downhill why were we walking uphill for hours yesterday?" she asked.

Raphael was tired, hungry and annoyed at being questioned when he had brought them so far without getting caught by the militia. He had watched over her protectively during the night as she slept. Why couldn't she just accept that this was difficult and a job for him, not for a ten year-old girl?

"Because we had to get away from the soldiers, didn't we? Because we had to find Mama, Laurent and Christine, didn't we? Because we had to hide from the men who killed Baba."

There was a pause and then Keisha's face just folded. She sat down in the dirt and tears began to pour down her cheeks. Her shoulders shook convulsively, but for a moment she made no sound, then a tiny cry started deep in her throat and swelled until it became a shout of torment. Her soft cries of "Baba" became ever louder as she repeated his name over and over in a way that added to his own distress and anguish. He wanted to comfort her but when Raphael tried to wrap his arms around her she wouldn't let him. Keisha was stammering through her sobs to say something. "Why, why, why didn't you tell me? What, what happened?" This was all she could manage and then the tears took over again.

Raphael hated himself. In his exhaustion and his anger at her reaction to their hurried escape he had blurted out the one thing from which he wanted to protect her. "I'm so sorry," was all he could say and his own tears began to fall beside hers. He repeated the words to her time and time again, until she could not tell if he was sorry for breaking the news to her inadvertently, or for their shared loss or both.

She kept asking him what happened and as he began to tell her a shortened version of their father's death so it gave him something to focus on and he started to regain some composure. For Keisha, hearing the story was no consolation, it was all so new and so horrible. Nothing here and now could dull the pain of her father's murder, the separation from their mother and being lost in the forest. She cried and she cried until there were no tears left in her. Little by little she allowed Raphael to put an arm around her and draw her close to him. And there they sat on a log, just holding each other in the forest shade, while above them the monkeys went back to their search for fruit.

Chapter 2
Boston, USA
Six Months Ago

It didn't matter getting wet at the cab rank, James was out of the office at last and he had plenty to occupy his mind. He should have been home by now but he'd been caught in a hell of a meeting – one for which, with hindsight, he should have been better prepared. One-on-one meetings at 5.30 p.m. on a Friday with Heather Nash, his department director, seldom meant good news. It had started with a grilling over his 'screw up', as she put it rather appositely.

"Is there something you want to tell me, James?" was all she'd said at first. That was when it had dawned on him that she knew, but he feigned ignorance, playing for time.

"I beg your pardon?"

She heaved a sigh. "OK, I'll spell it out. Are you having an affair with Selina?" Heather studied him closely, saying nothing and waiting for a reply.

"Ah yes. Well, we were. But not anymore," he said. He tried to sound relaxed about it.

"Dammit!" she exclaimed. "You just blew your last defence."

His brow furrowed, "You'll have to explain that." He was puzzled, but he wasn't going to roll over for her, not on account of an office fling. "I don't think we've done anything illegal." James ran through a mental checklist of his relationship with Selina. Unwise, probably. Even implausible, but certainly not illegal.

"I was hoping I could say that this was the start of a long and loving relationship that would take you both up the aisle. Hell, I'd have given you away myself. All too willingly, as it goes."

For a moment he lost his British reserve. "Marriage? Jeez, are you kidding?"

Heather stared him down and he felt knee high.

"Anyway, who are you planning to say this to?" He was puzzled and irritated at this intrusion into his private life.

"The top floor, Mr Reynolds and his banking buddies."

"What's my …" he paused, "my thing with Selina got to do with the Old Man?" James was now baffled; why would the Executive Chairman be interested in the love life of a mid-ranking staffer?

Heather sighed as though trying to explain quantum theory to a five year-old. "It's going to come up when he reads your file from HR, before he decides whether to give you the London job."

"No kidding. London?"

"Do I look like I'm kidding? You've probably wrecked your opportunity and my plans because you can't keep your hands to yourself. And there's no one half as qualified as you to take on the mess in London!"

"Thanks."

"It wasn't meant as a compliment. You're in a truckload of trouble, and so is this department. You've no idea how angry this makes me. She's your secretary, for Chrissake. Apart from this being a stupid career mistake for you personally, it's going to unsettle this entire department – I'll have to find someone more discreet than you to sort out what's happening in the British office, even if they are less experienced."

He cursed himself inwardly for not seeing that the London job might be on the cards, he'd just had so much on his mind since Lisa's death. He'd kept his head buried in his work for a year and a half, then it had just happened out of the blue with Selina and she had been the perfect, no-strings distraction. Heather had no right to dig around in his private life like this. Anyway, was her private life so damned spotless?

"Why didn't you tell me about London?" he asked. But he knew the answer even as he said it.

There was a second's pause as Heather looked squarely at him, "Because, James, I was hoping you would prove to me that, despite suspicions to the contrary in some quarters, you have the vision for such a helluva step up. Clearly, I was wrong!" She held his gaze levelly.

"OK, I deserved that. What happens next?"

Heather didn't reply at first, preferring to stare out of the window in search of some solution. She turned towards him, "You've put me in an impossible position. I could just write the report that I was planning to write, and risk looking totally out of touch with my own team if Human Resources tells the top floor about your extra-curricular adventures. Or I could spare HR the trouble, tell the top floor myself and start searching for someone to go to London in your place. Right now that's the most attractive option." Heather went back to ignoring him and continued to stare out of the window while she thought.

"Anyway, it's over," he ventured again, showing considerable economy with the truth. "With Selina, I mean."

"Well, that's not how Selina sees it. In fact, she's telling everyone in the Ladies restroom how great you are, what a fantastic time you're both having, and how she sees this going 'all the way'."

James's look of puzzlement rapidly turned into one of horror. "Why the hell would she do that? Does everyone know?"

"Waddya think?"

"Holy shit!" Well, that explained the unexpected grins he'd been getting from one or two colleagues.

"When was she saying this?"

"In the last day or so, I guess," said Heather. "What does it matter? Your secret's well and truly out now."

He couldn't be mad at Selina; he was angry at himself for not seeing this coming, and for getting into this mess in the first place. His mind was racing as he tried simultaneously to anticipate the next question and to review what he and Selina had said to one another.

Hadn't Selina always agreed with him that this was a bit of fun for them after they had both come out of serious relationships? She had finished with what's-his-name, and it wasn't two years since he'd lost Lisa. Now he thought of it, he couldn't remember her actually replying to that idea lately, but then she hadn't denied it either. Surely, she couldn't have thought this was a forever thing? Hearts and flowers? Wedding bells? He'd never tried to give her that impression – on the contrary, he'd been pretty open that this was just fun. He was still in Recovery mode, he'd clearly said so, used those words. Not very flattering to her in hindsight, but clear enough. Damn, she must have thought she was the cure.

On reflection, perhaps she could be that mistaken. She had looked great last Sunday morning, just drifting around his apartment in one of his blue shirts, reading the newspapers and showing those long brown legs – one thing led inexorably to another.

James tore his mind back to Heather. "… so, what do you think?" she was saying.

He struggled to recall what she had said. Nothing at all came to mind. "I don't know," he ventured non-committedly.

Heather stared at him. "Brilliant. You're supposed to be one of the brightest minds in the department and you don't know. Have you been listening to anything I said?"

He began to reply but she interrupted him. "On Monday, the Board will decide who takes over as General Manager in Northern Europe. Whoever it is will be running a small team that – I might add – is made up almost entirely of women. And the best candidate the Board have before them is shagging his secretary, didn't know that he was the butt of every office joke, and now hasn't a clue how to break it up. Assuming you want to, that is?" Heather left the question hanging. "Because if you prefer Selina to a career move back to London, and next stop a vice-presidency then just say so and I'll take your name off my recommendation."

"No, no. No way." He wasn't at his most eloquent today.

"I thought not. Then you have the weekend in which to sort this out with Selina. Let her down gently too, and whatever you do, don't mess it up, James. She may not have your experience but she's damn good at her job and she doesn't deserve a dick-for-brains boyfriend like you. Get out of here," said Heather without turning to look at him. "I don't want to see you again till 8.00 a.m. Monday." As he left, she continued to stare thoughtfully at the street outside while the rain pounded the glass.

******

The wind blowing off the Charles River almost tore the street door out of his hands when he reached his apartment. Close to the Boston waterfront the block's exterior looked much like the old warehouses around it, but inside his apartment was bright and modern with a mezzanine floor for their one large double bedroom. Well, he still thought of it as their bedroom. He liked it just as much now as he had on the day that he and Lisa discovered it three years ago. At the time he was still flushed with the excitement of a promotion and a good salary raise, and they were euphoric that at last they were getting a place of their own together. His feelings for the apartment hadn't even changed after Lisa died. It always reminded him of her but in a good way, like a favourite photo or a cherished birthday gift. He might never get used to a rent that was so high though, when there was just him left to pay for it. In fact, he didn't know how much longer he could manage it, but if the job in London came off he'd be moving anyway. *If*, he reminded himself. Yesterday he didn't even know about the vacancy, and now he'd gone from favourite to rank outsider, all in twenty-four hours. The job had to be in serious doubt now, unless he could sort out the mess he'd made.

James knew he was seen as a personable guy, laid back while always getting the job done. Getting the best from a team had served him well in his public relations career. At home he still savoured the luxury of closing the door on the world and some evenings he would just sit by one of his large front windows, cradling a bottle of beer, mulling over life. And loss.

The windows allowed a warm glow from the street lamps to light his way across the living room as he moved about. He turned the heating up high, switched on some lights in the kitchen and his bedroom, and dumped unopened post on the kitchen table. He draped his dripping raincoat over a stool before heading to the bedroom to strip off his sodden suit and shoes.

The shower was burning hot, just how he liked it and within minutes he began to feel a little more human, washing away a bloody awful day. James shifted to let the hot jet play over the back of his neck, warming him to the core and restoring some energy. Sharp needles of water massaged his back and prodded some life into him. It was a luxurious few minutes later that he stepped out and grabbed a warm towel from the rail.

As he dried, he looked at himself in the full-length mirror. Wavy, mid brown hair, clean shaven and although not exactly model boy looks he wouldn't frighten the horses either. Broad shoulders and a tall frame. Then the picture was not so good. It had become a reflex reaction lately to suck in his breath and tighten his stomach muscles. *You can't hold that forever*, he thought, *and exhaled*. OK, so that's the real me. There was no getting away from it, in recent months he'd become overweight and out of condition. Not fat exactly, but there were pounds around the waist and chest that shouldn't be there and hadn't been even a short while ago. Not bad for forty, he kidded himself; just a shame you're twenty-eight.

He knew he hadn't been in his best shape since he played rugby at university back home in England. Was that really six years ago? He'd even made the first team a couple of times through other people's injuries; he'd been strong and fast for a big guy. It had always amused Lisa that someone so large could be so light on his feet. She loved dancing and they sometimes went clubbing with friends or just turned up the music at home. Dancing had always helped him with girls, especially as a teenager when he was too shy to chat easily. You didn't have to talk to girls so much while you danced, unless it was a slow number and by then she was either in your arms anyway or heading back to join her friends.

It was at moments like this that he missed Lisa most. In the past eighteen months James had often turned to tell her something, ask her opinion, or share a laugh. She had a huge sense of fun – he still felt it was disloyal to describe her in the past tense, as though he was somehow relinquishing her – but her common sense had helped to rein in his wilder flights of fancy. Lisa had never put him down, she'd just helped him scrutinise his more impetuous ideas keeping him on the straight and narrow when she said nothing at all – her silences spoke volumes.

That made her seem negative but nothing could have been further from the truth. James had been captivated by her laughter, her positive outlook, her sense that the glass was half full and never half empty. That, plus the brightest smile he'd ever seen and a figure for which he'd have crossed mountains. His favourite photographic subjects as a keen amateur prior to meeting Lisa had always been landscapes, but then his hobby had extended to endless shots of her captivating smile, so many that he never had enough places to put the photos and many still languished on his computer seen only by James and his screensaver.

He sat silently on the end of his bed for a minute wrapped only in a towel, his elbows on his knees and his head down. God, he needed her strength and good sense now. But at moments like this all he could feel was the pain and hollowness inside him where once his heart had swelled with pride at being with her. At times like this he could only focus on what was gone, what was forever taken from him. The sense of what they had shared was something for his brighter days – he could never again feel her arms draped across his shoulders, enjoy the impromptu hugs, or the way her hand snaked around his waist while they were talking with friends or walking through Boston.

He longed for the easy silences at home. She had always been the first person he shared his news with, she was forever texting him at work with silly messages, and he still silently wished her good night before he fell asleep.

The pain was still there – he guessed it always would be – just lurking in the background waiting for his mind to take a turn down an unexpected path and suddenly there she'd be, right at the front of his thoughts, there but not there. He wondered if he was weird; a few times he had found himself crying for no apparent reason and it had stopped as quickly as it started. It wasn't hard to work out the underlying reason. He didn't always picture her face in his thoughts, it was more a sense of her presence, her dependability that he'd never found in previous girlfriends, something that distinguished her so quickly for him.

Maybe he should be thinking of her face more clearly. Was there a right way to deal with losing her? He had no idea, but occasionally it worried him that he found it harder these days to call her features to mind. Of course, her smile was always there to remember when he needed to, and he had a passport-sized photo in his wallet but there was an unspoken worry deep inside that if he tried too often to picture her face then the memory would blur and pale through over-use and he would find it even harder next time. At these moments he would refresh his memory with the snapshots he kept around the flat. The photos were good, but he had looked at them so often they were like someone else's memories, the best images of Lisa were his and his alone. The photos were poor substitutes but he still needed to look at images of her all the time, and when she'd died he'd bought more picture frames, hoping that surrounding himself with her image would hold on to her. That phase had passed, but the apartment bore witness to his constant need to remind himself their two-year relationship had been real, deep and precious to them both.

James missed Lisa's sense of humour as much as anything. She was never deliberately unkind, but she'd been a brilliant observer of life around her and was happy just to sit with him 'people-watching' in a pavement café. In the early days they'd found a favourite Italian place in Boston's North End where they could sit for ages cradling cappuccinos while they watched the world go by, until finally the owner moved them on because they weren't eating his extravagant but excellent pastries. James looked at himself again in the bedroom mirror. Well, he could see where the pastries were going these days, it was time to get back into regular exercise. Occasional games of tennis or squash were evidently not keeping pace with his corporate entertaining.

He put on a T-shirt and jeans and went through to the kitchen. Opening the refrigerator James pulled out a bottle of beer, then paused and looked down at his waistline in the harsh white light of the fridge. The beer went back in and instead he took out a small carton of juice. He couldn't be bothered with a glass and drained half the juice in one go. The unopened mail lay in front of him on the counter. He was feeling stronger, but not that strong.

******

James had been planning to take Selina to a movie and a meal tomorrow. He'd suggested a time and place to meet – but that would all have to change. He'd try to break it to her gently. "It's not you, it's me. I don't feel ready to be part of a relationship. I'm still too cautious for anything serious."

This was true, but he hadn't expected to extricate himself from anything like this. Maybe he'd been kidding himself, wasn't an office fling always going to end like this if it wasn't serious? And for him it never had been. He really had thought he'd made that clear to Selina. Were his communication skills so off or had they both heard only what they wanted to hear?

Selina had known about Lisa from the start, of course, how could she not? Lisa's photo was on his desk at work and all over the apartment. In fact, it was Selina's kindness and compassion towards him after the accident that had brought them closer, although it was a long time before anything physical followed – over a year, in fact. To begin with Selina had avoided mentioning Lisa in case it hurt him, but later she saw that he was OK to talk about it occasionally – it made him feel Lisa was real and not a figment of his imagination.

He'd tried not to talk about losing her too much and anyway his relationship with Selina wasn't exactly based on long walks and meaningful conversations. In any event, his stoicism seemed to have won Selina's sympathy, and now a lot more besides if Heather was to be believed. From Selina's early understanding had come small kindnesses – an unrequested coffee or a Danish, sometimes she'd stay late to work on their projects without being asked. She would stand close beside his chair to see what he was asking her to work on. Then late one evening he'd heaved a sigh of exhaustion and before he had even registered what she was doing Selina's hands had started massaging his neck and shoulders. When he'd protested – rather feebly it had to be admitted – she'd slapped away his protests and he'd given in to what proved to be the first of many treatments. At this late hour they were alone in the office and he had soon abandoned any further concentration, spinning his chair around and catching Selina's hands in his. For a long moment they had looked at one another wordlessly until he stood up, still holding her hands. Selina had gazed up at him and by now the silence was electric, then he had leaned down and kissed her for a very long time.

When he opened his eyes, hers were still closed. They had left the office very late that night and Selina still giggled about it when she reminded him of how they got together. *That should have been another clue*, he thought, *it was something that she talked about more than he did.* She had recently ended a relationship and – although he'd had no interest in anyone else – he hadn't wanted Selina to build up her hopes. As he saw it, she was on the re-bound and he was only just emerging from somewhere very dark.

In the early days they had definitely both professed that they were just in this for fun. *But perhaps her feelings had changed and,* now he thought of it, *she hadn't said what she wanted from him for a long time.* He'd just assumed that it was all the same as before.

It was a shame because he was genuinely fond of Selina but he couldn't see it going the distance and now he'd have to end it with the inevitable tearful scene; he had no idea if she would accept it or try to hang on to him. The relationship had been convenient, strictly contained – or so he'd thought – and great fun. Lately he had been quizzed for the first time since Lisa's death by his friends – mainly the women and the married men – who wanted to know if he felt ready to see anyone now that more than a year had passed. This was easy enough to answer initially as James could not imagine wanting anyone new. The next time someone asked he had been more evasive and, while he didn't lie to them exactly, he had allowed them to conclude he was still not ready for dating. Well, he couldn't very well shout about his office affair.

To be fair, Selina hadn't asked him to commit to anything either, but if she was saying all that to the girls at work then this might have become an even more complicated scene somewhere down the line. Selina was fit and she was a laugh, but she wasn't someone he would take home to Mum. Enjoy the weekend, he muttered to himself ironically. Damn, this was going to make things awkward at work. Why hadn't he just resisted the temptation? Perhaps there hadn't been any temptation in his life for a while. He hadn't even guessed how much he had needed companionship until it had all just happened. He hadn't made a pass at anyone because he hadn't noticed any women for a long time. If any other women had shown an interest in him during the last few months, he had been totally unaware of it, then again he'd never been good at reading the signs.

That was more his big brother's strength. Neil had never been shy with women. At fifteen or so, James had finally realised that if he didn't confront his fear of saying the wrong thing and start asking girls out, his brother would never let him live it down. Eventually he'd been more worried about the banter than of saying the wrong thing to a girl, so he guessed Neil had helped him out of his shell – although he wasn't about to thank him.

James had made more of an effort at parties, and since he could make people laugh he'd opened up. Eventually he had realised he was still in touch with many of the girls he'd dated, while Neil was forever moving on. A couple of James's ex-girlfriends were among his oldest friends and they had been supportive when Lisa died. Two years older than James, Neil had been touring the world with the British Army and his closest friends were all men, guys he'd served with in Germany, Kosovo, and Sierra Leone.

James dragged his thoughts back to the present. He'd better text Selina to meet him a bit earlier tomorrow for a drink instead of at the cinema. At least that would be neutral ground and if it all kicked off then they could just leave.

He really wanted to blame Heather, too, but he knew it wasn't her fault. He'd broken the golden rule – don't mess on your own doorstep. Well, he'd messed up big style, Heather had given him a bollocking, and he'd probably deserved it. All right, he had definitely deserved it, but it didn't make it any easier to take.

And what was all this about London? How come he didn't even know there was a vacancy there? His information sources were useless. The Northern Europe manager wasn't due for promotion yet, so maybe he was being fired or had quit. Either way, it was the best job in the company at his level, it would take him back to England and his roots for a while, and give him some travel opportunities in the region. James spoke reasonably good French which would be needed, he also had good contacts in other European territories especially Germany and Scandinavia. He had no mortgage or family commitments so he would be able to drop everything and fly wherever the clients needed PR support, at a moment's notice. He could see it made sense from the company's point of view, as well as his own – if he could only secure the job, and that meant getting past this problem. James grimaced at the prospect of tomorrow's conversation with Selina.

******

At 8.00 a.m. on Monday, James was at the door to Heather's office but he could hear her on the phone so he sat outside and waited. Her personal assistant arrived a couple of minutes later and remained silently and stubbornly immune to his welcoming charm. She must have seen or heard that Heather's call had ended. Without even looking up, she simply said, "Go in!"

"Well?" said his boss, "What happened?"

James told her how he'd met with Selina on Saturday and had explained that he wasn't ready for a more serious relationship. But he spared Heather some of the grizzly details of their conversation.

Selina hadn't asked what he meant by a more serious relationship, but they had both known what they were talking about. When she arrived at the bar and found him waiting for her, she had been smiling and cheerful, giving him a kiss on the lips to which he had hardly responded. It was then that she sensed his mood, and once he had ordered their drinks he had wasted no time in breaking the news to her.

Afterwards James was not sure how he had expected Selina to react. Tears? A big scene? Probably not. She had sat silently while he told her how he felt and how he was unready for any deeper commitment right now. The air just seemed to go out of her and her buoyant mood had evaporated instantly. She had looked long and hard at him while she seemed to be assessing him as a man or gauging his honesty, or both. It had made James acutely uncomfortable until she broke the silence.

"I'm not gonna beg you," she had said. "I've told you I have feelings for you, and I'm sorry if it's inconvenient now."

The clear implication was that James had changed his mind, but he didn't say anything.

"I'm sorry if this is more than you wanted. I've tried not to rush you." She had bitten her lip there and looked down. Selina was having trouble keeping her composure and even at this late stage James was learning that there were depths to her self-possession and forward thinking of which he had been unaware.

What else don't I know about her, he wondered to himself. He reckoned he'd done enough talking and more than enough damage, it was Selina's turn to speak or to leave and he would just have to take it on the chin. She did neither, she simply raised her head, and stared straight into his eyes. "Is this about the Europe job?" she asked.

Jeez, that really threw him for a moment. For Heaven's sake, had everyone known about this except him? "No," he'd said. Then seeing the look on her face he added, "Well, not directly. I guess if I ever did get a job overseas I would be leaving the States and I don't want to hurt you … any more, I mean." This time it was up to her draw the inference, that he would not be taking her if he left. He didn't like this talking in riddles but he was trying to say as little as possible while not walking out on the conversation. After all, they were going to have to face one another again starting Monday.

Selina had been studying his face but now she looked down again. "And there's no one else. You're not seeing someone else?"

He was on safer ground here. "Absolutely not. I just need some time to myself for a bit. I'm sorry if... I'm sorry that I've hurt you."

"You have," she said, "but I'll bounce back. I have before." Selina stood up suddenly and he struggled to do so too, though trapped by the cocktail table. "I won't kiss you," she said, "but I *will* always care for you. I can't help that, James and I don't think you can stop me." She pulled her bag higher onto her shoulder, turned on her elegant heel and he watched this attractive woman, who was tougher and smarter than he'd ever understood, walk away.

It was, of course, a rather truncated version of these events that James gave to his boss on Monday morning.

"So, is she coming in this morning?" asked Heather.

Ignorance did not seem an advisable policy. "I think so. I believe so," was all he could truthfully offer.

"You believe so. Well let's hope so, because the sooner things get back to something approaching Platonic normality around here, the sooner we can get some work done. Leave me James. I need to talk to the Board at 10.00 o'clock and I still have no idea what they will say."

As it happened, Selina did not come in on the Monday. She called in sick on Tuesday and Wednesday as well, and she wouldn't answer his calls or texts. He carried on without a personal assistant pretty well, but there was an unmistakable chill in the atmosphere when he spoke to some of the women in the office. The guys on the other hand were variously oblivious to it, ignored it, or wound him up mercilessly.

On Thursday, however, Selina was back and her first destination was Human Resources where he learned later that she had asked to be transferred. There were no tears, no public scene – perversely he felt it might have been easier if there had been. She came up after an hour or so, simply cleared her desk without looking at him and went to work downstairs – by lunchtime it was as though she'd never been there. The female frost lingered all week though, and so did the male ribbing, which was all the more intense because he'd had a pretty spotless image until now and this gave the wags some rich and unexpected new opportunities.

On Thursday afternoon James had an email with a party invitation from one of the sales team, addressed to "James + PA", which he did his best to respond to without being defensive, along the lines of "Can't come, haven't got one". He knew he would have to face this for a while. By the following week it appeared to be old news and, though Selina's friends were quick to move away from the coffee machine when he approached, he just got his head down and focused once more on his clients and their public relations problems.

The killer blow landed as he arrived at work on Friday morning though. "Sorry, pal," said someone in Accounts whom he hardly knew, even before he reached his desk. *He's a bit behind the curve on the break-up*, thought James. Then he noticed that one or two pairs of eyes were on him as he read his emails.

"Shit. Shit. I don't believe it," he muttered aloud before he could control himself. He got up, swore silently and more eloquently then strode the few yards to Heather's office. Her PA seemed to be pleased with something today and waved him straight in.

"I see you've given the job to someone else," he said. "You don't think that's being a bit short-term, Heather."

"Good morning, James. Sit down."

"I don't want to sit down. What the hell's going on? I sorted things out like you said, and this is what I get for it."

"Sit down and calm down or this conversation ends here."

James took a breath and sat opposite her. Heather looked him firmly in the eye, "I haven't given the job to someone else, the Board have. It's theirs to give, as you well know. Do I think they're being petty or short-termist? As it goes, I don't. I explained to you that you've been under the management microscope for some time, I'm actually surprised you never sussed that. And while there was a lot to like about you and your work, they were hoping to find a greater degree of stability and maturity in your personal life."

"But we both know that I'm the best qualified person in the company to take on this role in Europe..."

She interrupted him, "... Which is why we have had to go outside the company to fill the post when the Board expressed understandable concerns about your readiness."

James was thunderstruck. He had honestly expected that by sorting out this affair the Board would acknowledge his commitment to the company and the post they were considering for him, and conclude that he was the obvious candidate.

"Maybe you've forgotten, James," she continued, "how much importance a family man like Carl attaches to domestic stability. He sees it as a solid platform from which to manage the inevitable stress of a job like Regional General Manager. I'm genuinely sorry for you, as I think you could do it very well, but in time there will be other opportunities for you."

"Did you vote for me?" he asked bluntly.

"James, I could tell you that Board proceedings are confidential, but I won't lie. I proposed you to the Board, made a strong case for you, reminded them how well you had recovered from losing Lisa and your genuine focus on your work. It seems HR had been asked by Carl to line up one or two other external candidates. I voted for you, but on balance the Board preferred another candidate to deal with a sensitive situation in London following Roddy's unexpected departure. They reckon you will be more ready in a year or two, and maybe they're right, it's just unfortunate for you that this opening came up now," she concluded.

"That's all I needed to know," he said standing up.

"You're a talented guy, James. We both know that. So, don't blow it. I'm glad you've sorted things out here, and you will move past this, but you still need to get yourself together. If you want some time out, I'd be happy to arrange it. After which I know you'll prove to them that you'll soon be ready to be a GM somewhere else."

"Some time out. Yes, maybe that's the answer," said James as he stood up. "Thank you for your vote at any rate," he said ruefully, and with an expression that did nothing to hide his anger and wounded pride, he turned and walked out of her office, through the building and left the world of PR for good.

Chapter 3
Barcelona, Spain
Five Months Ago

Axel ignored the mobile phone that buzzed in his pocket, knowing what the text would say. "Welcome to Spain. Your calls are charged at…." He wasn't interested. As he queued for passport control, he had too much time to think, and he idly wished he had travelled in the 1930s, crossing continents in style aboard flying boats and ocean liners, with stewards who never served claret chilled in tiny plastic bottles. At least he had no need of a porter today, most of his belongings were at his crash pad in London and he carried only a wash kit and a change of clothes in his laptop bag.

At fifty years old and above average height, Axel was still in good shape. He was tanned and his blond hair was receding into a widow's peak but he brushed it straight back from a high forehead that only accentuated the retreat. His confidence was not the result of time spent in front of a mirror. A close observer at passport control might have noticed there was no wedding band, his only adornment being an expensive Heuer watch, a gift from a girlfriend with motor racing connections.

The immigration queue shuffled forward and Axel's view of a sunny Barcelona airport was obscured. There was little that he needed to prepare for today's meeting, the information was in his head and he intended to do more listening than talking. His attention turned to the passengers around him. Judging by the number of tablets, slick suits and sharp haircuts he guessed that most were heading to the cell phone industry's giant, week-long event advertised everywhere in Arrivals. It had made his search for accommodation harder.

The queue split into several channels and picked up speed until eventually Axel was through the throng and striding to the taxi rank. He had plenty of time to find his apartment on the Carrer de Mallorca close to the Sagrada Familia, Gaudi's stone-carved church famed for its coloured towers, inscribed buttresses and anguished statues. Axel often stayed in apartments, preferring them to the rictus smiles and forced politesse of hotel staff – besides no one saw your comings and goings or those of your visitors. In any case, his booking had been made at the last minute, long after eighty thousand members of the mobile phone industry had snapped up most of the city's hotel rooms and airline seats.

He wouldn't have chosen Barcelona amid the throngs of people and the abnormally high prices at show time but this potential client had intrigued him and it was a mutually convenient time and place for them to meet. Axel stretched out in the back of the black and yellow cab letting the warm air of the Catalan capital blow in through his open window, and wondered how much the surly young driver was going to try and stiff him for. Compared to London in February this warmth was relaxing – not like Africa of course, but welcome all the same.

Axel was standing on the kerb twenty minutes later folding his wallet back into a safe inside pocket. The 'dips' here were notoriously brazen, but pickpockets and muggers evidently came in all shapes and sizes. The taxi driver had told him the meter was broken but thoughtfully offered to charge him only seventy Euros for a fifty Euro ride. Instead Axel had climbed out and stood on the kerb with his bag, waiting for the driver to come to him and simply handed him a 50 Euro note as he stared the man down. Then he picked up his bag and walked away. They both knew it wasn't a sum worth getting in a fight over, and the driver had enough sense to see he'd met his match. He swore loudly in Catalan, spat on the ground where Axel had stood and departed with a squeal of tyres, knowing that an early return to the airport for a more pliant passenger was his best bet. *Sure, welcome to Spain*, thought Axel as he rode the lift to his apartment.

One hour later the efficiency of the metro service made up for the cab driver's welcome, delivering him quickly to the heart of town. A few streets away from the metro stop Axel made his way up the highly polished steps of an otherwise anonymous looking five-star hotel. A brown-coated doorman emerged, saw Axel's unremarkable arrival among the steady stream of Mercedes, and opted to ignore him in favour of better tips from departing VIPs. At the front desk a dark-haired girl asked in fluent English how she could help.

"I'm here to meet a Mr Hendriks of CCV. I don't have his room number. Let him know Mr Terberg is here."

"Certainly, sir," she said scanning the monitor in front of her. "Yes, Mr Hendriks has a meeting room on the fifth floor. I'll call him for you."

There was a brief conversation after she was connected and then she turned back to Axel. "He is running a little late, sir, but he'll send someone down shortly to meet you. Would you like a coffee while you wait?"

"No, thanks. I'll be over there." He gestured to some sofas across the lobby. Axel sat down and once more ran through in his mind how he came to be here. It was less than a month since he had received a call in London. Although Axel's name was not shown on his own company website a serviced business line could be reached by any online visitor. This call, however, had come through on his private mobile phone, a number he gave only to a select few. That and the fact that he didn't recognise the caller's number had been enough to arouse his interest. The call had come early in the morning while he was in the shower, perhaps it was from an Asian or African time zone, and a brief voicemail had been left.

"Mr Terberg, my name is Hendriks and I've been given this number by a mutual business acquaintance." The accent was South African, the delivery terse and clipped, and the name suggested an Afrikaner. "I represent a number of businesses interested in alternative sources of certain key minerals. Can you give me a call soonest?" and he left a London number.

The return call that followed had been similarly uninformative. When Axel had rung back later that morning, he could tell from the change in dial tone that the call was being diverted, and then it had been answered 'CCV' by a woman who said she was unable to put him through to Mr Hendriks at that time. After agreeing a ring back time that evening, the call ended with few niceties. Maybe CCV wanted to disguise their whereabouts, and they preferred to call him.

An internet search for CCV found no relevant business but this only piqued Axel's interest, nor was there any reference to them on social media. As arranged, at exactly seven o'clock that night, Axel's mobile rang again. "Is that Mr Terberg?" a woman asked. He was sure that it was the same person he'd spoken to earlier.

"It is."

"Just one moment, please wait while I connect you to Mr Hendriks."

"Terberg?" This time the Afrikaans accent seemed more pronounced. His manner was peremptory as though Axel had dragged him off the golf course.

"Yes," said Axel.

"Good. I don't want to go into details on the phone, but I'd like to talk to you in person about your thoughts on potential alternative supplies of certain…," there was a pause, "... key minerals for communications device manufacture."

"You mean mobile phones?" asked Axel. The man sounded like he was reading from an encyclopaedia – was he naturally pompous or was he straying outside his comfort zone? This wasn't exactly Axel's area of expertise either, although he was close enough to it to guess that Hendriks was referring to cassiterite, the most common tin ore, or columbite-tantalite better known as coltan.

Axel had made his money trading in diamonds, emeralds and other stones, but he knew something about it and knew a few people working in tin and coltan. Cassiterite's translucent brown crystals were widely available in Russia and parts of Asia. Coltan was rarer; it was a dark grey, tar-like mineral containing tantalum that went into vital components for cell phones, laptops, game consoles and defence systems. Axel knew that growing sales of smartphones and limited supplies of coltan had seen the price rise a thousand percent in Europe in less than a decade – fortunes were being made and lost.

"OK, before we go any further, which minerals are you talking about?" Axel asked.

Hendriks hesitated, perhaps because he was on the phone. "Mainly coltan. Look, there's no need to discuss this in detail now, but I'd like to meet you as soon as possible. Can you join me in Barcelona next month?"

Axel was tiring of the man's cloak and dagger attitude and was ready to tell him to get lost but something puzzled him. "Tell me first how you got my private number."

"Sure, I was given it by Joshua. He said you'd know who he was."

There was a pause while Axel digested this. He hadn't heard Joshua's name mentioned for a while, but if this guy came to him via Joshua then he may be worth talking to after all.

"Terberg, are you there?" Hendriks was getting impatient.

Axel ignored the man's tetchiness. "This isn't really my line and I hadn't planned to go to Barcelona in February. Make your pitch."

"I understand all that. But we'll pay your air fare and put you up for the night, of course. But we think you might be interested; there's good money to be made in this area, and our access to new markets could help your traditional business in the gem trade."

"I have all the contacts I need in that line," said Axel brusquely.

"One can never have too many friends in business, Mr Terberg. But in this case I wasn't thinking of your African or European connections, more the other end of the supply chain," he paused for effect, "with customers in China and the Far East."

Axel said nothing but his silence must have betrayed his interest. He hoped it also hid his confusion. Everyone in business in Africa knew of China's growing interests and influence from the Mediterranean to the Cape, but there was still minimal Chinese involvement in Congo's Kivu provinces, a region he knew well and the source of most of the continent's coltan.

As for his existing business, Axel had long wanted to develop diamond supply routes into China to meet rising demand among the country's *nouveau riche* who wanted high quality stones at competitive prices. He would need convincing that organisations in the coltan trade could really help his diamond business though – unless they were evading the Kimberley Process, the initiative by governments and the diamond trade to stem the flow of 'conflict diamonds' mined in war zones.

Hendriks was obviously keen to see him. "A ticket will be waiting for you at Heathrow's BA information desk, Mr Terberg. There's a flight at 6.00 a.m. on February 24th. Is that agreeable?"

It wasn't much to go on, and it would mean changing his travel plans to get to Barcelona, but Axel wasn't too busy to discuss a new line of business. He had some contacts and knowledge to offer in this area, and the clincher was the recommendation from Joshua. Underpinning it all was a growing certainty that the Cousins would be interested in this unsolicited approach. Anything with a Chinese flavour tended to catch the Americans' interest quite quickly.

"OK, I'll be there. Text me the address and a time to meet you. Use this number. Don't worry about accommodation, I know the city and can organise my own but I'll use your ticket." His decision about accommodation was just habit, he preferred to control his own whereabouts, and had no wish to let Terberg know where he'd be, and it was a precaution that had saved his life on one occasion. He saw no reason to break the habit.

"OK. Until we meet then. Good day, Mr Terberg," Hendriks said, and he was gone.

The meeting time and address reached Axel's phone within the hour and he spent the rest of the evening wondering why he'd agreed to fly out to see someone he'd never met on the basis of so little information. *It's a strange business*, he had thought to himself as he downed the second beer that night in his local pub, and that's probably why he liked it.

******

After ten minutes there was still no sign of Hendriks or his staff in the hotel lobby, and Axel had skimmed all the news he wanted from international papers on the coffee table in front of him. Then the lift doors opened and a severe-looking young woman in an expensive and conservatively cut business suit crossed the lobby. There were other men and women seated around him but she made straight for Axel. "Mr Terberg, my name is Lorette. Would you follow me?" Her English was almost accent less, but her name and the way she pronounced it made Axel think she was French. No smile or handshake were offered, and she was evidently used to having her requests met. These people would win no prizes for charm, but it was consistent with Hendriks' presumption that Axel would drop everything to join him in Barcelona.

The lift doors closed behind them, and there was silence all the way to the door of 529. She stepped back and ushered him into a suite that Axel could see had been turned into an office with the removal of the bedroom furniture. As he looked about him, he caught sight through the connecting doors of a stocky young man on a mobile phone. His glance was noticed and Lorette closed the door, while gesturing to a sofa and chairs.

"Please be seated. Would you like a drink? Mr Hendriks will be with you in a moment." He was tired from the early flight and the journey, so Axel Terberg accepted a coffee knowing that in Spain it would be a strong one. He was not disappointed, but he'd no sooner taken a sip than the connecting door opened and a small, unsmiling man in his late fifties, with a considerable girth came in. A crisp blue shirt strained to contain his midriff and he wore bright red braces without which his shirt and trousers would have headed north and south. Hendriks had a pink complexion, an air of great purpose and, despite the air-conditioning, was showing small beads of sweat along a stubbly grey hairline.

"Greetings Mr Terberg, my name is Joost Hendriks of CCV." He pronounced his first name in the European manner, starting with a Y. "Thank you for making the time to come to Barcelona." He extended a small, pink fist and the handshake that followed was damp, weak and memorably unappealing.

"Let's just say your invitation intrigued me," said Axel. He looked again at Hendriks – somehow he imagined there weren't many who called him Joost. Perhaps not even Mrs Hendriks, although Axel noticed he wore a signet ring and no wedding band. Hendriks was almost a head shorter than Terberg's five foot eleven inches. His hair was cut so short that it bristled and the skin beneath it was red enough to suggest South Africa might not be his ideal habitat.

Axel found himself being studied in turn over half-moon glasses by a pair of pale grey, unforgiving eyes. Hendriks sported the kind of beard that seemed so pointless, with a thin strip of close-clipped hair following the chin from ear to ear while clean-shaven skin folded above and below. Perhaps Hendriks hoped it accentuated a weak jaw line and strengthened an ill-defined curve from cheek to jowl. He seemed to be a man of soft curves trying to show a harder edge.

Axel could be wrong but he already felt there might be more amusing companions to share a few drinks with, in fact he struggled to picture Hendriks relaxing at all. The man had the air of perpetual activity, whose every minute was filled with trying to get what he wanted.

"Be seated," said Hendriks. His manner made the civility sound more like a command. Axel settled into a soft sofa and waited for Hendriks to take the lead. "Tell me, Mr Terberg. What do you know about CCV?"

"A bit more than I did when we last spoke. I know that you are a privately owned, limited company registered in Durban, South Africa."

"Come, come, Mr Terberg. Surely that's not all," clearly it amused Hendriks to test his guest's research.

"OK. You are the General Manager, and a minority stock holder." The smile that had been emerging on Hendriks' face disappeared at what he evidently took to be a slight. Axel continued, "CCV has had various business interests over the years from property to shipping, but today you act as commodity brokers or intermediaries for several original equipment manufacturers." Axel allowed himself to slip into the jargon that reassured some people they were dealing with an industry insider.

"These OEMs make components for computers, personal navigation devices, avionics systems but mostly mobile phones. Some of your clients are household names, some by contrast make little-known electronic components in devices sold by well-known phone makers or mobile network giants like AT&T and Vodafone, or smaller networks in less developed markets."

"The companies you mention are not our customers..." Hendriks began.

Terberg interrupted him, "I use them only as an example. Would it serve any purpose for me to list your top 10 clients? Presumably we both know who they are." Axel was growing tired of this game, and rattled off the names of two North American and two European companies.

"Quite so, quite so," said Hendriks, holding up his hands for his guest to stop. Clearly, the examination had not only been passed, but was now causing the examiner some discomfort. "You have been doing your homework, which is entirely as we were led to expect. People speak highly of your knowledge and contacts, and Joshua says you have often worked well together."

You don't know the half of it, thought Axel. He and Joshua had been together in Afghanistan as young men when the Russians were still running the country, and the two of them had helped some trigger-happy Afghan warlords to smuggle out the dark blue semi-precious lapis lazuli stones. That was before Joshua had received a bullet through the foot from a Russian border guard and decided it was both safer and more rewarding to concentrate on diamond finishing in India and Egypt, a trade that had always been close to his family's heart. Meanwhile, Axel was getting involved in carrying quantities of emeralds northwards out of Africa, but only sometimes with the formal blessing of the local police and tax authorities. They had both been independent-minded, young and far too sure of themselves. The pair had been living on their wits, operating in markets dominated either by corporate giants or organised crime – sometimes Axel had struggled to discern the difference.

The twenty-five year-old, Dutch-born Axel Terberg, whose family had no financial interest in his business and fortunately little knowledge of it, had found common ground with a young Belgian called Joshua Mokotoff. It was true, Joshua could be a rogue when it came to his dealings with others, but perhaps because of their similar outlooks he and Axel had hit it off well from the start, developing a friendship and a mutual respect. It was preferable to work as a team, so their dealings together had always been straightforward. Joshua's Jewish ancestors had lived in Antwerp for generations and, in contrast to Axel, his family were the financial mainstay, the network hub and the *raison d'etre* of his gem trading and finishing business.

Axel hadn't come all this way to dwell on reminiscences though, he wanted to get down to business. "Mr Hendriks, we're both busy men and you have brought me here at some expense. How do you think I can help you?"

"Indeed, let's cut to the chase, as the Americans say. My clients are looking for alternative supplies of coltan from which to extract the metal tantalum, as you rightly said on the phone. They need larger quantities, and more competitive pricing. For this they are prepared to deal flexibly with alternative suppliers, and will pay handsomely to whoever can facilitate this."

Axel recognised the end of the explanation for the bait that it was. Someone at the start of the coltan supply chain was about to be squeezed hard to drive down the raw material costs, but the clear implication was that Axel wouldn't suffer. His mark-up could still be substantial provided the final price at the factory gate was lower and the supply was steady and strong. The 'flexible' dealings with suppliers that Hendriks referred to suggested few questions would be asked about the sources or methods of supply. It took some direct questioning but five minutes later Axel had confirmed these assumptions despite Hendriks' reluctance to speak plainly.

Before he could take this much further Axel needed to know more about their current arrangements. "I don't want to waste your time or mine so tell me which coltan markets you've tried so far in your search?"

"This is commercially sensitive, you understand," Hendriks did not like having the initiative wrested from him.

"Mr Hendriks, my presence here is commercially sensitive, so let's not piss about." Hendriks winced at the comment, but Axel could see where this was heading and he needed CCV to spell it out for him. Hendriks was not a man who surrendered information lightly.

"Quite so. We have had various sources up to now. For years we have met all our clients' needs from Australia and China, and in future Greenland may also be a possibility. The prices from large suppliers in Australia, Brazil and Canada are sometimes prohibitive, while smaller producers are unable to offer us the quantities we need. So these markets are less attractive to us, and in any case, we do not wish to leave ourselves at the mercy of a single source, so we're looking further afield."

"If you're trying so many sources, you must be in need of a great deal of coltan ore."

"Mr Terberg, we require 100,000 kilos of tantalum by the end of December and twice that next year." He watched impassively as Axel reacted in astonishment.

"Christ! A hundred tonnes ... and two hundred tonnes next year?" Axel shook his head in disbelief. "The whole of Congo's official output was only 100 metric tonnes last year."

"Then it's just as well that we will consider all sources of coltan, not just the open market," Hendriks replied and Axel studied him again more closely.

"Even including the black market, that's a helluva lot of phone capacitors! They only weigh a few grams each." Part of his homework before coming to Barcelona had been to gauge the size of the global market. Some experts scoffed at the official figures, insisting that these massively under-estimated the illegal trade, but Axel knew that American estimates for global production of finished tantalum were less than 700 tonnes in total in the previous year. Yet here was one company looking to buy more than a quarter of the world's legally mined output next year.

Hendriks was still frowning at the profanity but said nothing, and continued to study Axel's expression. Axel was a useful poker player but the quantities were so much more than he'd expected that he had momentarily given up on nonchalance. "And you have confirmed buyers for that much coltan, do you?" Axel mused aloud.

Hendriks just looked at him for a moment. "I would not waste your time or mine if I did not," was all he said.

Axel began to think through the supply chain. Where would the coltan be needed? The high quantities meant accessing a large part of the black market supply which would then have to be trucked across the border into Rwanda and shipped or flown to Europe for processing. Ostend or Antwerp in Belgium and ports in Germany provided a frequent back door route into the legitimate coltan trade for illegal shipments that were not government certified. The columbite-tantalite ore could be processed in Europe and smelted into tantalum powder or ingots which would then be shipped to Asia to make parts for phones and computers.

"Where do you want it consigned to?" asked Axel.

"Macao." Hendriks offered this information with a smile, knowing the puzzlement that it would cause.

"Surely China has its own reserves of coltan. You could buy it there more easily, and maybe as cheaply. Why go to the hassle and expense of shipping it from Africa?"

"First, Mr Terberg, we would be employing you so that there is no hassle. It can easily be processed in China, but you can leave us to worry about its final destination," said Hendriks enigmatically.

Axel had initially suspected that Hendriks and CCV might be acting as front men for Far Eastern manufacturers. China's electrical goods factories were still booming, exports may be down but domestic growth was far stronger than demand in the West. There was a market in China for tungsten that helped mobile phones vibrate, for tin to replace the lead once used in circuit boards, and coltan for making corrosion-resistant tantalum capacitors.

Axel was puzzled though. There seemed to be a dynamic at work in this deal that he did not understand, and that unsettled him. It made him wonder what angle he was missing, and if he didn't understand CCV's motivation how could he weigh the risks and rewards of being involved? Where was the greatest demand these days for Congo's tin, tantalum and tungsten? Answer; in the electronics factories of southern and eastern China. And if Chinese manufacturers could get the tantalum they needed at home why look overseas?

No, whoever wanted to control so much of Congo's coltan trade was either unable to rely on China's reserves, suggesting they weren't Chinese, or the Chinese needed more coltan than ever before. It would help his negotiating hand if he could find out more. If North Americans were behind this, surely they would manufacture their devices closer to home, maybe in Latin America.

So, who were CCV trying to cover for – Germans, Scandinavians, Brits? The European manufacturers were unlikely candidates if the ore was being processed in China, it would just add to the shipping costs. The most likely answer was someone in Asia; perhaps they were phone and laptop makers in Japan, Korea or Taiwan. Guesswork was no good, he needed more hard information and he wouldn't get it here.

He did a quick calculation. Even with Congo's low costs of extraction the commission and delivery charges he could expect would run into millions.

The trade would certainly present him with political and security problems in the area, and he would have to consider these long and hard. On the downside there were buyers in the region who would be seriously angered to find a hungry competitor like him coming in with huge new orders, and few questions asked about the sources of supply. If you were ready to compete with these people, you'd better be ready to face their reaction, they were not the kind to upset lightly. Of course, he could expect some protection from the *comptoirs* and their protectors selling the coltan; the last thing they would want to see was their new customer being scared off or eliminated. He'd need to have his own security in place though, for close protection. That could be arranged through the usual channels.

At the moment the price was fluctuating wildly as tantalum supply frequently outpaced demand. The makers of phones and DVD players in Europe and the US had come under scrutiny in recent years from fair trade charities and a few journalists filming stories on human rights and the illegal trade in 'conflict minerals', the ores extracted from areas held by warring factions across lawless parts of central Africa and Latin America. Now the UN had become involved in efforts to stem the conflict minerals trade, and phone makers in the West were starting to demand proof that their mineral purchases were 'conflict-free'.

There was little pressure on manufacturers though, in India, China and South East Asia – in fact, quite the contrary. They were keen to break into the lucrative Western market for smartphones and other electronic devices that couldn't function without cassiterite, columbite, tantalite and other minerals. These were mainly private companies fighting for survival in competitive electronic device markets, whose owners expected growing profits and market share first, and worried about ethical supplies later if at all. New phone makers were coming into the market all the time and they looked for a cost advantage wherever they could find it. Axel knew that there were two costs most likely to be cut, in labour and raw materials. This was why smartphone makers had moved step by step to poorer and poorer countries with cheaper workforces, beginning in Japan and Singapore in the 1990s, before setting up in Malaysia, China, Indonesia and The Philippines. So Axel was not surprised to hear that CCV's clients were in China – assuming that was the truth. There were factories all over southern China from Shenzhen to Shanghai that might need supplies of coltan, and probably tin.

Hendriks' reply brought Axel back to the matter in hand. "Of course, with your help Mr Terberg, we won't be paying anywhere near as much as the open market rate," said Hendriks. "Our costs will be substantially lower, even after we've paid you a good commission."

Axel studied the South African for clues to his thinking. "Well, US production has stopped completely, and Australia and Canada are marginal producers at best with the price of tantalum where it is. Brazil and Mozambique don't have the capacity suddenly to increase production. So, I guess there aren't many places left for you to go. The DRC, the Democratic Republic of Congo, is your best bet." Terberg blew out his cheeks. "Of course, you could try the official route through the Ministry of Mines in Kinshasa, but I guess the reason I'm here is either because that's not attractive politically or economically, or because you've already talked to the Kinshasa authorities and drawn a blank. The Kinshasa option has failed."

"Not failed exactly, Mr Terberg, although you are correct in your overall analysis. I prefer to say we have not yet succeeded. The political situation in the tantalum producing regions of the DRC is … how shall I put it? Fluid. Kinshasa might like to pretend it still controls the east of the country, but it doesn't fully control the cities and the mines are changing hands all the time. We would be delighted to place our business through official government channels – it would make everyone's lives much simpler. But, although they cannot say so publicly, the Congo government in Kinshasa does not control much mineral extraction in its eastern provinces. And, since this represents conservatively twenty-five percent of the world's coltan reserves, we can't very well ignore this region, can we?

"It is of course, regrettable that we must deal with some of the lawless elements who hold these mines, Mr Terberg, but tell me what choice do we have?" Hendriks spread his hands wide and shrugged his shoulders. "We are not the world's policeman," he said, "We are just businessmen who must deal with the situation as we find it on the ground. We must leave it to others who are better qualified to right the wrongs of the world."

The argument was not a new one, in fact Axel had said the same sort of thing on other occasions, and Axel could see that he had that much in common with CCV. They weren't just dealing with the political instabilities on the ground, like him they were benefiting from them. These were the ways you found a profit margin here, an opportunity for your clients and yourself. He knew that life was tough in the mines and the camps around them, he'd been in the region's gold, diamond and tin mines often enough to know what life was like there. And what he saw had made him more determined never to be so poor or weak again that someone could take advantage of him. When his father had thrown him out of the family home at sixteen with no money and nowhere to go, he had told Axel this was the best way to learn to look after himself. It was harsh but he'd learned quickly that survival was what mattered first. Over the next year and a half, until he'd been able to sign up for the merchant navy, Axel had found out what it was to be poor and homeless. He had had enough of that to last him a lifetime and he would make sure it never happened again.

His mind had wandered from Hendriks for a moment, and the South African was still talking. "These are lawless areas, Mr Terberg, as I hardly need to tell you. There are new players, new device makers emerging all the time but the one thing they have in common is their need to beat the costs of the established household names." Hendriks paused reflectively and made a steeple of his fingers. "May I be frank with you?"

"That's what I'm here for."

"Our clients are very clear in their objectives. They have a strong and growing demand for coltan, for tantalum. Our task – and yours if you'll assist us – is to ensure that they get it. For this you will be handsomely rewarded. You could also benefit just as much from the many doors that my clients can open to you in diamond imports to the Far East. These people are influential players in other markets. They would make valuable ambassadors and investors in your various business interests – from Congolese diamonds to Afghan lapis, from Brazilian gold to Zambian emeralds," said Hendriks with the flourish of a card player revealing his hand.

It was Axel's turn to be surprised at the depth of their homework on him. None of his trades could be followed easily, and not even Joshua knew all his business interests. Someone had been checking Axel's résumé thoroughly before they contacted him, and yet he had heard nothing of their research on the grapevine. That concerned him, too.

Hendriks continued, "Perhaps we have not had the right – how shall I say? – Support until now. One of the reasons I'm here is to find out if you might be our vital ingredient, Mr Terberg, the link in the chain whose contacts and ability to work with all kinds of partners will get new coltan supply lines running. Are you that person?"

Axel paused and silently stared at the ceiling for a long time as he weighed his options. Despite his research he was under no illusion that he knew much about CCV, and he still knew nothing at all about their client. The part of the world he was being enticed into was very familiar, he might almost call it home, but he would be working in a mining sector with which he had had few dealings. His contacts were mainly in the diamond and emerald trades and, as Hendriks had pointed out, the region lived with constantly changing alliances, tribal jealousies, and political in-fighting. He smiled inwardly, that kind of melee was a world where he had always operated well.

Also on the plus side, Axel knew that whoever 'owned' the customer in this market was king. Kinshasa may not be able to control the region militarily, but one day soon the work being done by high tech companies in the West would make it possible to identify coltan extracted from individual mines and then it would be nearly impossible to find buyers for illegally mined ore. He knew that just from a single day trawling the web for information on coltan, so he could be sure the Chinese would know it, too. This might be one of the reasons they were stockpiling cheap supplies now, it could become harder to obtain later.

Campaigners were putting more pressure on phone manufacturers and other tantalum users to prove their products came from legitimate sources and, without the right certification, few of the big manufacturers would now touch an unverified supply although the smaller makers might. He figured that within ten years the buying public would have forced the electronics industry to do what politicians had tried and failed to do – buy only from certificated suppliers.

Did someone powerful see this as the last chance to seize control of a huge supply of minerals critical to many industries, from aerospace to defence to mobile communications? In the process a few people would certainly get fantastically rich, and it might even be a step towards achieving monopoly control of a vital commodity in twenty-first century life. Axel was no Ernest Oppenheimer but he couldn't help wondering what had gone through the man's mind when the mining company De Beers was on the brink of its global diamond monopoly in the 1920s.

Axel began cautiously. "As I say, to the best of my knowledge, Mr Hendriks, the whole of the Congo exported less than 100 tonnes of coltan last year, so what you're asking for is monopoly control of that market. Even allowing for the inaccuracy of official figures, you want to control one of the world's most valuable assets in one of the poorest and most unstable African countries. I guess it'll be no surprise to you if their government won't let it happen easily."

Hendriks raised an eyebrow. "You assume, Mr Terberg, that the trade is theirs to control. We don't believe the Ministry of Mines in Kinshasa could deliver that much coltan – whatever they claim. *Ergo* we have to talk to someone who isn't in the government, or who doesn't play by their rules," he added, and this time there was a conspiratorial smile.

"What you're proposing, Mr Hendriks, is enough to upset the government in Kinshasa for decades to come. If they even guessed that either of us was involved, they'd find a very deep hole and drop us in it forever. As if that wasn't enough, I'm sure other countries, global powers consider this to be a strategically vital material for everything from mobile phones to missile control and space exploration – they won't allow CCV or any other company to control a strategic market."

"Mr Terberg, even the Americans haven't managed to control it so far – what makes you think the West can do so in the future? We're grown-ups and we both know that coltan and other minerals are already flowing steadily out of the eastern provinces of the DRC into Uganda and Rwanda. We're not creating this trade, Mr Terberg, we're simply asking if you feel that you could use your contacts in the area to turn this market to our mutual advantage. We will play our part by guaranteeing much larger orders than have been possible hitherto, and still at prices that are attractive for all concerned. Surely that benefits everyone, except for the handful of small-scale buyers we displace. My clients would get the coltan at a better price than they now pay in other markets, and in the larger quantities they require. You secure a handsome and sustainable commission, and the traders in the region receive a good price and a more reliable market for whatever quantities they can deliver. Is that so bad? I'd say this is win-win all round."

This time it was Axel who said nothing. That rosy view of CCV and its largesse towards the coltan traders would not be shared by the Congolese government in far off Kinshasa, for whom no mention of taxes had been made. Kinshasa had long failed to control the illegal export of all kinds of mineral wealth – gold, diamonds, tin, cobalt, copper, columbite and tantalite. Even after two long wars and the death of over five million people, Kinshasa had still not been able to bring North and South Kivu under its control. The wealth continued to walk out of the country, almost literally.

Axel knew this was happening at present, and it showed no sign of stopping. He could either walk away stating that this was outside his previous experience, and let someone else earn the commission and win new business partners outside Africa, or he could work with CCV and their clients himself.

He was used to reinventing himself. He had been a copper miner in Australia's toughest mines, he'd sold lapis lazuli in India for Afghan warlords, and he'd dealt in emeralds, gold and diamonds. Axel was like mercury; he could slip this way or that and easily re-form his business wherever it suited him. He had done it before, why should this be any different? Of course, there was Langley to consider. As much as he would have liked to, he was no longer able to act on his own impulse. He was pretty sure what they'd say but he'd need to talk to them soon.

Axel had not been tempted to work in this market in the past, he'd been busy enough building a precious stone trade. Lately, however, the gem business had pretty much run itself. He had a reliable network of suppliers in Africa, cutters and finishers in Europe and India, and buyers just about everywhere – and in truth he had been looking for a new challenge. Just because this approach was unexpected was no reason to reject it and the money was certainly appealing. Just as significantly he was also attracted by the challenge of dealing in a new industry and the prospect of opening new markets with some influential backers in China and the Far East.

The more he thought about it the more he believed that Hendriks' suggestion that China wasn't the coltan's final destination was a crude attempt to obscure some Chinese clients. He didn't know yet why CCV felt the need to be so furtive but for now it wasn't important, and maybe it would become clearer in time. The way he looked at it, Hendriks was being employed as a mask to hide his clients' identity, and who buys a mask that looks the same as themselves? If these coltan buyers were Europeans, South Africans or North Americans, surely they would have approached him directly.

No, he was convinced that the mysterious and reportedly powerful clients to whom Hendriks eluded, and who he said were capable of opening up new markets for Axel, were Far Eastern and probably Chinese. The intermediaries, CCV, had clearly done their homework on his own company and its contacts, and they knew where he was strong and weak. That would have taken some thorough investigation.

The lure of new business opportunities outside coltan had been an extra inducement in case the money wasn't enough to win Axel's co-operation. And he had to concede that here they had played their cards well even if, in describing new market opportunities for Axel, Hendriks had betrayed more than he imagined about his principals.

Axel reflected on what he could bring to the partnership. First there were his contacts. Publicly, people in the region's gem trade knew he was a buyer of precious stones, mainly rough diamonds from Kasai in northern Congo and from North and South Kivu. They would know he paid competitive prices, honoured a handshake, and expected others to do so too. Axel was a bit old school like that, and he was happy if people knew it. He had built around himself a network of agents and shippers in the region who were more than averagely reliable. His network worked above and below the line – he numbered senior officers in the Army, Police and Customs authorities among his close connections, crucially on both sides of the Rwanda-Congo border.

Bad business experiences in Australia and Zambia among others had reminded him to stand his ground and occasionally to meet force with force. It wasn't his preferred way of doing business but from childhood he'd learned to confront bullies. As a twenty year-old, he'd had to look after himself in the copper mines of South Australia before he volunteered to serve in the Koninklijke Landmacht, the Royal Netherlands Army. Although he was identified as suitable for officer training Axel had grown bored with soldiering and left the army shortly after.

He was not a man who looked for violence but somehow in his line of work it found him. For sure, Axel could be ruthless when necessary, especially with people who crossed him; but violence was not his *modus operandi*. To him it was a business tool, neither welcomed nor avoided, just another way of ensuring that his interests were protected.

Over the years, Axel had become a man of influence in South Kivu and its capital, Bukavu. His charismatic public style and business largesse also enabled him to move easily across the border from his beautiful house in the Rwandan capital Kigali, to comfortable rented accommodation in the eastern Congo cities of Goma and Bukavu. Few men could claim such strong connections on both sides of the Rwandan border, and yet were still able to move unhindered in Kinshasa, a thousand kilometres to the west. The reason was simple; Axel made things happen. Although some people envied him, others in business and politics found him useful for his contacts with Rwandan generals, Congolese border officials, Lebanese diamond agents, Indian financiers, British shippers, and Saudi customers.

Nevertheless, Axel knew he was taking a big step. Even with his connections, he had never considered entering the coltan trade, not least because he didn't have a significant customer base that would make him a major player. He certainly hadn't planned to start a coltan supply chain from scratch – that was a young man's game – but when a business opportunity like this landed in his lap … well, he was never one to look a gift horse in the mouth.

Axel had paid little attention to Hendriks' glossy description of the coltan business, he was well aware of who would benefit, and who would not. There would be no increase in the prices paid to the miners themselves. When Axel thought about it at all, it was to acknowledge that he couldn't change the way the whole industry worked and nor would he waste his time trying. He was not a man who dwelt on issues that he could do nothing about – he was fully aware that the miners were being exploited but, short of becoming another warlord, what could he do about it? He hadn't listened to very much that his old man said, but he did remember him once saying 'Worry about the things you can change, and have the sense to recognise the things you can't'. It had been a rare meeting of minds for the pair of them.

Control of the scores of small mines worked by forced labour or cheap, artisan miners constantly shifted from one armed group to the next, and the fighters were getting rich on it. Axel was contemptuous of the way they all described themselves as 'rebels' – their leaders wanted nothing to change, this was not a political rebellion. They were getting rich from controlling the mines and it funded their arms purchases, which in turn enabled them to fend off rival groups fighting for control of the exports. The small scale, mine side traders would be lucky to see even a meagre benefit from any price rise but the armed factions holding the mines and comptoirs, the trading houses at the border, would benefit far more.

The comptoirs, literally counting houses, had long dealt with shadowy American and European companies. This had enabled unscrupulous coltan and tin buyers in the West to claim for years that they knew nothing of the exploitation of displaced villagers. Nor did they accept responsibility for the region's large number of orphans, some of whom were being forced to work in the mines with no pay and little food. The war had swept through other remote areas leaving people with no way of earning a living, forcing them to work in local mines and to sell the tin or coltan they had dug to middle men who sold it on to the comptoirs. Even worse, the miners were constantly at risk of having their coltan stolen by armed gangs before they could sell it.

Axel knew that some of the comptoirs were protected by corrupt officers in the Federal Army of the DRC, the FARDC. Headquartered in Mpama, officers of the 85th brigade of Congo's army roamed the region without effective command from Kinshasa. Ever since the notional end of the Second Congo war in 2003, a posting to North or South Kivu province had become a sinecure for army officers that was far more lucrative for them than staying in the capital, Kinshasa.

It was not that they turned a blind eye to illegal mining and mineral sales, senior army officers and members of the government were directly involved in the illicit trade. Everyone knew that FARDC officers controlled much of the illegal mining and trading. Brigades operated some mines, area commanders controlled the supply chain of *negociants* or small traders, and the FARDC supplied security and protection to other mines – for a fee.

Even that complicated picture, was further muddied by interference from the armies in neighbouring Rwanda, Burundi and Uganda. Congo was so administratively feeble, its civil service so corrupted that it could not pay its soldiers a regular wage, nor prevent its military, customs and border control officers overseeing the continued looting of the country's huge resources. Knowing that they and their soldiers were unlikely to be paid, the officers took what they could. The government in Kinshasa knew this too, so they wasted little effort on paying their wages.

This *realpolitik* was one of the factors that concerned Axel. The trade would need to be handled carefully in political terms; he would have to ensure the right connections and protection on the ground for himself and those working for him, something that was always dangerously unpredictable.

For his plans to work he would have to convince the comptoirs that he could broker a deal with long-term customers. And it would have to be based on more than price, otherwise CCV could end up in a bidding war with other foreign buyers of coltan like the Thais and Indians, which would just erode their price advantage and the very reason they had come to him in the first place. This was going to require a carrot and stick approach with the colonels who controlled the mines and miners, the police and customs officers who took their cut along the forest supply routes and managed the trucks and aircraft carrying the coltan out of the jungle, and the comptoirs buying their output. For that kind of palm-greasing and arm-twisting he would need to get out there soon, with a ready supply of dollars and finished diamonds in his pocket.

"How strong are your contacts in the east of the DRC, I mean outside Kinshasa's control?" Hendriks was asking.

It was a pointless question, like how long is a piece of string. Axel smiled to himself. They would not have flown him here if they doubted he could do business beyond the reach of Kinshasa's ministries. Axel bit back a rebuke, he needed to humour Hendriks for long enough to get the deal done. "They are good, and quantities like that would give me another bargaining chip."

"I must warn you, Mr Terberg, my clients are not accustomed to delay, and they believe it shows a lack of respect. We called you first because we believed you have the necessary people and connections already in place from your diamond and other interests. If we were wrong in this belief, you had better say so now."

Axel smiled. "You said it yourself; my people are there dealing in other commodities and it will take a short time to position people where we need them and to recruit any more skills that we require." He used the first person plural to encourage Hendriks to think of this as his own team. "There will be no delay, just a few necessary preparations in operations and security."

Hendriks relaxed visibly but it had given Axel a clue to the time pressures the man was under, pressures that would soon be passed on to him if there were supply problems.

"Mr Terberg, let us not divert ourselves into matters that are not relevant today. Can you help us with this project or not? I am sure there will be others who can assist us if you cannot."

Axel stifled a snort of derision; he knew how few people there were with his experience of the shifting sands of power among warring factions in North and South Kivu. Even fewer people had as many resources to call on as he did among mineral traders in the DRC's eastern provinces. His connections ranged from the Minister of Mines in Kinshasa, whom he had helped to promote, to several senior figures in the FARDC, the Congo's army. They even extended down the supply chain to the negotiators, comptoirs and international trading companies on both sides of the Rwanda-Congo border. Although he was closely identified in Rwanda with the despised Kinshasa government, Axel's business dealings along the border over the years had won him some powerful friends. His business was appreciated and his involvement in a deal carried some weight, whether he was dealing in diamonds, gold or now perhaps in coltan.

Eastern Congo was rich in so many rare minerals and gems that it was a magnet for anyone with even a passing interest in these trades, and while Axel preferred the refinement of trading precious gems, it was hard to resist the buzz of dealing in something new. Of course, there were some who had worked with the Rwanda-backed militias; but their control of the mines came and went as the war that had officially ended years earlier continued to flare up. Axel could think of no one who matched his degree of official influence in Kinshasa, the country's capital, fifteen hundred kilometres to the west, while benefiting from unofficial influence among the Congolese generals in the east.

"Well, I need to make a few calls of my own," said Terberg, "but I can certainly help you. I'll call you in the next few days after I've talked to my business partners in the area. I'll need you to send me a target price that you're prepared to pay, and some firm numbers on shipments and the dates you require them in Macao?"

"OK," Hendriks replied. "I will have these emailed to you tonight, but I suggest we keep our identities under wraps whenever possible. We should encrypt all messages to remove the risk of casual interception. Of course, more determined interception is still a risk, but at present no one outside these walls knows about our meeting."

"I've told no one," Terberg replied. Which was true, for now.

"Good, let's keep it that way, eh?"

The room was barely warm but Hendriks was still perspiring as he got to his feet awkwardly and with a grunt of exhaled breath. Axel rose with him.

"I appreciate your coming all the way to Barcelona, Mr Terberg. And I hope that we can do business to our mutual advantage." Joost Hendriks extended his hand. "We'll be in touch, and my colleague will show you out." Lorette must have been listening for she appeared at the half-open connecting door as Hendriks said this, but she didn't utter a word as she saw him into the lift across the hallway and the doors slid shut. He said nothing; he had plenty to think about.

Chapter 4
North Kivu Province, Democratic Republic of Congo (DRC)
Two Years Ago

The birds might be quieter now but the monkeys above were always at their busiest this late in the afternoon, and the forest inhabitants called and shrieked incessantly. The daily violence and tragedy of nature continued to unfold around and above them but the children paid no attention.

They had neither heard nor seen a single person all day and the expected smoke from cooking fires had been worryingly absent. Of course, that had its good side, if anyone had followed them the children had surely escaped by now; and there was now nothing to suggest that any soldiers were in the area. For a while last night they had heard intermittent gunfire after they had fled, sometimes single shots and sometimes long bursts that, from this distance, sounded like a shirt being ripped into rags. These sounds had long since ebbed away though, and the natural noises of the forest were consolingly familiar.

To begin with Keisha had held his hand tightly, and in truth it had been a comfort to Raphael to feel her presence. When holding hands became impossible because the path was only wide enough for one, he would take the lead with Keisha close behind him, keeping up a string of questions.

"Who were the soldiers, Raph? Were they Mai Mai?" she had wanted to know. To Keisha, all armed men were Mai Mai, the local Congolese militias originally created to fight off the regular incursions by Rwandan-backed gangs filtering across the border into Congo. Since then, everyone had watched as the Mai Mai leaders used their armies like all others, to make themselves rich and powerful. The violence and robbery they had used against their own people now made it impossible for them to go back to civilian life without risk of arrest or reprisal, even if they wanted to. This was the region's seemingly inescapable cycle of poverty and brutality, with killing piled on killing and theft on theft. The Mai Mai were divided into local factions – Baba had said they always did this as they took to cattle rustling and looting the villages of defeated rivals. Sometimes they just

58

demanded protection money from the villages they had set out to defend – either way the villagers suffered.

Raphael couldn't remember the names of all the groups. Most of the militias were known by their French names or just initials, groups like the Rally for Congolese Democracy and the Movement for the Liberation of Congo. Besides, the village elders laughed at them, saying the names were often changing anyway, as new leaders took the places of the old ones.

"I don't think they were Mai Mai, Keish. The Mai Mai speak the same as us, but I didn't understand these men. I think they were bandits from Rwanda or the FDLR." Even at 13 years old, Raphael was well-versed in the ethnic divisions that underpinned much of the fighting and political chaos, and he knew about the battles for control of gold, tin and coltan mines scattered throughout North and South Kivu. He had not been to school, his family could not afford the teaching and they needed his work in the fields. One thing he had learned long ago was that those with guns could get what they wanted, but it meant taking it from families and villages like his own, people who worked hard for their food.

When his father got together with his friends, they talked about it and sometimes wished aloud that their country did not have the gold and diamonds that people fought over. These brought only wars and fighting that continued long after ceasefires were talked of and political deals were signed in foreign countries. It seemed to him that so-called peace agreements were just stories made up by liars on the radio. Nobody believed that there would be peace, not even the grown-ups he spoke to in the village. The elders said that too many powerful people had too much to lose if they gave up their armies. This was how it had always been for his village and the whole province, with Tutsi tribesmen killing Hutus and Hutus killing Tutsis. No one knew how it had begun, and no one knew where or when it would end.

Certainly, Keisha was not interested in who they were, she had wanted the shooting, burning and shouting to stop. Now she just wanted to find Mama and the twins. Raphael knew from long experience looking after his younger brother and sisters that the only way to get them to change a subject was to give them something else to think about. "Can you see the sun?" he asked.

"Of course, I can," answered Keisha indignantly. "Well, the trees and clouds sometimes hide it," she conceded.

"Well, your job is to make sure that we take only paths that keep it on that side." Raphael knew perfectly well that the sun would move but they had to keep walking along jungle tracks, with only occasional glimpses despite the clearing cloud, and he needed something that would occupy her mind and help her feel in control.

"Right, let's go," he said with a certainty he did not feel.

"But where are we going? Where is Mama?" she persisted.

"We must go to another village and see if she has gone there or has left us a message." He was making this up as he went, but one thing was already clear to him; after what he had seen they could not stay where they were or even hide in their village, and the family had already fled ahead of them. But where had they gone? Where would Mama hide with two small children? Laurent and Christine could walk and run in the village, but the twins were too small to walk very far in the forest. He needed to find another village and ask a grown-up for help.

Raphael was still looking for the river, he did not want to go too high again and was searching for tracks or routes through less dense parts of the forest that kept them lower down. It had once led them into marshy ground where the water smelled bad, and although they were tired they had been forced to retreat and look for another way around. His father had taught him to gauge the position of the sun, seek out the routes the water took, and look for smoke from villages if they were lost. Of course, without smoke plumes to follow sometimes you just ended up in a marsh as they had now.

Several hours' later food and water were uppermost in the minds of the children. Raphael and Keisha had now been walking with little rest for the best part of a day. They had managed to sleep a little before dawn and later had sat quietly in the forest after they had discussed Baba's death. They had even drifted off for a while, but they were continually disturbed by insects buzzing around their mouths and eyes or landing irritatingly on their skin. Both had been bitten uncomfortably so that sleep had been impossible. Eventually thirst had driven them onwards once more; Keisha had cried so much so that she was now faint with hunger and dehydration. For her the plodding act of walking was now becoming too much.

Raphael could hear frogs close by, making a noise like a creaking door. There was the whirr of flying insects and from time to time something would fly into them which annoyed him but Keisha was now beyond noticing. Raphael was becoming more and more concerned that they should find water and enough to eat or else she would be unable to continue. He had no idea what to do if that happened. He encouraged her as much as he could but sometimes she did not respond and seemed unaware of his presence.

Whenever they stopped to get their breath, something that he tried to avoid now in case she was unable to restart, the silence would give way to the sound of small animals rustling through the leaves on the jungle floor. They had both jumped earlier when a sharp cry rang out close beside them; they could not identify the predator but it was only interested in an unseen, unfortunate prey.

Several times in the night the jungle had almost enveloped them but in his mind's eye Raphael was looking for a waterfall and a river that his father had spoken of. This had been a rough goal before but now their need to find a drink was so urgent that the river consumed his every thought. If their luck changed, they might even find a village where they could rest and ask for food.

Time passed and they walked on, their feet sore from the stones and rocks beneath them. He had long since taken over responsibility for carrying her blanket. The trees here were smaller and the forest more open than before. Around them, all that they could hear were occasional noises from the undergrowth that stretched unevenly away from the path. Drips of water fell onto nearby leaves, and once they were startled by the sound of a falling branch. A minute went by before it dawned on him; *that was it*, he thought. There was water from cloudforest condensation dripping onto leaves here and somewhere it must be collecting. He turned towards the sound and saw drops of water falling from high in the trees. They were striking the leaves close to the ground and making damp patches in the piles of debris and leaves on the ground. He looked around to see where it was going. Ten feet to his left there was a small rock buried in the wet ground. Raphael tried to dislodge it but it was stuck firmly in the clay. By scraping around it with the edge of a stone and using all the strength he could muster, he was able to dig it free. In the hollow it left behind, trickles began to create a bowl of water.

"Quick, Keisha. Here," he called. She was sitting listless and unmoving where he had left her not even watching him. So he cupped his hands and carried a little water to her. She drank it even though she looked asleep, and as she drank her eyes began to open wider. She looked at Raphael's hands as though they had wrought a miracle and turned her gaze to where he had found the water. He put an arm beneath hers and they moved across to the water bowl. They crouched down and drank from it in turns and slowly it was replenished allowing them to drink a little more.

A long-time of drinking and replenishing passed before Raphael became aware of how strongly the forest here smelt of decay. In his village the pervading smell was the soil, particularly when it rained or in the heat of mid-day. In the morning and evening this would be overlaid with the smell of charcoal and cooking fires. Now he could smell the freshness of the leaves, and the smell of damp wood and rotting fruit lying on the ground. There was something else. He could smell a cloying sweetness in the air. He turned around to study the area where they sat and then he caught it again, an unmistakable scent that reminded him of his childhood. In the clearing stood a custard apple bush and beneath it the yellow-orange fruit he had enjoyed as much as a small boy. He picked up two fruits and just pressed their skins to tear them apart. He gave one to Keisha who recognised it straight away. The custard-like fruit inside was creamy and sweet. To Raphael it seemed the best thing he had ever tasted, and there was more fruit on two bushes beyond. Some had been eaten by wasps or insects, but many were still unblemished. He could remember his mother collecting custard apples from bushes near the village and feeding them to the twins when they were being weaned onto solid food. Of course, she had had to remove the black seeds as they were doing now, but spitting them out was easy enough, although Keisha complained that she wasn't very good at spitting. Nonetheless, she ate several apples in quick succession but then her stomach began to hurt and she stopped.

He was relieved to see that Keisha continued to drink and he helped her wash her face and neck to revive her. Eventually they stood and he filled his pockets with fruit before turning back to the path. She may not have been thinking of it yet but although it was only mid-afternoon Raphael was hoping to find somewhere to sleep, for it now seemed unlikely they would reach a village by nightfall. With some food inside him and having drunk his fill the light-headed feeling had receded. His senses were alert again, sensitive to threats behind them or rescue and safety ahead. For now, there was no sign of either.

The path widened slightly as they walked, and once again it became clearer to discern. Raphael began to wonder if this meant they were near a village. So much had happened and it was all going round and round in his head. Was this really only last night? The sudden bursts of noise in the darkness outside their home, the burning thatch, the shock of seeing his elderly neighbour on fire, the disappearance of his family, and above all else what had happened to his kneeling, unprotected father.

He had never before seen his father being made to do anything he didn't want to. Then there was the image of Baba urging him to run, before the bullets hit him from behind. The last picture in his mind of this big man, this tireless worker, his smiling father who wrestled and tickled him when they played together, was of Baba lying face down, unmoving in the dark dirt. Raphael could feel the tears now running down his face again but he did not cry aloud. Keisha must not see him; they must get to a village and see if Mama was there.

Then it was clear why the path was wider, for he could see water and hear a stream. The animals must use this track on their way to drink. The sky was now darkening, and he felt suddenly overwhelmed with tiredness. Somewhere above him in the humid air a warbler began its call and soon it was answered by another.

Normally it was such a common sound that he would not have noticed its call, but tonight as his world was being turned upside down he was glad of its familiarity. Dependable elements of their journey like this, plus the continued responsibility of leading them to safety, occupied Raphael's mind so totally that for now he had no time to dwell on their loss and separation from the rest of the family. They just concentrated on putting one foot in front of the other.

As they approached the water, he could see that it was not a stream but a river and much, much wider than it had first appeared through the trees. Was this the river his father had spoken of? Was there a waterfall here? He wondered if the river might lead them soon to a village. If not, they would have to find somewhere to shelter for the night as it was starting to rain and they needed to keep dry because he couldn't make a fire. He just hoped that daylight would show them a village or help them to find someone who had news of Mama.

The path went straight to the water's edge. For a moment the pair stood silent and still beside the river, watching the light fading quickly and listening intently for sounds of human activity. There were none, and Keisha shifted irritably, feeling cooler now that she had stopped walking. "Where can we stay? Is there a village?" she asked.

He was about to reply when they both spotted a dark pattern on the riverbank just a few yards ahead of them. It seemed to undulate and Raphael put a hand on her arm to stop Keisha moving. It was alive but even in the failing light he could see that it was not the snake he had feared. A thick stream of ants was moving out of the long forest shadows and down to the water's edge. "Be careful, Keisha!"

The driver ants were not dangerous as long as you were able to move out of their way. They could only cover twenty meters in an hour but their marches were relentless when they left the nest in search of food. The soldier class within the nest were bigger, with massive heads and could occasionally sting, but Mama said that they usually relied on hundreds of powerful bites. There were horrible stories told by the older children in his village of sick people and tethered animals, unable to get out of their way, being suffocated by ants and their bodies stripped to the bone. Raphael had never been sure if this was true and none of the grown-ups had seen it, but he preferred to keep a respectful distance just in case.

The children stood still, and they did not disturb a hidden bristle bill calling its song. Then the bird flew into their view, hopping and dancing just ahead of the advancing column of ants, catching any insects that moved to escape the oncoming army. Then the bird sensed their presence and vanished as quickly as it had arrived. But Raphael had now noticed the ants' prey. In the shallow water at the river's edge the carcass of a mature Sykes' monkey had been washed up, or at least part of it had. Its lower half was missing altogether. The top half of its grey body lay face down on the mud, its startlingly white collar and chest markings smeared with brown silt. A few ants had already reached it and the main column continued to wind its way down the bank to feed.

"Why are you staring at the monkey?" asked Keisha. "I want a drink and something to eat," she pleaded. "I want to find Mama."

Raphael was looking at the monkey, but the mental image he was seeing was his father. The boy was now tired beyond anything he had ever known; he was chilled from walking half the night and throughout the day. The fruit they had eaten had been welcome but they were still hungry and thirsty. Above all, he had witnessed his father's murder just a few hours before. Suddenly he found himself bent over, one knee on the ground and retching from the lowest reaches of his stomach. The custard apples came back as he vomited repeatedly, until there was nothing left to retch. Bile came into his mouth and he spat on the ground to clear it.

Keisha was scared. She had been relying on her big brother's strength and now he was sick. She placed one hand on Raphael's back and crouched beside him to comfort him as she had seen their mother do when one of them was sick at home. "It's OK, Raph," she soothed. "Do you feel better?"

It seemed so strange to Raphael to hear the kind words that their mother used with him in the past being uttered by his ten year-old sister. The incongruity of the moment brought him to his senses, and he knew he could not weaken now.

"Fine," he managed. "I'm fine. We can't drink here," and he pointed to the monkey's carcass. "We'll go upstream a little to get clean water, somewhere away from, from that … and then we'll see if there's a village or somewhere we can cross."

They stood together and, holding hands in a way that they had now done more in one night than they had for years, they stepped onto a log and jumped easily across the ant trail. Neither of them looked back at the monkey as they followed the riverbank around the bend to a flat rock at the water's edge. Here they were able to drink and wash their hands and faces, just as they had been taught to do every evening at home.

It seemed to Raphael that there must be a village nearby otherwise there would be no track, but he couldn't see any footprints. Maybe the rain had washed them away. This was too clear a path to have been made by animals, anyway they would not follow the riverbank in search of a drink.

As the darkness descended, they huddled together on the river's sandy edge under the exposed roots of a tree, wrapped in the shared blanket, hungry, scared and lost. They talked to one another of the food they would most like to have or what they would tell Mama they had seen and done when they found her.

The moon was already visible above the treetops for the second time since they had run away. Muddy river water kept their thirst at bay, but they needed warmth, food and rest. Keisha's complaints about the growing darkness, their loneliness, and her hunger finally gave way to silence. When Raphael next looked at her, he was amazed to see she was already asleep, curled up in a little ball. He prayed that the forest spirits wouldn't take them away then tucked himself into the small blanket beside her before succumbing to exhaustion.

******

Breakfast had been the last of their custard apples washed down with water from the river. As they set off, Raphael tried to deflect any questions about where they were going. "Let's whistle," he said.

"You know I hate whistling," said Keisha. He didn't, and he suspected that what this really meant was that she didn't know how.

"OK, I'll whistle," he said and began to make up a tune in his head. It owed a little bit to one of his grandfather's favourite songs, songs they had listened to as

64

babies and that they had joined in with as they grew older but Raphael, as was his skill, added his own flourishes to the rhythm.

"You're not doing it right," said Keisha irritably after a while. "You always change things."

It might seem weak to stop now, so Raphael continued for another minute or two singing softly to himself to show that when he stopped it would be his own idea. And then they both heard it.

A steady thrumming that wasn't coming from Raphael. They stopped walking and strained to identify the sound.

"I think its water, it might be the waterfall," said Raphael and they began to run. As the next curl of the river unfolded before them, the noise went from distant hum to intense drumming with nothing in between. Now they could see that rapids stretched the full width of the river, for more than a hundred paces. From bank to bank there were rocks spread out above and below a waterfall that stood higher than a house. The rocks were of all sizes, some only as big as a man if he curled into a ball, some as big as a truck, and others were as tall as their home. The distances between them varied just as much. Some were a simple step, others looked much bigger. Choked by the tumbled rock, the river raced through the constriction with far greater force than normal before returning to the sluggish state they had first encountered downstream. It looked as though the path they were on ran directly to the nearest rocks while another smaller path came down to join it from the forest to the right.

"We can use it to cross the river," said Raphael. "If we step from rock to rock, we can get across."

"I don't want to," said Keisha.

Raphael looks at her in confusion. "What do you mean, you don't want to?" he asked.

"I don't want to. I want to cross another way. This is boring," she said enigmatically.

"What do you mean 'boring'? There is no other way. You've walked along the river with me, you've seen that."

"Then I want to stay here," Keisha said folding her arms.

Raphael recognised the signs. "You're scared, aren't you?"

"No. I just don't want to cross here," but her face told a different story.

Raphael knew that winning the argument was less important than getting her to accept the idea, otherwise they would be stuck here. "Listen," he said, "this is a proper path. There must be a village near here and I bet the boys and girls from the village walk across these rocks all the time. We can't stay here; Keisha or the soldiers might get us."

Keisha cast an involuntary glance over her shoulder along the way they had come, but there was nothing to see. She said nothing.

He sensed she was wavering. "Tell you what; we can hold hands all the way across if you like. And then we can look for something to eat."

Fear is a powerful motivator when you're ten, but hunger is also a force to be reckoned with, and now that they had spent a day and two nights in the open and on the move it was hunger that won. She said nothing but Keisha slipped her hand back into his and allowed herself to be drawn toward the water's edge. Raphael did not let her pause there in case she lost her nerve. He stepped straight onto the first rock which had a flat top and room enough for them to stand side by side. Her grip tightened in his but he kept her moving as they worked their way higher and higher towards the tallest rock near the middle of the river. Keisha clung more forcibly to his hand or to the back of his shirt and patiently, one rock at a time, he coaxed her upwards and out into the middle of the river until looking back they could see around the bend from where they'd come.

Until now Raphael sensed that she had been fearful of falling into the river. They could both swim but Keisha lacked confidence in the water, whereas he felt quite at home after years playing with the other boys in pools near the village. Now he realised he had made a mistake. If he had stuck to a lower route across the maze of rocks, it might have been different but from here there was a dizzying view of the rocks and the rapid water pushing, barging and surging its way through the narrow gaps below.

"I can't do it," she said. She was gazing at the water twisting and turning twenty feet below them through a darkened gap between the highest boulder and a sloping shelf of rock beside it. If they could make it onto the shelf, they would be able to get down close to the river level on the other side where it would be less intimidating and further away from the fastest water race.

Raphael tried to reassure her. "Yes, you can make it. You've been over bigger gaps already."

"It's not the same—" she began but he interrupted her.

"Come on, we'll do it together." And he walked her back a couple of yards to give them a run up. "Ready?" he asked.

Keisha didn't reply and Raphael understood that this was a big jump for someone so much smaller than him. But having crossed so much of the river they were committed now. "Are you ready?" he said again.

He saw her lips move, but if she said anything it was so quiet that he couldn't hear it over the rushing water below. He tugged her hand and with Keisha grimacing they ran the few steps together to hurdle the gap.

Strangely, it was Keisha who cleared the distance with the greatest ease. Like Raphael she was a fast runner and her spring carried her over the divide with at least a foot-length to spare. Raphael was not so lucky. Whether it was in his effort to hold onto her hand in case she didn't make it, or whether it was a slight stumble on the uneven rock just as he jumped, afterwards he couldn't be sure. In any event, his left foot landed on a sloping surface of small loose rocks, his right hand lost the grip on Keisha and his body twisted sideways from the uneven landing. He did not have time to protect his head which struck the rock face hard just above his left ear, leaving him dimly aware of the impossibility of grabbing anything to stop his fall. As he slid backwards through the gap, he could hear Keisha's scream recede and he had a twirling view of dark rock, blue sky, more dark rock and then the slap impact as his back hit the cold, deep river and he was pulled under by the torrent of brown frothy water.

******

The first thing he heard was sobbing, then Raphael felt some very strong fingers squeezing his jaw and someone kissing him on the lips. Then he turned his head sideways and was watery sick. All over the kisser. Which served him right really, because it was a man and he smelled disgusting.

Someone cheered, which seemed a strange thing to do in the circumstances and then the brightest sunlight he'd ever seen made him screw his eyes tight shut until it was obscured by a face very close to his. "You OK?" said a man's voice that he didn't recognise. But Raphael's mind was too busy to frame a reply. And his head hurt. No, his head really hurt – even the sunlight made it hurt. He thought he might be sick again, but the dizziness seemed to come and go, and then everything went spinny and grey and he passed out.

He had no idea how much later it was when he came around but there was a lot of excited chatter above him and he realised he was lying on his back on a river bank. "He'll live, but that bruise on his head is going to make him puke for days. You'd better wrap him up and stick him in the back."

Raphael could hear a car engine revving too fast, and there were more shouts and bangs as doors were opened and slammed. He hoped they'd stop doing that soon whoever they were. Judging by the voices the same someone was taking charge, but he seemed to go away. Raphael only realised that he hadn't moved when Keisha's face swung into view upside down. Just thinking about it made his head hurt more. She was wiping her tears away but still crying and she picked up his hand which was resting on his chest.

Raphael did a mental check around his body. He could feel his hands and feet and could certainly see and hear, but speaking was not his top priority right now – even the thought of it made him nauseous. Everything seemed to be there so he tried sitting up, which turned out to be a huge mistake. The world rocked violently, there was a sudden rushing sound in his ears and everything he looked at went yellowy-green, even the sky. He tried to be sick again but there was nothing left in his stomach, so the retching hurt even more.

He waited for the river and the rocks to stop sliding left and right in his vision, and then he heard Keisha explaining to someone out of sight that he had fallen down a hole in the waterfall. He wasn't sure that was exactly right, but now that she said it he remembered the backwards tumbling sensation as he disappeared through the gap between the rocks and he recalled the heavy impact as he hit the water. The rest was blank after that until he heard her sobbing, and he would prefer not to remember the next bit.

Raphael put his right hand flat on the ground and tried to stand up but everything wobbled again and the view from inside his head went all fuzzy so he dropped that idea. He sat still for a while longer with Keisha chattering to him, paying little attention to what she said. His input didn't seem to be needed in this conversation, which was just as well. He couldn't stand up and he didn't want to lie on the sand any longer, so there he was propped up on one arm.

He would have been there a lot longer if the driver of the pick-up truck hadn't started revving his engine. Men were climbing into the back of a red four-wheel-drive Toyota, similar to the one he'd ridden in to Bukavu. With his Dad. And instantly he remembered that his dad was dead, and he almost fell back, his head dropped and he felt utterly alone again. Alone and responsible, even among all those busying people. Then strong arms went under his legs and back and he was lifted onto a hard-looking pile of canvas that lay on the bed of the pick-up. There were things underneath the tarpaulin but they weren't so hard and the bed that they had made for him was more comfortable than it looked. Either that or he was too exhausted to care. Keisha was lifted in beside him and the tailgate slammed shut with a bang that made his head hurt again.

"Get some rest. We'll wake you when we get close to the mine," said the Kisser enigmatically. Raphael lay still and watched Keisha to begin with, then despite the bouncing movements along the road he fell asleep before they'd covered a kilometre.

He woke once when it began to rain on his upturned face. But someone pulled the tarpaulin over him and around Keisha and he went to sleep again, but it was a fractured rest in which he swam underwater beside a monkey that appeared to have no legs.

******

When next he woke, the pick-up engine and the rain had stopped but the shouting was back again. His head felt little better and Raphael's legs were desperately weak. He still had no idea what had happened to him after that or who these men were. Keisha just called them 'the men' and didn't seem to know who they were either. Neither of the children understood where they had been taken and

68

no one offered to explain, but there was a buzz of activity around the back of the truck where backpacks were being filled with enormous loads.

The dirt road along which they had driven was bordered by high grasses and the land was flatter here so that no hills could be seen from where he lay in the pick-up bed. The men were all old, in their twenties or thirties and unarmed. So, they weren't militiamen – he was relieved at that. Everyone was too busy to pay much attention to Raphael or Keisha but one of them kept smiling at the children and saying something to them in a language they didn't understand. No one else replied so Raphael figured that the comments were intended for them.

Food and other essentials were being bagged and strapped to eight or nine lightweight metal or bamboo frames. From each frame hung two slings for the men to put their arms through and there was also a large loop at the top surmounted in each case by extensive foam padding. The children had never seen backpacks this big before but when they saw the amount that was to be carried the need for their size was obvious. More and more bags of rice were being added, along with cooking oil, salt, sugar, dried foods, pots, pans, torch batteries, even rubber boots. And there was constant but good-natured banter among the men that seemed to be about unequal distribution of their loads.

The porter who kept grinning at the children, was pointing at his handiwork. He had taken a white plastic chair from the bed of the pick-up and lashed it to the back of his frame while some of the provisions he'd been due to carry were being re-allocated to other grumbling porters. Their loads looked impossibly large and heavy, in most cases they must have weighed over fifty kilograms, probably even more than Raphael weighed.

As the children watched, the first of the loads was lifted upright. A slender, wiry porter who looked the oldest of them squatted in front of it and slipped his hands through the shoulder straps. Then he pulled forward the head strap until his forehead took a share of the load and made as if to stand. The sinews in his neck bulged, the load was so heavy and so precariously balanced that he staggered for a couple of paces until his legs were properly braced beneath it. Then with a wave and a shout to his colleagues he set off along a scarcely visible path and into the tall, grassy undergrowth which quickly swallowed him from view. Within seconds another two porters had lifted their equally heavy burdens and followed him out of sight.

The man who had rescued Raphael and resuscitated him banged his hand on the tailgate for their attention and the children's gaze swung back to him. He was not given to smiling as much, but what he said was clear enough and in their dialect. "You cannot stay here, and we could not leave you at the river because the villages are all empty, burned, gone. Phut!" he gestured airily as though the occupants had vanished like spirits. "You will have to walk some more," he said nodding to Keisha, "at least until your brother is strong enough. For now, he will ride on the back," and he jerked his head to indicate Smiley's backpack frame which had now been turned into a chair borne litter.

Raphael was about to argue that this was not necessary when the man added, "We have been watching you and you will need more time to recover. You can get medicine at the mine if you have money. It's only a day from here. If she gets too tired to walk," he said, pointing to Keisha, "you can give her your chair for a while." They looked at one another in silence for a moment. "OK?" he asked.

Embarrassed at this attention, Raphael was about to protest that he was strong enough when the man forestalled his objection. He pointed to Smiley, "He is pleased, last week he had to carry a pregnant woman back to here." He laughed, "She weighed more than he did."

It was Keisha who broke the quiet first. "Thank you," was all she said. The man coughed and thought better of whatever he had been about to say.

"Where are we? Where is this mine?" Raphael asked. "We really need to find our mother, she will be worried about us."

The man's attitude was awkward now. "You're two hours' drive north of where we found you. I'm sorry but I don't know where your mother is, many people are on the move again. There is more fighting at the moment – who knows when it will end? We could not stay there and nor could you. This is as far as the road goes so we must walk to the mine and you can decide what to do next when you get there. Now come here," he held out a rough hand to Keisha. She hesitated, but when he held out both hands it was obvious that he was simply offering to lift her down from the bed of the pick-up.

Then, with the porter resting the plastic chair against the back of the truck, Raphael was lifted and guided into the seat. There was a strap running across the top of the backpack frame and when he sat back he was able to rest his head on this. The chair was comfortable and he had an unusual upward view of everything they passed, the birds above the grasslands, the heavy clouds as they crossed some open scrubland and then, as they climbed the first low hills, the first signs of the dense forest canopy closing in. *It looked a bit like home*, he thought, *as the rocking motion jogged him to sleep again.*

Chapter 5
London, UK
Six Months Ago

James was calling from his apartment. "Have you got a spare bed, Bro? I'm coming back."

"That's great. How long for?" asked Neil.

"For good."

"Blimey, that's a bit sudden. What's up? I thought you were all set out there."

"I'm fine, I'll tell you about it when I see you, but I need a place to crash till I can sort myself out. Is that OK?"

"Sure, just text me when you're arriving," said Neil. "The spare room's yours and there's a key in the usual place. You got any plans? What comes next?"

"Yes and no. That's one of the things I want to talk to you about."

"Sounds like there's a woman involved, kiddo. You got the Sopranos after you?" Neil chuckled. His understanding of James's life stateside had always been shaped by his TV viewing.

"Not quite. I'll tell you over a pint, but I've been doing some thinking about what's been going on and where I'm headed."

"Sounds a bit heavy for me, anyway email your flight details and I'll try to be in. Gotta rush there's billionaires to skin. See you," and Neil was gone, back into the world of investment portfolios for high net worth individuals.

Even three days later with his belongings in long term storage and the apartment left in the hands of a letting agency, James sat at the airport and realised he had absolutely no idea what should come next. And the surprising part was that it felt good. He could be a bit impetuous at times but walking out of the firm had seemed the obvious thing to do, and, in hindsight it still felt right. Screw them. If they couldn't see what they had in him, then it was their loss, not his.

Later, as he boarded the plane he was in a less punchy frame of mind. It was all very well this sense of righteous indignation, but it wouldn't pay the rent. He was lucky he could crash at Neil's, but that couldn't last forever. They got on well, but that was probably because they had lived apart ever since they were adults, they were too different for it to work well long-term. Besides, Neil had a bachelor life to lead. He was making good money in the City, many of his friends were in London, too, and he seemed to be mining a rich vein of attractive women, none of whom lasted very long – or maybe they just saw through him. The last thing he'd need would be his kid brother leaving his socks in the bathroom or otherwise cramping his lifestyle. They were friends so he'd put up with it for a while, but to stay on good terms, James would need to find a place of his own. That meant finding a job. He could go back into PR, he had the contacts, but he was hacked off with that life and felt in need of a complete change; the question was 'what?'

The agents in Boston seemed to think that sub-letting the apartment would be no problem, leaving James with enough in the bank to live off for six months or more. By then he'd need a new job. He hadn't touched the inheritance he'd received when his father died a few years ago, but he'd sooner save that in case it was really needed some day.

None of which gave him any answers about his next steps. He guessed he would make the obligatory duty call, offering to visit his mother when he got back, and she would politely decline. Afterwards, they would both heave a sigh of relief, knowing it would be months before anyone felt the need to repeat the call. Neil had given up calling her altogether, but James still made the occasional effort.

Their father's premature death at the age of sixty-five had robbed the boys of the one constant figure in their lives. He was more mature and worldly wise than their mother. In Yvette he had married a beautiful, self-obsessed actress who had not been particularly famous, although that wasn't how she portrayed it. She had achieved some success as a leading lady in provincial repertory theatre before making the transition to a couple of unremarkable appearances in London's West End. With the miles on the clock beginning to show for a romantic lead, their father had fallen for her elegance and saved her from further critical oversight. He whisked her away to a life of financial security, genteel boredom and prolonged domesticity in Sussex, for which she was manifestly ill-equipped. Ultimately, the sadness was not hers but that of a decent man who loved her too well to curb her selfishness.

Their parents had been unable to have children – such medical twists in life were common and still poorly understood. Above all, they were seldom discussed. There was no shortage of children for adoption, however, and at John's persistent urging the boys – though two years apart in age – were adopted simultaneously from different families. Until now James had not stopped to consider why they were adopted at the same time; perhaps John Falkus had sensed this was a battle with his wife that he could only win once. At any rate, once ample nursery support for Yvette was in place, the boys were adopted. Overnight the family grew from one-plus-one to four. Of course, the boys could remember nothing else. For them this was their nucleus, their globe, and a happy one at that.

With maternal care for the children supplied by nannies, and Yvette frequently staying in London, John threw his energies into life with the boys as well as his career as a stockbroker. He was able to provide her with the liquidity she expected. For her part Yvette danced her way gracefully through a succession of lovers in London, each more shallow than the last, with little thought for the injury inflicted on her diligent husband. From an early stage he opted to turn a blind eye to her other life, although he did manage to control her more reckless spending.

John doted on the boys and they never lacked affection or encouragement. As they reached the age of eight, nannies gave way to boarding school and by the time they emerged from public school at eighteen they understood the limits of their mother's love for them and their father. What he gained from the relationship apart from the occasional glamour of having her on his arm, kept conversations alive at many Sussex dining tables.

Yvette knew how to hold the attention of a room, the men with envy, and the women with loathing. She could enliven any party and took martinis, lit cigarettes and compliments as her due. She always had the energy to play till dawn, long after their father had called it a day. In short, Yvette had married into an old Sussex family that conferred on her respectability, security, and some social standing. These she accepted willingly, even as she sidestepped the attendant obligations of wife and mother.

In stark contrast, the affection that the boys felt for their father, John Falkus was total. Himself a boy at heart, John was at his happiest playing cricket with them in the garden or taking them to Lords to watch England. He could lose an entire weekend helping them to glue and paint models of old sailing ships and still wonder where the time had gone. As they grew older, the three of them would take their battered model ships, planes and tanks into the garden and shoot them with an air rifle until there was nothing left but plastic shards, tangled rigging and three hearty appetites.

Although a well-respected broker in London, James suspected that his father's life really began each time he got off the train and was back in the country with his boys and his spaniels. In another age he might have spent his life outdoors as a gentleman farmer or a man of the cloth but, with his family's fortunes in crisis as he reached maturity, John had found himself commuting daily to London. So it was no surprise that Neil had followed so adroitly into the City when the time came, the conditioning was all there even if the genes were not.

James watched the cabin crew going about their duties after take-off and ignored the book he'd bought in the airport as he considered his own life. He knew he was immensely lucky. His mother's deficiencies had been amply compensated by his father's affection. There was no favouritism, he applauded their individual and shared triumphs, and came down hard on any failings in manners or duty. One of the last in Britain to do his National Service in the army, John used to say that it had taught him to peel potatoes and whitewash anything that couldn't be saluted. Neil and James used to catch one another's glance whenever an army story emerged and, rolling their eyes to the heavens, would vie to deliver the punch line before their father.

John Falkus was never a man to show regrets and he was a stoic to the end when he suffered for eighteen months with Motor Neurone Disease, a debilitating muscle-wasting condition with no known cure. For a while he had managed to hide it from everyone, but eventually his difficulty in holding cutlery and a pen became apparent. The diagnosis, when it came, was brutally blunt. He had no more than twelve months to live and there was no telling what muscle groups would deteriorate the quickest. He knew he might lose the power of speech or his mobility. In the end it was his arm and chest muscles that failed him first. It became impossible for him to perform even the most basic tasks to care for himself and he required around-the-clock supervision and regular nursing.

To everyone's amazement, Yvette had risen to the occasion, showing him a level of care and concern so notably absent for all the years before. Ever the more cynical of the boys, Neil insisted that she had simply found a new part to act, and one that this time could be relieved would have a limited run while still winning her applause.

In the end the old man's troubled breathing, and the pain and difficulty of swallowing had been more than any of them could bear to see. He didn't complain, but allowed himself a black sense of humour that made light of difficult situations. "At least no one's going to make me eat all those bloody grapes you keep bringing," he'd said.

During his last three months he could no longer speak at all. It had been agony for them to watch the frustration in his eyes as this quick-witted man was unable to share a quip or a joke. He couldn't write down his thoughts, he couldn't speak or even mime, and from this moment onwards the boys had simply wanted it to end for him. The nurses had warned his sons beforehand that pneumonia was the most likely outcome, but, curiously, they referred to it as 'the old man's friend' for it carried away many who would otherwise suffer a protracted end. James was shocked when he first heard this description, but long before his father succumbed he began guiltily to wish that it would come and end his suffering.

It was a perverse source of pride to Neil and James that the old boy as they referred to him long outlasted the doctors' initial prognosis. He finally succumbed one night to pneumonia, dying quietly in a hospice, without them and without drama. John and the boys had had time to say their goodbyes; there were few tears left in them now. When the call came in the night from the ward sister, James and Neil had hugged one another hard for a while and in that moment a bond of mutual reliance had been forged between them. From now on that assurance, that dependability was unspoken; there was no need for words, in fact mere words would cheapen what they felt. They both knew that.

James sat in the half-dark of the aircraft cabin and blinked. He hadn't realised until now that he was crying. He was silent but huge warm tears were slipping down the side of his face and he rubbed them away before anyone else should notice. Some of the passengers around him were absorbed in their movies while others were falling asleep amid the aircraft's roar. James was relieved that no one had seen his emotion; his face was now cold and the drying tears tickled his skin. He realised once again how much he missed his father's dry wit and solid advice. This unspectacular man had created in both his boys a depth of respect that James hoped one day he could emulate. There had been few heroics in John's life, just a sure-footed, daily effort as a parent that spoke of love far more than duty.

It made James feel once again how lucky he and Neil were to have been adopted into this family. It had also helped to cement their own relationship, of course. James kept returning to this. He certainly wasn't looking for more from his brother, but somehow he felt that there had to be more in his life than Neil, his disinterested mother, the loss of his father and then Lisa. Perhaps he was only thinking like this because he'd quit his job, but the poverty of his remaining relationships seemed to define him at the moment. He couldn't help wondering how it would have felt if his mother had ever showed an interest in her sons. Slightly weird, was the first thought that came to mind.

OK, she wasn't a good example. He was struggling to frame this thought. What if Yvette had been his birth mother? Would she have loved him better? He had often thought about his birth mother in the past, wondering who she was and what she was like. Was she even still alive, and if so, where was she now? She could even be on this plane and he'd never know. It was a strange feeling knowing that there was this vital someone out there and that in some ways you could be just like them. Maybe he had similar interests or skills. He'd tried to discuss it once with Neil, but the conversation had been unusually awkward and Neil had changed the subject. James had no idea why. All he could think was that for some people it opened up questions so profound that they needed to come to them in their own time, if they ever came to them at all.

He hadn't discussed his adoption much with his father either. He could clearly remember Dad telling him when he was eight or nine years old that he was adopted, and immediately he'd wanted to talk about it with Neil only to find that he wasn't interested at all. It wasn't just that Neil wasn't interested, it was more than that; he was angry that James had even broached the subject. James certainly couldn't discuss that kind of thing with his mother, so it soon became a family taboo, everyone knew but no one discussed it. Of course, it didn't stop him being curious and he had hoped that the passage of time would make it easier to raise it with his father; but if anything it seemed worse. James could see that it pained his

Dad to describe someone else as their mother or father. He had simply called her James's 'birth mother' and had passed on a few snippets of information that adoptive parents were given in Britain in those days. James knew that the name given to him by his natural mother was David, and his father said that he had been born in South London and adopted at three months old. But, when pressed for more details, he seemed unsure if it was James or Neil that had been born there. And that was where the discussion had ended.

It was strange that this should occur to him now. James hadn't even thought about the conversation with his Dad for years, but now it seemed much more important. He wondered if this was because his father was no longer there. It seemed disloyal that he should even be thinking about someone else as his parent, but he had never pursued it at the time so he guessed no harm had been done. His mother wasn't really a consideration, so he could try to find out a little bit more if he wanted. Or at least, he could make some enquiries about what information there might be. He didn't know even how you went about the process of finding your birth parents, but he knew from the careful way that Dad's papers were always organised that there must be some information in there. There must be a central body in Britain – maybe in London – that held information like his birth certificate; that would be a logical starting point.

It was the red wine with his meal or perhaps the emotional exhaustion of the last few days; for whatever reason, James slept better than expected during the rest of the journey back to London. He awoke bleary-eyed when they brought up the cabin lights and the cabin crew circulated with hot face towels.

******

London in a snowy winter was usually one of James's favourite sights. But the snow was three days old and had turned to dark grey slush. London was now just cold and wet. Miserably, consistently, February wet. The collective mood in the capital reflected the outside temperature and long faces seemed to be the fashion as people bustled on their journeys with heads bowed against the weather. Almost as soon as James had arrived at Neil's apartment his brother had announced he was off skiing, taking some clients to the company's chalet. One client, Kara, called him frequently out of hours – how much work was being done was anyone's guess.

James now had time on his hands for job hunting, interviews with recruitment consultants, catching up with old friends from his London days, and trying not to re-visit the places he'd shown to Lisa which was just too painful.

He really had no idea what kind of work he should be considering. Logic suggested that he use his PR skills and experience, but he was finding it hard to motivate himself. In the back of his mind was the thought that he should have been coming back to London in triumph as the newly appointed European head of a leading US public relations consultancy. The truth was harder to describe, and he would prefer to avoid too many awkward questions about his sudden return. In truth, part of him was beginning to regret his spontaneous walkout. It wasn't like him to quit anything and he still wondered if he'd acted rashly. He would never have done that if Lisa was around. Sure, he might have left but only after they had weighed up the options together.

He needed to start thinking analytically like that again, to be a bit more strategic in planning his next career steps – except he hadn't a clue which way to go.

Instead of job hunting he'd spent some time finding out about the General Register Office and their Adoption Contact Register. He hadn't told Neil about this and he wasn't sure at what stage he would. There were numerous hoops to jump through first so he had time to decide. There might be nothing much to discuss anyway.

With his brother away, James settled at Neil's computer and searched online for the General Records Office. There was a site dedicated to birth, marriage and death certificates, and 'Adoption records' was one of the menu options. He was entitled to apply for a certificate of his original birth registration form, and his 'birth relatives' as they were described had the right to apply for permission to contact him as he was over eighteen.

James downloaded a form from the UK Government's Identity & Passport Service to apply for access to his birth records. As a person adopted after 1975, he selected the option to see an adoption adviser. He or she would explain the procedures to him and, just as importantly, counsel him on the range of possible responses that he might encounter from his birth parents.

James had already given some thought to who to search for first, as he assumed that his natural parents were not together. It seemed more likely that they had separated – although he knew there were many reasons why he might have been put up for adoption, besides being born to a single parent in the 1980s. Then it occurred to him that his birth father might not even know of his existence. Then again, he could be the kind of shit that just walked out on a pregnant girlfriend or wife. James didn't like to think that neither of them had wanted him, but he knew it was a possibility. In fact, the number of possible explanations for his adoption was so vast that it was hard to keep his mind focused on the first steps, and sometimes it literally made his head ache.

Would his natural parents want him to contact them or would he simply learn that they had never wanted to know him? Were either of them waiting for his call or would it cause them embarrassment, even distress? What if his birth mother had never told her husband or partner that she had had a child adopted? What kind of trouble might it cause for her and for her family?

No, this was none of Neil's business, thought James. The boys didn't even share birth parents, so this was his decision to make and his alone. Maybe nothing would come of it, maybe he wouldn't be able to find her – he vaguely remembered reading once that finding a father's details was very unlikely – but at least he had to try. Without some information on who his family were and where they came from he would always feel …, he searched for the right word, incomplete, that was it. He wanted a history, he wanted to know where his ancestors came from, who they were and what they did. Above all, he wanted to know why he had been put up for adoption. Hadn't his mother wanted him? Was she too young, or couldn't she afford to keep him?

Neil had kept a whole filing drawer filled with their father's papers, photos and other odds and ends, although judging from the dust on it he hadn't opened it in a long time. Just as he would have expected of his father, James found a folder inside that must have been there all along when they cleared out John's house, although James couldn't recall seeing it before. The folder contained a letter from an adoption agency confirming James's placement with the Falkus family. It confirmed his date of birth, his original forename, David, and even gave his place of birth as Clapham in south London, but that was it.

He was originally called David. Thinking about it with hindsight, there had been a history of James's in the Falkus family so he might have guessed. He kept hold of this file as it was solely about him, but he was suddenly aware that most of the drawer's contents were Neil's. This would be intensely personal for him, so he closed the drawer and settled down to re-read more carefully the meagre details of his own adoption.

Frustratingly, at the end of it he had learned nothing new of any significance. So, what was the next step?

At least James was able to complete the form. He gave the surname of his adoptive family, Falkus and his first names, James Peter. There then followed his birth date and country of birth, plus the date of adoption. He ticked the box to say he wanted to see an adoption advisor at his local authority in London. The form seemed simple enough, he had half-expected to have pages of information to fill in.

The form went into the mail that afternoon and James lay awake for hours that night wondering what he had started. Each of his birth parents had had ten years since he reached eighteen in which they could have applied for permission to contact him. And clearly they hadn't done so. What the hell did that mean? Nothing good that he could think of before he finally fell asleep.

Over the next few days James went back to his round of recruitment agency interviews, cycling and running to get fit, as well as seeing old friends. Neil returned from skiing on the Saturday, with a tan but without Kara who had wanted more of his time and less of his investment expertise. "I had to try and keep the whole party happy, and she couldn't hack that," he said that night as James made them both spaghetti Bolognese. "I needed to spread myself around more evenly," he added "so she took off." James sensed a degree of self-justification going on – as far as he could tell Neil had done little else but spread himself around London's available females for the last few years, but he said nothing and the conversation turned to snow conditions and the nightlife.

"So, how have you been, Bro?" asked Neil eventually. "Got anywhere on the jobs front yet?"

"I'm OK," said James. His words were neutral but his tone was downbeat. "Nothing much to report on jobs, but I'm combing through the ads and my name's now on the books at several recruitment consultancies. Hope to be out of your hair before too long." James didn't want to be in Neil's way any longer than necessary.

"No problem," said Neil. "Good spagbol, by the way. Didn't know you could cook like that. As you can see, I'm in and out of here all the time, so it's good to have someone keeping an eye on the place. I'm not sure if it's your running socks, kiddo or if you've trod in something, but the bathroom needs a bloody good airing. We might have company later." He pointed towards the bathroom where James's sports kit, part of his work to get back into shape, was lying in a pile.

"OK, point taken," said James. He'd never been into running but he was starting to see a positive effect on the bathroom scales and had shed three kilos in a week.

"Talking of which, I'm meeting some friends in Fulham later. Are you up for a drink? We won't go crazy but it'll be a laugh."

"Thanks. I may just stay in and catch the football later."

"No need, it's a sports bar so we can all watch it and I can record it anyway." It seemed that staying in the flat was not an option and James hadn't had a boys' night out since he got back from the States. Thirty minutes later a black cab deposited them both on the pavement outside the pub and Neil led the way in to find four friends who had evidently been propping up the bar for a while. They had to shout over the music but the place was busy and interesting, with giant screens on all sides showing today's matches without the commentary.

A latecomer who James didn't recognise joined the group just after them, and was clearly well known to everyone else. More beers were lined up and as James was handed a pint the introductions were done. He recognised one of Neil's old army pals and since he was the only person being introduced he reckoned that many of the others must also be ex-forces. Neil shook hands with the latecomer, then turned to James. "Evans, this is my little brother who's annoyingly bigger than me. James, this is Evans."

"Brainier, too, I dare say. Good to meet you, mate," said Evans, holding out his hand. James shook his hand and almost spilled his pint. His eyes went down and up again in confusion, and everyone in the group burst out laughing around him. The hand James was now shaking was cold and latex-covered. He could feel the metal mechanics beneath the rubber skin.

"Christ!" James was lost for words and could only splutter. "Sorry, I... er, I didn't realise."

Evans was grinning at him. "Just my little joke, mate. Not much point in being bionic if no one knows it. It's pretty useless otherwise – I'm much better with a hook. I can open beer bottles with that; it makes the specialists go spare but that's why I do it."

"Take no notice, he does that to everyone," said Neil. "It's the only pleasure he gets these days, isn't that right Evans?"

"Well, let's just say I've learned to use me other hand for most things, Roop."

"It's his party piece. He says it goes down well with the ladies, but so far none of 'em could stand his face long enough to check out his hand."

"Take no notice of him," said Evans looking around his friends and then at James. "We certainly don't, not since his operation." There were a few knowing smiles from the group.

"Operation?" asked James, looking baffled.

"Yeah, he's just back from having an arsehole transplant. Unfortunately, there was a cock-up and they threw away the wrong bit."

Neil just grinned and shook his head. "Now, how about putting a glass in that hand of yours instead of frightening people?" and he passed a spare pint over to the Welshman.

James was laughing with the rest of them. "What d'you call him, Evans? Roop, was it? What's all that about?" James asked.

"I'm guessing you wasn't in the Army, Jamie-boy," said Evans.

James took another swig of beer and shook his head.

"Probably why you haven't had your nose broken three times like 'im," he said, gesturing at Neil who was now part of another conversation. "All officers are chinless Ruperts. All other ranks smell. All short guys are called Lofty. All Welshman are Taff or Evans. All Scotsmen are Jocks. And all women are fair game, even the ugly ones."

"Especially the ugly ones in your case," said Neil over his shoulder.

James laughed aloud and began to forget about his unsuccessful job applications.

"You still got that ace Triumph of yours, Roop?" Evans asked.

"Yeah, but I've hardly ridden it for months. Work keeps getting in the way." A slow smile spread across his face. "I'd lend it to my kid brother but I'm not sure he's got over his last bike experience."

James groaned loudly, knowing where this was going.

"Oh?" said another, sensing a story, "what happened there, James?"

James exhaled in resignation. "Neil and I were going to a party, he was driving and I was riding pillion. We stopped at a pub somewhere on the way, I don't know what Neil had but I took in a few pints and … what can I say? I was young and even more foolish then, so we rode to the party and that's when the world started spinning. A lot. Of course, I blamed the dodgy sandwiches Neil had bought but OK, bottom line I was pissed as a newt when we got to the party."

"Two pints in those days and he was shit-faced," added Neil helpfully.

"But somehow we got there OK and I didn't fall off the back. It was a summer night and everyone was hanging around outside when we arrived. Y'know admiring the cars and bikes, chatting up the girls. I got off the bike still wearing my helmet and walked towards them. And suddenly I knew I was going to puke. I started struggling to undo the strap on my helmet, but I still had thick gloves on and I couldn't find the release button. Anyway, you guessed it, I couldn't get my lid off and just threw up into it."

"Ohhh," said Evans, wincing.

Neil and another guy began to laugh. "I tried running to the gents while I was frantically pulling at the chinstrap, but I didn't know where it was and I could hardly see out. Then I was sick again and the beer level inside my helmet rose behind the visor and I thought, *Holy Shit, I'm going to drown. In my own puke.* It was over my mouth and nose before I finally, drunkenly realised what to do. I leaned forward and opened the visor, and two pints of old beer and sandwiches landed on my feet, and all over the girl standing next to me."

"Oh, man. That's disgusting," said someone else.

"Yeah, that's pretty much what she said," added Neil. "I can confirm her fella also tried to punch his lights out. Fortunately, James was still wearing his pukey helmet so the boyfriend didn't get very far."

"No, I didn't drown, I didn't even get beaten up, but when I finally managed to get the helmet off my hair was standing up on end. I even had to wash the beer out of my ears." James shook his head, "I don't think I pulled that night."

"At least that night you had an excuse."

"Thanks, Bro. The next worst bit was putting my helmet back on to go home. I'd filled it with water and bleach and left it for an hour but it still reeked, it was soaking inside, and the bleach made my eyes water. "

"At 60mph I could still smell him sitting behind me. Stupid sod," he added affectionately.

Later in the evening, Neil appeared at his elbow while James was talking and watching the match, half in and half out of a conversation. "OK, little brother? Must stop calling you that, you're inches taller than me. Don't mind Evans, you know earlier. He does that to everyone."

"Hey, no problem. It was funny, but I nearly spat my pint over him."

"Would have served him right. We've seen worse, one poor girl fainted. It was a laugh seeing your reaction. Anyway, it's good to see you out and about, I haven't seen much of that from you since you got back. Beginning to think you'd left your sense of humour stateside."

James sighed. "Ah, be fair. I've had a lot on my plate lately, what with losing my job and Lisa."

"Listen, I've given it time before saying this but you need to move forward now! Sure, losing Lisa was terrible. No one would deny that. She was an absolute honey and frankly far too good for you. What it must have been like losing her when you were planning everything together... well, I guess you can only know that if you've gone through it. But one thing's for sure, eventually you have to come out the other side," he said.

James grimaced and put the drink he'd been about to take back on the bar. But he didn't interrupt Neil.

"Sure, life really kicked you in the nuts there, but as they say, shit happens. That was what, eighteen months ago?" Neil asked rhetorically. "You can either stay in, watch the telly and dwell on what might have been or you can get off your overweight arse – which it would be my pleasure to kick at squash or the sport of your choosing – and get on with the rest of your life." He paused and looking very directly at James, he added more quietly, "I only knew Lisa a little, but I think I knew her well enough from your years together to know that she grasped life with both hands in everything she did. Do you think she'd want you moping about when you could be taking the world on?"

"And, just for the record, you didn't lose your job. You walked out of it – there's a difference. Beats me why, if I'm honest, but you did. Now you're here and I'll be proud to have you around, but fucking pull those shoulders back, pick your chin up, and kick the world back a bit. Find what you like doing and just go and bloody do it."

James blew his cheeks out, but before he could respond Neil added, "Listen, Bro, I've got no agenda tonight, you know that. The only reason I wanted you to meet these guys was 'cos they're a laugh, they know how to let their hair down – well, those that still have it. And I thought they might give you a boost which I think they have already. But hey, while we're here, look around you. You think you've got worries! Evans's got one arm, the other was taken off by a bastardy Talib IED. Nick over there came back from Afghanistan to find his missus shacked up with the guy that fitted his satellite dish. And one of them can hardly hear a thing and only then in one ear, but if I didn't tell you who it was you'd never guess, would you? Well, would you?"

James shook his head. "No, course not," said Neil. "Actually, it's Si over there. He's learning to lip read and already helps out at a school for profoundly deaf kids. So stop sodding well feeling sorry for yourself, get up there and get another bloody round in before they think you're as mean as me." With that James was left talking to thin air.

Christ, he thought, *don't sugar the pill, will you?* But deep inside he already knew Neil was right. He could either sit here in London moping about like a kicked puppy or he could start taking charge of what he did next. James stood up, took a very deep breath, and said "Bugger it" loud enough to make the women at a nearby table put their heads together and giggle at him before he headed straight to the bar. Seven pints of amber nectar were needed, pronto.

******

Neil's words were still going round James's head the morning after, along with a well-built hangover wearing heavy boots. He lay awake for a while thinking about the night out. Neil had said what needed saying, of course, James knew he had a lot going for him. He was young enough to start afresh. He was old enough to have some qualifications, and to know what he did or didn't like doing. He had a little bit of money in the bank, he was healthy and getting fit again. He even had a base in town whenever he needed one, and now he had the chance to re-invent himself if he chose to.

What he had intended as a seamless transition from a US career path to another in Europe, was in danger of coming unpicked and he needed to focus his efforts. He might never have the chance again to do something radical with his life. Neil didn't mind him being there, the flat was big enough for the two of them and he was frequently travelling anyway. The only trouble with that was James felt cooped up in London and knew he needed to find a different challenge. Public relations had looked like a promising career till he chucked it in, but it had never been his passion.

So, what did he really like doing? He ran through a mental checklist but couldn't see how he could get paid to watch sports, play rugby badly, eat out, or go to the movies. But photography? Well, why not? He'd always had an interest in it and he knew he had some talent, he just wasn't sure whether it would measure up against the professionals. He'd even been on a couple of courses in his spare time to learn about travel photography. Most of the people on the course had been current or aspiring professionals, he had been one of only two amateurs and he hadn't paid as much attention as he should to the section on selling your work. But he might still have his notes somewhere. What if he could turn that into a profession? After all, his tutor had been enthusiastic, saying that what he lacked most was experience.

James's portfolio now consisted of photographs taken on holiday, although these were no beach snaps. They included some good images of Caribbean island life, a two-week tour of Guatemala and Mexico and another series on volcanic eruptions from a trip to Iceland. Come to think of it, there were some good urban photos taken on business trips in Latin America and the States that he should incorporate. If he put these together, he might have enough to get his portfolio seen. He'd need to go back to his notes and maybe ask his old tutor how to take it to the next stage.

As he lay there, he thought about what Neil had said; Lisa would expect him to go out and take on a new challenge and that's what he wanted to do. He could picture her smile, that wicked look that came upon her sometimes. There was a direct gaze from those green eyes as big as saucers. He could remember their first night together as though it was yesterday. Several dates had led them to a party near her parents' house where they were staying the night. They had come in at two or three in the morning to find her brother, Philip, in the kitchen. He had just got back from another party and was unsteadily trying to make himself some cheese on toast. The man was thickset, the same height as James and with an aggressive attitude. His drunken handshake was like being gripped by a vice and he hadn't let go, trying to intimidate his little sister's new man. James was untroubled by rough greetings but he was glad of the distraction when Philip's toast began to burn.

There was an undeniable protectiveness there. He made his food and studied James. It wasn't a warm or even neutral assessment. He asked him what work he did, his expression turning to one of puzzlement and then disgust that any man should choose to work at something so effete. Philip opened another beer for himself without offering anything to them, muttered angrily and unintelligibly before weaving his way out of the room saying he was off to bed. They saw him later, lying face down asleep on a sofa that was barely half his body length. He looked twisted and uncomfortable and James was content not to wake him.

Lisa and James had stood and kissed in the kitchen after her brother had gone. Knowing that her parents were asleep upstairs though James was just sober enough to see how awkward it might be to spend the night in her room, and somehow doing the right thing mattered more to him now with Lisa than it had mattered with any woman before. She led him by the hand through the darkened house, once pressing a cool finger to his lips for silence. She wore a scent he didn't recognise but would now remember fondly forever, and her honey-blonde hair that had been piled up all evening had escaped during the last hour in a glorious cascade. James wasn't sure if it had fallen down while he kissed her or whether she had shaken it free deliberately. Either way, the effect was bewitching and at that moment he would have followed her anywhere.

The large house was old, the beams were low enough for him to bang his head on, and the ancient floorboards creaked as the couple walked along narrow corridors panelled in dark wood. A little light filtered down the landing from the staircase. Lisa stopped and turned to him, still holding his hand and pointing theatrically to the door beside them. 'Mum and Dad' she mouthed theatrically. Even with a few drinks inside him, he knew it would be a bad start to their relationship if he was to meet them outside their bedroom door as he tip-toed past with their daughter. Besides, Lisa had already told him that her brother was a pussycat; it was her father that was over-protective. Having seen the size and nature of the pussycat, he had no wish to meet the top dog now. A few steps further on, she gently turned a door handle and showed him into the spare bedroom. It had an inviting double bed that sadly would see no action that night. Soft lighting indicated everything he might need. "The bathroom is across the corridor, you'll find spare towels in there. Sleep well, Jamie," and with that she stretched up and kissed the tip of his nose before slipping silently out of the door.

He sat on the bed and cursed himself for not asking her where her room was in this long and rambling house. He went to the bathroom, brushed his teeth and splashed water on his face which made him feel a lot more human. Back in his room he considered corridor creeping but, while he knew where her father and mother were, he had no idea where Lisa might be. The thought of meeting the old man with his shotgun was a passion killer to put it mildly.

He undressed and lay in bed with the light off. The room was warm and the bed extremely comfortable but he'd forgotten to close the curtains. There was bright moonlight shining across the floor and onto the corner of the bed so that he could still see clearly. And then he heard the latch lift slowly on the ancient door and when it opened Lisa slipped silently into his room. He sat up in bed but she held a finger to her lips and he said nothing. She looked stunning in a pale silk kimono that reached to the floor. The only sound was the susurration of sliding silk as she stepped towards the bed.

"I couldn't sleep alone, knowing you were here," she whispered.

"I'm glad you came," he managed hoarsely. His voice sounded like someone else's, his heart was thumping in his chest and he saw and heard every detail around him with wonderful clarity. The light of the full moon stretched across the carpet lending everything a warm glow, and then he caught that scent again. This time he reached out for her, putting his hand around the back of her neck and drawing her gently down to him. As their faces drew close, she paused and simply stared into his eyes and then her green eyes closed. His lips brushed hers and his hands stroked that beautiful body through the silk. The kimono was smooth to the touch and Lisa's skin beneath was softer than any he had ever known.

She pushed him back into the pillows and as she did so the kimono slid down a little on one side allowing him to admire the curve of her neck, the turn of her shoulder. "Surprised I came back?" That teasing smile was playing at her lips.

"You bet. I wanted to find you but I had visions of clambering into bed beside your Dad."

"Do that and he'll kill you," Lisa said. He smiled. "You think I'm kidding? He's bigger than you and he knows how to handle himself, with or without the shotgun."

"OK. I'm getting the picture. This isn't doing much for my libido!"

"Sorry," she giggled, "just thought you ought to know. We have to be silent or you're toast." Then she leaned away from him and for an awful moment he thought she was about to leave, but she simply looked at him in the moonlight. "I just want to remember this moment."

He smiled slowly at her. "Take it off." There was a delicious hesitation, as she looked long into his eyes. James held his breath and said nothing; all he could hear was the pounding of blood in his ears. Slowly Lisa looked down and began to unfasten the knot at her waist. She stood up beside the bed, reached up to the lapels and slowly drew them off her shoulders. The neckline widened, James kept his eyes fixed on hers, then the silk fell sweetly to the floor and Lisa stood naked before him. The deep shadows cast by the moonlight left her partly hidden and partly bare to his gaze. Her golden hair seemed silver in the light, her skin looked almost white and the shadows moved so kindly around her that no artist could have done her justice.

There was no need for further words as he lifted the cover and she slid in beside him, settling perfectly into his arms.

Chapter 6
Barcelona, Spain
Five Months Ago

Axel was back on Barcelona's streets within minutes, doing some serious thinking as he headed for the Metro and his apartment. He knew he had to scrutinise the risks from every angle, not just the rewards. First, he needed to talk to the *comptoirs* about this new demand in the market and with orders of this scale that had to be face to face. He needed to confirm lines of supply and build the team around him, in Europe and Africa. He would have to move funds and set up a new delivery chain. Moving large sums was getting harder following anti-money laundering legislation in the US and Europe, so his preference was to move diamonds for their high value and portability. And as a gem dealer he had rough and finished stones in safety deposits from Cairo to the Cayman Islands.

His contacts would need to find him two new bases to rent in DRC and Rwanda, but first he would have to spend enough in the right quarters over the next few weeks to seize the attention of factions in the Congolese and Rwandan military as well as armed groups. A lot would depend on the impression he made in Congo's Bad Lands where he was already known. With others he'd have to start from scratch. Once that was done future support would be secured by continuing to offer attractive prices and solid demand for the minerals they controlled.

He also needed to consider the political and reputational risks. Here he had an advantage over any rivals that CCV might have approached. He could think of no one else who kept so many lines of contact open with people on both sides of the conflict. In the DRC capital Kinshasa, he had spent a lot of time over the last twenty-five years building networks in the government, civil service and the military at all levels, getting to know the rising stars, those who could make deals happen and those to treat with caution. He had come to see how quickly the faces could change, even within a supposedly stable regime, as one power base gave way to another. One month he could be dealing with a senior general with influence throughout the region, only to find the next month that he had been replaced or retired to his Paris apartment to enjoy the benefits of office, leaving behind a colonel eager to do the same.

Axel had developed a blameless way of cultivating influence; simple but very cost-effective – his parties were legendary. He would rent a house in one of the best neighbourhoods in Kinshasa, somewhere secure, with influential neighbours, a good pool and plenty of garden. Then he would throw the most generous parties that anyone could recall, with internationally famous entertainers, the best local bands, good food, and fine wines flown in from the Cape. There would be fireworks and dancing by the pool. The parties would start as playful, daytime family affairs, with his affluent and influential neighbours prominent among the VIP guests, and when the children had left and darkness fell the hardcore partygoers began to enjoy themselves. Then, having made his mark in Kinshasa, Axel would repeat the whole process a few weeks later in Kigali, the Rwandan capital.

The only complaints were from those not invited; if you weren't there, you probably weren't anyone. In this way, the reputation Axel established for himself was that of a successful, well-connected, legitimate businessman, specialising in gems and gold, with strong social links to the leaderships of the largest half dozen parties in each parliament. He never involved himself in party politics, figuring that any advantage would be short term. It didn't stop him courting senior politicians, with invitations to dinners, weekends at whichever house he was staying in, and lavish parties that lasted all day and long into the night. His invitations became highly sought after among senior politicians and business people. "I'm not smart enough to keep up with the world of politics," he would flatter his guests, "so I stick to business." It was good business sense to give equal donations to all of the leading parties; consequently his political stock in both capital cities was as high now as it had ever been.

Axel inserted his ticket into the reader at the metro station gate and the clear plastic passenger barriers swung open. It was not yet rush hour but the station was fairly busy. His train eased quietly to a halt at the metro platform and he stepped aboard to find a spare seat in the brightly lit modern carriage.

The trickier part would come in balancing his position in Kinshasa with his business in eastern Congo where Kinshasa's authority was weak and foreign influence, from neighbouring Rwanda and Uganda regularly counteracted the distant Congolese government. The answer was always the same, to make himself indispensable. He had done business with a succession of rebel leaders in North and South Kivu, men more or less dependent on the Rwandan or Ugandan armies. Politics in the Kivus was even more mercurial than in Kinshasa as alliances came and went.

Deals like this one with CCV meant that Axel could, however, show rebel leaders they needed to do business with him because his connections in Europe,

Asia and North America would guarantee them a better price than with rival British, German or Thai exporters. Nor would this be a flash in the pan. Axel would be offering rising demand and secure prices. Years ago Axel had established a trading company in Goma, close to the Rwandan border and with no obvious links to his business in Kinshasa. Although his name did not appear above the door in Goma or on the list of directors registered in Kinshasa, businesses locally knew that Axel Terberg was behind it.

Ironically, by appearing to separate himself publicly from the region's politics as far as any businessman could, he made himself all the more valuable to all parties. He had even been able to pass information between warring factions and host meetings between people who couldn't afford to be seen in the same town. Without ever joining them at the table, he had offered his rented home or hotel suites to host clandestine meetings, and on this platform he had built a small but flourishing business as a broker across Africa's Great Lakes region. He was a commodities trader and occasionally a power broker, too.

Picking up a local paper as he exited the Barcelona metro at Sagrada Familia Axel made his way down the hill and into the park. It was getting dark, there was a light rain and he was enjoying the prospect of a long hot soak in a bath before going out for a beer and a meal.

As he walked back through the park, he considered the last element of the deal, the physical risk, which in this part of Africa was about as high as it could get. This was still an undeclared war zone, even if it suited most parties to pretend the peace accord and elections after the Second Congo War had spread harmony throughout the region. The continued presence of the UN Stabilisation Mission, MONUSCO reminded anyone who needed reminding that the peace was fragile and fighting was continuing between the Congo's Federal Army and the Hutu rebels.

Going into the region armed to the teeth and with heavy support was always an option, but it was costly and still uncertain. It wasn't really Axel's style either. In an area where arms were so cheaply available he and his guards could still easily find themselves outgunned. And while a show of force would play well with the more impressionable men he'd be dealing with, for others it would only antagonise already tense negotiations. No, he preferred to have an armed driver and wherever possible he would trust to his wits, his bankroll and his connections.

People still needed his business, his contacts and his help with negotiations – these were the key reasons for his bi-partisan success. It may have looked to some as if he was riding two horses in the race, but his race was different from theirs. For many people here politics was the game. In truth, politics bored him immeasurably. He saw it as a feeble, transient means of power, with poverty before and impotence afterwards. What interested Axel was doing business, outwitting his rivals, staying one jump ahead of corrupt authorities, growing his network, and above all doing deals.

If he could only extract himself from entanglement with the Americans, his life would be a load easier, but for now he couldn't see that playing out. When they had their claws into you, they were wouldn't readily let go. Which reminded him, he needed to bring them up to speed on developments before his silence became hard to explain.

At least he had no one else to explain himself to. No wife or girlfriend, no family. His parents, now dead and buried in the Netherlands, had been strict members of the Dutch Reformed Church with a family history of mission work. They had given him a love of Africa and a strong work ethic but that was where their mutual understanding ended.

They never understood where Axel's fascination with business came from, or his pleasure in a successful deal. He couldn't work it out either; he certainly wasn't a fifty-fifty product of his parents' genes. Somewhere in his DNA there lurked a trader, a broker, a dealmaker. The first sign of the trouble ahead came at eleven years old when he was called before the Headmaster and beaten for selling sweets in school. Even afterwards, Axel was unsure whether the headmaster was more affronted by the introduction of frivolous foodstuffs to the puritanical school diet, or the fact that Axel was doing something as vulgar as making money at school. His 'crime' was to have used his pocket money to buy the biggest blocks of chocolate he could find, which he cut up at home before selling squares to his class mates at a three hundred percent mark-up. Axel would have sold more but demand was so strong he ran out of chocolate before he could sell to other year groups. The headmaster was sure he had learned a lesson. He was only half right, Axel had learned that next time he must meet demand or raise the price; his love of trading was born.

The headmaster's cane had hurt, but being forced to give back the money had hurt more. The only consolation was that he had cut his losses by telling the headmaster his mark-up was only one hundred percent, which he then paid into the school's charity box in an apparent gesture of remorse. None of the pupils dared complain for fear of being identified as the guilty customers. If Axel had been searched as he left school that day, the remainder of his two hundred percent profit margin – neatly folded into a sports sock hidden in his underpants – might have landed him in worse trouble. His profits had truly protected his essentials. Meanwhile, his contempt for his teachers only grew as they failed to grasp the importance of supply and demand.

The headmaster's wrath was as nothing to his father's, as he demonstrated later with his belt. His father's anger was a righteous indignation, for one of Axel's customers had chosen to eat his purchase during morning prayers. This was also the day when Axel learned not to rely too heavily on his customers' intelligence.

The gulf between Axel's God-fearing father and his atheist son grew with each passing year. It tortured his mother, but she was too scared to confront her husband's fierce temper and harsh tongue. He wasn't physically violent towards her but he didn't need to be, he had long ago crushed any resistance in her. By the time Axel was a sturdy 16-year-old they stood toe-to-toe in their arguments. The boy's refusal to stay on at college or to follow any of the career paths chosen for him by his father in medicine, law or the church, led to a final split between them that was still unreconciled when the old man died. With no room for agreement on his future, Axel's father threw him out of the house after his sixteenth birthday when he still refused to enrol in college. If the older Terberg hadn't forced the issue, Axel would eventually have walked out anyway, but the die was cast and deep within him Axel still bore a burning anger. He and his mother remained in occasional contact by letter but they had only met twice since the day he left, once when she asked him to visit his father in the hospice (which he declined to do) and once to be with his mother at the funeral.

She still viewed his thirst for adventure, travel and commercial success with a mixture of concern and distaste. Axel repeatedly tried to share with her some of his financial success, but she would have none of it and in that sense she clung to her late husband's views. Axel's mother seldom showed her emotions but she loved and protected him. Perhaps she never understood his motivation, where he saw the thrill of the chase, the deal itself. Prospecting and mining, cutting, polishing, finishing, trading, they were all enjoyable aspects of his work.

He knew he must be tired; this kind of introspection was a weakness, not normally his style at all. He needed to stay focused a little longer tonight. He had to contact several groups in Africa, and he'd better start tonight by emailing his people in Goma to check that the senior army staff in North and South Kivu were unchanged. He guessed he would have heard if there had been any major upheavals, but he'd better be up to speed. Axel also wanted to call a couple of people in Rwanda tomorrow morning before his flight back to London and talk about supply routes, and the availability of aircraft and pilots. There were usually east Europeans with the time, skills and heavy-lift aircraft but if not he'd have to get them in from elsewhere. Then he'd better get on a plane out there himself.

He knew that he could make a lot of money here. If he played his cards right, the work could easily carry on for a year or two, although in this market you couldn't plan too far ahead. He'd just had a good year but this one deal could eclipse that completely – or it could swallow up everything he'd made if it went belly-up. He would charge CCV a hefty commission on the coltan he delivered 'FoB Macao'. Under these terms Axel's fee would cover the costs of shipment from the mine to Kigali airport in the Rwandan capital, plus loading, customs charges and air freight to Macao. CCV would then pick up the tab for all further handling and transportation – wherever the coltan was headed afterwards.

Axel crossed the road, dodging some of Barcelona's mopeds and bikes in the cycle lane, as well as the cars. He was directly in front of the Sagrada Familia which was already illuminated. There were orange cranes on three sides of the church and dense green netting draped across some of the middle levels to protect the public as the craftsmen continued their seemingly endless work on the masonry above.

He cut diagonally across the park in front of the church. It was almost dark now and the church looked even more striking than it had in daylight. The yellowed stone appeared greyer in the harsh floodlighting but the windows and alcoves in the four spires above cast deep shadows, giving the church a definition it lacked by day. Tired as he was, he paused to look again for he had never seen carvings like these anywhere else. A huge Christ nailed to the Cross stood just within the church's front portico, while disciples knelt beneath his tortured feet. Thirty metres or more above him, where the arc lighting was gradually lost to sight in the night sky, Axel could just make out some high figures like angels seated or standing in alcoves. He'd have to come back and take a look inside sometime, even if it wasn't on this trip. What was it that the in-flight magazine called Antoni Gaudi? 'God's Architect', that was it. Subservience stuck in Axel's throat, particularly where it concerned the Church. Despite his parent's best efforts, he felt utter disdain for those who relied on religion for their daily guidance. *It was superstition,* he thought, *dressed up in two thousand years of repression and clerical hypocrisy.*

Some people even wanted to make Gaudi a saint, for pity's sake. The place had been started in the 1880s, it still wasn't finished and it wouldn't be ready for another twenty years. He snorted in derision as he followed his route to the apartment. I guess that's what they mean by *mañana.*

Rain was falling lightly, the pavement now glistened and the sand pathways in the centre of the park no longer kicked up dust as he walked. The evening air felt fresher than when he'd landed that morning and the streets were starting to look well washed. Axel let himself into the building and stepped into the lift. He could hear someone talking on the first floor landing but he was too far away to make out their words.

CCV wanted him to manage the whole process from soup to nuts, starting from the mines in DRC to the quayside in Macao. Four million dollars in the first year would more than cover the hassles and expenses he would have, but he'd need to see some of that money upfront. There would be wheels to grease at first, he could see that. He'd have to insist on a commission that was high enough in the first year to cover the set-up time and costs. Once the supply route was in operation it would be a hell of a lot cheaper to run and his profit margin in subsequent years would be enormous; so this had to be a multi-year deal to justify the lower profits in year one.

The lift doors opened for him at the second floor just as a man and woman in their early thirties came up the stairs opposite him. Whatever the discussion had been about it was murmured as they saw him, and they were taking turns to point at a tourist map.

"Buenas noches," said the man. Spanish did not come easily to him. The dark-haired woman didn't acknowledge Axel at all. "Say, can you help us, we're a bit lost here," the man had switched to American-accented English, and he turned to gesture to the street map she was holding. As he swung back, Axel's attention was gripped by the black eye of a gun barrel that stared at him from waist height. The man allowed Axel to register the gun before withdrawing it beneath a light brown raincoat draped over his arm. The black muzzle was set in a squared off, steel grey handgun, something heavy like a Walther or XDm.

Any reply stalled on Axel's lips, and he cursed himself for getting caught like this. He didn't recognise them, but at this stage that wasn't important. Time seemed to slow as his military training made him prioritise fight or flight options. Escape was unlikely, two trained people were blocking his exit via the stairs, and he had to assume they were both armed. At that moment the lift door beside him closed, removing the high-risk option of diving back into the lift and hoping to outrun his attackers. Out of habit he already had the apartment key in his hand pointing outwards just below his knuckles – that was about all that he'd got right so far. As expected, the woman drew a gun from the back of her jeans, it was a smaller piece but he recognised the Kahr .45 pistol she was holding and it simply confirmed these were professionals. It would pack a punch, but was small enough to be carried in a front pocket or handbag, and slim enough not to show. There wasn't time yet to wonder who they were so he concentrated on the moment-by-moment threat they posed as he gauged his options.

"Suggest we all go in now, fella. It's not very welcoming out here," said the American.

Once inside his apartment Axel would be out of public view, there would be more room for his attackers to back away and neutralize his threat, controlling the situation with easy lines of fire. The noise of any assault or even gunshots would also be muffled or dispersed. There were only seconds left before the apartment door would close behind them and his few remaining choices would vanish.

He had to distract them or get them to lower their guard, and the best way he could think of was to appear less of a threat; it might sow a doubt in their minds, a doubt that they had found the right person. They were evidently expecting an English speaker, and someone used to armed confrontations, so he began to stammer a reply in his crude Spanish, all the time looking at the man who posed marginally the greater threat. "¡ por favor, no me lastimes!. ¡Por favor!"

Axel began tugging theatrically at the strap on his watch in an apparent effort to give them his valuables and save himself from a mugging.

Until Axel Terberg spoke the dark-haired man had been relaxed, he looked absolutely in control. But as Axel's words sank in, his arrogance evaporated and

93

confusion flickered across his face. He'd been told the mark was a Brit. Yet this guy was jabbering at him in excitable Spanish. In his eyes there was puzzlement and then concern. Surely they hadn't got the wrong guy? He'd fucking kill someone at base if they'd given him the wrong target. The guy in front of him seemed to match the grainy blown-up photo they'd been shown, and this was the right building wasn't it? But no one had said anything about him speaking the lingo. Shit, maybe this wasn't their mark after all.

While this doubt spun through the man's mind the woman made a basic mistake. In her eagerness to take the key from Axel's hand she reached too far forward and partially obscured her partner's line of fire. She was already stretching towards him just at the instant Axel broke into a torrent of Spanish.

The man was struggling to understand Axel's reply, and had to lean to his right to keep any view of his target. As Axel pleaded loudly that he had little money and began to undo his watch to buy them off, he grabbed the woman's left sleeve and tugged her sharply towards him, pulling her further off balance. Her gun hand was now pointing aimlessly away from him. Axel's arms were already raised in front of him so he pivoted on his right foot and met her face with his left elbow as she stumbled towards him. It sent a shooting pain through his lower arm but he connected hard with her nose and she screamed in agony. Her forward momentum had been stopped and she was instinctively bringing the gun up in her right hand but he was able to grasp her right wrist and turn it away towards her partner. The movement twisted her arm backwards and might give him the chance to fire at the man behind her.

Her companion had been momentarily wrong-footed, stepping back to avoid contact with Axel and looking for a clear shot. The American's training had overcome his momentary doubts and he was now reacting to the threat.

If the woman had managed to keep her feet, she would have been a vital human shield, protecting Axel from the torso downwards and leaving only his head exposed. Maybe it was just the twisting motion that made her stumble, maybe she slipped in her own blood now flowing down her chin and hitting the floor; whatever the cause, she fell sideways into the lift door. Her nose was bleeding hard and her left hand went up to protect it, but in another split second she could probably recover enough to strike back with a punch to his groin from where she knelt on the floor.

Axel managed to hold onto her gun hand as she fell away from him but it was in his left hand, upside down and pointing downwards. He started to turn the gun towards the man but even as he did it he knew he was too late. The rush of adrenaline made every movement he made seem dangerously slow, and Axel had time to wish that life was like the movies where the gun always falls neatly into the hand, but he didn't have time to react before the man raised his pistol again and yelled, "Stop! Or I shoot your knees."

There was nothing else Axel could do.

"Nice and slow, fella, nice and slow," the man said. "Put the gun down and gently push it over here with your foot. No kicks or sudden moves. And no fucking Spanish! Now, how about you pick up the key you dropped, open that door of yours and we all go inside before we attract any more attention?" Axel bent and placed the gun on the floor before slowly straightening up and raising his hands. He pushed the gun across the floor with his foot.

The man ignored his injured colleague and kept his distance, giving Axel no further opportunities to rush him. Axel knelt to pick up the key and, holding it where it could be seen in case the man had a nervous trigger finger, he put the key in the lock and stepped through the apartment door into the darkened hallway.

"Keep the main lights off, fella. You," he said without looking at the woman, "turn on the table lamp and close the blinds." She had retrieved her gun from the hall floor and now moved sullenly to comply, all the while holding her bleeding face. As soon as there was a soft light in the room she turned back to Axel and her look told him he'd made a brand new enemy.

Axel felt a solid prod from the man's gun in the small of his back, and he moved forward slowly into his own living room. "We'll keep the lights low for now." The man stood close enough behind him to press the gun into Axel's back when he wanted to, but far enough away to see Axel's hands and feet if he struck out. They shuffled forward together in ungainly fashion like a pantomime horse. Axel heard the street door downstairs slam shut and brisk steps reaching the foot of the stairwell as the woman watched the hall from inside his half-closed front door. The three of them stood still for a few more seconds until another man, taller and in his forties, was let in at which point the woman put the front door on the chain before taking up a position out of Axel's line of sight. Anyone who glimpsed them from across the street before the blinds were drawn shut would simply have seen a party of friends arriving at their apartment in Barcelona. Since her gun had hit the ground the loudest noise had been the slamming of the street door – the block was quiet once again.

The tall man pushed past his colleagues, ignored the low sofa and chairs, instead pulling out a dining chair before removing his dark topcoat, draping it over the table and settling himself. It was then that he noticed the woman tending her bloody and swollen face; he grunted and said nothing before turning his gaze back to Axel. Tall Guy assessed the heavily built blonde man before him and sighed. "I thought we'd been through all this, Axel?"

"To the best of my knowledge, we've never met," Axel replied tersely.

"Don't jerk me about. You know who we are and why we're here. You've caused the Centre and me a load of hassle, and the doctor says that's not good for my stomach." The boss studied the woman's nose for a moment, "It hasn't been good for her either."

Axel had half-expected a pistol-whipping, but the gunman remained still, so he was caught unprotected by a rabbit punch from the woman who was now standing behind him to his right. The blow to his kidneys was practised, powerful and undefended, and it blew the air right out of Axel's lungs. He collapsed to his knees, gasping for breath and his right hand automatically went to protect his back, thereby giving her a clear view of his torso and head. She could have put his lights out with a single kick to the temple but they obviously wanted him to talk, so she directed it at his torso and he felt a rib break, one that he'd broken before. His mind raced ahead and he was simultaneously calculating the best way to defend himself from further blows and the time his rib would take to heal. If she'd wanted to do him visible or lasting damage, she had already missed the opportunity while he was on his knees. This was evidently going to be a more discreet warning.

Axel was now lying in a foetal position on the polished wooden floor, his left cheek pressed to the cold veneer. His lower back felt as though it was in flames, and his rib made it painful but not quite impossible to tuck his right elbow close to his body on belated guard duty.

Curiously, Axel now found time to notice fine details. Through gaps in the blinds he could see the rain was leaving small droplets on the large window pane and the drops sparkled whenever he moved, something he was trying hard not to do. Some drops had run together and made small rivulets of water down the window pane. The windows were very well polished.

He even noticed the woman's shoes. Bizarrely, he now remembered one of the more useful pieces of advice from his father. To flatter a woman always compliment her on her shoes. These were low-cut brown walking shoes, with tough looking toes and heels set on top of flexible soles. Ideal for the job in hand but never likely to be complimented, and the white socks didn't go well with her shoes or her pale Rohan trousers either. *Bloody Yanks*, he thought, *always cocking up the details.*

Axel could now see the gunman more clearly; he was in his early thirties, about six foot two, dark-haired and mean-mouthed. He committed the face to memory and admitted ruefully to himself that he should have been this alert a few minutes ago, although it was hard to see how things might have played out differently. It was clear now that this was the Agency, they were long overdue a chat and if they wanted to talk to him they would always find him eventually.

The tall man, the only one of them seated, was now able to talk down to Axel as he lay on the floor. "I'm very disappointed, Axel. That was all quite simple, and we were led to believe you could be an awkward customer."

"Well, I guess you missed the first dance," said Axel through teeth that were clenched against the pain, and he thought he detected the tall man smiling at the woman's expense. "Why the big entry? All you had to do was ring the bell."

"I guess we couldn't be sure what reception we'd get, given you've been holding out on us. Just call it a message from Langley; they're real pissed with you." Axel was still winded and could only manage short sentences, so he said nothing. At least they were CIA, it could probably have been worse.

"Let's start with a simple question; how long have you known Mr Hendriks?"

"We just met today," was all Axel managed before a much heavier kick from the young man caught him in the backside. It just failed to connect between Axel's legs but the gunman wouldn't miss next time.

The Tall Guy sighed heavily. "You've been in touch with these people for four weeks and somehow you still forgot to mention it to us. You didn't talk to State, not even the London embassy, for Chrissake. Don't you think we've got enough to do without chasing round Europe to learn what should have been in your last postcard?"

"Yeah, sorry."

"Well, like I told my eldest when he totalled my car, sorry isn't always good enough. He put him and his girlfriend into ER, and caused his mother a shitload of worry. And I'm out a classic Porsche." With a Texan drawl he said it like Portia, and it was clear his son came a distant second in his affections.

"What Langley needed was advanced notice, time to react, the chance to re-position assets. Your silence robbed us of that time. And State are double-pissed with you 'cos they're playing high stakes chess and you left 'em blindfolded. Hell, we don't even know for sure who the other side is, though smart money's still on the Chinese. We're playing catch-up on this one and you still ain't told us who or what we're up against." He sighed heavily and Axel expected another blow but it didn't come.

"Get off the floor and sit here like a grown-up." He kicked around a low armchair and after an uncomfortable climb Axel tumbled inelegantly into it. As he did so the pain in his rib made him clench his teeth; *Jesus*, thought Axel, *this sort of thing was a lot harder these days.*

"We opened a lot of doors for you, Terberg, literally. We've dug you out of a few holes, too. And that's OK. That's what friends do for each other. Except, right now, seems we're doing all the digging, and you? You're admiring the view. Want me to remind you of the Zambian shithole where we found you? It'd be so easy just to drop you back in jail there next time we have a flight passing through. You'll have heard of Extraordinary Rendition." He leaned forward and Axel could see the leathery, sun-worn skin. He almost whispered, "I don't care what you may have read in the papers, it still goes on y'know, especially when everyone's focused on Guantanamo. I believe the Zambians still have a warrant out for your re-arrest – I bet they're just itching to know where you are, boy." He paused and leaned back to study Axel's face which was twisted in pain.

"So, why don't you tell me everything you know about Mr Hendriks and CCV. Then we just move onto everything you've found out or guessed about their principals. First off the bat, who are CCV fronting for?"

And for the next thirty minutes Axel laid out most of what he knew about CCV and the private company's manufacturing clients. He told them of their plans for his role, their stated reasons for contacting him, their need to access the maximum output of coltan from artisan mines in eastern DRC, the structure of the deal, and the transport he'd planned into Rwanda and beyond.

As Axel explained it to them, the CIA man asked something that was still baffling him, too. "Why would the Chinese be moving into this market in a big way when they could get all the coltan they need at home? Unless it's not really the Chinese behind it, or there's something wrong with China's supply. Is there something wrong with the quality or quantity of their resources, or even the cost of extracting it?"

"Maybe they want to monopolise the coltan market," offered Axel.

"But there are still other sources, aren't there. You've mentioned Brazil, Australia and Canada," said Tall Guy.

"True but you don't have to own a hundred percent to control a market," Axel replied. "And I don't buy CCV's line about the cost of extraction and the proven resources from these existing markets. There's nothing I can put my finger on but I have the feeling there's more to it than that." Axel had to hand it to these people. Moments ago the CIA were beating the crap out of him, now they wanted him to join a tutorial on global market economics.

He tried to take shallow, even breaths to lessen the pain in his rib and kidneys. "Don't they have a growing number of their own manufacturers of DVD players and medical equipment, even cars? I mean, mobile phones aren't the only use for coltan. OK, the tantalum in it is important right now but maybe everyone will need something else in a few years' time. You know, like tin has replaced lead in electronics."

The American said nothing and studied Axel Terberg at length. "At last, you're starting to think, which is what we pay you for."

"You don't pay me," said Axel moodily.

"Don't we? Is that what's eating you?"

"I don't need your money. Anyway, that was the whole point of setting me up like this, what with Congress legislating against anyone supplying conflict minerals. I think your London colleagues enjoyed the English term 'set a thief to catch a thief'. And if you did pay me the CIA would be conspiring to commit a felony, and that would be unprecedented wouldn't it?"

"Drop the sarcasm, Terberg." There was a long silence while he thought about what Axel had said. "The Chinese have a reputation for playing the long game, strategy over tactics, they say. But if they can dominate some of these industries for a few years it may be enough to finish some rival companies in the west. Look at the mess Nokia and Motorola got into. Perhaps the Chinese reckon this could speed their rise to the top of the industrial pile, in mobile phones, autos, defence, whatever."

Axel didn't say any more but he couldn't help feeling that if this was what the US State Department was thinking then their view was narrow and short-term. The Chinese were being patient, ingratiating themselves in Africa with massive investments in roads, dams, railways, and never asking African leaders too many questions about democracy, human rights or corruption. Everywhere you went from Egypt to South Africa these days the Chinese were replacing western companies on key projects.

Tall Guy was keying something into his phone, maybe he was texting someone. "I'm going, but let's be clear on something, Terberg. If I have to come looking for you again 'cos you've forgotten how to pick up the phone, it'll get serious. I don't generally do warnings, they sound so lame. They aren't necessary if we understand one another from the get-go. You're useful to us – as we are to you – but if you stop being useful...." he left the sentence and put away his phone. "You are replaceable. I sense that Richie here hasn't had his share of the fun yet so, unless you want to be his punch bag, you call your handler real regular from now on, make him feel wanted and keep us in the loop. Right now, we're feeling sadly unloved by you and I can tell you that makes the higher-ups twitchy, makes the desk-jockeys feel like you don't take 'em serious. Thin skins and fragile egos, if you ask me, but that's the way it breaks for you. Don't make this mistake again," and he paused to look around the modest apartment, "frankly, I don't want to see you or this cold, wet dump again. Got it? And clean up that blood outside, it'll draw attention."

Still clutching his rib, Axel nodded but said nothing. He didn't envisage doing much bending and cleaning for a long time. He was quite keen to lean in the opposite direction in his chair but he thought better of making any sudden movements while he was still within reach of Richie and the sartorially impaired woman.

Richie's expression of resentment had ebbed, and he was now sporting a sneer. He leaned closer. "See you soon, ... Axel baby," Richie exaggerated the last two words for some private enjoyment and, preceded by a still-silent and blood-smeared woman, the unwelcome trio left the apartment closing the door quietly as they went.

Axel exhaled carefully, something he would be doing much more of in the days to come. He gently frisked his own pockets, momentarily surprised that no one else had done so today. *Marks deducted for Richie and for CCV*, he thought. Perhaps they knew that in a foreign country for just twenty-four hours he was unlikely to be armed. Had they searched him they wouldn't have found a firearm, but they would have found a miniscule microphone, even smaller than those favoured by TV reporters. It was wired through his shirt and into a voice-activated digital recorder, about the size of a cigarette lighter. He'd carried it to record the meeting with the South Africans. As it turned out, he'd recorded more than he'd bargained for.

He unzipped his fly awkwardly with his left hand, and carefully peeled away the duct tape holding a small, black commercially available recorder taped to his leg just below his crotch. Normally, removing the heavy silver tape from his hirsute leg was a low point of the evening, but he had shaved to ensure the tape adhered all day. Right now this pain seemed a lot less significant than usual. He thumbed the manual 'On' button and the recorder screen came to life. Finding the last file in the list he pressed 'Play'. "Buenas noches," said Richie clearly. Axel then went to an earlier file to listen to Mr Hendriks.

From the last time he'd broken a rib – climbing a wall a couple of strides ahead of some guard dogs at a detention centre, and then falling off the far side – Axel well remembered that the most painful parts were getting in and out of beds, baths and low chairs. Right now he needed to get out of this low chair, run himself a bath and get into bed. All thoughts of food and drink were forgotten; his relaxing evening had just gone to hell in a handcart.

Chapter 7
Coltan Mine, North Kivu, DRC
Two Years Ago

Long before they arrived at the mine, Raphael asked the porter carrying him to set down the chair and take Keisha instead. She was dirty, wet, and hungry and she stumbled more frequently than she had when they left the truck, falling a couple of times and suffering minor cuts and bruises. She must have been tired for she put up no resistance when he told her to take his place in the chair, and once the porter had tied his thin jacket over her she soon fell asleep with the rocking rhythm of his stride.

Even when she awoke she spoke little, only staring into space before drifting back to sleep. Raphael's head still hurt but there was no point in telling anyone since there was nothing they could do about it. From time to time he felt so giddy that he had to stop walking and sit down. He took up a position near the back of the line – they wouldn't let him bring up the rear in case he fell behind and got lost, so he just had to do his best to keep up with the porters. Together, the nine men set a punishing pace. Raphael had only been fully awake for some of the time that he was carried. The porters had stepped and slithered their way through the pale brown mud, crossing streams fed by regular rain, and were now skirting marshland that to Raphael seemed endless. In all that time, he never saw a porter fall.

Raphael smelt the camp before he saw it. The wind was blowing in their faces and he caught the unmistakable scent of human filth as he stumbled along the path, followed some time later by a more welcoming waft from burning campfires. It stirred his thoughts of food and his stomach growled at having nothing on which to work. But it was another fifteen minutes or more before they crested a rise and saw the mine spread out before him. He was too tired to take much of it in, but he followed the man in front until they reached a collection of rough adobe buildings where they were greeted by some of the camp's occupants, eager to see what provisions they had brought. Raphael sat down and hoped that the world would stop spinning. He detected a murmur of concern and curiosity among the surrounding men at the sight of a small, sleeping girl being carried in a litter, and he was dimly aware that one or two similar glances were coming his way.

For the past hour or so Raphael had become more and more concerned at Keisha's lack of response to him, yet what he saw in her was simply a reflection of his own deteriorating condition. He was perpetually hungry for they had eaten little in the previous few days, and had walked as far and fast as most adults could have managed. Their diet had consisted of occasional finds of nuts and fruit when they had fled the village. Then, after meeting the porters, they had received a small share of the rice meal prepared by their rescuers. One young porter had complained that they already had too little food as it was, without collecting stray children, but he was hushed by the others – maybe they had children of their own somewhere. In any case all the food was cooked together and small portions were given to the children.

The whole party was exhausted from walking hard and eating too little. They were all accustomed to sleeping outside, but Raphael was still suffering the after effects of his fall into the river, with cuts and bruises on his back and legs, and periods of giddiness and nausea. Fatigue and hunger were already making the children listless and causing them worse stomach pains than either had ever experienced before.

This was the picture that Mama Dawa saw when she came to greet the porters and collect the medicines and supplies that one of them had carried in for her. Raphael sat down and looked around. He was too tired to keep up with the conversations going on above him, although he could tell that a disagreement had broken out between the porters and the man to whom they answered. Slowly Raphael became aware of the arrival of a tall, angular figure wearing sunglasses and a clean, pressed black shirt that demonstrated he was above manual labour. He was angry that one of them had carried a child instead of bringing in goods that he could sell. The porters explained that nothing had been left behind and they had redistributed the contents of the pack that had been made into a litter. They had only carried the children one at a time when it became clear that they were too weak to walk. But Jean de Dieu's attitude was dismissive; he waved away their explanations and said that they must have been carrying too little in the past if it was so easy for eight men to carry the load of nine, so they would each have to carry more from now on.

When they protested that their loads were heavy and he didn't always pay them anyway, De Dieu simply shouted at them that he, not they, controlled this mine, and they would do what he told them. The men were hungry and desperate to be paid with the usual cash and food. As they all began to surround him and continued to argue, he grew more angry and effusive, refusing to back down.

Amid the clamour he announced that he had decided he would only pay them for the work of eight porters not the nine who had travelled for him. There was an outburst from the men whose anger swelled and seemed likely to turn to violence, until one of De Dieu's guards stepped up behind them and fired a burst of automatic gunfire into the air. The noise caught all of them by surprise and the men lapsed into silence when the shooting ended, their mood tense, bitter and resentful. No one dared take this dispute any further with him, knowing that the next time there was any firing it would not be into the air. De Dieu smiled with the arrogance of a man who knows he can always get what he wants, and turning on his heel he made his way through the sullen porters back into the adobe hut nearby that served as his office. He knew, too, that the porters would have to do as he told them or go without work and food entirely – he did not need them, even in a small mine like this miles from most villages there would always be other porters to take their place.

The men and the few families at the camp were free to come and go as they pleased, in theory. They were artisan labourers, paid – if they were paid at all – on a piece rate for the coltan they mined. In practice though, many were heavily indebted to the traders and most of all to him as the mine manager. Others were simply as hungry and penniless as Raphael and Keisha, their homes and livelihoods had also been destroyed and work at the mine was all that was left to them. One way or another, escape from this unending cycle of work and hunger was well nigh impossible.

When Jean de Dieu re-emerged twenty minutes later, now unaccompanied by his guards, the porters had received their food allocation from the windowless and heavily shuttered stores next door before returning angrily to their homes. Only one of them – the ambulance man – had given the children even a backward glance, but the trouble that they had caused and the very real cost to the porters and their families in lost food payment meant that none of them wanted to be responsible for the children any longer.

De Dieu's curiosity was evidently pricked by the two children who sat motionless, tired and alone on the ground before him and he could see an opportunity to conscript them into his workforce. He could sell those materials and food and, since they would be unable to pay him, he would sell them the things that he told them they needed, building up a debt that it would take years for them to repay.

The mine manager stood over Raphael and kicked the boy's foot to get his attention. "Who are you?"

Raphael was so tired that there was a prolonged pause before he could give the mine manager their names.

"You owe me money for the ride in my pick-up truck," he said abruptly. In fact, the truck belonged to the Army but they weren't to know that. "My men tell me they saved you and brought you from the river, though God knows why," he added.

"You have taken up the time of one of my porters for two days. You owe me money for that, too." Before they had even arrived it seemed they owed money to a man they'd never met, and now that debt was beginning to mount. "You will need food, tarps for a shelter, bedding blankets, two spoons and two cups," he said tallying the costs in his head. De Dieu could see that they would be working unpaid for him – apart from their food – for a long time to come, it would not be hard to string this out this when dealing with a boy who was barely a teenager.

Then unexpectedly the mine manager attempted a smile, which Raphael found almost as unsettling as being glared at. The smile played around his lips, never quite reaching his eyes and then evaporated before it had the intended effect of making them trust him. De Dieu had much to learn about the art of smiling.

"Make sure that they have everything they need," he said without even looking at his assistant who immediately began to make a pile on the ground outside the store. Two blankets were brought out, and a trenching tool to dig a latrine although the smell around them suggested that many people relieved themselves in the bushes. This was followed by two steel pans with lids, assorted tins of food -- many without labels and some bearing the dents and rusty edges of an already long life. On top of these were piled two torches only one of which had a bulb, bags of sugar, salt, tea, rice, flour and enough tarpaulin to cover a house.

Raphael had never had to buy much in the way of provisions and now, without ever asking for it, he suddenly found himself the ill-prepared owner of almost as much as his parents had acquired after fourteen years together. Until now the only things that he and Keisha possessed in the world, had been the clothes they wore. The children were too exhausted and naive to understand the debt with which they were being saddled. Nor could they possibly have known that it would only get worse as their clothes wore out, or they needed more food, soap, batteries or equipment. Without even knowing it they were teetering on the edge of a life enslaved.

They would surely have followed this inevitable path had not a large and commanding figure seen what was happening with the mine manager and taken them firmly and unquestioningly under her wing. Mama Dawa stepped forward and embraced the by-now bewildered children. "My loves, how did you ever manage to get here? It's so good to see you at last! I thought we had lost you both forever." She turned and swallowing her anger beamed her most beatific smile at Jean de Dieu, whose face had creased from an unaccustomed smile to a look of puzzlement.

"Are these your children, Mama?" Behind his sunglasses he searched her face for some clarification.

"Not mine, of course. They are my poor dear sister's children. I am sure you can see the family resemblance?" De Dieu turned a baffled look upon the children but was not quick enough to question this baseless claim.

Mama Dawa did not pause. "Quickly, children. Gather up what is yours and follow me," she said, urging the exhausted pair to their feet.

"Well, if you are responsible for them then you can pay me for the ride in the pick-up truck and for the porters who carried them here for the last two days," he asserted.

Mama Dawa stopped what she was doing and turned slowly to face him. This time the smile had gone and there was an edge to her voice as she spoke. "When I see those fine officers whose pick-up truck you have been using, I will be sure to thank them for making room for these children among all your supplies."

The self-assured swagger seemed to drain from him in an instant. De Dieu began to realise that perhaps he had misjudged her. He straightened to his full height to deal with this threat – they both knew that the army had never intended that he use their truck for his own business, it had only been left at the camp temporarily. He was in no hurry to explain to them how it came to be transporting men and materials many miles away, close to the river and the fighting. He could only bluster, "Well, if these kids are with you, then I suggest you take them away and keep them out of my way and out of trouble before I find them something useful to do."

He cursed at this sudden reversal and humiliation by the woman. She had whisked away the prospect of extra earnings and cheap labour just as it had been dangled in front of him. He turned and made his way back to his office, barking commands at two young men he passed, ordering them to clear up and return the untidy pile of supplies to the stores.

Jean de Dieu had been taken by surprise. Although he was vaguely aware of her before, Mama Dawa had never openly challenged his authority and both knew there was a grave risk for her in doing so. There had been a moment when he stared into her eyes with such intensity that she thought he might take his stick to her. The sunglasses he wore at all times had made it hard for her to predict his response, but also meant she couldn't see the depth of his anger and this had given her the courage to rebuke him. In truth, her intervention had been a reflex action on seeing the children being misused. She had acted first and thought second.

If Jean de Dieu had held little opinion of her before this, there was certainly no love lost between them now. Although a civilian, he was appointed by the army in Goma to command the work at this uncertified mine and the camp that had grown up beside it, and as far as he was concerned no self-appointed camp nurse was going to undermine that position. But Mama Dawa was tall as well as broad and she had held his gaze at length. He would never know how much her hands had trembled at the thought of what might happen if he called out his soldiers. All she knew was that she needed to get the children away from him before he started asking awkward questions, like what were their names.

"Come, children, let's go home quickly, before he returns." And without further discussion she took them both by the hand, stepped around his pile of unwanted belongings, and led them with her head high in case he was watching during the short walk to her tented home.

Jean de Dieu angrily kicked the soldiers out of his small, dusty office and sat at his empty desk brooding at this unexpected challenge to his authority. At least it had not been too public – the soldiers were lounging out of earshot on the front step of the office and his young staff standing behind him had paid little attention to his conversation with this troublesome woman.

Well, he would remind her soon that she and all her fellow miners were only there because he allowed them to be. After all, had he not been appointed by the army to manage the mine, to extract as much coltan as possible and deliver it to the Walikale Express? He would make sure that happened and that the mine paid him and his army bosses well for their trouble. It had already cost him hundreds of dollars in well-placed gifts to secure this position. And he had paid much of this direct to his army patron, no less than the FARDC's second in command at Goma barracks. It was time that people in the camp remembered who was in charge and to whom they should show loyalty in return for the privilege of working in such a lucrative new mine.

For the hundredth time he thought it would make more sense if the soldiers guarding the mine reported directly to him, Jean de Dieu, not to some never-seen officer in a distant barracks. Instead they were commanded by someone they never saw, who seldom paid them, and who they he had now forgotten to fear. These soldiers – he almost spat out the description he was so contemptuous of their abilities – had fought no real battles and could neither read nor write as he did, yet still they failed to show him the proper respect. Whether it was the fault of corruption and incompetence in Goma or further away in Kinshasa, he knew they were paid so infrequently by the army that inevitably they earned their living by stealing from his miners at gunpoint, and the miners blamed him.

The lesson the soldiers had learned was simple: if you were armed you were strong, and if you were strong you made yourself rich by taking from those who were weak. Hadn't the world always been like this? Wasn't this also what countries did to each other? He knew his Congo history. Just remember the millions of francs the country had been forced to pay the King of the Belgians. Just look at the fortune the old President Mobutu had stolen from the country's diamonds, copper and gold traders. Well now, in a small way, it was his turn.

Instead of being paid what was due to someone in his position, de Dieu had been reduced to squabbling with a camp wife like some kind of market trader, haggling with one another across a pile of blankets, tarps, pots and pans. He was angry at losing the chance to tie two youngsters into his private workforce, but Mama Dawa was clearly a more tricky character than he had realised. She held the respect of many in the camp, and it irritated him that she could use her experience as a weapon against him. Now she seemed to have appointed herself as the unofficial doctor and pharmacist for the camp, bringing in modern medicines from Goma and Bukavu and offering her own treatments and bush remedies for every imaginable condition from worms to miscarriage. Even her worst enemies, and the mine manager now counted himself at the head of any such group, could not fault her industry. People had noticed that the camp was now a healthier place than it had ever been before.

Mama Dawa was not accustomed to taking No for an answer. Having forced de Dieu to take back everything that he had tried to sell to Raphael, when she got back to her tent she instructed her eldest son, Mubalango to help Raphael rig up an extra tarp as a shelter for the children. The young man stretched the spare tarp across a long pole that was tied to a tree at one end and rested on the ground at the other. With rocks to hold the tarpaulin in place it made a quick and effective tent beside hers, in a space that until then she had used for drying clothes. She quickly despatched another child to retrieve two cardboard boxes from behind Jean de Dieu's storage hut and these were quickly flattened to give them some insulation and keep the sleeping children off the cold, damp ground at night. Mama Dawa had plenty of space, she said, and warm children were more important than dry washing. For her this was elementary logic, but for the two children it was the first sight of her strength, spontaneity and undemanding kindness, and it showed a degree of care that had been missing from their lives for days.

She was determined to keep them out of the clutches of the mine manager but with the newly expanded family it became obvious a day after her showdown with de Dieu that they would have to purchase some essentials from him. She hoped that by sending her eldest son, Mubalango, she might avoid the inevitable confrontation that would have occurred if she or Raphael had been forced to buy items from de Dieu. But when Mubalango returned with extra tarpaulins, two blankets, some cheap candles, mugs, bowls and other essentials it came as no surprise to find that the price for his monopoly supplies had doubled. Worse still, de Dieu was well aware that Mubalango was her son and instead of taking her money as she had expected, swore he would have his satisfaction a piece at a time if need be, starting with a new debt for Raphael and Keisha.

Two days after his arrival Raphael was alert enough to see that she and her husband Patrick had obtained some new essentials for them and he was embarrassed that he could not pay her for them. *The children would have to learn in time that such debts were not easily expunged in full*, she thought, but for now she decided to leave further discussion of his new debt until he was stronger.

Mama then set about the process of restoring their strength and health with porridge and hot bush tea sweetened with precious honey. Her concern for them was, if anything, even stronger on the second day when she saw their filthy and bruised condition in the daylight. Both children were despatched to the stream to clean themselves thoroughly and when they returned they were each given a mug containing a special infusion of Congo wood bark. Only when they had finished this soothing natural rinse for their stomachs were they allowed a bowl of plain rice mixed with chopped dried nuts from the same tree. Rich in fat, the flesh had been pared from the inch-long nuts leaving only the kernel. Mama Dawa then boiled them in the rice to add protein to their meal. The mild, sweet flavour of the nuts and the comfort of the rice was instantly popular with both children and, when added to their evening meals for the next two nights, went a long way to restoring their strength. On their third day in the camp each managed a full meal and their first smiles in a week.

As the first few days went by, the children settled into the rhythms of this large and bewildering camp. The sporadic shade of enormous trees around the mine kept the heat down but ensured that the camp was always gloomy. The smoke from cooking fires wound its way up into the highest branches where it appeared to linger like mist. The camp's most notable feature, however, was its pungent smell. This was a cloying mix of densely packed, unwashed humanity, wood smoke, tobacco, strong meats roasting over the fires, and when the wind was in the west the unmistakable scent of human excrement coming from beyond the treeline. Raphael thought there must be hundreds of tents and makeshift shelters here, but he was too tired to count them.

On the fourth morning Patrick thought the boy was showing strong signs of improvement so he appointed Raphael the final member of a new three-man team of miners led by Mubalango. The boy's evident weakness prompted inevitable protests from Mubalango at having an inexperienced thirteen-year-old on his gang, but as the days passed his resentment faded when he saw the willingness and determination that Raphael brought to everything he did. It was clear to them all that his small size and lack of stamina would count against him in the mine, at least until he built up his strength, but he had nimble fingers, and was learning quickly how to wash and sift the coltan from the mud and rock that bore it.

To begin with, Mubalango and his partner on the team, Bahati dug the rock and worked the streams to expose the precious columbite-tantalite ore. Determined to prove his worth to the two older boys, Raphael threw himself into the task of sifting and cleaning. At the end of his first week, and at Patrick and Mama Dawa's urging, he made his first small repayment to Jean de Dieu although all of this money was swallowed up in re-paying the interest. The couple had made it very clear to Raphael from the first day that the sooner he extracted himself from the mine manager's debt trap the sooner Raphael would be able to find his family.

Raphael's mind was still in a whirl and he understood little of what was happening to them, but the couple seemed kindly and protective towards him and Keisha so he took their advice. It was still hard to take in all that had happened to them since they had fled through the forest and been rescued by the porters. It might have ended so differently, Raphael knew that now. Keisha's cries and the noise of his fall had alerted the men who had been resting at the riverbank and re-filling their water bottles. The nearest village had emptied as the rebels retreated, so if the porters hadn't stopped him being washed down the river he would not have survived. And if they hadn't carried him to the mine Raphael guessed that they would have died from exhaustion and exposure.

Raphael felt weighed down by his responsibility for Keisha, and was torn between the need to find the rest of the family and the fear that he could not feed and clothe them both if he left the mine. Keisha was constantly asking him when they would be leaving to find Mama, and he hated this place as much as she did. All he could do was change the subject or tell her that they needed more money before they could resume their search. Keisha had replied that she wanted Mama not money, but at ten she had never been responsible for finding food to eat each night and somewhere warm and dry to sleep.

He thought of his missing family, of food and little else. There had been no means or opportunity for Raphael to search for his mother since the night they fled the village, and he felt it as a stabbing pain in his gut every time he thought about it. Curiously, there seemed to be a tacit agreement with Keisha that this agony must remain unspoken for now, but soon their search must begin again if they were to stand any chance of being reunited. Raphael knew, however, that without money to live on their search could not start for weeks or even months.

Chapter 8
London, UK
Two Months Ago

When it finally arrived, James almost overlooked the letter. He had been out all day taking photos to build his portfolio; there had been no interest in his work so far and his morale needed a boost. A message from Neil when he got in said he'd had to change plans and wouldn't be able to destroy James at squash that night, but he'd be happy to kick his butt tomorrow night.

It was all the more irritating for the truth it contained. At least the games had been less one-sided lately as James got back into shape, but losing six kilos hadn't turned him into a better ball player. He left his camera on the bed and dragged on his sports kit for a run. It was only then he remembered that he'd dropped the unopened mail on the kitchen table. Aside from the usual takeaway pizza delivery offers, it was inevitably all for Neil, save for one brown envelope addressed to James and marked 'General Records Office'. Inside was a letter inviting him to meet a counsellor to discuss the details of his adoption.

James was surprised how nervous he felt at the prospect and spent the intervening days trying to imagine all the outcomes. He was still apprehensive ten days later when he sat down with the counsellor in a small room at the local authority office in Kensington & Chelsea. Mrs Darshna Khan introduced herself with an encouraging smile but he was on edge, toying with his papers as she talked. Briefly, she went through his reasons for wanting to see his adoption records and confirmed the little information that he already knew, then Mrs Khan silently folded her hands on the table and looked him unwaveringly in the eye.

"James, these are the records you requested." She slid a small folder towards him, "but I'm afraid we have some sad news. Your mother's details are shown here, of course, but I regret to say she passed away more than twenty years ago."

James had been in the process of opening the folder but he stopped and let out a long breath before closing his eyes. He felt the tension wash out of him only to be replaced instantly by a suffocating tide of disappointment. He said nothing and waited for her to carry on.

"Her name was Sophie Callender and she's listed as a spinster. So, this is her maiden name." James was unable to take in the completeness of this loss at once, it was only now that he realised how many hopes he had pinned on a positive outcome. Mrs Khan's voice filled the silence, "It's there in the file, there's a copy of her death certificate as well as your birth certificate which gives us a bit more information. I'm very sorry."

It might sound weak to anyone who knew their family background, but it had taken him years to build up the courage to confront this gaping hole in his past. Now, just as he had felt on the point of identifying his true family, he found that his mother had died when he was only two. It felt as though a curtain had been lifted on the most important scene in his life, yet before he could see the faces of the actors on stage it had dropped again.

Suddenly he had questions and they all came at once. What happened? How did she die? She can't have been very old. Where's she buried? The pent-up curiosity spilled out of him.

"I think she was twenty-one when she had you, she must have been about twenty-three when she passed away. From what we know – and the records don't tell us much – she was travelling in the United States and fell ill without warning. As she was on her own, it was a couple of days before the Embassy in Washington was notified that she was in hospital and she died before her family could be told, much less be at her bedside. The death certificate says it was a coronary. We don't know of any history of heart problems – it must have come out of the blue. She passed away in a California hospital, and because of the sudden and unexplained nature of her death the records say there had to be a post-mortem, or an autopsy as the California records put it. I've checked what I can with the Foreign Office who organised for her … her repatriation, and they told the post-mortem found it was natural causes, she may have contracted a virus affecting her heart. In any case, her remains were flown back for burial in the UK. The details of where she was buried are listed in there," she gestured to the file. "I'm so sorry this isn't better news."

James sat stunned, staring at the small pile of copied reports and letters in front of him. Viewed now, her life seemed so fragile, so short and to have little to show for it. She had died when he was only two years old – God, she had been younger when she died than he was now – and now he would never be able to ask her the questions that burned inside him; why was he put up for adoption, what were her feelings towards him, was she angry at getting pregnant, who was his birth father, how had they met, what had happened between them? It was all too much to take in, too bitter to swallow and he felt more crushed than he would have expected.

James had understood all along that his mother might not want to see him, but thinking that she would probably be in her early fifties he had never considered that she might be dead. He had hoped for at least one meeting and maybe the answers to some questions that gnawed at him. Now he just felt deflated, emotionally exhausted and utterly empty. He had to admit that he had quietly nursed hopes of being reunited with a mother who might care about him, hopes that had been snatched away, and this time forever. In the past, finding her had always been a tantalizing possibility and now that was gone. Her legacy suddenly seemed so small; her mark on the world had been washed away before he'd even glimpsed it.

It seemed ridiculous to feel emotional at the loss of someone he'd never even met. He tried to focus on the present. "Is there anything else you can tell me about her?"

"Well, we have her address in London at the time of your adoption. I don't know whether it's her family's home or just somewhere she was renting, I couldn't say."

"OK, but what about my father, my birth father that is?" he corrected himself. "Is there anything in there about him?" James gestured to the slim file, but even as he said it he knew this was a long shot.

Mrs Khan shook her head. "Nothing at all, I'm sorry. He doesn't appear on your birth certificate, all of which is quite normal for the period. Unfortunately for many children born at this time, if their birth parents weren't married there was no requirement to name the birth father, mostly they didn't."

He hadn't expected the moon and the stars, but James had hoped at least for some clues to his history – if only to know where in the world his parents came from, who his family were or what they did. Yet, it seemed he would never know more than he did now.

He tried to focus on what Mrs Khan was saying. "... and if you have any other questions that you think I may be able to help with, do please contact me, James. We will do whatever we can to shed light on this. Perhaps if you look into her family's history. Callender is not an especially common name in London. Scottish, I believe."

James picked up the file and stood. "Thank you," he mumbled and walked out in a daze. The sun had come out in London for the first time in weeks but it didn't even register with a bitterly disappointed man.

******

To James's credit the outward evidence of his disappointment did not last long, but the feeling of a lost opportunity ran deep within him and he thought it would linger forever. He felt a visceral pain for his birth mother who had died alone and so far from home. While he was thinking about it, he decided to drop the term birth mother for her; he would call Sophie his mother, regardless of the continued existence of Yvette who certainly hadn't earned the title. Maybe Sophie's death had been quick, but he couldn't shake the feeling that she must have felt frightened and lonely at the end.

A few days later James found himself knocking on the door at Sophie's last known London address, rehearsing how to introduce himself to people who might be his family. No one there knew anything about her, which wasn't surprising given that she had left more than twenty-five years ago. Houses and flats changed hands all the time in London; there could have been dozens of occupants since Sophie had lived there.

James was determined to keep a positive attitude and he was helped by a growing excitement at the portfolio he was creating, and he threw himself into this work with an almost febrile energy. It took a few days longer than he had anticipated but eventually James had assembled and edited a portfolio that he wanted to show. Having uploaded a selection of images to an online folder he emailed his former tutor whose photographic opinion he respected above all others. His tutor's delight at seeing his protégé, hitherto a student amateur, taking his first tentative steps into the professional arena had been infectious and his advice invaluable. Although James would have preferred to offer more images and wider variety, it didn't look too bad as a starting point and his tutor was encouraging.

James drafted a covering email which he sent to commissioning editors at several international image banks, and one came back that evening – thanks, but no thanks. Two took longer, with the same result. A week later the others had failed to reply and he sent polite reminders.

He wasn't disheartened; at last he felt there was a new direction in his life. James was quietly convinced that someone would like his work if only he could get them to look at it.

******

The message that really shook him came out of left field. James was going to the gym early every day; it woke him up, cleared his head, and he was getting into shape again. When he'd finished breakfast at a deli near the gym, he strolled down Sydney Street towards Neil's apartment, ignoring the wind that hurled itself around him today. He felt as physically strong as he had in years, and looked less like the desk jockey of the last two years.

He was about to start work on submissions to other image agencies and publishers when the front door buzzer sounded and the postman asked him to sign for a letter. It was a surprise to find the letter was for him, once again marked 'General Records Office' and bearing a 'Confidential'. What else there was to discuss?

Inside a typed letter was attached to an envelope that had been opened already. The covering letter was printed on UK Home Office paper and read:

Dear James,

Further to our meeting last week, I am very pleased to report that we have uncovered some further information relating to your adoption. I should explain that the private adoption agency managing your case was wound up several years ago and its correspondence was found to be in a poor state.

Since then our office has come across several cases where old documents were wrongly filed, and occasionally we still discover items that have been misplaced. As a precaution following our meeting, I asked to see all the old adoption agency's records beginning with serial code C for Callender and, knowing what has happened in the past, under F for Falkus. We looked in that year and for the next two years to ensure that we had given you every piece of relevant information. There was nothing wrong with the first file, but a letter addressed to you and intended for the Callender file had been received several months before the death of your birth mother. This had been misfiled under your adoptive surname and was not found again until today, for which I sincerely apologise.

The letter was opened when I came across it; I presume this would have been done at the time of receipt to work out what action to take with it and ensure it was appropriate to be kept on file. Since it was addressed to you, I am enclosing the original (we have retained a copy).

I hope it helps to shed light on your adoption and I will be very pleased to discuss it with you at any time. Once again, please accept my apologies on behalf of both agencies for any distress caused by our delay in getting this letter to you, and let me assure you of this department's continuing commitment to supporting you in any way we can.

Yours sincerely,
Darshna Khan (Mrs)
Identity & Passport Service

James hurriedly pulled open the attached letter. It had been written on flimsy blue airmail paper and folded to create an envelope, but it was so discoloured with age that it now had a greenish tinge to it. Though still legible the writing in a feminine hand looked faded. On the outside there were two simple stamps, bearing a portrait of some guy he'd never heard of and the legend USA 50. The letter was addressed to David, the name he had been given by his birth mother.

The Palace Hotel
Market Street
San Francisco
California
4th January, 1984
Dear David,

I guess this letter is going to come as a bit of a shock, whenever you get it. Maybe I should start by introducing myself, I am your natural mother, Sophie Callender. I've wanted to write this letter ever since I had to give you up for adoption, but I've put it off because you may be so angry with me for not keeping you. I just want to tell you how sad I was to let you go, and how much I miss you every day – even now.

That must seem strange when I only had you for a few weeks, but any mother will tell you what her new baby means to her. So being told by everyone that I couldn't keep you, and seeing there was no way for me to provide for you it seemed the only solution. If there had been a way to keep you believe me, I would have found it.

My family say that I must not write to you, that I'll confuse things for you when hopefully you've found a good home with people who love you too. It's taken me a long time to work out that I don't agree with them. I think every child should know where they come from. I mean your blood family. One day I'd love to meet you if you'll let me so I can explain what happened.

If I don't write this letter now, maybe I never will. If you're reading this, it must mean you've tried to contact me. I'm sad to say that I split up with your father before I came to America. In fact, being on my own was the main reason I couldn't keep you – I had no money and I needed a job. We were very much in love once but we couldn't work out how to be together and still do the things we planned to do in our lives, with his business and my art. It sounds pretty stupid or stubborn by both of us, but we didn't know you were on the way when we broke up. We thought we were just making decisions about our own futures.

I met your father Axel Terberg, while I was studying for a Fine Art degree in London and he was travelling around Europe on business. We travelled together and then we tried living together for a time, but that was less happy. Your father was very special to me and the time we spent together was exciting, but my parents just thought I was wild. My Dad didn't like him, he thought he was too ambitious and didn't come from a "good family" and they wanted nothing to do with him. I had to choose and I loved him so I chose Axel then they stopped talking to me. I'd never had an easy relationship with them, so I don't regret the choice I made.

I'm sorry, this sounds like I'm making excuses for having you adopted. That's not what I mean at all, it was my choice and it was the hardest thing I have ever done, or ever will do.

For a time Axel and I were happy living together, but his work kept taking him abroad. London didn't offer him the right opportunities for buying and selling gemstones. He worked in Antwerp and sometimes needed to travel at short notice to where the gems were being mined or finished. I tried going with him a couple of times, once to Bombay in India and then to Zaire in Africa. We stayed in Kinshasa, and I was able to paint and photograph the people and the markets. Axel loved it there and it's where I last heard from him.

Maybe I slowed him down because he stopped asking me on business and anyway I was starting my own career. I wonder if you are artistic? I'd love to know what you will be when you grow up, but that's a long way off. You're still only two years old and it will be many years before you read this letter, if you ever do.

James paused to take this in. She was writing a letter to a small child, not knowing if he'd ever receive it when he was older, and obviously fearing that – even if he did – he wouldn't try to get in touch. The cruel irony was that he knew now he would have loved to meet her, but it was all too late. She was gone. James tried to read on but his eyes were burning and he angrily wiped them with the back of his hand. He was being pathetic; he'd never met her and here he was upset by a letter she'd written twenty-five years ago. He looked down at the letter again.

I really hope you will get in touch with me when you're old enough, because I'm not allowed to contact you. I don't even know where you are – just somewhere in Britain was all they would tell me.

It might have been different if Axel and I had stayed together. We've lost touch now and I don't know how to find him and tell him about you. I hope I can one day. All I can say is that we were too young to settle down, our lives were pulling us in different directions and there was a lot of pressure from my family.

I've had time since you were born to do a lot of thinking. And I still think of you every day, David – that's not an exaggeration. I know I always will. I wonder where you are right now, if you're happy, and who is looking after you. It makes me so sad that I can't find you. All I can do is hope that this reaches you and one day you'll want to know where you came from.

I'm not sorry that I had you, I was very proud of you. You were the most beautiful baby I've ever seen and it tore my heart into little tiny pieces when the nurses came to take you away. I think about you all the time and I just hope we can meet one day, I hope you are having a happy childhood, and I'm sorry for the mess I made of your start in life. There will always be a hole in my life that's shaped like you. Until we meet please be safe and be happy. With all my love,

Sophie (Mum)

Xxx

He knew it was the most important letter he'd ever received, one that had so nearly been lost forever, and one that he would have to read and re-read.

Beneath her signature she had written in print, Sophie Callender and a phone number. It was too short for a London number these days and he knew the numbers had changed a lot over the years. Even if he had a working number she was dead and her parents would be dead too. *And, if not*, he thought wryly, *the shock of him turning up after all these years would probably finish them off.*

James sat down. He stared at the letter, skimming through sections and trying to find connections in his character with his long-dead mother. He nearly hadn't received the letter at all thanks to some idiot misfiling it years ago. It was only thanks to Mrs Khan that he'd seen it at all.

He leaned back in his chair and stared at the ceiling which helped to clear his eyes. How did he feel about his mother now? He paused. He wasn't angry, how could he be? She hadn't had a choice, he knew that. Attitudes to single mothers weren't the same then as they were now. He felt sorry for her; she had been in an impossible position with little or no family support and had taken the only course open to her. She was studying Art and now he wanted to see her work.

As the thoughts stumbled into his head one after another, James knew he was lucky. He hadn't suffered; he'd gone to a wonderful home with an amazing dad and brother. OK, his mum was a waste of space as a parent but he had a good relationship with Neil when his bro wasn't telling him what to do.

All this information was too much to take in at once. After years of nothing, suddenly he knew so much more about his mother. Despite its serious message he felt she was almost chatting to him, and telling him everything as openly as she could. It must have been a hell of a difficult letter to write after what she'd been through with the adoption, with her family and Axel.

Now, for the first time in his life, he knew something about his father. It wasn't much, but at last he had a name and an unusual one – at least it was unusual in Britain. James knew his father's occupation, he was a gem dealer or miner, and he even knew a bit about one period in their lives. In fact, James knew more about this period than his father did; Axel had never been told Sophie was pregnant. He also knew that his mother and father had been serious, together, an item. That mattered to him; he wasn't just the result of some one-night stand.

Axel Terberg. What kind of name was that? It sounded German or Swedish or something. He had obviously cared about Sophie if they'd lived together and travelled together when he was starting up his business. He'd been based in Antwerp. There could be tons of Terbergs in Belgium – even if you only looked in the gem trade. OK, so their relationship hadn't lasted, but he hadn't walked out on her because she was pregnant, which had always been James's suspicion. Axel had never even known about James.

He opened his web browser and typed in Axel Terberg. How many could there be? Did this make him half German? Or Belgian?

The first thing to come up online was a link to a truck manufacturer in the Netherlands called Terberg. Next was a *YouTube* video featuring someone called Axel. Then a load of Dutch language sites; did that mean that Terberg was Dutch not German? He kept searching; more trucks and spare parts. Some Terberg software he wasn't interested in, and more links in Dutch. But nothing on Axel Terberg, dammit. Surely anyone in business these days would appear somewhere online, wouldn't they? Unless he was hiding, or was he dead, too?

He tried another search engine; same result, then a Dutch search engine. Not a bloody thing. James put his head on the desk and banged his forehead hard three times. He didn't feel any better afterwards, worse actually, but it gave him something else to think about for a moment.

Yes, Axel might be dead by now. He'd probably be in his fifties, so perhaps not. All these possibilities were doing his head in, and there were still more loose ends than answers. James stood up, grabbed his coat and went for a long walk to clear his head before finally drinking alone in a pub he didn't know, where no one knew him, miles from home.

******

It was later that night while he was mulling over the letter that he realised he didn't even know where Zaire was, much less Kinshasa. Axel had obviously enjoyed spending time there but James knew nothing about it. He'd heard the name, but he couldn't place it on a map so he opened the laptop.

What came up, though, became increasingly difficult to read. Wikipedia reminded him, if he'd ever known it, that Kinshasa was the capital of the Democratic Republic of the Congo, or DRC. Zaire was the name given to the country by the late President Mobutu who had taken over in a coup. The Belgians left what they called the Congo after its largest river, they had brutally colonized the place for its rubber, and their Prince Leopold didn't mind who suffered in the process. Then the story became even more grim and complicated. There had been decades of Mobutu's corrupt dictatorship, backed by America's CIA and France, followed by years of civil war. Just when he thought it couldn't get any worse James read that it had turned into a regional war with up to five million Congolese people killed, and the people still seemed to be suffering even though the war was supposed to be over.

How could one country be so unlucky? The stories were so harsh James found it hard to read on. The two Congo Wars had been hellish for almost everyone, but for women and children it was beyond belief. Rape had been used to intimidate whole regions, in fact it seemed it was still being used as a weapon against civilians. Women and young girls were systematically being raped by fighters on all sides – even by the DRC army who were sent in to protect their own people. The UN said that mass rape was still happening on an almost unheard of scale to make populations leave their land, or to cow them into supporting one armed group or another. Videos on *YouTube* showed innocent civilians – even children and babies – who had been mutilated, having their arms or legs cut off with axes and machetes by soldiers. And sometimes these attacks were happening unchallenged just a few miles from the nearest UN outpost. The UN forces were heavily outnumbered and often outgunned, so no one was being brought to justice for these crimes and he had no idea why this was allowed to continue.

He couldn't work out whether the UN peace-keepers knew about these attacks but feared to intervene, or were genuinely unaware of mass rapes of hundreds of women and girls happening near their bases, sometimes for days on end. The first time he read about an attack James had to stop, he was so shocked at the savagery. Yet somehow it seemed cowardly not to learn more. He'd only gone online to find out about Kinshasa, the Congolese capital and now he was learning about attacks continuing to this day because nobody was willing or able to stop them.

Why wasn't this on the TV news? He watched it most nights and was sure he'd never seen anything about this. Weren't there any journalists there reporting these things, or didn't the editors think it was newsworthy? One link took him to some harrowing videos and a few organizations' names kept coming up when he scoured the web for news reports. Oddly, it wasn't the BBC or CNN; it was human rights groups, charities, even freelance reporters who seemed to be risking their lives to report on the front line.

As he lay in bed that night trying to sleep, images kept coming to mind of this beautiful looking country that seemed to have extraordinary wealth in copper, gold and diamonds, yet for some reason it was still poverty-stricken and caught in unending war. It was only in the small hours that James finally fell into a restless and troubled sleep. The airmail letter from his birth mother in California was still open on his bedside table. He had read it and re-read it several times searching for any morsel of information he might have overlooked. The airmail was crumpled from its transatlantic journey, yet in the blue light from his alarm clock the faded twenty-six year old letter looked almost new.

Chapter 9
A Coltan Mine, Walikale District, North Kivu, DRC
Two Years Ago

Darkness would soon cloak the mine, but Raphael and his fellow workers could not afford to stop while there was still light. The rain that had earlier cooled the miners as they sweated over their shovels and picks was falling harder now, as though determined not to be ignored. Raphael could scarcely lift his arms he was so tired, his shoulders were like lead weights, and the muscles in his forearms felt as though they were on fire. The rain ran down his forehead and into his eyes, carrying the sweat salt and mud with them. It made his eyes sting and they watered so that he could see even less of the earth and rock in front of him.

His T-shirt stuck to his back as the rainwater trickled down his body and filled his yellow plastic boots. To a casual observer they might have seemed incongruous footwear, but many around him were wearing something similar, while others were barefoot or shod only in flip-flops. Periodically Raphael would stop to empty his boots but the effort seemed so much harder this late in the day. The sun's heat was disappearing fast and the rain was chilling him through. Barely a teenager, Raphael found that his energy – so strong earlier in the day – usually deserted him by mid-afternoon. It was then a case of getting through the remaining hours as best he could. The older miners complained of aches and pains in the chill morning air when he was at his liveliest, but by this time of day their stronger frames carried them through the remaining hours, leaving him going through the motions at barely half the speed he had managed earlier.

Droplets of water ran off his nose, falling to join other rivulets of water in the dirt around his feet. His shorts were soaked through, but Raphael noticed little of this. He was only concerned at his failing strength. It was bearable for now while his mind was focused, but from time to time as the day expired he had simply felt overwhelmed. When he grew dizzy and then faint, he was forced to sit down. Hunger only made it harder to concentrate, and cramps squeezed his stomach like a twisted, tightening rope before leaving him as quickly as they had come. Torpor stretched over him again today weighing him down like a sodden blanket, but for

Keisha's sake he could not allow himself to stop. If they were to be paid, then he and his team would need to finish digging and sifting another bag of coltan tonight.

At moments like these his mind would wander into daydreams while he continued rhythmically and listlessly swinging his shovel, digging it into the rock and sand below the water line. The stream had been diverted by other people earlier in the day. The heavy drops of rain that fell all around him flowed down the thirty foot slopes of the gulley to his left and right. As the trickles slowly merged into rivulets, they gained momentum and joining forces began to dash more eagerly into the stream where he stood. The light was dimming rapidly. Raphael feebly pushed his shovel forward, feeling the tip strike the tell-tale rough ridges of coltan in the stream bed.

He lifted the spade's handle and turning it at right angles struck again at the dark grey rock, dislodging small quantities amid the yellow ochre sand and muddy water. A piece of rock almost the size of his own fist came loose and he grasped it before it could be swept away by the stream. Around them it was mostly sand-coloured rock but darker chips or even lumps of coltan could be seen within it and this one he passed to his neighbour to be pounded with a hammer, revealing its vital cargo. Below him a muddy mix of water, coltan ore and sandy rock was being rinsed and sifted by the third member of their gang to reveal and separate the precious minerals. The young man scooped the ore that he'd already retrieved from the rock into the open top of a battered plastic measuring jug and beckoned to Raphael and his partner who was further up the stream. They had enough to sell and before it was dark they needed to get the coltan to the *negociants*, the mine-side dealers who sold the ore in the cities on the border.

Together they struggled up the loose soil of the bank to the lip of the open mine, and there they drooped exhausted at the top for a moment. They might just be in time for they could see a coltan trader standing under the trees. Finishing a deal with another crew, he handed over the dollar bills to the head of the gang and stowed the bag of coltan in his backpack. They started down the hill to meet him but as he saw the boys arriving he began to wag his finger from side to side indicating that they were too late, he was leaving for the day. But this *negociant* was on good terms with eighteen year-old Mubalango, and when he saw who it was beneath the floppy-brimmed hat he relented. In truth it was not just their relationship that stopped him leaving; the extra profit was a strong influence on his time keeping. He had debts to pay, too, and this had not been a good week or two, with new soldiers arriving in the area demanding extra taxes from him. So he preferred to take the late coltan now rather than risk losing it to another trader in the morning. It didn't stop him grumbling loudly over the delay they were causing him, but everyone knew it was for his benefit as well. With an elaborate show of impatience he sat down again and took out his scales to view and measure the coarse and uneven grey-black granules.

The small charcoal-coloured stones that made up their haul of coltan for the day came to two and a half kilos in weight. The boys were not to know it, but in Europe or the United States, that would be worth over three hundred dollars, and the price had briefly been three times higher a few years before. But here in the forest close to Walikale there would be no such largesse. As the trader packed away the coltan and left them, they were relieved to share ten dollars between them. No one traded here in the local currency, the Congolese Franc. US dollars or food were all that the miners would work for. Until he came here Raphael had never touched a dollar bill, these days each dollar represented a little more hope for him and for Keisha.

This was harder work than any of the three boys had ever experienced, but Raphael knew that his share would have been close to two weeks' farming income for his father. That went some way to making up for the blisters on their hands, the dirt that rhymed every fold of skin, and the aching backs they felt each evening and morning. Raphael thought for a moment of the work that his father would have had to do if he was to earn three dollars as he had, and knew deep down that he needed to make every cent count if it was to help them search for the family.

Raphael grew angry at these unguarded thoughts of his father, a man he had looked up to, whom he had followed in all things and lost so suddenly. His bitterness was focused on the murderous fighters who had killed Baba for no reason, and he was struggling every day with these emotions knowing that he would never be able to avenge this. He would never see them brought to justice; there would be no payback for their indiscriminate theft of his father's life. Although weeks had now gone by, he could not escape the image that slipped unwanted into his head time and again. His mind kept revisiting the memories of his former family life, and once the sequence started in his head it was almost impossible to stop. That life was now so far behind him, not just in miles but also in experience that it seemed to belong to another Raphael and another Keisha. They were two children who had played in the village, who tried to avoid the chores their mother found for them, collecting water from the well, sweeping the floor of their house, rounding up the chickens at night and counting their eggs in the morning. Each memory of his father ended the same way in the flickering darkness as their village was torched and Baba was shot from behind, as he urged Raphael to escape with the family.

The boy's anger was spurred on by the feeling that he should have done something to protect his father from the cowards who shot him in the back. He could have shouted a warning at least, but he had stood still and done nothing that made a difference. He hadn't even found the rest of the family, all that he had left was Keisha and he was all that remained to her. In his tiredness his thoughts of despair were less focused but no less painful. He wondered if his parents would now have struggled to recognise their children had they found them today in this vulnerable state. Raphael's hair was longer and more tangled. His hands were scraped and scarred from clashes with the rock and, though he knew that it must apply to him too, he was worried for Keisha who had lost so much weight. Her fragile hope of finding Mama easily became over-optimistic and then was brought to despair. With the benefit of his extra years he had come to realise that it might be many weeks or months before they found the rest of the family – he simply would not allow himself to think that it might never happen.

Raphael had spent every cent that he had earned so far in feeding them both and paying off the soldiers for his licence to dig. The licence had cost $20 – that was if you had a spare $20. If you didn't – and Raphael and Keisha had arrived with nothing – then the mine owner, whose pick-up truck they had ridden in, would lend you the money and you could pay $40 for the licence, paying a part of it each month. There was nothing left by the time they'd also paid him for food and a few other essentials they hadn't been able to borrow from Mama Dawa including a pan, two blankets, soap and matches at a similarly extortionate interest rate. Tonight was the night when, exhausted as he was, the boy's hard work would begin to pay off; they would be fed and still have some money left over. Most days they managed only one meal, usually a maize porridge or broth before going to bed. Many times in the first few weeks he had gone to work with no breakfast and come home to find no supper. Those had been the worst days, but now he intended to begin saving for their journey, even though he had no idea where it might take them.

He had planned it all days and days ago. Raphael knew that he couldn't leave money lying around, and carrying it on him risked either robbery or losing it during the day's hard work. So he had saved an empty coffee tin that one of their neighbours had thrown out. He washed it in the stream before stowing it in their camp. Sure enough, although empty, one day when he got back from work he found that it had been moved. He questioned Keisha about it, but she could hardly have been less interested in his empty can, and said she'd never even seen it before. He knew then that this was not like their village where everyone was either family or friends – he knew that he could not trust to luck or the honesty of those around him.

Many people passed through the camp on their way to the mine and he would not always be there to protect his money, so one day he had taken a detour when he had gone to the latrine. No more than ten paces from the main path he had been able to drop down out of sight behind the bole of a large and distinctive tree whose roots spread left and right along an earth bank. Just as he'd guessed he might, he had found a hole dug by an animal and here he stowed the tin can as deeply as he could reach and well out of sight of anyone passing by. Although the mouth of the hole was as wide as the top of his leg, there were no new tracks nearby and it appeared abandoned. The tree was set back from the path, and the steep bank on which it stood faced away from anyone using the path. In any case, many of the miners never took the path to the latrine, simply relieving themselves in the bushes close to the tents – in some parts of the camp the stench was over-powering – so he was confident that this would be a safe hiding place. The latrine gave him a reason to be going along the path day or night and, once off the path and into the undergrowth, he would be well screened. Nor was there any reason he could see why anyone else might wander into the area; even if they happened to stop by the tree the tin can would be hidden well out of sight. He knew he must ensure that he was never seen leaving or returning to the pathway or it might raise suspicions.

Raphael's mind swung back from his plans to the present. As the trader repacked his backpack and left them, the three boys, Raphael, Mubalango and Bahati shared out the dollar bills and joked among themselves. "I am saving for a girlfriend," Mubalango laughed. "When she sees how much money I have, she will be so, so nice to me." Bahati grinned and the older boys slapped hands in a street handshake that Mubalango had learned in Bukavu. "She's gonna look so fine, walk with her nose in the air like she don't even see you other guys. You all are just something she'd step around. But me, she'll treat me fine. Cook me meals with meat every night, bring me beers that are cold and make all my nights so warm I won't even need a blanket."

"How's she gonna do all that if she's so blind," asked Bahati impishly.

"She ain't blind … hey, come here and say that, Bahati."

As usual, Bahati was one step ahead of Mubalango. He danced out of reach as the eighteen year-old boy tried to grab his shirt. Bahati was older than Raphael, heavier and stronger but would be no match for Mubalango even in a play fight. He knew it, so he used his speed to dodge the bigger boy. Raphael didn't know where he found the energy. Ten minutes earlier they had all been on the point of collapse but now, with money in their pockets and the prospect of a good supper ahead their spirits had risen and their energies with them.

Afterwards, Raphael could not be sure whether it had been the noise of their horseplay that had made him slow to see the threat, or whether it was just exhaustion. Either way, the first thing he knew of the armed gang's presence was a metallic clack as a large weapon was readied behind him. Within moments he heard other weapons being readied in the half-darkness on all sides. Dark faces and dark uniforms emerged from the bushes behind and beside them. Raphael naturally associated these soldiers with the men who had brought savagery and destruction to his village. His knees went weak and he was ashamed to sense it but he instantly felt a warm dark patch spread across the front of his shorts as his bladder prepared him to run. But his legs would not co-operate, they felt as weak as water while two, three, no … Four figures came closer to them. He could hear blood pounding in his ears and his mouth went completely dry.

Mubalango had also had his back to the first soldier who emerged from the bush, while he had tried to grab hold of Bahati and remind him who was the gang boss. Raphael, who had begun to relax and feel secure in his gang, was instantly more scared than he had ever felt in his life. The only one to react quickly was Bahati. He had been dancing on his toes to dodge Mubalango's grasp. Seeing the grasses part behind Mubalango and a shadowy figure with a huge rifle rise like a spirit from the ground he spun around and fled. Bahati was a quick runner, and although he had been hard at work all day his fear gave him a speed that might even have surprised him. The gang would have shot him down without hesitation if they had had a clear view. Perhaps those closest to Bahati were slow to react, or maybe he was away so fast that they couldn't loose off a shot in time. Either way, the boy named for his lucky nature managed to sprint clear of the group and disappeared in the dusk among the bushes and trees, leaving Mubalango and Raphael to their fate.

By now all the soldiers' guns were levelled at them and, nervous lest they let go of their remaining catch, they ordered the boys to kneel. A rifle barrel was pushed hard into Mubalango's stomach and there were shouted commands for him to put his hands in the air. He wanted to rub his stomach but he knew he could not risk it, so he raised his hands and beside him so did Raphael. Tension crackled in the evening air, and Raphael thought desperately of Keisha and how she would soon be alone in the world. There would be no one to protect her, one day to lead her back to her village and help her find the rest of their family. Nobody would hold her when she had nightmares, wash and comb her hair or nurse her when she was sick. This was the job that Baba had entrusted to him and suddenly it was clear to Raphael that he had failed within a few short weeks. He had no time to think of his own loss, he just felt the piercing agony of a responsibility unmet, a tacit promise to his father that he had not fulfilled. He felt a slap across the back of the head and knew he had missed something.

"… Give it to me!" said the soldier standing in front of Mubalango and Raphael looked up. The figure behind the gun was little more than a boy. He was older than Raphael, but probably no more than sixteen and clearly younger and smaller than Mubalango. Two of the other soldiers hid their expressions behind dark glasses but you could look into the eyes of this boy. Except there was nothing there to see. Raphael's mother had once told him that you could learn a person's history in their eyes and he had never found a reason to doubt it, until now. This boy was different. Of course, the natural dark brown of his eyes was compounded by the failing light but this close he would have expected to read a story, to gauge his character. The boy's pupils were enormous, and the whites of his eyes were reddened and tinged at the corners with an unhealthy yellow. Although the eyes flicked left and right between his hostages, in the depths there seemed to be no life remaining, no compassion, not even a human recognition. He was also angry.

His body language told Raphael that this young man was not in charge, but he was certainly the most vocal and agitated. The other soldiers behind him were tense but said nothing. They seemed eager to be away but this one, the smallest of them, had swung a gun that was too large for his slim frame onto his back. Secured by a sling that not only stretched across his chest but also hung to his hips and thigh, the gun was clearly heavy and awkward for the boy soldier to manage while he searched the first of Mubalango's pockets. Whenever the boy leaned forward, the heavy butt of the gun swung unbidden to his front so that the muzzle pointed to the sky and the gun appeared to control the boy's movements. At this the older soldiers began to laugh which only made the youngster more self-conscious and angry. Raphael wished they would stop for he was sure that the boy would take out his anger on his prisoners. Clearly, he knew that Mubalango and Raphael were both watching him closely and this earned the nearest, Mubalango a heavy backhanded slap across the mouth. By now the soldier had found a small roll of dollars in the bigger miner's breast pocket. It wasn't much, but it was everything that he had managed to save.

"How much have you found, Little Bean?" called the furthest soldier.

Little Bean didn't respond at first, perhaps keen to prove his independence, or resentful of his nickname. Eventually he shouted back, "Nothing. Maybe ten." He turned to Raphael, "What about you? It's time to pay your taxes."

With a dry mouth Raphael found it hard to speak. He made to say something but he was scared and no sound at all came out. The younger soldier must have taken this as resistance for he kicked at Raphael with his left boot. Raphael was now kneeling and the young soldier's blow struck the top of his right thigh. It did, however, serve its purpose for Raphael found his voice. "I have only three dollars," he managed to say, "but I need to feed my sister."

The soldier grinned, "You can do that after you have fed my brothers." And he made to reach into the pocket of Raphael's shorts at which point he saw the unmistakable evidence of the young miner's terror. He hesitated as he stood above Raphael. "Give it to me." Raphael waited a moment too long and the long gun came off the shoulder and was turned on him. "Give it to me or I will take it and your sister."

Raphael reached into the pocket of his shorts. The money was there and somehow still dry. Even in his exhaustion the dilemma seemed simple, he could be hungry again or he could be dead.

A hiss came from Mubalango beside him, "Bloody give it to them, or we'll both die."

It was enough to focus Raphael's mind and he passed the folded bills to the boy with dead eyes who made to put the money into his own top pocket only to receive a shove in the back from the soldier behind him. The money was reluctantly passed on. The soldiers stepped back a pace or two and suddenly

Raphael could tell that Mubalango was worried, too, for he shifted uneasily where he kneeled alongside. They could not have been satisfied with their haul, and they would have known that catching a *negociant* would have brought a far better result. But, for whatever reason, they had emerged too late and that had not happened today. The soldiers stepped backwards cautiously, watching their prisoners all the while, before melting silently away into the darkness as softly as they had emerged.

Mubalango let out his breath very slowly, and Raphael did what any boy of his age might do in the circumstances, he began to cry.

******

Keisha knew immediately that something was very wrong when Raphael and Mubalango arrived in the camp after dark, and without Bahati. This was later than they'd ever returned from work before and she was growing scared despite the calming influence of Mama Dawa.

Raphael had been excited that morning when he left their tent. He'd hugged her unusually hard as she carried water for washing clothes, nearly making her drop one of the big plastic bottles, and had told her that today they would start to get out of here. To be honest, she hadn't really understood what he'd meant by that but she'd been glad to see him so upbeat. She couldn't remember the last time he had smiled so much, and she had just been happy for him.

For his part Raphael had simply wanted to re-pay some of the kindness shown to Keisha and himself by Mama Dawa and her family, and bring in some money instead of forever borrowing from them. More than anything he'd wanted to feel that he had provided food tonight instead of living off charity.

Now, however, Keisha thought that she had never seen Raphael so disheartened. For weeks now they had both been too busy surviving to collapse into despair. Then when they had reached the mine they began to feel safe for the first time under the wing of Patrick and Mama Dawa. Today, as the family listened to Mubalango describing the theft, it was a shocking reminder to them all just how vulnerable they were to government soldiers, the fractious local Mai Mai militia, and the numerous rebel forces.

Raphael now sat quietly, several yards away from the fire. After the rain had stopped the night air had grown cold, but he made no move to cover himself. His knees were pulled up and he rested his chin on them, staring long into the flickering flames, saying nothing at all. Mama Dawa had heard what had happened from her son and was worried that the soldiers would be back tonight or tomorrow having taken so little in taxes. And if they came this time it would be the camp that suffered, she was equally sure of that. She had hidden most of her money but always held back something to give them. Most of all she feared that she could not protect herself and Keisha.

"Come on, Raphael," she urged him, "you're still soaking from the rain. Put on these old things of Patrick's. The shorts will fit you if you tie the waist up with a belt, and you're almost big enough for the shirt. I have something here that you can use as a belt," and she ducked into her own tent and emerged a moment later with a short length of rope. Still Raphael made no move to go until she approached him with the shorts. Then suddenly he stood, and grasping the proffered clothing, Raphael disappeared into their little shelter and returned later changed. Mama Dawa offered to wash his clothes for him, but this time he refused. It was unlike Raphael to be so taciturn, but although Keisha had not understood, Mama Dawa had been close enough to smell the ammoniac scent of his earlier fear and now she chose to leave him the space to find his own solution.

When the boy joined them a while later, she silently offered him a bowl of hot soup with beans, rice and peppers to fill his stomach and enough chillies to take his mind off his misfortunes.

Normally, at this time they would watch the fire and tell stories old and new with Raphael an eager listener and a ready participant. Tonight, one thing above all others was different: Keisha stood behind her big brother as he sat on a warm stone close to the fire. She hugged him without saying anything and talked quietly to him without embarrassing him where normally he reassured her. Tonight he was the first into bed under their plastic bivouac. And tonight he dreamed that it was he, Raphael who had the power to command the world around him, the power to protect, provide, decide... and, most of all, to punish.

Chapter 10
Kinshasa, Capital of the Democratic Republic of Congo
A Month Ago

There hadn't been any good hotels in Kinshasa the last time he visited and as he crossed the threshold Axel could see nothing in the Palace Hotel to change his sweeping judgement. He remembered the hotel when he first visited the city more than twenty years ago, before President Mobutu's corruption and incompetence led to his downfall. You could stay there fairly comfortably then, even if sometimes you found the DSP security police using nearby rooms for their own parties. It was best not to complain about the noise, whatever it was you heard. These days, his contacts told him, it was over-priced, dirty, and even more unsafe than it had been under the DSP's control. Today it was busy with foreign and local politicians, senior civil servants and army officers in wind-down mode, which did nothing to lessen the aura of an expensive bazaar. You couldn't move in the car park for brand new Mercedes and BMWs, and it wasn't surprising that these were the only customers in the city who could afford the drink prices. A poorly cooked steak here would cost more than the average monthly wage in Kinshasa.

It was all enough to ensure that Axel stayed elsewhere, although he could keep his finger on Kinshasa's pulse more easily here. If you wanted to get things done, find out who was climbing the greasy pole and who had slid off, this was the place to do it. You couldn't throw a stone in here without hitting a member of parliament on the take. Come to think of it, mused Axel that might not be a bad plan.

As so often in such outwardly smart hotels, the lobby gave a thin veneer of opulence. One hotel he'd stayed at in the old East Germany had had a foyer lined in black marble and crystal chandeliers, but he had had to collect his small daily ration of toilet paper from the front desk. Upstairs, the guests plugged their basins with little strips of rice paper stamped with the words 'People's Republic of Viet Nam', which had singularly failed to stop the water escaping while he shaved.

Here, a chequer-board of cream and brown marble slabs covered the Reception floor, and uniformed staff weaved in and out of the throng to help with bags and drinks. A first floor gallery restaurant looked down on walls adorned with Congolese art that hung above white leather sofas and smoked glass coffee tables.

Sebastian Luaba, the private secretary to the Minister of Mines, was waiting for him at a reserved table, and rose to greet him with a warm smile as he approached. "Mr Terberg, it is good to see you in Kinshasa again. How are you?"

"I'm very well, Sebastian. Are you looking after yourself?"

Sebastian beamed contentedly. "How do you English say it? I'm 'on top form', thank you. My eldest girl is nine now and already asking for her first cell phone, which worries her mother. Sit down, please. What can I get you to drink?"

Axel ignored the supposition that he was English. His name would have informed most people but his colloquial English gave some that impression. One or two detected a twang from his time in Australia, and Rhodesia before independence, but to many people in Africa he was as English as roast beef.

Over the years some people had laughed at his English politeness to junior staff. "You must treat them firmly," an Egyptian politician had once said to him, "These people are just here to serve you. You'll get more out of them when they fear you."

Axel did most things for a reason and had ignored the comment. Those who worked with him knew he had a fierce temper, but it was seldom seen in business which made it all the more effective when it was. He had learned that you never knew who might have been promoted the next time you met. So he continued to network in his own way. Besides, it was the same the world over, career success did not always depend on talent – the politician in Cairo had eventually proved that. He'd met plenty of well-connected fools in senior posts and better-informed underlings; it was just bad business not to have people you could call on when you needed them.

The two men had met several times before and talked comfortably until the beers came. From habit, Axel always drank straight from the bottle; it was safer to avoid ice and glasses in Congo. "The Ministry's Special Adviser is running a little late, I hope you are not in a hurry, Mr Terberg."

"There's always time for a cold beer in this heat, and if he's only a little late we can both be silently amazed." Sebastian smiled awkwardly and refrained from commenting as they settled to discuss Axel's recent travels and the growth of Sebastian's family. In the end Moise Businga was almost an hour late, which was considered prompt for someone of his standing in national politics and business.

The first indication of the VIP's arrival came with a flurry of activity among the front of house staff, with the Duty Manager buttoning his jacket as he hurried to greet the general at the front door. Two black Mercedes pulled past the large glass entranceway. While the rear door of the second stretched Mercedes was being opened by the hotel manager, one security man waited in the shade of the portico and another strode into the hotel foyer where he looked around before heading over to where Luaba was silently sweating.

Even from a distance the general's entourage appeared to be wilting in dark suits, but behind them a tall, portly man with heavy jowls was dressed in a garish blue patterned silk shirt. The lively design of his long-sleeved shirt was slightly incongruous on a man aged about sixty, but at once it proclaimed his pride in Congolese crafts and his effortless seniority.

He marched towards the entrance and the doorman was only just quick enough to avert a general and glass door interface that would have ruined everyone's afternoon. The focus of all this attention walked briskly through the foyer and, following his security detail, he was guided towards the sofas where Axel now sat and from which Sebastian was urgently rising.

The former soldier's head was shaved close and his dark scalp glistened – it may have been these grooming oils that wafted a strong musk scent to those nearby and, with his aviator shades still in place, contributed to the aura of a man at ease rather than at work.

Conversation in the lobby and reception had stilled and heads turned to identify the commanding figure at the eye of this whirlwind. Some eager young politicians rose to greet him as he passed and were happy to be seen exchanging pleasantries, while a senior air force officer saluted and was acknowledged with a firm handshake. One or two figures at more distant tables rose in hope of recognition, only to subside in disappointment hoping that no one had noticed their rebuff.

If he was conflicted by his twin roles as Special Adviser to the Ministry of Mines and recently retired senior officer of the Federal Army of the Democratic Republic of the Congo (FARDC), he didn't show it. General Moise Businga reached Sebastian's table and Axel stood to meet him just soon enough to show respect and late enough to suggest he was in no way beholden. There was a particular African etiquette about these matters; timing was everything to avoid someone's loss of face. It was a ritual that the two of them had been through before, and it was clear to even the lowliest observer – and there were many – that honour was satisfied and the scores were even. No hands were shaken. As the local French slang had it, a *Grand Legume* or big vegetable had arrived and everyone else had better defer to him.

They all sat and Axel waited silently. Businga raised a hand to beckon briefly without turning his head, and his personal private secretary who had followed him closely from the car was immediately at his side. There was a brief whispered conversation before the secretary stepped back and Businga raised his eyes again towards Axel, looking at him in steady, wordless appraisal for several seconds. There was no warmth in the assessment. "Remind me, when did we last meet, Mr Terberg?" he said eventually.

"It must have been two years ago, General."

"I have retired from the armed services since we last met, so perhaps Dr Businga would be more appropriate."

Axel inclined his head in acknowledgement. He knew that the man was no medic, Moise Businga had earned the title of Doctor of Musical Arts and Axel vaguely recalled it was from an American University, but it was the first time this had come up in their conversations. It seemed an unexpectedly cultured qualification for a man known for his unforgiving nature, his brutal way with dissenters, relentless pursuit of power and his enthusiastic involvement in the Congo Wars. The brigade of almost 3,000 men he had drawn mainly from his own tribe in the south east of the country had only ever existed under his direct command. Although they were now disbanded and scattered, many of these experienced fighters were rumoured still to be armed and ready to move at Businga's order. These troops had once been among the most feared in two Congo Wars, by their allies as well as their enemies.

Curiously, Axel had also heard tell that Businga played classical piano at his own candlelit soirées and he had been known to fly in renowned American and European concert violinists and cellists to play for his guests. Certainly, money was no object for him – a position he had achieved early in his army career and one that owed little to the modest and unreliable pay of a captain in the FARDC.

"I trust you are well, Dr Businga."

A drink arrived unbidden at Businga's elbow – perhaps it had been the subject of the confidential discussion earlier. "Thank you, yes. My doctor – a real doctor," he laughed at his own humility but his tone said this was a joke that only he could make, "tells me that I must take more exercise but there never seems to be the time." He paused to take a sip. "How long are you planning to stay in Kinshasa, Mr Terberg?"

"Just a few days, then I need to head east." Axel knew better than to give too much information.

"And what, may I ask, takes you there?"

"I have business in the gem trade that needs my attention."

"Gems? Really? I heard you had other interests these days."

Axel's face didn't flicker and he gave no ground. "You are well informed as ever, Gen ... Dr Businga. My business interests have always extended to gold but diamonds remain my passion."

"Gold *and* diamonds. Really, Mr Terberg is there any precious stone or metal of ours in the Democratic Republic of Congo that you don't have your eye on?" he cocked a quizzical eye of his own at Axel and the gaze did not waver. Sebastian, however, shifted uncomfortably, and Axel realised that he hadn't been acknowledged or even dared to speak since the general arrived. Everyone present knew that Sebastian reported directly to the Minister of Mines, the Special

Adviser's political rival and the adviser saw his presence here as a spy for the second largest party in the coalition government. Evidently, Luaba's presence at the meeting would be tolerated for now but participation would not be encouraged.

In the recent political turmoil ministers and deputy ministers had come and gone, but Dr Businga had made sure that his appointment more than five years ago was as Special Adviser to the Ministry as a whole, not to any transient minister. To an outsider it might seem a subtle distinction but it meant that while political fortunes waxed and waned, the Chief of Staff would still control the ministry's actions with the help of his old army friend, the Special Adviser. Together they liaised informally whenever they pleased with the office of the President and senior Cabinet Ministers from their own party.

Axel smiled slowly, ignoring the implied rebuke. "I feel sure that my professional contacts in the wider world will continue to find markets for much of your nation's excellent output. And my company continues to ensure this is to everyone's advantage," he added gently. Over the years Axel had paid as much in commissions to senior ministers and advisers for his export concessions as he had ever paid in taxes – it was just the way it was in politics and business here.

"We shall see whose advantage it is," said Businga, giving little away. "So much depends on the market and the price. There is also the question of who is your supplier." He didn't pose the question directly but it was clear that he wanted to know more about Axel's partners. It was less clear whether he was talking about gold and diamonds or if, as Axel suspected, Businga was aware of his new interest in coltan.

Axel took a long, unhurried draft of his beer as he pondered his next remarks. He couldn't be sure how much Businga already knew or how much he was kite-flying. Clearly, he was aware of some changes in Axel's interests, so someone was talking. It would not be advisable to openly cross the Ministry of Mines, or come to that the Army which Businga still represented. In addition Axel knew something about the General's family that was causing him some concern, but he'd keep that to himself for now.

Businga's initial wealth was rumoured to have been achieved by levying a ten percent private tax on rough diamonds being smuggled out of the country. He had been a mid-ranking army officer at the time, but had made his men available for armed protection and escort duties, the fees for which had been payable in diamonds. There was no reason to suppose that this personal enrichment process had stopped now that he was advising the ministry responsible for all mining in the country. Axel knew from a contact in Rwanda that Businga was enriching himself from the mining industry controlled by Kinshasa, as well as some parts outside the central government's writ. So, he, too, was playing a dangerous game by working with the government here in the west and the rebels in the east.

In these circumstances, disclosing a little bit of the truth might corroborate whatever Dr Businga already knew, while not declaring Axel's hand in full. "I am sure you already know all the people I deal with from my previous visits," Axel began. "But if I can be of assistance to the ministry in any way while I am out there then I hope you will let me know. I would be happy to put my contacts at your disposal."

"If that is the case, we will be sure to call on you. While the security situation remains so volatile in the Kivus, Mr Terberg, I would advise you to tread most carefully in your dealings with third parties. Sadly, not everyone these days comes with the cast-iron reputation that one might wish. I would hate to see you get into difficulties by keeping the wrong company. At times of uncertainty like this I tend to rely on those I know best, the long-standing relationships that I have come to trust, don't you?"

It was Axel's turn to study him closely. If Businga had been about to declare a detailed knowledge of Axel's intended export of coltan that was the moment when it might have been expected, yet it had not come. Did that mean he knew too little to confront Axel or that he was waiting to see who Axel dealt with? The verbal sparring continued as he asked Businga, "Are there any people in particular that you think I should speak to?"

Businga turned to Sebastian. "Leave us now. I will call when I need you." Sebastian seemed about to protest that he was here to represent the Minister, but knowing Businga's reputation he clearly thought better of it. Avoiding Axel's gaze he stood and left them without a word.

The Special Adviser resumed his pondering until Sebastian was out of earshot. "Who to recommend?" He paused to suck in a breath through clenched teeth, as though it was causing him physical pain. "Such matters always come down to a question of trust on such sensitive subjects and are best discussed with those who need to know." There was no need to refer to the Minister, but Businga's languid gaze drifted towards the Minister's eyes and ears in the shape of Sebastian Luaba.

"Well, I find one's family is always a known quantity. It's easier to allow for their strengths and weaknesses and they can be a rock in times of hardship," said Businga. Sitting comfortably in the city's largest hotel, with a cool drink at his side and staff hovering just out of earshot, it was difficult to say what hardship he was referring to. Perhaps it was a comment on the times in general.

Axel was in no rush to be tied into an open-ended commitment that benefited Businga's family above all others. He attempted to deflect the conversation. "Are these times harder than they have been recently?" Axel asked.

"They are as hard as ever, Mr Terberg, and I should hate to see them become more so, for either of us," he said pointedly and paused to sip his drink. "You are venturing into extremely dangerous territory and I recommend that you remember who your friends are. I will have someone contact you when you arrive – they will easily identify themselves – and they will be able to act on our, that is to say our nation's, behalf."

Axel hadn't said where he was going, but that clearly hadn't bothered the Special Adviser who obviously felt able to keep tabs on Axel's movements. I take it that you will be working in coltan and cassiterite? It would make sense, tantalum and tin prices are very favourable at the moment."

So there it was, the old soldier had saved his trump card until the end. Axel was only known for his interests in gems and a bit of gold trading in his youth. The money and connections had been tempting but the critical reason he was working in coltan now was because the Americans had cornered him into feeding them information on parts of the trade not sanctioned by Businga's own government. Spying was another word for it, but Axel tried not to dwell on that or to think about what the Congolese would do to an American spy. Yet here was Businga calmly talking about involvement in illegal coltan and tin mining. Axel couldn't work out how the general had learned that he was now involved in this trade. It had either leaked from CCV in South Africa, the US embassy, or from one of Axel's own contacts near the mines in the eastern Congo. He filed this thought for later scrutiny and focused on how to deal with Businga. There no longer seemed much point in denying his involvement.

"You are well informed, as always. The diamond trade is not what it was, and I guess we all have to keep our eyes open for new business opportunities." He left it there. They both knew that tighter regulation of the diamond industry through the Kimberley Process had made it harder to sell uncertificated diamonds. The lack of independent monitoring in Congo had left the door open for some of the trade to continue in diamonds from conflict zones like the eastern DRC.

Businga paused again and surveyed the room carefully. Was he looking for threats, for eavesdroppers, or just taking time to play his hand? "I feel sure that someone of your accomplishments … and *many* contacts," there was great stress on the word, "will not lack for opportunities, Mr Terberg. But as so often in life, it is a question of finding the right partners. Shall we be able to …" he was choosing his words carefully, "count on your continued support for the elected government of the Congo? Our beautiful country is at a delicate stage in its growth and like a fragile plant it needs careful tending. In some respects I consider myself the Head Gardener, clearing and preparing the soil while weeding out those elements that might harm its growth. I'm just wondering which category to put you in. Are you a grower or just a digger, Mr Terberg? My country has no use for the latter. The wider world, as you put it, has too many of those to offer us and too few who plant anything of lasting value in this country." He savoured his own metaphor and continued to study Axel.

Axel stifled a laugh. This man had played a bloody hands-on role in the first Congo war while serving in the Federal Army, had risen to colonel and amassed a small fortune by controlling districts beyond the reach of Kinshasa. He had been promoted to general during the second Congo War and helped to negotiate the peace that followed, in the process securing for himself a senior and seemingly enduring post in one of the most notoriously corrupt and lucrative ministries. And all the while he had been turning his small fortune into a large one and eclipsing several strong political rivals.

Seen beside this record, Axel thought his own digging was almost amateur. But he also knew that to succeed in his plans he would need allies here in the capital, to keep him informed of any threats of intervention from the army, the UN Mission, or others. That meant winning allies and binding them close to him with financial incentives. This was not an occasion for using threats or force, but for employing greed and ambition.

"I can only rely on my track record. I'm sure you'll agree it shows how much I have done to enrich Kinshasa's Treasury through taxes that my company has paid directly, through the people we employ and the taxes they pay, through the export levies paid to your Customs authorities and the inward investment we bring in with our international partners. Of course, along the way I have also helped to make wealthy men of many Congolese business partners."

"Indeed?" said Businga, already tiring of this list of financial contributions. "As a public servant, I know little of such things."

"Of course, if these skills are no longer required then, regretfully, I shall have to turn to other markets." Axel knew such a warning was only effective if it was credible, but he was counting that the DRC government knew little about the extent of his activities in other countries. He could be sure, too, that whatever information they did have in the Ministry of Mines, would be jealously guarded from the separate fiefdoms of the Treasury, Customs, and the Army.

Businga sighed, "It is sad that the situation in North and South Kivu remains so lawless, and hard to control from Kinshasa. I will certainly keep in contact by whatever means necessary, to ensure your safety. And don't forget that – remote though you may be – my associates can be by your side in no time at all should the need arise."

Axel smiled, "I shall bear it in mind." He had seldom been threatened so elegantly. It was clear, however, that these 'associates' would not be coming in suits and carrying briefcases. There was an implicit threat in everything Businga had said. I know where you are, I know what you're doing, I know who you work with, and I will be paid handsomely by you for non-interference. The alternative is that you involve me in your export operation or you will be shut down by force – and you will vanish with it.

Without warning Dr Businga rose from the chair and straightened his blue silk shirt as Axel stood with him. The general did not even bother to look at him as he said, "Bon voyage, Mr Terberg. We shall be in touch." From his position out of hearing, Sebastian half raised a hand in farewell and smiled weakly at Axel. The nearest security man was already clearing the minister's exit path as Businga swept out of the hotel. Amid a worried-looking entourage he moved as serenely as an ocean liner surrounded by puffing tugs.

******

The Avenue des Aviateurs in Kinshasa is host to numerous diplomatic missions to Congo, from Israel, Portugal, the People's Republic of China, even the UN and, at number 310, the Embassy of the United States of America. It was at their main entrance that Axel Terberg presented himself early one Tuesday in May. To avoid unpleasant surprises and enable them to confirm his *bona fides*, he had arranged an appointment with a Mr Powell – no first name given – in the office of the US Defence Attaché.

The marines guarding the entrance were expecting him and once the online identity check was complete he was ushered down a flight of stairs and into an unmarked interview room below ground level. Axel waited for five minutes with a coffee in front of him and reflected on the improved tone of this meeting compared to his last encounter with US officials in Spain.

At one of America's smaller embassies such as this he might have expected to see a local official to give them an update on his movements and meetings, so when the door was opened to admit three officials he slowly sat up. He recognised none of them but they knew plenty about him. Mr Powell, or David Powell as he now announced himself, had an East Coast accent that Axel couldn't quite place and described himself as the local NSA liaison. Whether the US National Security Agency considered him one of their own was not confirmed as no IDs were being shown. He was in a secure room in their embassy and the details would be explained when they felt necessary. Powell took the lead, perhaps because this was his home turf, introducing Axel to an athletic thirty-something white Ivy Leaguer from the US State Department named Nick Johns, and an older African-American, Payne Rawlings of the CIA. Powell led the introductions but a bluster and nervousness in his demeanour made Terberg sure he wasn't in charge.

It was Rawlings who held Axel's attention. He was around forty, with thick hair cut short, the same solid build as Axel, and glasses with a graded tint that obscured the upper half of his eyes. Axel had no means of knowing if these were their real names, but it didn't matter to him either way. In his growing experience of their world of subterfuge, handlers came and went without explanation – no matter which department they claimed to belong to – and there would be others to meet next time.

The one irritating thing that never changed was the way that, however well briefed they were, they always needed the story retelling from the beginning. This work was becoming Axel's own private Groundhog Day. These three were no exception and forty-five minutes and two more cups of coffee were wasted confirming the notes they had probably carried in. Still, Axel was in no hurry. He now knew this was how it worked and he walked them through the phoned approach from Hendriks, CCV's invitation to Barcelona, the request for a price and service quotation from the South Africans, his subsequent proposal, and their acceptance with no haggling – in itself enough to raise suspicions.

Axel's description of events moved on and he shared his thoughts that CCV had had fewer than expected questions and the price had proved so easy to arrange by phone and email that he was left wondering if he should have charged more for his commission, much more. Never mind, he had agreed the terms of a contract review for next year so there was scope for his prices to rise.

When the three agents had finished asking questions, Powell said, "You'd better tell them what happened in Zambia, as a bit of background."

Axel sighed; this was going to take even longer than he'd anticipated. "About four years ago I had a misunderstanding with the authorities in Zambia."

Powell snorted, "Misunderstanding? Is that your famous Limey understatement? I heard they strung you up and were using you for baseball practice with heavy electric cables." And with a stage wink to Johns and Rawlings he added, "They have a *lot* of copper there." The local liaison was clearly amused at his own wit but neither of his colleagues reacted.

Axel looked him up and down slowly and in the silence that followed Powell shifted uncomfortably. "Do you want to tell this or shall I?" asked Axel. Powell waved his hand airily for Axel to continue. The reluctant agent took a deep breath, "OK, I was working with a local company in Ndola, about ten kilometres from the DRC border. To cut a long story short, my Zambian business partners fell out with some influential government people, but the first I knew about it was when I was hauled out of bed in the middle of the night and taken to a police station for questioning about some missing emeralds. These were supposed to be part of a deal with a company in Europe. What I didn't know was that the packets of stones had also been promised to some senior figures in Zambia. If it was cash they'd been offered, I might have been able to sort something out, but my partners – I shan't call them friends – had done a moonlight flit north across the border taking the stones into Congo and leaving me to face the music."

Terberg paused. "You're right, Mr, er … Powell. They worked me over pretty well. Then they had me transferred to Lusaka, where someone else started all over again." Axel didn't like being made to relive it. These were ugly memories he now managed to keep in a mental box, one that was seldom opened.

Perhaps Powell was too inexperienced in this posting or too unimaginative to understand what this experience might have been like. He was now idly doodling circles on his notepad and occasionally looking up at Axel incuriously, as though he'd heard the story a hundred times from Axel's lips.

In contrast, the men from the State Department and the CIA were silent and attentive as he retold the tale.

"Of course, the novelty of jumping on a white guy's bones was intense to begin with, but it didn't last much more than a couple of days at each jail, and then they left me alone. I couldn't give them the answers or the stones they wanted and I guess my story as the fall guy for the Zambian company matched what they were hearing from the police and business contacts in Ndola. But they didn't really know what to do with me. They couldn't show me to any embassy officials looking like that, and my Dutch passport didn't mean much to them. If I'd been American, I might have got out a bit sooner. But then again, with a name like Terberg I was lucky they didn't think I was Afrikaans, or I'd still be their punchbag."

Rawlings smiled and Johns snorted a breath. Powell tried not to look puzzled.

"Anyway, I was transferred to a prison hospital for a couple of weeks to recover while the bruises subsided and I started to walk again – the soles of my feet and my fingers were badly infected, you see." Johns winced slightly, but Axel continued, "I thought I was back to looking my best when they finally let me out of hospital but there weren't any mirrors there so perhaps I was still a bit of mess when your people showed up, but that was much later." He nodded to Rawlings of the CIA who said nothing.

"When I say 'let me out', all they did was transfer me back into the top security wing of Lusaka's Central Prison, but after my previous experiences it was OK. The food was bad and there wasn't much of it, but I got to see the light of day occasionally and the beatings stopped – at least from the guards."

"So, how were the other prisoners towards you?" asked Johns.

Axel hesitated at first and then didn't answer directly. "I don't blame them really. I must have stood out like a prick at a christening, plus they figured if the police hadn't found out where my emeralds were then maybe they hadn't tried hard enough. I stood my ground as well as I could but I wasn't in the best shape." He grimaced.

"That was when State heard about you, was it?"

"Not quite. The powers behind the scenes had decided by then that, if they couldn't have their gems, and they couldn't find the guys who did have them, then they would have their satisfaction out of me some other way. So a pre-trial hearing was held *in camera*."

Rawlings anticipated Powell's question. "Behind closed doors," he murmured and Powell nodded as though that was what he'd expected.

"Although they weren't allowed to attend the trial, the number of unanswered questions about who I was and what I had done attracted the attention of several embassies, all of them wondering if I was one of their citizens. That was when the

US State Department turned up in my cell. It was already quite crowded in there so I was taken for a closely supervised interview in a prison office and they came back two days later for a more private chat and with a proposal. The food improved in the meantime, and the kicking had stopped. I think one of your people had had a quiet word with the higher-ups."

This time no one said anything as Terberg spoke.

"If you want me to share the proposal now, I can." No one demurred so he continued. "It was quite straightforward. Langley had an information deficit in Africa at the time, you probably still do, and there was nobody who could give them details about how well the Kimberley Process was being observed – you know, eliminating the trade in illegal diamonds. Your guys needed some hard intelligence from within – how shall I put it? – some of the diamond business's murkier recesses and they figured that with my gemstone experience I was just the man to fit in and find out what was going on. If I co-operated, they would see that the charges were dropped and that I was released."

Terberg paused for a while. "Well, your guys didn't keep your side of the deal, at least not all of it. Emeralds are one of Zambia's key exports so, not only was this theft seen as very damaging to their Treasury's reputation, they found it politically unacceptable to have a European waltzing off into the sunset without a backward glance leaving them with no one to punish. Plus there were probably some Zambian officials who still believed I had the stones. I was politically friendless there, the US State Department didn't discourage them, and so the Zambians gave me a 25-year sentence for smuggling, embezzlement and money-laundering and handed me over to your colleagues at the US embassy a month later when the headlines had died down."

There was another long pause as Terberg silently studied Nick Johns, the representative from State, who returned his gaze directly. If Axel had been hoping for a sign of embarrassment, he was to be disappointed.

"Anyway, now I have a 25-year prison term hanging over my head for someone else's crime, and I obviously can't go back to Zambia," said Axel, "because the sentence still stands and I don't expect I'd get out of Central Prison a second time. But your Department did get me out of there once, for which I have since shown my gratitude by turning over a few metaphorical rocks and shining a light on the diamond business beneath. I thought that would be the end of it, but I was wrong. It seems there are always some more rocks to turn over and the debt to Uncle Sam is never fully paid."

Axel Terberg looked up and stared at each one in turn, as CIA and State returned his gaze without flinching. The local NSA liaison busied himself with another doodle. "You can call me naive, but I didn't imagine when I agreed to this deal that it would automatically segue into a lifetime helping you guys with every local or strategic difficulty you find in precious metals, stones, and minerals. My mistake, I guess, and there's not much I can do about it now," Axel lapsed into silence. Nobody disagreed with him.

Johns spoke first. "Thank you for your candour, Mr Terberg. We didn't come here to dig up old memories that, by the sound of them, would be best left buried. But I can tell you it sure helps us to understand some things that the files barely even hinted at." Rawlings grunted in agreement.

"Well, as you can imagine, I've no wish to revisit this. But I'm surprised that after the work I've already done for you I'm being put through the mincer all over again," said Axel.

"You mean working with CCV?" This time it was Rawlings who spoke.

"Of course I mean CCV. Look, I can earn myself a crust any number of ways, and a good one. I wouldn't have to re-invent myself as a coltan buyer. I can talk my way out of a lot of sad endings but I have to believe in my cover and right now I'm struggling to convince myself that my story will hold up in the Badlands out east. It already came under close scrutiny in Kinshasa. And if I'm not convinced by it, what chance do I have with people who know the business there backwards and are looking for reasons to distrust me. I mean, this industry is different from what I know, I'm a long way out of what you'd call my 'comfort zone'," and as he said it at least two of the Americans in the room tried to gauge whether this uncharacteristic humility was genuine.

"You've spoken frankly with us, Mr Terberg ... Axel," said Johns. "Very frankly. Let me be equally clear. We need that information from the eastern Congo and there is more riding on this than you can know. There's layer on layer of reasons why this is important to us. All you need to know is that at the micro level we have to see whose hand is uppermost in the east. We can get any number of reports from diplomats and NGOs, but there's no substitute – as we've found to our cost in the Middle East and South East Asia – for having people on the ground that understand the region and work in it daily. Sometimes the industry they come from doesn't matter overly. In this case, though, it matters big time.

"I don't need to tell you the industrial and economic significance of this trade to the West – just stop and think what would happen if an enemy managed to get monopoly control of minerals that have economic significance way beyond their size or local value." Johns was getting into his stride, but it seemed that the fundamental question of who was friend and who was enemy was not going to be addressed. It was also clear to Axel that a US monopoly was one thing, but a foreign monopoly would be intolerable.

"Then there's the strategic significance of rare minerals that are vital, and I do mean vital, to our national security in aircraft guidance systems and satellite controls. You can forget the news headlines around the world on conflict minerals going into mobile phones and DVD players. That's just for the scribblers. There's a critical struggle going on here; it's not a war yet – it's not even an undeclared proxy war – although some day it could be. But when that day comes we want to know who we can deal with and what we're up against."

The State Department man sat back and looked at Axel appraisingly. Axel could see Rawlings eyes flick towards Johns. He raised himself from the slouch he had assumed throughout the meeting and coughed, it seemed meaningful to Axel, perhaps he was concerned at how much of their thinking Johns was sharing. Johns must have heard Rawlings but he ignored him.

Axel smiled inwardly at the silent power play going on. He sat calmly, the picture of relaxed co-operation. For now, it seemed sensible to let bygones be bygones where the Americans were concerned. Even with the extra space of business class the flight out had been uncomfortable, but his rib was mending, and he had no wish to put new doubts in their minds about his willingness to comply. So far he could manage to deliver what these people wanted from him, it wouldn't be easy but he was experienced at developing business in new markets. Axel was still a free agent financially, and the Americans might be useful in opening commercial and political doors now or in the future. Besides, the alternative of a return to jail in Zambia was a threat he still took seriously.

"Tell me, Axel, what do you make of CCV as a company?" asked Johns. Axel's eyes darted briefly to Payne Rawlings, the CIA rep who was maintaining a curious silence given that Axel was nominally Langley's agent. Rawlings gave an almost imperceptible nod, more a blink of half-covered eyes, so subtle that the men beside him would not have noticed. A tacit understanding had just been confirmed between him and Axel that he could report to others only with CIA approval.

"Of their executives, I've only met Joost Hendriks, and I've given you a report on him," said Axel. "To recap he seems a little out of his depth, either in the calibre of client he's dealing with, or the subject matter. I'd say he's used to swimming in a smaller pond and is uncomfortable dealing with these minerals, phones or any technology come to that. He doesn't understand either aspect particularly well, he stuck out like a sore thumb in the European theatre, or he's not as good a poker player as he'd like to believe."

"Hmm, probably not a bad analysis from what we know. But," Johns persisted, "what about CCV itself?" The other two just watched Axel.

"It's hard to say. They're small – probably fewer than fifty people – keep a low profile, as you know. I've spoken to the guy who gave them my name..."

"Remind me, who's he?"

"I'm sure you have it in there," Terberg nodded at the manila folder in front of Johns. "Joshua Mokotoff. He's an old friend, a dealer in diamonds and semi-precious stones. He knows little about CCV, he did some work with them in South Africa's diamond industry and they were always keen to avoid contact with governmental authorities and tax regimes. He tried tracing their ownership years ago. It appears they're based in Cape Town but he gave up when he ran into a mess

142

of Panamanian and Cypriot holding companies each more opaque than the last. Joshua knows little about coltan and cares even less, so he pushed them in my direction just because I know the region and in case I wanted the business or to pass it on to someone else – you know, to earn a commission or do a favour. I think he also wanted to get shot of them, to be honest. He knows this isn't really my subject area but we make introductions for one another from time to time."

"Understood, Axel. So, what can you tell me about CCV's client?"

"There isn't a lot of evidence to go on – I was hoping that you'd tell me."

"All in good time. You first, Axel," said Johns, and Powell nodded as to show that he had been going to suggest this.

"Well, it may be easier to start by saying who they aren't. They aren't one of the regular coltan brokers, they don't have the knowledge. Nor one of the processors, same applies and there aren't many of those anyway, so it's been quite easy to eliminate them. Then I thought they might be an intermediary for a big name European mobile phone manufacturer or a US electronics maker, but the market's changed a lot in the last few years. Human rights groups have put so much public pressure on governments and on the big name device makers that they all need to have audited suppliers so that they can prove their gold, coltan, tin or tungsten only come from conflict-free regions." Terberg paused to marshal his thoughts.

"The price of coltan in Congo has fallen dramatically in recent years. For anyone unscrupulous enough to buy conflict minerals in bulk quantities it's a buyers' market here now. But these will be buyers who don't answer to shareholders nervous about their reputations and being fined by the US or EU governments for illegal trade. Whoever is behind them will not be too worried about facing pressure groups like Global Witness. That immediately reduces the number of countries where the end products (and I don't know if they're smartphones or satellites) are being made."

"You can look at it from the other end of the telescope of course, and ask yourself which country has the money and manufacturing capacity, who has the growing demand? And on the balance of probabilities I expect you'll come up with the same answer I did. China."

"As I say, Western electronics brands have already been seriously embarrassed by publicity over their previous supplies from this part of the world. For years they didn't ask any questions and stuck their fingers in their ears when people asked awkward questions about inhuman working conditions or the proceeds going to fund conflicts. Suddenly they're all desperate to show how clean they are. Of course, there are still plenty of smaller device makers, especially in Asia, many with big ambitions and some of them are growing mighty fast. To keep that growth going they'll need larger and larger quantities of coltan, plus an aggressively low price. So a secure supply for such a critical and rare mineral would help them grab a share of mature markets that are still dominated by the likes of Samsung and Apple."

Johns spoke for the first time in a while. "We gotta look at the geography as much as the market dynamics. If it was some Korean new kid on the block, why ship the coltan to China? They'd send it where it could be processed closer to their factories. The same probably goes for Taiwan, why send it to their over-bearing neighbour, China?"

Axel paused to sip his coffee, but it was cold and he wished he hadn't. He continued, "CCV and their clients want the coltan flown to Macao to start with, at least until they've got a small stockpile. Then they'll be happy to have it shipped. That was the first surprise. I wondered if this was a bluff, and Hendriks was certainly keen for me to believe that. But, if the coltan's going to be forwarded on to somewhere else it just adds unnecessary cost and delay, both of which seem to be critical factors for CCV in this deal. No, my bet is that it's being processed in China for use in Chinese-made phones or whatever. Before you say it, I know coltan has other uses besides the obvious, so perhaps it's not going to the mobile phone industry, at all. You mentioned aircraft guidance and satellite control systems. That's way outside my experience, I wouldn't know.

"My guess is that CCV are Chinese-backed, and are being used as a cut-out, so that I'm not talking to oriental faces. Hendriks kind of over-played his hand on that one. It wouldn't surprise me if this stuff was destined for a manufacturer in the Middle Kingdom."

"Middle Kingdom?" asked the embassy's Powell.

Axel looked at him again. "You're not a Sinologist, are you?" Powell's face flushed. "Zhōngguó the centre country or Middle Kingdom; it's the traditional name for China. The emperors believed China was the centre of the world, hence Middle Kingdom." Now Payne Rawlings was definitely smiling.

Axel continued, turning his gaze back to Johns and Rawlings. "It's still a hunch. Without firm evidence it's based on probabilities, so call it a gut instinct, but I've learned to trust my gut. My feeling is that either for tactical or strategic reasons China needs extra quantities of coltan, over and above what than they can extract from their own mines and they don't want to buy it openly through the usual channels. I don't know if this is to keep the purchases hidden or to keep the cost down – or both. That's for you to judge, not me. It could be to meet a short-term need, like a new technology from one of their companies, or something more long-term like strengthening their manufacturing base with an in-built price advantage over Korean and Japanese competitors. Or it could be to dominate the global market ahead of the West."

"They may have heard about some technical advance coming in the West that they want to try and control. They can't prevent Western manufacturers using alternative coltan supplies – there are smaller producers all over the place, in

Venezuela, Australia, even Greenland from what I've read, but the costs are higher than the Congo." Terberg was tired from all this talking and rubbed his face thoughtfully. "Perhaps it's a bit like De Beers with their diamond stockpiles; they just release those slowly onto the market. In a monopoly market CCV and their masters could dominate the world supply for years, controlling who makes all sorts of consumer devices from auto parts to smartphones and how much they can charge. Everyone else would have higher costs. It'd give Chinese manufacturers a huge advantage."

Axel looked down at his coffee and thought better of it. "Anyway, that's about as far as I've got, except to say that this is all against the background of China's aggressive diplomatic and economic push into Africa. You've all seen it; every new road, dam or rail line from Cairo to Cape Town seems to be made by skilled Chinese labour these days. So, whatever advantage in coltan reserves China achieves in eastern Congo – and I'm assuming it is the Chinese – is being sanctioned by the government in Beijing. That's a brave policy, because it risks seriously pissing off the regime here in Kinshasa if they can't control their own country's reserves. These minerals are being illegally exported every day and the profits are disappearing with them. Maybe that's why the Chinese need a front company, to give them deniability." Axel had said his piece, and sat back folding his arms.

"We will have to consider what you've said, Mr Terberg." Johns looked at Rawlings to see if he had anything he wanted to ask while they had him. There was a small shake of the head. "OK, right now, as there are no firm answers we can give you," *or that you want to give me*, thought Axel, "let's consider our next steps. How ready are you to supply CCV, what are your next steps and what meetings are planned?"

"I'm not ready and I'm already getting some unwanted interest from the Doctor of Music." Johns and Rawlings both looked surprised, Powell just looked perplexed.

"What did Businga have to say?" asked Rawlings.

"He was on a fishing expedition. He clearly knows something, for instance he knows where I'm going, but he's not saying much more than that. I don't think he's got much on me otherwise our meeting wouldn't have been so polite, and he wouldn't have asked so many questions. He knows I'm not here for my health, and he seems to know that I'm working with new partners. More worryingly, he also knew that it's in coltan, so that tells me there's a leak somewhere in the information pipeline. That'll be on your side."

Powell bridled at that. "How do you know it's on our side?"

"Jesus, because I haven't talked to anybody except the guy that told me, Joshua Mokotoff, and he couldn't give a stuff about coltan – he'd probably think it was barbecue charcoal and about as interesting. He has no reason to blab and I

145

have learned to trust him over the years – with my life. There's nothing from me about it in writing or online and I've made no open reference to it in any calls. So it doesn't take rocket science to work out the leak came from somewhere else."

Terberg was getting angry now and he turned to Rawlings. "Listen, I'm not going to piss about here. I'm the one putting my neck on the line when I go into North Kivu, which is more than I see you guys doing. So, it stands to reason I have a greater interest in keeping my mouth shut and in sniffing out the leak. I'm telling you it's coming from your side of the table and it's time you got a frigging plumber in. Right now we're collectively getting our butt kicked by intelligence officers from the world's 176th largest economy, and one of the most corrupt regimes in Africa at that. What I want to know is why it takes me to tell you that, and what it is you're going to do about it?"

"OK," said Johns, "let's all take it down a notch shall we? There's risks being shared all round, Mr Terberg, and just because you don't see them it don't make 'em any less real. We have people on the ground in the Kivus right now and, yes, we do have a clear view on Chinese and other states' involvement but unless and until it impacts your role we won't be burdening you with it. Got that?"

"And before you leave, which in the light of this conversation should probably be by the back door to avoid further upsetting our Congolese hosts, I suggest we spend some time working through your next steps. Now, David, I think we can take it from here, thanks."

Powell sat up from his note taking, "Hey, wait a minute, this is my turf and I need … NSA needs to know what's happening."

Rawlings spoke for only the third time. With a languid drawl that nevertheless conveyed his command he said, "Mr Powell, this has now become a multinational matter and therefore lies outside your level of responsibility. Thank you for your input; you have just received a direct order from a ranking officer within State. It's time to be about your business."

Powell looked from Rawlings to Johns and back again before turning a hate-filled look on Terberg, the only man present whom he dared confront. He stood and gathered up his notes. The door slam that he intended would have been more effective if the hinge had not been on a gas strut. As it was, it closed silently ten seconds after he swept out in a humiliated rage.

"That guy will go far …." said Rawlings, "with any luck." And the three men went back to deciding who to work with in Goma, who to avoid, and which palms to cross with silver in North and South Kivu, over the border at the airport in Rwanda, and at the seaport in Tanzania. An hour later a marine was called to walk their man down to the basement garage where an unmarked van was waiting.

******

146

The tone of his meeting with the CIA was noticeably calmer after Powell's departure and once Axel had got some of the frustrations off his chest. He was no nearer to feeling happy with his cover story or his involvement in their geopolitical and commercial mess, but clearly it wasn't going to change and there was sod all he could do about it. He nodded to Johns and Rawlings before climbing into the back of a dirty white delivery van driven by a black marine in civvies. Another marine – judging from his crew cut – climbed in, slammed the door shut and told Axel to lie down out of sight. Ten minutes later they dropped him miles away, far from prying eyes and an irritatingly long and hot walk from his house. There were no taxis to be seen which Axel would not have minded were it not for the fact they had given him an envelope filled by Uncle Sam with $10,000 in hundred dollar bills to cover his expenses, and Kinshasa's streets can be mean places even in daylight.

******

"Do you think he can deliver?" Johns asked when Axel had gone.

"Guess it depends how much we want from him," said Rawlings. "He's been in business long enough to be convincing, but he's seldom traded in these minerals so his track record's kinda weak. But he's tough, I'll say that. You wouldn't know he's still carrying broken ribs from, let's call it a disagreement with one of our field units in Spain. And anyone who comes through what he faced in Zambia is no pushover. If he can make the right contacts in Goma and do it well enough to convince CCV, then we'll have a line into coltan shipments. We may have to help him get started, but for now we're going to stand back and let him make the running. We'll know a lot more about Mr Terberg's value to us when we see how he fronts up when he gets out East. He's useful but not indispensable. He knows dick about our operations here so he can't give much away even if he's exposed."

"What d'you make of his assessment of CCV and the conflict minerals trade?" asked Johns, trying to coax a bit more information out of the CIA man.

"Dunno. Langley's been kicking ideas around and the analysts have been doing some of their thinking aloud," said Rawlings.

"Sounds dangerous," Johns smiled to put Rawlings at ease. There was supposed to be total transparency on this between America's two largest spy agencies, but you could be sure the other side always held something back.

"Langley wishes it was all as simple to follow as the old days. The legally-mined coltan may have changed hands between dealers five or six times as it was shipped but the route didn't change; it was often shipped via Dar es Salaam in Tanzania to Antwerp in Belgium. Then it was transported to a tantalum processing plant owned by someone like Bayer subsidiary, H.C. Starck. It was easy to monitor if you needed to, but in those days nobody much cared," said Rawlings.

"Then the warlords realised how much they could make out of the trade. Various comptoir trading houses and shippers were happy to help them, and suddenly you had rival armies springing up like mushrooms, all trying to win a slice of the action. The trade went underground and now you can't tell who's behind it. You just know from the cars and houses that a ton of people are making big money at it."

"What's the latest thinking on the Farm?" asked Johns.

Rawlings seemed happy to continue. "At Langley?" He puffed out his cheeks as he considered his reply. "A few of the boffins are arguing that if it walks like a duck and quacks like a duck, then maybe the damn thing *is* a duck!"

"What the hell you talking about?" Johns demanded with a growing sense of frustration. He wondered why the Agency man always talked in riddles.

Rawlings paused again to weigh his words carefully. "To the naked eye the coltan deals CCV are proposing fly in the face of everything China wants out of its cosy new relationships in Africa. That begs the question, are CCV really dealing for the Chinese state? Is it China at all? If it is China, maybe this isn't being done officially. That's what the analysts are saying in Langley. Maybe it's being done through CCV *without* the Chinese Communist Party's knowledge."

Johns looked puzzled. "Re-wind a second; why's the agency so all fired up about China? I thought the issue here was coltan, and threats to American supplies. I thought most of the coltan out of DRC was going to Europe. Isn't that where the problem is?"

Rawlings smiled. It was a slow process that lacked the key ingredient of warmth; in fact it reminded Johns of a snake baring its fangs. "You want the line we're giving to the Senate Intelligence Committee?"

"Don't piss me about, Payne. We bring you the Intel, if you want more and if you want quality you can share more. Otherwise next time you ask you may find our satellites looking the other way."

Rawlings grunted, and said nothing for a moment. Disclosure did not come naturally to him and he liked to weigh every ounce of information before revealing it. "OK, as far as the Senate's concerned the US end of the supply chain is all taken care of. The Dodd-Frank Act that Obama signed took care of that. And in Europe there's a growing lobby to get the EU Parliament to force all users of tin, tantalum, tungsten and gold to show where it came from. So, of the major players, that just leaves China. They're the largest manufacturer of electronic devices."

"And the Senate Committee go for that shit, do they?"

"Seem to, so far. You just have to mention China to some on the Hill and they start foaming at the mouth."

"Meanwhile, the real reason for CIA interest is …" Johns left the sentence hanging.

"Ah." Rawlings stopped and stared at an uninteresting flake of paint on the wall.

"Hey, I got all day," was all Johns said, and he leaned back in his chair to emphasise the point that this time he would wait until he got an answer. They were finally cutting to the chase and he sensed the CIA Supervisor had clearance to talk; he just wanted to say as little as possible.

"It's about taking the Long View." Johns was bracing himself for more evasion, but Rawlings continued. "We need to know who we're dealing with, in China. I'm talking about the big picture, who's in charge. Not just now but who'll be in the driving seat in ten years or more."

"And you'll find that in a hole in the ground in Africa?" scoffed the NSA man.

Rawlings said nothing for moment, just looked harder at his questioner as if re-assessing NSA's value as informed partners. Johns shifted in his seat under the scrutiny, feeling the initiative leaching away from him. "I believe we could." His Southern drawl gave him a laconic air. "The next twenty years will be dominated by different battles to the last twenty, or so the strategists and game players tell us and I have no reason to doubt them. Wars won't be fought over religion or race, not to the same extent. People's concerns the world over will be about resources. Water, oil and gas to some extent, fishing and exploration rights. Minerals." He said the last with a flourish, like a poker player laying a winning hand.

"If we wanna keep our place in the world, we gotta plan now how we'll get the resources we need, that means identifying who or what we're up against."

"You mean in China."

"Sure I mean China. We're not losing sleep over the Russkies or Europe. Europe's a frickin' museum. You been there lately? It's washed up – even Germany's too small to play major league. We know what we're dealing with now in China, but who knows what's coming down the pike."

"OK, back up. You said maybe the coltan trade was being done through CCV without the Chinese Communist Party's knowledge." Rawlings just nodded.

Johns frowned deeply and considered this for a moment. Then he looked up, and his unblinking gaze showed he was wondering what his CIA colleagues had been smoking. "You mean, you think there's a crime syndicate or a company in China big enough to stockpile enough coltan reserves and maybe other minerals, to sell millions of high-tech devices. Some group suicidal enough to risk going behind the backs of the Politburo in Beijing. I don't buy that. Not for a second. China's State Security would hang 'em up by their wieners if they found anyone jeopardizing their long-term African geo-political strategy. It's taken them over a decade to develop, and it's bearing real fruit now."

"Hey, you can't assume the Commie Party machine knows everything going on in China. Don't see how it could. The Communist Party's made up of regional party machines, and just like any giant organisation it has rival factions jockeying

149

for power. Stands to reason, one day there's going to be a challenge to the Party old guard. Maybe, just maybe, this is part of it."

"You're shitting me!" Johns exhaled loudly in contempt and stood up.

Rawlings shrugged, as if to disown the notion. "It all seemed a bit wacko to me too first time I heard it. I'm just sharing their analysis. The brains back home are looking at the evidence, asking the questions and searching for answers and patterns."

"Jesus, if that's the best Langley can come up with we're all screwed. Might as well just shut up shop, you and me. Let the Ruskies and Chinese have this continent to themselves." He threw his half-finished coffee in the bin and stomped out.

Chapter 11
Coltan Mine, Walikale District, North Kivu, DRC
Two Years Ago

Raphael had woken in time to watch the dawn light spread. He lay still in his bed neither wishing to disturb Keisha's sleep nor lose the moment to think, and there was plenty that he hadn't been able to figure out. He tried to imagine how his parents would react in his situation but his troubles kept crowding in upon him. As far as he could see, they had few choices; they could leave the camp, but where would they go? They had no money, they had no friends or family to turn to, and he was frightened by what he'd heard about the cities. At least, they had been accepted here and had even been taken in as part of an extended family and given food, shelter and encouragement.

If they left the camp, he knew he would not find work in the fields; many farmers had already been scared off their own land just like his family as they tried to avoid one army or another. So how would he make enough money to feed them while they searched for their family? No, the answer must be to work with Mubalango and, now that he had returned, Bahati. He would have to save every cent that he could, and hide it as he had planned. But he still didn't see how he could protect himself and Keisha while he did it.

The blows of having their money and food stolen he felt like a physical pain that squeezed his heart and crushed what little hope he had. He knew so little of how to look after them both; the only thing that was obvious was that he must learn from those around him if he was to reunite the family.

He was sure that Patrick would not have been caught as he had been. The man was smaller than his wife, Mama Dawa, and like the other miners he was unarmed and vulnerable to these thefts. Patrick was smart and quick-witted though; and it was he who had advised Raphael to be ready for the soldiers' visits. Give them something that they want, he had said, but save everything you can. Raphael hadn't understood him at first – it was clearer to him now though. Don't leave your valuables where the soldiers or anyone else in the camp might find them. In his mingled fatigue and excitement at finally earning some money that he might keep,

Raphael had not had a chance to follow his advice. It frustrated Raphael that there had been no time to hide any money but, if he was honest with himself, he knew he would have held on to the money overnight so it would have been stolen either way. His gang would have to be doubly alert when soldiers were in the area, and be ready to hand over enough to look like they were co-operating, while hopefully the soldiers were robbing elsewhere.

It was hard to see anything far in the future, but he knew they had to get out of the camp forever as soon as they could, taking with them enough dollars to last for several weeks of searching. He didn't know how he was going to find the answers he needed. He didn't know where his family might have gone; he didn't know how long their search would take, so he couldn't work out how much money they would have to save. He didn't even know how to begin looking. It was all too much for a thirteen year-old to understand – how could he manage it alone? It was even harder to imagine how he could tackle it while looking after Keisha.

Everyone at the mine seemed to be at the mercy of soldiers demanding money for protection. Only the week before they had killed a digger who refused to hand over his last coltan. They shot him dead on the spot, in front of his workmates, took the small amount of money he had been saving for his family and left his friends to dig his grave and mourn him before they went back to dig for their survival.

Sometimes the army disappeared for weeks at a time – according to Patrick this either meant that they expected a battle with an armed group or they feared missing a pay day, one of those occasions when the Federal Army in Kinshasa arranged to pay some of what it owed its troops in North Kivu. No one at the mine knew how the troops found out they were to be paid but occasionally soldiers could be seen winding their way through the jungle on their way back to barracks.

Anyone who had spent long in the camp knew that their supposed protectors could vanish at any moment. The army would spend days or even weeks at the mine, with soldiers helping themselves at gunpoint to the coltan worked by the miners or stealing their food. The small traders tried to make themselves scarce, but their livelihood was inextricably tied to the coltan coming out of the mine and sooner or later they had to return and then they too were at the gunmen's mercy.

By sheer good fortune Keisha and Raphael had stumbled into a welcoming family circle. They watched as men – there were fewer women and children – queued at the door of Mama Dawa's tent almost every morning to explain their ailments to her and ask for help. There was one price for bush remedies and a higher price for the neat boxes of European medicines; nobody studied the use by dates very closely. Either way the demand for her medicines and her skills was constant.

Even the soldiers came to her door for treatment when they were in the camp. They pushed their way to the front of any queue but their swagger and confidence often deserted them when confronted by Mama. She had an almost mystical reputation for her cures and the soldiers would sit and wait to see her with their guns resting across their knees. It amused her no end that the soldiers with conditions of a more personal nature often used Patrick as a go-between to describe their symptoms. He had become particularly skilled at describing the symptoms of sexually transmitted diseases.

She had always insisted that they pay for their medicines and, though the soldiers could easily have withheld payment, there had seldom been any trouble in getting them to pay for treatment. Her skills and experience were revered by these uneducated men, and were a rare reminder of their healers at home. All in all, it was a respect that Jean de Dieu could not comprehend.

If Raphael's reaction to his new job and friendships was thoughtful, Keisha's was much more dramatic. At home in the village she had done her share of the children's chores, but here in the camp she threw herself into the work that needed to be done. Mama Dawa had assumed enormous importance in the little girl's life – she was an island of kindness and stability in an ocean of misery and confusion. It was inevitable that Keisha should have fixed on such a strong maternal figure. She had children of her own and work to do so there was a limit to the support she could offer the child, yet Mama Dawa had been generous with her affection towards Keisha. In truth, she was also concerned that she might be adopted as a surrogate parent by Keisha – what would happen if they managed to find her mother again?

The sound of pouring water brought Raphael back to the present, and he realised one of the boys was taking a morning leak behind the tents. Whoever it was, they'd better hope their mother didn't catch them. She had already told Raphael to do his business in the trees, not here in the camp where she was trying to make a home and keep it clean. Then he heard Patrick's voice murmuring something to one of his children as he went off in search of some breakfast.

A little further away, probably the other side of the tents, Raphael could just make out the sounds of pots being moved to and from the fire. She was making porridge for breakfast, but hungry as he was he found it hard to get out of the blanket that he shared with Keisha. His sister was still sleeping silently beside him, her small back turned towards him. He willed himself to get up and slowly crawled out of the mouth of the shelter, before standing for a few moments studying the camp.

Even with the morning mist still hanging heavy in the air there were signs of movement all around. The camp was mainly filled with men, who were emerging like him to stretch, scratch and find themselves something to eat. For up to a hundred metres in every direction people were moving quietly between the shelters, and from fires stoked to life again after last night's cooking the smoke was drifting up towards the high treetops and the grey sky above. It wasn't raining at the moment but it was only ever a matter of time in this part of the country.

Most of the shelters were no more than plastic sheeting stretched over saplings or branches bent into the ground. These looked stronger than his makeshift tent and he decided to ask Mubalango for help later with making a stronger, more weatherproof home. They had rebuilt their shelter shortly after they arrived when they found that the rain blew in too easily and the makeshift doors flapped noisily at night if the wind backed around. Lately he'd been so tired he had scarcely noticed. Waking up to find the cardboard on which they slept was wet and the water had reached their blanket was still sometimes adding to their discomfort. He would try to finish work earlier tonight, take down their makeshift tent and build a strong new shelter if he could find some help. It would all have to be done before darkness otherwise they would have no place to sleep tonight.

Not far away people called out a greeting to one another and Keisha stirred. Raphael looked at her small frame and wondered how on earth she had coped with separation from the family, the dreadful news about Baba, their escape through the jungle, and then her distress at seeing him fall into the river never knowing if he would resurface. Perhaps she hadn't had time before or since to consider the consequences if he had suffered a serious injury or worse. She certainly could not have managed on her own, and the thought renewed his determination to get them both home to their family.

It was remarkable how Keisha had adapted to her new circumstances. In the relative security of this strange family circle, she had accepted Mama Dawa as though she were a favourite aunt. Keisha worked hard for her, fetching water, helping to prepare food or clean clothes. The whole family had embraced this bright, busy and precocious little girl as one of their own and praised, cajoled or gently scolded her as necessary. Keisha had never once complained to Raphael since they arrived and the petulance and stubbornness that had tested him in the first few days on their own was mercifully still absent. She still had it in her nature though, and he was sure that he would see her temper again sometime soon. For now though he was secretly proud of her and grateful that she was trying to fit in for it gave him one less thing to worry about.

Although Patrick was no substitute for his father, Raphael soon found himself turning to him for advice. He knew instinctively that he could trust him, and share his worries. What Patrick lacked in height and teeth, he made up for in hard work, grit and common sense. He also had an impish sense of humour that often kept the family smiling when everyone's spirits might otherwise have failed. Patrick must have been almost a head shorter than his wife, Raphael had thought when he first saw them together, and probably twenty kilos lighter, but theirs was a strong relationship. Having heard the children's story, the couple encouraged them to keep busy with work and domestic chores. Perhaps it was just their way, or perhaps they understood that any time spent alone with their thoughts would be distressing and demoralising for Keisha and Raphael.

It had never been voiced, but from the evening that they arrived and Mama Dawa had intervened with the mine boss, she had fed them both and watched over them as they washed their clothes and cleaned their tent. She might have supervised their ablutions too had Raphael not made it clear on day one that he and Keisha were quite capable of managing for themselves. So she had been content to buy them a single comb, one that Raphael had never used and that Keisha now treasured as her finest possession. The shiny steel comb, missing only a couple of teeth, was now kept safely in their blanket for Keisha found it hard to sleep until it was secure in her grasp. Raphael couldn't begin to understand the attraction of a comb and was sure she would inadvertently jab him with it in her sleep, but with so few other belongings he was glad of anything that made her life a little more tolerable.

Keisha had made herself useful from the start by fetching water from the stream for washing and cooking, and by helping Mama Dawa and her daughters to earn a few cents by washing miners' clothes. Raphael felt frustrated that he didn't know what Keisha was thinking but she showed surprisingly few outward signs of their recent trauma, aside from asking almost everyone she met if they had seen her mother and the twins. As the days went by, it certainly wasn't easy for Raphael to lay down his emotional burden; whenever his mind was unoccupied thoughts would crowd in upon him and he found it easy to become tearful or slip into an introspection that was entirely out of character. He found that the answer was to make sure he was so busy during the day that there was no time to think about everything they had lost – their family, home, neighbours and friends, even his prized chickens. At first he had hoped he might be so tired he would simply sleep each night, but it was weeks before he slept for a full night. The darkness was still punctuated by frequent and recurring nightmares in which faceless soldiers burned his house and his parents were not there to stop them. He frequently woke in shock from these black dreams, only to find that his parents really were gone and unable to comfort him as he cried and trembled. Then all he could do was put an arm around his still sleeping sister and hope that the waves of miserable thoughts crashing over him would subside. Every night he had vivid thoughts of his father's death, his mother's abandonment of them – for this was how it now felt to him – and the hardships of their unwanted new lives. Although physically tired, Raphael was often unable to sleep for a long time during these nights until finally exhaustion took over.

He and Keisha had been fascinated by Mama Dawa's family; in fact it had been days before he was sure he had met them all. She had told him quite plainly when they met that she had five surviving children, but there was such a constant stream of children and young people arriving at her tent that he had begun to doubt

155

her. From here she dispensed hugs and stern advice for the few girls and frequent reprimands for the boys, plus food and – in dire cases – some homemade medicine that Patrick had warned Raphael about with an unusual air of gravity. After their misfortune Raphael began to realise how lucky he and his sister had been to fall into Mama D's embrace.

But that protection couldn't remove the debt that they owed to Jean de Dieu, the mine manager. It was his vehicle that had brought them there, they were his tools that Raphael had needed to buy, it was his camp in which they rented tent space, his plastic that now kept the rain off their heads, his pots they stirred, and his spoons they licked clean. Had the manager known it, it was even his cardboard that they'd taken on the first night to make their bed. Had Mama Dawa not arrived it would have been so much worse but they still needed to repay him and save money to search for their family.

So Raphael worked every hour that he could, filling a plastic container with the dark grey rocks and chips of coltan ore. To him it looked like shiny charcoal, although it weighed a lot more. He still had no idea why people wanted it so much. One man said it went to Rwanda to be made into jewels. Another said that the Americans wanted it to re-build the twin towers in New York. To be honest, he didn't really care, as long as they could earn money from selling it to the traders then he could plan their escape from the mine.

They would be sad to leave their new-found friends, but he was now sure that the mine was too dangerous a place for them to stay; they needed to find their mother and get back to their village. Raphael couldn't bear to think too much about losing his father so for now he had almost wrapped up these thoughts and put them away at the back of his mind. Maybe he would open up these thoughts later, once the family was reunited.

Except his family never would be fully reunited, would it? It never would be the same again. Something huge in his life that used to be as solid and fixed as the ground he played on had cracked and shifted. Like a broken pot his world could never be put back together again. It had only taken a few minutes but everything that Raphael had loved and relied on had gone. Everything that had once been done for him, all the work at home that he'd never really noticed, now had to be done by him and Keisha – finding firewood, drawing water, bringing in Mama Dawa's chickens, sharpening tools, mending their shelter, everything.

He didn't know how he was going to manage it but when he did find his mother and the twins – and he was adamant that he would – he now realised that he could never again simply run out of the door at home and leave her to worry on her own about food, clothes, tools, seeds or medicine. He had never thought much about these things before, but now he thought about little else. For the last few months his mind had worked endlessly on the fact that his father was gone, and sometimes he was angry at the way his mother had left him looking after Keisha.

He knew it wasn't fair to blame her, but he felt so alone, hurt and resentful that he had been put in charge when he was still only thirteen. Most boys of his age were playing football or fishing when they weren't helping in the fields – not looking after little sisters.

Raphael also felt ashamed at owing money to Jean de Dieu, something Baba would never have allowed. He was still struggling to come to terms with the way it had all happened so quickly – to be honest, he didn't really understand about the money and that too made him feel afraid. It was so frustrating that this prevented him from resuming their search; all he wanted right now was to be rid of this debt. He had thought about taking Keisha and just running away, but he'd been told the nearest town was a long way and he didn't even know in which direction. Besides, Jean de Dieu had wide influence in the area, so where would they hide? What would they eat? At least Raphael had begun to pay off their debt to the mine manager, although it was a slow process. It would take him months to complete even if he bought nothing else, and he could see now that that was unlikely. The thought that he might never finish paying the man back hadn't even occurred to him.

Raphael hadn't admitted it to Keisha, he probably never would, but there was also a deep anger inside him at the injustice of Baba's death, he could feel it like a burn in his chest. A couple of times at night before he finally fell asleep he had imagined one day catching the soldiers who killed his father and the soldiers who robbed him here at the mine. Only this time in his mind's eye he had a gun and they were the ones unarmed. He never knew that he was capable of hating anyone so strongly. Once he had been the calmest of boys, now he was forever finding bitterness and frustration inside. He nursed a fierce protectiveness towards Keisha, he felt anger and bitterness towards the militia who had killed Baba, and the soldiers who had stolen their money, and an acid frustration at their weakness. These were feelings that he couldn't share with anyone at home in the camp, he hadn't even voiced them to Patrick. *And wasn't it strange*, he thought, *how quickly they had come to call a cardboard bed and tarpaulin 'home'?*

******

That evening the transition from daylight to darkness was as swift as always and, with no moonlight, the blackness was total. His plan to finish work a little earlier and re-build his shelter had been over-ruled by Mubalango, who reminded him – as if he needed it – that their entire earnings for the previous few days had been stolen and they had better bring home some money soon or none of them would be eating. It meant staying in their rough tent a little longer, but if the choice was that or go hungry then that was an easy decision.

157

Raphael's new torch was precious and he used the batteries sparingly in camp, so it was better to be out of the mine before sundown. He made his way with the last of the older miners back to the camp where he collapsed exhausted onto the cardboard bed he shared with Keisha.

Covered in mud, dust and sweat he eventually sat up and used a little water from one of Patrick's buckets to wash his hands, neck and face. He was tempted to just lie still and sleep in the hope that it would all feel better in the morning, but he knew that he needed food to face another day like today. Raphael was only just strong enough to manage the physical labour. Although he hadn't analysed it, there was a precarious daily balance between the amount of food he put into his tall, skinny frame, and the enormous physical demands he placed upon it every day. All Raphael knew was that he was perpetually hungry by day and exhausted by night, and there seemed to be time for little else.

He didn't know if it would ever get better but by the end of his work each day Raphael's shoulder muscles and forearms were always knotted and bunched, and his hands tightened so much that they felt like claws. He spent the first few minutes in camp each evening just stretching his fingers, trying to get some movement back into them. He looked down at his hands and hardly recognised them. There were blisters and callouses on each palm from swinging the shovel, as well as cuts where he had been handling rocks. He was glad the day was over because it was painful to work with his hands in this condition, but he couldn't see how he could avoid repeating it all tomorrow. He looked at Patrick and Mubalango; their hands were hard and the skin was tough and scarred from years of mining in all weathers. Mubalango was only five years older but even with his shirt on Raphael could see his shoulder muscles tense and relax as he went through his evening tasks. How Raphael was supposed to keep pace with Mubalango's work when he was so small by comparison worried him constantly. He didn't dare voice such fears, but right now he was wondering if he could cope with the workload much longer.

Raphael knew that in the morning he would have to return to the monotonous noise of the digging and shovelling, the painful rasp of rock on skin, the agony of using a shovel with blistered hands and dealing with the regular rain that made their work so slippery and awkward amid the high sloping banks of earth. And all the time the miners knew that the army or rebel soldiers could appear without warning to take from them by force every gram of coltan they had wrested from the soil. The risks of hunger and robbery competed to be uppermost in their minds, yet for the miners it was just the way that life had always been – the strong get fat and the weak starve.

******

Apart from soldiers, and porters arriving every five days there were no visitors to the mine and nothing to relieve the tedium. For eleven hours from a little after daybreak until sundown at six o'clock the three-man gangs would work, taking time off only for a drink of water or to relieve themselves. There were no meal breaks for there was no spare food. Their main meal of the day would come at sundown, and they might have a little porridge or some bread in the morning. The rest of each day was spent digging rock and earth, sifting out the coltan-bearing earth, breaking the rocks, washing away the loose soil, before separating and collecting the columbite-tantalite. Mubalango told them to swop tasks periodically, but his build made him more suited to digging than Raphael. There was little to occupy their minds other than the songs they sang.

One August day dawned that could not be distinguished from any other by its work or the boredom of their routine. It was routine until voices could be heard coming from the lip of the mine above them. Everyone's first nervous thought was that more soldiers had arrived but the voices spoke a different language and soon the miners could make out the tops of a few heads, white people's heads. The groups around Raphael stopped their digging or sifting and looked up at the strangers. It was a novelty for all of them.

At the edge of the mine stood Marc and Marianne Audousset, a middle-aged French missionary couple and Emmanuel Salumu, a visiting Anglican priest from a congregation in Kinshasa that supported the Audousset's mission. What they saw was causing them a great deal of concern, and all three were already determined to prevent this abomination continuing. Despite his name, Jean de Dieu had never been baptised, indeed he had not set foot in a church since he was a child. So his experience of missionaries was second-hand, and he was suspicious and defensive in the face of his uninvited visitors. He was attempting to explain to his unexpected guests why it was that he had so many people working in a mine that was said not to be controlled by Kinshasa's Ministry of Mines. Who were all these people, he was asked? Who claimed to own the mine now, they wanted to know, and who was he answerable to? But above all, he was having great difficulty explaining the presence of so many children amongst the miners.

Had he been intellectually capable of it he might have tried to bluff his way through the encounter by referring them to one or other office in Kinshasa in the hope that this would delay or dissuade them from pursuing their awkward line of questioning. The mine manager was, however, neither quick-thinking nor resourceful, so his only possible response was to threaten and attempt to browbeat them. It was a policy that Marc and Marianne were used to from local and national government officials, so it did not even dent the resolve of a couple who felt answerable to an altogether higher authority.

From time to time the couple had heard tell of existing mines in this area expanding as well as new ones opening up. To that extent this mine was quite typical; as it had grown and delivered more coltan to its custodians so word had spread of the work to be had there and exaggerated reports of the money that artisan miners could make had lured the desperate. What they found was a disorganised dig where in theory the successful miner could make tens of dollars for every small bucket of coltan they found. To dispossessed farmers and shopkeepers in the region, especially those unfamiliar with the hazards and hardships of mining, the prospect of regular work was not just appealing it was a lifeline. The fragility of that lifeline would have been plain to see had they been able to witness the working conditions before setting out, or if they had witnessed the threat from marauding soldiers. Instead, every week brought new recruits to the mine, hoping to make a living for their families left far behind.

News of this steady influx of miners reached not only the surrounding villages but ultimately was heard by a small group of missionaries – doctors, nurses and teachers – working outside the town of Walikale. The two Congo Wars had forced many missions to take UN advice and leave the Kivu provinces altogether, but since the latest peace accord a steady trickle of Christian missions of varying denominations, including Baptists, Catholics, Presbyterians and Salesians, had returned. Some were focused only on preaching, others such as the Audoussets were caring for children orphaned by the fighting and the growing number of rape victims. Their orphanage now had over thirty children and more were arriving every month, so that Marianne had serious concerns over their ability to cope with the numbers. If Marc shared such practical fears, he would not admit it. Every new face at the mission house encouraged him to renew efforts in his fund-raising back in France, and prompted Marianne to find ways to extend their care to new arrivals. The support they received from Emmanuel and his church in Kinshasa was invaluable but if anything the expanding headcount was accelerating. The mission had little income of its own except from the clothes that were made and sold by the women. In the circumstances, the prudent policy might have been to care solely for those able to reach the orphanage. To Marianne and Marc, however, prudence meant abandoning any chance of protecting the children they had heard about at the mine.

Marc, a doctor and a lay missionary, had been in this part of Congo for long enough to know that the mine's earnings would help to fund the continued fighting and killing. With Emmanuel there to translate if necessary, they had followed the porters until they came upon this open wound of pale earth spreading across the undulating grassy hillside. They had not been there long before they were confronted by Jean de Dieu, demanding to know what they were doing at his mine.

"Who are you exactly? You do not have permission to be here, this mine is private and you must leave immediately," De Dieu blustered.

Marc sidelined his protests with a question of his own. "By what right do you keep children working in this mine?" he demanded. "You are not licensed by the

Ministry of Mines, this camp is illegal, many of its workers are just children and you must cease their work immediately."

"This is my mine," de Dieu shot back. "I take no orders from you, whoever you are."

"Really? Then that makes you legally responsible for this illegal activity. We are here on an official fact finding mission and will be reporting back to Kinshasa in the morning."

He was stretching the definition of official to breaking point, but he suspected that the mine manager would know little of the workings of a Government department in the capital, somewhere that he had probably never visited.

"You will, of course, be able to show me your Permis d'Exploitation Minière from the Ministry of Mines in Kinshasa." Marc had moved on from questionable definitions of his role, and meeting little solid resistance he was now making this up as he went along. One thing he did know was that any legal mining operation would have some documentation to use in dealings with local authorities or the Army in the provincial capital of Goma.

Jean de Dieu looked momentarily blank before regaining his composure. "You will go now or my soldiers will force you out at gunpoint." He jerked a thumb over his shoulder at the handful of teenagers in motley uniforms lounging in plastic garden chairs behind him. Only one held a gun, two were asleep and another wearing fake Ray-Bans was slowly and reluctantly getting to his feet. The soldiers did not appear to be dancing to Jean de Dieu's command; sleep seemed to be a higher priority. Marc knew, however, that their apparent indolence could change and the situation quickly become threatening. They had hoped to find no guards here but that was always going to be unlikely, and they had discussed just such an eventuality.

Emmanuel Salumu stepped forward and switched from French to Kiswahili, knowing that his words would be more widely understood by the growing crowd around them. "My Brother, you may indeed have authority from Kinshasa to mine here, although you still have not shown us your permit. But these are important people, with the ear of many people of influence in Goma and Bukavu, so do not upset them. If you want to avoid a visit from the Governor and many foreign soldiers of MONUSCO with their helicopters and machine guns, then perhaps you should ask yourself if it is still worthwhile employing these children in your mine. Whoever your masters are, they will not take kindly to interference in their work from the blue helmets, is this not so? Do you think they would want such a visit, and all the questions that would inevitably be asked? They would rightly hold you responsible. Think how much money they would lose from all this outside interference and time wasting. Once again, who they would they hold responsible, eh? You, I suspect? Consider this wisely."

Salumu paused and they watched as Jean de Dieu digested the idea that UN forces might be brought in. He might well feel it was unlikely, but everyone knew they went everywhere in helicopters and you never knew where they would turn up next. If these whites decided to make trouble for him with the blue helmets because he didn't co-operate about a few children then he would also be getting a visit from the Army in Goma. That would be much worse than any trouble these three might cause him now.

Jean de Dieu knew, of course, that he could deny responsibility for the children but that would make him look powerless in his own camp and he would certainly lose face. They were not really his responsibility, after all, but many of them still owed him money and, whatever the priest said, they earned the money to pay him from their digging. "What is it you want?" he said, not meaning to give ground but merely playing for time.

Salumu, however, was a skilled negotiator and he had the benefit of forward planning on his side. He smiled broadly and, lifting the manager's un-proffered hand, he shook it warmly. "That is most helpful of you, my friend," he said, making a loud and public assumption of de Dieu's co-operation that had never been intended. "We are here to…" and he paused for he had been on the point of saying 'rescue the children'. He began again, "We are here to help these children find their parents if they are still alive, and to feed and clothe them if they are gone. You are indeed wise not to attempt to shoulder this responsibility alone any longer, we are sent by the Lord God who is the Master of us all to assist you in their care. Amen."

There was a murmured response of Amen from some of the men and women now grouping around them, and De Dieu began to sense that matters were slipping out of his control. The Anglican priest continued, "I am sure their food must be costing as much as they make for you, so we will identify those who are in need of our support and help them on their way."

Jean de Dieu could not quite understand how he had reached this position in a few short sentences, and the prospect of seeing even a few children leaving him with unpaid debts immediately alarmed him. Salumu's assumptive closure in this discussion had worked, but only up to a point. "I have not agreed to their going yet, they owe me for their food and shelter. Who will pay these debts if they go? No, they will stay and you shall have them when their debts to me are paid."

Salumu made a calming motion with the flat of his hand. "One moment," he said and turned to Marc and Marianne. In rapid fire French he explained the turn the conversation had taken but this too had been anticipated by the trio. They knew that to have secured even this measure of agreement already was an achievement but that it could all be lost if de Dieu was allowed to ponder on matters overnight or – worse still – to contact his superiors, whoever and wherever they might be.

The missionaries needed to act swiftly if they were to secure his acceptance of the proposed departure.

"That is understandable. We are in the service of the Lord and our humble church is not rich. How many children are orphaned here and what do they owe?" asked Salumu. He already had a figure in mind that the group was prepared to pay if they had to.

Jean de Dieu's eyes narrowed in suspicion. "Why would you pay for these children? They are not yours. Where are you planning to take them?"

"All of us are God's children and through his infinite goodness He will help us to provide a roof over their heads. Now," Salumu continued, "how many are there and what do they owe you?"

As de Dieu paused, Salumu sensed his greed taking over and could feel the conversation assuming a new commercial slant. "There are five that owe me money, but only three are without parents. Between them they owe me much money, above a hundred dollars."

Salumu sighed theatrically. "Oh dear. Is it really so much? That is a pitiable debt that we would be unable to settle on their behalf. We must leave them to you and hope that you can resolve their debts with them before the blue helmets come calling. I imagine they will have heard the same reports that we did. They may be getting into their helicopters right now to come and take these orphans away, then you will receive nothing except maybe a big fine from the governor for this illegal mining. Or perhaps he will just throw you in prison for failing to pay taxes to him and to the government in Kinshasa."

Salumu gave a slow Gallic shrug that his white colleagues could not have read more clearly had they been native Kiswahili speakers. He turned back to Marc and Marianne, shaking his head extravagantly, while starting to turn them away with him and lead them back along the path that had brought them. Jean de Dieu could see cold hard cash getting ready to just walk away and, although he could not be sure that the blue helmets would fly all this way for a handful of orphans they did do strange things. This was yet another risk to the mine's future that he could easily prevent, thereby earning the gratitude and respect of his soldier masters in Goma, while also settling their debts in hard currency.

He called out to Salumu. "How much do you bring me to pay for their debts?"

Salumu stopped and affected disinterest. "It is clearly not enough for a wealthy man such as you," he shrugged dismissively. "No matter, we thank you for your time."

Jean de Dieu persisted, "So, how much will you pay to settle their debts? They owe me $150."

Salumu, his arm draped consolingly over Marianne's shoulders, stopped and turned and raised an eyebrow. "This debt seems to be rising all the time. It's gone up even since we arrived. Perhaps the interest you charge these *children*," he emphasised the word, "is too high for a churchman to pay. If I'm to agree a price with you, first I must talk to the children."

Jean de Dieu was getting impatient and with uncharacteristic boldness he ordered the standing soldier to send someone to find the three orphans. The soldier began to protest but seeing that there was talk of money changing hands he thought better of it and kicked the legs of a teenage gunman lounging beside him. "Get up and bring all the children with no mother and father. Tell them they may soon go to school and play with other children if they come quick. Go on, go."

The gunman got to his feet and made to collect his gun but his leader barked at him to go immediately, and he headed for the camp muttering at this sudden and unwelcome workload. Perhaps it was just as well he went as he did, for few children would have willingly accompanied any of the soldiers had they been armed. The missionaries smiled benignly at Jean de Dieu and sat down with their guide and porter to have a drink from their canteens. They knew that this could take a long while, but if it was to be done at all it would need to be done in time to leave before sundown.

Marc passed a packet of cigarettes around and he and the guide who had brought them to the mine lit up. The odd little party of church folk and guides settled down for a leisurely drink and a smoke while they watched the digging that had long since resumed below.

Far below, Raphael of course knew nothing of these discussions. The novelty of the white people and churchman visiting the mine eventually gave way to the necessity to dig out more coltan. He, Mubalango and Bahati resumed their tasks and he followed their example while the visitors talked to the mine manager somewhere above them. He was still busy thirty minutes later when he heard Keisha calling frantically to him as she ran perilously fast down the open side of the dig before dropping into the stream in front of him. "You have to come now, Raph, Mama Dawa says so. You are to bring Patrick, too."

Patrick who was barely ten yards away had already stopped and was leaning on his shovel when she approached. It was very unusual to see Keisha in the pit, although she often came with Mama to the mine's edge. Now, hearing his name, Patrick studied her closely. "What is it, little one?" he asked in concern. "Is someone hurt?" Clearly something important was happening and he was instantly anxious for his family. "Is it the soldiers? Have they hurt someone?"

Keisha managed to take a deep breath. "Mama says that you and Raphael are to come immediately with me to the camp. She's worried about Jean de Dieu, he's up to something bad and she needs you both there."

Patrick looked at Raphael and turned to speak quickly to Mubalango in a low and urgent tone. Mubalango nodded in agreement and, calling to Raphael to keep up, both men began to run up the steep bank. The loose earth gave way but they angled their run to intersect a hard packed line of steps that had been worn into the

164

mud and rock and which was the fastest way out of the long, deep pit. Mubalango reached the steps just ahead of Patrick and bounded up the rough pathway with Raphael and Keisha following behind. Raphael had no idea what was happening, but he knew that it concerned him directly for Mama Dawa had said so and he was not sure whether to be frightened or not. If Jean de Dieu was involved, it would not mean good news. They expected to head for the camp but Mama and a growing group of bystanders were waiting for them near the top of the path. Patrick tried to catch his breath at the top of the slope as he came up after Mubalango who was now listening to his agitated mother.

She bustled through the throng of people and grabbed Patrick by the arm of his dirty shirt. Her usual calm had deserted her and she was talking so fast that her husband could scarcely understand a word she was saying. He took both her arms and held them tightly, staring into her eyes. "Tell me, slowly," he said, "what has happened, who are these people?" He nodded in the direction of the missionaries who were standing once again and watching with concern the growing hubbub that now surrounded their discussions with the mine manager.

"They are pastors from Walikale and they want to take away the children who they say should not be working here. Jean de Dieu is trying to sell Keisha and Raphael to them because they have no parents – we must stop them."

"But pastors don't buy children, and they are not de Dieu's to sell." Patrick turned to stare accusingly at Jean de Dieu who was now surrounded by miners' families in a growing clamour for information. There were many people talking at the mine manager at once, but Patrick's deep voice bellowed above the confusion. "What is happening here? I ask you why you think you can sell our children. They live with us, we look after them and they work with us. You know all this very well. And who are these people, anyway?" he gestured to Emmanuel, Marianne and Marc.

Jean de Dieu began to reply, but, seeing the way things were developing and eager to calm the growing sense of panic, Emmanuel Salumu stepped forward. A smile was never far from his eyes and clouds of tight grey curls above his ears gave him a distinguished look. His voice showed all the command and experience that could be expected from decades spent holding church services outdoors or in open-sided meeting houses. "My friends," his voice boomed and the hubbub subsided noticeably as his years and his calling earned him a respectful hush.

He began again. "My friends, it is good to meet you all here today and we thank you for this warm welcome. We bring you greetings and the love of God himself from our church in Walikale. I have with me two dear friends in Christ who have travelled all the way from Europe to be with us in our work, Marc is a doctor and Marianne a teacher."

Jean de Dieu was fidgeting for he had long since lost control of this meeting and its heady mix of negotiations, sermons and talk of salvation on earth. He looked uncomfortable with all this church talk and he was increasingly aware that Emmanuel's oratory had the capacity to turn the still growing crowd of people in ways that he could not influence.

"It is our task as God's lowly disciples," the priest continued, "to do everything in our power to protect the lives of the weak and humble. Just as you do with your children, we protect our children from those around who would sleep while they work, or who would steal the very food from their mouths." His eyes rested on Jean de Dieu who looked away knowing what inference the watching miners would draw. While some of those listening might have been unable to keep up with his rich vocabulary, no one could fail to see that Emmanuel Salumu had identified himself with the swelling crowd of fifty or more people now surrounding him. From his broad smile and widespread arms to the easy delivery of his words and the confident way in which he looked into everyone's eyes, it was easy to see that he represented no threat.

"We cannot sit comfortably in our church in Walikale, singing hymns and just teaching the children who have already found their way into our care when we know that there are others out here," again he emphasised their proximity with a slow sweep of his arm, "even children here among us this minute, who need God's protection and love."

There was a rumble of agreement from the assembled miners. Some of them had visited churches in Walikale and a few knew of the work done by foreign missions to shelter and educate children orphaned by the fighting. This was a dramatic day for them as it was the first time anyone could recall seeing the Anglican mission step out of its gates to search out children who might need its care.

He hadn't moved but Jean de Dieu was sweating now. There were murmurs of anger from the many fathers present at the thought of their own distant children being exploited as these orphans were. "My friends and I wish only to provide them with shelter from the sun and rain, to give them meals, to see them grow, and school them that they may learn under the protective tree of God's love. If there are any here who already know our church, let them vouch for our work."

There was loud assent from a few of the miners. De Dieu looked about him but now there was no sign of the soldiers and he felt increasingly exposed as he guessed the turn that this monologue was bound to take. He began to sidle quietly towards the edge of the group. At first people made way for him as they concentrated on Salumu's words.

"If you know of such children in this camp, whose parents have perished in the fighting, or children who are separated from their families please let them know that we are here today to protect them. We can look after them today, taking them from this camp and this mine, to a place of safety and learning where there are many other children to play with and there is food for them to eat twice a day. But we need to get word to them now, while there is still the chance for them to go."

At the edge of the group, two men were in hurried discussion and the younger of them broke away and ran down to the camp. De Dieu could guess what message he was carrying. Salumu had the crowd in the palm of his hand and, lest he lose them, he did not pause. "It is urgent, send word to them now and with your help we can find protection for them."

"As we all know, there are those who try to exploit them, to take the money that these children earn. They wrench it from their hands and keep it for themselves. Then there are those who lend them a franc and ask for five francs in return. It is up to all of us to do what we can to protect Congo's children from this abuse, this theft, this violence. Now, do we have any such children here? Or do you know of any in the camp?" The rumble of discussion that had continued throughout this peroration swelled as soon as he stopped speaking, for most of the miners knew children to whom this might apply.

Behind him Raphael could hear Patrick and Mama Dawa deep in conversation. She sounded anguished but he was calmer and seemed more assured. He came over to where Raphael stood and placed a hand covered in dried earth on the boy's shoulder, drawing him to them. "Do you know what this means Raphael?" he asked as gently as he could. "These people, these priests are offering you – and Keisha, of course – a choice to spend the rest of your lives in mines like this working with us for little money and watching as the soldiers take what you earn. Or you can go with these priests and start again with Keisha. They will feed you and school you every day. You can learn to read and write, and then you can send letters to ask if anyone has seen your mother."

Raphael could hardly take in the enormity of what he was saying. "But what about both of you, and Mubalango? And Bahati?" He looked from one to the other in search of comfort or certainty. In Patrick's eyes he saw only kindly concern, and when he turned to Mama Dawa she was doing her best to hide her crying but her hand would not let go of Keisha's and the tears could clearly be seen on her cheeks. She wiped them away repeatedly with the back of her hand but her face was soon wet once more.

"You are not to worry about Mubalango or about us. You have seen we can take good care of ourselves. And one day we may be rich from all this coltan or the gold we hear of."

"But I can take care of myself, and Keisha … here at the mine, with you," said Raphael clinging to the one certainty that remained to him.

"You have done a fine job already," said Patrick, "and it has made a good man out of a young boy. But none of us can prevent the soldiers taking what they want, whenever they want it. Not me, nor Mubalango for all his strength. Not even you. Keisha will not always be a little girl, and you will not always be there to protect her." There was an involuntary little cry from Mama and, without quite knowing why, Keisha was suddenly crying too. You understand me, don't you?" asked Patrick pointedly. Raphael nodded. He had heard the stories of gang rape and even abduction – the boys being made to fight and kill while the girls were kept as sex slaves.

"You must make this decision not just for yourself, but you must be as brave as your father would have been for Keisha if he was still here. We can offer you so little, and these people are known to many of my friends. They can give you food every day, new clothes, even a real bed. You won't have to work in the mine, you won't have gunmen taking your food and money, and they can even teach you both to read and write letters. This could be a start of a better life for both of you and maybe with their help you can find your mother."

Raphael could not bear the thought that he might be parted from this warm family that had taken them both in, cared for and fed them, and sheltered them from the harm that would surely have befallen them otherwise. Now that same family was urging them to leave. His eyes were filling with tears and Mubalango, who for so long had treated him as a little brother, would not meet his gaze.

Emmanuel spoke again, "Is there any child here that would like to come with us, to leave behind this work and come to school to learn and play?" He was talking in general terms, but with so few children among the miners it was easy for his eyes to rest on Raphael and Keisha. He could see the anguished discussions that had broken out among the group and must have sensed that this was not quite the family circle that it might have appeared.

Marianne and Marc too were smiling warmly at Raphael and seemed to represent a happier, more positive future – and, above all, one in which they might have the chance to search for the rest of their family. Although he didn't feel ready for such a drastic change, and it had arisen without warning, the prospect of quitting the mine, its painful, heavy drudgery, the constant atmosphere of threat and the debts that they owed to Jean de Dieu was appealing; no it was more than that, it was exciting. It was just that it came so suddenly and at such a high price in parting from their new friends and losing the one network of support they had found since they had fled the village.

Keisha pulled hard on Mama Dawa's hand in an agony of incomprehension, knowing only that something momentous was happening. "What is it, what is it?" she kept asking. There was so much talk among the adults that she hadn't understood, but she was acutely aware of their distress and Raphael's stricken look of indecision. Mama Dawa knelt to look her in the eye and explain to her as best she could, and Keisha's tears began to flow freely as she understood. All the time she shook her head at the prospect and hugged Mama's arm.

Salumu was not finished yet. "We still have one problem that must first be resolved before we can bring these children safely to our church. This man," he said, pointing to Jean de Dieu who had broken free of the group that had swelled to almost a hundred people, "this man claims that these children all owe him a great deal of money. Can this be true? These are children, after all."

There was a roar of anger from the crowd. "He is a thief," shouted one man. "He takes all the money we earn," screamed another. De Dieu was looking about him but the soldiers who had earlier been sleeping nearby were now eyeing him from a distance. They felt no allegiance to him, they were not paid by him, he had no power over them and they would be just as happy without him there. Jean de Dieu felt every centimetre of the ground that separated him from the soldiers, and knew deep down the gulf between them. The crowd of miners sensed it too. The only factors that were preventing them taking direct action against him were the side arm that he carried in the waistband of his trousers and which he was now fingering and, as it turned out, the emollient actions of Emmanuel Salumu.

"I am sure that now he has had time to reflect on this debt, your manager," at this he paused and a growl of anger swelled within the crowd, "would like to make his own gesture of goodwill towards any children who want to join us in Walikale. Is that not so, my friend? How about if you were to wipe the slate clean? Send them on their way with no debts to pay. Doesn't that sound good? Think how your reputation will grow, how people will tell one another of this great thing you have done."

All De Dieu could think was how his largesse would be viewed by the army if his reputation reached Goma barracks. But Salumu was a good judge of character – even if he was unaware of De Dieu's fear of his masters he could see that the manager knew he could not carry the soldiers with him. Salumu knew that an appeal to his vanity was the surest way of enlisting his agreement. It would be far more effective than a threat or a promise.

When Salumu proposed that the manager release the children from their debts, there was a roar of approval from the miners. Jean De Dieu began to protest. It still wasn't clear to him how many children might go, and he could picture a stack of dollars walking out of the camp. Yet he knew now that he was powerless to prevent it.

"Is that agreed then, my friend?" Emmanuel pressed home his advantage better than any market trader. De Dieu paused and the crowd's murmurs started to swell to anger again. There were calls from some of the miners to take all his money and one invisible speaker urged them to string him up if he would not agree. But Emmanuel Salumu was having none of it. "We do not want this man's blood, what Jesus wants is for him to show his strength and generosity."

There were whistles and howls of derision from the crowd at the thought of this devious man willingly giving up what he plainly saw as his entitlement. "What is it to be, sir? Will you waive any further claim to the wages of these children?

Will you bless their new start in life, and allow them to leave here without further hurt or loss or debt?" Salumu almost spat out these last words.

His challenge to De Dieu was now direct, and even the Audoussets who did not speak the language needed no translation. De Dieu said nothing, and the crowd began to seethe and move closer to the two protagonists.

"We do not have all day, my friend. What do you say?" asked Emmanuel.

"Very well," mumbled De Dieu.

"I beg your pardon? We could not hear."

De Dieu was angry and spoke up, "I said, very well. The children can leave without paying me back."

"You mean their debt to the mine owners is cancelled, I think," the priest prompted him.

"Yes, that's what I mean," and with that De Dieu turned on his heel and pushed his way out of the crowd to jeers and laughter from the throng.

"Now we need to see these children and ask them if they would like to join us in Walikale. Where are they? Children, please come forward, do not be afraid for your debts have been settled. We offer you the protection of the Lord our God, his son, Jesus Christ and of the Holy Spirit. And we will join with you every step of the way to your new home and your new school in the safety of our mission."

A boy, who could only have been a year or eighteen months older than Raphael, stepped out of the crowd smiling nervously. Marianne came forward and put a hand on his shoulder, she spoke to him softly in French and Emmanuel translated for her. The grey-haired priest looked up in Raphael's direction. "Are there any others?" he asked quietly.

There was a silence and as everyone turned to look at them a channel seemed to open through the crowd. Raphael was in agony. He looked at Patrick who just shook his head as if to say this is your choice, I can't help you here. Until today he had never seen Mama Dawa show any weakness nor shed a tear, but now she was speechless. She seemed to lean against Patrick and by her left side Keisha stood quite still, uncertain who was in charge. Keisha turned to Raphael with a pleading look, but he couldn't be sure what was in her mind. Did she understand at all the choice that lay before them? Or was she simply longing to stay with Mama Dawa and Patrick? So many confusions were tumbling after one another in his head. Her stricken look suggested that she understood through a ten year-old's prism that her life was changing once again and might be whisking away the few certainties that remained to her. This tableau might have continued unbroken had it not been for the breathless return of Mubalango who pushed his way from the back of the crowd to stand at his father's side. Under his left arm was a blanket-wrapped bundle and his right hand was clenched. Slowly he opened his hand and proffered it towards Keisha as a grin spread across his face, for concealed in his huge fist was a small, shiny steel comb.

She looked up at Mubalango and held his gaze for a second but seemed unwilling to speak. Then, looking down again at her comb, Keisha sucked in a breath and started to slip Mama Dawa's hand, before stopping. She turned to face the woman who for these few weeks had behaved like a mother to her. Keisha reached out and Mama pulled her close, wrapping her in a last strong embrace. Keisha's may have been a small frame but she squeezed the woman harder than either of them would have believed possible then, with tears running freely down her face, the young girl took a step backwards and moved through the group of miners to join her brother.

The inertia had been broken and Raphael now knew more clearly than he had for many weeks that they must get away today or risk never having another chance to do so. Mubalango had had the presence of mind to grab a few essentials for his young workmate. There was no sentimentality in their parting, just one last handshake in their accustomed style and then the bundle of belongings was handed over.

Patrick managed a final smile for Keisha and raised a hand in salute to Raphael, but the last goodbyes were being hastened by the need to leave the camp before the light failed. None of the newly enlarged party of visitors wanted to stay a moment longer than was necessary and risk losing their advantage over Jean de Dieu and the guards. As they filed away towards the only track out of the camp, both the children looked back, but Patrick had turned his wife away from the departing missionaries and children and the couple were making their way silently back down the hill to the camp. With the confrontation now over most of the crowd had already gone in search of their supper. Of their surrogate family only Mubalango still stood in the fading light and watched as Raphael and Keisha disappeared once more into the bush.

Book 2

Errors, like straws, upon the surface flow;
He who would search for pearls must dive below.

All for love, Prologue
John Dryden
1631 - 1700

Chapter 12
London, UK & Kinshasa, Democratic Republic of Congo
A Month Ago

London's Shepherd's Bush Arena was a strange place for an epiphany but for James that was where it began. He had been called by a couple of friends with a spare ticket for a gig, and as he stood with them in an audience swept away by the music, the most challenging and exciting idea he'd ever had washed over him with the haunting first line of the song Square One. *'You're in control, is there anywhere you wanna go? You're in control, is there anything you wanna know?'* By the time the song ended five minutes later James Falkus had decided something, and as the words *'It doesn't matter who you are'* drifted away he suspected that he was taking a path that could change his life forever.

He hadn't known it when he arrived but the gig was a charity fundraiser and it was the huge AfriCan Care banner at the back of the stage that planted the seed of an idea. He'd never heard of AfriCan Care before, but they were said to be working in four countries, one of which was the DRC. The charity's name kind of spoke for itself.

As he left the event with his friends, he was quieter than usual, and after a drink together he was quick to make his excuses. He certainly wasn't tired; he just wanted time to think as he walked the mile or so from the pub to Hammersmith Tube. All around him there were people spilling onto the street from pubs and takeaways. Some were walking arm in arm, either for warmth or support. Across the road in a bus stop there was a catfight between two women too drunk to land a blow on each other or to feel it if they did and the noise of traffic here was as loud as most rush hours. Yet James took little of it in. His thoughts were on Africa, the equatorial heat of the Congo, imagining the desperate street life in Kinshasa. In his mind's eye he was walking through a shantytown or flying into the country's interior to photograph children in the war zone. His head buzzed with mingled feelings of anticipation, fear, and excitement that were only slightly tempered by the inconvenience of having no job there to go to and the fact that his plan was less than half-formed.

By the time he got home, Neil was asleep and James was more awake than he'd felt for weeks. He wanted to go for a run, or stand on the roof and shout. He had this crazy idea and there was no one he could call at this hour to share his plan. Instead he found AfriCan Care's website and looked at videos and photos of famous supporters, mainly musicians, but also well-known models and artists. For now, he skipped past the information on their projects and fund-raising activities until he found the charity's address. There, North London; that wouldn't be hard to get to. At 3.00 a.m. he sat down with a strong black coffee and drafted an email introducing himself, his photography, his interest in the DRC with a link to an online sample of his portfolio where they could review some of his work. He was simply asking for a chance to meet them, to see if there might be photographic work he could do for them in Congo in the near future. He sat back when it was drafted and re-read it, before adding a couple of sentences. "I have been shocked by what I have read and seen about conditions in the DRC. A family connection in the country means that I'm doubly keen to help raise awareness of the effects of war here. I am a widely travelled photographer and can offer experience of meeting tough deadlines, often in challenging environments. I would also be willing to undertake this work on an unpaid basis for three months. I only ask that you cover travel and other reasonable expenses." Then he hit SEND and went to bed.

That was on Tuesday. On Friday there was a brief email reply asking him to contact the AfriCan Care office to come in and have a chat. That was positive, he guessed, but they were giving nothing away and when he sat down at their office in a side street in Kentish Town the first comment from the tough-looking young woman opposite him was, "Let me just say we have a large number of photographers already on our books. But," and she finally cracked a smile, "I'm grateful to you for coming in, we liked your images. It's always crucial to meet the people behind the camera; there's only so much we can learn about you from your photos."

James was wondering if her caution was because he didn't have a portfolio of previous charity or commercial work to show her. She hadn't asked about his experience yet, so he hadn't flagged it up. Or was it a query about his portfolio's quality? James held on to his optimism and just nodded.

Twenty minutes later, when he left their offices he was no nearer knowing if they would use him. She had complimented his work but also emphasised his lack of experience working amid such poverty, the hard task of getting to some of the locations, the sometimes distressing situations and their impact on people's ability to get the job done. While James couldn't claim to have been in a war zone before, he was not naive and, as he pointed out, surely every photographer they'd ever taken on had to start somewhere. If she was impressed by his reasoning, she didn't show it, and on the way home he wondered what else he should have said to show his readiness to work in harsh circumstances. He shrugged to himself, they weren't the only people working out there; he would just have to approach other charities in the area and improve his message.

Meanwhile, he hadn't told Neil the type of work he was trying to do because he wasn't ready to open up a conversation about his birth parents. It was strange really, in every other way Neil was the one person in the world to whom he could tell almost anything, but his sensitivity in the past on his adoption made James very wary about discussing this with him.

******

Buffing up his portfolio and CV wasn't going to keep him busy and it certainly wouldn't pay the rent. James was watching his bank balance fall daily, and continued to contact as many charities and research organisations as he could find in Europe and North America with an interest in the DRC. There was a real danger that he would run out of money and time before someone offered him any work, so he began to concentrate harder on his initial plan of supplying photos for a stock image bureau. It seemed incredibly dull in comparison but he needed a back-up plan, and at least there was no shortage of agencies.

It was a fortnight later, after he'd been for two more unsuccessful interviews with image bureaux and had been rejected or ignored by several others, that he found an answerphone message waiting at the flat. It was as brief as before and just asked him to call AfriCan Care. Since he still hadn't discussed this with Neil he was glad to have picked up the message first.

"Sarah Page speaking," said the voice when he called back.

"Sarah, its James Falkus, the photographer." He felt a fraud calling himself that without ever having had a paid commission, but if he didn't believe it nor would she. "You left a message earlier."

"Yes, James. Thanks for calling back. We've been giving your proposal quite a bit of thought here. To be honest, normally we wouldn't take on someone unproven in one of our four key regions but your visit was more timely than you could know."

"Oh? How's that?" he asked.

"One of our regular photographers is unavailable and we need photography to cover a visit to Kinshasa by some of our senior staff. There's also the regular need for new material from Goma and the refugee camps. Would this sort of thing still be of interest?"

"You bet."

"You also generously offered to work unpaid for a few months. Given that we haven't worked with you before and we are taking a bit of a risk – as we appreciate you are – we'd like to take you up on that offer, but we can review this at the end of the first month and discuss it with you then. Does that seem fair? I mean, if all's going well we may be able to offer you a short-term paid assignment then. It wouldn't be much but…." she left the last sentence hanging. "The other advantage is that you could go in on a tourist visa since you're not being paid, which may speed the process of getting you out there."

"That's fine." James couldn't quite believe it. For the first time in weeks he felt he was moving forward again. And, even if no money had changed hands, he'd just become a professional photographer.

******

Parting with his brother had never gone worse. Neil had been travelling in Europe on business and came back in a foul mood after experiencing problems with the project he was working on and delays caused by air traffic control strikes. James decided to put off announcing his plans until they could have a more positive discussion. So, in the end it was another forty-eight hours before they were in the flat together and he could tell Neil what he was planning.

"I don't get you," said Neil. "What's wrong with the parents you have, or had? Why do you need to go digging up the past for some people who gave you up? I'm damn sure I don't want to."

James resisted the temptation to describe what was wrong with their sole surviving parent. "Well, that's where we're different, I guess," said James. "I've always wanted to know who my blood family are. It's nothing to do with Mum, and certainly no reflection on Dad. He was brilliant. But he's not where I came from."

"Why are you doing it now then, why didn't you search for them before if it was so damned important?"

"Maybe I should have done. Maybe I was just happy to carry on with what I had at the time. But things can change." James didn't want to say it in case it sounded maudlin, but Lisa's death had made him review so much in his life and quitting his job had been the final catalyst. He suspected they both knew this anyway.

"You wouldn't have done this if Dad was still alive," Neil said bitterly. The implication that James wouldn't have had the guts to do it was clear.

"Actually, I think you're wrong on that. It's not as though I never discussed it with him, just that I was content to leave the matter alone at the time. I wasn't mature enough or ready to find out for myself. Well, I am now." James was angry now, he didn't want Neil's approval but it would be good if they could just discuss the subject.

"So, I'm not mature enough to deal with it, is that it?" Neil shot back angrily.

"No. I never said that, so don't twist my words. I was only talking about me."

Neil shrugged his shoulders dismissively. "Anyway, what's got you all fired up about it? It doesn't affect you. They're my parents not yours." And even before he'd finished he wished he hadn't said it, laying bare as it did the taboo that they were not blood relatives. It had never seemed to matter to them before, yet suddenly James felt that he had opened a small but important gap between him and his brother. Worse still, he wasn't sure if it could be closed again.

Neil looked at him without speaking for a second and in that moment James saw that he was hurt but wouldn't say so. "OK, let me get this straight, your mother gave you up, then died when you were two. And she wrote to you – or to the adoption agency – from the States, what, twenty-five years ago? Now you're going to the hotel in Congo or wherever it is to see if he's still there over a quarter of a century later? D'you think he's been sitting there waiting for you to reply? And what are you gonna do, help him pay his bar bill? It should be a tidy sum by now."

"You can drop the sarcasm. I don't know where he is now, and that's not the point. I just want to see where he lived and worked. But now that I understand a bit about what the country has been through maybe I can help bring people's attention to the impact of the war on the children there. If I can show the work being done for them, others may want to support it. I don't think that's a bad thing, do you?"

"Very noble. But war is shit, little Bro." What had once seemed a term of affection suddenly felt very patronising. "I've seen it first hand and any sane person would be running as fast as they could in the opposite direction. People get killed and worse. We all know it's happening there, it's not a bloody secret. It's in the papers and on the news every night, for Chrissake. What makes you so special that everyone's going to sit up and hear what you've got to say about it?"

"Perhaps because I'm filming the guys who aren't running the other way." James paused. "Anyway, that's where you're wrong. This war's been going on, one way and another, for longer than the Second World War and it's *not* on the news tonight or any night." He drew a long breath, trying hard not to preach to his own brother.

"Listen, I'm not doing this for effect or a medal. I'm not a fool, and I do know that it won't be easy there. But I'm not like you, I've played it safe all through my working life. I've never done anything that was worth a damn. I've never worked on anything of real, lasting value. There's nothing I can put my hand on or point to and say, 'That's where I made a difference to the world and people will remember what we did'.

"You can probably point to any number of lives saved or battles won. I can't and suddenly it really matters to me. I don't want to look back later at a life just spent on the 6.45 train to London Bridge. This is a chance for me to learn new skills, see if I can cut it as a photographer, visit a part of the world I've never seen before and maybe, just maybe, I can come back thinking I've done something that mattered more than buffing up the image of some crappy software company." James subsided, he'd said most of what was eating him up.

"Nice speech, kiddo, but I don't think it'll be anything like you imagine. You do what you have to do, I'm off to bed. I'll see you in the morning."

"I'll see you then, and don't call me kiddo." James turned on his heel and went to bed but not to sleep. In the morning Neil was already gone when James got up and started planning his inoculations and travel arrangements.

******

The first view of Kinshasa as the plane came in to land was the yellow painted concrete of the control tower and buildings at the Aéroport de N'djili. He had filled the hours from London via Brussels nervously checking his cameras and doing some more reading about his destination. When James landed, it was late afternoon. It wasn't the heat that struck him first, it was the humidity that clamped your shirt to your skin in a soggy embrace. There were puddles of rainwater in the shade; Kinshasa was still in the midst of thunderstorms and the skies were impressive with tall dark clouds looming, beyond them a line of pale grey clouds was approaching. He'd never been anywhere in Africa before and the smell of wet grass and hot dust that greeted him was strong and intoxicating. It soon gave way, however, to intermittent wafts from overloaded drains struggling to carry away the latest rains.

He walked down the steps to a waiting bus, its doors mercifully open. The breeze tried and failed to relieve the heat and he began to melt as he and his fellow passengers waited to go. The bus doors closed, the bus moved off and swung around before coming to a halt after a journey of no more than a hundred metres.

The Australian businessman who had been sitting next to James on the flight grimaced at him, "God knows why we couldn't walk. Jobs for the boys, I guess." James half-smiled, unwilling to be dragged into a negative view of the place before he was even officially in the country. The man was immediately behind him in the queue for Passport Control, and put down his bag with a sigh. "This is where the fun starts," he muttered wearily. "Where's my bloody protocol got to?"

"Protocol?" asked James.

The man turned to study James. "Of course, this is your first visit. You need a protocol and mine's late, they're the guys who smooth your path through Security, Passport Control and Customs. And whichever other thieving bastard takes a shine to your luggage and valuables. Don't tell me your people in London didn't warn you! What the hell do they do for you back there? Listen mate, if you don't have a protocol now you'd better get one for the journey home – fifty US may seem a lot, but it's a damn sight cheaper than shelling out for every sodding 'security officer'

– he mouthed the words with contempt – on the take, and basically that's all of them. I've always used Simon, but they all have their strengths and weaknesses. Simon gets you through and my company pays, of course, but his weakness is women, sometimes he just forgets to get dressed and come down here. Ah, speak of the devil, he's here … Listen, it was good meeting you, er…"

"James."

"Right. Good meeting you, James, hope the photography goes well, mate. I'd better be going otherwise he'll wander off, then I'll be bloody stuck here. See you on the flip side," and he nodded at somewhere beyond the security officials.

The Aussie left the passport queue and followed a young beanpole of a man across the hall. The protocol had a swagger about him, perhaps it was his height but he moved with a languid grace as though thinking his way through a few dance moves as he went. In one hand was a mobile phone, and in the other a set of car keys on a chain. On anyone else the ensemble could have been very camp, somehow he just looked cool – Simon was in his element. He opened a frosted glass panel door and without looking back held it for his Australian charge. The pair went through and the last James saw was a porter taking the man's bag and guiding him into what looked like a lounge with armchairs and a huge indoor plant.

There seemed to be two lines, one for special people and the other in which he stood. Periodically an official would take someone from the long line and put them in the shorter special one. "Come!" said a voice nearby and James turned back to see an officer beckoning irritably at him. He was keeping a Health Control officer waiting, which wasn't going down well. He handed over his passport and vaccination card and the man studied it, grunted loudly and then just stared at him. "La date de vaccination. Ce n'est pas bon," was all he said at first.

"It's new…" James was surprised, but he didn't know what was expected.

"Yellow Fever. It is *too* new. Ten days only," he said with menace. James shook his head in incomprehension as the man demanded sixty dollars.

Here we go, he thought. James grimaced and pulled out his wallet. The charity had warned him to take dollars – everyone preferred their dependability. Every street kid here knew the precise value of a greenback and claimed to offer the best exchange rate in Kinshasa.

James had expected that banks would be few and far between and the hotel exchange rates extortionate, so he was carrying mostly dollars in a money belt and wallet. He slid three twenties across the high counter. There was no receipt. James looked about him, he wasn't being singled out – everyone in line was being treated in much the same way, one passenger was becoming increasingly angry and aggressive but it certainly hadn't helped him.

The next queue was for Passport Control desk, with another uniformed official sitting in a glass cubicle. The man snapped his fingers, demanding more documentation.

James quickly dug it out of his pocket and showed the unsmiling official.

"Visa," said the man. Evidently, there were problems with this, too.

"It's stamped in there. Look," and he gestured at it in his passport, but the passport was out of reach and he guessed what was coming. He had to have a ninety dollar 'special visa', again no receipt. The man flipped the passport back to him and gave James a beatific smile.

******

Ninety minutes and five controls later he finally emerged into the Arrivals Hall with his bag. God only knew how the luggage had moved more slowly from the plane than he had, but it had finally made it onto the only working carousel. James was a little older, wiser and poorer. He waited a moment but no welcome party was visible until he emerged from the shade of the ugly yellow concrete building. A dented once-white minibus was waiting outside with an AfriCan Care sign in the windscreen; the local driver was all smiles but Serge, the promised European contact for the charity seemed not to know how. His ill temper matched James's mood, he wondered if he could have been better prepared for the officials who so expertly extorted money from him. *He had travelled with enough money to get by on*, he thought, *and those plans had just gone to hell*. The only positive was that he had his passport back, now with a smudged 'new' stamp on the Visa that filled most of one page, and he had learned his first lessons on life in the Congo.

He had no idea why his contact was so surly. Serge's clothes matched his demeanour, he was dressed in a dirty blue T-shirt, worn down clogs made of wood and leather, and jeans that were torn but not in a good way. After a couple of attempts at conversation had been ignored or rebuffed James left Serge to his own mood and, intent on putting the airport experience behind him, he stared out of the window absorbing every bit of his first sight of Africa. There was a lot of chatter going on in front of the minibus before the driver finally took his seat, fought the reluctant gearbox into an uneasy submission, revved the engine and kangaroo-hopped the van out of its parking space in second gear.

To begin with the kerbs were all neatly painted red and white but this soon petered out and along the dual carriageway trucks and cars were parked nose to tail at the roadside with people milling around them. As the road grew clearer, the minivan picked up speed along tarmac that was surprisingly smooth and in better repair than he had expected. He was close to the rear window and the rush of warm wind through the vehicle was a welcome relief from the airport's stifling heat. He was able to watch people walking beside the road, making their way home from work or the market. The earlier wide grassy central reservation had turned to dust here and hawkers were selling drinks, cigarettes, newspapers and even jerry cans of petrol from the roadside under the shade of brightly coloured umbrellas. A young pedestrian took a crazy risk running across the road in front of them, trusting more to their brakes than was wise. Women and men in equally bright printed skirts and shirts walked slowly in the heat along the Boulevard Lumumba, beside a succession of vividly painted and poster-covered walls and billboards.

Ahead of them an old green Peugeot estate wallowed along so low on its rear axle that a whole new suspension set-up must have been overdue, and its cracked exhaust announced its passing to one and all. Two men were standing on the rear bumper on either side of the half opened rear door, and leaning forward to avoid falling off. From James's seat he could also make out three pairs of legs dangling out of the back of the vehicle and occasionally he glimpsed more passengers inside.

Where the N1 road turned northwards stood a tall statue and he recognised the distinctive glasses and profile of Congo's first elected President, Patrice Lumumba. He remembered reading how the president had been overthrown by Mobutu and then assassinated, reportedly with help from the CIA and Belgium's secret service. Politics here was clearly dirty and he wondered how much had changed in the intervening fifty years.

They skirted a smaller airport close to the city centre before passing the modern-looking Stadium of Martyrs. The van flashed past a market that looked chaotic and filthy, and which James would have loved to photograph. He was tired, in need of a wash and happy enough to be taken to his digs wherever that might be. He had no idea where they were going but Serge discouraged conversation in English and James needed time to regain his confidence in French. Eventually they pulled up outside an anonymous looking grey concrete apartment block in the Avenue des Huileries. There were one or two embassies in the area and he'd spotted a few multinational company headquarters so he reckoned they must be in one of the capital's better areas.

"This is it. You get down now," said Serge. "You *habits* here. We return for you 20.30. Ce soir."

James looked at his newly acquired cheap sports watch, as recommended by the charity. "OK, in one hour, yes?"

"Of course," said the charmless Serge.

James turned back to look at the building. It didn't seem to be a hotel. "Where do I go? Which way?"

"In, in," said Serge with ill-disguised impatience. Then James saw the driver pointing to a woman further along the pavement; she was beckoning to him from a doorway at the end of the building. He picked up his kit bag and his cameras and slid the van door shut at the second time of slamming. Serge was already looking the other way and giving directions to the driver. James turned back towards the woman and headed for the doorway as the van hopped away.

The second floor room to which she showed him was basic but fairly clean, and better than he'd feared. The sheets and blanket were OK, and the mattress still had some give in it even if the springs beneath were noisy. But the single overhead light worked and he had a view of two neighbouring apartment blocks much like his own, some trees and a deserted side street. There was a bathroom across the corridor but no sign nor sound of anyone else so maybe he'd have it to himself. James was tired from the flight and eager to freshen up so he stripped off his T-shirt, pulled a small towel from his bag and crossed the corridor.

Inside, many of the floor tiles were cracked and viciously sharp-looking edges so he kept his shoes on, stepped inside and turned the topmost tap. Nothing happened. He heard a bang somewhere in the building but it could have been a far off door slamming, he didn't think it was the pipes. *At least there was no shower curtain to get in the way*, he thought. The bottom tap brought a torrent of brown water, dirty and cold enough to make James step smartly out of the way. The colour improved but the temperature didn't. "Soddit," he said to himself and winced as he stepped under the meagre flow until he emerged clean and invigorated.

With a new T-shirt, jeans, still-damp shoes and a growing thirst James was waiting on the kerbside with his camera bag when he heard the minivan approaching. The sound was unmistakable, particularly among the surprisingly large number of Mercedes and Lexus cars with blacked out windows that were oozing through the streets in this part of town. He hadn't expected that either.

It was dark now, and despite the almost total absence of lights in this street, he was able to make out the face of Mournful in the front. The van pulled up beside him and Serge cast a disparaging look at James over his half turned shoulder as he opened the rear door and climbed in. "Bonsoir," James ventured and the driver's warm response in French made up for the Frenchman's silence. "Où allons-nous?" James tried again.

"MONUSCO," was all he caught from Serge's brief reply. James's French was rusty and he hadn't caught it all.

"MONUSCO?"

"Oui," said his colleague. And left it at that.

"Qu'est-ce que c'est, MONUSCO?" There was puzzlement in James's voice.

"Vous plaisantez."

"No, I'm not kidding," said James in English, beginning to lose his temper. "In case it escaped your notice, I only landed here a couple of hours ago."

Serge shook his head and sighed theatrically. "It is headquarters of MONUSCO, you know United Nations? You hear of UN?"

"Course I've fucking heard of the UN. But I don't know MONUSCO yet 'cos it's my first visit, you arse," he was failing to control his annoyance. He still wondered what this guy's problem was. He hoped he wasn't going to have to spend too much time in Serge's company but it wasn't looking good. He wasn't about to be patronised, but James knew he'd have to get along with him somehow.

"Comment?" Serge had turned in his seat and was straining over the noise of the engine to hear what James had called him.

"I said it's my first visit, since you asked." And James settled back into his seat. "And you couldn't have told me all this before?" he said in English.

"You have not ask," Serge said with his first smile of the day. "You take photos of *les ambassadeurs*, OK? Clic, clic." And he mimed photography at James over his shoulder and turned to grin at the driver looking for someone to share the joke. If he understood, the driver was uninterested and Serge shrugged his shoulders before turning back to watch the road.

James looked down at his T-shirt and sandals – if he'd known he was meeting ambassadors tonight .... *Screw it*, he thought, *if that's how you want it, we can both play.*

The van's windows were all shut making it as hot as hell, and it was a minute or two after they'd set off that it dawned on James the closed windows were for security. He hadn't noticed the doors locking while he was exchanging words with Serge. Before he left London he'd read that street robberies were on the rise in Kinshasa, and now he realised that standing on the kerbside in the half-darkness had not been the best idea for a stand-out white guy carrying expensive camera gear. Lesson three, he said to himself, after the airport protocol and the brown shower and he'd only been here a few hours.

It only took a few minutes to cross the district of Gombe in Kinshasa but in that time the heavens opened up and rain started to fall harder than he had ever seen before. The van's wipers were not man enough to clear the screen and the noise of hundreds of heavy rain drops hitting the vehicle's roof sounded like someone was attacking the minibus with a fire hose. When they reached the UN headquarters close to the Congo River, James and Serge made a dash for the front door in a futile attempt to avoid a soaking. James was immediately sodden again and Serge, now infinitely smarter in a collared shirt and jacket, was drenched across the back and shoulders.

James may not have been expecting MONUSCO, but they were expecting him. The doors of the UN Stabilization Mission in the DRC were opened as soon as James and Serge approached, and he could see that they were invited guests. Security gave him a waiting badge and he was ushered in, collecting a welcome cold drink as he went. The reception room was already filled with over fifty smartly dressed guests of varying nationalities. There were Congolese and other Africans in suits and army uniforms, women in saris, men and women in full length local dress, high ranking Indian and Pakistani military figures to judge by the gold braid, and business suited men from East and West. The noise level was high and from somewhere he could hear a live jazz band playing *Summertime*. He had to pinch himself that he was in the capital of one of Africa's poorest countries, and one beset by continued fighting in the east.

Serge pointed to his camera which James had readied in the van and took him by the elbow, steering him towards a nearby group in close discussion. He instantly recognised Sarah Page from AfriCan Care and was introduced to three members of a band she had flown out with the week before from London on an awareness-building mission for the charity. Obviously, James had been in the States too long, because he had never heard of them, and they seemed slightly put out by his low-key reaction to their name. Serge urged him again to photograph the group and then to get pictures of the whole event. So he busied himself with taking photos of Sarah talking with her VIPs and local colleagues, and caught the charity team as they mingled with UN officials and guests in other groups. James was more comfortable in this role anyway; they may not have been images of African scenery or the refugees they were working for, but he was now engaged in his first professional commission and he was determined to make a success of it.

He moved slowly around the room capturing each group from several angles, and paying particular attention to the mingling guests from AfriCan Care. From time to time he would switch from camera to camera. When these photo opportunities were exhausted, he followed the sound of the band through to another room where guests were collecting a buffet supper or already enjoying the food at tables. The smell of food reminded him how long it was since he had eaten on the plane but he needed to get the job done first, in case people started leaving the party. So he moved around the room, taking shots of those still talking, and sparing those who were eating.

As he looked for the next angle, he saw someone sitting alone at the table to his right typing on a laptop. He was just making conversation, but it was only when he spoke that he truly noticed her. Afterwards he couldn't even remember exactly what he'd said; something fairly innocuous about being under-dressed for the occasion as he pointed to his jeans and scruffy shoes. She looked up, still engrossed in her task and evidently not interested in chatting, and James thought that she was the most exotic person he had ever seen. She smiled briefly, memorably, and went back to her work without a word of reply, clearly not inviting small talk. He put his spare camera down on the corner of the table and tried not to stare at her, but his eyes were drawn back. Was it the long flight today that made it so difficult to concentrate on camera settings and reviewing the images he'd taken? He'd lost interest in moving from this spot. He just wanted to talk to her but he didn't know what to say that wouldn't simply be an unwelcome interruption or a dumb chat-up line.

What was it about her that was so captivating? He sneaked a glance at her again; her skin was the purest cafe latte, and was flawless from neck to brow. It was her eyes, though, that had stopped him in his tracks. They were the darkest brown, in this light you couldn't see where the iris ended and the pupil began, which gave the impression of dramatic size. Her teeth were contrastingly bright and very even in a wide mouth framed by generous lips the colour of chocolate. The overall effect was dazzling. Her dark hair was braided tight to her head in rows of multi-coloured beads, and the braids hung down her back to shoulder level. Wisps had escaped by one ear and James resisted the urge to replace them. He could hear the beads click gently together as she turned her head to read a notebook beside her computer. James couldn't have told you what she was wearing, all he could think to do was ask if she wanted a drink. She didn't but her soft voice when she thanked him was one that he wanted to hear again. She could have read him the fire drill and his attention would have been total.

He loitered a while longer. From her eye movement as she typed he sensed she knew he hadn't gone far away, and he was just summoning inspiration to talk to her more meaningfully when Serge appeared again in the doorway, gesturing to James to follow him out. For a second James was tempted to tell Serge where to go, but this was Day One in Africa and a sense of duty won through so he picked up his cameras, glanced back at the woman behind the laptop screen – was that a little smile playing on her lips? – And he went to see what was needed. The group from the charity had joined another table and a place had been saved for him to eat with them. The conversation was flowing, with the VIPs eager to share their new-found knowledge after a visit to a children's education project in the city, and the rest of the group provided a willing audience. The enthusiasm of the whole party for the work being done was palpable and James was swept up in the conversation, listening to the challenges and successes, asking a few questions of his own or just learning from the expertise around the table.

Throughout it all he had one eye on the door to the other reception room, but the band had stopped and there seemed to be less activity in there now. He desperately wanted to go through and start a conversation with her, any conversation. He could offer her food, a seat with their party, ask her what she was doing. Why hadn't he thought of these before? Leaving the table was impossible now if he was to give the right impression just as his work was starting. Serge's mood had improved with food and alcohol but James was clear that the man had an issue with his new photographer – even if it was impossible to decipher it at present. *They would tackle it somewhere down the line*, he thought, he certainly wasn't going to spend weeks walking on egg shells because some ugly French dude had issues.

When the reception and dinner began to break up, the group left their table and went through to the lobby to find their lift home. James wandered to the doorway as casually as he could and looked into the next room; by now it was virtually deserted and she was nowhere to be seen leaving James to rue a missed opportunity. Shit, why hadn't he just said something to her, anything? She must have been aware he was killing time in there, maybe she guessed why.

He stood with the others in the lobby chatting as they waited for their minibuses, and when the first vehicle arrived the VIP guests were ushered under umbrellas through the heavy rain while James, Serge and Sarah waited inside.

"Did you get good shots of the band?" asked Sarah.

"Yeah, I'm happy with them. I'll know more when I've downloaded them and can see them full screen, but they seemed good." He knew she needed to hear confidence, to reassure her that they had chosen the right person, and she seemed pleased with his answer.

"So, what do you make of the country so far?"

"It's probably too soon to say, I've only been here a few hours. It's wet and hot, and maybe not really as broken as I expected, but obviously I haven't seen much," James replied.

"It's an unfair question but I always like to get people's impressions and see how they change during a trip. And this place isn't representative of Kinshasa, much less Congo as a whole. You wouldn't have to go far in any direction to find the kind of poverty I'm sure you imagined, not that I'd recommend doing it on foot. It's a dangerous city and, if anything, it's getting worse. There are more kidnappings now than there were two years ago and robberies are up, especially by gangs of street kids – and some of them aren't so small. I guess they have nothing left to lose, and the police are brutal towards these kids – robbing them of whatever they have, beating and sexually assaulting them, even killing them sometimes – so maybe it's not surprising if that's how they learn to survive. We plan to do more work in the capital as soon as we can but we need to raise funds and for that we need to raise awareness; so, you see your photos will be crucial. It's just a shame we couldn't have got you out here last week, for the band I mean."

"Oh? I didn't know you wanted me here last week."

"Well, I guess it would have been a bit short notice since we only met you recently but we thought we'd be able to cover things with a local photographer until you got here," she lowered her voice. "A friend of a friend, if you get me?" James followed her gaze, as it swung towards Serge sitting a few feet away. "But it didn't work out, we didn't get all the shots we wanted, in fact we didn't get much at all," she looked away. She was obviously annoyed at whatever had happened but she wasn't going to say any more. *Well, that explained a lot*, thought James. I'm treading on laughing laddie's toes, no wonder he's pissed off with me.

A taxi arrived and Sarah said, "That's for you. Serge and I are going in a different direction. A taxi will come for you at eight o'clock tomorrow. Bring everything, we're flying to Goma in the morning but we'll get some breakfast and talk it all through first thing. Good night," and she held the glass door open for him. There was no one ready with an umbrella for a mere photographer, so James put his head down and dashed through the pouring rain towards the taxi waiting at the end of the path. With his head and shoulders bowed over to protect his camera bag he didn't notice a woman racing to the cab door from the rear of the car. Within a few steps of the front door his head was soaked, rain was in his eyes and he saw her too late to stop, cannoning into her left shoulder. His camera bag connected squarely with the laptop she had cradled in her arms as she crouched to run, and the computer flew out of her grasp, across the boot of the car and he heard it land on the tarmac. The woman herself was thrown against the side of the taxi and losing her footing sat down in a puddle, just as he fought to regain his balance and teetered over her.

"My God, I'm so sorry," he said. It was as he bent to offer his hand and lift her to her feet, that he realised it was the young woman who had so mesmerised him at the reception.

"My laptop, where's my laptop?" she said, brushing away his hand and getting quickly to her feet. Under the flood lights at the front of the building he couldn't help noticing the seat of her leggings was soaking wet, and there would probably have been better times to admire her neat shape. She danced nimbly around the rear of the cab and picked up her laptop; it had been carried in a lightweight neoprene sleeve, but the fall had broken open the zip and the computer was already wet from the rain or the puddle. His thoughts were swept aside as he looked at the crack across one corner of her computer and the water collecting on the lid.

"Jeez, I'm so sorry," he repeated. Galvanized to action, he looked down and saw a folder lying on the tarmac, surrounded by papers already smudging in the heavy rain. He picked these up and held them out to her.

"Shit, my laptop. It's got everything. You damn idiot," she said with an American accent, "don't you even look where you're going?" She was scrabbling to pick up another paper beside her at the same time as sliding the computer back into its broken sleeve.

"I'm really sorry," he began. "It was my fault, of course I'll pay for any damage."

"Damn sure you will," she said. Her head was still down and he could see the multicoloured beads above a high forehead and strong cheekbones. He continued to pick up her papers and re-fill the folder as best he could.

The rain was running down her face and the driver hit the horn, presumably unaware of the collision and urging one of them to get in. The rain was collecting in the tiny curls of hair at her brow and had already trickled down her neck, and he knew he really shouldn't be noticing that right now. Her eyes were narrowed – was it against the rain or just with anger at his carelessness? He couldn't tell, but he found he was still talking. "Let me help you get this stuff out of the rain. We can dry off these papers before all the ink runs."

She was rigid with anger. "I think you've done enough damage." With her computer back in its sleeve and safely in her grasp she held out a slender hand for the remaining papers that he had picked up. She breathed deeply and seemed to control herself, "That won't be necessary."

"Well, please take the cab and at least send me the bill for any damage to your Mac. It looks nearly new," he volunteered.

She had opened the car door and turned to look at him as the rain ran down his face and his now sodden T-shirt clung to his body. If she was aware of him at all, she might have seen an open face, an apologetic smile, a strong chin and curls of brown hair now plastered to his head. She seemed about to say something but thought better of it. "It's insured."

"If it needs repairing at all, send me the bill, I'm James, I'm a photographer with AfriCan Care." For once he had the sense not to react in the English manner and look for a handshake. In all other respects, though, he could hardly have made a worse impression.

Turning to the driver he said, "Revenez-vous à moi, s'il vous plait. Tout de suite," and he turned to go back inside and wait for the cab to return. There was no longer any point in running, he was wet through. As he reached the door, he glanced back and saw her in the rear seat, but she ignored him completely as she instructed the driver.

Sarah was still in the lobby and smiled as she looked at him. "Well, you certainly know how to get a girl to notice you."

"Oh, don't even go there. I nearly flattened her, and God knows if her computer will ever work again. Anyway, the cab's going to come back for me."

"You'll be lucky," said Sarah. "They're not all that reliable here. You can come with us and we'll take a detour."

"OK, thanks."

"You'd better hope she doesn't put you in one of her articles. She's an American journalist, works for several US and European business papers, it's quite punchy stuff. Does a lot of TV as well, I hear."

"Right." James held his breath and tried to sound nonchalant. "What's her name?"

Sarah grinned at him. "Jessica. Jessica Tsiba. You can Google her." And before he could protest his innocent interest she added, "Here's our car. See if you can avoid hitting anyone this time."

Chapter 13
Taweza Road Mission, Walikale, North Kivu, DRC
Two Weeks Ago

For a long time Marc and Marianne Audousset found it hard to take in the enormity of what they had discovered. Together they had fallen in love with Africa and together they had explored so much of it in their early years of marriage; Cote d'Ivoire, Ghana, Kenya, and Maroc had been visited in quick succession. Africa had never seemed to fit the TV stereotypes of poverty, corruption and famine when they visited from France – every holiday was such a mixture of experiences, but they were just holidays. Following some harrowing reports in the French media, they were moved by what they saw of the war in Congo and knew they could not ignore it and carry on with their lives. Five years ago, the atrocities committed against civilians had reached such a pitch that Marc, quit his surgical post in Nice and came here to see what he could do for the rape victims. Marianne had been equally determined to deploy her teaching skills, and they had made two fleeting visits to support medical and educational charities, only to return to France bitterly disappointed at leaving so much work unfinished. Gradually their plans had evolved from assisting local charities to founding and running their own mission, and now they were sure it was the only way they could have a lasting impact here.

The Audoussets had searched far and wide for a suitable mission site when they arrived, throwing their net further every week from their temporary base. They needed to be close enough to the affected villages to offer shelter to the people in most need, while avoiding routes regularly taken by the fighters. They arrived in Walikale soon after the end of the Second Congo War, and everyone involved in the mission had hoped the fragile peace would enable the couple to provide much-needed schooling and healthcare for the area. When, despite the peace accord, the fighting continued the couple had been had forced to change plans, providing more medical services and only latterly building up the pupil roll.

Their search for the right location had taken them north a dozen miles up the River Lowa from Walikale, to a place where the unmade road vanished altogether. Long before they reached the signposted settlement of Taweza, somewhere in a village with no name, beside a road that went nowhere, the couple had found an abandoned church and school. To many people its emptiness would have been a warning. However, when Marianne had heard that Taweza meant 'we can' in Kiswahili she felt this was meant to be and had prayed on the spot to take over the buildings and begin their work. With numerous villages nearby and no healthcare to be had in a day's walk the need was obvious. No one could have known that five years later their location would put them close to one of the worst attacks on unarmed civilians in the region, but when it happened the presence of the mission and the dedication of its staff were invaluable.

Adapting to life in the orphanage had come more easily to Keisha than to Raphael. The sadness they had felt almost two years ago at leaving Patrick, Mama Dawa and the family had been agonising for them both, and was tempered only by the end of their harsh work in the mine and the camp. The transformation in their lives was extraordinary. At the mine they had risen every day with the sun, worked throughout daylight with no food and little rest, before returning to camp for a meal followed by sleep in a makeshift shelter. Today they slept in their own camp beds, had breakfast and dinner, wore clothes they had been given, and were schooled six days a week. And when they weren't in school Keisha played with other mission children, while Raphael played football or tended the enormous vegetable garden.

Inevitably, they felt the loss of their surrogate family keenly. At first Raphael and Keisha stayed close to one another at all times, refusing even to be separated into classes according to their age. As Keisha had had no schooling at all and Raphael only little, this presented few immediate problems. Their teacher, Marianne, was already confident that they would be more settled by the time it was necessary to separate them; they were intelligent children and seemed to learn quickly.

Keisha's friendly outlook meant that she was quick to find her feet in their new surroundings, and at last she had other girls to play with. In the absence of her mother, she was comforted in the mission by a large circle of women. Some of the patients were too physically or mentally damaged to play any part in the children's lives, and were confined to bed or to chairs on the veranda from where they could watch the mission's activities. Alongside the hospital, the school's dynamic, happy mood was infectious.

The boys' dormitory was upstairs in the main block while the girls slept on the far side of the mission from the hospital. Most of the children's time was spent in class, after which there was time to clean the mission followed by singing, games and sports organised on the dusty square in front of the concrete buildings. There were no uniforms yet, although the Audoussets planned to introduce them when funding could be found, but in many respects Taweza Mission looked like any other Congolese school.

Raphael had grown fast since leaving the mine. The stress of constant hard work and meagre food supplies had been lifted and, although the diet here was simple, food was not in short supply. The fertile country around Taweza was once again being tended by artisan farmers who found the mission a ready customer for their crops of rice, beans, peppers, potatoes and manioc. These staples were augmented by occasional goat meat and bony fish from the River Lowa that Raphael and Keisha neither recognised nor liked.

In the mission's own vegetable gardens Raphael found solace in the steady work of a farmer, work that he had learned to do for his father. Truth be told though, Raphael was not the same jovial, carefree boy his parents had known, these days he was much more withdrawn, untrusting and prone to bouts of anger and frustration. Feeling their loss acutely, he clung every day to the belief that their twin brother and sister, Joseph and Grace – who would now be seven years old – were still alive somewhere and living with their mother.

He had never been discouraged in this belief until he reached the mission, where the practically-minded adults in the orphanage, looked kindly on his conviction in the early days. But as the months went by and there were no parents to link Raphael and Keisha to, they appeared to staff to be like any of the other orphans under the same roof. Raphael would only refer to it as the mission or school and refused to call it an orphanage; accepting that term would mean he had accepted the loss of both parents. The team at Taweza Road struggled to understand that such a determined child could not write off any lingering hope that the rest of his family had survived.

Marc Audousset had tried talking to Raphael about it, but the Frenchman was better suited to administering physical than psychological care; he saw only the practicalities of two more children without parents, lost and barely afloat when he and Marianne had found them. He knew that Raphael appreciated their rescue from the mine, as the Audoussets described it, but in his view the boy was simply in denial of the glaringly obvious conclusion that his mother, sister and brother had not managed to escape from their village. To begin with Marc ignored Raphael's intransigence, but lately he had begun to feel irritated by it. After all, the boy was unquestionably intelligent and resourceful so it was clearly time he understood this reality. Marc decided he would tell Marianne when the topic next arose that Raphael must bow to the inevitable and shed these false hopes that must be damaging to his well-being and distracting him from his schoolwork.

"I don't think he is lazy, he's certainly clever and yet he clearly isn't applying himself intellectually which is having a bad effect on his own results and on those around him," Marc insisted.

Marianne felt that Marc was over-reacting but she kept her opinion to herself for now. Raphael was still one of the best senior pupils of fourteen years or above. If he was having trouble adapting to the harsh realities of his new life, he certainly wasn't alone, and there might still be time to set him straight. They could school him and care for him for one more year, after which it would be time for the boy to decide on his future. They would surely help him in that, particularly since his sister would still be in their charge. She confined herself for now to suggesting that Marc allow the fifteen year-old the time to grieve, time that had been denied him when he was bereaved. "He will come out of himself," she said. "Give him enough time, you'll see."

Her husband gave a heavy sigh. His doubt was obvious.

Raphael was certainly enjoying his studies; at last he felt that his brain was being employed and not just his muscles. Physically he was filling out fast and becoming a strong young man. Aside from sports, one of his greatest pleasures these days was bringing on seedlings from small pots in the mission garden and planting them out to grow squares of maize, or rows of peppers, chillies and onions. It was a side of him that marked him out from the other boys and they teased him for it, but he enjoyed the sense of achievement in growing food where before there was just dirt.

The boy's relationship with Marc had started warily and still had not progressed beyond awkward and formal. Raphael had recently exploded in frustration with Marc and Emmanuel Salumu when they had referred to the mission as an orphanage. The Frenchman had downplayed it to Marianne afterwards but he and the boy clearly disagreed over the whereabouts of Raphael's family. Matters had only worsened when, with growing concern at the boy's slower than expected academic progress, Marc had threatened to reduce the amount of time he spent in the garden so that he could extend his studies. In the end, Marianne had stepped in and pulled rank on him – the clinic was primarily Marc's responsibility, but the school was hers and she worried that Raphael was approaching a crisis point. Reluctantly and with much grumbling at wasted talent, Marc left her to it and the moment passed.

"I don't belong here, neither of us do," Raphael said later to Emmanuel when they were alone during one of the latter's infrequent visits.

"I understand what you feel," ventured the priest.

"No you don't, Keisha and I still have a mother. She's not dead."

"All right, but we don't know where she is, even if she's still alive," Emmanuel persisted.

Raphael shrugged, indifferent to their lack of knowledge. As far as he was concerned, it wasn't the point. "Maybe, but that doesn't mean she's dead, does it? So Keisha and I aren't orphans. Anyway, nobody's looking for her, so what chance do we have of going home? We've been put in an orphanage and we don't belong here." He was bitterly angry that they were over-looking this critical distinction. It had nothing to do with semantics and everything to do with being found, and there were tears of frustration in his eyes that he hated himself for showing. "At least in the mine I was earning money, then I could save up to look for them. Now I'm stuck here with no money and no chance of finding her, and if she's looking for us she obviously won't look here, will she?"

Nothing Emmanuel could say would placate Raphael, and Marc only made things worse when he tried later. The men were adamant that Raphael and his sister were in the best place for children with no other means of support, and the boy found it hard to answer that. He knew that their efforts for all the children at Taweza Road were sincere, but it was impossible for him to see how this could be resolved. Unless he ran away, but he couldn't do that to Keisha, much as he now wanted to. In the end it took someone from outside the orphanage to prompt a solution.

******

Visitors to the mission were few and far between, and this was how the team of carers and teachers preferred it. The medical and psychological care needed by the patients at the mission benefited by complete isolation from the dangers and worries of the world outside. The small medical staff led by Marc had built up a modest but effective operating theatre and hospital to deal with the physical and psychological consequences of the fighting. Marianne and two Congolese nurses dealt with trauma counselling, while without Marc's surgical skills many rape victims would have faced critical infection, or a life of incontinence and infertility. The skill of the small team dealing with these conditions had become well known in the province, and the churches in Africa and Europe that supported their work were constantly being called on to raise further funds for surgical facilities, generator fuel, medicines and anaesthetics, as well as the costs of lengthy after-care.

The fighting had not reached them here – although recently it had come much too close – but somehow its victims had. The mission's isolation in this valley was critical, lying as it did near the end of the road to Taweza, almost equidistant from Walikale's airstrip and villages to the north and east that had recently seen some of the worst attacks. In reality, the airstrip was just a two kilometre straight section of the tarmacked N3 national road but this was usually enough to keep them supplied. Traffic along the road itself was often halted by fighting or the sudden return of road blocks where robberies and killings were commonplace. Flying to Goma was the safest way out of the area.

So, when a journalist arrived at Taweza Road Mission one afternoon in October the staff were intrigued and nonplussed. Marc was in the operating theatre and Marianne came only as far as the door. She had not scrubbed and could not risk entering but she called to him to let him know. He had to ask for his favourite jazz to be turned down so that he could hear her, which didn't improve his mood in the middle of a challenging procedure.

"I said, a journalist has just arrived," Marianne repeated.

"A journalist?" he said with incredulity. "What on earth does he want?"

"I don't quite know. And it's not a 'he'."

Marc looked up from the deep perineal tear that he was trying to suture. "OK. Find out what she wants and send her away. Journalists, in my experience, are just trouble."

"Does that include female journalists?" she asked impishly. "And what exactly is your experience?" One of the nurses giggled until she caught Marc's look.

"Look, just let me finish and I'll deal with her when I get out of here," he said, "but trouble follows these people. You mark my words."

With a strong black coffee in hand he was feeling a little better when he emerged half an hour later; he deliberately hadn't hurried himself and he was ready to send this woman packing. He came out onto the veranda in his surgical greens and there was only one face there he didn't recognise. The terse dismissal that he had been rehearsing suddenly seemed somewhat churlish as he looked at the smiling face of a young black woman, who was enjoying a long cold drink with Marianne.

"Cherie, je te présente Jessica Tsiba," said Marianne. "Elle parle bien le français. She's an African-American journalist who's come up from Goma to cover the work of carers in the province following these recent attacks. Jessica, this is my husband Marc. Forgive me, I need to go and check on the children in school for a while. I'm afraid he has not had good experiences with journalists, Jessica, so I wonder if you can make amends?" she turned to Marc and smiled archly.

Marc affected not to notice his wife's gentle teasing as he sat down, but there was no denying that the young woman was unlike the few other scruffy and unkempt reporters he'd met. He was about to speak again when Marianne turned at the door, "I don't know what your plans were but please stay for dinner, Jessica, the heavy rain will make the road dangerous in the dark, and it would be good for us to have some company. We can easily put you up for the night, and one of us can drive you back to Walikale in the morning. I will see you both in a while," and she left before either of them could disagree.

Jessica shrugged her shoulders and smiled at Marc, "That is very kind. It looks like I'm staying. Anyway, it is good to meet you, Dr Audousset. I have heard a lot about the work that you and Marianne are doing here."

"Really? I shouldn't have thought it was known beyond Walikale," said Mark.

"On the contrary, I have been with some of the major aid agencies in Goma and they are not only aware of what you are doing, they value the way it keeps vulnerable patients close to their homes. It's better for the patients, and reduces the displacement of whole villages. But why am I telling you this? You are both something of a phenomenon in Goma."

Marc looked at her steadily, trying to see if he was being given the soft soap treatment but her smile seemed genuine and she was correct about some of the benefits of their location. "Well, it avoids submitting the most vulnerable patients to lengthy journeys, too. Far too many would not survive or their condition would deteriorate, and it would be agony for many of them."

The woman was a practised inquisitor. She knew enough to ask informed questions without affecting any expertise, and critically she also knew when to keep quiet. Once he began talking about the work that he and the team were doing at Taweza Road it never occurred to Marc to restrict his comments. He was not being indiscreet in any way, but his earlier hostility began to evaporate and any reticence about talking was forgotten as they discussed the fighting in the area, the dreadful consequences for the whole population and the way in which women and girls were being singled out for systematic and atrocious violence as a means of displacing entire communities.

Coffees and soft drinks gave way to cold beers as Marianne returned to the veranda and, although the rain had stopped, any half-formed thoughts of leaving that Jessica may have had vanished with the sunset. For the Audoussets this was a welcome chance to glimpse the outside world through the eyes of a well-travelled woman, and for Jessica it was the prospect of good conversation and welcoming company after a prolonged diet of politicians, world-weary hacks and exhausted aid workers. Marianne even found a couple of precious bottles of South African pinot noir to have with their stir fry of peppers, chillies, goat and rice.

"And you say these vegetables are all grown at the mission?" asked Jessica. "I haven't eaten this well for weeks."

"Yes, we have a number of people involved in the gardens, it's very therapeutic for the patients – as well as being vital for our income. We can feed the patients and students at little cost and sell any surplus, though there isn't much," said Marc ruefully. "One of our best gardeners is a fifteen year-old boy. He used to be a farmer until his parents were killed."

"His father was killed, Cherie," interjected Marianne. "We still don't know about his mother and the rest of the family, apart from Keisha, of course. And we probably never will." She turned back to Jessica, "It is very hard for these children to adapt. The hardest part for some of them is not knowing." Marc sipped his drink and said nothing.

"I can understand. So, does he run the whole garden?" asked Jessica.

"Yes, he's playing an increasing role here. As Marc says, his family were farmers so he has a lot of skills and a natural way with livestock and plants. I think it surprised him how good he is at it, and he certainly enjoys working outside with the chickens and goats," Marianne replied.

"I should like to meet him before I go, if that's possible?"

"We'll see, maybe if there's time before his classes. I don't want his schooling to suffer any more," said Marc.

Jessica was alert to his comment, "... anymore?" she asked.

Marc toyed with his glass and was about to speak, but Marianne stepped in. "He is a naturally bright child and we are still concerned that the enormous disruption to his life following the loss of his father is causing him to fall behind. It would be a shame for him to lose the benefit of the education we can give him before he has to leave."

"When is that?"

"Normally we school them until fourteen but with the most able pupils we can sometimes keep them until sixteen," said Marc. "More wine, Jessica?"

"Thank you, yes. But what happens to them afterwards?"

"We can't find work for them all here but occasionally there are local labouring jobs or even openings with the aid agencies in this area, particularly if they speak more than one language," said Marianne. "And they are comparatively well educated, most of them leave here able to read and write and they learn a bit about raising crops and livestock – as you can see we have a few goats. So there is sometimes work for them in the area or in Walikale. Sadly, too many of our school leavers are under-employed."

"Which is why some of them end up going to Goma, which we do everything we can to avoid," said Marc. "You'll have seen why, it's not always a good place for a young girl or boy on their own. In some camps they're at even greater risk of violence than they are in the mountains. A few of them end up in the tin and coltan mines, either because they have no alternative work or are hoping to make their fortune. As you probably know, it doesn't usually turn out like that. Above all, we try to teach them the life skills to keep them out of the fighting, not just literacy but skills to get them a safe job, such as typing, book-keeping, hairdressing, brick-laying. Whatever they're interested in if we can."

"That must be hard to see, I mean when they do end up in the wrong place," said Jessica.

"Fortunately, to the best of our knowledge it hasn't happened much. The fighting tends to draw in less educated or skilled boys from the cities and camps, plus all of those that the soldiers capture in the forest. It's not as bad as it was during the war, but children are still being kidnapped and forced to fight, and it's happening all the time. Sometimes they're made to kill a friend or relative just so that there's no way for them to go back. It's hideous. Mostly, though," added Marianne, "the children here have learned from their own experiences in the mines or in the fighting. They've no wish to go back to it. "

"I'm intrigued by one other thing; how did you two come to be here?" she asked.

So Marc retold the story of their growing concern at what they were hearing in France, about this beautiful, broken country, its irrepressible people, and the needs that the couple felt they could meet. They described how they had tried to make a difference in their short, preliminary visits, only to be shocked at how their efforts seemed to be no more than a drop of water in an empty bucket.

"One thing changed everything for me," said Marc, "and that was coming back on a later visit and recognising a woman I had treated before. She had been attacked for a second time by a gang – they call themselves soldiers, but they're no more than murdering thugs, high on pills, weed and liquor – anyway, this time it was worse for her. Far worse." His voice cracked as he spoke these last words and he stopped, momentarily unable to say more.

"Cherie," Marianne's concern was palpable and Jessica felt that there was much more to say but before she could ask anything he got up and, silently gathering their plates, he left the room. Marianne paused, "I am sorry, Jessica. There are some things that we have witnessed here that no person should see, no person should ever suffer, and it's tempting to say that only a monster could do these things to another human. But, of course, they are not monsters. They are people; damaged, broken, uneducated, badly led by other dangerous people. I don't know if you believe in God, Jessica but the Bible taught me that even when we don't fully understand God's actions, we should still trust him. It says, 'His thoughts are not our thoughts and his ways are not our ways'." There was an awkward silence.

Jessica had never believed in God and everything she saw in her work here made her doubt the existence of a merciful Protector even more. But she said nothing, she had no adequate words of comfort for her hosts. There was a long silence that Jessica decided not to break.

Marianne had been staring at the oil lamp that lit the table with a warm yellow glow, but she raised her head suddenly. "I'm sorry. We are out of practice at receiving guests, and here we are laying our troubles on you. Perhaps you'll be kind enough to put it down to the wine and relaxed company. We've only talked about ourselves. What brought you to DRC?"

"Well, I won't bore you with the whole story but I wanted to be a foreign correspondent – for CNN or NBC – but I only spoke one other language besides English and that ruled me out. I couldn't get a job and my dad said he wouldn't support me indefinitely, he told me to choose something else. He's very ambitious for me and always wants to decide my next move for me – I guess he means well, but he still can't accept I'm not twelve any more. He was splitting up with Mom at the time and I'm a bit stubborn so I kinda ignored him. Reckon I get that from him, it's his Italian blood. Mom's from Somalia, her family came to the US when she was small. She's a bit more laid back and likes to have her family around her for security – you'd think she was the Italian one," Jessica smiled at the recollection.

"Eventually I found a job on a business magazine and got some experience before going freelance a couple of years back. It was hard financially at first but the works more regular now. That was when I read what was happening here and the way some western businesses are buying conflict minerals and effectively funding the continued fighting. I was surprised how few people I talked to knew anything about it so I decided to come out here and see for myself, and maybe make folks on Main Street USA see what goes into making a cell phone, through the tin and the coltan trades. Mom wishes I'd stay home, my dad wishes I'd get a "proper" job. Me, I just wish I could understand what's going on here a bit better. I still find it confusing at times."

Marianne grunted in acknowledgement. "Apparently, they used to have a sign up in one of the western military bases in Lebanon twenty years ago; it said, 'If you think you know what's going on here, you haven't got a clue!' Except I think they added a few expletives. It's much the same here, just when you think you know what's happening, the rebel groups change, the alliances change and it all gets more complicated."

"How did you come to be here?" Jessica persisted.

"Well, the patient that Marc mentioned died in theatre and this affected him more than any other patient I have ever known. He called her his failure. I don't think he meant in surgery, he meant in being unable to protect her from returning to danger in her village.

"It became obvious to us that the only way to have a lasting and positive impact was to be here full time. So we sold our house in Provence and came to live and work here, and every day we're glad that we did. We had no parents or children to worry about, so it was easier for us than it would be for many people. And then we lived out of our suitcases for months until we found this place. It almost drove me crazy – but I don't think Marc even noticed his crumpled T-shirts and old shorts, although I certainly did," and Marianne smiled again. "When we got here, we felt as though this had been home all along, and we look back at our lives in France as though they happened to someone else."

"Our outlook changed so quickly from our first visit. We soon discovered that most of the armed gangs in the Kivus used indiscriminate killing or mass rape as weapons against the local population. At first we couldn't understand why the militias and the army weren't protecting them, then we discovered it was worse than that. They were also subjecting the very people they claimed to be protecting to this nightmare. You have to recognise that most of the armed groups are incapable of holding territory they take – even the Federal Army has only recently begun to hang on to areas that it's won. The front line is constantly shifting as the fighting moves this way and that. And while it's just low-level skirmishing – I've never really understood that phrase, I bet it doesn't feel low-level when your village is in the middle of it – anyway, the world can hide its face and pretend it's not happening. It also helps the West that a ceasefire is still in place – on paper at least."

"Anyway, after a while, mass rape became just another factor in the political chaos, and nobody was telling the truth about what was going on here. I hope you'll bring some honesty to what's being written. I mean, if you listen to the politicians in Kinshasa you'd imagine that Congo's army was in complete control here and there were no security threats from army deserters and thieves calling themselves rebels. You'd never believe there are foreign-backed militias still moving in their hundreds across the Rwandan and Ugandan borders.

"Of course, once we got here we found what everyone else here already knew; it wasn't as simple as the Congolese fighting a Rwandan invasion. The violence is partly tribal with Hutus fighting the Tutsis, it's historical after Rwanda's Hutus attempted the genocide of the Tutsi minority, and underneath all that it's economic. There's just so much natural wealth in the ground here and there's little or nothing to stop the rebels and Congo's neighbours helping themselves. Certainly not the army – their officers control some of the worst illegal mining of diamonds, tin, gold, copper, coltan …, you name it. All these factions are like locusts, stripping the country of its inheritance."

"What about the UN forces? Can't they do more to stop it?" Jessica asked.

"The West expects too much of MONUSCO, the UN force here," said Marc who had rejoined them. "Listen, I'm sorry I left you earlier – I'm afraid my emotional armour still isn't complete," he placed a hand on Marianne's shoulder. She rested her head on one side briefly to touch her cheek to his hand but said nothing.

For the first time since she'd met them Jessica felt she was intruding. "Please, Marc. You have every right to feel this deeply." It seemed inadequate, presumptuous even, but it was all she could think of.

"I don't know why the UN doesn't support its MONUSCO mission better, although I guess it's got something to with money and international priorities," said Marc. "You might think sixteen thousand troops would be enough to act as peace-keepers, but what you had was a great big lie that all the leading parties, for their various reasons, had signed up to. In truth, there's been no real peace here to enforce. The UN contingents were thinly spread, they still are although it's better now; for heaven's sake, this country is the size of Western Europe. On the whole they're lightly armed, and in the Kivus they're hours away from any logistical support and have little air cover. Plus they can only stay here as long as the government in Kinshasa wants them, and the regime there is divided over doing deals with Rwanda's leaders to keep them quiet. It's just a bloody mess, Jessica. Everyone involved seems to have a hidden agenda. You can't quote me on any of this. You understand?"

Although the discussion hadn't been off-the-record she had no wish to abuse their hospitality or endanger the mission. But she could certainly use the information as unattributed background, naming no names. "I understand," she said.

"You promise?" asked Marianne. "We can only work here if we remain invisible, and if we were thrown out …," she puffed out her cheeks, "well, what would happen to all these children, and all these women."

"It's OK, I won't quote either of you, or name the mission. I just needed to understand why things are as they are, and you've done a lot to help me. Up to now all I've had is a diet of government bull … excuse me, propaganda. And some of the aid agencies peddle extreme views of their own. I needed an independent viewpoint. And talking of diets," said Jessica, "thank you for an enjoyable meal."

"We're glad you came," said Marianne. "It's been charming to have your company and to hear a bit about the outside world. I don't think we've given you a chance to say much at all. I didn't mean to preach, it's just that this is such a wonderful country, with amazingly resourceful people. Imagine if France or the US had suffered as these people have, with two long wars, five million Congolese people killed, and a million refugees arriving on their doorstep from Rwanda. And all the time there was a vicious conflict going on around them. Well, I don't know how we would have handled it."

"You have to understand that the government in Kinshasa cannot control this part of the country," Marianne added. "The army officers here see this posting as a get-rich-quick scheme. Whatever they can get out of it for themselves will be their pension, and since the soldiers don't always get paid by Kinshasa, it's hard to blame them."

"But why does the West encourage this?" Jessica persisted.

"I think the West feels it can't win here. The problems are so intractable and the areas affected are so large that it would take billions of dollars to make a difference and tens of thousands of boots on the ground. Voters don't want that and you don't see anyone asking the colonial powers to come in and help. There's no upside for all the hard investment it would take, nobody would thank them. And the Americans are seen as just another coloniser in the region – you only need to look at the way they undermined the first elected president and supported Mobutu, the dictator who overthrew him. The CIA was implicated in that and carried on backing him for decades, long after everyone else realised he was a cunning crook.

"At least the UN has realised that white faces would be unacceptable in a country that suffered so much under the colonial power. I mean, what Belgium did here in the early twentieth century or to be more accurate what King Leopold did to ensure he sat at Europe's top table alongside Britain and France, well it was as bad as anything we're witnessing today. Maybe worse."

"Yes, I read a bit about before I came here." It wasn't hard for Jessica to see parallels in the brutality still afflicting the country.

"So, you have a power vacuum here, in a naturally rich country that desperately needs better government. And over the border is a country that is led more efficiently but it's … well, it's ruthless. There's no real opposition there and dissenters disappear. Rwanda has far less mineral wealth than Congo, the government blames the Hutu refugees here for the attempted Tutsi genocide. The UN can't be surprised that Rwanda has quietly helped itself to so much of Congo's wealth, making millionaires out of its leaders," Marc added.

"The Rwandans deny they have a single man here, but even the UN has finally reported that they do. I don't expect you've seen Rwandans in uniform in Goma, have you?" asked Marianne, and Jessica looked shocked before shaking her head. "For the most part, Rwanda has left the fighting to its proxies which allows their government to blame Congolese rebels. The UN has reported their support for the rebels but nothing ever happens and some western governments still vie for influence in the region. Britain, France, and even some Scandinavian countries sent millions in economic aid to Kigali though it's stopped now. That just freed the Rwandans to spend their own money on the war. And the regime may be led by a charismatic guy but it's amazing how many of his opponents are silenced or end up dead at home or abroad. Yet somehow he's been the West's poster boy, its economic success story."

"We haven't travelled much this year, but some friends told us recently that they'd come across senior Rwandan officers a long way into Congo. You couldn't call it an invasion exactly," and Marianne paused to find the right words, "but they seem to be playing a major role in their neighbour's civil war."

As the three of them savoured the last of a second bottle of wine, the conversation turned to the number of children the mission had taken in over the years and the changing needs of patients at the clinic. The three of them had already talked comfortably for hours, and then they wanted to know about Jessica's programmes for independent TV producers and her syndicated stories for newspaper groups in the US and Europe. She hadn't expected to say much but perhaps it was the wine and the sympathetic company; whatever it was, Jessica opened up telling them about the dangers and beauties of travelling in the Horn of Africa, especially Somalia where her mother was born, and of her own upbringing in New York.

"My father was a banker, well he still is, but we haven't spoken for a long time. It became hard between us when he and Mom split up. I was twelve and he said he'd visit me all the time when I went to live with her in upstate New York. He promised, and he does meet up with me occasionally but he never comes to our house; it's not much of a relationship. I can't talk to him easily – maybe because I don't trust him – and he's sure as hell not interested in what I do. Whenever I ask her about their relationship and what went wrong, Mom tells me it's complicated and if I persist she gets angry or withdraws into herself, so now we avoid the subject. I guess I've backed off 'cos I don't want to lose her, too. It's all a mess, and something I never wanted to confront, until now." Jessica paused and no one said anything as she stared into her glass pensively. "But I guess I've learned a lot about families since I've been here and it makes me sure that I'm going to confront them separately when I get back. Damn sure. I deserve to know what happened, 'cos it's affected my whole life."

She lifted her head and smiled briefly at Marianne. "Listen to me. Hey, I can't complain; I was lucky, I had a very comfortable upbringing, a good education and I had pretty much everything I needed – except a dad, that is."

"At the time I thought he didn't want to have much to do with me, but now I think maybe Mom kept stuff from me. Who knows? She flat out denied it when I challenged her once and he never showed up at home. I used to look for him among the other parents at school plays and singing competitions if I was performing, but I never saw him so I guess his work was more important. To begin with I got the odd post card from him, he was always travelling. Then even that stopped. I read about him online sometimes, he's often speaking at conferences in the US and Europe." Jessica's voice trailed off.

"What made you choose journalism?" Marc asked.

"Oh, I was good at English in college, so I guess I used my writing to do some travelling of my own. Mom didn't want me to go, she wanted me to stay nearer to home, settle down and have kids but there's time enough for that later. I need to see what's out there, and I like reporting what's going on. It makes me feel in touch. I reckon I've been real lucky, certainly luckier than some of these kids!"

"You said that some of the children were rescued from the coltan mines," said Jessica. "Are there many children still in the mines or is that over?"

"I'm afraid there are many still there," replied Marianne. "We last visited a mine a year ago with one of our friends, an Anglican pastor from Kinshasa, Emmanuel Salumu. "He was amazing, wasn't he, darling?"

"Brilliant," Marc agreed. "We came away with three children that day, in bigger mines it might have been more. But without him we would have left empty-handed, of that I'm sure. It can get ugly when dealing with the people who run these places. Sometimes you're negotiating at gunpoint with people who feel they have everything to lose by co-operating – money, respect, position." His thoughts went back to the last confrontation at a mine.

"I know children have to work at an early age here, but is it true that children are being held captive in the mines and made to work unpaid?" Jessica asked. "That's slavery." She fell silent for a moment, looking from one host to the other as they nodded in turn. "This is awful," she breathed. "Isn't the government able to do anything about this? Or the UN? Who knows about this?"

Marc snorted and Marianne just sighed. Despite her travels Jessica seemed so naïve about the life of ordinary Congolese. *Perhaps it said more about how they had become inured to what was going on around them*, thought Marianne, *that they had to see it through her eyes in order to be shocked by this exploitation of children in the mines.* Marianne shook her head, "The government in Kinshasa is part of the problem, Jessica, not the solution. The army still can't, or won't, control this region. When it does take control of a mine from the rebels, the troops sent to guard it are seldom paid so it's not surprising that they steal from the people they're supposed to protect. They have guns after all; what else can you expect? They take what they want, money, minerals, and girls."

Marc leaned forward, trying to get the point across. "Honestly, it's worse than the Wild West in the mines. The troops don't get paid for months at a time because somewhere between the Treasury in Kinshasa and the barracks in Goma or Bukavu someone is siphoning off their money. The soldiers just know that if they keep control of the mines they can survive, and the officers may even get rich by stealing tin or coltan from the miners. The miners just work for themselves, you see. They're not organised or employed by anyone, they're just artisans. Who are they going to complain to?"

"On the rare occasions when the authorities like the Ministry of Mines or senior Army officers turn up to assess the situation – or occasionally when journalists arrive at a mine – the soldiers just shed their uniforms and hide their guns until they've gone. They just look like any other miner. Anyway, from what we hear the Ministry of Mines is too busy with political in-fighting in the capital to make significant changes. The people we've talked to in Kinshasa say that the Minister is just a figurehead, he was appointed after the last election in the horse-trading over portfolios that goes on between the Presidential Alliance parties. And his deputy was only put in his post by the President to watch the Minister. The real power lies with the Chief of Staff, Businga, he's been there for years and is ex-military – very well connected," added Marianne.

"Did you say Businga? Hold on." She stood up and went over to her bag where she pulled out her laptop and quickly showed them a series of images. "Do you mean this guy?" She turned the screen around on the table for them to see.

"Well, I've only seen his photo in the papers once or twice, but yes, I think so," said Marianne.

"I'm the same," Marc agreed. "But I do remember when we first came out here he was in the news a lot because he was high up in the Army. This was a few years back and of course he was in uniform, not that awful shirt. I think it's him though."

"Yes, he seems to like these shirts. I found a few photos like this."

"Even if they all spoke with one voice at the Ministry of Mines I doubt they could control the FARDC, the Congolese Army, and certainly not this far from Kinshasa," said Marianne. "Once army officers get posted this far away they usually become a law unto themselves. There's not even a proper road between here and the capital. They're a thousand miles from any serious discipline or supervision, so it's no surprise that they see this as their chance to make a fortune, just like their predecessors. It's a pretty rare individual in any country who can withstand that kind of temptation when they start so poor. It's no surprise that they 'fill their boots' – isn't that the American expression?" Jessica smiled in acknowledgement.

"As a result, very little tax revenue goes back to the state coffers. And a lot of the tin, coltan, gold and diamonds find their way onto the black market, far more than anyone likes to admit. A few senior people in the army and in ministries like mining, finance, customs and border control are getting incredibly rich – even by Western standards – while most of the population can barely survive on two dollars a day."

There was a silence. It was getting late and the two were exhausted, while Jessica was overwhelmed by what she had heard. She had thought she knew how bad the situation was in North and South Kivu. But all this detail was beyond imagining. "Obviously, I don't want to quote you or I'll put the mission in danger, but is it possible for me to get to one of these mines to see for myself?" Jessica asked.

"No, you mustn't publish our names or any details about the mission," said Marc. He appeared shaken at how much trust they had placed in this woman whom they had only known for a few hours. "We can only tell you this because we believe it is wrong and would like to see it changed. But nothing must jeopardise the future for these women and children."

"I understand," said Jessica. "I have no intention of risking your work here. But if I can get to see a mine like this it might help me bring pressure for change from the outside world." She wasn't bargaining with them exactly, but Marc sensed that a mine visit might take her mind off covering the mission.

"Believe me, the tin mines are just as bad if not worse," replied Marianne. "It's not that the adults or children are held there at gunpoint exactly. It's the poverty, the isolation and lack of alternative work that traps them. I mean, how else can they earn money to keep themselves or their families once their village has been destroyed by looters? In the mines they can end up working for the very people who burned their villages."

The French couple looked at one another. Marianne spoke first, "I can only advise you as one woman to another. Do not set foot in one of these mines. They are extremely dangerous places. I only went to a nearby coltan mine because we knew enough about the people there before we set out to know it was a risk worth taking. I strongly urge you not to try, Jessica. Or, if you must do it, go in only with a well-armed and trusted group beside you."

"Marianne is right," said Marc. "These places are more dangerous than you can imagine. Normally I would hesitate to visit one myself and I would not allow Marianne to come too. I'm sorry if that sounds patronising, I don't mean it to. I'm sure you are very experienced and capable in threatening circumstances, but sometimes it's best to know what you can get away with if you are alone and unarmed. Why don't you sleep on it, and we can talk further about it tomorrow if you're still determined to go. I certainly won't arrange it for you, but I can tell you where some of the mines are."

Jessica nodded and said nothing further on the subject but her mind was turning over everything she'd heard about the cruelty and injustice that their conversation had confirmed. She had not seen any reporting of this in the West and her instinct was to bring it to the world's attention; at least she had to try. And at the back of it all, a small, insistent voice inside her head was arguing that this might be a story like no other she had ever covered – the kind of story that, in the right hands, won awards and shaped entire careers.

With the wine exhausted and fatigue creeping up on all of them, she thanked them both for their hospitality and helped them wash the dishes before Marianne showed her to a spare bed upstairs in the main building.

******

In a comfortable room after too many nights in a tent, Jessica fell deeply asleep and was only awakened the next morning by the sounds of youthful exuberance all around. The boys' dormitory was near enough for her to hear children chasing one another, laughter and shouts in an unfamiliar language and somewhere downstairs a constantly banging door. *The wind was up but it was more likely*, she thought, *the result of lively children being readied for the school day.* She dressed, repacked her small rucksack and went downstairs.

There was no sign of Marianne or Marc and she was about to follow the noise of the children in search of them when she saw two boys tending to a tripod frame up which a healthy stand of beans was growing in the garden.

They were engrossed and did not notice Jessica's approach. "Good morning," she spoke formally to them in Kiswahili and treated them as adults. The boys straightened immediately and turned at the strange voice. "Good morning, Miss," said the larger boy politely, while the other just looked at her.

"What are you doing? Did the wind blow this down?" she asked disarmingly.

"Yes, it must have happened in the night," said the older boy. "We need to check all the poles otherwise the beans will be damaged." The younger boy said nothing but continued to stare.

"Are you both in charge of the whole garden then?"

"I suppose I am, partly," said the same boy.

207

"Well, my name is Jessica, I'm just visiting," she said. "What are your names?"

"I'm Raphael," said the more talkative of the two, "and this is Ben."

"Good to meet you, boys." She hesitated and then, expecting no better opportunity she continued, "Do you mind me asking how you came to be living here?"

There was a silence and she thought she may have over-stepped the mark with them. The boys looked at one another and Ben said nothing, Raphael looked at the ground and then raised his eyes to hers. "They killed my Father," was all he said.

"Who did, Raphael?"

"The soldiers." He said it matter of factly, without any intended drama. "They shot him in my village. We escaped through the forest, I mean my sister and I, and then we had to work. That was where Emmanuel found us, in the mine. Then we came to live here with Marc and Marianne." He seemed about to say something else but perhaps his nerve failed him.

Jessica was staring at him. "I'm sorry to hear about your father. You must miss him very much."

The boy looked at her intently for a second and in the pause before he replied she felt he was assessing her motives for asking. "I miss him every day." He glanced sideways at the vegetables he had planted. "He would never have let these beans fall over," and the boy sighed so deeply that Jessica just wanted to put her arm around him. "Baba knew everything about growing. I always make mistakes and so I have to learn that way."

"Well, they look good to me. We had some of your vegetables for dinner last night, they were very good. I mean it, I was telling Marianne." She was eager to keep the conversation going, to understand a bit more about their lives and what they'd been through, but she did not want to upset the boys or scare them away. She guessed this must be the child that Marianne and Marc had mentioned over dinner the previous night. She had expected a much younger lad, but Raphael was turning into a young man and was tall enough to look her in the eye. She didn't want to give the impression they'd all been discussing him behind his back, so she asked, "Do you have any brothers or sisters here?"

He looked closely at her again. "Yes, I have a little sister called Keisha."

It was him then. Jessica tried to keep their conversation alive but knew that asking this was risky. "What about your mother?" Ben shifted to the other foot and Jessica hoped that he would not suddenly find his voice.

For a boy who appeared so strong, when the reply came his voice was suddenly very faint and she realised how young and alone he really was. "We are still looking for her, but…," his words trailed away.

"That must be very hard for you, I'm sorry…." She was about to continue when Marianne appeared at her elbow.

"Boys, why are you not in your class? You are already late for lessons. Go on, you can finish this later." They hurried off and Marianne turned to Jessica. Now there was anger in her gaze and Jessica could see a storm coming. "I don't know what that was all about, but I would hate to think you were interviewing them."

Jessica shook her head. "No, I was talking to them about the garden and thanking them for the vegetables we ate last night."

Marianne raised an eyebrow, "Then what was all that talk about Raphael's mother?"

Jessica raised her hands in surrender, "OK. I shouldn't have asked them that. I was just trying to understand what it's like for them. Being without their parents, I mean. I apologise, I shouldn't have let the conversation go that far."

"You are correct, you had no right to ask them such things. I'm surprised at you and very disappointed. If Marc had found you, he would have thrown you out and made you walk back to Walikale. You have been agreeable company and I like you, Jessica, but if you abuse our hospitality or the trust of the children in any way by bringing in your newspapers and TV to scrutinise these children you will never be welcome here again. And I dare say things might be very difficult for you with the NGOs in Goma," she continued to stare at the young woman. "Do I make myself clear?"

"I understand. As I explained yesterday, I only came here to see if I could profile your mission's work. And since you've made it clear last night that you don't want me to, I won't publish a word about you. It's just that, I hadn't expected..." and she gestured to the garden around her and the protective walls around the clinic, orphanage and school, "well, all this. What you and Marc, and Emmanuel of course, are doing is remarkable. And one day I'd like to tell the story in a way that you're comfortable with, but sometimes we – I mean journalists – kind of forget that if we bring it alive with a colourful setting or a sympathetic character, we're treading on people's lives. I am sorry."

Marianne held her gaze for a moment, assessing the sincerity of her words, then she smiled, a decision made. "Come, you haven't seen the clinic or the school. I'm afraid we can't have any photos in the clinic, but I expect you could take some unidentifiable pictures of the children from the back of the class."

As the pair started to move off, Jessica put her hand on the older woman's arm for a moment. "I know this is in danger of being misunderstood, Marianne, but I really would like to help. I was thinking about it last night after dinner. I never expected to meet Raphael; I mean, I didn't even know his name then. I do have a lot of contacts, as I'm sure you do, at the aid agencies in Goma. It's just that," she paused seeing the particular sensitivity surrounding Raphael, "if his mother and family *are* in the area it might still be possible to find them. I'm sure you've already tried, but one more effort using a different set of contacts surely can't do any harm, can it? And it just might do some good. I just keep thinking of that brave young man and his little sister. What was her name, Keisha? I just keep thinking of them and wondering if I could do something to bring their family back together. Would you let me try?"

"I don't know. We have tried so hard for well over a year, we've exhausted every avenue we can think of and I would hate to raise false hopes in him. He's vulnerable enough as it is. I don't think Marc would allow it, in case it's one disappointment too many for them both. After all, Raphael has been through so much, and so has Keisha, that we couldn't bear to cause them any more hurt. Right now, he needs to pass his exams and we are already worried that he may be falling behind. Thank you, but no." Marianne smiled sadly at her and Jessica thought of protesting, but she was already on thin ice and it seemed the Audoussets were of one mind on this.

It was only after saying her goodbyes and as she climbed into the mission's elderly Toyota Land Cruiser just before lunchtime, that Jessica noticed Raphael and a little girl standing together, watching her from deep in the shadows of an outbuilding. Marc was busying himself loading empty baskets to carry provisions on the return journey and when he went back into the kitchens the boy beckoned her vigorously towards them. Jessica looked about her but there was no one else to be seen. She got out of the vehicle again and went over to join them. "What is it?" she asked.

"This is my sister, Keisha. We want to ask if you know people in Goma?" said Raphael and the pair hung on her reply.

Jessica looked down at the slim, bright eyed girl who could not have been more than eleven or twelve, and then back at Raphael. "Of course," she replied.

"We need to find our mother. She is still alive, we know it, but we don't know where. Aren't there people in Goma who can find families and children who are lost?" There was desperation written across Raphael's young face and his small, silent sister looked equally anxiously at her. They had been standing side by side but now as they waited for Jessica's reply Keisha put her hand in Raphael's. For once in her life, Jessica did not know what to say. She felt hideously torn between betraying the promise she had only just given to her two new friends, and devastating the fragile hopes of these life-battered children. She kidded herself that she would decide what to do with the images later as she brought up her camera and rattled off four photos of Raphael and Keisha standing together quietly in the shadows. She glanced over her shoulder, worried that the flash would have caught Marc's attention, but he was still inside.

"Listen, I cannot promise you anything at all. Do you understand that, Raphael? I will try, I will ask some people I know, but Marianne and Marc have already tried hard and I don't think I will be more successful. One thing, tell me what was ... what is the name of your village?" As she asked the question, she could hear the kitchen door banging shut, Marc must be returning.

"Nyasi. We lived in Nyasi," and the pair turned and ran off.

"Are you ready, Jessica? Is anything the matter?" a voice came from directly behind her. Marc had loaded the car and was walking towards her.

"No, just looking around," she felt bad at how easily the lie came. I'm OK to go, now," she added. There was a breathlessness to her voice that she hoped he did not detect.

Marc turned back to the car and she walked behind him so that he could not have seen her switch off her camera and scratch 'R & K Nyasi' on her notepad as she went. By the time they bumped out of the mission she was composed and listened as Marc chatted on about the roads. She paid him scant attention; Jessica was mentally listing the people to whom she could email the photos.

Chapter 14
Goma City and Kanyaruchinya Camp, Eastern DRC
Two Weeks Ago

Mount Nyiragongo, little more than ten miles from the airport, filled James's view through the aircraft's tiny window. He had been looking for a view of the city of Goma but it was the mountain that first held his attention. He could clearly make out the chocolate dark lines of lava that the volcano had spilled across the valley and on through the city only a few years before. At the northern tip of the sixty mile-long lake the pilot swung the plane eastward and crossed the mid-line marking the border between the Democratic Republic of the Congo and neighbouring Rwanda. From about five thousand feet the volcano was now clearly visible although the sky around them was filled with puffs of pale grey cloud and a thin haze softened every inch of the shoreline beneath them. Today Nyiragongo looked benign, coated in an innocent velvet greenery that belied the destruction wrought on the city's half a million inhabitants, people already traumatised by war. Out of the mist a dusting of bright metal and red-tiled roofs shone up at him looking like silver and scarlet confetti, and the houses and roads began to spread further inland from the lake. Gradually, the buildings organised themselves into lines and grids around roads and folds in the land, until the view disappeared as the plane passed over Goma port nestling in the half-moon embrace of a sharp volcanic rock spur.

The pilot dallied briefly with Rwandan airspace before banking the plane north again and skimming in low over the northern tip of the enormous Lake Kivu. The colours below were totally unexpected; James hadn't anticipated the neat red roofs, clean white walls, green gardens, shiny lava-hued roads, even blue swimming pools. After ten blocks of prestigious housing the plane eased its way over the city centre's roundabouts, a few hotels and office blocks, and whisked across some poorer, greyer neighbourhoods before landing as soft as a bird on Goma's single runway. From the air it had seemed to be one big city, but he'd seen on a map that as the border emerged from the lake it ran north dividing the jumble of buildings into two cities. To the West, Congo's Goma took up two thirds of the urban sprawl, and Rwanda's Gisenyi made up the remainder to the east. The two cities were not just idly touching, James could see they were fused together on either side of a single unpaved road that threaded its way northwards from the lake, and skirted the airport perimeter by a whisker before arrowing north and east into the Parc National des Volcans.

The airport had clearly been affected as much as the city by recent political and geophysical upheavals. It was less than a decade since the volcano had erupted, violently spewing out lava that flowed south for ten miles across the intervening rich arable land before the rolling wall of molten rock – sometimes as much as six feet high – had tumbled hissing into the lake where it had disappeared from view. The lava flow had also punched long arms of liquid rock into the city centre, and one of these arms had reached out to cover the northern third of Goma's two mile runway. Although most people had escaped its onrush a few of the unlucky or unwary had been killed, burned by lava or overcome by toxic gases escaping from deep underground.

The airport terminal had even been cut off from the runway. Aid flights for refugees fleeing the continued fighting, already stretched to breaking point bringing in relief supplies, were suddenly complicated by relief efforts for those injured or made homeless by the eruptions. To some in Goma at the time it seemed that the city was being punished beyond endurance, with almost half of the city covered by the tide of lava, killing an unknown number of people and obliterating thousands of homes.

In the circumstances, James was amazed to see such an apparently normal environment as he came down the aircraft steps. It was easy to see where the lava flow had finally abated, as well as the work that had since been done to add a new concrete taxiway from the terminal to the runway. There were signs of civic pride here too, with small, tidy lawns separated by box hedges and a smart new sign welcoming visitors to the Aéroport de Goma. Its modern terminal buildings of concrete and glass wouldn't have looked out of place at a regional airport in the US or Europe. Only the large number of white-painted Indian Air Force helicopters parked nearby when not being flown for the UN suggested anything out of the ordinary. He counted eight but there could have been more.

Smartly uniformed Congolese soldiers from the FARDC wearing combat olive greens sauntered in a loose single file across the apron to a large waiting chopper. Most of them ignored his party, but one or two grinned towards them as the line of troops snaked its way past. This was the first indication for James of the amount of work being done by the UN, the Kinshasa authorities and other non-governmental organisations in the area as they tried to restore Nord Kivu's provincial capital.

Inside the terminal the military use of the civil airport was made even clearer by the number of UN officers and other ranks – all from the Asian sub-continent – awaiting transport. There were men from India, Pakistan and Bangladesh and all of them saluted as an Indian general passed through on his way to a meeting. A few more soldiers were chatting and smoking outside in the sunshine, others preferred to sleep on the floor in the terminal's shade. There was no sign of a contact for the group from AfriCan Care, so they settled down in the airport to wait for someone to collect them, lounging against their kitbags just as the assorted soldiery were doing nearby.

James knew that his brief view of Kinshasa in the far west of the country had not been representative of the city. He had been there for little more than a day which had frustrated the photographer in him, for he had hoped to find a driver and get around the city. There should still be time for that on his return journey but he had had to be content with the sights of one of Kinshasa's smarter business districts. He fully expected to get a better look at real life in Congo here, and a lot more images to go with it. Flying a thousand miles to Goma on the opposite side of this vast country had already given him a sense of the enormity of their task. To fly for three hours and see so few signs of life had made him even more aware of the difficulty of making a difference in such a large country, especially one split apart by conflicts, some of which were centuries old.

Goma was surprising, it didn't neatly conform to his mental image of a war-ravaged city, and in a few places it was unquestionably modern. His expectations had been low before arriving; yet what confronted him was entirely different. Construction work was under way in many areas. While most of the houses they passed in the taxi that they had finally rustled up were roughly made in concrete or breeze block with corrugated iron roofs, many were not. From the air he had seen two and three storey villas, and some smart hotels and lodges on the lake front that were set behind lawns and well-tended gardens running down to the water. There were low-rise concrete office blocks huddled together in the business district, and the roads ranged from smooth asphalt in the city centre to rough and pot-holed laval surfaces further out. His preconceptions of Congo were being shattered all the time.

It wasn't a long journey to their temporary guest house but what they found was more comfortable than he would have expected, and more comfortable than most of them were used to as it turned out. Four-wheel-drive SUVs and pick-up trucks stood on the asphalt drive, and there were a couple of umbrellas set over tables in a tiny garden at the front. Tiered blue-grey gabled roofs perched over newly-painted white walls, and inside a football match was showing on a flat screen TV. James made an effort to junk all his remaining notions of Goma. He was struggling to understand a city that was showing more ambition than he had anticipated. Yet he knew from what he'd read before flying here that just a few miles away people were enduring extraordinary suffering, just surviving in temporary camps that were showing signs of permanence.

He was sure that tomorrow would bring its shocks, but he was keen to get started. He desperately wanted to justify his presence here with stills and video images showing how the charity was tackling life in the camps edging the city.

"Make the most of it, bud."

James turned to see the grinning face of Aidan, one of the charity's workers in Goma. "I guess we won't be here long," said James.

"Just tonight, man. Then it's mostly tents for a few weeks as we get out and about. We just need to meet with some people from Rwanda. A team from MONUSCO has left early and given us their rooms for the night, all paid up courtesy of the UN. So, tonight we can enjoy a cold beer and hot water. You're sharing with me, and Sarah's got the other room. Perks of rank, pal." His smile was infectious.

"Well, I'll dump my kitbag. Then you can lead me to a cold one."

******

As their battered, once-white SUV left the guest house the following morning, Sarah turned in the front seat to talk to James. "Did you manage to get your head down last night or did Aidan lead you astray?" She was smiling but he sensed she was only half-joking.

They both glanced sideways at the slumped figure of their Scottish-born liaison in Goma. His head was resting on a battered kit bag and it looked as if he'd been wearing the same T-shirt for a while. James didn't know where Aidan had got to after he'd turned in. They'd had a few beers together in the guest house bar, but both of them had been fairly sober when James called it a day. It could only have been around midnight, but he'd been pretty bushed from two lengthy journeys in forty-eight hours so he hadn't been looking for a late night.

Aidan O'Dowd had, it seemed, matched some European pilots in the bar drink for drink, and when he came back to their room James was so deeply asleep he hadn't even heard him. Aidan was still stretched out on the bed in his clothes when James got up at seven o'clock in search of breakfast.

"Yeah, a couple of beers and I had a good night's sleep, thanks. What've you got lined up for us today, then?" he said, keen to take the spotlight off his sleeping colleague.

"Well, you may have read about this one already but we've set up a project for vulnerable girls in Goma, in fact it caters for girls from all over North Kivu, as long as they can make it here. Sadly, many can't. Our project is targeted at vulnerable girls and women from all parts of the province. Some have been separated from their families, either because of the fighting or they've been forced into prostitution to survive. It's horrible, but, even if they escape this, many are

215

rejected by their family or their village and end up back in Goma living on the streets to survive."

"A lot of them have children of their own, even though they may only be fourteen or fifteen. And then there are the former girl soldiers conscripted into rebel groups. Sometimes they're in the worst position," said Sarah, and she paused to collect her thoughts. "Conscription can go one of two ways, the youngest ones – pre-puberty – often end up fighting. Many of them will have been forced at gunpoint to commit atrocities; killing people, sometimes even having to kill members of their own family."

She saw James' shocked expression. "I know, it's designed to bind them into the militia, to give them no way out. Other times they're forced to kill other children who have tried to escape, or adults whose village they've captured. The leaders tell the children they can't run away after this because the authorities will imprison them for what they've just done. So, boys and girls as young as twelve are made to beat these people to death with rocks or clubs. It's pretty hard for anyone to get over the mental scars of being forced to do something like that, but we help them as much as we can."

"Jesus!" James was stunned. For this to be happening to children was beyond anything he'd imagined. "So, what happens to them after that?" he asked.

"If they don't manage to escape, and most can't, they are trained to use an AK-47 rifle and a bayonet. They learn how to handle grenades and set booby traps. By the age of fourteen some of them are so damaged that – even with the best psychiatric care we can give them – they may never fully recover. Most of them do move on, though, as long as we can give them a way out by teaching them work skills and helping find a job when they leave us. Some of them can go back to their village. For others that's not an option – the village may have been burnt out and deserted or perhaps their families are dead or scattered.

"That's the youngsters, of course. Like I said, conscription can go one of two ways. You've probably read that the older girls are often kept as sex slaves and cooks by the militias," said Sarah. "When the soldiers tire of them or get fed up having their kids around the place, they throw them out with their children. And these women – well, many of them are still girls – end up in the camps around Goma, sometimes suffering from HIV and sexually transmitted diseases, as well as mental scarring."

"A million people have now lost their homes here in the east. Many people flee to Goma, although it's not always much safer, and life is pretty precarious in the camps. Various militia operate openly there and the Kinshasa government can't stop them; the gangs and the army are extorting money from people who have nothing, looking for young fighters who have escaped, or just battling other groups for influence."

"God, I'd read a bit about Congo before I came, but I had no idea it was like this. Who's supposed to be running the camps? Is it the Kinshasa government or the UN?" asked James.

"Well, the UN administers the healthcare and food distribution and organises education, and they are nominally supported by Congolese troops. The troops are supposed to be loyal to Kinshasa, but in reality they only answer to the local FARDC officers."

"FARDC?"

"Yeah, confusing isn't it?" Sarah nodded. "There's a lot of abbreviations here, and just when you think you've got it nailed, new groups spring up with new initials. FARDC is the French abbreviation for Congo's army. And like most of them, what they say and what they do are light years apart."

"How do you mean?"

"Well the rebels are frequently called Free-this or Democratic-that, when nothing could be further from the truth. These groups aren't rebelling to form a government, they're just run by thugs who can get guns too easily," said Sarah. "At their best the Congo Army can be highly disciplined, loyal to their officers and pretty effective. Unfortunately, that's still the exception. Most of them are poorly-trained, ill-equipped conscripts. They seldom get paid properly by Kinshasa, so it's no surprise that they steal food at gunpoint to survive, and loot any valuables to get money. And the further the officers are posted from Kinshasa the more they just look after themselves. Corruption here is endemic and it's anyone's guess how it will ever be brought under control." She held on to the back of the driver's seat as they hit another massive pothole and somehow rolled out the other side.

"Of course, that has an effect on the UN forces – you know, MONUSCO. Mostly they come from countries that aren't much richer than Congo, so the temptations here are obvious." Her expression was tight-lipped.

James sat in the back of the battered jeep and tried to take all this in. He wondered if his photographs could ever do justice to the beauty of the scenery or the calamity unfolding around its people every day. *All he could do*, he thought, *was try to get the best shots of whatever confronted him.* And listening to the suffering that was going on, he knew it wouldn't be long before he started.

When they reached Maison Christine, the women's refuge in Goma, Sarah disappeared inside. James had been warned at the last minute that photography was not permitted anywhere at the refuge or in the grounds, to protect the women's identities, so there seemed to be no immediate role for him. Nor would he be allowed inside. But within minutes of their arrival one of the cooks had found him leaning idly against the vehicle and signalled he needed his help in carrying a new oven into the kitchens from where it had been left under a plastic sheet in the yard.

Men may not have been allowed in most parts of the modern, concrete block but there seemed to be no objection to getting James to help in the kitchen, where he was at least able to meet some of the staff. Some of these women and a few men were providing counselling for thirty young women, many of them former girl soldiers and their children who called the refuge home. Several were teachers giving the girls the schooling they had missed on the streets. A few doubled up with ancillary work as cooks and cleaners. In such a lean organisation there seemed little room for job demarcation and many of the staff had more than one role.

There was a vibrancy and sense of purpose about the place that was palpable. The kitchen was small and sparsely equipped but it was clean and recently painted, and at last it boasted a new and hopefully more reliable oven. Clearly, the charity had created a refuge that did much more than shelter the girls, it was educating and rehabilitating them, as well as giving them the skills to create their own, more positive futures.

The taciturn man who had called James in to help carry the oven flicked his fingers imperiously at the British interloper as he straightened from his removal task. George the caretaker had only one eye, the other socket was protected by a piece of bright yellow fabric patch that kept drawing James' attention. Periodically, George would lift the patch to rub the empty socket which evidently irritated him. Maybe this was the cause of his sombre demeanour, he was certainly not one for long speeches, but he instantly found James another job sitting in the yard on a chopped log beneath a lean-to shelter. From his position near the kitchen door, George could keep his one eye on all the comings and goings at the business end of the house, and here the two of them began to peel and chop an enormous pink mound of sweet potatoes before putting the bright orange pieces into two large black, water-filled buckets.

It was here thirty minutes later that Sarah found James chopping the last of the vegetables. "Ah, there you are. Sorry to drag you away but we've got other work for you to do," she grinned.

James willingly put down his knife, "I don't think they'll be taking me on here any time soon, anyway," he said. "It takes me twice as long as George to peal a bucketful." He wiped his hands on his shorts and waved a goodbye to the caretaker before picking up his unused backpack and heading to the car.

A few minutes later they were on their way again, this time headed to Kanyaruchinya camp, outside the city. As they left the refuge, the street scene around them began to change; the condition of roads, shops and housing deteriorated more with every mile. Except the others didn't seem to notice. James took photos as they drove, but already he could see a stark contrast to the tree-lined comfort of Gombe, the embassy district that had been almost his only view of Kinshasa when he arrived in Congo.

Here in Goma the roads were hard packed earth or murram, and on both sides there were stagnant pools which, to judge from the stench, were made by streams of raw sewage and soapy waste water that seeped out into the roadway from swollen ditches and pipes set into the nearby buildings. This was still no shantytown. They were surrounded by solid looking two and three storey concrete buildings on either side, shops with plate glass windows, and advertising hoardings promoting mobile phone networks, sweets, fizzy drinks and beer. As they drove further on, more of the windows were broken or missing their glass altogether. There were fewer cars, and he noticed they were generally smaller than the ones he had seen in the centre of the city. Now there was the constant buzz of small Chinese-made motorbikes, usually carrying two people, or sometimes a family of four with children wedged between Mum and Dad or held precariously in place between the driver and the fuel tank. The bikes wisely negotiated their way around the pools of effluent, seemingly oblivious that the detour took them into the path of an oncoming bus or truck. Clearly, the first requirement for driving here was a working horn, to signal the driver's displeasure as much as his whereabouts.

The deteriorating streets were a far cry from the elegant lakeside houses and hotels that had surprised him as they flew in to Goma. Dangerously loose-hanging electricity cables were slung across streets or from house to house, and even as he passed at ground level James could see that the wiring owed more to Heath Robinson than a functioning utility company. There were bunches of extra wires tapping into electricity inspection boxes; it must have been a long time since anyone could close the door. Festoons of disused wires hung down to street level, creating a hazard for even the smallest passer-by, assuming the foetid pools of excrement didn't get them first.

Loud Congolese rumba and soukous rhythms boomed across the streets from bars that were already busy at eleven in the morning. Groups of men stood and chatted idly with one another beneath the drinks vendors' garish red or yellow umbrellas. Further on, half a dozen children as young as five or six played football back and forth across the road, barefoot and filthy, and all of them excited.

As they travelled further from the city, he began to see the kind of shantytowns he had always expected. These one room buildings were made of rough wood planks, with corrugated iron roofs, and shutters instead of windows. In front of the larger shacks, there were walls of lava that had been cleared to make a small, flat front yard. From time to time, James passed tarpaulins spread out across these spaces and chillies, spices, nuts or fruit were being dried on them or prepared for sale. The wealthier homes had brightly coloured motorbikes parked outside, most did not.

The SUV paused to allow a large bus to pass and a hot, dusty backwash blew into his face. Through an open door he glimpsed three women laughing as they worked at a bare kitchen table covered in pots and pans. By this stage on their route the huts were more thinly spread. Each still had a patch of cleared ground at the front but the broken lava that had spilled across the plain from the erupting volcano a few years before here encroached a little closer on each home. They were not far from the centre of Goma, but, although still fifteen kilometres from Mount Nyiragongo, James could see that these homes must have been overrun by molten lava. The inhabitants had only managed to clear the rock from small patches of earth for cultivation – he was beginning to see what an enormous task it must be to roll back the damage done to a hugely fertile plain. Years later, people were still struggling to unpick at the margins, what Nature had done in a matter of hours.

Close to the houses a few tall and spindly thorn trees and acacias were flourishing, their bright green leaves twisting in the breeze and beneath them there were a scattering of scrub bushes. The rest of the land had been inundated in lava the colour of dark mud. Here and there the craggy rock had set into flat areas that looked like a level terrace, but mostly there were folds and ripples in the hard, angular ground. It would be useless for farming or even smallholdings except for tiny patches where back-breaking labour had broken up the rock and carried it away.

Their vehicle bounced along the road past poor and unremarkable homes and businesses. Beneath a tree that was bent almost double and now spread over a corrugated iron roof a sign on a bright blue shed caught his eye. WIRA CORP GOMA – WIDOWS SEWING PROJECT and underneath in French, ATELIER DE COUTURE POUR LES VEUVES. There was no immediate sign of the widows who perhaps were sewing inside. Ever since they left the guest house this morning he had seen enterprise, thrift and hard work. Further on he could see a gang of kids playing beside the rough dry-stone lava walls, watched by women preparing vegetables piled high in coloured plastic bowls. But even the bright bowls were eclipsed by the vivid blues, greens, reds and yellows of the kikoys they wore, wraps which shimmered and dazzled the eye as the women moved.

In contrast, most of the huts were built from heavily stained dark wood planks, covered here and there with small pieces of flattened tin in a nailed on patchwork of repairs. These children were better off than some he had seen in Goma, all of them wore shoes and were dressed in clean, well-fitting clothes.

At this point the lava road began to widen to thirty or forty metres – with no defined edges the roadside simply finished at someone's front door. James was finding the heat oppressive, and the humidity was a trial to a European who had yet to acclimatise. Although the day was bright and the sun was out, the sky hung a heavy grey curtain ahead of them in a solid line of clouds.

Electricity pylons were placed sporadically along the route and yet the power lines still drooped dangerously low across the roadway. Now that he thought of it he couldn't remember seeing any street lights since they left. An array of trades was being conducted at the roadside. He saw two men transporting a beautifully made wooden front door, neatly crafted with diagonal panels, and strapped with thin ropes to a large wooden scooter made with wooden wheels. It was a type that he had already seen in Goma. The pair were struggling to move the door across the broken ground and, with an air of resignation, one of them had his hands thrust deep into the pockets of his baggy, dirty brown trousers, while the other wrestled to tighten the ropes.

Just beyond them, two teenage boys were manoeuvring a bicycle carrying four full five-gallon jerry cans. He couldn't tell if they were filled with petrol, water or paraffin for cooking, but it was clearly hard work. Little cameos caught his eye all along the road to the camp and they kept him busy taking photos through the car's open window.

It might have seemed impossible at first but slowly the road began to deteriorate still more. The only other vehicles around were tough-looking little motorbikes and now there were fewer of them. Huge muddy, brown puddles occupied the centre of the road and mostly their Congolese driver skirted around them, but sometimes they were unavoidable and the stench of faeces as the car splashed through these run-offs from nearby houses made him gag and lean back from the open window.

It was only after another twenty minutes of slow progress over increasingly rutted roads that the gates to the camp came into view and the car pulled up at a prefabricated entrance block. The building itself was a work in progress, with wooden walls covered in white plastic sheeting bearing the blue markings of UNHCR, the UN High Commission for Refugees. Young men dressed in jeans and assorted football strips hung around outside the door, watching them with passing interest as the charity group got out to stretch their legs and register their arrival with the UN officials inside.

A large white metal sign had been set into concrete blocks beside the gate, declaring in bright blue paint beneath the UNHCR logo that this was CAMP KANYARUCHINYA. The roadways were filled with large puddles that had yet to evaporate from the previous night's rain, and they stretched from the camp gate for a hundred metres or more past a storage area with plastic-covered pallets neatly stacked and labelled. There was a sense of order here that James had not expected.

The camp was now home to over fifty thousand people who had fled the fighting engulfing their villages and homes. As his group drove deeper into the camp, the rain re-started and suddenly umbrellas began to pop up around them. Many of the people they passed had no choice but to ignore the rainfall and carried on with their business. The elderly Toyota had been in its element negotiating the vast potholes and ridges on the unmade road out of Goma, and now it gave them some temporary shelter as the wipers struggled to shift the heavy rain.

It wasn't long before they reached a large market place set in an open area the size of half a football pitch. At the margins surly looking youths stood in the lee of larger tents, hunched into their light jackets against the weather. They were neither going anywhere, nor did they appear particularly interested in buying or selling. They just stood and watched as the party climbed out of the vehicle.

The market was filled with men and women, old and young, selling cooking utensils and small amounts of food, or drifting among the colourful cloths and hessian sacks on which the goods were displayed. Perhaps it was the warmth of the air and the certainty of drying off quickly, perhaps it was the urgency of their purchases in the market – in any event the majority without umbrellas seemed in no hurry to take shelter. James continued to photograph the market activity, wandering among the vendors and ignoring their calls for him to buy. He continued to be watched from a distance by the young men, but no one moved to challenge him or prevent him taking photos.

Then he heard Sarah call and turned to see her beckoning. She left the group of UNHCR officers and her local liaison colleagues to come across to him. "James, you're going to have to be sensitive here. We need some images that convey what conditions are really like for families living here. Don't be fooled by this normal market scene, what you're about to see is the reality of life here when people arrive. There simply aren't enough tents or shelters for each family and I need you to capture that. But remember that people are inviting us into their home, or what passes for one and try to imagine how you would feel if someone came into your house to record the moments of your greatest vulnerability and desperation."

She looked searchingly into his face seeking his acknowledgement and he nodded. "Sure, I'll be careful," he said, "but if there's anything in particular you think I shouldn't shoot just tell me in advance. Otherwise I'll try to be invisible." That, as it turned out, was harder to do than to say.

A Congolese official with a UNHCR badge attached to his neat brown suit, smiled warmly at the visitors and led them to the curtain door of a tall, plastic-covered wooden structure. At three or four metres tall it was far bigger than a tent, and the translucent plastic walls and ceiling made it brighter inside than he had expected. But what surprised James most was the number of people it housed. The shelter must have been about ten metres long and six metres wide, and the plastic roof was supported by a dozen rough-cut wooden poles. The walls were simply made of clear plastic sheeting draped over a structure of thinner wooden struts that had been built into a flimsy-looking lattice.

What caught and held his attention, however, was the way it was crammed with families. Wherever he turned in this makeshift shelter there were people sleeping on mats laid on the bare ground, or wrapped up in blankets and coloured sheets. At first he thought it was entirely occupied by women and children until he noticed one or two men among those resting or sleeping. The occupants seemed to be grouped into three or four extended families, with little space between them. Children no older than two or three stood or sat staring at him as his group came in to witness the scene. A little girl near him, clearly new to walking, held herself upright on one of the central poles, a smear of mucus running from her nose. She was wearing only a T-shirt and her chubby legs, which had yet to lose their puppy fat or grow strong through walking, wobbled ever so slightly as she stood. A woman who might have been her mother lay beneath a blanket on the ground and occasionally her whole body was convulsed with coughing that went on for twenty seconds or more before slowly subsiding. The little girl sucked idly on her fingers, carefully taking in every move that James made.

There were clothes, wraps and blankets hanging over every horizontal strut within reach in the shelter. The pungent smell of drying clothes and unwashed bodies was almost overpowering at first, but within minutes he hardly noticed it. The team from the charity began to talk to a nearby group who were resting after their journey. They appeared exhausted and listless but Sarah struck up a conversation through an interpreter. "Where had they travelled from?" she wanted to know and the UNHCR representative translated for her as she made notes on a clipboard. "How many were in their initial group and how long had it taken them?" It seemed the group was comprised of two families, two mothers and seven children in all but so far there was no mention of the fathers. The families had walked for six days to escape the fighting that had broken out close to the Rwandan border, during which time they had exhausted the small quantity of food with which they had fled. The little rice they possessed had gone to the children, but one woman's five year-old son had contracted diarrhoea shortly before they escaped the fighting and although he had been carried all the time he had died on the third day. The mother appeared too exhausted to grieve and her friend described in a voice so soft that it was almost inaudible how together they had buried him in a dry ditch under heavy rocks to keep the animals from digging up his body.

Sarah put her hand on the woman's shoulder as her friend explained this, but the mother seemed not to notice, continuing to lie motionless staring blankly at an empty blanket on the ground in front of her.

"Have you managed to eat any food since you arrived?"

The official answered Sarah for them. They had arrived with twelve others the previous evening and two of their children had been taken immediately to the medical centre, where they were still under observation – weak but no longer in immediate danger and likely, the doctors had told him, to be released tomorrow. Their treatment would not be finished, but the bed they were sharing was needed urgently for more vulnerable cases that continued to come out of the north and west where the fighting was at its worst.

All of them, children and adults, had been given high energy rations on arrival but the group was plainly worn out, and James sensed there was additional trauma that had yet to be described. He spoke to the official for the first time. "Can you ask if it would be OK to photograph them in here?" He had been thinking how to go about asking, and didn't want to explicitly say he would be filming this group, but he didn't want to begin until he had checked.

The Congolese official seemed to notice James for the first time, and he began to ask the women. James hoped the man would phrase it as carefully as he had, and perhaps he did for the woman who was answering shrugged her shoulders and nodded at James. He began to work quietly, turning away from them initially to take shots of their surroundings, but he knew that the images would only work if there were pictures of the people here and he slowly picked his way around the shelter until he could take shots of the group, of the children individually and the exhausted women. They were powerful images, he knew that instantly, but he didn't want to dwell solely on these two women so he carefully stepped through the people sleeping on the ground nearby and made his way with what he hoped was a reassuring smile towards another group resting a few metres away.

They just looked at him nervously in return and sat still, not reacting to the camera when he took their photos nor showing any reluctance to be photographed. He couldn't imagine what these people had been through in recent days – the fear, hunger, thirst, desperation, the loss of family members and homes, and of course the sheer physical challenge of walking for so many days with their children and meagre belongings. He wondered if they had felt a sense of safety and relief when they had reached the camp, been accepted into it and their identities processed before being fed, given new blankets and taken to this shelter. Their losses in the last few days and weeks must have left them feeling isolated and bewildered. In the circumstances, he wondered if he would have submitted to being photographed had his life reached such a low ebb. He didn't want to take advantage of them but he knew that AfriCan Care's work could only continue if people at home saw what was happening here.

He'd been so struck by the plight of the people inside that he'd completely forgotten the rain, and when they eventually left the shelter it was falling harder than ever. James took a spare T-shirt out of his backpack and wrapped it protectively around his camera.

The reek of overflowing toilets that he'd noticed before was even stronger now; the rain probably made it worse and a small rivulet of filth ran from beneath one canvas wall of a camp latrine before reaching a bright green pool of excrement and rain water. It was only a few metres away but James had barely registered it before. In truth it was just three small, white box-like tents with UNHCR markings that had been erected over a structure of wooden poles. The doors were loose flaps of tarpaulin that constantly blew open in the wind, emitting an appalling stench. James knew he would avoid using it, and then realised he hadn't seen anyone else use it either – it would surely be preferable to go in the scrub somewhere.

Nearby a boy of eight or nine years old stood hunched against the rain in the lee of the shelter James had been in. The lad was wrapped in a thin piece of black cotton material and wore some kind of kilt or wrap beneath. His feet were in flip flop sandals that were much too big for him and the rain was running down his face. The boy's gaze wandered to others who were scurrying for shelter but still he stood unmoving in the rain. James took a few photos of him and smiled at him when his gaze returned but there was no response. He could easily have found shelter nearby yet he stood alone, and his feeble protection from the elements struck James forcibly.

Why wasn't he looking for some shelter, didn't he have anyone to go to? Surely, he must have some friends or family in the camp. The boy didn't react at all when James offered him a piece of chewing gum. He allowed it to be pressed into his palm but made no effort to unwrap it. James pointed to his own mouth and mimed an elaborate chewing action. Still the boy said nothing, looking only briefly at the gum before returning James's gaze. It dawned on him that the boy had never seen gum before, so James took the stick out of the wrapper for him and put it back in his hand, before pointing at the boy's mouth once more. This time the boy raised it to his lips and put the stick in his mouth.

A look of concentration flitted across his tired features, and a fleeting smile came and went as he began to chew. Belatedly James tried to mime that he must not swallow the gum, but he gave up after a few efforts when it clearly puzzled the boy again. "You ready?" said a voice behind him and James swung round to see Aidan.

"Sure, I'll be right there." By the time James turned back again the boy was walking unhurriedly away. James wanted to ask him a hundred questions, but there was a language barrier, and the momentary connection had passed. He still had a job of work to do; all he could do was take some poignant images of a lone child walking away oblivious to the rain that continued to fall on both of them. James was looking into the light which made it more challenging to get the right image. The sun was still high and it shot bright blades of light through narrow gaps in the heavy clouds, creating a brilliant halo around the boy that contrasted with the lowering dark grey and silvery wet backdrop of the huts and the hills beyond. The rain was driving hard but he was satisfied that one or two of the images were truly striking. Yet James could not feel pleased – he wondered where the boy would sleep tonight, who if anyone would look out for him and whether he was still at risk here in the camp. James was still thinking of him a long time afterwards.

No words were exchanged when he rejoined Aidan and the group; they all seemed weighed down by their thoughts as they began to move off on foot. For perhaps the first time since they had arrived he looked about him with the eye of a layman and not a photographer, and as he did so he began to take in the magnitude and character of the camp. The lines of shelters were highly regimented, and yet confusion and chaos were being held back by frail defences.

As the rain diminished, they passed a couple of cooking fires being urged back to life. Both fires were alarmingly close to the plastic shelters, presumably to give protection from the wind that whipped through the lines of tents and huts. It wasn't cold but it threw stinging rain into their faces as they walked, and it was hard to imagine how anyone could stay dry for long in these circumstances. Young children stood watching and waiting for their meal, occasionally helping the adults bring up enough logs to keep the fires going through the night.

A few metres further on the group passed a woman selling stacks of thin brushwood that she had set out in bundles. They were piled up beneath tarpaulins on the driest piece of ground in sight, and she was surrounded by buyers and casual watchers. All about them stood an assortment of bright blue, green or orange tents pitched closely together with little room to move between them. This proximity gave them modest shelter from the strong wind which swept north from the lake, buffeting these fragile shelters hard before sweeping away across the few kilometres of flat land leading to the volcano.

As the charity group walked, the road opened without warning onto a vast open space bounded on three sides by a scattering of small trees and scrub bushes, and on the other by a long, uneven line of tents and shelters. The UNHCR must have cleared the land here with bulldozers in readiness for more refugees. Soon, he suspected, most of this ground would also be covered in tents and toilet blocks, homemade shelters, rough market squares and water tanks. The trees at the edge of the cleared ground were immature; this area would have been one of the first to be overrun by the lava flow from Nyiragongo's last serious eruption barely a decade before. He realised he had no idea what the forecasts were for future volcanic activity but there were arguably more pressing matters to attend to on this fact-finding visit, and after discussions between Sarah and two UN officials his party had turned sharp right and was making for a health clinic in the heart of the camp.

He would be needed there but he hung back behind the group for a moment photographing the volcano and the camp's setting as best he could in the grey morning light. The sun was about to break through the clouds above the mountain top, but there would be better opportunities to capture its drama. He had been so absorbed by all that he was learning today that this was the first time since reaching the area that he had really taken in the enormity of the volcano's looming presence.

Here at ground level he could begin to understand the terror that must have been caused by the first explosions and the clouds of smoke and ash. It was hard, though to imagine the panic that would have followed a full-scale eruption making the sky as dark as night, and obliterating everything in the lava's path, starting ten kilometres north of here and running all the way to Lake Kivu the same distance south.

He pulled his thoughts back to the present, but when he turned back to his party they had disappeared. Shit, where had they gone? He knew roughly which path they had taken but from this distance the tents all looked the same and so did the paths between them. He sprinted after the group, trying to re-wrap his camera in the T-shirt as he ran, but when he reached the point on the tent perimeter where he thought he'd seen them go there was no sign of them.

He sprinted down the alleyway, past a smiling boy who was stepping carefully over the guy ropes as he carried his young brother on his back. A heavily pregnant woman waddled slowly along in front of him blocking James's path for a while until eventually he was able to squeeze past with an apology and ran on, looking left and right down every side route in case his group had taken a detour. Then he was held up by a crocodile of ten or twelve small children holding hands as they slowly followed a teenager through the alleyway. At any other time each of these obstacles would have made great photos but he was starting to imagine how hard it would be to locate his party among more than fifty thousand people if he didn't find them soon.

He carried on, dodging between two women who chatted as they carried toddlers in slings on their backs. Two men approaching from the other direction laughed at him as he rocketed past. Then he saw some people heading into a tent further down the pathway. There was a green cross sprayed on a white panel over the door. *Thank God*, he thought, here was the clinic, and he burst in through the doorway, only to find himself surrounded by a startled audience of women and children. Aside from the two women who had entered just ahead of him, everyone was seated in a circle on the ground where they were breast-feeding their babies. It might have been a clinic, but evidently it wasn't the one he was searching for. His colleagues were nowhere to be seen. On a table at the back of the tent scales were being used to weigh the infants. A nurse in a white jacket stopped moving among the mothers and turned towards him at the sound of his intrusion.

Some of the mothers laughed loudly, one child began to cry at the interruption to its feed, and James babbled an apology in English. He was blushing, which only made him more embarrassed. He started to back out of the tent only to find his exit blocked by two large women trying to come in behind him. "I'm sorry," he said, "sorry, I didn't know you were …, I mean …" It was only then that he noticed one other occupant of the tent. She was staring at him coolly, and as he recognised her, Jessica Tsiba slowly began to shake her head in amazement at his entrance.

Oh God, this wasn't happening. She already thought he was a jerk for barrelling into her in Kinshasa and damaging her laptop. His attempts to apologise or make good the damage that he'd done just a few hours earlier had been completely rebuffed, and who could blame her? James had hoped that if they ever met again – and he now realised he had thought about that possibility a lot – he could make it up to her, or at least show her that he wasn't the clumsy oaf he had appeared. *It wasn't even a fair way of describing him*, he thought, but he knew that she would now have this unshakeable impression of him.

"I'm searching for someone," he began feebly, "well, a group. They're from a charity visiting the health centre." He stopped and took a deep breath. Still she said nothing, looking from him to the feeding mothers, many of whom were staring at him. "It's Jessica, isn't it?"

A look of puzzlement crossed her face and she frowned at him. "How did you know that?" she asked. Suddenly there was no warmth at all in her voice, and he knew he must seem like a stalker.

"I asked around." That sounded worse when he'd said it aloud than it had in his head. "I mean, when we met before, when I damaged your laptop, I wanted to pay to get it fixed but I didn't even know your name so I asked someone at the reception. They gave me your name, but we left for Goma before I could find you to apologise."

For the first time she smiled slightly. It wasn't much, but in that instant her face lost its stern, professional shell and he glimpsed the woman beneath. "I'm glad you explained," she said, "I was beginning to wonder."

"I can't blame you; I mean what were the chances of meeting you again so soon a thousand miles away? Anyway, I'm just a bit lost. I have to run, I've got to find these people or I'm in deep sh … deep trouble. I'll see you around." It sounded trite to his ears, but this time that casual phrase was sincerely meant.

"Well, whatever your name is …" she began.

"James. James Falkus. From AfriCan Care."

"Well, James Falkus from AfriCan Care, I suggest you leave but this time *don't* run. It only seems to get you into trouble." Jessica nodded over his shoulder and he turned to see a tall, thin, angry-looking nurse making her way to him through the throng of mothers and babies sitting on the ground. The nurse was stepping carefully through groups of breast-feeding mothers, and as she waved him away with irritable, dismissive flicks of her hand she was making the kind of shooing noises that one might save for a dim-witted sheep.

James turned back to Jessica and returned the smile. "Something tells me I'm not needed here."

"You think?" she teased, and raised one immaculate eyebrow. It made the whites of her eyes even brighter in the perfect caramel skin. He took in as much of that face as a mind could absorb in a few seconds and then pulled himself together.

"I really have to go; I'm already for the high jump for keeping them waiting."

"I'm not keeping you," she said and turned back to her notes.

"Actually, you are," was what he wanted to say, but the thought was never voiced. All he managed was a wave goodbye and then he backed out of the tent, dodging late arrivals coming in behind him. He willed Jessica to look up at him one last time but she didn't and he exited, pursued by the nurse still making shushing noises as he offered his apologies. The whole episode had lasted barely a minute and yet again it had been characterised on his part by speed but little thought. As the tent flap closed behind him, he heard a shrill ululation from inside, followed by gales of hysterical laughter.

He didn't have time to dwell on his *faux pas*, he dragged his mind back to the problem confronting him. James still had no idea where the rest of his party were. He turned to continue along the path he had been taking, then stopped. Having sprinted in their general direction he felt he must be much closer to them. Would he be able to hear their voices? He stood still for ten or twenty seconds; there were noises from each direction but nothing to indicate which way the party had gone. He slung the backpack carrying his cameras over his shoulder again and walked quickly on, keeping his ears open as well as his eyes.

The path between the tents opened out into a small square, with few distinguishing features other than an extinct fire at its heart. He pressed on until he reached a roadway. This was more like it, maybe this would help him see them or at least get his bearings. With the mountain at his back he knew that he must be heading towards the entrance. And then he heard a high-pitched whine, a noise that he recognised but at first couldn't place, until he realised it was the sound of a dentist's drill. And where there was a dentist, he reasoned, there might well be a general practice health clinic. The sound was intermittent and had carried on the still afternoon air so that it was a couple of minutes before he was able to track it to its source.

Sure enough, when he reached the clinic there was his group and a distinctly frosty reception from Sarah and Aidan. The UN officers, on the other hand, grinned from ear to ear as he was given a public dressing down for getting lost and wasting their valuable time in the camp, time that he was told could have been well spent taking shots of the clinic, the doctors, the single dentist, and a harassed team of nurses trying to cope with another influx of desperately weak new arrivals at the camp. James set to work capturing the scene and the next two hours flashed past; he paused only to change memory cards or swop cameras, and later on to accept a welcome drink of sweet black tea and some unleavened bread that helped to allay the hunger pangs starting to nag at him.

Sarah had meetings to get to and she left him to get on with his own job, with strict instructions not to wander off again.

"We need ya here gettin' on with the job in hand," said Aidan, "we've nae time to nurse you or send out search parties, so bloody stay on it." The boot was definitely on the other foot now. This morning on the way to the camp, James had been the blue-eyed boy while Aidan was being watched like a hawk by his boss. Now, the metaphorical mud had hit the air-conditioning and suddenly he was the one being lectured on his duties and work rate by the erstwhile bad boy.

When he had exhausted the possibilities for further shots inside the clinic, James went out to get some air. The clouds now appeared even heavier, lower and leaden grey. The humidity was becoming oppressive and although there was still direct sunlight the low angles and harsh contrasts were making photography harder. James had been given another cup of tea – it seemed to be the staple drink here – and he was blowing on the surface to cool it when he saw a large black car passing down the road less than twenty metres away. Then another followed it and behind that came a military jeep with a soldier standing in the back manning a heavy machine gun.

James paused with his drink. He didn't understand this, he'd been told that the Congolese army, the FARDC, was forbidden by the UN to enter the camp. Surely it was a UN agency running the camp, wasn't it? How had they let these guys in, and who the hell were they?

Both the cars were large modern Mercedes saloons, or sedans as he'd known them in Boston, highly polished and with blacked out windows. That alone would have marked them out here among the few dusty, mud-spattered vehicles. James lost sight of them for a moment but could still hear the deep rumble of the accompanying jeep's engine. He burned his lips on the tea as he sipped it too quickly, so he set it down on a nearby stack of pallets.

Then he saw the vehicles again. They had now turned sharp right off the central roadway and were making their way more slowly along a narrow lane between the tents and huts where they came to a halt. His curiosity was aroused by the incongruous sight of smart, new limousines and armed guards in such a godforsaken setting. James took a few steps to his right and the arrivals were in sight again twenty to thirty metres away. He wasn't needed in the tent now, he'd got all the shots he could get inside and Aidan had told him to wait here for them so that was what he would do.

Evidently, other people had been waiting for this entourage. Several men stepped forward into his view to open the rear doors of both cars. Three smartly suited men stepped out of the first Mercedes, then uniformed and senior military officers climbed from the second car. Not only did the brass buttons and cap badges show they were senior officers, but it was immediately clear that the new arrivals were no strangers to their hosts. There were brief salutes from the military men then broad smiles all round, vigorous handshakes, some back slapping and a bear hug between two of the figures at the centre of attention.

It seemed that one of the visitors was a guest of honour, and looking through his telephoto lens James had the strongest feeling that he'd seen a couple of these men somewhere before, but he had no idea how this could be. Then it came to him, at least partially; one of the men that he recognised in this welcoming party had been at Goma airport; his size and commanding attitude made him quite recognisable. He was a tall, well-built Congolese colonel who had been dealing with MONUSCO's top brass at the airport. Yet, oddly, here he was in one of the UNHCR's refugee camps.

James knew from the conversation with UN officials when they arrived that the Congolese army was not allowed in the camp. Although it lay well within Congo and miles from the Rwandan border it wasn't even open to senior officers from the host nation. Perhaps that rule might not apply to UN soldiers, but they could be readily identified by their blue flak jackets, helmets and berets. And they drove in white vehicles – these guys were not from the UN. They were Africans, not the Asians who made up a large part of the MONUSCO force here.

As a senior army officer – and a uniformed one at that – UN regulations forbade him even to be here. What was more, he was greeting guests in different uniforms as though he was the host. The colonel welcomed one suited figure as an old friend. This was now bugging James, who prided himself on his photographic memory for faces; he was sure he'd seen the guest too, but it hadn't been at the airport. James knew so few people in Congo that he thought that he must be mistaken.

He was up-sun from this group and in the dusk they didn't see him step back into the darkened doorway of a tent from where he could watch the mysterious arrivals. He'd taken so many photos today that it had become second nature to record everything he saw, and as the sun began to go down he adjusted the camera to the failing light and kept shooting.

One of the striking features of the group was their obvious warmth with one another and their laughter. Although it was clearly a serious gathering with everyone dressed in either business suits and ties or parade uniforms, it was evident that many of them knew one another well. Their open display of friendship was in marked contrast to their secretive arrival in limousines with blacked out windows. Add to this the meeting's curious location in the middle of a refugee camp and it was hard to escape the feeling that this gathering was furtive, even secret – in which case they probably weren't keen to be seen by outsiders which intrigued him more. The heavily armed jeep, the soldiers and black-suited security guards surrounding the vehicles simply added to the mystery.

He continued taking photos until all the introductions had been made and welcome formalities were completed, at which point the hosts ushered their VIP guests into one of the larger tents out of his line of sight. Two soldiers climbed out of the jeep, and joined the Mercedes drivers who were partially obscured as they talked with the security detail on the door. This left one soldier manning the machine gun, and he was only interested in getting one of the cigarettes that were being handed out. Although James couldn't hear what they said, there was occasional laughter as they exchanged banter and waited for their masters to reappear. One of the soldiers went back to the jeep's passenger seat, pulled his cap over his eyes and settled down for a snooze; it looked as though this could be a lengthy meeting.

He wasn't entirely sure why he'd taken so many photos of them, except that they aroused his curiosity. He had spent the day trying to blend into the background in order not to affect the charity team's work or the reactions of those they were supporting. So, it had seemed only natural to stay in the background as he shot the VIPs' arrival.

The whole thing was odd, but he could ask his team later if anyone knew who they were. He needed to stay with his group now, so he put the cameras away, hoisted the backpack onto his shoulder and emerged into the lane to hook up with his colleagues in the clinic. If he considered it at all, James would have thought that he was just one more white guy moving around a health clinic, and would attract no particular attention. The hope was misplaced. One soldier nudged his neighbour and gestured with his cigarette towards the tall young white man who had emerged from a tent less than thirty paces away and shouldered a pack onto his back. Unlike the few other white officials in the vicinity, this one wore no white lab coat.

******

When the AfriCan Care delegation approached their waiting minibus outside the camp entrance block, a handful of men were standing nearby, watching them with bored expressions. They must have seen hundreds of visitors come and go; there was nothing special about these.

James waited for the formal goodbyes to finish, but he was surprised at himself. Despite all the harrowing photos he had taken throughout the day of homeless families, sick mothers and under-nourished children, it was the final images of a meeting of powerful men in an incongruous setting that now stuck in his mind. He couldn't unravel the enigma of their meeting, in a refugee camp of all places. All he knew was that it didn't look normal.

The guns had made him nervous and James was relieved to find there was no one at the gate to quiz him about what he had seen of the meeting in the camp. All the same, he was keen to get into the minibus and be out of here. Photos of refugees on his camera were one thing but he imagined that his final photos in the camp would take a bit of explaining.

The handshakes and thanks were eventually finished and at last the driver came out of the entrance block, and threw open the van's sliding doors. Sarah, Aidan, Serge and their two interpreters climbed in ahead of him and he was just about to follow when a man's voice rang out behind him.

A question had been asked but James had no idea whether it was in Kiswahili, Lingala or something else. He was anxious to be off and began to climb into the vehicle. But the shout came again, this time louder, much more insistent, and there was the sound of running feet behind him. Suddenly, there was a tug at his elbow and a strong hand stopped his progress and pulled him around.

He half expected to be confronted by soldiers, but there were no troops. A short stocky young man in a dirty green vest and shorts stood before him and he had the attention of everyone around. He was smiling and jabbering a question at James who could not understand a word and simply shrugged his shoulders. The man was also waving something in his hand so excitedly that it took James a moment to identify a memory card that he had been carrying in a side pocket in his bag. It must have fallen out when he'd put his bag down. It was slim enough to slip out underneath the flap and that was why he generally put them together in a zipped pocket, only today he'd kept an empty card spare in a more readily accessible side pocket.

From inside the van, one of the interpreters said, 'He wants to know if this chip is yours.'

"It is. Please thank him for me." He was embarrassed at this evidence of further apparent disorganisation. "It's an empty card, a spare," said James, trying to make light of his slip up. "But please thank him very much." Serge just stared at James and shook his head in disbelief.

A few moments later, as the van bounced through the puddles on its way out of the gate, Sarah said, "I reckon that's what we'll call you."

"What's that?" asked James, then wished he hadn't.

"Chip." It was said more in resignation than humour. And she turned around in her seat and went to sleep.

He couldn't blame her; looking back on today his performance had been lamentable. Until she saw the striking and harrowing images that he knew he'd nailed, what was she supposed to believe? He was eager to improve his standing in the group and perhaps that would start when they got back to their rooms and he was able to show them the photos on his laptop.

He was normally an efficient person but he'd had a run of bad luck since he got here, and it troubled him to be misunderstood like this. Perhaps it was because he was feeling his way into a career as a photographer, instead of staying in his comfort zone in public relations.

Had he known about it, however, James would have been far more concerned by a phone ringing in the gatehouse a few miles behind them. The UN official there could only tell the soldier who was shouting down the line at him, that the group from the charity had left at least ten minutes earlier and it was too late to stop them. Who did he want, the official asked, but the caller had already hung up.

Chapter 15
Gisenyi City, Rwanda. Close to the DRC border
Two Weeks Ago

Few cities in the world are as intertwined with a neighbouring country as Congo's Goma and Rwanda's Gisenyi. Viewed from the air you might never know these are two cities. The border runs through the middle and there are only two crossing points between the two, Grande and Petite Barrière, the Great and Small Gates. Life is seldom straight forward here, as Axel knew well, so perhaps inevitably it is Petite Barrière that is the larger and busier crossing point. A disparity in wealth between the two cities is soon evident; the Rwandan side boasting a purpose-built border control office and a paved road, the Congolese side having neither.

It was through this border gate that Axel had crossed into Rwanda in the early afternoon. He crossed on foot with a minimum of delay, being greeted as arranged by Martin, his long-time driver and bodyguard. The house Axel was renting in Gisenyi was set in the immaculately tended grounds of L'Arc en Ciel Hotel on the north shore of Lake Kivu. He was well known here and would sometimes take a house for himself. If he wanted to have guests or to meet people discretely, there were other houses in the gardens where they could stay. On this occasion, Axel had chosen it for its comforts during what promised to be a lengthy stay and for its ready access to Gisenyi and to Goma across the border. Best of all was the privacy that the hotel afforded some of his guests who would rather not let it be known they were meeting him. Deniability, wasn't that how Washington politicians put it?

As soon as he saw Axel, Martin shouldered his way through the throng, batting away any interference from the Rwandan Customs authorities and ushering him to the hired white Mercedes that waited outside. It was far from new but spotlessly clean, unlike the vehicles that surrounded it, and Axel relaxed into the back seat. He knew his way around Goma, but it was bigger, dirtier and altogether more stressful than Gisenyi. Besides, the business he needed to do would demand discretion, patience and access to senior figures from both sides of the border.

The smart but elderly Mercedes' air-conditioning was unequal to the task of dispelling the midday heat and humidity, so Axel put the window down and enjoyed the breeze as they made their way from the crossing to the lake shore. Soon they had left the paved road and were driving through the hot, dusty streets of Gisenyi. Just looking out of the window confirmed his earlier impression that ordinary people here seemed better dressed and the shops were more prosperous than their counterparts in Goma. Most of the shops were shut at this time in the afternoon, a 'Papeterie' or stationers announced itself in italic script on an elegant signboard as his car sped by, and its shutters of vibrant blue were only outdone by the intense azure sky above.

He was tired, he had been on the move for most of the past week, staying in cheap hotels around Goma and keeping a low profile as he flitted from office to office talking to the comptoir owners about their coltan business, seeing whose mining connections might be flexible enough to take the conversation further with him.

A couple of firms had played their cards very close to their chests, searching for information on his client. One comptoir owner had been openly dismissive of his prospects of bringing anything new to the table, focusing only on his meagre experience outside the gold and gemstone trades. That had been a short, frustrating meeting. One of the counting houses had immediately shown interest in the new business that Axel promised to bring them, but on closer inspection Axel doubted their ability to provide the quantities of coltan he was looking for.

The Mercedes was able to make good time to the hotel. There were few cars around but their journey was frequently slowed by trucks, motorbikes and pedestrians. Axel could tell they were close to the lake as he could still make out the tops of the harbour cranes.

Then the car swung left beside a scattering of single storey concrete shop fronts and began to head eastward again up an unmade road. Gradually the busy streets gave way to high walls built around large houses. The roads narrowed slightly and were edged by storm drains, dry now but deep enough to swallow a scooter. There were occasional trees behind the walls and the foliage grew thicker and thicker as they made their way further from the city centre. At this time of day it was mainly women walking along the roads, many of them carrying large loads home from the market. One had a huge bundle of rags on her back, while her companion somehow balanced a stack of blankets so tall that they seemed bound to topple. A group of men dressed identically in workmen's blue overalls strode along together, deep in conversation. They drove past the Alpha Computer Centre, its doors wide open to keep the air moving but probably spreading a film of dust over all the hardware.

The road they were on began to deteriorate yet curiously the houses behind the high walls were growing in size and status the further they went. There were driveways here protected from prying eyes by elegant, white wrought iron gates backed by brown or red painted sheet metal. Even the perimeter walls in this part

235

of Gisenyi began to show greater wealth, and sections of crisp white-painted railing were backed by shining new sheets of galvanised corrugated iron. The determination to keep out uninvited guests was emphasised by the size of the spikes that topped the panel-effect gates. The gates were steel, mounted on heavy rollers and with an inspection window let into one side. Less mock-tudor, more mock-welcome.

******

When he reached it, the hotel and villa was everything Axel remembered it to be. His luggage was being taken to his room by porters in brightly coloured uniform shirts, but he stopped for a moment to take in his surroundings and stood on a path that wound its way through the immaculate gardens. He had no idea what they were but he wasn't oblivious to the hydrangeas that spilled over the balcony of one of the villas or the pink and white frangipani that lined the garden.

It was the hottest part of the day but he could hear fishermen on the lake chanting to synchronise their paddling as they drove their canoe through the water almost a mile away. Their harmonious voices carried clearly to him across the water, the notes rising and falling above the constant buzz of insects and hum of birds in the plants at either side of the lawn.

The long lush grass sloped down to the lakeshore. From his vantage point on the upper pathway Axel was able to look for miles out over the lake, across the top of a row of thatched shelters built on the beach to shield sun-worshippers. The vast lake continued out of sight to his left before curving back into view on the other side of a large bay. It was hot and the air was hazy at this time in the afternoon but he could make out some large houses on the far shore, embraced by trees on three sides. The signs of affluence were unmistakable and completely at odds with the impressions of Africa he regularly saw on European and American TV.

To his immediate left low palm fronds moved idly in the welcome breeze. Beneath them a vivid array of flowers was set in well-tended beds that bordered the close clipped grass. He was the only guest in view, and it would have spoiled the moment to have shared it. He could hear a couple of the porters talking in the nearest villa where they had taken his bags. Otherwise, the gardens and the shoreline were his to enjoy alone. Tiny waves, more like ripples, lapped at the beach of brown sand, and he could make out a man working in the hotel's speedboat that he remembered using on a previous visit. Its black hull rocked slightly from his movements and he watched as the boatman washed down the pale deck.

Two long fishing boats came into view from the west; they were being paddled but their large size made him wonder if they could be described as canoes. The boats were clearly working in tandem with long poles suspended from their midpoints and dangling over the heads of the forward paddlers.

Martin had gone ahead with the bell boys to check the house was secure and soon he reappeared further down the pathway, signalling with a circled thumb and index finger to his boss that all was OK. The building was as comfortably appointed as the hotel; the hall was wide and opened up to a galleried first floor landing. The immaculate white walls contrasted with sand-coloured polished stone tiles. The furniture and fittings were all modern and would not have been out of keeping in a luxury Mediterranean villa. A small infinity pool was shared with the empty guesthouse next door and a glass-fronted fridge behind a bar appeared well stocked with white wine, beers and soft drinks. The luggage was taken to his room upstairs and once they had checked that Axel needed nothing more the staff melted away as only good staff can.

******

Axel was never entirely comfortable with a security man around him. Invariably he found their intrusions too much or too little, but he had worked with one local company many times and found their international mix of staff well trained, discreet, and affordable. Martin was no exception. Until recently a sergeant in the Rwandan Army, he spoke French and English in addition to local languages including Kinyarwanda. He carried a sidearm, was a good shot, trained in unarmed combat and was a formidable driver. Best of all in Axel's book, he wasn't in your face.

Martin preceded Axel to dinner in the hotel on the first night and after a word with the Maître D, he found Axel a table in the corner with easy access to an escape route through the kitchen. Axel wasn't expecting trouble but he was working in a sensitive sector and it did no harm to be prepared. Martin sat in the bar from where he could see anyone approaching or leaving the restaurant while he nursed a long cold tonic water. The only time he stood up was to check the kitchens when someone dropped a plate.

When it was time to leave, Martin left first while the bill was presented to Axel for signature. Axel followed at a slower pace, savouring the night air as he ambled through the gardens. It was only when he passed through the open French windows from the terrace that he knew something was wrong. Martin lay motionless on the stone floor; he appeared to be unconscious and a large cut on his head was bleeding heavily on the floor. There was no time to react before two heavy-set men with machine pistols stepped out of the shadows on either side of the entrance and pointed their guns at Axel. One gestured to him to sit down on the sofa with Martin on the floor beside him while the other gave a soft whistle.

The kitchen door opened and a tall man with a ramrod-straight back walked in and wordlessly sat on the opposite sofa. His dark black skin was in marked contrast to the white leather sofa on which he sat, and although he was dressed in a business suit he carried a swagger stick in his right hand as if he had just stepped off a parade ground. Occasionally he tapped it against his elegantly tailored trousers.

"I'm unarmed and I'm going to lean forward now and dress that head wound," said Axel. There was a stirring from the two men by the door, but their boss gave a contemptuous flick of his stick in acknowledgement. Axel took a cotton throw that lay over the back of his sofa, ripped it down the middle, folded it into the width of a bandage and bound it firmly around Martin's head before tucking the loose end in at one side. It wasn't perfect but it would apply some pressure to the wound and might help stop the bleeding. Head wounds were always messy. The security man was still unconscious but Axel checked that his breathing was steady and moved his leg to put him in the recovery position.

The intruders watched all this with silent disinterest.

"OK, who the fuck are you and what do you want?" Axel was not about to let them intimidate him with their nocturnal invasion.

"Let's start this way," said the seated man in a deep and strangely familiar voice. "Are you Mr Axel Terberg?"

"I am. Who are you?"

"We haven't met, but I am the eldest son of General Moise Businga who you met recently in Kinshasa." He scanned the room as he said this, as if looking for recording devices. "I am Major Louis Businga. For security, just confirm for me where you met my father?" He spoke English with a South African accent; presumably he had had some education there.

"In the Palace Hotel, two weeks ago."

"Good. I didn't want to talk over the phone but my father says it's important for us to meet and from what I hear I think he's right."

"And what have you heard?" asked Axel.

Businga didn't answer directly. "I want you to meet someone who I think will be a good business partner for you."

"I choose my own business partners," said Axel.

"Well, when you have met him I'm sure you will choose this one," said Businga calmly. "Alternatively, we can take this man away with us and send him back to you a piece at a time, until you learn to co-operate."

"Do what you like, he's just the hired help."

"Your little display of first aid tells me that you aren't the kind of man who would want to see him suffer unnecessarily. So shall I continue?"

Axel said nothing and waited for Businga to continue. "We want to ... no, we expect to play a leading role in your new trading venture, Mr Terberg. You have been of passing interest to us in the past, but frankly your impact on our gemstone markets was too small to be of much concern. Now you appear to be playing with the big boys, and you're doing it in coltan which is a key national asset."

Axel snorted in derision at Businga's concern for national assets. "What is it that interests you about our trade in particular?" he demanded.

"Oh, just about everything in this deal, Mr Terberg. From the mines that supply you, through your would-be partners in the comptoirs, to your choice of transport links out of Congo and your transport agents in Kigali. We have friends in all these areas who are only too willing to work with you, for the right price of course."

"Of course," said Axel.

"Our contact will come here tomorrow at eleven o'clock. His name is SK Zaidi. You will be here." The last was a statement, not a question. Businga Junior was clearly used to getting his own way.

Axel wasn't going to give him the satisfaction of seeing that he could walk in and take over the deal. Then again they held the guns and the aces. "I'll think about it," he said noncommittally.

"Of course, you will. And then I am sure you will sensibly come around to my way of thinking. We both know that if you do not, Mr Terberg, you will lose the up side on this deal, and there will be a very costly downside to pay. If you decide to work through us, not only do you get to keep some control of your trading but you will find that you are suddenly playing in the big league, you will be dealing with the strongest partners in the region's coltan trade – partners in the mines, in the comptoirs, in logistics, and in smoothing the path through official channels."

"You are a business man, playing at a higher level than before, so you see it really is that simple. There will be no hard feelings among your customary partners; they will see that they have been outbid. We share our supplies with you, and you share your customers with us. Believe me; the alternative would be very distressing. You may be out of your depth but I don't think you're a fool Mr Terberg, so I hope I don't have to spell it out to you."

Axel was about to speak, but Businga Junior raised a finger. "Of course, if you are unwise enough to reject our offer of support, not only will all these avenues be closed to you but we can and will ensure that not a single kilo of coltan reaches your clients." He smiled, "You know, it's funny. I already think of them as our shared clients. Anyway, I presume that's clear enough for you, Axel." There was a heavy emphasis on his first name. Perhaps it was meant to demonstrate that they knew him intimately, but whatever the objective, Axel was immune to it. He was simply struggling to see a way around this intervention.

He urgently needed to talk to the Americans and in particular to Payne Rawlings. They had got him into this, they had insisted he immerse himself in the grubby end of this market, buying and selling a mineral that bored him shitless. Without them he would probably be enjoying a long cold beer right now with a stunning view over Dubai, and maybe with some equally attractive company. Instead he was listening to threats from the psychopath son of a murdering bastard, knowing that he couldn't just tell him to stick his deal. If he did, Businga & Son would probably see he ended his days at the bottom of Lake Kivu, or the Americans would escort him onto an early plane back to Lusaka and a very unpleasant reception.

The money he was promised was nowhere near enough to make it worth swallowing this much crap from Louis Businga. Axel wondered if the Americans would accept this major change to the deal. On the upside, it demonstrated where the real power lay in this market, which was partly what the Yanks wanted to know. He would still be able to demonstrate to them how quickly a major new customer could tap into big supplies of coltan. It was then up to someone else at the Agency to follow the supplies and see where they led, to see if – as Axel still suspected – the corporate customer was in China. What they'd do with that information he had no idea; he was already in over his head and just trying to keep a deal, any deal, afloat for long enough to hand over to Langley and get the hell out of here with his pink skin still in one piece and carrying whatever remuneration he could take with him.

Axel would be able to show them where the real power lay in eastern Congo, assuming they didn't already know. Of course, Rawlings would demand to know how Axel had so quickly lost control of the trade they'd asked him to set up. All he could say was that this way he was on the inside of the deal instead of being carved out of it completely. He still 'owned' the customer, as it were. They hadn't demanded the customer's details from him. Well, not yet. But Axel was under no illusions that they would want that soon. Then his role would be over as far as they were concerned; that would be when it became truly dangerous for him and some insurance would be necessary.

If the CIA dug their heels and rejected the Busingas' approach, he'd need some strong protection. On the other hand, if the CIA agreed the change of deal the only benefit that Axel could see for himself personally was that all the political and logistical hassles he had been wrestling with would land in the Busingas' Inbox. The Congolese would squeeze him out of the deal and he would know too much for his own safety; that's when things would get even more dangerous for him. Once Axel had divulged CCV's identity and perhaps effected an introduction, he would be surplus to requirements. He would swiftly lose his status as an asset to the Busingas and their partners, and become a liability at which point he'd either need some life insurance in the form of future value, or some fast wheels.

Neither scenario was looking good for a happy retirement.

There was a groan from floor-level as Martin began to come round. Axel guessed he'd been pistol-whipped by someone here who didn't care how hard he hit him. If Martin was to be OK, he'd need a doctor and an X-ray soon, and Axel would see that he got them. The man was part of his team and he'd saved Axel more than once in the past – he still owed Martin plenty.

"Rest assured, Mr Terberg," said Businga, "SK has complete authority to act on our behalf – I won't get involved. Unless I have to, that is." He looked pointedly at Axel and his gaze dropped to Martin whom he regarded with distaste before quietly rising to his feet. It wasn't just Louis Businga's facial resemblance to his father that was striking, the major was every bit as physically imposing and just as contemptuous of others.

There didn't seem much left to ask that wouldn't be better discussed tomorrow with their agent, so Axel said nothing and just watched as Businga left through the French windows, at which point another man emerged from the darkness holding a semi-automatic rifle. They formed an envelope around the major, and the two in the room melted away into the darkness as quickly as they had appeared, taking their lead from their leader's speed of movement which increased noticeably as he stepped outside.

This was a highly professional team, but it was clear that Major Businga was keen to be out of the area and maybe to slip back over the border. Axel checked on Martin then stepped outside in time to see a single black Mercedes SUV swing out of the main gate above the house. He heard the large petrol engine rev as it sped off into the night.

For someone based in Kinshasa, General Dr Moise Businga's reach seemed pretty effective 1,000 miles to the east, and in a foreign country at that. Axel had been warned by General Businga himself that he would be keeping a watch on Axel's business; he had obviously under-estimated the man's power as well as his greed. What had appeared to be an arm's-length interest in Axel's business had turned into a forcible demand to control the trade. He knew these were not men to be lightly ignored, certainly not on their home turf. He could pursue his own routes to market and ignore them, of course, but Uncle Sam wanted to see who the key players were and this time the players had come to him. Now he needed to discuss the proposed change of plan with the Americans but he could do that over the phone later, and he had a feeling they'd agree to it for the information it would bring about both ends of the mineral supply chain.

Meanwhile, Axel went back into the house and placed a call to his office in the capital, Kigali. The call was diverted to a mobile and answered immediately by his personal assistant. "Listen hard, this line's not secure but I've got Martin here, he's semi-conscious and he's had a nasty fall. He needs medical attention and soon. You know where I'm staying, I'm in villa 5, and it would be better all-round if whoever you send comes in the back way when they collect him. I'll wait with him, but I need to leave in one hour for another meeting; I'll call you with my destination details as soon as he's gone. Oh and Franca, I need you to find me a replacement for Martin. Hopefully temporary, but," he looked down at the man's recumbent form, "you never know. I don't care how much it costs; make it someone good, OK?"

Axel put the phone down and checked Martin's pulse again, it was surprisingly strong. The bleeding had stopped but the floor was a helluva mess. "Tough old bastard, aren't you?" he muttered, and poured himself a scotch while he waited next to his prone bodyguard.

******

The meeting with SK Zaidi the following night could have been an anti-climax after Businga junior's melodramatic entrance. Instead Axel found himself having a surprisingly convivial dinner in his villa with the managing director of one of Goma's leading coltan wholesalers, Comptoir Gosomines. SK Zaidi proved to be a very different kettle of fish from his client and protector, Louis Businga; first of all he came in through the front door, and second he brought no heavyweight enforcement. He clearly didn't feel he needed it.

A small, wizened man of Indian extraction, SK appeared to be in his late seventies, maybe more. What he lacked in height or youth he more than made up for in intellect. He was razor sharp and a great deal more cultured than Businga Junior. Far from the business being a challenge, it proved surprisingly easy to transact. If he didn't know the Businga's better, Axel might have relaxed his guard.

'SK' Zaidi said little at first, asking only for the details of Axel's requirements. They shared an excellent fish while talking at length about the diamond and coltan markets, and the challenges that politics placed on their respective businesses. To Axel's surprise there was no haggling and no mention at all of the Busingas who had thrown them together; to the casual observer this would have seemed a business dinner like any other.

The older man took the conversation in his own direction. He quizzed Axel closely on his upstream business links, while wanting to understand the strengths and weaknesses of Axel's company and the extent of his political connections. He would have been able to judge Axel's connections in Kinshasa through his introduction by the Businga family, but this last part of the conversation involved polite but persistent probing and SK seemed sceptical until Axel revealed a little more about his contacts on both sides of the border, as well as in Europe and the States. Then the older man asked about the end user, but Axel would only say that the coltan was being flown to Macao in China.

"It may seem impertinent but I have to ask you, Mr Terberg," said Zaidi, "how is it that you come to be involved in this market when most of your experience lies in other areas – albeit with some business crossover?" The old man's eyes twinkled with a smile, but Axel was glad to have kept a clear head for he knew every word would be analysed and could be repeated to the General. Axel had learned as a

242

child that to lie convincingly it was best to stick as closely to the truth as you dared.

"It's very simple really, SK. I was made an offer that I could hardly refuse. An old friend in Europe recommended me as an agent for a new client who is eager to make an impression in the market."

"I think we can both agree they have already done that," Zaidi smiled as he spoke. "Certainly my principal is adamant that we shall do business together and he is not accustomed to being let down." SK's quiet sigh was pregnant with meaning.

"I understand. My client's primary expectation of me was my business and political connections here – at all levels – so I'm glad to meet you. You and I have a price, we've agreed a delivery schedule that could give the quantities my client requires. So, unless there is anything else we need to agree, shall we conclude for now with a toast? I suggest Long Life and Happiness."

"I have the advantage over you, Mr Terberg. I have already had a long life, but there is always room for more happiness." And with a frail hand he raised his glass of lemonade and the two men toasted one another watchfully.

Chapter 16
Goma, North Kivu, DRC
Two Weeks Ago

James couldn't remain the unidentified photographer at the camp for long. A few questions at the clinic showed that they had been visited by AfriCan Care, and the Entry Log at the camp gatehouse listed the five people from the charity who had entered. One was a woman, and the guards had identified a white male photographer. One was a local interpreter. Of the three remaining charity workers, the health centre staff identified the photographer as James, they didn't have a surname. The Entry Log showed a James Falkus. They had no photo, but now they had a name and the cover he was working under.

When they took their information to the boss, he put his coffee down slowly on the desk as they explained why they had been looking there and showed him mobile phone photos of the log book at the camp gate. He had been kept aware of their search from the moment they first hesitantly raised their concerns that a photographer may have been filming their meeting. His temper and brutality were legendary.

"This is just a precaution, sir. We don't know that he was photographing us, but we know that he could have and no one in the clinic can explain what he was doing in an unused tent overlooking the guests' arrival area. We thought we should investigate further, given the meeting's sensitivity." The head of security appeared calm, but he watched for the tell-tale signs of his boss's imminent explosion. It was not unknown for him to punish people who brought him bad news, so it was critical to present it well. The security officer knew that the consequences of any security breach would be disastrous for all of them and probably terminal for him.

"What are you doing about it, Gahiji?" Major Businga looked him directly in the eye and held his gaze. The boss still liked to use his military title even though he had resigned his commission in the FARDC, the Federal Army of the Democratic Republic of Congo some time ago. It still helped in his line of business.

"We have a man finding the headquarters of this charity. It may be a hotel, an office or a private house – we don't know yet, sir. But we're working on it urgently."

"Dammit, right now he could be sending those photos to whoever he's working for. Right now, you hear me? We cannot afford that to happen." He turned a malevolent gaze on his security officer. "*You* cannot afford that to happen. Is that clear?"

"Yes, very clear sir," said Gahiji.

He did not intend to suffer the same fate as one of Businga's earlier lieutenants. The police were finding pieces of him all over Bukavu for days after he disappeared, but parts of him were never found, probably carried away by the wild animals that occasionally came into the suburbs. No one ever questioned Major Louis Businga officially about his missing aide, but everyone on the base in Bukavu noted that his father made a sudden unannounced visit to the barracks, and not long later the Chief of Police found his daily commute was made more bearable when he took delivery of a brand new BMW.

"Get on with it then."

"Sir." The security officer stood to attention, old habits die hard. Then he turned briskly and left the boss to his thoughts. The driver jumped up as Gahiji left the boss's study.

"Where are we going, boss?"

"Right now, anywhere. Just drive, I've got some calls to make."

******

James was physically exhausted and had fallen asleep straight away. But something had woken him and now he couldn't get back to sleep as his mind replayed episodes from the previous day. Getting lost had been a low point and then he had been berated in front of his new colleagues and the charity's guests. Of course, he'd deserved it by allowing his attention to wander with so many striking images around him. The one saving grace was that he'd had time to look at his photos in the minivan on the way back from the camp and he was confident they included some of the best shots he'd ever taken. He'd need to play it cool, as though these were routine photos for him, but he was quietly hopeful that some of the pictures of refugees, their desperate condition on arrival and their grim existence in the camp would prove his worth to the team.

He continued to turn over in bed, seeking the rest he needed but after another hour James was still wide awake and eager to do something productive. He was sharing a room with Aidan so he got up quietly, put some clothes on and gathering up his laptop and camera gear he tiptoed through to the dining area in their temporary headquarters. He plugged in his laptop and phone to recharge and began transferring all the images that he'd captured during the day. *It must be almost four-thirty in the morning now*, he thought, but he didn't look at his watch, it would only irritate him that he wasn't asleep. It was still dark and he was glad to have time to go through the photos, deleting any that were no use and backing up the rest on his laptop and a separate hard drive. This belt and braces approach had come in handy in the past. When he was a teenager, he'd had his first decent digital camera stolen on a beach. It was only because he had copied all the images the night before that he hadn't also lost the photos, these were far more precious to him than the camera.

He had intended to back up the photos before going to bed, but over supper the team had begun to relax together and to talk. He knew he had a lot of ground to make up with them so he had listened and taken part in the easy-going conversation whenever he could, injecting a bit of humour and learning from their experiences. By the time everyone turned in it was late and he felt a little less like the black sheep of the group than he had before.

With nothing to disturb him, he now worked quickly and silently editing images, discarding those that didn't meet his expectations, cropping a few to remove clutter or extraneous people, and correcting orientations so that the best pictures could be shown to Sarah in the morning as a slide show. He created date and location files so that he could find images quickly when he needed them and by the time the sky began to lighten with the dawn he was happy with most of the shots he had taken since he had arrived. The only ones he had yet to file were the ones he had snatched of soldiers and smartly suited figures arriving for their meeting.

He needed a coffee to wake him up so he found a mug and a jar of instant and put a pan of water on the stove in their sparsely equipped kitchen. It looked as though it would be another hot day. Yesterday's clouds had vanished and the sky was marked only with a few parallel streaks of cirrus. The view across the yard from their ugly little bungalow was enough to show him the sky, but he would have to wait for another day to photograph an African dawn. While he waited for the water to boil he picked up *The Economist* magazine he had bought in London and which he still hadn't finished. He was just about to discard it when something caught his eye.

"Bloody hell! That's him," he said out loud. Staring back at him from a review of recent world news was a photograph of a man he recognised, someone he had seen only yesterday. He took it across to his laptop and pulled up the file of unsorted images from the meeting he had witnessed. He knew it wasn't in the early shots of the cars and jeep arriving. He carried on flicking through the folder. There, among the other suits getting out of the first Merc ... there it was. He enlarged the image. It was him, surely. James snatched up *The Economist* again. Their photo was black and white and quite small but it was a head and shoulders image of one man taken in three quarter profile. He was smiling at someone out of shot, and it was similar to one of James's own images.

He recognised not only the heavy-rimmed glasses and close-cropped hair with a widow's peak, but also his trimmed moustache and a mole high on the left cheekbone. The nose and eyes were the same. There could be little doubt. James's instinct had been right yesterday, he knew that he had seen the man before. So who was he?

He scanned the article on Congo's war-ravaged economy. At last there was said to be more hope that several military successes against rebel fighters could be translated into economic progress. The man in the picture was one of the rebel fighters now being pursued by the Congolese Army and the UN.

That didn't make any sense. How the hell was he able to move around openly here in Goma? And why was he meeting senior Congo army officers so cordially if they were hunting him? And if he was negotiating his surrender to the government, wouldn't it be done like all these things in a foreign country such as Kenya or South Africa, and among politicians not soldiers. They certainly wouldn't meet in a UN refugee camp where access for any military forces was expressly forbidden.

The neglected water was boiling furiously by now and he made himself a coffee before taking it back to the table and re-reading the article. Then he went online to search for more images of the man. James wanted to confirm his identity before he made an ass of himself with any questions. The search revealed few photos of him, and one was taken years ago when he was in the jungle. But the more he looked, the more certain James was that this was Didier Toko, the rebel leader and said to be involved in the Rwandan genocide twenty years before. This was baffling to him.

It was too late to go back to bed and anyway James's head was buzzing with questions so he went back to work. Thirty minutes later he heard footsteps elsewhere in what they laughingly called the villa, followed by the sound of running water. He found a few stale croissants in the fridge and had one to keep himself going, then he closed his computer and went to the bathroom for a shave. Aidan was grumbling to himself as James dug a clean T-shirt out of his kitbag and packed away dirty kit at the bottom where it could protect some camera gear that wouldn't fit in his camera bag.

By the time he got back to the living room, Sarah was moving in and out, drafting emails to her colleagues back in London. She nodded at him but said nothing for a while and taking his lead from her he busied himself by copying and sorting the images that he'd been puzzling over. A period of business-like silence from him wouldn't do any harm.

With no one else appearing she eventually closed her laptop and asked, "You ready for today?" There were no niceties and it was clear that she was still assessing him.

"Certainly," he said.

"You know you were one almighty fuck-up yesterday, don't you?" and it was only now that she raised her eyes and looked long and hard at him. He was startled to hear her talk like that which seemed out of character from the little he knew of her. "There was a point when I was ready to cut you loose, y'know leave you behind at the camp."

"I wouldn't have blamed you," he looked back at her steadily. "I let you down and I'm sorry, it won't happen again." She seemed about to say something more, but he added, "If it's any consolation, I've got some of yesterday's photos to show you. You got a moment?"

Sarah glanced at her watch. "Well, no one's ready to leave yet and I can't talk to London for at least a couple of hours, so why not?"

James turned the laptop to face her and started the slide show of his images of refugees in the camp. Sarah was unsmiling and leaning back in her chair, with a disconnected air. Slowly she began to relax. He knew the images well by now so mostly he watched her. After a minute she unfolded her arms and put her hands in her lap. Then almost imperceptibly she began to lean forward until her elbow was resting on the table and she was entirely focused on the photos fading, scrolling and wiping their way across the screen before her. He could have given it some background music but he was glad he hadn't for the silence between them was much more powerful. When it came to his last and most evocative image of a small boy silhouetted as he walked alone towards the setting sun with the darkest clouds imaginable above his head, she sat staring at the screen for some time. Only then did she look up again and hold his gaze for a moment.

She stood up and at first, her face betrayed nothing. Then there was a smile. "You'll do, Chip!" was all she said, and she turned on her heel, gathered her PC and went back to her room.

******

It took Edouard Gahiji only two calls to locate the charity. His office gave him the number for the UN High Commission for Refugees, and in the second call a helpful UNHCR official looked up the Goma address for the charity team and read it out to him over the phone. Within thirty minutes he and his driver were parked up a little down the road and were watching the anonymous long, low residential property for signs of life.

A couple of windows of the one-storey building were open. He saw someone moving about in one room. He was caught between his boss's fear that the spy would be communicating immediately with whoever sent him, and his own caution about drawing attention to himself. He would have to pretend he was out of range on the mobile if Businga called. So Gahiji and his driver settled down to wait and watch.

******

The charity team left much later that day than they had intended. Even Aidan was up and ready at the planned departure time, but there was no sign of the minivan. Aidan had a smoke and another coffee to kill some time and was evidently bored until he saw James editing some images.

"Are those the pics from yesterday, pal?"

James didn't feel very pally towards him, but he certainly needed an ally. "Yeah, you want to see them?" He didn't want to push it too hard but it wouldn't hurt for Aidan to have a better opinion of him as well.

"Sure, why not?" Aidan stubbed his smoke out in his coffee and leaned closer. James wasn't sure which was worse the coffee breath or the waft of old cigs.

A few shots went by in the same slideshow and the Scotsman had said nothing which worried him. James had been looking at the images, but now he looked sideways at Aidan. He was grinning. James was baffled; there was nothing amusing in the slide deck. The smile persisted and eventually he had to ask. "Why are you smiling?"

"Oh, it's no' the photos, pal. They're good, no they're bloody great. I canna help thinking what Serge will say when he sees 'em, 'cos these shots are everything his pal's weren't. Jeez, they're in focus for a start. But no, seriously, they're good. Have you shown Sarah? She'll be stoked."

"Well, yes and no. I showed her earlier and she said she liked them, but if she was thrilled she managed to hide it well."

"For a smart guy you can be pretty dumb, can't you?" said Aidan with a huge grin.

"How d'you mean?"

"For feck's sake, man, last night she was ready to get shot of you. Sarah was gonna kick your sorry pink English ass right out o' here. Even though she likes you – and I don't mean like that – she was going to get rid. Got it? Now suddenly she finds she's got someone who can actually take a decent photo, the kind that her marketing team in London have been crying out for. You're a regular Don McCullin, aren't you? A Mario Testino for the camps. I guess she was changing her opinions. Like I just did. Last night she asked my advice and I said to get rid o' you."

"Thanks," said James.

"C'mon, look at it from her point of view. We always knew we were taking a risk with you, and you were turning into a liability, a charming one but a liability all the same. You were an unproven snapper in a highly sensitive environment

249

where one wrong move could get us slung out of the camps for good," said Aidan. And as he did so James was thinking about the other photos he'd taken and was suddenly very glad he hadn't shown them to anyone.

"If that happened, we'd probably have to shut up shop here altogether," Aidan continued. "Can ye imagine how that would 'a affected the bairns?"

"The bairns?"

"The kids, man. Maybe we could carry on in Kinshasa but what good is a children's charity in a war zone if it canna get near the children. Until just now you'd given us nae reason to believe you could do the job – in fact, we all reckoned you were shite, worse than Serge's mate. It looks like I'm going to have to eat my words, pal. You're a no' bad lens man … for a half-wit, at least." He gave James a huge smile, added a playful slap on the cheek and walked off whistling.

James shut down his laptop, thought better of leaving it behind and slid it into his kitbag. He might be able to work on it later when he'd got all the images he needed. He almost forgot to swop the full memory card from yesterday for a new one, so he did a quick mental check, he had the laptop and both cameras. They were a bit of a weight in this climate, but it was best to keep them with him and he couldn't be sure which he'd need.

"OK, where to next?"

"Mugunga One, Chip," said Aidan from the kitchen, through a mouthful of bread. "Grab whatever you need and let's go, it looks like the van's arrived. And if you thought Kanyaruchinya was bad yesterday, it's a bloody model of organisation and security next to the Mugunga camps."

James put yesterday's memory card with all its photos on his bedside table – he was carrying a back-up on the laptop so it would be better to keep them separately – and he was the first into the van ready for the drive. He pulled out his phone, plugged in his headphones and found something to listen to. They were away in under a minute.

******

Gahiji made his choice. It was either follow the minivan with the charity workers as they carried out their work and hope to see who Mr James Falkus spoke to, or get inside the house and take a look around. He'd seen one young guy who fitted the guards' description getting into the van with a backpack. *So you're the spy, are you?* he thought. It was always good to see what you were up against and he'd seen nothing there to worry him. The guy looked like any another white aid worker, to that extent his cover was good. Judging from the way the van filled up with people and the care with which the front door was locked and checked, they had all left the house and would be gone for a while. It was time to earn his wages.

He looked at the other houses in the street, but at almost eleven in the morning the workers had long gone and there was no sign of movement. It was all about looking like you belonged there. He told his driver to go past then reverse into the drive as though he owned it. Seconds later Gahiji, dressed in a suit and business shirt, got out of the car, ignored the front door and walked casually round to the back of the building. It was ideal; he could only be seen if someone leaned out of a neighbouring window. No one did.

He carried a long flat-blade screwdriver but in the end he didn't need it, one of the occupants had obligingly left a small rear window open. Crouching on the window ledge the tall Tutsi was able to use his long reach to open the adjacent main window. He was through this in seconds and left it open in case a quick exit was required. He was in a rear bedroom, a man's room to judge from the shorts and T-shirts lying on the floor. He wanted to scan all the rooms quickly before taking his time wherever seemed most promising. Next door was a woman's room.

Back through the living room; a mess with laptop cables, mugs and empty beer bottles on the low table, then the kitchen – not much to see – and just one more room. With two single beds and two sleeping bags, this appeared to be shared by two men making it the odds-on favourite for a first search. A large canvas bag on one side had a label on it – Aidan O'Dowd. There was no bag by the other bed, but on this side of the bedside table was a camera case containing a spare lens. On the bed were a photography magazine and a paperback; poking out of the top was the stub of a recent airline boarding pass being used as a bookmark. He heard a car door slam outside and holding the book Gahiji crossed the living room in three strides to look outside over the roof of his own car. Nothing happening in either direction. His man was still sitting quietly in the car, engine off as instructed to avoid attracting attention. It must have been another house.

He went back to the bedroom and studied the boarding pass, issued in the name of James Falkus. Got you, Falkus! He stuffed the pass back into the pages and replaced the book where he'd found it. It was only then that he noticed, partly obscured by the lamp base, the type of memory card used in laptops and cameras. The card went into his pocket and he spent some time going through the cupboards and drawers looking for Falkus' computer but without success. He paused and went back to the bed, lifting the mattress and checking within the base cavity. The cupboard was a fitted unit offering few hiding places and none containing what he was looking for.

Gahiji moved quietly into the main room and scoured this from end to end. There was no sign of a computer in the kitchen or utility room either and he drew a blank in the other bedrooms. It seemed they had all their equipment with them. Time to go, same way out as in. This was less easy in a suit than jeans but he had had plenty of practice. He stepped from the bed onto the outer sill and swung the window shut behind him. Gahiji reached back in through the top light window to secure the handle – force of habit really, it was worth the extra effort to avoid detection – and in ten seconds he was back in the car.

"OK. Switch on and drive slowly, like you've got your mother-in-law in the back." Gahiji felt in his pocket for the SD card. He sincerely hoped this had something on it, otherwise he was facing big trouble. Who are you working for Mr Falkus, he wondered. South African intelligence services, the Rwandans, the British? He gave up for now. First let's see what's on this card.

Chapter 17
Walikale and Bisie, North Kivu, DR Congo
Two Weeks Ago

True to his word, Marc Audousset had driven Jessica all the way to Walikale. Soon after crossing the Lowa River he deposited her outside a little church by the main road. The church was almost indistinguishable from all the simple houses around it, except for a small cross made from two straight sticks fastened above the door. Evidently as far as the French missionary was concerned, it was the epicentre of Walikale. Jessica would have preferred to be dropped outside the nearest bar or general store.

Like all the other buildings the church was set back twenty metres from the N3, the best paved road in the area and one which bore the only white road markings for a hundred kilometres in any direction. She sat down in the shade to one side of the tiny church, and began to reorganise her backpack leaving her camera out of sight but easily accessible. She took a long swig from the stainless steel water bottle she carried and began to think of where she might refill it. There were high clouds and the day was hot, but it was the humidity here that left her feeling like a damp rag. There would inevitably be a thunderstorm later.

A woman washing her child nearby gave Jessica directions to the nearest store where she could buy a drink. She had a small parcel of food from Marianne at the orphanage and sat down in the sun to read about the endangered gorillas of Walikale. It was frustrating to Jessica that she was so close to one of the last remaining breeding grounds for Mountain Gorillas and yet she didn't have time to explore it or write about it. The gorillas were less than two days climb from here, high in the mists of the National Park beneath the Virunga Massif. With the benefit of hindsight she knew she could have paid for more of her Congo journey if she had had some articles commissioned on the endangered silverbacks, but that would have to wait for another time. There was at least more hope for the gorillas than there had been five years ago. Then they were being shot for food by rebels or the starving villagers fleeing from fighting in the forest. The animals were shot, trapped in snares or killed by land mines deliberately placed on jungle paths used by the huge primates. With the fighting between rebels and government troops moving further north, the gorillas stood a chance of being left in peace. It was early days but there were signs of an increase in mountain gorilla numbers. With outside help some returning villagers were now making a living by farming pigs and goats.

In search of better shade Jessica found the bar and a warm beer, while she wrote up her experiences with the Audoussets and copied some recent photos to her laptop. There was only one other customer, a young soldier with a crewcut who looked briefly at her as she arrived then paid her no further attention.

"Parlez-vous français? Or do you speak English?" she asked him.

He snorted derisively and with little interest said, "Français. Bien sûr."

"When is the next plane coming?" she asked in French.

He shrugged his shoulders at the question. "No time. They here soon. But you not get on."

"Why not?" She looked concerned.

He gave a dismissive grin that made it clear she was foolish for even asking. "They have cassiterite to carry, much cassiterite. You must pay more than …," he struggled for the word, "more than they are pay for a sack of rocks. Or they not take you." He looked her up and down. "Maybe two sacks," he laughed.

Cheeky bastard, she thought. "We'll see about that. I can pay for a seat."

"Seat?" He laughed derisively at her. "This is Walikale Express, lady. You sit on rocks – if they take you at all. They Russians, not liking passengers." And he laughed again at his wit and turned back to his beer, his shoulders shaking.

She tried to ignore him and read some background information on the area, only looking up when she heard a chair being shifted, and seeing him take a long swig from his bottle. He called for another beer, tilted his chair back and went to sleep with his feet on the bench in front. She had no idea how he could sleep like this in these still and humid conditions. A strong, foetid, rotting smell pervaded everything here and wafted in from the forest that barged its way right up to the backs of the line of clay and thatch houses on either side of the road.

Half an hour later there was a sudden squawk from a building nearby. Then she could make out bursts of static and a tinny voice that marked a VHF radio. That would explain the constantly running generator engine she could hear at the back of the buildings. Someone had started it soon after she'd arrived; she guessed it would be too expensive to run the whole time.

Then came a shout of "Max, Max," followed by the sound of a door banging nearby. She looked up from her screen to see a very large woman moving as quickly as she could in her flip flops across the dirt yard between this and the neighbouring building. "You must come, you come. There is trouble."

The young man drained his bottle and stood up. "What is it?" he asked with studied indifference.

"You come," she repeated in French and turned on her heel and headed back to the radio hut.

It was almost thirty minutes later when he emerged and came back to the bar. He banged on the wooden wall to gain attention and called out an order to the owner who was out the back, then hearing no answer he went through and Jessica could hear a dispute starting. She wasn't sure what he was speaking about but thought he might be trying to order some food. The argument got louder and only ended with the banging of pans.

Max emerged a moment later with a moody expression and still muttering to himself. Then to Jessica he said, "There is a flight in twenty minutes. Be on it when it leaves or you are stuck here for a long time."

"Is there a problem?"

"Sure, there's a problem. A big rock fall in Bisie and miners are trapped. How many?" he shrugged theatrically. "No one knows, but is serious." Jessica could only just keep up with his accented French. "A big group comes to help from Goma tomorrow, but I must take the first people to the mine today. The porters can guide the others."

"How far is it?" she asked.

"Fifty kilometres, maybe sixty. Why?"

"Because I want to come." The thought was ill-formed in her head, but she knew immediately that this was a good way of bringing the attention of the outside world to what was happening here. "I'm a journalist and I want to tell more people. Maybe they can help."

"*Vous* êtes journaliste?" He looked amazed, possibly he had thought she was a tourist, albeit one who had strayed a long way from the hotels in Goma and Gisenyi. "We don't need journalists. We need doctors and engineers, strong men who can get the injured out to hospital. We need helicopters."

"I understand that, but the safety at this mine will only be improved if pressure is put on the people who run it."

He gave an involuntary snort of derision. "The army runs it. Will you put pressure on the army, with your writing?" he scoffed. "I'm a soldier, I can't take you. So you can't go."

Jessica continued to argue the point but she knew he would be in trouble if senior officers discovered he'd taken a journalist to witness the aftermath of this mine collapse, particularly since it was confirmed as an Army-run mine. Nor could he tell her this without losing face. When a plate of chicken and beans arrived, he lost all interest in her and set about his food. Clearly he didn't know when or where his next meal would come from, and seeing this she ordered a meal for herself. A plan was forming in her head and she needed to be ready soon.

*****

Jessica didn't like armies. The stark truth, however, was that sometimes a freelance foreign correspondent needed a war. It didn't sound good, when you put it like that, but it was the truth. Her dislike of soldiering wasn't a principled objection, just based on poor experiences, starting with an officer cadet at college on whom she'd had a crush. They had gone out together a few times until a friend found he was running a sweepstake on when he got to first, second or third base with her. That was when she'd gone off soldiers.

She knew that if she was ever going to break into the tight-knit ranks of America's globe-trotting foreign correspondents she would have to deliver her editors something extraordinary. Only then would she be able to prove her doubting father wrong. She would sure enjoy watching him eat humble pie, knowing how he had underestimated her. To do that she needed to prove herself under fire – preferably somewhere under-reported where her copy could stand out. Ever since she'd learned that the fighting was still going on here, long after the signing of the peace accords that brought senior rebels into the government, it had looked like the Democratic Republic of the Congo fitted the bill.

Thus, within an hour Jessica had visited the tiny general store at the near end of Walikale town and bought herself a nylon poncho, a bowie knife, rolls of nylon line and tarpaulins, a second water bottle, an ageing box of malaria pills with Spanish and French labelling, a battered bush hat, toilet roll, trowel, plastic lighter and a spare pair of ill-fitting trousers. She also found rice, salt, loose tea, and sticking plasters. It wasn't much but she had limited space in her backpack, and with the right guidance it should see her through a few days away. The key to her plan were guides and she began to ask about the porters.

Soon after she was at the end of the airstrip standing among the porters looking for one who spoke French, and she was ready to haggle. There were several men there, but it was only after some blank looks, embarrassed discussions and flat rejections that she found one, Ben, who would guide a woman on her own through the forest to the mine. Ben smiled little and said even less. He was clearly more porter than guide, but as he was the only one prepared to take her there for five dollars upfront and another ten at the other end. It was easy money for him; she was paying the equivalent of three trips.

Ben lay down to rest after the arduous, heavily-laden journey down from the mine, so Jessica unrolled her tarp under a tree a few metres away, made a pillow of her jacket and closed her eyes.

Later, the noise of the day's third plane approaching overhead woke her and since she had missed the others she stood up and wandered onto the wide grass verge beside the road to watch it circle. The plane was bigger than anything Jessica had imagined could land on a road in the jungle. The twin-engined transport circled a second time, before disappearing to the south. Then she saw it as a white speck above the trees to her right, the wings set above its fuselage made it look like an ungainly giant seabird. It crested the trees at the end of a long straight section of tarmac road then dropped lower, its wings far exceeding the road width and spreading out across the high grass at either side. The pilot dropped the aircraft until its undercarriage skimmed the road and gently placed her on the highway heading straight towards the waiting loaders. The aircraft slowed with plenty of space to spare, although Jessica imagined they might need every straight metre of the roadway to take off once they were laden with tin ore.

A man in blue overalls stepped forward in front of her, hands held aloft and signalled professionally for the pilot to approach closer and then to turn the aircraft's nose towards the jungle to his left, as far as the roadway would allow. The engines began to slow and as the noise subsided it was replaced by the revving of a battered green pick-up truck carrying a load of cassiterite rock to the plane. Six loaders walked forward and began to manually push the aircraft around, led by the man in overalls who now pulled the plane by its nose wheel with the aid of a long steel pole. When he was satisfied, a young boy ran forward and slid a chock in front of one wheel to prevent it rolling down the camber.

With the silent aircraft now facing the way it had come, the truck pulled up beneath one wing and after some men had exited the aircraft and been escorted away by the soldier, the loaders began to lift the fifty kilogram sacks through the passenger door. Jessica could see loaders inside sliding the tightly bound nylon bags forward in the aircraft where they lay in a single layer that started just behind the pilot and co-pilot. Neither of the crew had emerged and she could just make out two white faces in the cockpit. Two blue-uniformed policemen had appeared from somewhere and were actively overseeing the loading although neither got his hands dirty. This was clearly a well-practised routine; within twenty minutes of touching down the aircraft doors were closed and it emitted a high-pitched whine as the props started to turn. The wheel chocks were pulled away and the aircraft lumbered down the roadway, slowly at first and bouncing heavily on its undercarriage before picking up speed. Jessica watched anxiously as it seemed to use up the entire straight and just as she thought it must hit the trees it began to lift and immediately to bank left. There wasn't enough room for the plane to carry over the trees ahead and it was still only thirty metres off the ground as it slid sideways in mid-climb and took the bend in the road, disappearing from view for a second or two before emerging above the tree tops a long way past the corner in the road.

Jessica let out a breath that she didn't know she'd been holding and Ben, who had appeared beside her, grinned at her reaction. "C'était trop proche," she said. That was too close.

He just shook his head. "Normal, c'est normal."

Beside her a policeman removed the flimsy wooden barrier he had earlier placed across the highway and waved through a motorbike taxi to reclaim it as a road. Heavily laden with two men, the little bike puttered down the road in the bright sunshine making more noise than speed.

"Allons-y," said Ben. "Let's go," and with that he was on his way.

Jessica was glad of her walking boots. Ben was shod, like most of the porters who were accompanying them, in white wellington boots. He was setting a strong pace and she concentrated hard on finding a rhythm that, while it may not have matched his lengthy stride, kept pace with him. For the next three hours he paid her little attention, only once did she see him look back. They were climbing through sparse trees on a muddy zigzag path and there were two other porters between them. He didn't stop but she wasn't concerned at that as long as she could keep up with him. After an hour the long-threatened thunderstorm finally broke and she was glad of the poncho that covered her backpack and torso. She liked the bush hat but was glad her Manhattan friends couldn't see her now.

God knows what they would make of this. As soon as she had gone to college, Jessica had begun writing for the newspaper, quickly moving into online publishing. She had discovered she had a natural talent for presenting short video and thirty minute programmes that few of her colleagues had mastered. Perhaps her ambition stemmed from her cosmopolitan background; her first generation immigrant Somali mother had been a successful New York catwalk model who married a young man with strong Italian roots.

One thing eluded her when she graduated though, the chance to break into a national TV network or newspaper group as a foreign correspondent. There was nothing wrong with Jessica's writing or interviewing, the problem was that she had graduated with only one foreign language, French and even that wasn't fluent.

When she realised her shortcoming, it was too late. Jessica was in a hurry to start her journalistic career and had no wish to go back to college and learn another language, so she had to self-fund her first few trips in Europe as a freelance and sell feature articles to editors on her return. She thought back to how badly it had paid, but at least she had gained a foot in the door. After that she never left home without a series of commissions. Not that anyone had commissioned this particular diversion – this was all of her own doing. Her mother would say she was being typically impetuous. Who knew what her father would have said – she hadn't spoken to him for a couple of years.

The tough terrain brought her mind back to the task at hand. None of the porters spoke, and on the few occasions that they were on open ground there was no time to admire the view. She had no intention of falling behind, but Ben set a determined pace that seemed unaffected by gradients or changes in terrain. He made much the same speed climbing a hillside as he did negotiating the tree roots that snaked across their level paths and provided a slippery hazard for the unwary. By the end of three hours Jessica was wondering how much longer she could keep this going, when they came up to a large, flat grey rock. All the porters put down the frames on which they carried the supplies for the mine and refilled their water bottles from a stream that trickled underneath a nearby overhang.

Jessica replenished her bottle, and looked at the group. They seldom spoke to one another, even at rest, but they walked together and stopped together. When she returned, the men were picking up their packs and once again they were on their way.

This continued for another hour until the light was fading and she feared they might walk on in darkness. Just as she was considering how to ask Ben where and when they would sleep she smelt something, something foul. The group walked into a clearing in the trees and they were greeted by the pungent smells of wood smoke and human excrement.

It seemed to be a glimpse of prehistory. Here in the jungle, miles from any contact with the outside world, still a day's march from the mine and the disaster that had struck it, a hundred men and now one woman were starting to cook their only meal of the day and to find whatever rest they could. The rain continued to find them through gaps in the tree canopy and although she had a cigarette lighter Jessica cursed herself for not thinking earlier of finding dry kindling for a fire.

She had been fortunate in her choice of companions though. Ben and his followers had a fire burning before she had even taken off her pack, and soon they beckoned her to join them beside it. She took off the poncho which had spared her from the rain but left her soaked with sweat beneath its cover. The sweat was cooling and she was chilled for the first time today. Huddled with her guide and four others they warmed themselves in front of the fire that was now burning well and above which they had suspended a pan of boiling rice and dried beans. She offered her rice to the group but they would not take it. "Demain," said Ben, waving it away till they had need of it tomorrow. She wanted to contribute so she dug out the tea and it was accepted with nods and placed beside the fire to drink later.

Within minutes of their arrival it was dark. With the cloud overhead no natural light reached them and they were all reliant on firelight and the occasional torch. When the rice was strained, they put the pot in the middle of the group and took turns to scoop out a handful. As they ate, they talked with Ben translating into French for her.

"Who's running the mine now?" she asked.

There seemed to be two answers. Some said it was the FARDC, the federal army. Others said no, it was Nduma Defense of Congo, who had pretended to assimilate their group into the FARDC after the last peace talks. They had received new uniforms from the federal army, then carried on taxing the local miners.

Jessica tried a different tack. "How do they take money from you?"

One man waved a cigarette in the air and mimed drinking from a bottle. Apparently, their leader had monopoly control of all cigarettes and alcohol sold in

NDC-controlled mines. Another said he had gone back to portering because his family had to pay a huge tax for the pit they had dug. It was fifty dollars per week. Jessica did some mental arithmetic. If they had twenty pits, and she'd heard the mine was big, that was a thousand bucks a week in protection money. Over fifty thousand bucks a year from one mine. She could see why the minerals were at the heart of the region's conflict. The money was attracting anyone with a gun and the will to take control. All they had to do was start another militia and chase away the other groups.

"Who controls NDC?" she asked. She had half-expected to be met by silence but they were happy to tell her. His name was Sheka Ntabo Ntaberi. Apparently, he used to be a mineral trader until he saw the real money was being made by the men with guns. So he opted for a career change, re-inventing himself and his colleagues into the NDC. Of course, they had had to fight for control, but he had been ready for that. He had thrown out the local Mai-Mai militia, de-capitating those that they captured in the mine.

The men said all this matter of factly. There was an air of resignation, if it wasn't this group it would be another for as long as the Kivus had minerals in the ground that could be sold. It didn't matter if it was gold, tin, tungsten or tantalum. It gave them work when any other work was unreliable and hard to find.

Eventually, they tired of her questions and the group fell silent. The rice tasted of little but there was just enough to fill them, and after passing around a bowl of hot tea the porters curled up to sleep on the ground where they had sat. She was the only one with a ground sheet and a poncho to cover her, but she was unused to the constant drip of water and the snores of the men around her made her the last to fall asleep.

She was also the last to wake. They shared out bowls of tea, this time with some sugar and the porters were waiting for her when she hoisted the pack onto her aching back. Jessica had repacked the poncho; the cover had been more useful while sleeping and in the heaviest rain but her clothes would stand some chance of drying now.

The group started downhill which seemed counter-intuitive but the path was clear enough and porters moved along it in both directions like so many termites on a nest. The pace was metronomic, it never varied whether they were climbing or descending, but one thing that was new was the occasional view of the country around them as they crossed ridges on rising ground. They walked all through the day, stopping infrequently for a short drink before pressing on towards the mine. She was feeling faint by two o'clock but she didn't want to think they could walk further than she could on an empty stomach, and preferred to attribute it to the altitude and heat. Jessica passed scores then hundreds of men heading in the opposite direction carrying large sacks of cassiterite strapped to their backs. She had heard they weighed fifty kilos, and looking at them she didn't doubt it. That was almost her bodyweight and she struggled to understand how they managed this day in, day out, bringing three or four loads to the airstrip per week, and all for five US dollars per load. She couldn't begin to imagine how tiring that must be or the long-term effect it would have on their bodies after a few years. Jessica also knew, as the men probably did not, that their loads were each worth hundreds of dollars on the market in London.

As their path rose and fell through the trees, sometimes wide enough to drive a truck along, more often so narrow that two men could scarcely pass, the mud beneath her feet turned into drier soil and it began to segue in colour from chocolate brown to a sandy red. They traversed a steep slope and came through an opening where a landslip had carried away the tree cover. It was the best view so far and Jessica allowed herself a few moments to stare out across the top of the jungle canopy. The valleys were deep, some of them hundreds of metres deep. There were more shades of green in this view than any place she'd ever trekked through and the uniform cover of foliage was broken only once by the sight of a muddy brown river far below them. Several men in her group had overtaken her by the time Jessica resumed and she made a renewed effort not to fall behind.

An hour later they passed from the jungle into a clearing, smaller than last night's rest stop and, after the noise of birdsong on the lower trail, eerily still. The path wound its way between rectangles made with low wooden rails, and then she spotted that some of them bore crosses. With a shock she realised that this must be the cemetery for Bisie mine. Here they buried those who succumbed to exhaustion and starvation, to malaria, cholera, and the other diseases and dangers affecting the mineworkers. If the reports were true, she feared that the latest rock fall might have caused more fatalities.

"Not far now," said Ben beside her. She hadn't even noticed him; he must have waited for her. He wasn't talkative and she was about to leave when he pointed to a grave not far away. "Mon fils. My son, Joel." He said nothing more and she turned to him in shock.

"Je suis désolée," was all that she could manage. She was about to touch his arm in a compassionate gesture but something made her hold back and then he had moved past her to stand at the graveside.

Ben said nothing. Not a muscle moved and his face betrayed nothing of his feelings. Jessica stood some distance behind him, not moving as he contemplated his loss. Eventually the guide turned and returned to where she was standing. He did not look directly at her and his voice was low so that she struggled to catch his words. "Many of us have someone here," he said and then he simply shrugged before turning back to the trail.

Jessica had plenty to think about for the last thirty minutes of their journey. Ben's loss, his stoicism, the prospects for his life and the way this mine seemed to continue in perpetuity, regardless of who controlled it. The Audoussets had mentioned there were about ten mines in the area and that this was the oldest and largest. She also knew that Marianne had said not to come here, but that was before she heard the news of the accident. Jessica could have turned her back yesterday and flown down to Goma but what kind of journalist, she asked herself, would ignore the chance to tell a human story like this. She was still thinking wider thoughts when they began to see daylight through the trees ahead.

As they continued to climb, still underneath the tree cover close to the mine, she could make out the dark red earth bearing the tin ore. It was a steep route and below her she could see men and boys in a deep hole dug in the sand and rock. Many of them were standing and looking into the bottom of the pit and she could just make out a few figures moving in and out of an opening, no larger than a crevice in the rock. Jessica turned and resumed her climb with the group. As the trail emerged from the forest and wound its way among the mine workings, all around her men stopped what they were doing and stared at her. She saw boys no more than ten or maybe twelve years old, and dozens of teenagers. As with Ben, it was hard to gauge the men's age. Their mud-streaked faces were weathered and lined from exposure to sun and rain, and there was a dull look in the older eyes that said nothing now could shock them. Few moved quickly in the heat and all seemed more interested in watching Jessica and her party arrive.

She wanted to pay Ben the other ten dollars he had asked for and had bills ready but he did not stop. "Come, come," was all he said and beckoned her to follow. As they came to a wide rocky ledge, the other porters stopped, but Ben called her to follow him up a smaller path. It was not so well trodden and there was grass and rough vegetation on both sides. At the top of the slope, was a narrow flat piece of ground on which was perched a long, thatched roof hut, open at the front and sides. In the shade sat an army officer, recognisable by his beret and shoulder flashes on his immaculately clean and pressed shirt. All the other soldiers wore ill-fitting tunics, caps, and white rubber boots, and none were as clean.

Jessica had heard plenty about the Federal Army of the Democratic Republic of the Congo and its years of ineffectual fighting against the rebels. Now with some UN support and outside training the FARDC had at last begun to remove some rebel groups from the mountainous regions of North Kivu. Their reputation was still bad; there were frequent reports of atrocities committed by the army against its own people, and civilians were still forced at gunpoint to pay 'taxes' to pass through army checkpoints.

There was a moment's surprise on the officer's face at the sight of a solitary woman in the mine. It wasn't enough to get him out of his chair and his soldiers stood around, guns slung idly at their sides and all their attention on this unexpected visitor.

"Who is she?" the officer jutted his chain in Jessica's direction but he spoke to Ben.

"She is a journalist from America," said Ben, "and she's come to rescue the trapped miners." There was a roar of laughter from everyone within earshot and the officer slapped his thighs with both hands in delight. Ben looked confused and Jessica could make out enough of what they said to blush angrily.

"That is not why I'm here. Yes, I have heard of the accident, but I know the army runs this mine and they surely won't need the help of one woman. I am here to report for newspapers in New York and London; I hope I can tell them how the mine operates securely now that the army has thrown out the rebels." Her flattery was shameless, but she'd been reporting from the front line for long enough to know how to get through roadblocks. This, she reasoned, was just another.

The laughter subsided and the officer took a closer look at her. "Come here," he said in French, still lounging in his vividly striped garden chair. "What is your name and who do you work for?"

Jessica hesitated, then stepped forward. "My name's Jessica Tsiba and I write for the New York Times and The Times of London."

"Well, Jessica Tsiba from the New York Times, you can just turn around and fuck off back to wherever you came from. Understood?"

She paused, but the officer's gaze was unflinching and the eyes hidden behind sunglasses made him hard to read. Jessica had half-expected this. "That's a shame. The Editors of both newspapers will be sad not to have your story and your photograph on their front pages." She waited for this to sink in. "They have heard about this accident, Commandant, and will be reporting on the rescue that you've made. I guess they will use someone else's photo on the front page and on the internet; someone else will get the credit for the rescue."

The troops looked at her with renewed interest and some turned to see how their leader would react. "I am Captain, not a Commandant," was all he said at first and he continued to stare at her, chewing idly on something.

"This accident, it is complicated. There are many people trapped."

"You mean they're still in there?" asked Jessica incredulously. "How many? Do you know? How long have they been in there?"

"Nobody knows how many were down there. Fifty, maybe sixty? It is not our job to mine, it is our job to protect the area from attack by bandits. There are many bandits here and if we leave they will take control again. Then the miners will have nothing," he said. "There are people down there digging to get them out, but so far …" and he shrugged, "no success."

"Can you show me where?" Jessica noticed that the conversation had skipped past her presence there and she wanted to keep it that way.

"One of my men can show you, I must stay here for news from our headquarters in Bukavu. We have radioed for help and they are sending a team, but it takes a long time as you know. Tomorrow you will come back here and we will talk about your article and your photographs." He waved her away imperiously but for now she had permission to stay.

The officer gave brief orders for two soldiers to lead her and they started back down the path. But Jessica was not quite ready; she turned to Ben and shook his hand firmly holding it in both of hers. Ben guessed what was happening and did not react as twenty dollars was pressed into his palm. She wanted to hug him but knew it would not be right. "Thank you," was all she said then Jessica turned and finding new energy she walked quickly away to join her escort.

They were at the top of a giant red scar on the deep green mountainside. Every tree had been felled for a width of five hundred metres as though a vast avalanche had carried them away. From where they had started to the foot of this giant quarry Jessica estimated to be a slope of a thousand metres or more, but their progress was slow. The few paths between the digs wound circuitously down the mountain skirting enormous holes in which men sweated as they dug in the last heat of the day. These men seldom looked up; those that saw her stopped to watch Jessica pass, then went back to their work with a shrug or a comment to their neighbours.

It took longer than she had expected to reach the scene of the disaster, and as they approached the throng of miners grew thicker. There was a melée of activity around a cleft in the rock. It staggered her that just a few metres away other groups were digging tin ore from more holes in the ground, regardless of the plight of others nearby but perhaps it was wrong for her to judge the situation. She knew enough of the conditions here to know that miners who didn't mine didn't eat and nor did their families.

Workers around her stared curiously at this lone woman who had demanded that the soldiers take her to the mine entrance. She ignored them and focused on the rescue efforts beneath. The ground opened ahead in a dark scar between two huge rocks and the entrance to the mine was crowded with the sweating backs of men. It was now more than a day since the tunnel had collapsed and the miners had had time to bring some order to their work. Soldiers stood on the rim of the excavation along with a few onlookers. Ten metres below them men had formed a chain to pass up rocks and baskets of sand. Their faces were dirty and grim, exhaustion written across their features so that there was little talk between them.

"Who can tell me what's happened?" she asked aloud. Faces turned towards her, and at first no one answered. Then one man spoke up. "The rocks fell on us," he said. "Some of us got out, but there are many still in there."

"When did this happen?"

"It was yesterday morning, early. We were changing over and some of the miners were getting ready to come out. Many had been underground for two days and they were due to come up."

"Two days!" she exclaimed. "Do they always stay down there for so long?"

"Most of them, yes. Especially the younger ones who are digging the rock out."

"Oh God. How old are they?" She almost didn't want to know.

He shrugged. "Maybe twelve years, some a bit older. They are small, they can work in the tunnels more easily than us." He looked around him and the men nodded.

"Has anyone been rescued?"

"We have pulled out seven, but they were all dead. Crushed by the rocks or suffocated by the earth that fell on them. We are opening up new holes and tapping on steel poles we have pushed through the cavities to let them know we are coming. But we have not heard anyone tapping back."

"Someone told me that fifty are missing. Is that true?"

"No one knows. Maybe less, maybe more." The man shrugged. "It's not the first time this has happened, but this is one of the worst collapses anyone can remember."

Another man pushed to the front of the men surrounding her. "Who are you?" he asked.

"I am a journalist, from a newspaper in America. I'm here to tell the world what is happening here."

"Can you bring help? We need America to help us. I need help to get my boy out."

"Your boy is one of the diggers?"

"Of course. He has been in there for three days now and he has just two bottles of water. He is only young." The man looked down, unable to say more.

"How old is he?"

The father shrugged. "Fourteen," he said but he didn't seem certain.

"All I can do is try to get this news out to Europe and America, and that will take a very long time. But the army have asked for help from Bukavu." The man steadily raised his eyes to her and she knew that what she said offered him no hope of a rescue at all. He was too upset to say anything else to her and turned away.

Jessica could do no more than note the heroic but so far futile efforts going on around her. She spoke to the man who had first answered her. "Can I take photos for the news? Is that OK?"

He looked at his neighbour then back at her and gave a weary sigh.

"Take your photos, but bring us help." With that he resumed his place in the human chain, and Jessica placed her backpack on the ground and took out her camera. The men watched in fascination as she struggled to capture the enormity of the challenge they faced without any mechanical support.

Eventually, as the sun began to set, she packed her bag again. For once in her life, Jessica didn't know what to do or say. She was shattered, though she couldn't tell if it was from the walk, the lack of sleep in last night's rain or the emotional scenes she had just witnessed. She needed to find somewhere to sleep, something to eat and to reach somewhere with internet access as soon as possible.

In the event, her return came sooner and faster than she expected.

******

Jessica awoke to excited shouts coming from somewhere below her in the darkness. She could see the bobbing lights of torches so she grabbed her own and her camera and pulled on a jacket as she hurried towards the commotion, in the darkness negotiating perilous drops to left and right into some of the digs.

As she drew closer, she could see that people were bent over a figure, she could only catch glimpses but it was a teenage boy who had been pulled alive from the mine. Even from the back of the group she could hear his tortured, laboured breathing presumably affected by lack of oxygen or choking on the fine sand. His slight figure was caked in dirt from head to foot, and when they shifted him his head lolled and she could see that his eyes had rolled back. He was barely conscious now and there was no movement in his limbs.

Desperate to help, the miners tried to give him water, but he could not swallow and the water just spilled back out of his mouth. He lay motionless on a strip of grass as one of them gently cleaned his face with water poured from a bottle onto a folded T-shirt. Just as she began to think he had died the boy began to shiver uncontrollably in the cold of the night air and they quickly wrapped him in a blanket. Having taken photos of the group bent over the slim frame Jessica snatched a few close-up shots of the frantic efforts to revive him – no one objected, no one appeared even to notice her. She looked at her watch, it was just after midnight. As the shivering wracked his body, the diggers were galvanised into renewed efforts to hold on to this young miner's life. The rescuers' hopes for his safety hung tantalisingly out of reach, and all the while she could see work continuing below them to extract other trapped miners from the hole. She noticed the father she had spoken to earlier when he lifted his head from the work being done at the entrance to the mine. He cast a glance up the hill to where they worked on warming and reviving the teenager; clearly this was not his son. Jessica wondered how many of his age were buried in the rock and soil below them.

There was little change in his condition, but eventually those caring for him were successful in trickling a little water into his mouth which this time he swallowed. A minute later he retched up the water and some mud, and a couple of minutes after that he began to bleed from the mouth. Jessica couldn't bear to watch. Another boy, possibly his older brother, was kneeling by his side but he was too shocked to speak. There was no doctor, no nurse, and no first aid. The men were talking of getting him carried out by porters to the nearest free hospital run by the French medical charity, *Médecins Sans Frontières*. It had recently re-opened in

Walikale having been forced to close for a month following heavy fighting in the area and working under the constant threat of rebel attacks on nearby villages. The men knew he would be too heavy for one man to carry, so they would have to make a hammock on a pole and hire two porters to take him.

Two men went off in search of materials for a hammock and another rejoined the group at the mouth of the mine into which men were still disappearing and returning with basket loads of spoil from the rock fall. They were saying little but there was an even greater sense of desperation about their work, as though the boy's removal from the tunnels and galleries below had reminded them of how little time was left in which to effect any more rescues.

The group around the now-unconscious boy had dwindled to three; Jessica could only watch as they talked to him and told him how they planned to carry him to the hospital. She felt useless, wanted to do something, anything to ease his shallow, rasping breaths and help him recover. All she could think to do was hold his hand, and so she sat beside him with his cold, hard, muddy hand in hers. The darkness was punctured by a solitary torch beam and even that was weakening and flickered occasionally. A little after two in the morning there was a change in his breathing which seemed to stop and start while the pulse in his wrist became more difficult to detect. The men returned from their search for the makings of a hammock and she shifted out of their way. One of them nodded at her, perhaps thanking her for her gentleness with him, and once more he washed the boy's nose and mouth removing further traces of soil. A few minutes later, and with no drama or other outward signs, his breathing stopped altogether and he was still.

Jessica wanted to resuscitate him, but she cursed herself for not knowing how and so, helplessly, she watched the boy die, a boy too young to be doing this job, who should have been in school or at home with his family. The bitter sadness that she felt was giving way to a blistering anger, at her own inability to care for him, at the fact that mines like this existed at all, that people like him had no other work to go to when they had fled their threatened villages, and that soldiers who could have helped had sat just metres away doing nothing while he suffocated.

He had been the only one pulled alive from the mine so far; uncounted others had been killed outright or were still trapped below ground with little air, water, food or hope. Jessica was simply too tired to cry, she stood and placed a hand on the brother's shoulder but he didn't seem to know she was there. She wasn't even sure he knew that his little brother had gone. There were no words to say, and no one to say them to. Jessica silently made her way back to her bed not far from the sleeping porters where she had felt safer.

******

She put her camera away in the bag and dug out her poncho for warmth. As she did so, she rediscovered the bag of bread and fruit that Marianne had given her so many hours ago. Jessica blessed her kindness and ate the bread with a voracious appetite and a strong sense of guilt that she was alive and the teenager was not. After the bread she tried to savour the fruit more slowly and washed it down with some water. Her supply was getting a bit low but she'd be OK tonight. In the morning she would make some rice for the journey and follow the porters back along the trail to Walikale to tell the world of the horror she had seen.

Chapter 18
Bisie tin Mine, North Kivu, DRC
Two Weeks Ago

Jessica never had time to fall asleep before they were on her. She was about to switch off her head torch when two large figures hit her simultaneously from behind and one side. The surprise was total and they made no attempt to be quiet. Amid the shock she could discern two uniformed men wearing caps and heavy belts as they pummelled her with punches. As she instinctively rolled away from the blows, her torch criss-crossed them and she could see they were soldiers. She couldn't identify them; all she could do was curl up into a little ball.

Oddly, her next thought was to prevent them taking her camera and laptop which held all her work. They had other intentions though. One man punched her in the back of the head and she felt as though a door had slammed on her. Her vision was momentarily split by a diagonal white light and then she was able to focus again. In front of her, one man now held her by the throat. This was the most terrifying thing she had ever known; for the first time she felt that her life was ending, that someone overwhelmingly powerful had the means to finish her there and then. He was going to do it and there would be nothing she could do to stop him.

Then the man behind her grabbed her collar and pulled her back so that she fell from a throttled kneeling position to lie on her back. Perhaps because of the darkness they weren't working in concert, the backwards wrench had loosened the other attacker's grip on her throat. That may have been the first time she screamed – she couldn't be sure – but she certainly yelled then at the top of her lungs. She heard her cry ring right around the rocks above but there was no answering call or challenge to the soldiers.

One of the men took hold of her kicking boot as she lashed out at them and continued to shout, and he tried to drag her away towards the edge of the forest where her shouts would be muffled and their attack hidden. She screamed again but it was as if she was now mute. Nobody came, there were no lights or alarms, Jessica was on her own against two men and there could only be one outcome. She could see something bulky and inanimate lying half beneath her now and she realised that having been thrown one way and then pulled back again she had been moved closer to her backpack.

She was certain the soldiers would be armed and if they pulled a gun she'd be dead because she would not stop fighting. It was strange, Jessica felt a swelling sense of indignation that nobody was coming to her aid, although the men who had been sleeping all around her must be able to hear the attack. She knew the miners around her were too scared to intervene, and it was this indignation that kept her going.

The one who had pulled her by the foot swung a kick at her, but she was a moving target and in the darkness he would have had little idea where to strike. She couldn't see the blows coming, the first she knew about it was when his boot hit her shoulder and though painful she was surprised that it hardly affected her.

The attacker in front of her was much more of a threat. He had the advantages of surprise, weight, reach and training on his side as he threw himself forwards and smothered her movements so that she was pinned to the ground. He struck at the left side of her head but misjudged Jessica's height and the blow glanced off the top of her head. It hurt, but she was sure the next one would be worse once he'd corrected his aim.

She screamed again, loudly and he put his forearm over her mouth to silence her. He leaned his weight on her upper lip and she felt it split as it was caught between his downward force and the immovable position of her head. The pressure on her top teeth was so great that she thought they might cave in.

Then they started to rape her, both men now tearing at her clothing. A few minutes earlier, while she was eating her food, she had folded her shirt back into the bag and put on a thin fleece for warmth. Now the man on top of her began to rip it and the seams gave way easily, exposing her shoulders and the straps of her vest. With his arm still over her top lip she could not breathe through her nose and air came only in gasps through her mouth.

Jessica could feel his hands ripping open her belt buckle and starting to undo her jeans. She reached out to one side searching for something, anything with which to defend herself but there was only hard-packed soil and not even any rocks with which to strike him back. The soldier lay on top of her and she was disgusted at the smell of his neck and body, while his stubble scratched at her face and his fingers pulled furiously at her trousers.

The man's weight made it impossible for her to wriggle free, but she did manage to roll her head to one side and the muscle of his forearm slid into her mouth. She could taste her own blood in the back of her throat and she wanted to cough away its warm saltiness, but now Jessica could repay him. She bit down hard and then harder still, feeling her teeth pass through his shirt, then through his skin. His blood hit her face at the same moment that his scream almost deafened her. The amount of blood in her mouth increased dramatically and she wanted to heave. She could hardly breathe and thought she might choke. His agonised shriek continued and it just got louder as she rolled her head like a terrier killing a rat. She could feel her teeth pass through his flesh and wondered if her jaws would meet.

Even as she flailed around she recognised him as one of the men who had guided her to the mine disaster. He now tried to reach her eyes with the fingers of his right hand but Jessica was rolling her head so much beneath his forearm that he missed repeatedly, but she was totally unprepared when he head butted her. Her head torch shattered, plunging them all into darkness, and the blow left her giddy. She had time to think that the head butt would have been much fiercer if his arm had not been in the way and she feared what the next would do to her. The head butt made her involuntarily relax her bite and with a howl of agony he tore his ravaged arm free.

She lay there battered, exposed and desperately searching to see where the next attack would come from. The second attacker had been blocked from reaching her by his larger companion, but with the latter nursing his arm somewhere out of reach she heard the next man move in to take over and sensed from the few sounds he made that he was less than a metre away. She was still lying on her back but she kicked her right leg across and felt a satisfying crunch as her heavy walking boot connected with something that moved. From the way he yelled she hoped that she might have hit his kneecap; whatever it was, she heard him fall to the ground beside her. In the darkness it had been a wildly lucky blow and she knew she could not repeat it. Her right arm shot out in search of her precious bag and she hoped that its contents might give her some protection, but instead of grasping a shoulder strap her hand fell straight into its opening where some of the contents were spilling out of the top. She could feel the water bottle and the plastic bag that had held her food. Her shirt had been folded near the top of the bag and underneath was something hard. The knife. She could only grasp it through the folded shirt and it had snagged on something so her grip was compromised. With one hand at the limit of her reach Jessica tugged again and suddenly the knife came free pointing upwards just as the first attacker lunged at her again. She thrust upwards blindly in the darkness but with little force in her strike for she had barely been able to grasp the handle. Yet the man's onward rush at her ensured there was some power in the blow and Jessica felt the ten centimetre blade strike something – she couldn't tell if it was a bone or a belt buckle – then she knew from the way that it twisted it had sunk home into flesh. In the struggle she felt the knife handle being torn from her meagre grip. Jessica was now completely defenceless.

There was a dramatic exhalation of breath and no scream but the man squirmed away from her. "Putain" he breathed, and now she could just see him outlined against the sky as he started to move towards her once again. That was when a very large boot landed right beside her head and, before she could work out who or how, out of the darkness above her a high kick connected with the assailant's chest. Her attacker was thrown backwards and tumbled into the dirt.

All she could see of the new arrival was the boot as it lifted centimetres from her ear and landed in a new position a little further away. The second attacker had fallen close beside her and with her eyes now adjusting to the darkness she could make out that he was half kneeling, trying and failing to rise with the use of only one knee. The figure above her did a long-legged pirouette and the back of his right boot swung around to catch the kneeler in the face; he went down and didn't get up.

She lay there too stunned to see what happened next but somewhere beyond her feet there were the sounds of a very brief tussle before she heard someone approach at a walk. She had lost her knife as soon as she had used it and there was nothing left to defend herself with, but she need not have worried. A man reached down a hand and a familiar voice said, "This is why I don't take women into the mines." It was Max, the soldier and guide she had encountered in Walikale. "Up here, you're more bloody trouble than you're worth. Didn't I tell you not to come here?" he said in exasperation. "Because this is what happens."

******

"I'm leaving in two minutes; if you're ready you come with me. Otherwise I leave you to explain what happened to the Captain, and he deals with you."

Jessica was sitting up now, still dazed and shocked. She couldn't see it in the darkness but there was a curious stickiness that suggested her vest was covered in blood, and she could feel it caking, drying and cracking on her face and neck. God only knew what she looked like, Jessica could feel that her top lip was badly torn; it felt swollen, was increasingly sore, and seemed to move independently. Although she couldn't see it in the darkness she could feel that her fleece was torn and virtually useless for keeping her warm; and right on cue she began to shiver fiercely. Jessica hurriedly fished out the shirt from her bag and put it on, throwing the fleece away.

"De rien," he said ironically. You're welcome. Jessica realised that she hadn't even spoken to him since he turned the table on her attackers.

Through broken lips she mumbled an ill-formed response but he had already gone. When he returned a short time later, she was wearing her shirt and there was silence between them as she closed and strapped up her bag before hoisting it onto her shoulder.

"This is yours, I think," and he handed back her knife, handle first. He had wiped the blade clean but she hesitated. "It saved your life one time already, don't lose it."

So she accepted it and this time she thanked him more fully.

She felt a heavy numbness weighing her down. It could have been a result of the last few days, or just the last few minutes; with her head in turmoil, Jessica couldn't begin to analyse which. Something terrible had just happened, something even worse had been narrowly avoided and she was unable to process the thoughts fast enough – they were just a jumble of fear, relief, bewilderment, rage and self-blame that filled her head and vied for attention. How could Max be so calm after what had just gone on here?

Jessica held a tissue to her upper lip, fortunately the large cut was bleeding far less now although it still hurt like hell. Her mouth felt very swollen and she had such a lisp when she spoke that she hardly recognised her own voice. "What have you done with the men who attacked me?" she asked.

"They are unconscious but one is waking up so we must go. I hope they didn't see who I was," he added, "or that will make things complicated. The Captain is not my commander, but there will be trouble when these two wake up and tell their version of events." With that he turned around and made off down the hill towards the tree line.

When she picked up her bag, she found her hands were trembling almost uncontrollably and that didn't stop for another thirty minutes.

******

Dawn broke soon after they left, and the light above the tree canopy gradually improved visibility where they marched thirty metres below. They were an odd couple, walking wordlessly through the morning and stopping only to replenish their water bottles at a stream. Max ate some dry rations but offered nothing to Jessica. He did ask if she had any food and when she showed him the last of a bag of dried fruit he told her to eat it now or she wouldn't get through the rest of the day. She had clearly inconvenienced him enough already and he said he didn't want to leave a collapsed woman on the trail but, if that was what it came to....

They made better progress after they had eaten and continued walking until sundown with only brief halts to drink, but Jessica felt light-headed and unable to concentrate by late afternoon when finally they made camp with some porters heading up the trail. Without asking, Max took most of her rice and poured it into his own pot while Jessica stared listlessly into the fire that he had built in moments, and when it was cooked they shared it. By now Jessica's head was spinning with accumulated exhaustion and he had to dip her hand into the rice and boiled meat – she had no idea what it was but it looked like South African biltong and smelt only marginally better when cooked than it had when he took it from his pack.

Perhaps it was his army uniform but whatever the reason the porters gave them both a wide berth that night. For her part Jessica moved her sleeping mat closer to him than she would have considered before, and collapsed into a deep and uncomfortable sleep.

When she awoke, she had been bitten by insects and her lip hurt badly. She was sure she'd need a stitch or two to heal it properly and was anxious to get back to somewhere where that could be done well. She did at least have the energy in the morning to clean her face and remove traces of blood that lingered in her hairline. Nobody had taken much notice of her when they arrived at the overnight stop, so perhaps the covering was not as complete as she had feared. She cleaned her blood-stained vest in the stream as best she could and put it back in the pack.

Once again the track was so well worn and with thousands of porters on it she probably could have followed the route back to the airstrip, but Jessica was now aware that not only did she owe her safety to the man she knew only as Max, but she would never have managed the journey without him. Before they left he made her stand still in front of him while he examined the deep cut on her face. It needed iodine, he said. Otherwise he didn't speak much to her.

Around the middle of the day they heard a plane, and twenty minutes later the squawk of the VHF radio could be heard in the village. When they walked into Walikale, she was definitely more tense than before but they were met with indifference by the few soldiers they came across. If the injuries to Jessica's attackers had been reported, then their explanation had not involved the attempted rape of a foreign journalist. Jessica remained on edge though, her mind playing over scenarios in which the army would be looking for her, and she was desperate to catch the earliest plane possible.

She sat down out of sight in the back of the bar and drank a bottle of iced tea that she savoured like no drink ever before. Feeling stronger already Jessica knew that she didn't want to wait here any longer than was necessary and was about to go and talk to the crew of one of the planes when Max returned. "Get your bag," he said, "we're on the next flight."

"Are you coming, too?" she asked in surprise.

"*Bien sûr* that was my last trip for a while. Maybe forever with any luck." He hoisted his bag onto his back and strode off to find the plane, with Jessica doing her best to catch up. She was starting to find his secrecy irritating, until she realised that he knew as little about her.

There were a group of men hanging around the plane and they watched Max and his companion walk towards them, their interest growing as they saw this woman with a swollen and badly cut lip.

Both pilots had the broad faces and high cheekbones of Slavs, and they were chain-smoking much closer to the aircraft than she thought was clever. One of them nudged the other in the ribs and said something to Max that she couldn't hear. The men laughed loudly together before the second said in English, "You should look after your women better Max. Or is she a boxer?"

He smiled at them, "Truly, you have no idea." Max threw his bag into the aircraft and climbed in nimbly leaving Jessica to find her own way. As Jessica climbed aboard the plane, she heard the rhythmic thud of a rotor beating the air. Turning and shielding her eyes from the sun, she could just make out a large helicopter circling overhead as it prepared to land in the heart of the town, and she wondered if this was part of the long-delayed rescue effort for the trapped miners. Jessica desperately wanted to find somewhere with internet access to file her report on the collapsed mine and the trapped young miners.

She stepped forward carefully, negotiating her way over the tightly packed bags of tin ore. There were three hard and dusty seats in a row behind the pilots; a bulkhead obscured the view forwards for the middle passenger and Max had taken the seat on the left. She put her backpack down and collapsed into the right-hand seat, closing her eyes for a moment until one of the pilots tapped her shoulder. She winced slightly, it was bruised where she'd taken a kick only the day before. He rubbed his thumb and fingers together in the international signal for money. She sat up and dug some notes out of her wallet, which he looked at without expression before repeating the signal in a demand for more. She just wanted to be out of there and was prepared to pay double if only they would take off now, so she gave him some more notes. Jessica was unclear whether she had just paid double for herself or bought Max's seat for him – either way it would be worth it to be off and she knew she owed him a great deal.

Their plane was the first of three that was waiting in line to take off; clearly there was booming demand for this tin ore. All the other seats had been removed, and Jessica lay slumped across her pack and her eyes began to close as the plane's rear door was slammed shut and locked from the inside by the co-pilot. As he returned to the cockpit, the pilot completed his pre-flight checks. The engine fired immediately, the props turned slowly at first and then rapidly gathered speed.

Max was saying something to her. She cupped her hand behind her ear to hear him. He was grinning and speaking French again. His face came alive with a broad smile that she hadn't seen before, "C'est curieux, some miners say its bad luck to take women through the forest. Don't ask me why!"

She grinned back and then her badly damaged lip made her wish she hadn't; it was agony and her hand involuntarily went up to hide her mouth. She laid her head back down on the bag between them, too tired to take any notes about her departure. She didn't notice the policemen wave away the elderly twin-engined Russian plane. She was asleep by the time another two tonnes of Congolese minerals lifted off from the jungle for the thirty-minute run to Goma.

She never noticed the tiny thatched houses that crowded the edge of the roadway, or the long grass that blew back beneath their wings as they accelerated down the narrow tarmac strip, and she never saw how close the trees were at the edge of the jungle. It was probably just as well that Jessica never spotted the two broken aircraft that lay in the grass beside the last of the town's houses, silent skeletal reminders of the dangers of the Walikale Express.

******

As the aircraft came in to land, Jessica awoke with a frightened start and for a moment had no idea where she was. Then she saw the volcanic black ground and bright green grass of Goma airport and the last few days caught up with her in a rush. She gathered her things together and then just stopped doing anything while the aircraft taxied in. She thought about the last few days, the awful things she'd seen, the report she needed to file, but mostly she thought about how lucky she was to be here. Goma wasn't the safest place but at least here she had help at hand if she needed it. She looked down at the splashes of blood on her jeans and thought how differently this might have ended, were it not for the man next to her.

Jessica leaned over, touched him on the arm and he turned to look quizzically at her. "Max, I'm sorry for ..." her voice trailed off. "I've been a pain in the butt," she said in English and then attempted it in French. "I should have listened to you about Bisie when we first met, and there's someone else I should have listened to. I guess I just wanted to say thank you for helping me, you took a big risk," and she rested her hand gently on his arm. The engines were shutting down and the noise subsided into stillness as the pilots finished their work.

He looked at her sternly for a moment and she thought she'd overstepped some unknown boundary. Then that rare smile spread across his face. "Jessica, you annoy me when you don't listen. But I must be mad."

She looked puzzled. "Why's that?"

He smiled, "Don't ask me why but I would probably do it again." Max shook his head; he didn't seem to understand it himself and seemed embarrassed at what he had said. "I have to be in barracks. Take more care next time, because I will not be there." He stood up abruptly, slung his bag over his shoulder and stepped out of the rear door of the aircraft onto the baking lava. She watched him go, the long easy stride eating up the ground as it had through the forest only that morning.

She stepped down from the plane and could not dispel the tension in her body. Jessica expected a military hand on her shoulder at any moment and a world of trouble that would follow. Her heart was pumping as she made her way through the airport concourse but there were no shouts, no one called her name, and outside she fidgeted as she waited for a minibus to her hotel.

In spite of her exhaustion, at the first opportunity she had pulled the little laptop out of her bag. *Thank God it was light and strong*, she thought. Apart from a bit of dust on the neoprene cover, and the cracked corner it had sustained before there was no outward sign of damage.She would give it a thorough clean and one day she'd write the world's best testimonial for this piece of kit; it had survived being knocked to the ground in Kinshasa by that guy from the charity. Was he cute, she wondered, or just a klutz? Since then she'd used it in the camps, made notes on it at Taweza Road – damn, she needed to do something about the photos of those kids. She had carried it up into the mountains around Bisie mine and, although she hadn't used it there, it had survived the attack on her and even provided a pillow on the flight down from Walikale.

Her priority now was to write and post her report on the mine accident, and she began it soon after reaching her hotel room but she was so tired that the two articles took much longer to write than they should have. They were still unfinished when Jessica collapsed onto the sagging mattress in her cheap hotel and fell asleep as though this was five-star luxury.

It wasn't until the next morning after a cold shower (the hot water was out again), a long sleep and some food eaten very carefully that she began to feel halfway human. There was relief at being back in a world of modern communications but the fear hadn't left her that soldiers would come knocking with questions about dead or injured men. She kept her door locked and only went out for food at first, but she had a pressing problem. Her upper lip was badly cut and needed better cleaning than she had managed. The area around the jagged tear was more swollen and red but now it also felt hot, something that was beginning to alarm her, as she feared it might be infected. She knew she needed a doctor but was worried that anyone recommended by her hotel would not be clean or competent to stitch her wound. If she was to avoid serious infection or permanent scarring, she urgently needed some good medical help.

Jessica switched on the laptop and went to brush her teeth, something she had to do extremely gently. When she came back, the screen was still dark. She could have sworn she'd booted up. Jessica tried it again and still nothing happened, at which point a bit of panic set in. She had good reason to worry, she had so much writing and photographic work on here, and having been away from anywhere with internet access she hadn't done an online back up for a week.

Heaven only knew if or where she could get a Mac fixed in Goma, or how long it would take if she could. The problems were piling up and now her best link to the outside world was on the fritz. She fought back tears of frustration and tiredness, and tried to prioritise her problems. Doctor first, laptop second, then the rest.

Then there was a loud knock on the door. Jessica froze. Christ, if that was the Army what could she say? Should she deny all knowledge, or say that the soldiers attacked her. What about Max, she couldn't mention him without getting him into trouble, even though he had saved her. She said nothing and hoped they would go away.

"Miss Tsiba, this is the manager. I talk to you, please open."

Her heart began to return to a normal rate and she went to the door. Jessica still needed reassurance. "Who is it?" she asked and peered through the peephole.

"Hello, Miss Tsiba, I'm Daniel, I'm Hotel Manager. Can I have speak with you?"

She looked again through the peephole and this time instead of listening at the door with his head bent, he had stepped back. She had a much better view and recognised him from the Reception desk. There didn't appear to be anyone with him.

"One moment," she said and took the chain off before opening the door.

He smiled at her and his expression turned to one of concern. "You OK? You mouth …" and he pointed to his top lip.

"I fell yesterday," she said and found herself miming a trip which instantly seemed idiotic. "I'm going to the doctor soon."

"Yes, or it be …" he struggled for the English word and settled for, "bad."

"I am worried you go for many nights and we don't know where you to go. I am happy you …" he was about to say OK, but looking at her lip, he started again, "I am happy you here."

"Thank you, yes I'm OK."

"Sorry, but we charge you for room when you not here." He spread his hands in the international gesture of regret. Is policy of hotel, Miss Tsiba. "If you go away again, you must to tell and we store you bags."

"Thank you, er … Daniel. No, I understand. I was away for longer than I expected. I will pay you for these nights too. But is your email working now?"

He spread his hands out again. "Sorry, not email today. But very soon, we have an engineer coming. He come soon. Is big engineer and he make email OK good. He fix hot water, too."

Sounds like a real specialist, she thought, *but kept it to herself.* At which point Jessica had an idea, one that might help her tackle several problems at once.

"You pay for room now? Before you go, again," he said pointedly. She just nodded and closed the door. She needed to find a card that she hoped was somewhere in her luggage.

******

After a week or more spent on the road, shooting videos of numerous refugee reception centres in the Mugunga camps, then photographing the charity's work at a women's refuge and rape care centre, and an orphanage further south in Bukavu, James was back at their lodging in Goma. It wasn't lavish but it was home for now, and drier than their recent overnight stops.

For the first time in more than a week they didn't have any appointments and James was lying in bed, enjoying the comfort of his sleeping bag. He'd get up later and update the charity's blog, but for now he listened to the unfamiliar birdsong that was only interrupted by someone boiling a pan of water. *A coffee would be great,* he thought, just not quite yet and turned over. It had been dark the previous night when they had driven up to Goma from South Kivu, a journey made slower and more stressful by the number of army checkpoints along the way. They were all tired. There had just been time for a plate of pasta, before he had plugged in his phone which had died the day before, and gone to bed.

The last thing he expected was for his phone to ring early the next morning but it sounded like his ringtone. He had been out of the UK for weeks and it was even longer since he had been in the States. Who even knew his mobile number? Neil? He wouldn't call except in emergency. Nor his mother, she wouldn't call again till Christmas.

A shout came from the other room "Is anyone going to answer the sodding phone?"

James recognised the music sample, it was definitely his ringtone. "Bugger," he said and wriggled out of his comfortable cocoon. The fact that the day's warmth was starting to make him hot in the sleeping bag was no consolation.

He stumbled his way into the living room, his hair tousled from sleep and dressed only in boxer shorts. James picked up the fully charged phone and pulled the cable out of it before gruffly mumbling hello.

"James, is that you?"

He didn't recognise the voice. American accent. Who would be calling him at this time from the States?

The woman's voice continued before he could reply. "I don't know if you remember me, my name's Jessica Tsiba. We ran into each other in Kinshasa. Literally."

The phrasing had suggested a chance meeting, but his heart went bang as he recalled her. Big eyes, big smile when he'd seen her in the maternity tent at Kanyaruchinya camp. Beautiful, really. Now he was awake and bizarrely she was on the phone, calling him.

"Sure, I remember." He tried to sound cool, though he didn't feel it. He was straight out of bed and his voice croaked. He unconsciously brushed back the hair that had flopped into his eyes and stood up straighter as though she could see him. Dressed this way, it was as well that she couldn't.

"James, I don't know if you can help me but I've got a couple of problems and I couldn't think of anyone else to turn to. I hope you don't mind me calling, but you did say you might be able to help if I had trouble with my computer and you left your business card." For the first time he heard vulnerability in this interesting, spiky woman.

His pulse had gone from standstill to racing in the time it took him to clear his throat. He couldn't for the life of him remember what he had said to her in

Kinshasa, except that she'd been understandably angry with him for a few seconds before she calmed down a little. In those moments he'd glimpsed someone who was passionate about what she does, and who had seen it jeopardised because he hadn't spotted her as he sprinted through the pelting rain. He'd been clumsy and then she hadn't let him help which he'd found frustrating as he genuinely wanted to make amends. So he'd had the presence of mind to push one of his new photography business cards into her papers as he handed them back, it had made him feel less guilty. She'd obviously found the card, and hadn't thrown it away. That in itself was a surprise.

"My computer has died and I desperately need to get an article out. Also I wondered if you or your colleagues know a good doctor? Someone good with a needle and thread."

"Bloody hell, what have you done to yourself?"

"It's a long story, but I need to get cleaned up and to get some stitches."

"Where are you? Are you still in Goma?"

"Yes, I'm at my hotel but it's pretty bad and I don't think it's a good idea for me to stay here much longer. Like I said, it's a long story."

"Hold on," he said. "I'll just ask." He put his hand over the phone, and called out, "Have we got a doctor? A good one? I've got someone, a friend here who needs to see a doctor and get some stitches."

There was a pause, then Sarah poked her head round the corner. "Of course we have. He's not far from here. What's happened?"

"Thanks, I'll tell you more in a moment."

"Jessica?" It felt good saying her name. He'd thought of it often enough. "Are you still there?"

"Yeah, I'm here."

"Are you mobile, can you get over here?"

"It's not that bad. I just need to see someone I can trust."

"We're near the hospital by that big roundabout," and he waited while she jotted down the full address.

"Thanks, James. I'm sorry to lay this on you."

"No worries, catch a cab and we'll see you here in a while."

By the time Jessica arrived over an hour later, James had not only showered, shaved and tidied his room and his room-mate, but the living room too, much to the amusement of his colleagues.

Aidan was up now, wandering around in a pair of blue Y-fronts that had seen better days. They were so old the elastic was failing and he kept hitching them up. "So tell me, James, you say you hardly know this girl, right? And yet she calls you out of the blue to help her find a quack. Don't they have a phone book where she is?"

"There's a bit more to it than that, I think she's got PC problems."

"When did you become an IT nerd?"

"I'm not, I was going to ask you, mate."

"Oh really?"

"And you say you saw her in Kanyaruchinya? In a Post-Natal Unit? You're getting a bit ahead of yourself, aren't you?"

Sarah walked in to the kitchen. "Not at all. He's already had the poor woman on the floor the first time he met. Personally, I reckon she's serving him an injunction." James grinned and had to take it. He knew he could expect a lot more of this before the day was out.

Serge just made himself a coffee, ignored their banter and trudged back to his room in his ill-fitting cotton suit.

They heard the taxi arrive and when the doorbell rang, James answered it to find Jessica on the doorstep clutching a backpack and frequently touching her fingers to an upper lip that was jaggedly torn, bright pink and thickly swollen.

"Jeez, Jessica, come on in. Here, I'll take that. What the hell's happened?"

Sarah was standing just behind him and her look of wry amusement at James's unexpected visitor immediately turned to one of concern when she saw Jessica's face. This was her metier and she knew what to do.

"Hi, Jessica, I'm Sarah. You won't remember me but I was at the MONUSCO reception in Kinshasa where you two first met. James, look after her bags. Jessica, bring anything you need, 'cos, girl, you're coming with me," and she turned her right around and led her back to the door. There was an authority in her voice as she called out, "Serge, get the car. Now!"

******

With the women gone James was at a loose end. She hadn't given him her broken laptop and he didn't want to go rummaging through her belongings. Since he was up and dressed he might as well deal with his own work and be free to help Jessica when they returned. He put his laptop and cameras on the dining table, and went back for the memory card he'd put by the bed. No sign. He got down on the floor beside the bed and searched properly but it was nowhere in sight. Then he opened the bedside drawer but drew a blank there too.

"Aidan, have you picked up a memory card from the bedside here?"

"Wossat?" said Aidan from the next room.

James could see where this conversation was likely to go, if he confessed to losing a chip. "No problem," he called back, it would be best not to cement his reputation for losing stuff. But he was baffled by this. He knew where he'd placed it and he was sure that Aidan hadn't used the bedside table between them once while they had shared the room. He picked up his book to see if the card had slipped between the lower pages. There was no card and his bookmark was in it, but it had moved. It was now upside down and in a page that he'd read days before. Maybe Aidan had knocked the book onto the floor. There was no harm done, he knew he had back up images, but James couldn't shake off an uneasy feeling.

******

The others hardly saw Jessica when she returned later. Sarah bustled her straight through saying that she needed to rest, and immediately set about making a bed for her in the box room. That meant commandeering the sofa cushions that Aidan and James were sitting on, to use as a mattress. She clucked around settling Jessica in to her temporary new home then returned to the living room where she busied herself saying little.

Aidan and James exchanged glances but the enigmatic mood showed no sign of lifting. "How is she?" ventured James.

Sarah looked up at him as though she'd only just noticed his presence. "Much as you'd expect." For a moment it seemed as though that was all she would say before she added, "Tired, sore, embarrassed, and a bit scared."

Another glance from James to Aidan. "What's she embarrassed about?" asked Aidan.

Sarah put down her pen with a sigh, as though she were a schoolmistress explaining algebra to a class of five year-olds. "She's embarrassed about turning up here and asking for help. She's embarrassed about the stitches in her lip and how they make her look. She's embarrassed at having to explain herself to people she hardly knows. She feels professionally embarrassed that she hasn't filed her articles yet on an important story because her computer isn't working. Is that enough to be going on with?" And Sarah went back to her work.

James was glad that it was Aidan who had asked the question. "Well, I've got good news for her then," said Aidan. "Her Mac's running fine now. It's a bit scuffed and there's a crack in the casing but I've got rid of the error screen and it seems to be finding the internet again OK. It's ready whenever she wants it."

For the first time since she returned Sarah managed a smile. "That is good news, we can tell her as soon as she awakes."

"Tell me what?" Jessica had come out of her room.

"What are you doing?" said Sarah. "You need rest and some real food, you heard what the doctor said. "

"Thanks, but I don't sleep easily in the day. What were you going to tell me?"

"Aidan here has fixed your computer," said James.

Aidan beamed at her.

"Oh, that's fantastic, thanks so much. I won't kiss you," she pointed at her lip and pulled a lop-sided smile.

282

"Another time," said Aidan cheerily, and James found himself wishing he had fixed it.

Her lower lip was unmarked but her upper lip had the distinctive purple traces of iodine on it, and three black sutures punctuated the once jagged tear. Only now the wound was clean and neatly closed. There was still noticeable swelling but some of the bruising was turning yellow as it faded and the red inflammation had diminished already.

"I'm not supposed to speak much, and I'm probably hard to understand at the moment, but I just wanted to say thanks to you guys for taking me in," said Jessica.

James shook his head. "Nope, didn't get any of that," he replied grinning.

"No' a word," said Aidan.

She started to smile and clamped her hand over her mouth, "Don't make me laugh. That really hurts. Now, can I have my computer?"

"Better give it to her Aidan, I'm not sure how long I can take this mumbling. Now who wants a coffee?" and he headed off to the kitchen.

"I'll have one, please," said Jessica. "It may help me file my reports."

******

It wasn't until much later that James found a moment to talk to Jessica on his own. With her articles on the mine collapse and the military control of the mine written and emailed she relaxed a little over dinner. She talked as much as she comfortably could about the diversion she'd taken on her journey back from the orphanage and how it had led her to the tin mine. She told them a little about the harsh, dangerous work in the mine, and how an unsupported shaft had caved in burying people alive, many of them children. She told them of the soldiers who controlled the mine and its output, and of the impossibility of rescuing everyone, but how one boy had been pulled out alive only to die in front of her. At this point she had found it difficult to go on, and had gulped back her emotions.

Someone asked her how she was injured and she made light of the attack, but James wasn't alone in thinking that there was a great deal more to the story. It may have been hard for her to speak with her stitches, or there may have been aspects that were hard for her to discuss at all – perhaps he'd never know. He sensed that Sarah knew more, but she would be the soul of discretion.

There was a lull in the conversation and Sarah stood up from the table. "I'm going to bed, and you should probably do the same, Jessica."

"I will. And thanks, Sarah. Don't know what I'd have done without you, all of you," she looked around them.

"You're welcome. See you in the morning."

Aidan and Serge turned in as well, leaving just James and Jessica at the table. "I know I should go to bed but I've got too much going round in my head," she said.

"Such as?" asked James.

"Oh, I don't know. A lot has happened in the last few days, it's hard to take it all in."

"Do you want to talk about it?"

"Not really. I think I need to process it a bit first."

"OK. If you change your mind, I'm a good listener."

She looked across the table and studied him silently for a second or so longer than he might have expected. "I'm glad I called," she said.

James smiled at her. "Me, too."

Then she added, "I mean, you've all been so kind to me."

"Oh. Yeah." James had hoped she was glad to see him, but clearly she was being polite about what they had all done. After all, she had needed the group's support, not his alone. For a moment there his heart had lifted and now he felt a swoop of disappointment. He tried not to show it, but it was a well-known failing of his, apparently; he always wore his heart on his sleeve. "Well, it was no trouble. We couldn't leave you like that." He didn't know what else to say, but he didn't want to end this conversation.

"I haven't seen any of your work," she said. "Would you show me what you've done?" Perhaps it was the fatigue, but James saw a gentler side to her now. "Sarah said it was really good."

"Did she?" James was pleased and astonished, which was enough for now to put aside his sense of let-down.

He pulled over his laptop and opened one of the folders. "This is unedited and a bit rough. There's a lot of deletion and cropping to do but I took these shots the day I saw you at Kanyaruchinya," and he started a new slideshow. "I'm going to have another coffee. Do you want one?" He stood up.

"No thanks, or I'll never get to sleep." Then she was silent, absorbed in the images.

He busied himself for a minute in the kitchen.

"What are these?"

"What are what?"

"These shots are all of soldiers. It looks like they're in the camp. That can't be right, can it?"

"Oh, sorry, I told you they were a bit rough. I haven't sorted those ones yet. Yeah, they were in the camp. I don't know what they were doing, it struck me as a bit odd at the time so I took the photos; I guess it's becoming a habit. I did it a bit surreptitiously because they had armed guards everywhere. I've worked out who a couple of them are though, I think that guy in the suit is the Rwandan Defence

Minister, I saw them both in *The Economist*. Here, look," he pulled the magazine out of his bag, "same people, I'm sure of it."

"Looks like it. They shouldn't be there, James. Even the Congolese army shouldn't be in the camp. Who're they meeting?"

"Not a clue, but it looks like the other new arrival may be Didier Toko, the rebel leader. There's a big welcoming party of Congolese army officers led by some bigshot. Here, this is him…."

"Oh, I've seen him before, in Kinshasa," she said.

"Really? You sure?"

"Definitely, he's the son of a very senior government fixer. General Dr Moise Businga, a nasty piece of work from what I hear, up to his eyes in the bloodshed during the Congo Wars, and did very well out of it for himself," she said. "People still don't like talking about him, he's real bad news."

"Blimey, so we've got the leader of Congo's FDLR rebels, backed by their neighbours in Rwanda, fighting the Congo government, having a secret meeting somewhere they shouldn't with a senior mover and shaker in the Congolese government. Interesting? Yes. Puzzling? Sure. But it doesn't tell us very much." James sucked his teeth as he thought it through.

"It may be perfectly legit," Jessica offered.

"Maybe, but why meet so furtively and why there?"

"He arrived in a convoy of shiny black Mercedes followed by a heavily-armed jeep. I wouldn't call that furtive."

"I haven't been here that long but I've seen plenty of high speed convoys like that zipping around Goma. And it's furtive in my book when you skulk behind blacked out windows and meet people where you definitely shouldn't – especially when it turns out they're your sworn enemies. I dunno, I guess it'll have to be a mystery. Have you shown these pics to Sarah?"

"No, I don't think she'd approve," he said. "I was only supposed to be taking photos of refugees not secretive politicians. To be honest, I think she'd go ape shit, and I'm only just back in her good books so don't mention it will you?"

"Not if you don't want me to. Listen, it's all catching up with me so I'm gonna hit the sack. I'm bushed. I meant what I said, I'm really grateful for the bed and the meal and all your kindness. You guys have been great," and as she stood she extended a slender brown hand and rested it on his arm. It felt cool.

James couldn't think of anything to say that he hadn't already said, so he just smiled and then she was gone.

Chapter 19
Taweza and Goma city, Eastern Democratic Republic of the Congo (DRC)
A Week Ago

The more Raphael thought about it after the newspaper lady had gone, the more sure he was that he couldn't just leave his family's future in her hands or any of the adults who had let him down before. Marianne had promised to help, but Marc had often stood in her way saying it was a waste of time and would raise false hopes. She had achieved nothing so why should Raphael believe that this reporter would be any different – she may have forgotten about them already.

He had even suggested to the Audoussets that he should go on his own, but Marc had dismissed the idea saying it was too dangerous and asking how he would find them among the millions of people now in Goma. OK, he didn't know how; all he knew was that he would never find Mama, Laurent and Christine if he stayed here. He wasn't a fool, he didn't need Marc to patronise him and tell him that it would be difficult and dangerous, and that the odds were stacked against him. He just knew he would never see a Man in the mirror if he didn't try. Anyway, hadn't Miss Jessica said that she couldn't promise to help. No, there was only one person that he and Keisha could rely on and that was himself.

Raphael was angry that he had wasted time and learned nothing from seeing those earlier hopes of finding his family dashed. You couldn't trust people – whatever they said at the time – they let you down later. He had really hoped that someone would help them when they were taken to the mine, but the place had been completely isolated and it was easy now to see that no one was even interested in trying.

He was a man and he had to act like one, instead of waiting and hoping for other people to solve his problems. That evening he sat down with a piece of paper and began to compile a checklist of all the things he would need. It was hard to predict everything, but it was a lot easier than thinking how to tell Keisha that he was going and this time she couldn't come.

Raphael knew he had to be practical and go prepared. He didn't have a lot to take, and he might have to borrow some items from Marc when he wasn't around – he'd give them back later. Meanwhile, he would pack everything in his blanket.

He would need money, too. Funnily enough, that wasn't quite the problem it would have been a year ago since Raphael had been earning some money. It wasn't much but it would have to do. As he was approaching the time when he would have to leave the orphanage, the Audoussets had sat Raphael down several months ago and explained that they couldn't afford to send him away with much when he left in a year's time. Nor could they pay him for the vegetables, poultry and goats he raised since these were the orphanages and he did it in school time. But they wanted him to go out into the world with more than their good wishes and the few tools they had set aside for him, so they asked if he would like to teach the other children what he'd learned about cultivating a smallholding from his father and since he had arrived at Taweza Road.

So that same week Raphael had begun to give lessons to the other pupils in the morning and every evening after school. With his enthusiasm for his subject the lessons proved popular, the children were able to look after the chickens and goats, and the fertile soil in the garden and on the floodplain beside the river encouraged their efforts. Now, months later, Raphael still hadn't spent any of his earnings – there was nothing to spend it on. He'd watched the coins build up, and been pleased that gradually they were augmented by notes. At last that saving had a purpose. He couldn't think further ahead to when he would leave the school; in any case he might have found his Mother by then.

Less than a week after Miss Jessica had gone Raphael playfully flicked Keisha's ear in assembly. She was in the row in front but she didn't need telling who it was. She didn't want to get in trouble for talking so she ignored him. "Keisha," he hissed twice. The girl next to Keisha turned and hissed back at him to be quiet. Raphael took no notice of her, "Keish, I need to talk to you."

"Not now," said the other girl out of the side of her mouth.

"I wasn't talking to you. Keish, I'll see you after in the garden."

"O-kay," said Keisha over her shoulder and in evident irritation.

Twenty minutes later he was picking the excess stems off his tomato plants while he waited. Fortunately, Keisha was alone when she arrived. "Beatrice says you're a pain, and she's very glad she doesn't have a brother."

He laughed, "I wouldn't want her as a sister. My goats smell better than her."

"I'll tell her you said that."

"Good. Maybe she'll start using soap."

"You're horrible. What do you want? I've got stuff to do."

"It'll have to wait, this is important. Sit down." She didn't move and he realised he was doing what she hated and being older-brotherish. "Please?" he added.

"OK, but just for a minute, I've got to do my French."

Then it came out in a rush. "Listen, I have to leave. The school. Not forever, but I've been thinking about the twins and Mama. All the time we're in here they may be looking for us, or they may even give up looking – I have to get out and search for them. And I don't mean the kind of search that Marc and Marianne have done. They've just asked their friends, we know that's not going to achieve anything."

He half expected her to burst into tears or to protest, but she did neither. Keisha was always a bit of a mystery to him, if the truth be told.

"What about the lady who took our photos? Isn't she looking for them?" she asked.

"She said she would, but I don't know. We don't know anything about her, she might forget or not try very hard. Or Marc and Marianne might tell her not to. Anything could happen. At least, if I go then I'll know I've tried. I don't know if I'll find them, but don't you see, I've got to try." Raphael couldn't keep the desperation out of his voice.

Keisha sat still and chewed her bottom lip as she always did when thinking hard. She looked up at him, "Actually, I think it's a good idea. You should go, but you have to come back. You mustn't leave me on my own."

"You'll be all right. You love it here." He smiled at her but she was having none of it.

"I mean it, Raphael. If you leave me here, I'll hate you forever, and I'll never speak to you again." There was a pause as they both took in the unintended logic of what she'd just said and, even though she wanted to be angry with him, Keisha began to laugh and so did he.

"Of course, I'm not going to leave you here." And he put an arm around her shoulders. "You're half the reason I'm going to search, right? Besides, I won't be gone long and one of us needs to be here in case Mama comes looking." Even as he said that, he knew he couldn't promise when he'd return. It was just one of those things you said that people wanted to hear, wasn't it? Of course he'd come back as soon as he had some news. He certainly didn't want to reappear empty handed and have Marc say, 'I told you so'.

They stood up and Keisha gave him a fierce hug around the middle. She stood there gripping him for a long time not letting him go and when she spoke it was into his shirt which he could feel was getting damp, "Have you told Marianne and Marc? When are you going?"

"I can't tell them, Keisha, they'll stop me. I'll go early tomorrow morning." Now that he'd put a date on it he felt both exhilarated and scared. He was excited at being out of the school and the orphanage, and at seeing Laurent, Christine and Mama again. The twins would be huge now.

"Come and see me before you go," she said and without waiting for a reply she turned and ran off so that he couldn't see how hard she was crying.

******

From the moment he stepped off the ferry in Goma, thought Raphael, *everything had gone wrong.* He had walked for hours to the main road without seeing any traffic. After that a few taxi vans overtook him and there were private cars but they didn't stop. He'd kept walking in the heat of the early afternoon and, just when he thought no one would give him a lift, a covered truck had pulled over in front of him. The back was filled with crates of empty beer bottles so he'd been allowed to sit between the driver and his mate in the cab. It was hot, noisy and bouncy up there and he loved it. This was the first time he'd ridden so high; you could see everything from up there, even looking down into people's cars and houses. He thought this would be a good job to have, driving people or things all over, seeing new places all the time. Somehow he'd have to learn to drive but he was sure he could manage it. He had watched carefully what the driver did beside him and asked a few questions. Raphael knew about the steering, the brakes and the gears, and he knew what the gauges on the dashboard should tell you – even though the water temperature and oil pressure dials were broken.

The road was signposted to Bukavu, a huge city standing on the shore of a lake so enormous that as they drove down through the hills towards it Raphael couldn't see across it, although he could make out an island in the middle. The lorry was unloading in the ferry port and it seemed this was his only way to Goma at the north end of the lake. So, reluctantly, he spent some of his precious francs on a ticket and walked on with all the traders taking their goods to the markets in Goma.

As the ferry left the harbour, Raphael was excited and just watched the scenery slide by in front of him, but once they had passed between two islands the lake began to widen and there wasn't much to see. He was tired and went in search of some shade. The heat was made more oppressive by the still air. The clouds were threatening to bring thunder squalls, but the wind was light and it felt hot on deck.

A blue and red flag hoisted above the ship's bow hung lifelessly and it was only when they were under way that there was any breeze to cool the passengers. The rhythmic thrum of the ship's engine soon sent him to sleep on top of his pack and it was almost dark when he awoke three hours later. He could see lights on the shore ahead and within an hour the ship had docked in Goma port.

Raphael stood at the rail and looked down on a crowd of people either waiting to meet someone or to board the vessel for the return journey early in the morning. Below him a man in a T-shirt and jeans looped a length of rope and threw the coil down to another waiting on the quayside who deftly tied it off. Cars and vans were lined up ready to meet the passengers, and motorbikes weaved between them revving their engines and using their horns to little effect. Beside them the blue and white ship MV Iko rolled gently in the ferry's wake and somewhere behind him a loud ship's horn announced the arrival of a smaller orange boat. A man with a bulging multi-coloured woolly hat stood next to Raphael staring at the quayside, searching for a face; Raphael couldn't take his eyes of the man's long hair that spilled from under his hat.

He joined the other passengers queuing to get off and walked down the ramp, and was greeted by the noise of vehicles and a powerful stench of diesel oil and rotting fish that stabbed his nostrils. As he reached the dockside, he found himself being jostled this way and that by people who knew better than he did where to go. Many were shouting and gesticulating to one another, urging their friends to hurry, rounding up stray family members, or haggling over fares with stubborn-faced taxi drivers. Raphael had never seen so many people all at once. In his village, people would be ready for their beds by now. The thought brought a pang of anxiety as he remembered his last view of the burning houses, and the shouts that surrounded him now blended in his tired mind with the screams that had followed him as he fled with Keisha all that time ago. He shook his head to dispel the images and walked on up the gritty black road in search of an area of calm in which to gather his thoughts and plan his next steps.

The noise of traffic swirled around him leaving Raphael bewildered and unsure of himself. He followed a line of people as the waiting vehicles dispersed, until after a kilometre or two he could see a few shop fronts and some concrete steps where he could sit down. A few of the shops were brightly lit and doing good trade in drinks and food. He was hungry but he knew he had to save his money so he moved away to somewhere where the smells were not so enticing.

At the end of the row of shops he found an old cardboard box which he ran off with before anyone could stop him. No one said anything. It would serve as a groundsheet tonight to keep him off the bare earth. He passed a barber shop that was still lit as someone swept up the hair that had fallen. A dusty road between tall houses led away from the lake and away from the ranks of streetlights. A dog the other side of the fence startled him with its deep bark as he passed by, and somewhere nearby another dog joined in. Behind the houses stood two shipping containers set back from the road on the black earth that looked so strange to him, their corrugated steel painted a dull colour that he couldn't identify in the pale wash from the nearest house lights. Occasionally a motorbike would buzz along the road, its rider weaving with practised ease among the puddles of water or worse. Between the containers was a space no more than a metre wide into which Raphael slipped to find a safe resting place, from here he could look up and down the street. There was only darkness at the other end of the parallel boxes. Each steel structure was longer than their home in Nyasi and almost as tall; he had no idea what they were doing here but they gave him a feeling of safety and an observation point from which he could see the street's coming and goings. He had felt vulnerable in such a large crowd and he wondered if it was a feeling he'd ever get used to. He would go in search of food first thing but for now he wanted to sleep and to think what to do tomorrow.

"That's Snake's," said a disembodied voice.

Raphael leaped to his feet, responding to the warning even before he'd registered where it had come from.

The sound of laughter came from somewhere close. He spun around, searching by his feet in the half-darkness but he could see nothing.

More laughter. It was coming from above. A face appeared over the top of one of the containers, and whoever he was he could hardly speak he was laughing so hard.

"No, you jerk," said the face. "That's Snake's." Then he rolled back out of view and gales of laughter echoed again under the trees. Raphael just stood there, staring up to where the face had appeared and wondering what the bloody joke was. It was obviously at his expense.

He was still staring upwards when two guys came walking round the corner, one from either end of the corridor in which he was lying. There was a swagger about them, and they looked at home. "Who're you?" said the one who had spoken before.

A year or so before Raphael would have been intimidated by them, but he was at least their size and physically strong. He knew it, too; there was no one at Taweza Road who could put him down. If nothing else, his time spent working in the mine had developed his physique and had taught him what it was like to be really scared. To him, being scared now meant being confronted by armed men carrying Kalashnikovs, it meant not being there if Keisha was in real trouble. It did not mean a gang of two boys, who appeared to be armed only with attitude.

"Who's asking?"

"Hey! We've got a player here, Snake," said the guy behind him. There was bravado in his voice, but now he seemed to be re-assessing Raphael.

The one in front of Raphael grinned and his sharp-looking teeth shone, but there was no humour in his eyes. "He's on our ground, and he wants to know who we are. He needs to learn some respect."

Raphael was cornered but he could avoid having one behind him, so he turned sideways, keeping his eyes on the larger of the two.

The one who had been behind him didn't wait to discuss it any more, he rushed Raphael from a couple of metres away. If he had moved, it might have been more effective, but Raphael had ample time to see him coming and stepped towards him raising his right knee as he did so. It almost didn't matter what it connected with, at that closing speed it was going to do some damage. The rounded muscle above his knee struck the guy full in the face and his attacker went down with little sound. The boy lay motionless on the dirt in the confined space between the containers and Raphael spun at right angles to face the next threat but the other guy wasn't even looking at him. He was looking down the street to his left and immediately put his finger to his lips. "Polisi! Let's go!"

Then Raphael, too, heard the growl of a big-engined 4x4 and simultaneously saw headlights swing across the trees opposite as a police car pulled slowly into the road and crept past their hiding place. It was white with blacked out windows, bull bars framed the front and there were spotlights on the roof. "Quick, take his other arm!"

A moment before these guys had been going to knock him out, now one was enlisting him to help them escape from the police. For reasons he could hardly explain – perhaps it was the perception of a shared and greater threat – Raphael put both hands under one arm, while the boy's friend did the same. He was heavy and Raphael needed to grip his upper arm tightly. He scooped up his blanket of belongings and following the other's lead they staggered at speed between the containers away from the 4x4. When they reached the end of the steel corridor, the boy turned left and Raphael followed. They heard a door slam and saw a beam of light from the car's roof sweep back and forth. Whatever the police had seen or heard, it was no longer there but it wouldn't take much to find them.

They stood there breathing hard with a slack weight suspended between them. Raphael hoped that he would stay quiet a little longer. *This was mad*, he thought, *I've done nothing. Why am I hiding?* But he was aware that these guys must know more about the police here than he did, so maybe it was best. They could hear a tinny voice squawking on a radio inside the vehicle, and whatever it said it was enough to draw the policeman's interest away.

"Polisi bastards! They'll kick you down the street if you don't pay them protection. Break your arm or leg. Sons of whores!" And he hawked up some phlegm which he spat into the dirt an impressive distance away. "They don't like homeless people; they'll take you in and you do not want that. That's a trip to the hospital, or the morgue. What's your name?"

"Raphael."

"Mine's Snake. You're not from Goma." It was a statement, not a question.

"Nyasi."

"Never heard of it."

"It's all right, I've never heard of you."

The guy paused. Then he burst out laughing. "I like you, man. You make me laugh. Well, this is my patch. Snake's patch so don't get no ideas. You hear me?"

"Your patch?"

"Sure, it is. You want to say something about that?" Suddenly a thin, sharp-looking knife appeared in his hand from nowhere.

"No, I just meant I didn't understand." Raphael was now aware of how close he'd come to being stabbed by someone much more dangerous than his friend. "This is where you live?"

"And eat, and earn, and sleep. So, no grafting here for you. No working."

"I was just going to sleep and then leave in the morning."

"You're not working?"

"No."

"Where you going then?"

"I don't know, wherever people go when they've had to run away. I'm looking for my family who had to leave our village."

"Well, you're bloody lost then. You want to be in one of the camps. They're north of the city, not here."

"I just came off the boat from Bukavu—" He was interrupted by a groan and the figure they'd put down between them and momentarily forgotten tried to get up.

"Leave him, he'll be alright." And Snake stepped over him and grasped Raphael by the shoulder in a brotherly way. "Let's get a drink."

"Shouldn't we ...," he began. Raphael pointed to the groggy but improving guy sitting in the dirt.

"Nah, leave him. Joe knows where to find us."

Raphael wasn't sure if the drink meant alcohol. "I don't have any money," said Raphael. *At least none to spare*, he thought.

"We don't need no money. They owe me, Raph." And Snake led the way through the streets to a drinks stall. Whatever the truth of it, he was served two beers, no money changed hands, and they sat on plastic chairs underneath a wide umbrella, and studied one another by the light of a few bare bulbs above the drinks stall.

"That was a move, taking Joe down like that. Where'd you learn that? Man, he's gonna have a headache for a week." He cackled with laughter.

If it had been my friend, Raphael thought, *I'd have stayed with him, never mind the beers*. But it wasn't his friend, so he said nothing and enjoyed the cold drink. Over his shoulder a plate of fried potatoes was placed on the little wooden table between them. Raphael reached for them eagerly then stopped and looked at Snake who was eyeing him. "Go on," he said, "they're for you." Raphael hadn't eaten all day and he was ravenous. The potatoes were some of the best he'd ever tasted, or maybe that was his hunger.

Neither of them moved when a chair was put down next to Snake and Joe lowered himself gingerly into it. He said nothing and looked down at the table, not at them. The whole situation seemed a bit weird to Raphael, but it was obviously quite natural to Snake to sit down and share a meal with someone he'd only just pulled a knife on. This was his territory, so Raphael went along with it.

Snake looked around then pulled a half-smoked cigarette from his pocket and lit it. The smoke from it was thicker than Raphael remembered from the elders in his village, and when it reached him it was more pungent. "You want some?"

"Nah, I'm OK."

Snake passed it to his friend. "Reckon you need it more," and he laughed. Joe didn't join in, he avoided Raphael's eyes as he took a couple of long drags then passed it back.

A man in a large and elaborately painted wheelchair came towards them. There seemed to be no obvious form of propulsion for this three-wheeler until Raphael spotted the small boy in ragged shorts behind who was pushing him. There was an old guy in the chair, with grey hair and a wispy beard. In one outstretched hand he held a plastic cupful of cigarettes. The other arm lay twisted, thin and useless in his lap. "You want smokes?" They shook their heads and a second boy appeared out of the darkness to take over the job of pushing the wheelchair to the next group of tables.

An hour later, Snake suddenly stood up. "I've gotta go see someone. Joe here will look after you and he'll see you right for the camps tomorrow." He held out a clenched fist; Raphael didn't know what to do with it but he did the same and Snake attempted a handshake that Raphael had never seen before. "Man, you've got a lot to learn," he laughed loudly again and shook his head at Raphael's naïveté. "Joe will show you where to kip tonight. I ain't here tomorrow but come back sometime and meet the others. You've got an innocent face, we could use that. And the girls will love it," he grinned.

Raphael had no idea what he was talking about; he just knew he had much to learn about street life. "I will," he said and he meant it. He'd enjoyed being taken seriously for once; too often people talked down to him or treated him like a kid and he'd shown that he could look out for himself.

"You coming?" asked Joe. It wasn't said with any warmth but there was respect, even a little fear there. Raphael wasn't sure he wanted to be feared but at least it gave him a sense of control and that was a rare feeling for him lately.

"Lead the way."

"Where's Snake gone?" he asked as they walked.

Joe didn't answer, and the conversation died. They walked for ten minutes and Raphael had lost his sense of direction in the dark and unfamiliar surroundings when Joe suddenly ducked through a hole in a wire link fence beside some waste ground and disappeared through a rough screen of bushes. If James hadn't been watching him, he might have lost the guy altogether. One moment he was there and the next he was invisible from the street. Raphael didn't have a lot of choices so he followed. He certainly didn't trust Joe, but Snake's offer had seemed genuine and Joe hadn't tried to pressure him into coming. A line of scrubby trees was growing up through the cracked concrete that lay ahead and a broken down wall to his right set the limits on the derelict plot. Joe cut across the space diagonally and hopped over a low rail. They were at the side of a large building and he could just make out some faded lettering announcing CINEMA, on top of which a large, brightly lit sign had been fitted. Manhattan Club it said, in illuminated blood red writing, the flowing kind of letters that you saw in photos of America. Raphael had never seen anything like it. There was just enough light to guide them to a steel door set low in the ground and partially obscured by a retaining wall beside it. If you wanted your entrance to be discreet, you couldn't ask for better.

Joe tugged open the door and it squealed on hinges that protested their age and neglect. There was a green glow inside from an Emergency Exit sign and they needed it to see the concrete stairs as they climbed. These brought them out into a long empty corridor and from there into one of the largest rooms Raphael had ever seen. It was almost in darkness but there were Exit signs shining over doors at intervals around the vast room. Large double doors at the far end were open and some light filtered through from there, but for the most part the place was in darkness. He blew a low whistle. "God, this is amazing. Is this place used much?"

Raphael thought he wasn't going to get an answer again, but Joe said, "Four nights a week; people here like their music. If you come back, you'll find us on the door. We handle the security." There was a stage to his right and on it stood musical instruments, set up and waiting for a band. There was a large drum kit, something he had dreamed of playing for years, but Joe wasn't stopping. He walked out through the nearest side door and up another flight of steps, before opening a door at the top and switching on the lights. At the back of the room was a bar with stools but no bottles and around the large room were three long sofas. Bedding was strewn over one of them and the other two were uncovered.

"Snake's gone to see his woman. He won't be back for days, and no more questions. You can have that one tonight," said Joe, gesturing at one of the sofas. "Toilet's not working, so it's outside. I'm bushed," and with that he pulled off his shirt, turned and collapsed heavily onto his bedding.

The surreal nature of the night was now complete as Raphael pulled his blanket over him. First he was nearly mugged by these guys, then one of them had bought him food and drink, leaving the other to put him up for the night. He had no idea what tomorrow would hold but as he fell asleep he wondered how it could be any stranger.

******

In the morning Raphael woke first and got up straight away to dress. Joe groaned at the noise and turned over. "Wossa time?"

"I don't know, not early. It's been light for a while."

295

There was a long interval and Raphael wondered if he should just leave. Then there was a muffled voice from beneath Joe's blanket. "D'you know where you're going?"

"North is all I know. I can find that."

"You won't see many signs, but it's called Kanyaruchinya. Just follow the white UN cars and trucks heading north and you'll be OK." And he turned over and went back to sleep. Raphael folded his belongings back into the blanket he'd slept in, retied it and walked downstairs. He stopped in the big dance hall and smiling to himself climbed onto the stage. He picked up the drum sticks and didn't hesitate, just began to play rhythms on the snare drum and the big bass drum pedal, before eventually finishing with a flourish on the high hat. Raphael was still grinning to himself as he slipped out the back way a few minutes later. If Joe wasn't fully awake before he would be now.

Raphael was on his own again. He liked that, he could move faster, there were no distractions and he sensed today could be important, for today was the day his search would resume.

Looking at the position of the sun he found north and settled into an easy pace. At the first market he passed Raphael bought a bottle of water and some bananas, two of which he ate immediately. The rest went into his pack along with some bread. The woman at the stall gave him directions to the main road; it was going to be a long walk.

Chapter 20
Goma and Bukavu, DRC and Kigali, Rwanda
A Week Ago

The line was poor. "You may not remember me, Jessica, my name's Ashok; I'm at the UNICEF office in Kanyaruchinya camp. You left your details here in case we had anything more to tell you."

"Sure, Ashok, I remember."

"We've been trying to reach you for a couple of days. There's a boy who's been coming in here. He's asking for you and says he's looking for his family. His name's Raphael, do you know him?"

"Oh, God."

"I haven't given him your details; I just didn't know what to do if he comes in again. What do you want me to say?"

"I know who it is, he must have run away from the Taweza Road orphanage. I said I'd help by circulating his photo and his sister's but I haven't had a chance to do anything about it yet." Well, the first part of that was true; she was still getting over the experience at Bisie. Although she'd written and sent two articles she hadn't had the strength to do much more. In fact, the children had slipped her mind for the last few days.

"What would you like me to do?" asked Ashok.

"I'll do it now. If you see him again, Ashok, tell him I've sent an email to all my contacts here to see if anyone recognises his story and I've posted his photo online. It's possible his mother is being helped, too."

"Hmm. Well, I guess anything's worth a try." Ashok sounded as unconvinced as she felt. "To be honest, I think his best bet is through us or one of the NGOs like Save The Children. Is there any other message for him?"

Jessica hesitated, neither wanting to offer false hope nor to let him down too roughly. "No, just say we've spoken and that I'm trying, and not to give up hope. Tell Raphael I'll contact him through you if I hear anything."

Despite her good intentions it seemed like a brush off which was not what she intended. "Can I take your number, Ashok, in case something comes up?"

Jessica put the phone down and immediately sent an email with a photo of Keisha and Raphael to her Africa group contacts for this trip, then she posted their photo and background on social media asking for help finding their families. Looking at it now, she knew that Ashok was right and her efforts were unlikely to have any impact. They didn't even make her feel better, she felt terrible for having wallowed in her own difficulties over the last few days when others out there had much larger problems.

She could hardly imagine how desperate Raphael must have been to have left the security and relative safety of the Taweza Road Mission and made it all the way to Goma in search of his family. She thought of her own Mom with her sister at home in Albany, upstate New York. She wondered if Raphael was living in one of the camps and what he was doing. Even allowing for the aid agency contacts that she'd added to her group since she'd been out here, it was futile to imagine that she could help him and she kicked herself for having raised false hopes in the boy. There was only one way she could really help and that was using her reports to get the message to the wider world about the ongoing conflict here, and the devastating human impact it was having. The face of the boy pulled out of the dirt in the mine kept coming back to her; it was one of the reasons she hadn't been sleeping much. In her dreams she gave him mouth-to-mouth resuscitation or washed the soil out of him to ease the breathing that was even more tortured in dreams than it had been in his final hours. In the dream she was either struggling to move through glue or was held back by chains that turned into the grip of her attackers. She had had the dream twice in three nights now and each time woke up sweating and terrified.

No, the best thing she could do to help would be to shine a light on what was happening here. That meant writing about it and completing the interviews she had planned before she came. She still wasn't sure how best to present all her information, but she needed to interview as many members of the coltan supply chain as she could. So far, she'd talked to mine owners, managers and the miners themselves. Jessica also had an interview in the bag with a shipper but not with anyone from a *comptoir*, the local trading companies that bought tin and coltan from the mines, cleaned and bagged it before selling it to foreign companies. There were also the phone manufacturers to talk to, but that could wait until she got back to the US and Europe.

It was while she was thinking of the mobile devices and DVD players that Jessica wondered if she could do a video, perhaps with camerawork by James. Apparently he had done some video work already for the charity. Would he film a short piece for her?

When she put it to him later, James was more enthusiastic than she had expected. Sarah was less happy about it.

"When are you planning to shoot this ?" she asked.

"Sometime in the next few days."

"I'm sorry to rain on your parade, but you're employed by us not her."

"Of course, I understand. I was just hoping to use my day off. It wouldn't take more than a couple of hours, maybe less. Jessica's got an interview to do in Goma and she's going to write it up anyway – she just wondered if I could manage the time to film the interview or for her to do a piece to camera after she's met him."

"OK, if you can finish the work I've already given you today you could do it tomorrow. If you can't do it tomorrow, that's it, I need you after that."

"It's a deal. Thanks Sarah, I appreciate it." It didn't give Jessica much time to confirm the interview but it was the best opportunity for filming that they'd get and by that night he was ready.

******

By 9.00 a.m. Jessica and James were leaving in a taxi for the interview. It had taken some persuasion to get Mr SK Zaidi to agree to a meeting at short notice, but Jessica could be persuasive. They might not have been offered the interview at all if she hadn't mentioned the names of his industry colleagues that she had already spoken to. It often opened doors with the more reluctant interviewees if they knew that they were not alone, or might miss out on some useful promotion. If all else failed, Jessica appealed to their vanity. That hadn't been necessary in this case, Mr Zaidi was not a vain man – in fact, for someone in a trade she found so complex he had sounded straightforward and polite on the phone.

The taxi was on time for once and she and James climbed in, keeping their bags close. They were so busy discussing their destination with the driver and their plans for the day that neither of them noticed the dirty white Toyota car that had been sitting outside an empty house nearby for much of the last two days. As the taxi pulled away, the Toyota's engine started and it followed slowly, its occupant content for now to keep their distance.

The office was easy enough to find, Avenue Beni was not long and there was a large Comptoir Gosomines sign over the door. Mr Zaidi was still in a meeting when they arrived so, having given their names and explained that James would wait for her outside, they sat in Reception. Eventually his secretary said, "Miss Tsiba? Mr Zaidi apologises, his meeting has overrun, he says he won't be more than a couple of minutes."

A little later Zaidi's office door opened and they both looked up. A blonde-haired white guy came out followed by the elderly SK Zaidi. The two men shook hands warmly and she noticed the middle-aged white man first as he was nearest to her. He seemed relaxed and confident, smartly dressed in blue linen trousers and an expensive shirt. Zaidi extended his hand and gave her a welcoming smile. "Miss

Tsiba, may I call you Jessica? Won't you come in?" and she stepped forward into his office.

"Thanks for agreeing to see me at such short notice, Mr Zaidi." She looked him up and down. He was tiny, several inches shorter than her, with a ring of white hair circling his bald, brown head. His gaze was quizzical, his manner unhurried, and his demeanour calm. This was a man who was sure of his ground.

"Come in, and sit down. Would you like some tea? I cannot offer you coffee, we don't keep it as it disagrees with me." He spoke with a cultured English accent. With wisps of white hair thickest around his ears he looked like a little gnome.

"No, thank you." Jessica sat and placed her voice recorder on the coffee table between them as the old man settled into the armchair opposite hers. "This is just to help my memory," she nodded at the recorder.

He spread his hands indicating relaxed acceptance. He must have noticed her damaged and stitched top lip but he was too gentlemanly to comment. "Now, let me just confirm," he said cautiously. "This is 'off the record' you say, yes?"

"Yes."

"And thus you won't quote me by name or identify my company in any way? I cannot allow any images that will identify me or my staff. It could be dangerous for me to say too much in public."

Jessica raised an eyebrow at this disclosure, but all she said was, "Correct."

"I do not say this for myself. What are they going to do, shoot me?" It was unclear who Zaidi meant by 'they' and Jessica chose not to interrupt his flow. "I am an old man already and one day soon I will die anyway. No, I am concerned for my staff who have been most loyal to me, and have stayed with me even when it was dangerous to do so, or when they could have made more money elsewhere with less work. Much more money."

"Sure. I just want to understand better what is happening in the tin and coltan trades. It seems to be a constantly shifting picture and it's hard to describe it to the outside world."

"Quite so. Which version do you want?" he smiled impishly.

"I beg your pardon?"

"Do you want the sanitised version given by the authorities – the governments, the EU and the UN? Or do you want the more complex picture?" His smile seemed innocent enough, but there was a challenge in his eyes.

"I'd like the truth, please."

"Ah, the truth. Even if your publishers may not like it?"

"I'll leave the editors to deal with the publishers, that's above my pay scale. I just report what I find and leave others to decide what gets published."

"Indeed. We are all but cogs in a larger machine."

"Can I start with where you buy your coltan and cassiterite, or more accurately who you buy from?"

"We buy columbite-tantalite – coltan ore, as you say – as well as tin and some gold and we only buy here. The sellers are traders, *negociants*, of all sizes who bring the minerals to us."

"Of course, we must pay ten percent of the coltan's value to local Congolese export agents. You will understand that I won't name them, even off the record, but I'm sure you know who the – how shall I say? – movers and shakers are here. Come with me, let me show you, and you can bring your cameraman, but remember what I said about not identifying people."

As they passed through Reception, Jessica beckoned to James who followed her and after a brief instruction from Jessica he began videoing as he went. Zaidi ensured that he was not pictured but continued talking quietly to Jessica.

"It would be better for business if there was no fighting," said the charismatic comptoir executive. "But as things stand, in my business we try to hold it at arms length but I am faced with a simple choice; I lose everything I've spent decades building and all of us lose our jobs or I pay a percentage to these people and I keep my business and my staff." He gave a large shrug. His smiling face displayed a row of perfect white teeth and his features seemed ever ready to break into an engaging smile. This was not the unapologetic face of the illicit coltan trade that Jessica had been expecting. He looked like someone you might happily spend time with at a business function anywhere in the world, and it undermined some of the prejudices and preconceptions that she had held.

In the workshop the comptoir staff were dressed in smart, clean blue overalls and wore masks to prevent them inhaling the coltan dust. They also helped to disguise their identity in the video. An electric mill stood to one side being continuously fed with lumps of coltan which it loudly ground into a dense, dark grey powder that was then poured into five kilogram bags.

"Is coltan radioactive? The ore is dangerous to work with, isn't it?" Jessica asked. She had heard that local doctors had linked this to birth deformities and Spina Bifida in the workers' children, but she had yet to find any research to support this. She had read anecdotal evidence of five centimetre round lesions and swellings on babies' spines. Some doctors had suggested this was because some families ate from the same bowls used for measuring coltan; they were the only bowls the families had.

Mr Zaidi shrugged his shoulders. "All I can tell you is that we have had no such problems here, but as you see we take precautions when handling it, and we insist that our staff wash their hands afterwards." It didn't seem all that reassuring but Jessica had no evidence that he was failing his workers.

"How do you know it's from legal sources?"

"No one who buys in North or South Kivu can know with certainty. Mines change hands between rebels and the army as the fighting swings back and forth. You could even have coltan extracted at an illegal mine, and by the time it reaches us the mine has been retaken by the government. Or vice versa. So is that legal or illegal coltan?"

"Isn't there a list of approved mines for you to work with?"

"Not yet, although the Ministry of Mines says it is planned."

"I thought companies in the West are now compelled to declare any minerals they buy from the Congo or from neighbouring countries like Rwanda."

"They are. So what should they do? If they choose to buy nothing from this region, they may protect their reputation, and the price of coltan collapses as it did here over the last decade. For a while, the government in Kinshasa even banned all mineral exports from the Kivus. All that happened was that many miners went hungry or moved away in search of other jobs, some even joined the rebel groups in order to feed themselves, while the coltan from rebel-held mines found new ways onto the market through unlicensed European buyers.

"There is no system for proving that the minerals are 'conflict-free', I think that's the favourite expression in the West, isn't it? It's not like diamonds, you see. An expert can readily identify the source of a diamond. Coltan and cassiterite have no reliable markers, life would be much simpler if they did."

"So, the problem lies in the rebel held mines and with the European buyers?"

"I didn't say that, my dear." He looked at her carefully. "Are you sure you won't have a tea?" asked Zaidi solicitously.

She shook her head, eager for him to continue.

"There are some elements in the Congo army who have always been more interested in mining than soldiering. Fighting was a means to an end, a way of ensuring that they continued to get rich, colossally rich. One of the ways of overcoming the rebels has always been for governments to offer their leaders a high-ranking position in the army, and to give their men the security of becoming a government soldier. Many have readily swopped sides in this way, changing allegiances overnight as easily as they changed uniform. One big problem is that the army's soldiers often remain unpaid for months at a time, and there's no incentive for the new officers to stop running the mines. So everything continues as before – the only difference for the miners is that their guards now wear new army uniforms. The revenue continues to go to these officers, not to the state. They can be quite open about it, sometimes they even fly the flags of their old rebel groups over the mine so that no one is in any doubt. Their troops receive just enough to stay loyal to the officers and not to Kinshasa."

"Doesn't Kinshasa do anything about this?"

He smiled wistfully and toyed with his empty teacup. "They try. The Minister of Mines has been known to confiscate truckloads of minerals found on the roads because there is no paperwork to show their provenance. Then as soon as his back is turned the minerals are released. No one can say who to, but some people get richer in the deal. Once again, there is no paperwork.

"The Minister was extremely angry recently when he heard that two illegal truckloads of coltan were stopped on the road to Rwanda. The minerals were allowed to continue but only after a personal arrangement had been agreed."

"You mean money? A bribe?"

"A bribe, certainly. Probably paid later in minerals."

"Who is supposed to enforce the regulations?"

"Ah ...." he said enigmatically. He didn't answer immediately. When he did, he appeared to be choosing his words carefully. "Again off the record ... the responsibility is the FARDC's, the Congolese army's. They are there to ensure that minerals are only sold through the official channels, the *centre de négoces* or negotiating centres."

"That's the same army that cannot prevent some of its officers running mines and paying its troops with this blood money."

"That is your phrase, not mine."

"Is this a *centre de négoce*?"

"But, of course."

"So you only deal with minerals from sources that are known to be government-approved?"

"I refer you to my earlier replies. Minerals and people are not always as they would have you believe. You see, my dear, it is hard for honest negotiators such as ourselves to be completely sure that everything we are told is true. Viewed from New York, Antwerp or London it must seem very simple. Importers should only buy their coltan and tin from secure mines, mines that are held and controlled by the army. And all shipments should have government certification. But in practice the monitoring is weak, the penalties are light, and the rewards for malpractice are vast.

"In short, if the world wants our minerals they will have them, whatever we do, especially when alternative legally-controlled sources of supply are more costly. The only laws that apply here are the laws of supply and demand. I would prefer to work in a different political and business climate, but this is the world we have not the world we might wish." He stirred from his position, "And now if you will permit me I have another appointment to which I must attend."

Jessica still had other questions but he was intent on concluding the interview and he had been more candid than she had dared hope. "Thanks for your time and for being so frank. If I have any other questions, do you mind if I email you?"

"Not at all. I will help you if I can. Please remember what I said about my staff, I would hate anything to befall them or their employment."

"I understand. Stay there, I can find my own way out."

"Actually, I have to tell my secretary something before I forget. After you, my dear."

In the Reception office his secretary looked up and smiled at them both.

James began packing his camera away in his bag as Jessica turned to him and spoke quietly. "Are you ready? He doesn't want to do a video interview, I'll explain later. I'll just do a piece to camera."

"Oh, OK," said James and he stood to pick up his camera bag and return the glass of water that he'd been given.

Behind them Mr Zaidi was speaking to his secretary, and Jessica waited for a moment to reiterate her thanks. "Ayesha," he said, "can you just send an email to Axel for me? I meant to ask him just now how long he'll be staying. I've pencilled his email and hotel address into your blue book; it's under T for Terberg."

There was a crash behind her as the glass hit the stone floor and shattered. Jessica turned to see a stricken look on James's face. He was staring straight past her at Mr Zaidi and the blood had drained from his face.

"James. James, are you OK? You look like you've seen a ghost."

"Excuse me, I need to get out of here," and he stumbled out into the street.

Jessica grabbed her bag and went after him. She ran down the steps of the building to where he sat with his head in his hands. "James, what is it? Are you sick?"

At first his lips moved but nothing came out. Then he murmured, "No. No, it's nothing like that. I can't believe it. It's him, it has to be." He kept repeating over and over, "It's him."

"It's who? What are you talking about? You're not making any sense."

"My father."

"What? Here? Who do you mean?"

"I was adopted. In Britain." He seemed to be short of breath. "I think that was my Father."

"Who was your father? I don't get it."

"The guy they mentioned in there, Axel Terberg. He's the guy that came out of the meeting when we arrived. That's the name of my father, my birth father. I found out his name only recently and I've been searching for his name online. It's very unusual but there was no sign of him. Someone sent me a letter from my birth mother, mentioning his name and saying that they had been in Congo together."

"My God, that's extraordinary. But can you be sure it's him?" she asked.

"No. Maybe. I don't know. I've never met another Axel, nor a Terberg. I know that he spent time in Congo, and one thing I do know is that he worked in the gem trade and in mining. And we're here at a mineral trading company. I don't know if we look alike. How old would you say that guy was?"

"God, I don't know. Fifty-ish? Fifty-five? How old are you?"

"Twenty-eight. So that would be about the right age, too."

"His hair was a bit lighter than yours. He was a similar height, and well dressed. I didn't notice much else." Jessica paused, trying like James to take in the enormity of this thought. "Does he know about you?"

"No, I don't think my mother, my birth mother, ever told him. They split up before she knew she was expecting me and they lost touch. She died later in the States a few years after I was adopted, so I don't think he knows," said James.

"My God. Hey, I know this is a big question, but do you want to make contact with him? Do you want to tell him, assuming it is him?"

James had been staring into the distance, but now he turned to face her. At first there was a look of confusion on his face, but there was something else that she hadn't seen there before. His jaw was clenched whether with tension or determination and he looked her squarely in the eye. "I have to talk to him. To find out if his name is just a coincidence or if this is really him. I can't just walk away, this may be my one chance to meet … my father."

She searched his face for more information. His determination seemed total. James stood up. "What are you going to do now?" she asked.

He breathed in and out deeply a couple of times. "I'm going to take a leaf out of your book and follow the only lead I've got." He climbed the steps and went back into the office, and Jessica followed him in.

When she caught up with him, James was already doing his best to explain his request to the receptionist. "I know this is going to sound a little odd, but I believe that the man who was seeing Mr Zaidi before Jessica, is … is a relative of mine."

The secretary looked blankly at him.

"His name is Axel Terberg, isn't it? Well, I think we are related and I need to contact him. Can you give me his phone number or his email? Please?" He tried to smile, but his tension got the better of him and it came out as a grimace.

The secretary pulled a face. "I am sorry. I am not allowed to say anything about our clients and partners. Mr Zaidi is very clear on this."

"But this is very important. I have never met him and this may be my only chance."

The secretary shook her head. "I'm sorry. It is absolutely forbidden. If you want to ask Mr Zaidi, he will be back in an hour or two."

"That may be too late. I need to know now!"

"I am sorry, you must wait for Mr Zaidi."

Jessica was about to say something when James reached over the desk and picked up the blue exercise book in front of the receptionist. He turned it around and his finger ran down the page. Nothing under today, so he flicked to the A-Z section and looked under Terberg. It was there in pencil, as the old man had said.

"Excuse me! This is Mr Zaidi's private appointment book, you are not allowed to have this. Give it here," and she tried to grab it back.

James took one step backwards out of her reach. "Here, Axel Terberg. Hotel Arc-en-Ciel, Gisenyi," and he took a photo of the page on his phone. "I'm sorry if I've alarmed you, but I have to speak to him."

He spun around and strode out of the building for a second time. Jessica tried to offer an apology to the secretary who ignored her. She was already dialling Mr Zaidi.

James was already striding down the road when she came out. Jessica hurried to catch up with him. "Where are you going?"

He didn't answer.

"James, hold up. Are you going to try and see him?"

When he turned around, he was angry. "Of course, I'm going to bloody see him. That's my father. It's too much of a coincidence to be anyone else." He held up a hand and counted off the elements on his fingers. "His first name is Axel, surname Terberg. He's in Congo. He's the right age. He works in roughly the right sort of business – well, he's not an accountant or a lion tamer, or something. How much more do I need in order to try and find him? And if it turns out he's not the right guy then I'll apologise and leave him alone."

"Let me help you. You're upset, it's understandable and maybe I can help." She wasn't quite sure why she'd offered, except she didn't like to see him so distressed.

"No, just leave me alone, will you? I've got to deal with this on my own. It's not just one of your stories, y'know, this is my life."

"I didn't mean I wanted to write about it." She was taken aback that he would think that of her.

He raised his hands in a gesture of dismissal. "Whatever," he said and turned to walk down the road. Clearly, he was not expecting her to accompany him and she had no idea where he was going. She suspected he didn't either, unless it was the Hotel Arc-en-Ciel across the border in Gisenyi. He'd better have his passport with him.

She watched him walk away. *I really didn't deserve that*, she thought bitterly. *Dammit, I was just trying to help. Well screw him*, she thought, *he could deal with his own problems*. Jessica looked in her bag to check her phone was there, she was going to need a taxi and she couldn't very well go and ask in Zaidi's office. Maybe she could find a taxi on the street.

As she was thinking it, there was a squeal of tyres on the tarmac and then another. She looked up to see a pick-up truck with a covered rear had skidded to a halt and was now parked diagonally across the road about fifty metres away, with a white car halted just behind it, half on the roadside, its doors open. She wondered if there had been a collision, but the vehicles didn't appear to be touching and it was hard to imagine where the pick-up could have emerged from unexpectedly, there was no side road so a crash seemed unlikely.

Then she spotted several men involved in a struggle. They were standing between the two vehicles, she stood still as one black fist was repeatedly being swung downwards at a target out of sight on the ground. She heard several shouts and she began to walk forwards. Jessica could see men leaning over something and then there was a muffled shout. Her mind was racing and she wondered if James was near enough to have heard what was going on, then instantly realised she couldn't see him. She started to run and at that moment three large men in jeans and T-shirts picked up a limp body and threw it into the back of the truck. It was James. Then they dragged an orange bag over his head. Someone inside the truck pulled him into its shadows and he was lost from view.

Jessica found she was shouting at them as she ran and it was only then that they noticed her. Two of the men vaulted over the tailgate and into the back of the pick-up. There was a bang on the roof and it spun back into the road, gunned its engine and roared away. One of the men walked straight past the car and continued striding towards her, it was only then that Jessica noticed he had his right arm outstretched and was pointing a gun at her. She threw herself sideways across the pavement and a shot ricocheted off the tarmac and past her. A second hit the dirt a few metres in front of her. The next shot surely wouldn't miss. Jessica lifted her head and over the top of her bag she saw him turn, stuff the gun into a side pocket and walk nonchalantly back to his car. He was muscular and walked unhurriedly with the waddling gait of a weightlifter. The man closed the rear door as though he had collected some shopping then eased his frame into the passenger seat and the dusty white car bumped back onto the roadway and accelerated after the pick-up.

The whole episode had taken less than thirty seconds and Jessica cursed herself as she realised she hadn't even noted the car's number plate. She could describe the car passenger well enough, but she would have little else to go on other than the barest description of the pick-up truck. All she knew for sure was that James had been abducted.

******

When Jessica finally returned to AfriCan Care after a difficult journey across the city, the living room had been transformed. Gone was the air of quiet industry, and in its place were four laptops grouped together on the central table. Behind each one sat a member of the team and there were two new faces. Sarah arrived by car soon after and instantly took control.

She clapped her hands for attention. "OK, everyone, listen now. This, as you know, is not a practice drill. We've rehearsed this kind of thing before, but unfortunately this time it's for real. We have one member of the team missing, James has been abducted in central Goma by an unknown group of … how many were there, Jessica?"

"I saw five men, no, six counting both drivers, but there could have been another person in the pick-up truck," she said.

"OK, we'll come back to you in a minute. For anyone who's just arrived, we have Derek Bromhead here from the British embassy in Kinshasa. Luckily for us, he was in the area and has dropped everything to liaise with us until a more permanent arrangement is in place or until this is resolved. And thank you to Karl here, who most of you know, for coming in so quickly from MONUSCO."

"Right, what do we know? Let's go in turn, starting with you Jessica. For those of you who don't know her, Jessica, is a freelance journalist friend of ours who is staying here for now, and was with James when he was taken. Serge has already circulated a briefing note on James, with his photo, description, the clothes he was wearing, and when and where he was last seen."

"Jessica, tell us what you can." So she retold everything that had happened. To keep it simple and because it didn't seem relevant she didn't mention yet the news that James had learned as they were leaving, but Jessica was going to share it with Sarah later.

"OK, thanks. I want updates from everyone else now on what they've been doing, who they've contacted. I want to know what we've said and what we've held back. Let's start with you, Aidan."

"Aye, cheers. Our first call was to Head Office in London, fortunately they were at their desks so we didn't lose any time," said Aidan. "We spoke to Alan, for those who don't know, he's our security officer, and he reminded us of the next steps. London is notifying everyone who needs to know outside DRC, including the neighbours in Rwanda, Uganda and so on. And for now we're responsible for dealing with everyone on the ground here in Goma. Serge got through to the British embassy in Kinshasa at the same time as I was calling the UK and about now they're circulating our briefing document to other embassies and the ministries of justice, defence, state, home affairs, and the PNC, the national police."

Derek Bromhead coughed meaningfully. "Sarah, can I ...?" She gestured to him to continue. "Since we don't know where he's been taken, do any of you have any thoughts on why? Why might someone have targeted him?" It was the first time that the British Embassy official had said anything, and Jessica realised that no one had told them what his job function was. "This is critical, it might tell us who has got him and maybe even where. Anyone got any ideas?"

Everyone looked at one another, and shrugged their shoulders. "OK, if we don't know who or why, what about ..."

"Excuse me," Jessica raised her hand as though she was in class then quickly put it down.

"Yes?" said Bromhead. His eyes squinted at her from a lined and deep bronze skin that seemed older than his voice. He was clearly not one of the Foreign & Commonwealth Office's desk jockeys, and from the look of him Jessica guessed that he spent little time in London. He had large, ringless hands, some feint tattoos on his right wrist and a plain but tough looking watch that seemed to reflect the man himself. No affectation, no wasted effort, and yet capable.

"I don't know if it's relevant, but have you looked at his photos?"

"Yes, I've seen them," said Sarah. "He showed me, but I don't see the relevance."

"Me neither," added Aidan. "He often takes his laptop with him but he had video gear to carry today so he left it behind, right enough. We could have a look."

"There's something on here you need to see, he showed me the other night," said Jessica. "Do you have the password?"

"Of course," said Aidan. "We have all the staff passwords. Hold on, I'll pull it up," and he looked at his own system before typing a string into James's computer.

"What was it you saw?" asked the embassy official.

"I asked to see his work and there was a slideshow which was mostly of children."

"Well, it would be," said Aidan impatiently.

Jessica ignored him. "At the end the slides included shots James had taken of a meeting he witnessed between soldiers and some guys in suits, and most of them we couldn't identify. The odd thing was that the meeting happened in the refugee camp, in Kanyaruchinya. There were heavily armed troops escorting several men, and one of them was treated like a VIP. The soldiers all mingled, I remember James said that they greeted each other like old friends, but they should have been enemies. Some were in Congolese army uniforms and others wore FDLR uniforms – yet they're sworn enemies, aren't they?"

"This is important. Are you sure about this?" asked Bromhead.

"You can see for yourself in a moment. Can you find those pics, Aidan? That's not all. The person leading the FDLR soldiers was Didier Toko. He was clearly identifiable and there should be a photo of him in a magazine lying around here somewhere for you to compare. That's what James did."

"Why the hell didn't he tell us?" asked Sarah. She was furious.

"I think he felt he was in enough trouble with you already, you know with his poor performance at the start."

"God, this just gets worse and worse," she said. Aidan pulled up the photos on screen and people began to stand up to get a glimpse.

Derek stepped forward to Aidan's side. "If this is what you say Jessica, this could be politically sensitive, highly sensitive. Sarah, is there somewhere we can go? You, me and Jessica."

He closed the lid so fast that Aidan only just removed his fingers in time. "Hang on a minute…" he began.

Derek Bromhead was unconcerned at Aidan's ruffled ego. "This is now a matter for the embassy to deal with, and I will let you know if we need any more assistance. Now if you'd just give me James's password I will deal with his photos from here. Thanks." He picked up the laptop and looked down at Aidan who had been about to protest further. Seeing Bromhead's attitude he said nothing.

Sarah stepped forward and whispered to her right-hand man. "Aidan, we need their help, but something is going on here that is way outside our remit. I'm not going to stop the Foreign Office accessing these photos, and nor are you. Just give him the password, discreetly, and let's get on with what is our responsibility and that's finding our team member. Because however much I want to kick his arse right now we need to find him first. That's our task. The rest can wait."

Aidan stood up and looked from her to Bromhead whose gaze did not flinch. He hesitated, then wordlessly showed the embassy man James' password stored on his phone.

"Sarah, we need to talk about this privately," said Bromhead. "And everyone in here needs to forget what they've just heard. No one is to breathe a word of this outside this room, is that understood? This information confirms that James' life is at stake, if what he saw leaks out his life expectancy will be measured in minutes. Is that clear?" He looked at everyone in the room in turn. They nodded one by one.

"Sarah, where can we talk privately with Jessica?"

"We'll use my room. Just excuse the mess," and she led the way through the building. Bromhead closed the door behind Jessica. He didn't wait for her to sit down, "Did anyone see him taking these?"

"I wasn't there. He didn't say so but," Jessica paused and shrugged, "I guess it's possible."

Sarah put her hands to her head. "God, if it gets out that one of our photographers is taking politically sensitive photos we'll be labelled as spies. We could be finished here, maybe other places too. This is a bloody disaster."

"Jesus, that's the least of it. People have been looking for this kind of proof of rogue Army officers dealing with the rebels for years," said Bromhead. "That alone could cause an almighty ruckus in Africa and beyond if it gets out. And if politicians in the region think the Brits are spying on them there will be some serious and lasting political repercussions." His crossed arms showed a very defensive body language.

Jessica sat down on the bed and looked at them both, lost in their respective worlds, thinking only of themselves. "Excuse me; can we keep a bit of focus here? Suddenly you're talking about the charity and you're going on about world politics. Why is no one thinking about a colleague and friend who's been kidnapped and is being held captive by armed men somewhere around this city?"

Sarah at least had the decency to look embarrassed, but Bromhead had opened up the folder again and was staring slack-jawed at one of the images. He was whispering something, and it was hard to hear what he was saying but it seemed to be, "Businga Junior? I don't bloody believe it!"

310

As far as he could make out, it was a warehouse. The drive had been short, which was a relief as he had taken a terrible kicking and stamping in the back of the pick-up. As James was being thrown into the truck, a bag had been dragged over his head. It still had dust and grit in which went in his eyes, made him cough and the tight weave of the nylon made it hard to breathe. A little air came in around the neck but a drawstring had been pulled tight enough to prevent the bag falling off so he was constantly short of breath and close to panic. He could taste blood in his mouth, and one nostril was blocked which further impaired his breathing. He guessed his nose must be bleeding too, and he felt something sharp in his mouth. A tooth was broken and his tongue kept going to it. The rest of the tooth had either fallen out or he'd swallowed it. He must keep his tongue still in case they punched him in the face again.

Punch after punch had hit him when he landed heavily on the truck bed. Fists and boots struck him in the face, on the back of the head, around the stomach and kidneys. Someone had repeatedly stomped on his left hand and it felt as though a bone was broken. He had curled into a ball to protect himself from what he thought were three attackers and there was a lull while they pulled his hands around behind his back and plastic cuffs were fitted and tightened hard. Every sideways movement of his body as he was rolled around in the back put greater pressure on his wrists adding to the pain.

He was starved of air, he couldn't see where his attackers were and now James's hands were bound. For a moment he curled up and tried to protect his vulnerable stomach, groin and face but every kick made him angrier. When one of his captors gave away his position with a punch to his torso, James swung his right leg up in the hope of kicking the man's head. He must have missed by some distance, he thought his foot had caught the man under the left arm and thrown him forward. There was a clatter as the attacker lost his balance in the swinging pick-up bed and crashed into the back of the driver's cab. Any satisfaction was short-lived as James took a boot to the head from behind that left him groggy and unable to respond. Other blows then hit him and he struggled for breath, teetering on the edge of consciousness. Gradually, as the journey continued, they could see that he was unable to resist further and the blows subsided.

He was breathless and lay still trying to get his bearings. He didn't know Goma well, but there was little else he could do. Blinded by the hood and the near darkness in the back of the pick-up, James was bewildered by what was happening. He had no idea who these people were, where they were taking him or why, and he hadn't the breath to speak.

Overwhelmed by events at the start of the journey he had lost all track of time, but thinking about it later he guessed it couldn't have lasted more than fifteen or twenty minutes. Towards the end of the journey there was a period of waiting in the pick-up with the engine idling, during which they beat him again and then ordered him in English to remain silent. Their warning was pointless; he couldn't recall saying anything since they had hooded him as they pushed him into the back. A heavy cover was thrown over him, perhaps a tarpaulin – so they were trying to avoid detection. The vehicle then drove more sedately and left the usual potholed lava ash roads, travelling over asphalt for a few minutes. Nobody in the vehicle said a word until they stopped again. There were voices outside speaking Lingala, Kiswahili or something, and then he heard a heavy object on steel rollers being moved away. It sounded like large doors or a gate opening.

The pick-up moved forward and there was a booming echo around them and he could make out a smaller second engine, possibly a car. Hadn't there been a white car behind when they first attacked him? He couldn't be sure, it had all happened so fast.

The vehicle he was in drove on and then swung around. This must be a big building and from the tinny echo it didn't sound to be of brick or concrete construction. The truck stopped and then the accompanying car switched off its engine after which he heard the sound of the doors, presumably closing behind them. Only then did the men begin to talk again and occasionally to give him a kick.

He heard them getting out, then talking animatedly nearby, there was laughter and the smell of cigarette smoke reached him. James tried to steady his breathing and take stock. He had no idea where he was, or what they wanted. He was injured but he was sure he could walk, and he was hooded – breathing was only manageable when he lay still. And his hands were bound so tightly behind him that he was worried at the loss of blood supply if this went on; the pain in his hands was also getting worse.

The tailgate of the pick-up went down and they pulled him out by the feet, inevitably his torso and head went down hard. Sensing what was about to happen, James tried to curve his back and protect his head, but with his hands tied behind him his skull took a large blow as he hit the ground and he blacked out.

******

As they settled on a chair and on the bed in Sarah's modest room, Derek Bromhead smoothed both hands slowly down his face and appeared to be mulling over the rapidly growing task he had taken on, and not evidently relishing it. "What happened to you?" Bromhead gestured to her lip. Jessica's bruising was yellowing and less obvious now. The infection had gone and the swelling had subsided, but she still had three very visible stitches and some scabbing along the line of the tear.

The stitches would come out in a few days and she hoped each morning that the sight greeting her would be less scary. The progress seemed slow.

"I had a fall at a mine near Walikale." Sarah raised one eyebrow and Bromhead said nothing, it was unclear whether he believed her or whether he thought that it mattered. Jessica was eager to change the subject. "There is one other thing about James," she said.

"God, not more!" Sarah whispered.

"It may not be relevant but I think you ought to know. I was interviewing a well-connected coltan trader this morning, the owner of a comptoir, Mr SK Zaidi. James was preparing to shoot a short video afterwards. Someone else came out of the office with Zaidi when we arrived and neither of us thought anything of it. He was a white guy of about fifty. When Zaidi showed me out later, he mentioned this guy's name to his secretary in front of James, and suddenly James went a bit crazy. I think he was in shock; long story short it turns out this guy may be James's natural father who he's never met. Apparently he was adopted, and one of his motivations for coming out here from Britain was to find out more about where his blood father had lived because Kinshasa was the last known contact point for him. I don't think he ever expected to meet him, and yet the two had almost bumped into each other. It really shook him up. He wouldn't talk to me and stormed off. That was when they took him."

Bromhead looked baffled. "What was this guy doing with Zaidi?"

"It seems he's a gem trader. Comptoir Gosomines deals with diamonds as well as coltan and tin."

"What's his name?"

"Terberg. Axel Terberg."

"Means nothing to me, but we'll run it through the system. Now, unless you've got any more bombshells, tell me about any other clues from the abduction," said Bromhead, and he scratched his close-cropped greying hair. "Describe each person and the vehicles. Did they look organised, professional? Or was it rushed and panicky? What were they armed with? What did they do to James to restrain him? It all helps. I gather James is a big guy so they may have had to work hard to overpower him. I want to see if there's anything else we can learn from what you saw."

******

When he came round, James could see nothing at all, despite the fact that the bag had been taken off his head. He could breathe again but he was in darkness and it was colder than before, much colder. And it was damp, he was lying in a puddle of water. James sat up. His hands were free and he rubbed the raw patches where the plastic cuffs had cut deeply during the struggles. There was a small chink in the

313

darkness above him, not a light exactly just a sliver of grey in the black. Then he saw another gap above his feet. Parallel lines of grey. *God only knew where he was*, he thought, *all he could tell was that it was a chamber and there was no sound.* He tried to stand up and banged his head. At six foot tall he had to crouch but he could at least turn around.

The chamber seemed to be brick-lined, with a damp dirt floor, and he ran his hand over the low ceiling then wished he hadn't. It was made of heavy timber, rough cut and unfinished. A couple of splinters went deep into his right hand. The chamber reminded him of something but he couldn't think what.

There was nothing to sit on, he couldn't stand, and his shirt and trousers were wet from lying down. He tested the floor. It was gritty and a space at the far end from where he had started was dry so he sat down there and took stock of what he knew.

******

"No, there was no panic," said Jessica. "In fact, when one of the kidnappers shot at me before they pulled out he was totally unhurried. I don't know how he missed me."

"Maybe he meant to," Derek replied. "If he was as close as you say, he wasn't interrupted, and his escape route was ready…" He didn't finish the sentence.

Jessica looked at Sarah and back at Derek. "Somehow that feels worse than if he'd missed."

"I reckon you're very lucky. Now tell me about James. Did he put up a fight?"

"It was hard to see, the car was in the way. Yes, he was fighting; it took three of them to get him into the back of the pick-up. I could just see some fists being raised and heads bobbing into view above the car, then I heard a shout and the next I saw of him they were throwing him into the pick-up truck and, yeah that's right … they put a bag on his head."

"OK, tell me about the vehicles."

******

Those blows to the head must have been hard, it took James a while to work out where he was. This must be a vehicle inspection pit, the kind of pit you saw in old garages where they didn't have a hoist. *One up for me*, thought James. Not a major triumph in the circumstances, but you had to take the positives where you found them. All that it told him was he was being held in a garage, a disused one it seemed. Then he heard an engine whining in the distance. He frowned in concentration; they must be very close to an airport or landing strip and since the engines sounded large perhaps this was near Goma Airport.

Thank God the bag over his head had gone, but that feeling of claustrophobia remained as he lay trapped in the darkness in this pit. He could breathe now and move his hands, at least those bloody cuffs had gone.

He called out but if anyone was there they didn't answer. The light had gone too, and no one came which told him they weren't overly worried about the chances of him escaping, or being overheard with whatever they planned for him. Not good. He didn't like that train of thought so he tried to find another, but that just made his head hurt. There were numerous bruises to consider, he didn't know which hurt most as he ran his hands over himself to check the damage. Ouch, yes, he did. The back of his head. Now he remembered his head hitting the ground as he came out of the pick-up. Neil had always said James was bone-headed and he should use it in rugby to break his fall. This time it was too close to the truth. Bloody hell, it hurt. His left hand wasn't too good either.

He hadn't thought of Neil for a while. What would he do in this situation? He'd say, stupid bugger; you shouldn't be in this situation. He guessed Neil's training would tell him to conserve warmth, it was surprisingly cold down here and he was in wet clothes. Find water and warmth. No sign of either here. The chamber was empty. Look for escape. Fat chance. Christ, was he going to die in here? Shut up. Think of something positive.

Most of the inspection pits he had ever seen were capped with lengths of timber like this. They couldn't all be removed at once but they could be taken away individually. His left hand hurt like hell but he tried lifting each length in turn. The first three didn't even budge; there must be something heavy standing directly on top of them. The next one shifted a few millimetres upwards which brought down clouds of dust and grit that set off a coughing fit. Then there was another that wouldn't shift at all, and the last two moved upwards a little but stopped after only a centimetre or two. James sat down again. That was no bloody good.

He was losing his bearings now, his eyes had adjusted earlier to what little light there was but now it was pitch black. Night had descended and there was nothing for it but to sit down and rest. God, he was thirsty. He could eat a manky pit pony, too, but it was the thirst that hurt. He could still taste the dust in his mouth that had fallen from the wooden ceiling.

He curled up at the dry end of the pit and closed his eyes. Wet and cold. Fuck these bastards, whoever they were. Until now he hadn't even thought about today's revelation about his birth father. He wondered if that really was the same Axel Terberg? How many could there be in Congo? He wished he'd paid more attention when Mr Zaidi had emerged with him, he had little recollection of the man except a pale blue shirt, dark blue trousers, and blond hair. That was all he could remember. Bloody useless, really; he'd struggle to pick him out of even the smallest line-up based on that information.

James wondered if the dampness at the other end of the pit meant water. He had to find a drink somehow. Stooping he walked to the far end and knelt down. The ground closest to one wall was wet and there was damp on the wall but no running water. He sniffed it but the whole pit smelt dusty and bad – heaven only knew what he'd get from licking the wall of a disused inspection pit. He'd look at the wall again in daylight if he could. He sat down again at the dry end and tried not to think of food or drink. The movement had warmed him marginally and he leaned back against the driest section of wall. What followed wasn't sleep exactly but he did doze. Wet and cold, scared and angry, and bits of him were hurting hard.

Chapter 21
Goma, North Kivu, DRC
Five Days Ago

Raphael wasn't sure what he'd been expecting but the camp north of Goma gave him little help and even less hope. The place was a confusing mix of organisation and chaos, with lines of huts in different shapes, colours and sizes. As you walked through it, these gave way to ordered lines of tents which then petered out into rough shelters made of tarpaulins stretched over branches. Many of the newest arrivals – and hundreds more like him were coming here every day – didn't even have this and they were forced to sleep night after night in the open, despite the pouring rain.

There was no local fresh water supply so drinking water was being trucked in every day but food supplies were sporadic and some families went for days without eating. The crying of the children was one of the constant features of life here. The newly-arrived were listless and hungry – children led by parents too scared to stay in their villages and too exhausted to leave the camp. Here they just existed, sitting all day on patches of grass in a lava field shadowed by the live volcano, Mount Nyiragongo.

Some people he spoke to were unwilling or unable to say a word, either traumatised by what they had witnessed at home, or despairing at their new-found conditions. One motionless father seemed resigned; Pascal told Raphael he had arrived the week before with his wife and seven children only to see three of them die here from disease and malnutrition. There were rumours that cholera was coming; Raphael had never heard of the disease before he arrived but everyone here was scared that it might strike. Doctors were treating scores of suspected cases in the clinics and there were reports of ten deaths locally in the last few days. He had no idea if this was true, but it was one of the many fears that constantly swept through the camp.

Raphael found a tent with some officials dressed in pale blue bibs marked UNHCR. Others in the queue told him this was the place to start by registering his name, and an hour later he had given them his name and Keisha's, and information about their village. His fervent hope however, that there might be news of his own family, was soon dashed. The experience was utterly anti-climactic; no one knew anything about his family who weren't to be found on any of the officials' lists. The authorities were so stretched they had no time to show interest in people who weren't there, it was a mammoth task just coping with the steady stream of arrivals who stood or sat resignedly in front of them. Eventually Raphael left the UN and went in search of some food, but there was none. Nobody could give him a firm answer on when supplies would reach the camp. There had been a delivery of high energy biscuits three days before, since then nothing.

Had the walk from Goma and the whole journey from Taweza been for nothing? Maybe he should have stayed at the mission. He sat down on an unclaimed stretch of grass, pulled his blanket tight about him and closed his eyes.

He wasn't sure if he could go on. He had invested so much hope in finding some news of his family here that he hadn't stopped to consider what to do if he was unsuccessful.

The one thing that drew people here was the relative safety of this position behind the front line that had been established by the Congolese Army. Now supported by a patchwork of armed forces from Uruguay, India, South Africa, and Tanzania, the UN was at last helping to bring some security to this area.

From what Raphael was hearing in the camp this left vast swathes of Congo's eastern countryside at the mercy of Hutu fighters who had been thrown out of Rwanda. He was sure it was these FDLR rebels who had killed his father, burned their village, and forced his family to flee.

His head was filled with confusing thoughts and fears. For the first time he began to believe that he might never play with Christine and Laurent again, might never find Mama or fulfil his promise to Keisha to bring the family back together again. He sat slumped and more dejected than he had allowed himself to feel at any time since they had fled the village. It grew dark and Raphael sat unmoving, oblivious to all the movements around him, a hunched statue in a pitiable tableau.

There was no rain that night and after an hour he lay down and fell asleep where he sat. When Raphael woke in the morning, his blanket was damp with dew and he was hungrier than he could ever remember. He had been so tired that he had fallen asleep without going back to the officials at the Registration tent to ask if they had heard any news about his family from the journalist, Miss Jessica. There was nothing else to do when he awoke so he walked back. It meant queuing again, but he was getting used to that.

******

The previously affable SK Zaidi sounded a lot less relaxed when Jessica called. There was no reason why he should talk to her, he said. Her colleague had

318

abused his hospitality, insulted his personal assistant and frankly he had not expected to hear from either of them ever again.

"I would like to apologise for that and please may I explain?" She was surprised she had even been put through and Zaidi still sounded ready to hang up so she just said it quickly to grab his attention.

"What do you mean kidnapped?" he asked.

"Something strange happened to my colleague, James, as you saw. He is normally a very calm person but something had upset him and it was only when I caught up with him after he left your office that I found out what it was."

Mr Zaidi said nothing, she even wondered if he'd hung up, but Jessica carried on.

"James was adopted as a baby. He never knew either of his real parents. But recently he found out about his mother, and received a letter that she had written to him just before she died unexpectedly in the 1980s. She was still very young. He knew little about his father, but he did know that the couple had travelled from London to Kinshasa, that his birth father worked in the diamond industry and finally the only other thing he knew was that he was called Axel, Axel Terberg."

There was another long silence, which eventually Jessica broke. "So you can probably imagine how shocked he was when he overheard you mention that name to your secretary. I doubt there are two people of that age, with that name, in the diamond business, and in Congo."

After a pause Mr Zaidi said, "Well, this Mr Terberg deals in coltan, not diamonds. And you said that your colleague has been kidnapped?"

Now it was Jessica who was startled at the news of Axel Terberg's involvement in the coltan trade, but she brought her mind back to the question. "Yes, moments after James explained this to me he stormed off. I think he needed some time alone to take in what had happened."

"He took an address from my private files." SK Zaidi was clearly still affronted.

There was no point in denying or glossing over it. "Yes, Mr Zaidi, and that was inexcusable, and seems out of character. I'm also sure if he was here he would be quick to apologise. I don't know him well, but it's not something I'd have associated with him. Aside from wanting to apologise to you and your PA personally, I wanted to call anyone who has local contacts in the police or armed forces just to make sure that everything that can be done is being done. We don't know why he's been taken but his attackers shot at me when I got too close, they are obviously very dangerous people."

"And you say you don't know why he has been taken?" Zaidi sounded sceptical.

"I don't," she said, although she thought she could hazard a guess based on James's photos that she had seen.

"What do you want from me?" The old man's warmth was returning slowly.

"I know how well connected you are, is there anyone you know in the police or the military that might be able to help us find James?" she asked.

Again, a hesitation. Perhaps it was a natural instinct to avoid police involvement, or maybe he wanted nothing to do with someone who had so upset his receptionist. "I make no promise but I will see what I can do. Was there anything else, Miss Tsiba?"

She was no longer Jessica to him, but at least he hadn't hung up on her. "No, except to say thank you for taking my call, Mr Zaidi. Not many people would be so forgiving and I want you to know that I appreciate it."

"Hmm, well, it wasn't your behaviour that I had an issue with. I must go now, but I will give it some thought as I'm sure time is of the essence."

"Judging by the actions of the kidnappers I would say so. You have my cell phone number, if anything should come up please let me know."

"I will," said the old man and without formalities he hung up.

Jessica noted that SK hadn't denied having good connections with the police or army; perhaps he would spread the word that they were looking for James. What really shocked her though was that James's birth father appeared not to be a diamond trader but a dealer in coltan. She put the phone down slowly after she heard that. Knowing what she now knew about that trade she found it hard to reconcile the person she had met in James with a father dealing in coltan or diamonds in the middle of a war between the Congolese and the Rwandan FDLR rebels.

Were these conflict minerals? If so, what kind of man would be involved in trading them? Did he have any moral conscience, or was he just a profiteer, greedily exploiting people without thought for the misery and suffering he caused? And then she thought of the avuncular figure of Mr Zaidi who seemed quite open about the difficulties of doing business normally during a conflict. Did she have double standards? Was she being a hypocrite if she respected one but not the other? The whole trade had seemed so much easier to understand back in New York; from that distance it had seemed easier to spot the good guys and bad guys.

If this Axel Terberg was in fact James's father, as seemed likely, he could be the embodiment of everything she was working to expose and bring to an end. Then she realised James must have guessed that this man was involved commercially with Zaidi, only adding to the shock disclosure of Axel's full name.

Once again she wondered where James had been taken, who was holding him, how they were treating him and whether he was able to confront such thoughts about the man he thought was his father. Terberg was trading Congo's coltan while a war raged around him; he seemed to be getting richer and more influential by dealing in blood minerals, ore mined by children working at the point of a gun. Did the charity really want to ask for Terberg's help in finding their missing man? Wasn't he part of the problem, not the solution?

******

"I wondered if I'd get a call," was his first response.

"Well, I nearly didn't call you, Mr Terberg" said Jessica, "but I'm staying with a London-based charity, and one of their workers has been kidnapped. We're trying everything and everyone we can think of to get him freed."

"OK, let's rewind a bit. Who are you?" asked Axel.

"My name is Jessica Tsiba, I'm a business journalist out of New York and I've been staying with AfriCan Care, that's the charity. One of their people, a Brit called James Falkus, was abducted in Goma in broad daylight earlier today by armed men and we're trying to find who has him and get him released."

"And what exactly has this to do with me?"

It shouldn't have come as a surprise but she couldn't get over how English he sounded. James did, too, but somehow Jessica had imagined that someone called Axel Terberg would seem more Dutch or Scandinavian or something. "I'm sure if you heard from Mr Zaidi that I was going to call he would have explained why," said Jessica. She sounded terser than she meant to but his offhand manner irritated her. She loathed what he represented but she had agreed to contact him for James's sake.

"No, he just said something about a family connection and that you might get in touch. So, since I don't have any family here you'd better tell me what this is actually about before I hang up."

"OK. It would be better if this came face-to-face from James – the guy who's been kidnapped – but these aren't ideal circumstances so it'll have to come from me. This may come as a shock, but he has good reason to believe that you may be his father."

There was a pause, followed by a derisive snort then one word, "Bollocks!"

"Excuse me? Listen, the only reason you're hearing this from me is because James isn't able to tell you himself. And I'd have left him to do that if it weren't for the fact that your obvious connections here may be able to save his life." Jessica was getting angry again. "If that's not enough reason to help someone you've never met, then you're obviously nothing beside him. So, maybe, just maybe, you might do something to help him if you know what I now know about the connections between you."

"And what are they supposed to be?" Terberg was bristling with hostility.

Jessica ignored the dismissive tone. "He was born in the early '80s – I don't have the exact date but we can find it from his passport – and he was adopted in the UK. His mother died a couple of years later. She sent him a letter, only to be

321

opened if he ever went looking for his birth parents, which he did. And in the letter she said that his father was Axel Terberg."

"That doesn't prove anything."

Jessica exhaled slowly in frustration and continued as though he hadn't spoken. "This Axel Terberg was a dealer in gems, working out of Antwerp and travelling all over Asia and Africa including Congo, or Zaire as it was then."

"So? Even if they meant me, anyone could say that," Axel insisted.

"Her name was Sophie Callender, I think I've got that right, and I'm sure James will have the letter. I might even be able to find it here, but I haven't been through his things."

There was a silence at the other end of the phone. Jessica waited for him to say something but nothing came.

"Hey, are you still there?" Still there was no response, but she could hear the line was open.

Then, "Yes, I'm here." Axel Terberg paused again, "What did you say his name was?" His tone was less belligerent.

"James Falkus. I guess the surname comes from his adoptive family. He's a photographer working at AfriCan Care. If you've got internet access, you can see his photo on their home page, reporting what's happened to him. I gather it's all over the news in London. We've got everyone we can think of here looking for him."

"And you say Sophie, Sophie Callender died in the eighties?"

"Yes. I don't know much more than that. Except James overheard your name being mentioned at Mr Zaidi's office and it freaked him. He'd come out here hoping to find out about the country that you – assuming that it *was* you – and Sophie Callender visited. He never expected to find any real trace of Axel Terberg, far less to run into you, well almost. Was it you that came here with Sophie, Mr Terberg?"

Axel didn't answer her directly. "Before we go any further I need to make a couple of calls. Then we should meet."

Jessica breathed out slowly. "So, it was you."

"You still haven't given me proof that I'm the father."

"Maybe not but, of the two of us, only you will know how likely Sophie was to tell the truth about the father."

He digested that, before saying, "Where are you calling from?"

"I'm in Goma, and you're obviously in Gisenyi. We can meet here if you like," and she gave him the address of AfriCan Care's headquarters and her number.

"And where was he abducted?"

"Less than a hundred metres from the Comptoir Gosomines office."

"I need time to think," said Axel.

"Well, time may be one thing that James doesn't have. He needs people with real influence working on his side, and I don't mean tomorrow. We've tried the official channels and so far we've drawn a blank. Now we need to use the, er … unofficial back channels."

"I hear you. I'll be in touch," and he hung up.

"Sure," said Jessica to herself. "Real nice talking to you too!"

******

"Why was he abducted, if he's just a charity worker?" asked Axel.

"Fuck off!" Aidan snapped. "He may be 'just a charity worker' to you, but he's a colleague and friend here. So if you want to help then help. Otherwise, just fuck the hell out of here." The assembled team glared at Axel, and there were mutterings of anger at his involvement.

"OK, that came out wrong. What I meant was why would a photographer be of value to kidnappers?"

To give him his due, Axel had contacted Jessica within an hour and agreed to a meeting at their headquarters, arriving one hour later. Jessica could have responded cautiously but they needed to persuade Axel and persuade him quickly. "We don't know for sure, but we think that James may not be valuable exactly, but he may be seen as a threat to someone. It could have been after he took some photographs." She glanced up at Sarah who nodded her assent for a fuller disclosure. The team had his computer ready. "We found these photos on his laptop and it's possible that the people involved may have seen him taking them."

Axel said nothing as he studied each of the images. "I guess you know who those people are then," said Axel. His expression hadn't changed at all.

"Well, we do now. Representatives of the FDLR rebels, plus some senior Congolese officers and a leading member of one of the most powerful families in DRC."

"Yes, these are not just any old representatives." He pointed to the tallest of them, "This psychopath is Louis Businga. He calls himself Major but he was due to be cashiered from the army, and he would have been if his family hadn't been so influential and quick to hush things up. To hear him tell it, he resigned his commission. In fact he ordered the dismemberment piece by piece of one of his closest aides with a chainsaw, someone who let him down. I've no idea what the man did or didn't do. From what I hear, Louis Businga played a leading part in it, just so that his troops would fear him even more. He's bad news. God help your man if the Major's got him."

"The other guy in that bromance," he pointed to the photo of two men in a bear hug, "is Colonel Didier Toko, or Loco Toko – except in his hearing. Things haven't been going so well for the FDLR rebels since the UN weighed in on the side of the Congolese. The UN used to just sit in their barracks before going out to clear up whatever mess was left after the fighting. Now they're a lot more hands-on, with some effective troops. Last I heard they had a tough Brazilian in command who took very little shit from anyone. Anyway, you think these people may have seen … James isn't it, that they may have seen him taking these photos. Is that right?"

"We don't know for sure," said Sarah, "but someone from the British Embassy took a look around here today and found fresh footprints coming in through a rear window, footprints that don't match anyone's here, and none of us had reason to come in through the window. The marks weren't there a week ago when the place was cleaned, besides it's rained a lot since then. It's possible that someone broke in to burgle the place but there's nothing missing as far as we can see, so we think they could have been looking around."

"What are your plans from here then?" asked Axel.

"More of the same. We're maximising the publicity through the official channels, we've briefed the local media, and our head office in London has lines into the British Foreign Office and US State Department."

Axel Terberg seemed on the point of saying something. Jessica found his coolness irritating and the feeling only increased as he drummed his fingers slowly and pensively on the table. Nobody had anything to add, so they waited for him to speak. Eventually he said, "You don't know where he is. You don't know for sure who's holding him. You have only one theory as to why someone's taken him. It isn't much to go on."

Sarah was about to protest, when he held up a finger to pause her. "On the other hand, your one theory is plausible, and it's better than no theory. We also have some names to work with. Not nice ones, but some names." Sarah and Jessica exchanged glances; both had noticed the shift from 'you' to 'we'. Axel Terberg seemed to be putting himself on the team.

"There aren't too many courses of action open to us, and from what we can guess time is against him. In other circumstances I'd imagine it would be better to play this softly, softly but James doesn't have that luxury. So we need to barge in through the front door."

"I don't understand," said Sarah. She was well out of her comfort zone and she knew it.

"I'm just mulling over our options. If Louis Businga is involved, then these are not formal or officially-sanctioned negotiations between the Kinshasa government and the rebels. If he wasn't present, I might urge a bit of caution in case you were revealing too much about secret negotiations by the government, say for a peace deal. But with Businga there we can discount that. Kinshasa wouldn't touch him with a ten-foot pole, far less entrust him with delicate negotiations. So, if the

Congolese government has no role here then there's only one person I know who does have any clout with Major Louis Businga."

"Who's that?" asked Jessica.

"General Moise Businga, now officially retired as commander of the DRC army's 5th Brigade, his dad. He is based in Kinshasa but very little happens out here without his knowledge, even in retirement. When his son's violent behaviour became impossible for the army to ignore and they wanted to court martial him, it was Dad who got him off with a slap on the wrists and an honourable discharge."

"Do you mean you know *of* General Businga or do you know him personally?" Sarah asked.

"Well, we're not friends, if that's what you mean. I'm a bit more choosey than that, whatever you may think of my line of business." No one tried to deny the implication and Axel continued. "We certainly aren't close but I have met him several times, in fact we had a meeting in Kinshasa only a few weeks ago. He is as deeply involved in business and politics here as he ever was. And don't believe everything you read about Kinshasa having no influence in the Kivu provinces."

Sarah chose her words carefully. "What approach would you suggest then?"

"Well, since you're not known to him, I guess you mean me." Axel studied her and Sarah returned his stare.

"I guess I do," she replied.

Axel drummed the table again. "Look, these people aren't Good Samaritans, they will either do something for their benefit or to save themselves some trouble. I don't think you've got any incentives to offer them, have you?"

Sarah let out a snort of contempt at the idea.

"I thought not," continued Axel, "I will try and get through to General Businga tonight to see if he knows anything about this. Not that he's likely to admit it, but if there is a connection here then maybe I can get him to see that it isn't in his best interests to allow this to go any further."

******

If there was one thing guaranteed to upset General Dr Moise Businga, it was being interrupted when he was playing the piano. Even in retirement the Doctor of Music found it hard to keep an evening entirely clear for practice. So hearing from his staff that Mr Axel Terberg was on the phone late one evening insisting to be put through soured his mood immediately.

"This better be important," came the old soldier's booming response.

"It is, otherwise I wouldn't have called you this late."

"Well, you've got thirty seconds. What is it?" Businga demanded.

"It's something that's blown up in Goma, where I am now, and is only likely to get worse."

"I'm listening." Businga was not a patient man at the best of times.

"A charity worker has gone missing, and …"

He cut across Axel, "Tell me you didn't interrupt my evening to bring me this news."

"What I was about to say was that he's a photographer, from a charity I know a little." There were limits to how much Axel wanted to share with Businga about his relationships. "They called me because they found something of interest when they checked his laptop after he was abducted. Something I think will be of interest to you."

"Ten seconds. What's that?"

"Among all his photos of refugees, there were photos shot in Kanyaruchinya camp in Goma this week; photos showing a more-than-friendly meeting between several senior figures I recognised from the FDLR and senior army officers from your side, from the FARDC."

"Mr Terberg, if this is news, give it to the newspapers. If this is a crime, call the police. They may be interested, I am not."

"Fine. And who would you like me to give it to if it shows your son giving man-hugs to Didier Toko, head of the FDLR?"

There was a pregnant pause. Axel said nothing while the father digested the latest follies of the son. "Where are you calling from? This is not a secure line." said the older man.

"Nothing is a secure line, we both know that. However, I'm calling you on a new pay-as-you-go phone I bought in a Goma hotel this evening. I can't speak for your end of the line," he said pointedly.

"And who else knows about this?"

"Ah, that's where it gets messy. I've put a lid on it here but I may be too late. The charity had already called in the British Embassy and MONUSCO, so it could be the talk of London and the UN in New York by now."

"If there is a funny side to this, Mr Terberg, I fail to see it," said Businga, his anger boiling to the surface again.

"It certainly won't be funny for the photographer concerned. The Brits believe that someone spotted him taking the photos, traced him to the charity's base in Goma, broke into it and confirmed the substance of the photos before kidnapping him. Is this ringing any bells yet?"

"I still don't understand why you are calling me and not my son. You say it was him in the photos." Ever the wily politician, the elder Businga was keeping his distance from any fall-out.

"Oh, I think you do, Doctor. We both know what happened to the last person who seriously upset the young Major. And I'm guessing a call to Louis from me would only hasten the young man's demise. Whereas a call from you …" Axel left the sentence hanging.

"Leaving aside the personalities in your allegations, it would be a shame to see the progress our government has made in the Kivus being undermined by some ill-judged friendships. I think it is better we end this conversation now and I will see what can be done at this late hour." Businga rang off.

******

James was waiting, cold to his marrow and seriously frightened when they opened up the pit. He had been awake since first light, shivering violently, hugging himself for warmth, and favouring his damaged hand. The first sign of activity had come with the sound of a large diesel engine starting right above his head. The fumes had quickly filled his jail leaving him choking and close to vomiting – only his hunger and his thirst prevented it. He had been relieved when the truck that must have been parked right on top of him was moved away.

As one man began to pull up two of the planks at the edge of the pit, he could see other men staring down at him. Two of the three guards were holding what looked like rifles or semi-automatic weapons, the one who wasn't appeared to be in charge. Even in the restricted light of the garage James squinted as he looked up at the men who stood framed against some high windows. They were tense and clearly wary of him; he hoped that at least one of them was still carrying bruises from him. What scared him most though was that they made no attempt to hide their faces from him; if they planned to release him surely they would have blindfolded him.

They gestured to the rungs of a steel ladder set into the side of the pit, a ladder that had been blocked all night by his wooden ceiling. He began the climb but it was too painful to pull on his left hand so he used only his right which slowed his exit and clearly demonstrated his discomfort. The air above ground was fresher but the garage still smelt of diesel fumes, grease and dust. Now he could hear more plainly the distinctive sounds of aircraft taxiing, as well as occasional landings and take-offs.

"I need a drink," he said through parchment lips. James could feel every movement of his tongue all the way to the back of his throat, his head was banging and his eyes were dry and sore. He was also finding it hard to concentrate. He might not have spoken for all the notice they took.

It was only then that he noticed someone new sitting in a camp chair at a small folding table. On the table was a leather-bound stick with a silver head. It looked like the kind of thing that colonels used to carry in the movies. The man's hair was cut short and he was dressed in an immaculately tailored dark suit and crisp white shirt. He could have stepped straight from the pages of GQ but he was tall enough to look slightly ridiculous in the camp chair, and there was another similar chair that stood empty across the table from him. There was nothing comical about the mood in the garage, however, and all eyes were on James.

"Sit," said the suited man. He smoked a cheroot nonchalantly and he pointed it towards the chair opposite him. James looked about him trying to get his bearings and take in his surroundings. The garage was probably forty metres long and thirty wide. His gaze made him slow to respond and he received a sharp jab in the back with a rifle barrel from someone behind him so he sat.

The moment he was seated strong hands on either side bound both his wrists to the chair's metal arms with plastic cable ties. His wrists were still sore from yesterday's cuffing and his left hand felt painful, swollen and weak.

The man who had spoken in English to him studied James's face; he was unhurried and appeared untroubled. He gave a nod and the truck that had been parked above James overnight was started up by one of the guards who began to rev its engine. The noise in the shed built quickly to an uncomfortable level. James sensed one of the guards close behind him, then felt a shattering electric pain run up his arm even before he registered the hunting knife that had been stabbed into the back of his weak left hand. It went in deep and blood instantly ran across his hand then down the chair leg. James jerked away in a reflex action but he couldn't escape the cable ties or the knife that had pierced right through his hand. He found his voice in a shrill scream of agony that was unrecognisable even to him. Through eyes squeezed tight in agony James stared at the long knife standing upright, its blade protruding five centimetres from just above his knuckle. The bone handle on top of it was well worn and showed that it was in regular use. He looked again with a hideous fascination at the hunting tool that transfixed his hand so deeply that it had cracked the plastic chair arm. In his pain he wasn't immediately aware of it but he was shaking again, this time in shock and he could hear himself shouting but his befuddled, dehydrated brain could not tell him what he was saying.

To add to his confusion the noise of the revving truck engine was so loud that James could hardly hear himself scream. He guessed that no one outside the garage would have heard anything amiss. Then mercifully the engine subsided to a noisy idle and now he could clearly hear his own agonised sobbing.

"Where are you from?" asked the man opposite. He spoke English with an American accent that James couldn't place.

James tried to reply but he couldn't speak. He sucked in short staccato gasps of breath, and writhed his head from side to side as waves of pain surged the length of his body. Then the words came tumbling out in short sentences, matching his breathing. "Listen. I'm a photographer. My name is James Falkus. I work for a charity, in Britain. I don't know … who you think I am … but you've got the wrong guy."

The man in the suit shook his head. Long-limbed and angular, he had bloodshot eyes that looked distinctly unhealthy with a yellow tinge at the corners –

they were staring unflinchingly at James. "Your true name is not important, we may come to that later. I know what you do, that is what matters. Now I want to know who you work for. That interests me very much. Who is it?"

"I've told you. I work for … AfriCan Care. If you don't believe me, you can call them. They will tell you who I am. They will be looking for me and so will the British embassy," said James more in hope than certainty.

"We have seen your passport details, they mean nothing." He nodded and the truck engine began to race.

"No," said James but the man behind leaned over his shoulder and twisted the handle of the knife, separating the bones in his hand, opening the wound wide and pushing the knife even deeper. The pain was worse than anything he had ever known and seemed unending. James knew he must have screamed again but when he noticed his surroundings again the engine revs had subsided. He must have passed out. The knife was out of his hand which was still bleeding from both sides, where it had passed right through his palm.

"I'm not … I'm not who you think. I really am a photographer. I'm British and I'm working for…" he began.

There was a loud bang as a printout of one of James's photographs from the camp was slammed down on the table in front of him. It showed two men in suits embracing; in the background guards in camouflage uniforms stood by a heavily armed 4x4. "Why would a charity photographer take this, or this? Tell me," he said and another photograph was banged down in front of him.

James didn't have time to wonder how they had found these photos. "I was just curious. I'd finished photographing for the day, all the mums and kids." James could hear that he was babbling almost incoherently. "I just saw this meeting happening nearby. It looked different, so I took some photos. It's just what photographers do."

"We can do this all day," said his interrogator stubbing out his cheroot.

"No, please. I've told you the truth. I can't tell you anything else. I shouldn't have taken the photos, I was curious because it was my first day in the camp or any camp. I've only just started with the charity and I was learning my way around, trying to understand what happens there."

The man in front of James just shook his head disbelievingly. He turned to look at the truck driver when somewhere a mobile phone rang; it seemed to come from inside the interrogator's jacket pocket. He pulled it out, looked at the screen and sat up straight before answering the call with a puzzled expression. There was a brief exchange that James couldn't understand, during which he cast glances at James and then at his men before he replied.

******

"You know who this is and this line's not secure, so don't use our names. Understood?"

"Erm, OK."

"You listen to me and you listen really hard, because I'm not going to say this again."

"What's the problem?" his voice was slightly muffled, as if the younger man was covering his mouth.

"Once again, you're the problem. Why do I have to spend my time clearing up your messes? How old are you? And just how fucking stupid? Not only are you still dealing with Toko after I told you to drop him, but you do it in broad daylight in the middle of a refugee camp. Then you wonder why someone takes photos of you."

"How did you know that? Anyway, it's all right, I've got that under control. The whole problem will be silenced very soon." He glanced back at James.

"Oh, have you? Are you wondering how I know about this? Now stop to think who else knows about this. Does it bother you that MI6 are already all over this, that they've told the Americans and the blue hats? It's far too late to just eliminate the problem, as you call him. It's not a leak now, it's a bloody river. Are you trying to undo everything I've built over the last forty years?"

"I don't understand how it could have got out!" The younger man's truculent demeanour was less in evidence now and he turned again to look at his captive.

"I don't know, and it's far too late to worry about that now. You need to put some distance between you and the problem. Go away for a while. Go abroad, stay with that woman you've got in Cape Town. I wouldn't go to London, if I were you, they may be waiting for you – but you've probably worked that out for yourself. Don't contact me or your mother for a long time. And if anyone asks you about this problem, deny it."

"What if they have evidence?"

"What do they have? Photos. Photos can be faked," said Senior. "Just deny it. And deny it. And deny it again. Say, it's all mistaken identity. You can always ask who took the photos. And ask why a so-called aid agency is spying on someone's business meeting. Start asking why the aid agency's doing this. Ask if it really is a charity, or something else, and if so why is it getting involved in politics and business? You could embarrass the hell out of them. That'll throw up a smokescreen for a while. They'll soon shut up. Meanwhile, find a way to release that photographer."

"I'm going to take care of the problem permanently."

"Christ, will you think? Just for one minute in your life think harder. At the moment you're stirring up a hornet's nest. If they don't get him back alive, that'll just get worse as it goes on. But it'll settle down if he comes back to them in one piece. He is still in one piece, isn't he?"

"Sure he is. OK, if that's what you say is best. I'll need time to arrange this."

"Don't take too long. We've spoken too much as it is. I can't come to Goma now, it would only create a link in people's minds. Just sort it out, shove him out the door then go to Cape Town!"

The son said OK, but the line had already gone dead. He still looked unconvinced and he had no idea how to spin this change of policy with his men. His father would know how to do that, and that annoyed him even more. He needed time to think.

******

With his expensive Italian shoes he might be in charge here, but judging by the body language James reckoned the tall man in front of him answered to whoever was on the phone. The interrogator stood up and moved away from the guards, he shook his head and said something heatedly, then he looked at this watch while he continued to listen. "OK," was all that James could make out before the call was ended and he put the phone back in his pocket.

He looked up at James and considered his words. "I have a meeting, we will finish this later." He waved his hand airily to the guards, "Put him away."

"Wait. I need a drink, and some food," said James.

"No food," he replied, then turning to one of the guards he said only, "Tu chupa ya Coke." The man nodded, before pulling the same hunting knife from his belt and deftly cutting the plastic ties holding James to the chair. James's head hung down and he hadn't even seen the knife coming out again, which was probably just as well. The noise of an airplane taking off somewhere nearby made any conversation difficult and they were urging him back to his hole in the ground.

James hugged the cut hand to him. It was swollen, still bleeding although less heavily, and now so agonisingly painful that he could hardly bare to touch it at all. The pain pulsed from his hand up the length of his arm, leaving little room for thoughts of his surroundings. The guards gestured with their rifles for him to walk back to the pit and James reluctantly followed. They were taking no chances and keeping their distance from him. His eyes scanned his surroundings; there were big sliding doors at one end of the garage – possibly the ones he had heard squeaking earlier. A small steel door was set into one of these. At the other end was a toilet and an office made of breeze blocks.

He looked at the pit as he approached. It was covered in solid planks of timber that looked like railway sleepers. They were heavy as he now knew and heavily stained from years of oil spills and tyre movements across them. There must have been about ten sleepers of uniform width, the only difference was that two in the middle were a little shorter. They were right under the truck and he couldn't have lifted them very far anyway. He sat down awkwardly on the edge of the pit and mimed a drink to them. One of the guards nodded but the other signalled him to climb down again through the narrow gap and into the darkness. With his left hand clasped to him he turned and stood on the steel rungs. "I need a drink," he said but they waved him down. "No," he said. "Give me a drink," and he tried again to mime drinking from a bottle. He almost lost his balance and grabbed the top rung to stop himself falling backwards. The opening created by removing two timbers was narrow and he sat down exhaustedly on the nearest plank that remained in place. "Drink," he said one more time, and his chin drooped on to his chest. One of the guards stepped forward threateningly but James felt something tap his shoulder. His reactions were slowing, he now realised that one of the sounds he had heard was the truck door slamming; the man behind him had retrieved a large bottle of Coke from the cab. Some of it had been drunk but there was plenty in there and he was giving it to James. James took it and before they could change their minds he held it to him with his injured arm and clambered down into the pit. It was damp and nearly dark in there, and it smelt bad but he had only one thing on his mind. As he fumbled the lid off the bottle and took several enormous gulps, the timbers were lifted back into place above him, darkness returned and the idling engine revved as the truck was driven back into place to bar his exit. The drink was such a relief that it was another minute or two before he thought again about the future that awaited him. A huge constricting feeling of self-pity welled up in his chest, but he pushed the thoughts away angrily and pulled the hem of his shirt around his hand to stem the bleeding before sitting down in the dry end of the pit. Through exhaustion and hunger his movements were clumsy, and the mere act of sitting down was enough to make him cry out with pain as he inadvertently jarred his left hand. When the pain subsided a little and he began to listen to what was happening above, he realised that the truck engine had been switched off and then he heard a steel door bang before it all went quiet. At least this time, he could picture his surroundings and as soon as it was silent above he stood up as straight as he could. There was something he wanted to test.

******

James snapped awake. He was sitting up with his back to the cold wall and his head had fallen forward uncomfortably. He was unaware that he had even been sleeping, but now he was able to recall some vivid snatches of a troubled dream unusually fresh in his mind. There were two things he needed to do and the first was to take a leak. There was no choice but to go in the furthest extremity of this long narrow chamber. He stood up and immediately felt light-headed, forcing him to sit again. For a minute James leaned back against the wall for balance, and saw stars in the near darkness at the edge of his field of vision. It reminded him that it was a day and a half since he last ate. What little sleep he had grabbed last night

332

had been taken sitting up in a cold, damp cellar, he was chilled to the bone, he had lost blood and been subjected to a beating and a stabbing. The bleeding had stopped, but frankly it was no surprise that he was feeling crap and still very scared.

When he returned to the dry end of the pit, he sat and listened intently for five minutes. They would probably have posted a guard but if last night was anything to go by he might not be nearby. James was worried that a guard could be sitting in the garage office but his shouts last night hadn't brought anyone out so, if someone was there, he might be outside the main doors.

James could still hear the occasional aircraft – some large, most of them small – taxiing, taking off and landing. He recognised the rhythmic thud of helicopter rotors as well as the steadier drone of planes. He wondered if he could use the noise to mask his efforts in the same way that his captors had. There was nothing else to do but go for it. He moved to the side of the pit by the ladder and stared up. The driver had parked in almost exactly the same place as before. He focused his attention on just two planks and crouched to avoid banging his head on the timbers above him as he fumbled one-handed in the darkness.

While he waited for the covering noise of an aircraft he thought about his family. They didn't even know he was in trouble, so he would have to think of the charity as his family and he offered a silent prayer that they were working to find him. James thought he had heard a woman's shouts when those bastards nabbed him and he wondered if Jessica had seen any of what happened. If so she could raise the alarm, but then he recalled some shots as he was being driven away – he didn't know how many. God, what if they had killed her? He didn't like to think of that, he had become fond of her. Then he thought what a total arse he'd been to her before he ran off. If she was still alive, she probably wouldn't be speaking to him, and who could blame her? Crap. Why did it always go so badly when he fancied someone, he wondered? He should carry a bloody health warning. Even by his own pitiful standards in relationships, this was a monumental fuck-up. Scratch that thought, move on.

He had something new to think about, if he could ever get out of here. Axel Terberg. He was alive and kicking and working in Congo, surely the man must be his father, his natural father. The age was right, the unusual name was the same, and his birth father had spent time in Congo. Surely that couldn't all be coincidence, there couldn't be two of them floating around this part of Africa. Could there?

Neil had said don't come. Well, to the extent that he was someone's prisoner and was being tortured for information he didn't have, Neil was right. *Yeah*, he thought ruefully, *but leaving that aside…*

James had no idea how Neil would face this, so he would have to deal with it in his own way. He took a long drink of Coke but kept some back in case he needed it later. He really hoped that was an unnecessary precaution, if he spent much longer in here he knew that thirst would be the least of his problems.

Chapter 22
Goma City, North Kivu, DRC
Four Days Ago

He tried to stand up but banged his head. At least his height meant James could try lifting the beams with his shoulders; then maybe he wouldn't need to rely so much on his hands, only the right one was fully functioning. He preferred not to think what they had done to his left hand.

After one last listen it seemed the coast was clear. He heard the gradual increase in background noise as a plane began to taxi out towards the runway. James could only hope that the noise would mask his efforts, as he put his right shoulder under one of the middle timbers and lifted. It went up OK for a few centimetres then stopped. He tried this with the one beside it. No movement at all, he must have got the wrong side. James shifted to his left by one timber and he managed to lift this one upwards a few centimetres too. There were no shouts from the guards, perhaps they were outside. There was no way of lifting them high enough to create a gap he could scramble through. Anyway, he wouldn't be able to lift himself out with only one hand. But what if he could slide one or both of the shorter timbers far enough along? He began to drag a timber forwards and it moved as long as he didn't try to raise it too far. He was picking up some small splinters in his shoulder, even through his shirt, but this time the pain didn't seem so bad. *It was all relative*, he thought.

He had moved the timber along by more than ten centimetres when it stopped. Bloody hell. He tried again. Nothing. James shifted position and worked on the second of the short timbers. There were no wheels touching this one either and it slid along even better. He wasn't sure how much leeway he needed but he just hoped that there was enough room. It slid fifteen centimetres, twenty, and thirty and suddenly the entire weight of the plank was on his shoulder. James tensed and held the position, listening for a shout, then slowly he bent down and put one end of the timber on the pit floor. Now the timber next to it could move more freely and he could help it along with a decent grip. It came free at the same end and again the weight pressed down hard on his right shoulder. Slowly and silently he let one end of the timber fall beside the first and now he could see daylight beside the truck.

He began to wriggle up this narrow ramp and found that although the truck was low slung there was just enough room to squeeze by its nose. It seemed to take an age, but it was probably no more than thirty seconds after he started to climb that James emerged into the daylight and lay panting on the concrete floor. He noticed the vehicle more clearly now, it was an airplane tow tractor, a powerful tug used for manoeuvring the largest aircraft.

Now he had to find a way out of the garage without attracting the guards' attention. He got to his feet and peered over the front of the tug. He couldn't see anyone, but he was sure they wouldn't have left him alone, his photos obviously made him a danger to them. James needed to know where the guards were before deciding what to do. There was no light in the small office and he couldn't hear anything, but if someone came to check on him he would need a weapon. He searched around; there was nothing on the ground, but a workbench next to the office had several tools on it. James kept low and ran over to the bench, making no sound and without being challenged. A selection of spanners lay scattered on the worktop, all too small to be of any use. He picked up a flat blade screwdriver and pushed it into the back of his waistband, he'd never been in a knife fight but it looked like this might be the next best thing if it came to it. Then he noticed a hefty torque wrench further along the worktop. Its rubber grip sat comfortably in his palm and the business end was heavy enough to do some serious damage – unless he was confronted by a guard with a gun, of course.

He still needed to know if there was anyone in the office. Peering through the window would leave him exposed if there was someone inside, so he ducked beneath it and scuttled round to the half open door. This was it, he stood up and spun through the doorway with the wrench raised to strike but the room was empty. James was both surprised and relieved. Then as he looked out of the office window he noticed the shadows of a pair of feet passing occasionally outside the main doors. Shit, if he tried to open the small door he'd be a sitting duck for anyone with a gun, and he knew from the noise they'd made on arrival that the big doors created a hell of a racket when they were opened. It would be enough to alert any number of guards and there was no other way out of the place.

Then he saw the answer standing right in front of him, the airplane tug. It would be low-geared for towing heavy aircraft and very powerful. He knew it worked; they'd manoeuvred it backwards and forwards twice leaving him coughing diesel fumes below. The biggest problem was he'd never driven one before and had no idea how it worked. He just hoped it was like the tractors he'd driven as a student on a holiday job. He ran across to the tractor cab. Beautiful, the key was still in it, ready for the next time they needed to get him out. He was going to have to reverse and try not to drop it into the hole he'd created in the inspection pit. James reckoned it would take him five seconds to get the engine running steadily, and another five or ten to cross the garage in reverse. That wasn't enough – the guard would come in fast through that service door the moment he heard the engine.

James climbed out of the cab and ran noiselessly across the open space to the door, willing it not to open. If the guard came in now, he'd be caught in open ground and either shot or recaptured. As he'd hoped, there was a small sliding bolt to lock the door from the inside. He slid it across as quietly as he could until the door was secured. That had bought him some more time to get this right.

He ran back to the cab. It was now or never, best to go while there was probably only one guard outside the door. Without starting the engine James checked the gearbox was in Park. He half-turned the key until a red ignition light came on. There was a yellow light shining beside it which he guessed was for the glow plug to warm the old diesel engine, and sure enough it went out after a few seconds. Now or never, James twisted the ignition key all the way and the huge engine thumped into life. Clouds of black smoke – all too familiar to him from his time beneath – burst from the rear and he slammed the shift into reverse. Christ, where was the parking brake? He hadn't checked. There was a shout from outside and he saw feet run from one side of the steel double doors towards the tiny service door. He'd done the right thing to lock it.

Then he spotted the handbrake and it was already flat on the cab floor. The driver had just left it in Park with no brake on. He pressed the accelerator and the tractor jumped backwards with startling force. The unladen tug's acceleration was so strong that he was thrown forwards painfully pinning his hand against the frame of the cab before quickly regaining his balance. He peered through the glassless rear window as the tug swiftly gathered speed across the empty garage.

Built to pull and push aircraft far heavier than itself, the tug's strongest part was the rear towing pintle, and it was this that struck the join between the sliding double doors a metre off the ground. Not designed to withstand such a lateral force, the doors' huge steel castors jumped clean out of their guides. The long flat rear deck continued unchecked through the doors that were now bent outwards and the tug emerged into sunlight like a twenty mile-an-hour sledgehammer swinging through tin foil. James kept low to avoid any gunfire but he could see the doors had burst open with such speed that the guard outside had been tossed aside by the impact like a discarded doll and was lying face down, twisted and motionless three metres from where James had last spotted him. His gun was nowhere to be seen.

There was a shout from the corner of the garage as two guards emerged into the sunlight. Then a rasp of gunfire which must have gone over his head. The next shots were more accurate, several struck the tug and James instinctively crouched lower; the cab he was in was open at the side with only a thick steel rail to prevent him tumbling out. He was completely exposed to the gunmen and still going backwards which was seriously restricting his speed. Then he heard an engine start somewhere nearby and the pick-up that had brought him here reversed hurriedly around the side of the building. There was one man with the driver in the cab, and as it made a three-point turn another jumped into the back.

James slammed on the brakes and the tug stopped surprisingly quickly. He braked and pushed the gear selector into Drive. This time he was ready for the surge of acceleration. By now the pick-up truck had swung around and was heading after him. James had no clear idea where he was going. He knew that the terminal was at the far end of the airport and he guessed that the pick-up would have a higher top speed so they would catch him long before he could reach it. If he made it there, he could be protected by all the Congolese and UN forces posted around it, but he'd never make it in a drag race and his pursuers only needed to get close enough to shoot him.

He emerged from the warehouses onto the perimeter road. To the right he could see the road surface deteriorated quickly and the 4x4 would have a big advantage so James swung left taking the better made route north towards the terminal buildings and the mountains. Already the pick-up truck was gaining on him and their shots were getting closer. The tug had a flat rear deck to give drivers maximum all-round visibility which meant he had little protection from behind, fortunately the seat was set low in the cab so James crouched down as far as he could while still seeing ahead. Even at his top speed they would overhaul him soon, then he saw a service road running upwards to the right and he took it towards the runway. The road surface was compacted dirt and there was a slight incline which began to slow his heavy vehicle. He felt the automatic drop a gear, the revs picked up and seconds later the tug burst out of the gully onto a rough road that ran level and parallel with the runway. He now had his bearings and seeing a better made track twenty yards to his right he swung the tug off the rutted and baked mud, onto the murram road. Loose stones of lava, some as large as his fist, pummelled the underside of the tug and he prayed that the tyres would survive this harsh punishment. He was gathering speed again but the pick-up had followed him across the grass with ease and the gap was closing once again. When he next turned to look back his heart sank. Someone on a large off-road motorcycle had joined the chase and was gaining on the pick-up truck behind him. As far as James could see, there was no one riding pillion.

The pick-up truck was still the nearest threat. They were shooting at him, but he couldn't hear anything over the roar of his overworked diesel engine, then gouge marks suddenly appeared on the tug's wooden decking and there was a whine as a shot ricocheted away. A moment later wood splinters flew everywhere and he felt something sharp strike him in the face but all he could think about was how to outrun his pursuers. Through his feet he felt three distinct thuds in quick succession, they seemed to be different from the random thrumming of gravel beneath his wheels. He ducked involuntarily and now could barely see where he was going. He could either remain invisible and take the chance of running off the road or continue to peer over the wheel and risk having the top of his head blown off. Not a great choice, but it would all be over anyway if he crashed so he steered and snatched a look every few seconds.

He knew the runway would suit his vehicle better than this packed gravel track but getting to it would mean crossing a grass divide and he couldn't tell if there were any hidden ditches or rocks that might tear his wheels off. If he stayed on this route, they'd soon catch him, he was sure of that. They might catch him anyway if he turned, but at least he would stand a chance on a better surface.

The tug bounced down the murram service road running parallel with the runway, doing brutal damage to the vehicle's tyres and suspension. Now he was able to build up speed again and steering one-handed he crouched low in the cab. If the pick-up truck was gaining on him, it wasn't as rapidly as before. He roared past a line of yellow landing lights, the runway was somewhere to his right. He had to reach that smooth surface otherwise he wouldn't stand a chance of finding safety.

The stretch of grass and low scrub separating him from the tarmac grew narrower now and he began to swing a slow right turn trying not to lose speed – he prayed that the grass wasn't too deep, the ground too soft or rocky, that there were no hidden obstacles, and he kept his foot down hard on the accelerator. The tug bounced jarringly as it left the gravel and then slowed a little as he ploughed through long grass before running down a slight incline and onto the runway. He had avoided any hidden obstacle, somehow the tyres had stayed on and now he was out on the runway gaining momentum while heading north at a speed the tug's designers would never have imagined.

He aimed diagonally across the wide runway knowing that all the terminal buildings and military checkpoints were on that side. Now he risked another backwards glance; the truck was close and when he looked to the front again he had to swerve violently. From nowhere, a woman with a baby tied to her back in a cotton wrap had stepped nonchalantly from the grass onto the runway. He was less than a hundred metres from her when she noticed him bearing down on her. She stopped in her tracks, directly in the path of the on-rushing tug and pick-up truck, which put her in the gunman's line of fire. The woman must have heard some shots for she spun around and began to run back the way she had come. A sandal spun off her foot as she reached the grass and she high-stepped through it, her long pink dress slowing her flight. The baby bouncing on her back began a high-pitched wail that carried to him over the engine's thunder. Then he flashed past and she was gone. Ahead he could now see more men and women crossing the airport. Didn't they have a bloody fence round here? On the left of the runway four schoolboys no more than twelve years old were slowly kicking a stone across the smooth asphalt apparently on their way to school, their bright white shirts and black trousers an incongruous sight in this shooting gallery.

One by one, James's towing tractor, the pick-up and then the motorbike came into view from the terminal, their engines screaming. It would have taken only a few seconds to see that James' pursuers were closing on him. The schoolboys stared in surprise and for a moment they grinned and pointed at the tug straining at its rev limits, until they realised it was losing a one-sided chase with a truck and a motorbike. Their amusement turned instantly to wide-eyed panic as they heard semi-automatic gunfire zip past them from the back of the pick-up. The burst was long enough to be unmistakably gunfire and close enough to make them sprint. Two boys broke left and raced away through the grass. The one who had been leading the way started running across the asphalt, then seeing that his friends were heading in the other direction he stopped, turned and ran back into the path of the tug. How James missed him he would never know, it could only have been by a split second, and then he was past and alone, totally exposed on the runway and very vulnerable.

The bike had caught the pick-up and started to close the gap on James's right rear side. It dawned on him that the rider would need his right hand on the bars to hold the throttle open. If he was right-handed, he would find it hard to shoot with his left. Looking back he could see the rider reach awkwardly into the back of his waistband with his left hand and emerge with a handgun. He was less than twenty metres behind and closing fast when he fired his first shots. James heard the reports clearly but felt nothing, then he saw the man was aiming at his tyres. That was the moment he heard a loud bang and the steering went stiff and heavy as the tug began to pull hard to the right. James fought hard to counteract it. Debris from the tyre spun wildly out of the wheel arch forcing the bike to veer away to the right.

They raced up the runway's right-hand side and began to pass aircraft parked in gravelled stands dotted among the grass margins; first a large abandoned four-engined jet, then a smaller twin-engined aircraft. They must be getting closer to the terminal but still it was too far for him to reach before they caught him.

There was a loud thrumming followed by intermittent bangs as the tyre began to disintegrate and strike the wheel arch. James leaned his full weight against the steering, holding it on course. He was still travelling but friction from the ruined tyre was slowing the tug even further, and now smoke began to belch from the tangled rubber and wire. From his time beneath the vehicle James knew there were two wheels on each side of the axle, all he could do was hope that the remaining wheel would not puncture or explode from the heat.

As he fought to control the tug and straighten its line once more, the biker swung back towards him; he was almost level with James now and he seemed to be grinning as he came alongside. James looked around for something to use as a weapon. There was a fuel can out of arm's reach in the cab so he stretched his left foot across and hooked it towards him. It was full and heavy. He tried to pick it up with his bad hand but he had too little strength to grasp it. By laying his body across the steering wheel he was able to keep on course and he reached down for the can, swinging it up and out of the cockpit towards the motorbike just as the rider began to come alongside. The biker saw what was coming in time to swerve the bike away again, and the fuel can bounced harmlessly on the ground between them before splitting open and spilling diesel fuel on the tarmac. All James had managed was to postpone the next shot.

Up ahead he could see a line of newer white aircraft in UN livery. By the look of the orange tarpaulins tied over their cockpit windows some had been laid up for the long term while others were being serviced. An elderly fuel tanker was gently making its way up the edge of the runway to the service area. Covered in rust and the marks of long neglect it was trundling along so slowly that even the wounded tug was closing fast behind it.

The biker swung back towards James to finish him off. He lifted his gun to take aim and James let go of the steering wheel that he had been fighting. Freed from his grasp it spun back wildly for a second and James was thrown against the side of the cabin just as the next shot was fired. Two bullets passed over the wheel where he had been standing seconds before. He put out his arm instinctively to steady himself and cried out as the pain from his damaged hand ran up to his shoulder. This time, however, the sudden change of direction caught the bike's rider unawares as he closed in from the right, his left hand was off the bars to prepare for the coup de grace. He was leaning to the left to swing the bike closer for an easier shot. The debris of one of two right rear tyres was now wedged into the wheel arch dragging the tug towards the verge, and as James stopped fighting the twisting motion the tug swung violently right and struck the bike broadsides. The rider was skilled and managed to keep it upright but he needed both hands and the heavy gun in his left was preventing him gripping the bars. To James it seemed to happen in slow motion as the bike went into a deadly tank slap motion with the front wheel swinging wildly left and right, ripping the bars from the rider's grasp and forcing the machine into the weaving motion that bikers dread. Even with both hands the rider would have been unlikely to overcome the violent swing to right, left and right again. He dropped the gun but held onto the handlebars for a fraction too long so that the swinging bars broke his right wrist at a sickening angle. As the bars snapped back again to the left, the tug drew level with the rear of the fuel bowser and the bike became wedged between two heavy trucks moving at different speeds. They trapped the rider's legs and James watched as its front wheel was dragged beneath the bowser's rear axle and then the rider went under with it. His scream was cut short as the tanker bumped heavily once and the rider was left behind in a tangled mess of two-wheeled machinery and a seeping stain on the runway. The tanker driver shouted something and hit his brakes but James was already swinging his steering wheel back to the left to separate the two vehicles. Somehow, they weren't entwined but plenty of paint had been exchanged and the fuel tanker now had some serious dents in its low storage lockers. The tug's momentum carried it forward and soon the bowser was somewhere behind him – James had no idea how he was still going, but the powerful tug ploughed on, continually pulling to the right as its injured driver fought to keep it straight ahead.

The pick-up truck raced past the fallen biker, and now the firing was more intense than ever. Two bullets smashed through the dashboard in front of him peppering James' shirtfront with glass and metal fragments and leaving dark holes in the controls. It didn't seem to affect the vehicle which blundered on.

James looked around him, there were no signs of any planes landing. Then he looked back and saw that the front seat passenger had climbed from the pick-up's cab and was sitting in the open window, pulling his gun into position. The man was sitting sideways in the window which placed James slightly behind him; it was an angle that made shooting difficult but not impossible so he was passing the gun to the man in the rear.

They could all see the terminal now but it was still half a mile away and James knew he would never make it that far, he wanted to take the fight to them but he was unarmed, he couldn't turn left and if he turned right he'd be on the grass and handing the speed advantage to the undamaged 4x4. He needed protection and then he saw it. Ahead there were another ten or more bright white planes and helicopters parked on an asphalt apron. Beyond them a wall of shipping containers stacked twenty feet high bore the French and English logo, ONU / UN. At the far end he could see a gate, inside which he could just make out some three storey stacks of prefabricated buildings and a UN flag on a tall pole.

They had already passed the southerly end of the long UN compound but the entrance was still two hundred metres away. Now his pursuers were so close that James could hear the pick-up truck over his own tortured engine, and when he risked another look behind he saw the gunman in the back struggling to reload as the 4x4 swerved to come alongside him.

The two vehicles were closing on the access road to the compound and as the pick-up truck finally drew alongside him James saw the gunman in the rear taking aim. There was a sudden blast of air from above mixed with flying grit that stung his eyes and skin, and with it came a rushing shadow and a deafening roar – James watched in fascination as a huge white helicopter swept over the gunman from behind catching them all by surprise. He couldn't tell whether the gunman was unbalanced by the rotors' downdraught as the helicopter passed close above him. Perhaps the undercarriage had struck the exposed man in the rear – it didn't matter. He pitched forward, his gun still clasped in both hands, and wordlessly tumbled out of the truck's flatbed into the roadway. Several shots went off before he hit the ground. Falling headfirst at speed from a couple of metres onto the runway he bounced but was never going to get up again. The pick-up truck slowed momentarily and James raised himself a little to keep it in view. He looked around in time to see the chopper climb steeply, bank at an almost impossible angle and then swing back to face the pick-up truck, hovering malevolently no more than twenty metres off the ground. Behind him the pick-up truck was stationary at an angle, isolated in the middle of the runway.

Another dirt roadway opened up to James's right and he relaxed his grip on the wheel enough to allow the tow vehicle to turn down the narrow route towards the gates. He could hear a siren wailing inside the compound and saw soldiers inside rushing towards the closing gates, pulling on flak jackets and blue helmets. "Wait, wait," he yelled and waved his bad arm while steering with his good. One more look back and he saw the pick-up swerve away from the helicopter and flee south for safety. With a final bellow from the diesel engine beneath him he swung through the fast closing gate and braked hard but not enough to stop him crashing into the back of a line of pristine white Land Rovers.

James slumped forward against the huge steering wheel. A black arm in jungle camouflage bearing a badge with the South African flag, reached past him and turned off the engine, removing the key as it did so. James lifted his head for long enough to see the soldier was pointing a rifle at him and stepping back warily; it was only then that he noticed a ring of blue-helmeted troops around him all pointing their guns at him. "Hands up!" yelled several tense voices at once. Amid the hubbub there had been a silence in his mind that suddenly gave way to a cacophony that must have been queuing for his attention. He heard the second gate close belatedly with a metallic clang, there were the clicks of safety catches going off, the banshee wail of the compound siren was rising and falling endlessly, engines were being started, there were the insistent shouts of rattled soldiers and officers yelling orders, then all he could hear was the ticking of hot metal, and nearby some idiot was laughing. God only knew why, but it was him.

******

SK Zaidi at Comptoir Gosomines had been as good as his word. Any doubts that Axel had harboured about his ability to deliver the quantities of coltan that CCV required had proved groundless. Of course, the Businga family were playing their cards close to their chest about which mines the coltan came from but the use of this comptoir in Goma indicated to Axel that their supplies must be coming from the surrounding area, most likely from some of the ten or more mines around Walikale. Other families might want to compete but the Busingas were still key players. This was one of the most lawless areas in North or South Kivu, with fighting continuing between the Congolese Army backed by the UN against the Hutu rebels of the FDLR. Politicians insisted that the fighting had ended years ago, but the FDLR still used the area as a base for raids into Rwanda as they tried to overthrow the Tutsi government. Axel guessed it must be more critical than ever for the rebels to keep hold of the hill country for its mineral wealth, slave labour and child soldiers. The once powerful M23 rebels, also backed by Rwanda, had been driven out of Goma by the army, but smaller bands had grown up in their place. Whenever he returned to the area, Axel found the politics initially bewildering.

He had had very little feedback from his client CCV since the first supplies began to reach them in Macao. Their silence was probably a good thing, you would always hear quickly enough from clients if they weren't happy. After some positive discussions with them and hints that next year's demand would be even greater than forecast he had let sleeping dogs lie.

Axel wished he could say the same of the Americans. The State Department's fascination – you could call it an obsession since it obscured most other considerations – with the influence of the Chinese in the region had not lessened. He hadn't been summoned to any more meetings in Kinshasa, but the CIA's man in the eastern provinces had taken to calling in, for "moral support" as he put it. It was another way of letting Axel know that he was always on their radar.

Axel kept wishing he was back in the diamond trade. He was learning to find his way round the coltan business, but he felt on more solid ground with gems and he enjoyed their complexities and beauty. Perhaps he wasn't quite the Philistine that some people told him he was.

******

Neutral ground seemed best for their first meeting. Axel sipped a good coffee as he waited in the sunshine at the Hotel Ihusi. High clouds blew over the mountains in Rwanda and across the lake on a quickening wind but here at ground level the breeze was light and warm, simply ruffling the umbrellas by the unused pool and rippling the dark waters of the lake. He saw Kris, his new security man, sit up at the other end of the terrace as they both heard movement and they each assessed the young man who approached. Kris intercepted James and introduced himself before asking if he was armed. You could read the surprise in James's face for, although assured that he was not, the bodyguard asked if he could frisk him and duty done he returned to his table a few metres away.

James shook his head and walked on grim-faced towards Axel who had stood to greet him. What Axel saw was a young man, marginally taller than himself, well-built and dressed in shirt and shorts. As James came down the steps, he flicked back the brown hair that was falling into his eyes, eyes that were concealed behind sunglasses.

The two men sized one another up before James asked, "Do you do that to all your visitors, or just your children?" If he had intended the remark to be humorous, it never became a smile.

"Let's not get ahead of ourselves." He waved James to a chair. "But I will apologise for the necessity, I have had some unwelcome visitors in recent weeks. As have you, it seems," and he nodded to the bright blue bandaged plaster cast on James's hand. "How are you? I heard they roughed you up a bit."

James studied his own hand for a moment, turning the cast this way and that as he grew used to it. "That's not how I'd have put it, but yes, I'm fine. I won't be doing pull-ups any time soon but I'm told it'll mend if I give it some rest."

"Would you like a real coffee? I thought this would be a good place to meet, with no one to disturb us. Not even waiters, it seems," said Axel ruefully.

"I'll have something when someone comes, I'm unemployed so I'm in no rush."

"What happened?"

"Apparently the London office took a dim view of my extra-curricular photography. To be fair, they seemed very pleased to get me back in one piece, or near as dammit. They did however mention something about unprofessionalism – I don't know, is that even a word? – And what else was there? Unacceptable risks to other staff, gross misconduct, etc., etc. To be honest, I was a bit tired; I didn't take it all in. Anyway, I'm looking for gainful employment again. So, if you know anyone who needs someone who was once a good PR manager but is now a high risk freelance photographer without a reference, I'm your man."

Axel smiled. "You're hard on yourself."

"It's OK, I'm not the only one," James replied. He sat up a little in his chair. "You catch me at a low point; normally I'm the life and soul of the party. I'll bounce back."

"I don't doubt it, if you're Sophie Callender's son."

"I am," said James firmly, "and I'd be happy to show you her letter that says so." There was a silence, and the two men eyed one another again.

"Do you have it with you?"

"It hasn't left my side since I got it, apart from a recent stay in a garage," James reached for the long wallet in his back pocket and noticed Kris's gaze swing quickly towards him to assess the threat. He opened the wallet and carefully removed an ageing airmail letter before passing it over to Axel.

"OK if I read it now?"

"It stays with me, so you'd better." There was a mettle to this quietly spoken young man that Axel was starting to see.

Axel didn't know what to say when he reached the part in Sophie's letter that said she might have been slowing him down on business trips because he stopped asking her to go with him. More than anything else he had heard in the last forty-eight hours this drove home what she had meant to him, and what he had been missing ever since. He preferred not to speak at this point so he carried on reading; he was not prepared to show his emotions to James.

Judging from the letter and the young man's manner there was no doubt in James's mind now that he was Sophie's son, but Axel found it hard to make that last connection and accept her implicit assurance that he was the father. And as he read he also began to think of what she had brought into his life: openness, affection, then love, but above all honesty.

No family or friend had ever demanded the truth from him so forcefully. His life until he met her had been one of confusion about who he was; he was so unlike his own parents. Disappearance and deception had always been his default modes, his protection mechanisms so that he could blend like a chameleon into any surroundings, not wanting to be noticed because it suited his life and his business to keep a discreet, low profile. Then he had met Sophie and for the first time he hadn't needed to pretend to be anyone.

The letter reminded him that, bizarrely in his view at the time, she seemed to love him for who and what he was. There was no need for pretence or deception. This was one of the facets of their life together that Axel had found so surprising and so liberating. He could be who he wanted to be. And it had made him a better man, all the time that he still had her.

And now it struck him with renewed clarity that this was exactly what he'd lost when he left her. He had missed her laughter, her gentleness, her teasing that combined to break down his defences. She had opened a window for him onto an unfamiliar world. It wasn't just her love of art and her creativity, although he had never noticed it before and, thanks to Sophie, it was a window which remained open to this day. No, what he missed, and above all what he had lost, was her honesty.

Now, all these years after they had broken up, all these years after her death she seemed to be challenging him to deny her, to say that she was untrue and this was not her son, and not his son. If he accepted this letter – and from the handwriting, the paper, ink and stamps, he had no doubt about its authenticity – he must accept what she said. The boy had become the man, the man who had searched her out through all the formal channels, he was hers. And he was Axel's too. Axel handed the letter back to James, and was wondering what to say when James spoke.

"How does an Axel Terberg come to sound like he's from London or the Home Counties?" asked James.

"My English-born mother insisted that I was educated in Britain, it was one of the few battles she won with my Dutch father. Through her father I inherited the right to apply for a scholarship to a public school in Sussex, a scholarship that eventually I won. She wanted to have a little English gentleman; you can probably imagine her disappointment."

James smiled briefly.

"So what does that make us? The unprofessional son and the unacceptable father?" asked James. "I reckon Sophie would have had something to say about that."

"Do you mean what was a man with no moral compass doing with such a principled woman?"

"I wouldn't have put it like that, but that's close enough," James allowed.

"I loved her. In fact, I loved her more than anyone I've met before or since, but I could never pretend to match her," said Axel.

"So it was easier not to try, huh?"

"I don't blame you for being cynical. I look at who I was then and sometimes I don't recognise myself. What I see now is not necessarily an improvement, but it's who I've become."

"That just sounds like a cop-out to me. You reverted to type, is that it?" James felt only contempt for this attitude.

"Not at all, as I said I learned a lot from your mum. But not all of it stuck, it might have been better for everyone if it had. I guess after Sophie, I went back to what I knew best. I never stopped thinking about her, if that's any consolation but I didn't know about you at all."

"Would it have made a difference if you'd known she was having a baby, that she was having me?"

"You mean a difference to my future with her?" Axel didn't wait for a reply. "I've thought about this a lot since your friend Jessica called. Yes, I believe it would."

James scoffed. "You would have tried again with her if you'd known about me?"

This time there was a silence. "It's taken me a bit of time to work it out," said Axel, "but I believe it might have changed things. I trusted her implicitly then and I've no reason to start doubting her now. Meeting you, and reading that letter makes it much easier to believe. It's reminded me, if I needed reminding, that she was always absolutely straight with me – even if it made my life uncomfortable for a time. I just think this is one of those times."

James grinned. There was a lengthy pause while he toyed distractedly with a drinks mat, turning it over and over in his hand as he considered how best to ask the next question. "Does having a son make you feel uncomfortable?"

"Too soon to say," Axel smiled and James realised that he hadn't expected to talk so openly with this stranger. "At the moment this looks like a pretty big challenge to me. But I suppose I try not to duck challenges."

This time the silence between the two men was a little less strained, and was eventually broken by James. "The biggest challenge round here seems to be getting a refill."

"I don't know about you, but I think this calls for something stronger."

"I have to ask; how can you work in the coltan business?" said James. "You must know what it does to people here. You know what happens in those mines – the forced labour, the children working for hours or even days in dark tunnels with no breathing equipment, no support when something goes wrong. I mean this isn't something theoretical or abstract, it's not some giant 'What If', it's happening right now while we're sitting here. People are being robbed of whatever they dig out. Women are being raped, right now. I don't get it – you're clearly an intelligent man. It should bring wealth to Congo but the wealth goes to people like you and it seems to bring nothing but pain and misery. Aren't you ducking a challenge right there?"

"It's not the coltan trade that brings misery to this area. It's the way it's run and the people it's run by," Axel replied.

"Oh, I see. Isn't that the gun lobby argument in the States? It's not guns that kill people, its people that kill people. So, this has nothing to do with you. Is that what you're saying?"

"I didn't say that. But I don't see how one man like me can change it. Sadly, I don't have your skills to inform and persuade people."

"Bull shit! If you wanted to help, you could make sure you buy only from government-certified suppliers," James insisted.

"On the contrary, that's the bullshit. Even the government doesn't know which mines it controls, and the list will be different next week or next month. People who argue for that don't understand that a certificate proves nothing. Forgeries would be easy to get hold of, and officials are bribed all the time to make conflict-area minerals appear OK. As for child labour, I'm sure you know what happens. Inspectors go into an area. The children all get moved out. The inspectors leave and the children get moved back in. And don't make out it only happens in this business. Children here work in shops and on farms everywhere; if they don't find regular work they're on the street hawking, begging or stealing. And before you jump in, I'm not saying I'm saving them from a life of crime; just that this is the norm here – don't apply Western rules when there's no Western benefits system for them to fall back on."

There was silence between them, and renewed tension.

Axel tried again. "It's not the coltan trade that's at fault, it's the politics here. I don't mean just domestic politics either, neighbouring countries are still trying to get their hands on Congo's mineral wealth, and global powers are always looking for some geopolitical advantage."

James snorted. "How can you talk about foreign interference? You're not Congolese and you're here making a fortune out of it."

"Well, we could argue about the fortune aspect, but ..."

James interrupted him. "I don't suppose you're doing it for a few dollars a day like most Congolese!"

"No, that's certainly true. But I put sellers in touch with buyers, that's just what I do. It's all I know, and if and when the Congolese can do that entirely for themselves, then I'll be out of a job or making a lot less than I do now."

"Oh, this just gets better. Now it's the old if-I-don't-do-it-someone-else-will argument." James looked away and wondered if he should leave. This conversation was going nowhere.

"To be honest, I didn't even want to get into the tin and coltan trade," said Axel. He thought about the CIA and all the secret aspects of his work that he could never discuss with James, or anyone else come to that. They lay at the root of his involvement in the trade, and James would judge him forever on a fiction, a subterfuge. He was no saint, but it was galling that he couldn't tell the young man the truth.

"You're a reluctant entrepreneur, is that it?"

"That's nearer the truth than you might imagine. In this business I am," said Axel and hesitated, choosing his words carefully. "I'd rather be dealing in diamonds or emeralds, and hopefully I will be again soon." *The reluctance was true enough*, he thought to himself, *even if the justification that followed wasn't.* "It's complicated but I got into this to help out an old friend."

"But there are people dying out there just to bring the minerals to you. And, reluctantly or not, you sell it in Europe or wherever for, what, fifty times what you pay them? A hundred times?" asked James rhetorically. "I'm still new to all this, but even I can see that you're either part of the solution here or you're part of the problem. I've been taking photos in the camps of kids as young as one or two who have been orphaned, and all because some bastard wants to make money by controlling the area around their village. There are kids of ten or eleven seeing their parents hacked to bits in front of them, then being marched off into the hills at gunpoint so that they can be trained as child soldiers or put into the mines to work for little or nothing. I've met women who have been gang-raped, and then their daughters have been raped in front of them. And all for the money these bandits can make from tin or gold or coltan." James shook his head in despair.

"I understand you're angry at what you find your father to be." It was Axel's first use of the F-word and it silenced James for a moment. There was no self-pity or false humility, it was just a statement of fact and the older man seemed to be choosing his words with exaggerated care. "All I can tell you is that sometimes in business things are not exactly as they seem."

"Have I misjudged you then or got the situation wrong in some way? Are you quite altruistic?" James stared hard at the older man, wanting to be convinced but struggling to find the redeeming qualities that had obviously attracted Sophie.

"Altruism and business can be uncomfortable bedfellows. I admire your charity and its ambitions. From time to time I even support them, but it doesn't mean I have to be one of you; it's not a crime to make a profit you know. All companies do it if they can," Axel was growing irritated at being asked repeatedly to justify his actions.

"Jesus, I'm not some teenage anarchist; I've spent years in business myself, I'm well aware of that. I just meant that I'm having trouble squaring one particular circle," said James. "I've known very little about you until now. All I knew about my blood parents before today was what I learned from Sophie, and that was precious little. You can't tell very much from a single letter, but she seemed to me to be a thoughtful person, very caring, and in love with a young guy trying to make his way in the world. I have a picture of a principled woman and I'm struggling to see any of the same principles in you. What I find when I meet you is someone who is no longer even in the gem business, who is working in the shitty end of a perfectly legitimate business that – if I understand it right – creates products we all rely on. It makes me wonder what Sophie would have made of you now."

Axel said nothing and looked at James before turning his gaze away over the lake. There were birds circling high above them, riding the thermals coming off the land and the wind was starting to pick up. James wondered if he'd gone too far and this was where their relationship would end with Axel walking out, but he was glad he'd spoken candidly. If he was ever to understand his blood father, this might be the best chance he'd get to ask these questions.

Axel continued to stare across the water towards the Rwandan shoreline as he considered what and how much to tell James. When finally he did speak, his voice was quieter, his tone more pensive. "Who can say what she would have made of it? Who knows if we could have stayed together under any other circumstances? One thing I can say for sure is that she was one of the best people I've ever met, so to have been loved by her is something that is still important to me. If you want the God's honest truth, I'm still amazed that she saw anything in me at all. I'm not sure I saw it myself, I know my family didn't! She's also the reason that I haven't married since. It's not that there haven't been opportunities – but I guess it's true what they say, once you've tried champagne it's hard to settle for lemonade."

In other circumstances that would have been pretty cheesy, but looking at Axel he could see that he was sincere. James said nothing, not wanting to interrupt the reminiscences about his mother.

Axel was silent again for a moment, lost in his thoughts. "I only know that she shone brightly in my life for a year or so. I admired her courage, her individuality and artistic skill. She stood up for what she felt was right, she wasn't afraid to put people straight – especially me – and she loved discovering new people and places. Sophie had a real talent for getting on with people; maybe you have it, too."

"She went backpacking in Europe when she left school, then travelled across India and parts of Africa with me, which her parents didn't like. She used to battle with them to do things her way. They were very traditional and didn't believe art could be a secure future for a young woman with a good education, plus they hated my nomadic lifestyle and believed I should have a proper job, a traditional career. We tried living in a flat in London together but we both needed to be on the move doing different things. She wanted to study art in Europe, and my work in the gem trade meant being in Africa and Asia a lot. I suppose that was when the trouble started between us. Eventually I went back to Africa, she stayed on in London and that was the last I heard from her. I'm just sorry for you that you never met her, James, she was funny, strong and exciting to be with."

Axel sat up straight. "Hell, I sound like an old man, rambling on."

"It's OK; you're my only link to her and what she was like. I like hearing about her." He realised he knew little about the man's life. "Where is home for you, Axel?" It was the first time James had used his name; he had no intention of calling him dad.

"I don't have one centre. I've got a couple of places I collect junk mail, one in London and one in Rwanda, but I travel too much to call one place home. I need London but I love Kigali. I can do business through my office there, but it's just as important for entertaining industry partners at the house."

Then he became more tight-lipped again and James sensed that Axel was wary of telling him too much, perhaps he was the same with everyone. He wasn't secretive exactly, but he was still being guarded about his life. James wondered if the man would ever truly open up – he very much doubted it. The strange thing was, now that he had met Axel, James was surprised at how relaxed he felt at the prospect of never knowing much more. He didn't mind the man's enigmatic approach to life, and he could see they would never share much in the way of values. It really surprised James how different he was from his blood father, and he genuinely didn't feel the need to know everything. He had had such a strong relationship with his adoptive father there was nothing lacking in this area, no burning need to find a father figure. In sharp contrast, it had become clear to him in recent weeks how much more he needed to know about his birth mother, Sophie – perhaps this was a result of the unsatisfactory relations he still had with his mother. This conversation, although awkward at times, had already doubled his knowledge of the woman who had brought him into the world.

James looked around and savoured the view, while drinking one of the beers that had eventually reached them. It was only now that they had spoken and James had asked what he wanted to ask that he realised he had time on his hands. In fact, he had come to another crossroads. He could head straight home, wherever that meant. Although he still had an apartment in Boston, he knew this really meant Britain. His family may be small but it was now clearer than ever how important it was to him.

He was still due to have a final debrief interview with the UN who had been reluctant to let him leave their base until more was known about the whereabouts or identities of his kidnappers. When it became clear, there weren't going to be any immediate arrests he had insisted on going. The authorities had been more concerned than he was – perhaps he was just becoming used to the goings on here.

As if reading his thoughts, Axel said, "I understand you had a rough time from your abductors. Any idea who they were?"

"No, but a little bird tells me I owe you for picking up the phone to some influential people. Nobody seems to know how much you were involved but I'm grateful for your intervention, whatever it was. If I hadn't escaped under my own steam, your involvement might have been critical, things were getting pretty hairy towards the end there."

"I've been in a similar situation myself. At times like that you need all the help you can get."

"Well, I'm glad to have the chance to thank you face-to-face. Your name seems to carry some weight round here."

"Sometimes what you say matters more than who you are," Axel replied. "I was just able to share a few home truths with some people." He didn't seem comfortable talking about his contacts and changed the subject. "So, where to now? Any plans?"

"First off I'm looking for work as a freelance photographer. If you know of anything, let me know. Apparently, I've been 'relieved of my duties' – which means 'fired' to you and me. When I made it back to AfriCan Care, they said how pleased they were that I'd escaped, but on the downside I'd cost them time and money that could have been spent supporting the people here, and worst of all I'd put their entire operation at risk in Congo and beyond. Anyway, my services were no longer required. I can't blame them; I wasn't cut out for this line of work. You'd think that as a former PR exec I'd be more used to keeping sensitive secrets but it seems I'm crap at that side of it. There was no possible benefit to the charity in what I did, I was just being nosey – maybe I should be a journalist? If it had become widely known that I was taking politically sensitive photos, they might have had to pack up and leave their work here forever.

"So, to answer your question, no, nothing concrete; I've got no work, a ticket to London and no money coming in, so the clock is ticking. And you know what, for the first time in weeks that feels bloody good."

James sat back, wondering if he should be pumping his blood father for more information in case he never saw him again. Who knew when they'd next be in the same country or if they would want to meet? He had wondered for so long what it would feel like to look into the eyes of the only man to whom he was genetically connected. And the strange thing was that most of the questions had quickly been answered or had melted away. They didn't seem quite so important now. He could remember all the thoughts he had rehearsed over the years, but somehow he now had all the information he needed.

There was no compulsion on either side to be best friends. He would take Axel's contact details if he was prepared to share them and James would meet him again if the opportunity arose, but the relationships that mattered to him were already banked. His father, Neil, Lisa; these were his life's reference points.

It was time to find somewhere new to stay and to resolve one more thing, for good or bad.

Chapter 23
Goma, North Kivu, DRC
Three Days Ago

News of the explosions in Goma did not take long to reach the camp. For months the city had appeared relatively peaceful compared to the fighting that forced the Rwandan-backed rebels to pull out. People had been saying for a long time that the war was over in the cities, even if not in the mountains. Here was proof to the contrary, the conflict was now reaching deep into Goma itself and several shoppers had been killed in one of the markets. Foreign nationals were being advised against all travel to the area and NGOs were once again looking for protection in locked and razor-wired compounds.

Raphael had learned enough French at Taweza Road to hear all about this at the UN camp, but still his mind was made up. He was achieving nothing and had not found his family by going through the normal channels. Even if these people had tried their best they hadn't come up with anything at all, he was still hungry and despite the UN soldiers patrolling the area he didn't feel safe in the camp. The way he viewed it he now had a choice to make; he could go back to Taweza and live with the humiliation and frustration of knowing he had failed. In any case, he knew he could only stay there for a few more months until he was sixteen, then he would have to leave Keisha all over again. Or he could go back to the city and continue his search there, to see if Mama had found a job or a shelter somewhere. He still refused to accept any darker scenario. He couldn't stay here, he was sure of that much, and whatever choice he made his route would take him to Goma so that, Raphael decided, was where he would head.

With a meal inside him and his belongings wrapped once more in his dirty blanket Raphael began the walk back to the city. He had been walking for miles and was approaching the outskirts when a boy offered him a lift on the back of his chikudu. There was easily enough room for two to perch on the platform of the tough, handmade wooden scooter. Raphael perched behind, holding on to the shoulder of the boy's jacket with one hand as he clung to his own bundle with the other and the wooden wheels squeaked loudly in protest at the extra weight. With much of the route flat or downhill, they sped along the edge of the road until their routes split and Raphael jumped off.

He recognised the area in which he'd been eating and drinking with Snake and Joe, he even recognised the old club where they had stayed, but his pride wouldn't let him go in. He didn't want them to see that he had failed. Raphael had no energy to make any more decisions and listlessly sat down in the shade of an old advertising board.

He was still sitting there when Joe appeared beside him two hours later. "Here, have this," he said, and passed Raphael a bottle. It was sickly sweet, but it was liquid and gradually a sense of the here and now came back to him, although he didn't feel like doing or saying much.

"What happened?" asked Joe.

"At the camp? Nothing."

"You didn't find no one?"

Raphael said nothing and stared into the distance.

There was a long silence between them. Joe stirred the dirt in front of him with a stick. "You going back home?"

"Don't have one." Neither of them spoke for a while, Raphael had no plans and Joe wasn't sure what to say.

"You wanna kip here, then?"

Raphael shrugged but said nothing.

"Snake won't mind. He's always saying he needs more people. He'll tell you."

******

With the fighting intensifying close to Goma and occasional bursts of shelling close to the border it was no surprise when the Rwandan military began to close the border crossings between Goma and Gisenyi at six o'clock each evening. They re-opened the Grande and Petite Barrières crossings between the neighbouring cities at six each morning.

It was an inconvenience that Major Louis Businga could have done without, adding as it did to the pressure on the border guards. They were now pumped up, nervous and alert with the ever-present threat of shelling from an unknown position in Congo. Most people assumed the FDLR rebels were behind the gunfire, but for the Rwandans this was a hidden enemy skulking in the plains west of Goma and retreating into the mountains whenever they were confronted by the Congolese Army. Rwandan frustration levels were running high.

Restricting the usual amount of traffic to a twelve-hour crossing period meant that queues developed quickly at the border in the mornings and tempers flared. Businga hoped that this would eventually make the guards eager to pass people through more quickly – so far it hadn't worked out like that. He sat brooding and watching from a distance in his blacked-out Mercedes SUV. The engine was running and the aircon was on, but somehow he was still sweating – after recent setbacks he needed this to work. His partners across the border were starting to question his credentials and that was something he wouldn't tolerate.

Louis Businga had never been very good at taking orders, which wasn't a good trait for a Major in the Federal Army or any other. The surprise was not that he had persisted as long as he had in the forces, but that the army had persisted with him. Perhaps it was because he was stationed with the 101st sector in Nyabibwe, an outpost so remote that he sometimes wondered if his superiors knew it existed. Then again, when your father is one of the richest men in the country and an influential, unelected member of the government, the normal rules of command don't apply.

Of course, all that came to an end with the death of his adjutant. The man had fundamentally misunderstood his role as a military administrator, and shown Louis the utmost disloyalty by reporting some discrepancies with the unit accounts to the higher ups. What was Louis supposed to do? Let some jumped up clerk throw him to the wolves over a bit of confiscated gold? Of course not, you had to teach these people a lesson, one that others would see and fear. Otherwise, they'd soon have the upper hand and officers would lose the men's respect. He knew he had been right to sort him out, it was just unfortunate that news of it had reached the wrong ears. Never mind, it was all in the past and he didn't have to take Army orders any more.

The posting had had its compensations though. He had had a steady supply of coke, scotch and cannabis to numb the days and any woman there that he wanted to keep out the night time chill. Above all, he had enjoyed total control of the area's tin mines. The locals did not have much in the way of food, but they had cassiterite to spare, and Businga had helped them share the supplies around. Global demand was still growing and there was an easy route to market through Rwanda so it was only sensible to help himself while he could. Who knew how long the posting would last? Then there had been this trouble with the missing adjutant and he had been forced to leave the army, but he still had all the contacts he needed in the area and there were plenty of people there who owed him favours so after a few months it was back to business as usual.

The amounts he had been able to smuggle out of the country had been small at first. Businga had begun with a few trial exports of cassiterite using a repainted Army jeep but he was now ready to do this on a more industrial scale. More accurately, he was not only ready, he desperately needed the cash. He didn't know quite where it all went, but as fast as the money came to him it was spent again. He had expenses to pay: cars, a big house, his security team – without these who would take him seriously in business around here? He had also had an expensive break in the States recently; he loved Miami and the Miami girls loved him but nothing in life was free so he needed to pull in a serious stash of dollars soon. This job would keep him liquid for a while but he would have to come up with something else in the long-term. It seemed he could expect nothing from his father these days. The old man was richer than God and almost as old, he showed a divine ability to stay alive, stubbornly refusing to have the decency to die and leave his vast wealth to Louis, his eldest son. Louis knew that he would be able to spend it much more wisely than the old man – for him it was all pianos and fine wines. The old man was turning into a loser.

Meanwhile, Louis had no choice. He had debts to pay and he had to make this scheme work, the alternative was facing his father for a loan which was certain to be refused, or facing his creditors empty-handed. He didn't even want to think about that.

The first part had gone well early this morning. The jeeps came roaring south out of the darkness, moving in a three-car convoy as fast as they could manage along the last section of the N2 into Goma. They bore FARDC camouflage with more Army markings and were driven by dusty looking soldiers, Businga's most reliable men. At this hour the UN were still safely tucked up in their barracks and there was no one to observe the unusual route taken by the military convoy. Instead of turning left onto the airport road for the barracks, the convoy hung a right and continued south into the commercial district. As dawn broke, the vehicles swept into the open gates of a private compound and parked out of site in a warehouse. The gates were swiftly closed and if passers-by noticed anything untoward they were sensible enough to keep it to themselves.

Businga was waiting to inspect the jeeps and their load. At the government-controlled mines these days' bags of cassiterite and coltan were more often being tagged, to ensure that conflict minerals did not enter the legitimate supply chain. Businga's answer to that was to siphon off as much of the mine's output as he could before it was tagged then transport it twice a month in vehicles that his men commandeered. They had to carry it openly in the jeeps, and if they were stopped by another unit it would be a major problem for them unless they could bribe their way out. This was why they only did it twice a month and at night. In the last month alone they had managed to take out two tonnes of tin ore and deliver it to the buyer in Rwanda. Conservatively, this would be worth forty thousand dollars on the open market, maybe twenty thousand dollars to him, for one month's supply with very little personal risk. He smiled at the thought then quickly composed his expression again.

Businga gave the minerals a cursory inspection, it all looked the same to him but demand for it was high and getting higher. He then sent his boys off with a couple of crates of cold beer, and told them he would pay them later. He had been up all night, excited and nervous but the job was half way through now and the ex-Major needed some sleep. They would all re-assemble here in the early afternoon.

"Aren't you going to tell me what happened?" said Jessica later.

James had been surprised by her interest in his personal life, and was trying to decipher what this meant. He had hoped briefly that she wanted to know more about him, but the more he thought about it the more sure he was that she was following a nose for a human interest story. He didn't want to be the subject of her next article, but lunch with Jessica was an opportunity he was not going to pass up.

She had made him promise to meet her later and when a colleague mentioned a cheap Italian restaurant popular with off-duty aid workers it seemed the best answer, he was certainly no longer welcome at the charity's headquarters. Renewed shelling and the deteriorating security position across Goma meant that Sarah was now urgently looking to find space for AfriCan Care in one of the larger agencies' secure compounds. James wondered if she was shutting the stable door after the horse had bolted but it was no longer directly his concern.

He was offered a chaste peck on the cheek when she arrived late, with breezy apologies for keeping him waiting. A floral scent that he hadn't noticed on her before was enough to make his mind wander, but she was business-like and preoccupied with the staff who made a fuss of finding her a cleaner glass and offering to protect her bag. Jessica wouldn't let it out of her sight, and James half expected a tape recorder to be put on the table.

"So, go on. Tell me, did you meet your blood father?"

"Sure. Do you want some wine? This red is surprisingly good."

"If you don't start telling me every last detail in the next five seconds, you'll be eating with two broken hands. Now shoot, fella."

"Okay. We met this morning at a hotel and I told him about the letter from Sophie, my birth mother. Can't quite get used to saying that yet." He caught a stern look starting to cross Jessica's face as he deviated from the subject. "He was there with his minder, which seemed strange."

"Minder?"

"His muscle, I guess you'd say. Anyway, he listened to the story of how I found out about Sophie, he confirmed that it was her handwriting and filled in a bit of background about her. But he didn't seem very keen to accept that I might be his son."

"Maybe that's not such a surprise," said Jessica. She saw James looking at her in puzzlement. "I don't mean anything against you, but it's a lot for anyone to take in – having a man claiming to be your son appear out of the blue like this. Did he give any reason for doubting you?"

"No, just that the letter proved only that she was my mother, not that he was my father."

"He's pretty direct then."

"Hmm, I guess you've gotta see it from his point of view. He knew Sophie but he doesn't know if I'm honest or some kind of chancer, you know, hustling him. And as you say it's a lot to take in all at once," James conceded.

"You're more generous than I would have been."

"Don't get me wrong, I didn't leave it at that. I pointed out that if she was everything he said she was – and he had been full of praise for her, said she was honest, caring, and fun to be with – then maybe he ought to trust Sophie when she said something that was this important to her. I reckon that made him think how she had always been absolutely straight with him. As soon as he accepted the letter and the hoops, I'd had to jump through to get it, he began to realise that Sophie was being just as honest with him all this time later as she had been when they were together. Once he accepted that he started to accept that I must be his son, after all. I think he just needed to see me and the letter in order to make the connections."

James was finding that describing the conversation made him sad again, sad that he had never known Sophie. She sounded fun, but no pushover where Axel was concerned. He said nothing and looked down, his good hand toying with his glass. His thoughts were roaming across a scene that had passed twenty-five years ago and for a second he forgot where he was. He was brought back to the present when he felt a cool hand being placed over his. He looked up and saw a worried frown on Jessica's face. Then suddenly she seemed uncertain of what she had done and withdrew her hand before he could stop her. "How the hell do you get a glass of wine around here?" she asked a little too loudly.

"I'm sorry, let me get the waiter."

"What is it with you English, always apologising for other people? Here," she raised a hand as a waiter came into view, and ordered them both a glass of wine. "How would you describe his character?"

"Direct like you said, business-like, intelligent, he was more charismatic than I expected, and he's obviously been in some scrapes, adventures – and I guess that's still going on otherwise he wouldn't need the bodyguard. He's certainly not pompous, he's got a very dry British sense of humour. That was another strange thing, he was brought up in Holland by Anglo-Dutch parents and yet he got a scholarship to a private school in Britain. He wasn't close to his folks and I don't know how much he enjoyed school; I think he couldn't wait to get out into the big bad world, but it sounds as though he's done OK for himself with a house in Rwanda and an apartment in London. Hey, you must be hungry. Let's get some food."

******

359

The truck was almost ready when Louis Businga returned to the warehouse in the early afternoon. Sparks were flying as a welder concealed the last of the tin ore in the vehicle. When that was finished, the final job would be to make the vehicle look old and dirty again before the run across the border.

Until now they had only used jeeps for the transfer which restricted them to less than four hundred kilos but the truck's capacity was five times larger. Businga clapped the nearest man on the back when he saw the progress, this was looking more promising. The man grinned at this unexpected approval from the boss and was told, "Be ready to go at three o'clock, I don't want the truck still waiting in line when the border closes."

The man nodded his understanding. They had been through the plan five times already, everyone knew the drill, but he wasn't going to say so. At quarter to three Businga could wait no longer, he ordered the roller door to be raised and the truck carrying a shipping container moved slowly out of the warehouse, the gates swung open and it turned onto the street to begin the short journey to the crossing. It was now liberally covered in newly-applied dust and dirt, and below the empty container the flatbed showed no signs of having recently come out of a workshop.

The driver gunned the engine, crunched into first gear and the truck trundled slowly up the road, the brick red container clearly visible above the surrounding traffic and looking every bit as beaten and misused as any others on this road. The container, truck and driver had been chosen for their anonymity. All was prepared.

Instead of getting into the back as usual, Businga climbed into his Mercedes' passenger seat and reminded his driver for the third time to keep his distance behind the truck. They were there only to observe remotely, not to become involved in any way. The less he had to do with the haulage at this stage the happier he would be, but Businga was a micromanager, trusting no one, and he needed to see that the job was done well. A lot of money and prestige were riding on this.

Ten minutes later his car was at the back of the unusually long queue at Petite Barrière. Businga was not making the crossing himself until tomorrow but he wanted to watch discretely as his delivery was made so he ordered the SUV driver to turn right and go around the block before coming back to a quiet parking position they had already identified within sight of the border. There they pulled over and settled down in the shade to wait. Barely fifteen metres away the border ran parallel with the road Businga was on. His vantage point under a roadside tree would be unremarkable to a casual observer, and from this position one block south of the crossing point they could see all vehicles approaching the border area. Businga could clearly see across open scrubland as the vehicles crossed the Rwandan border and approached the smart new customs buildings.

The traffic was backed up for over a kilometre into Congo, all the way from the Rwandan Customs & Immigration Centre. Car drivers had no intention of wasting their fuel, so whenever the queue made its way forward a few metres whole families would get out and push their vehicle forward until the queue came to a stop again. There was a comical inevitability about the low speed shunts that kept occurring when the driver was too slow to jump back in and apply the brakes, and once they witnessed tempers flaring in the hot sun as two vehicles collided at no more than walking pace.

The two men in the back put their handguns on the seat between them, rather than sit with them uncomfortably pushed into their waistbands, making the car look even more like a rolling arsenal than usual. Businga liked to keep automatic weapons in the back and from time to time was known to carry rocket-propelled grenades – they had become his trademark during counter-insurgency operations, earning him the nickname among his men of Major Boom-boom. He knew their name for him and did nothing to discourage it.

Time ticked by and Businga sat silently watching the slow progress of the queue, occasionally glancing at his gold Rolex or picking up a pair of excellent binoculars that he had liberated years ago from the Army quartermaster's stores. From time to time he would mutter an imprecation to the gods of immigration to be about their work, but it had no effect. By five o'clock the truck was nearing the border but it was going to be a close-run thing, Businga couldn't be certain whether his Trojan horse would make it through before the gate was finally closed for the night. He had a few of his own men in the border force on both sides of the line but there could be a snap inspection at any time, it was just one of the risks. He continually drummed his fingers on the centre armrest – it was irritating to the SUV's three other occupants but it would have been madness to say so.

******

"Does Axel look like you?" You had to hand it to Jessica; she was a journalist to the core and wouldn't let the subject go. James had tried several times to talk about her, but she seemed reticent about her own background and eager to hear more of his story.

"I'm a little taller and darker, but I guess there are similarities. He's doing OK for his age; he looked fit and still had most of his hair, so I guess there's hope for me in the future."

She smiled. "And do you think you're like him in any other ways?"

"Jeez, I hope not. I brought the conversation round to his work and I asked him why he works in an area of his industry that harms so many people?" James toyed with the cutlery, "He was a bit enigmatic. First of all he said that things are not always as they seem. I have no idea what that meant. I didn't have a chance to find out – then he said it was a dirty business but he couldn't change it on his own."

361

"Oh, I see, so he'll carry on without trying then, just making money from it," said Jessica. She shook her head in disgust.

"That's pretty much what I said to him, but he simply blamed the politicians. Then he said something like, 'you're wondering how a man like me with no moral compass could have got together with such a principled woman?' I wasn't wondering that at the time, but it seemed a fair question."

"What was the answer?" Jessica asked.

"It was quite surprising. He said that he'd loved her more than any woman before or since, but that he could never match her. I thought that was a get-out, an excuse for admiring her without trying to emulate her, and I told him so. I told you I don't want to be like him, Jessica."

"You aren't," she said. "How did he react?"

James shrugged. "I think he'd been expecting me to say something like that. How's your pasta?"

"Lovely, thank you, and quit changing the subject will you?" It pleased James that she had now relaxed enough to banter with him. He didn't know when he'd have the chance again so he studied her face intently. Her brown eyes were sparkling, the cut on her lip had healed well already and though it still showed it was no longer the first thing you noticed about her. He wondered what the first things were that he noticed about Jessica now. Probably her cheekbones, almost impossibly high, they were flattered by long lashes. Was her nose too big? Maybe to some, but to him it looked strong. He was looking for imperfections; she had a high forehead that just demonstrated the quality of her skin. He gave up and just allowed himself to wonder how on earth she was here with him, while he tried to not to show his true feelings. He could hear his brother Neil warning him to stay cool; women, he said, don't like being fawned over. Why the hell was he thinking of Neil when he was on a date with Jessica? Was this even a date? He'd like to call it that but he was equally sure she wouldn't.

"… do you know?" Jessica asked.

Christ, I've done it again, daydreaming when I should be listening. "I beg your pardon."

She grinned. "Sometimes you're so English. It's cute."

Cute is good, isn't it? he thought. As long as it's not cute as in 'let's be friends'. You had to avoid that at all costs, that was a slippery slope and he was sure that was where he'd been headed.

"I said, do you know if he's got any other children? Do you have any half-brothers or sisters?" She looked at him quizzically.

"Do you know, I forgot to ask! Somehow, with everything else to discuss it never came up."

"How could you not ask that? Jeez, men! You are impossible," she said in exasperation. "That would have been one of my first questions."

"I guess I was trying to establish that I was his son, anyone else on the family tree seemed a subject for another day."

"So there will be another day, you are going to keep in touch?" Jessica was intrigued.

"We've exchanged emails and numbers. I don't know if we'll ever meet up again, but he's in London from time to time so it could happen. Now, I've done all the talking. I want to know about you. Where is home and what brought you here?"

So Jessica told him. And finding he was a good listener she shared more about herself than she had expected with a relative stranger. He asked questions, but he didn't talk over her. He even remembered things that she had said or done. It was not what she had expected from the meal. Except that he didn't seem such a stranger now, she felt she knew more about his background than most people would, and unlike other men she had known he hadn't tried to be all deep and mysterious. You could see it in his green eyes; he was open and honest – just like his mother from all accounts.

She described her family's middle-class existence in Syracuse, New York. How her father and mother had divorced, how Jessica had blamed her father for not giving her mother or herself enough time. How he had taken little interest in her activities as she grew up and belittled her ambitions as a journalist because he had wanted her to go into law. A life in the legal profession would have crushed her, she knew that instinctively, but he couldn't see it and was more interested in her social status and how much she'd earn. Her father had been scathing of efforts to get into TV reporting and had felt entirely vindicated when she was rejected by the networks.

It seemed to James that maybe Jessica had found few occasions to trust the male of the species. Her father was disappointed in her and she conceded that her relationships seldom lasted – James took that to mean never. At which point it finally became clearer to him why the openness of their conversation over lunch had piqued her interest. It wasn't that she wanted to turn him into a documentary, as he had feared.

He started to wonder how often Jessica was with a man who wasn't trying to impress her, who didn't claim to know it all, who was reluctant to be the centre of attention yet prepared to share a life-changing moment. She was talking as an equal and there was no one like her father here to put her down. He didn't want to shower her with the usual vacuous and transparent praises, he just enjoyed being open with her and hoped it would make her more candid about herself.

"Something tells me they want to go home," said James. "I'll pay the bill."

Jessica looked around the room. They were the only customers left and the only people still at the counter were two taxi drivers from the cab company next door. Every tabletop had been cleared and it seemed that neither James nor Jessica had noticed.

363

"I don't know about you but I need a coffee and I know just the view to enjoy it with." He waited expecting her to cry off and tell him that she had an appointment somewhere else.

"Oh, and where's that?"

"A hotel across town with a terrace overlooking the lake, they serve barista coffee, cold beers, there's a pool and the best view of the mountains in the city. I hear they even play R&B in the bar," he sounded nonchalant but he hoped that he hadn't oversold the idea to her.

"Very tempting," she said, "but I have an article to write, and an editor to keep happy. I'm definitely not sober and I need a shower just to wake up."

His heart sank. He knew it had all been too good to last. "Come and have a swim, you can sober up that way. It looked so nice after the charity's base, I'm checking in there." He paused. "I'm sorry, that came out all wrong."

"It's OK. I know what you meant, but truly I am going to have to take a rain check." They stood up and he signalled to one of the cab drivers. "Please take this lady wherever she wants to go," and the driver beamed as James gave him a handful of dollar bills.

"You don't have to do that," she said.

"If I remember rightly, I still owe you for a laptop, so I think I'm getting off lightly. All the same," he said grinning at her, "It might be safest for you if we said goodbye here."

She smiled then reached up to kiss him lightly on the lips. They were both wondering what was meant by goodbye.

******

At half past five Businga couldn't take the tension any longer and climbed out of the SUV to take a leak against the wall of a house. As he relieved himself, a phone in the car began to ring. The other occupants looked at one another uncertainly until he bellowed at them to answer it. The driver picked it up and pressed to accept the call only for it to ring off just as he did so. "It didn't say who was calling boss, an unknown number, they just rang off," he explained as Businga got back into the car.

"That's because you were too bleeding slow, as always. Why am I surrounded by idiots?"

The driver knew he would have been in trouble for answering or for not answering – he was used to it now, it went with the territory when working with someone like this. Not that he'd ever come across anyone quite as mercurial or violent as 'Major Businga'.

His boss looked at the call register and was just about to call out when the phone rang again making every one of them jump. "Look at you all," said Businga, "you're like a bunch of frightened schoolgirls," and he laughed at his own wit. He evidently did not recognise the number. "Yes," he barked at the caller and listened for a moment before interrupting.

"What the fuck are you doing calling me, you asshole? I told you, you only call the warehouse? They can let me know if something's urgent. I don't care if you are worried, just sit tight and keep moving forward. Of course it's going to close at six – we all know that." The caller tried again to explain his concerns. "Well, if you don't get through," said Businga, "then you go back to the warehouse like I told you – we've been through all this a hundred times. Don't call me again or I will personally tear your frigging head off and send it home to Mama. Got that?" He hung up angrily. "Jerk off!" he added for good measure.

Then there was no need for further calls. They could see the truck emerging into view ahead of them; it looked like it might get through tonight after all. A few minutes later it was pulled out of the queue and waved into the Rwandan Customs' inspection area. The tension in the Mercedes went up another notch. "Why the fuck have they done that?" breathed Businga. He and his men were all leaning forward staring intently at the scene unfolding before them only a hundred metres away in another country.

"It's well hidden, boss," the driver ventured.

Businga looked at him with contempt, and as he did so, he looked past him and caught sight in the wing mirror of a blue helmeted soldier crouching and scurrying towards the back of the Mercedes. "Look out," yelled Businga and reached for the handgun he had left on the centre console. It was a foolish move, they were already surrounded and although his accomplices began to raise their hands he attempted to bring the gun to bear on the soldier nearest to him. Businga was facing the wrong way and the gun was on safety as he swung his body towards the two blue helmets on his side of the car.

They had clear rules of engagement and the nearest two did not hesitate; they opened fire from less than five paces away taking off Louis Businga's right arm below the elbow. The second shot passed over what remained of his arm and blew the contents of the driver's head all over the windscreen and the shattering side window. Two more automatic rounds went harmlessly through both of the front doors and the next tore a new opening in Major Businga's major intestine. By now there was an arc of Indian soldiers on two sides of the vehicle giving them clear fields of fire. It was testament to their discipline that only those who had been directly threatened by Businga ever opened fire, the others later cursed their luck that they hadn't been a few paces closer when he raised his gun so that they could have taken part.

The booming voice of a blue turbaned Sikh sergeant shouted at the car's occupants in English. "Hands up, now! Keep your hands high where we can see them." Even if they didn't speak the language the meaning was clear enough. Then came a bellowed order, "Cease firing!" The platoon had been instructed to bring in as many alive as possible in the hope that they could learn more about the network on both sides of the border and make examples of these ones.

Then someone was shouting, "Medic! Medic!" and the soldiers were pulling open the doors. One of Businga's guards in the back seat was shaking violently in shock, and the other one just stared slack-jawed at the soldiers while keeping his hands high and visible. A spreading stain announced that he was still in the process of wetting himself.

In the front, Louis Businga's breathing was already shallow and he was dipping into unconsciousness as the medics reached him, and from the level of blood loss and trauma they were already wondering if they could save him.

Chapter 24
Goma, North Kivu, DRC
Three Days Ago

James didn't feel like eating, he didn't feel like doing much at all. After a great lunch – no, a wonderful lunch – that owed more to the company than the food he was feeling deflated. He'd had her there, and then he'd let her go. Idiot, he told himself, bloody idiot. How could he have managed to bring the most amazing woman he'd met in years to a wonderful meal in an Italian restaurant and still not told her what he felt about her?

Jessica was the first woman in a long time who made him feel this alive, who intrigued him, stood up to him, listened to him and laughed at the same things. The first woman who could do that since Lisa – and now he realised how long it was since he had thought about Lisa. He felt he could talk to Jessica all day, and looking at her was no hardship either. Inwardly he cursed himself again; would he ever learn how to seize the moment? Surely he could have steered the conversation in a more romantic direction? Yet somehow it had never seemed the right moment and he hadn't wanted to lose the easy-going atmosphere by forcing things. In real life though, sometimes you had to make your own luck, seize the moment or risk being pigeonholed as just a friend.

He sat at the hotel's poolside bar, nursing a glass of wine and a brooding sense of his own romantic shortcomings. As the sun went down, its parting gift was the warm pink glow it threw over the mountain tops far across the lake, but the dying light matched his mood. There was a gentle breeze stirring the warm evening air, occasionally fluttering the fringes of the beach umbrellas. He could hear but could not see the palm tree fronds moving above him in the darkness. Apart from the barman he had the place to himself. Everything was almost right and yet it was all utterly wrong. He caught sight of his reflection in one of the hotel windows and felt ashamed at the stoop of his shoulders; why feel sorry for himself he thought. So he took out his phone and tried to remedy the situation.

******

It was weeks since Jessica had received a text, and she was momentarily startled when the phone buzzed on the desk beside her. She picked it up; the text icon showed one message waiting and she opened the message from James Falkus:

Lunch was not enough. Have dinner with me tonight. Got the best view, wine, music, table. Just missing you. Taxi coming in 30 mins. J x

******

Payne Rawlings was surprisingly talkative today. Perhaps the CIA man was enjoying the time away from his colleagues at the National Security Agency and the State Department. "We calculate that most of the illegally-mined coltan from North and South Kivu is being smuggled out of eastern DRC through regulated border crossings. And we suspect some of it's being shipped via Idjwi Island in the middle of Lake Kivu."

Axel was about to inform him of their own shipments through Idjwi, but Rawlings was in full flow and it would wait. Axel was suddenly aware of how long it was since he'd given Rawlings a proper briefing.

"Then it just gets tagged as Rwandan output and put into the market before coming out 'green and clean' in Europe and Asia," the CIA man added superfluously – none of this was news to Axel. "It's a long border, there are plenty of busy crossings and the Congolese don't have the resources to scrutinise them all even if they wanted to."

One thing puzzled Axel though. "If you're so worried where it's ending up, why don't you just cut off the supply at source. If you helped the Congolese government clamp down on the Army officers getting rich here, then they might begin to control this mess." Axel was tiring of the US government's politically-motivated posturing on conflict minerals. Publicly they called for the trade to be curbed or controlled; privately they must know enough to put a serious dent in the trade in tin, coltan, and gold out of Congo, yet they did nothing.

Rawlings stared at Axel for a moment, unhappy to be quizzed by a field agent. "If it were just a few low-level bums that woulda happened way back. Nah, these people are well protected politically. You know what it's like in Kinshasa. Even when the authorities do catch a smuggler he'll do bird for a coupla years and pay the fine before he'll reveal what he knows. Everyone knows what happens to a grass. We can tell them till we're blue in the face to clear out the senior officers but it's up to the Congolese – unless the smugglers or their bosses stray into U.S. jurisdiction, of course, and they're careful not to do that. You never know, one day they may slip up," said the CIA man. This was more than Axel had heard the man say in their entire meeting in Kinshasa.

The call for a briefing had come while Axel was busy preparing to head back to Europe and it had not improved his mood. He was under new pressure from his clients, CCV, following Louis Businga's arrest. No one seemed to know if he was dead or alive, but from all the rumours circulating in Goma it seemed he had taken a bullet or two. Either way, Businga Junior was now in UN custody and would be out of circulation for the foreseeable future. Even if he lived, Businga would be charged with abduction, conspiracy to defraud, and possession of illegal weapons, just for starters. He also seemed to be beyond the reach of his father's protection this time, so a quick release and comfortable exile was looking unlikely. CCV were getting extremely nervous about the implications for their coltan supplies flowing from Rwanda to Macao. Axel was going to have to meet and reassure them or they'd shop around for a new supplier and the Agency would lose its finger on their pulse.

For the hundredth time he wished he could ditch this bloody business and go back to the more straightforward world of the gem trade. You could keep your dirty bloody coltan, give him an emerald or a diamond any day. Rawlings seemed to carry some authority at Langley, so maybe it would be worth discussing an exit strategy with him before this meeting was through.

"The smuggling control measures have had some effect but Kinshasa's production figures show a huge discrepancy between what is officially produced and what is actually exported," said Rawlings. "We know that twenty tonnes of coltan were produced at five mines recently, but in the same period the government banned all exports. So where are those twenty tonnes? They aren't piled up in the negociants' offices in Goma, so the coltan has probably been smuggled out of the country. It's inevitable, for sure, coltan in Rwanda is almost double the Goma price."

Axel had viewed Rawlings as a man of action, but this discussion wasn't going anywhere. He interrupted so that he could drag the conversation back to the current situation. "Anyway, what was it you wanted to see me about? Because I've got a plane to catch and frankly I can't leave too soon – it's been a particularly shitty week."

Rawlings sipped his cold drink and studied his man. He was in no mood to be hurried. "Sounds like you need to remember the bigger picture, and it hasn't been all bad. You'll know by now they caught Major Businga and a big tin shipment he was trying to smuggle out."

Axel still hadn't told Rawlings that Louis Businga was the local coltan contact. He'd allowed them to believe that SK Zaidi was the one pulling the deal together from suppliers all over North and South Kivu. That was only partly true, Zaidi reported to the Busingas. This should have been the moment to mention it but a stubborn streak in Axel meant he still said nothing. He had the Americans on one side squeezing him for information, and CCV on the other pressuring him to deliver more and more coltan for a client or clients they wouldn't identify and a use they wouldn't disclose. There was no particular reason why he hadn't told

Langley everything; he was just fed up with everyone jerking him around. He had been forced to surrender control of every aspect of his life, so keeping an occasional silence or playing each card he held slowly and offering information only when it was necessary was his way of keeping some small degree of control. It was also exactly how the Agency had been treating him from the start. Deep down he knew this attitude was probably futile, it was certainly a dangerous gambit, but he was damned if these bastards were going to trample all over his life and dictate everything he did. He'd had enough of that in jail in Zambia to last a lifetime – he'd learned in prison to use information as another valuable commodity and occasionally a weapon. Axel put it down to the independent-minded Boer genes in his make-up – he didn't take it well when others intruded. "Yeah, I heard something about Businga," was all he said.

"Sure you did. I don't suppose it pleased his dad any, which is fine by us. He was a dickhead, a dangerous one, but a dickhead all the same and it seems he made a rookie error. He and his people sent an empty container through on a truck and Customs were left wondering why the tyres were bulging and it was down on its shocks. Didn't take them long to find the tin, of course. Louis never did have his father's brains. There's one unanswered question in it for us; word in Kinshasa is that General Businga wants to talk to the guy who told the blue helmets his son would be supervising the shipment personally. In fact, he wants to talk to him so bad he has a bounty on them being delivered alive to him … five thousand bucks. That kind of cash would go a long way here. You wouldn't know anything about that, would you?"

Axel shrugged and just shook his head. He appeared disinterested. "I kind of assumed he'd been shopped by a partner, either here in DRC or Rwanda. What about his father? Is he in trouble over his son's deals?"

"Are you kidding? He's spotless. It all came as news to him apparently, and he's every bit as shocked as the rest of us. I don't think anyone involved will say otherwise, do you? If junior survives the shooting, the UN may even get him Al Capone-style, y'know charge him with tax evasion. That is, if the Congolese government stays pissed at him long enough. The Rwandans can check how many of Louis Businga's trucks passed through its border posts in recent years. It's sure to be hundreds. Fortunately, Rwandan record-keeping is better than Congolese. There's even talk of re-opening the unsolved case of a missing adjutant. If he lives, young Mister Businga will be going down for a long time."

Then Rawlings voice dropped and he fixed his eyes on Axel as he continued. "Of course, whoever it was that yapped about Businga also endangered our entire surveillance ops here. If we don't have a supply route through Goma, we can monitor then we don't hear the buyer's intentions, and that would be … disappointing. Isn't that your British understatement?"

"I'm Dutch," said Axel.

"When it suits you," said Rawlings. He studied Axel Terberg from behind his shaded glasses, but the reluctant agent showed no nervousness or hesitation. "Was Louis Businga one of your suppliers for CCV?"

It was a direct question now, and Axel knew he should have told Rawlings about Louis' involvement long ago if he was going to. It was too late to mention it now so he'd have to play dumb. "I deal with SK Zaidi, like I told you. If Businga is – or was – somewhere in the coltan delivery chain, then he's been keeping well out of sight. But I thought you said he was smuggling tin."

As far as this went, he'd given the truth, but it was far from the whole truth. He also hoped to deflect Rawlings from discussing Businga with him any further.

"You know as well as I do that the people selling conflict minerals aren't too picky what the minerals are, so long as there's a ready market for 'em," Rawlings replied. Axel didn't like the way Rawlings was studying him, maybe he suspected he was holding out on him. It was unlikely that the Agency knew of Businga's clandestine visit to Axel's house in Rwanda and the assault on his bodyguard, unlikely but not impossible. It would also be much better for Axel if they didn't know of his intervention with Businga Senior on James's behalf, otherwise they'd want him to report on the General for them too, and that would make life even more dangerous. There was absolutely no upside in getting more involved there, and the downsides could prove enormous and painful.

For the time being Rawlings waved away whatever concerns he had about Axel.

Axel interrupted his train of thought. "Anyway, we have something else to discuss," he said. "I want to talk to you about something," said Axel. "I've delivered everything you've asked of me and I want an exit strategy. An early one."

Rawlings snorted. "This ain't a corporate merger, Terberg. We don't like people quitting the team, it makes us kinda jumpy, given what they know."

Axel was about to reply, when Rawlings held up a finger telling him to pause. "Unless ..." he said.

"Unless what?"

"Like I say, we're not interested in your retirement, but re-location – hey, that's another matter."

"Go on," said Axel.

"We have something we think you may be able to help us with. In Asia. All expenses paid, as before. And it would help you wash your hands of all this tin and coltan round here."

"Forgive me if the financial terms sound under-whelming. You'll have to do better than that. What do you have in mind specifically?"

"I don't have anything in mind at all, Axel." They were back on first name terms again. "However, my colleagues in London do."

"And if I say No? What then?"

"C'mon Axel. We've done OK together here, haven't we? And 'No' sounds pretty final," Rawlings laughed, but there was no warmth in it. "I'd hate you to regret not taking up a new opportunity. You had a helluva lot of time on your hands in Zambia to reflect on what might have been; surely you don't want to spend the rest of your life with those kinda regrets."

Axel looked at him. "You bastards, you people are fucking unbelievable. Nothing you say is real, is it? It's all just bullshit."

Rawlings didn't react. "That BS here has served you well, now hasn't it? You're way richer than when we started. You've met a son you didn't know you had – yes, we know about that. You've picked up a tan, and the ribs seem to have mended well. So, I suggest you see my colleagues in London in a couple of weeks. Take a break first, have a vacation, go lie on a beach. Just don't sign for any packages from a Dr Businga and you'll be fine."

"What happens with CCV?" Axel asked.

Rawlings was scribbling a note on a pad and didn't even look up. "Like you give a shit," he said.

"I mean, we haven't had a chance to discuss it yet, but they've called a meeting with me in Brussels next week. It's all a bit cloak and dagger, as it always is with them. All they would say was that they've had a meeting with their principal and he's got some questions for me. He'll be there in person apparently."

"We know."

"Of course, you do. And there was me thinking wiretaps were so Last Century."

"They have their place, but that can be your swansong. The Agency wants you at that meeting, to find out who this guy is and anything you can about his organisation. And we expect a full report before you leave Brussels and face-to-face in London after. You know how to reach us, and make sure you do it quick. You won't want the top floor getting jumpy again and sending people to look for you like before, or next time it may not just be a rib that smarts a bit. Got that?"

Axel nodded.

"Keep your eyes open, we've no idea how much they know about you, or us. Don't assume they're fools, they ain't. We think they wanna know if you're the real deal, and if you're really working alone. You didn't bring your work phone today, did ya?"

Axel gave him an old-fashioned look. "What do you take me for?"

Rawlings ignored the jibe. "Good. Message from NSA: they say you need to use that phone more, for social and business messages. They're worried it looks like you're keeping it as a spare, like you reckon CCV are bugging it. So have the odd scrap with people on it, call a girlfriend, surf the web, place a bet. Do whatever you might do."

"I do all that already. Jeez, I had this conversation with them. I just don't use any phone as much as their spotty nerds. If I suddenly start making loads more calls or sending more texts on it, that'll stand out even more. It's got to fit with my normal patterns of use. Why am I telling you people this? Don't they know anything?"

Rawlings grinned unexpectedly. "I expect you just told them yourself," and he looked meaningfully at his personal phone on the table.

For once Axel smiled too. He had nothing more to say on the subject. Messages received and, for his part at least, understood. He stood up and from habit checked his wallet, phone and passport were still in his jacket. It looked as though he would need them more than expected.

******

The Senate Foreign Relations Sub Committee had been in closed session for over an hour and tempers were beginning to fray. It was late in the day and earlier furtive glances at wristwatches were now frequent in some parts of the room. A few on the committee were even wondering whether they should be discussing this at all. Of course, there were liaisons present from the Senate's Africa and Global Health Sub Committee, but it was only now becoming clear why this matter had been shuffled onto their agenda. The Democratic Party's junior Senator for Delaware cast a look towards his colleague from New Mexico who raised his eyes to the heavens in search of patience.

The East Asia, The Pacific and International Cyber security Policy Committee, to give it its full title, was unusually blessed with intellect for such a subcommittee but not everyone was convinced their time was being well spent. Going into closed session might have been expected to encourage the committee and its guests to cut to the chase without fear of being quoted in the media, but little progress had been made so far.

One of the liaison officers from the Africa Sub Committee was coming to the end of a lengthy explanation about the battle between governments and warlords in Central Africa. "This has kept the fighting going on here for years, even though some of the rebels dressed it up as a liberation struggle. Which is why armed forces from Uganda, Rwanda, Zimbabwe, Burundi and others have all been pitched into the fighting in Congo at one time or another over the years. The region's politicians won't admit these were invasions, they prefer to describe them as peace missions or rescuing their nationals. It's like Canada, Russia and Mexico all invading us at the same time to get rich quick."

There was a barely-suppressed snigger of laughter from someone and the Chairman, himself tiring of the explanation, banged his gavel. "I don't feel that analogy is moving us forward."

"Mr Chairman, may I...?"

"Go ahead," said the chairman.

"I believe I may have strayed into the wrong committee room," said one of the Majority members. "The sign on the door said this was The East Asia & Pacific Committee. Could you tell me where I should be?"

"That'll do, John," said the Chairman with a sigh. "Can the State Department kindly get to the point?"

A new, younger voice spoke. "We are concerned, Mr Chairman, that Chinese influence in the region is expanding aggressively from industrial partnerships and infrastructure investment – the Chinese build more roads and bridges in the region now than all other foreign partners put together – it is expanding into areas that could critically affect the strategic and defence interests of the United States. Namely, minerals and rare metal ores that, although they can be found elsewhere, are in limited supply and may not always be available to Uncle Sam in the future, or not at the same price."

"The reason we're here, Mr Chairman, is to inform the subcommittee that we need to understand the extent of China's influence in Africa, particularly in countries rich with natural resources – not just diamonds and gold, but minerals with strategic importance for U.S. industries. We can't always predict the future political landscape but what we can say with certainty is that some mineral resources are already vital and will inevitably become rarer and more costly as global reserves dwindle. Knowing where they are now, in places like the Congo, gives us the chance to protect western interests, U.S. interests in the region."

"At last, thank you. And you are?" The chairman looked at the young man over his half-moon spectacles.

"My name is Nicolas Ortego, sir. I'm an analyst in the China Section at the State Department offices in Foggy Bottom. A junior analyst," he said looking hurriedly across at his colleagues. It was the first time he'd attended a Senate hearing *in camera*, and it was as much a surprise to Nicolas that he had spoken as it was proving to be to his colleagues.

"Huh, well at last we have some clarity from Foggy Bottom," grunted the Chairman. "We've heard a lot – too much if I'm honest – about the African perspective. Can you or someone tell me about the Chinese view?"

"Yes sir," said Ortego's boss, casting a venomous warning look at his junior. "As someone already pointed out, it is not illegal to trade these materials, but it is illegal to sell them here in the U.S. without an audit showing they *don't* come from a war zone, like the Democratic Republic of Congo. Which makes them conflict minerals. Most of the people involved in the coltan trade in Congo have committed no offence, and much of the coltan and tin ore comes from legit government-owned or controlled mines."

"What about the materials coming from these slave mines then? Who's behind them?" asked a committee member.

"We don't categorise them as slave mines, sir. It's a constantly changing picture, it's hard to know which ones are under rebel control at any given time. To answer your question, NSA believes there are tens if not hundreds of companies, from Europe, the Middle East and South Asia all taking part in the conflict minerals trade. The unrefined coltan – that's the raw mineral the tantalite comes from – passes through many people's hands on its journey from the miners to the smelters. The smelters can be in Europe, India, Thailand, China, you name it. It's impossible to track it all, because it's high value it is moved in relatively small quantities. It has no signature, no properties enabling us to identify where it comes from. And it can be mixed with minerals reclaimed from used devices – like old cell phones."

Payne Rawlings spoke up to move the discussion along. "One thing we do know, Mr Chairman, is that in recent months there's been a significant new buyer in the market. The spot market price has risen as someone has taken a chunk of the minerals from conflict zones, with no questions asked about its source."

"The question for agencies like ours has been, 'Is it organised crime behind this?' If so where from and why are they suddenly interested in this market? If not, who is doing this? If it's organised crime, I guess it'll become the FBI's concern, assuming it involves U.S. citizens or comes into the States. We still believe that the trade is likely backed by organised crime syndicates, probably in China."

"But you have spectacularly failed to come up with any evidence," said a previously silent representative of Risk Monitor Services. "Maybe, Mr Chairman, that's because there is no evidence." He looked challengingly at Rawlings.

Rawlings leaned across to his CIA neighbour, and whispered loudly, "Who in hell are Risk Monitor Services?" Everyone at that end of the table heard him and two junior observers stifled giggles at his bluntness.

Rawlings' neighbour was unwilling to be drawn into his boss's discussion but found he had little choice. "Another Washington Think Tank, mostly ex-Pentagon and State," he hissed. "Don't think they've ever stepped out of the Beltway. White House loves 'em apparently, that kinda explains their giant fees to Uncle Sam."

The chairman banged on the table and glared at Rawlings. "You want to take your discussion offline gentlemen? No? Well, shut the hell up." And he turned back to Mr Risk. "So, you say there's no evidence. Exactly what intel are we getting on this?"

There was silence around the table.

"Either I've gone deaf or you're not doing your jobs, any of you. We've got more theories on who's behind this trade than fleas on a hog, but no one's giving me firm answers. Mr Rawlings, all of a sudden you don't have so much to say. You must have assets in-country? What are they telling you?"

Rawlings coughed in surprise at being put on the spot about his sources. "Sure we got assets, sir. They're telling us the recent spike in all T3G trades is down to one South African outfit, but it seems they're a cover."

"Oh, Sweet Lord. Do you guys ever speak English? T3G?"

"Tantalum, tin, tungsten and gold. The analysts call it T3G, guess I picked up a nasty habit." His contempt for the nearby private sector analysts was clear enough.

"Cover for what?" the chairman interrupted him. "You said the South Africans were a cover."

"A cover for the Chinese."

"Are the Chinese doing anything illegal buying from the South Africans? I'm sure the West has been buying this stuff in Africa from other Africans for years, hasn't it?" said the chairman.

"Depends what they do with it, sir. If they use tantalum in tablets, radars and cell phones and sell them here then, yes, it is illegal. The Securities and Exchange Commission, the SEC ..."

"I know who the SEC are ..."

Rawlings battled on. "The SEC watches the sales into the U.S. If they sell them in China, then no, it's not illegal."

"Then can someone, for the love of Mike, tell me why we're having this conversation?"

"Because, sir. These minerals are a critical resource today, a finite critical resource that looks set to become increasingly important to America's technological lead. And if an enemy of ours, or someone who threatens one day to be an enemy, starts cornering the market in these materials it's our job, the CIA's job to notice, to investigate, to report it to you sir and if we're asked to recommend next steps."

The Republican chairman of the East Asia, The Pacific and International Cyber security Policy committee leaned back in his chair to appraise the speaker in front of him. "And what does the Agency recommend, Mr Rawlings? Apart from a budget extension." There was timid and dutiful laughter from some outside the Agency.

"If it is China, what they're doing here is still unclear, and since they have some of these natural resources of their own anyway, it is ringing alarm bells at Langley. We don't understand it, so we know we need to know more. The recommendation has to be deeper investigation, sir."

"There's no more money in this, Mr Rawlings. You got that?"

"We haven't asked for more money, sir."

"Hmm. Well, this committee's gonna need better answers next time we come to this. Way better answers. Have you got that too?"

"Sir," said Rawlings and began to sketch a map of China on his pad before animatedly scratching it out.

The air of danger and uncertainty in Goma had increased in the last few days following the sporadic shelling. It rarely seemed to affect the Federal Army but high explosive shells had killed scores of civilians and injured hundreds more. For an African war that wasn't happening it was awfully deadly.

The mood among Snake's gang was tense, and there was no sign of the warm welcome that Raphael had been led to expect. But with the promise that he was ready for hard work the outsider was accepted into their group. The nature of their work had still not been discussed but Raphael was pleased just to have a roof over his head and once again to sleep in the dry.

He had heard the occasional rumble while in the camp, but from that distance he had been unsure whether he was hearing thunder or gunfire. He had his own pressing concerns, and the noise had stayed far enough away that he didn't need to think about it.

This time Snake had two more men with him as they sat in the upstairs room where Raphael had slept before. Their banter only died down when two girls brought in a pot of food for the boys and placed it in the middle of the floor. There were enough plates for all of them and the boys helped themselves as the girls left. It was rice, fish and beans and Raphael devoured his portion.

"So, I feed you and you're working for me now," said Snake. It wasn't a question.

Showing gratitude might look weak so Raphael simply said, "OK. What's happening?"

"We'll go out later and I'll show you."

"Tonight?"

"Of course, tonight. That's when people are out, they've had a few drinks."

"Then what?"

"Then we go fishing," he laughed and the others laughed with him.

"I don't know anything about fishing," said Raphael uncertainly. There was more laughter.

"You'll catch on fast. We show them the bait, they bite, and we strike. Job done."

Raphael had some more questions but Snake seemed on edge. He had fidgeted as they ate and then stood dancing to some music that was only in his head.

There was an even greater unpredictability about Snake tonight, with none of the back-slapping bonhomie that he had received following their first encounter. Something had changed, although Raphael could not work out if it was a reaction to him or if something else was causing it. He had his answer soon enough though.

******

What had seemed like Gahiji's lucky day was rapidly turning sour. The job that the Major had sent him on meant he wasn't needed to oversee the truck's delivery to Rwanda. That had been the difference between arrests or, in Louis Businga's case, shooting and an easy afternoon collecting some debts. The first he'd heard about it was a panicked phone call from one of the guys at the warehouse telling him the Major had been shot and everyone with him had been arrested. Then he'd heard nothing more.

The surprise came early in the evening when the General himself had called. Needless to say he hadn't introduced himself, just asked Gahiji if he recognised who he was talking to. "I understand you were helping my son to hold a package, a valuable package but somehow you managed to lose it."

It was clear who he blamed for this. "That package is one of two that are of great concern to me. The one you were looking after before you mislaid it came from Britain and there is an older package from Holland that we have spoken of before. Both could help me a great deal. On the other hand they could help our enemies a great deal, and we can't afford that. *You* can't afford that," said General Businga with added emphasis. "Do I make myself clear?"

"Yes," said Gahiji.

"Find both these items," said the General before they walk out of the country, and let me know when you have them. Do not destroy them, keep them safe. If either package has left the country, then you will have to follow them and our people here will make the necessary arrangements for you from Kinshasa. Do not fail. Call me on this number when it's all in hand. Now repeat my instructions, I want to be sure you know what to do."

"Yes, sir." And Gahiji retold General Businga's instructions to him.

"Good." The line went dead.

You didn't argue with this guy, but how the hell was he supposed to find two foreign spies in a city of over half a million? He could get people to try the hotels but it would take ages, and they could be staying anywhere. What if the Brit was still in the hands of the UN? What if they'd left the country already? Or worse, if they'd gone in different directions? Think. Put yourself in their shoes.

Edouard Gahiji had a network but he didn't have enough people now to cover all the places they might be staying – he would have to look for the choke points, the places they'd need to pass through as they moved around and fortunately there weren't too many. Anyone leaving would be most likely to go through the airport or go over the border at one of the two crossings into Gisenyi. He would put men close to each of the border posts into Gisenyi and someone at the airport and the port. If the spies left the city, he would lose them for sure. His men only had a couple of advantages as far as Gahiji saw it; even if they were expecting to be watched the spies wouldn't know who to look out for, whereas his men knew their targets. The border crossing would open at six in the morning and the same with

378

the airport. They'd better get started; if he lost them … well it was better not to think about that.

******

James sat in the cab and went over his options. He was a patient man but the last half hour had crept by. He glanced at his phone for what must have been the tenth time. There had been no reply to his text, yet his phone showed that it had been delivered. Had she decided not to come? Was he rushing things? He didn't think so, if anything it seemed to him that he'd been a bit slow to show her that he really liked her, not just as a friend. Friends; the killer blow that waited in hiding for many a man. "I don't think of you like that, I see you more as a friend." How many times had James heard that line over the years? Even once was too many. Once she had pigeonholed you there was no way back from that. One of his mates had made it through the minefield of the Friends Zone, and look what had happened to him. He'd gone from Friend to Husband in one terrifying bound; that looked like a dangerous overshoot to James and he wasn't ready for that. This was one relationship that he didn't want to see going down the Friends route. Play things too fast and you were rushing her, too slow and one day you turned around and she was looking at you like a brother. There must be a right way to do this but he hadn't a clue what it was. Why didn't women come with a manual in ten languages? That was one instruction manual men would read thoroughly.

Where were they? James didn't recognise the neighbourhood but Hell that went for most of Goma. To make sure he got them home again safely he'd asked for the hotel's own car and driver, then given him clear instructions. Then he saw a couple of buildings he recognised and soon they were outside the AfriCan Care's building, only this time he was seeing it as an outsider. He had been expelled and here he was, back again on their doorstep. It could be awkward, but definitely worth it to see Jessica again.

The driver looked at him in the mirror and said something he didn't understand. James just said, "Wait," and made what he hoped would be understood as staying gestures before getting out of the car. There was no answer at first when he knocked on the door, nor was there a bell so he knocked again more loudly. A light came on in the entrance to the charity's office and eventually a voice said, "Who is it?"

"Serge, it's me, James."

"What is it you want?"

"Well, firstly I don't want to shout through the door!"

"I'm only supposed to open it on official business."

"Serge, don't be a prat, you know who I am. I'm not going to steal anything!"

379

There was a pause, then a bit of grumbling, and finally the chain and bolt went back. "What is it?" he said holding the door half open. "They are not here."

Over Serge's shoulder the place looked deserted and the only light came from the dining area beyond. "I'm after Jessica," said James.

Serge blew air out of his mouth contemptuously – it wasn't clear whether this was to dismiss Jessica or James's chance of finding her. It was amazing how many ways Serge had of being disparaging without ever saying a word.

"Do you know where she is?"

"No, of course not." He began to close the door.

James put his foot in the door then regretted it. It hurt more in moccasins than it appeared to in the movies. He tried again, "When will she be back?" Serge didn't even bother answering that, just shook his head.

James was wasting his time here and removed his foot from the door. "Fuck it, is there anything on God's earth you do know?"

"Fuck you, too, English. You wasting space."

James had been turning back to the taxi, but he stopped and swung back. Serge was already closing the door when the heel of James's hand struck the door hard above the handle. The door flew out of Serge's hand and swung heavily into his face. The Frenchman fell backwards, landing like a sack of sand and clutching his eye. Then he sat up, and one by one astonishment, humiliation and anger flitted across his face.

"Call yourself a doorman?" muttered James and walked back to the car. He heard the door slam shut behind him, but for once with Serge he'd had the last word. It was petty, but the little shit had had it coming from the moment they met. James climbed back into the taxi and was taken back to the hotel feeling more alone than he had for a while. The driver said nothing to him throughout the journey, but he kept shooting nervous glances at his passenger in the mirror and accepted the fare and the tip without a murmur.

******

James grabbed the phone when it buzzed. It was a text but it wasn't from Jessica. It simply read, "Call me. Urgent. Axel"

That was unexpected, and it seemed out of character for someone as laid back as Axel to talk of urgency. James was still far more concerned about talking to Jessica but he dialled Axel's number anyway. When he got through, the conversation was brief and worrying.

"Hi, it's James."

"Listen carefully. No names. The man who … took you away is either dead or in custody. I'm not sure which yet."

"Bloody hell! That was quick."

"It's for something else he did, but that's not why I called. The point is he has influential family here and they're blaming you for getting him caught and shot. You're also the only link between the crimes of the son who's been shot, and the father who is a big noise nationally and internationally. He's got a vast fortune and a big reputation to protect which means he wants you gone. Permanently. D'you understand?"

"Christ. Why me?"

"Grow up, will you? Because you were saved by the blue hats and just a few hours later the same troops arrested his son after a gun battle on the border. It's sparked a diplomatic incident – the neighbours don't appreciate people firing across their border. The family – I think we both know who I mean – are saying it was your information that led to the shooting and his capture. This is rapidly spiralling out of control. I can't stay on long and I have to leave for business reasons so I can't help you. I suggest you get out of the country, do it immediately. Grab your passport and go. Don't go back to Kinshasa, that's where they're strongest, cross over into Rwanda and go home that way."

"But my return ticket is from Kinshasa."

"If you take that route, you won't make it to the plane. Personally, I wouldn't risk it for a few hundred quid."

"How the hell do you know all this?" James demanded.

Axel hesitated. "Just call it networking. Text me when you get to London so that I know you're out." Then he hung up, leaving James staring in bewilderment at his phone. What the hell was life turning into? All he wanted to do was take good photos.

******

Life here in Goma was still a mystery to Raphael, and nothing felt safe or normal. The heavy gunfire had died down but he found himself constantly looking over his shoulder, and jumping at sudden noises. He also resented the fact that because he was alone he was forced to trust people like this, people who were street smart in a way that he knew he was not. Sure, he was a quick learner but deep down he hoped he might never be like them.

He was still analysing this and the underlying tension in the group when the others suddenly stood up at an unspoken signal. No words were said they simply headed down the stairs and out of the club by the usual back entrance. One of the new guys was slower, he had a weak looking leg and he walked with the aid of a single crutch. The girls had changed clothes by the time they joined the group on the stairs, and now they were dressed like they were going out. Raphael could only follow, leaving most of his belongings behind, and hoping they'd still be there when he returned.

It didn't take long for them to cross this part of the city and reach an area filled with hotels, shops and restaurants. It was smarter here, there were working street lights almost everywhere and close to the lake the air was cooler. The smell of dust, sweat and urine that lingered throughout the old cinema gave way to the smell of warm, dry earth, flowers and the comforting night sound of crickets in bushes by the road. As the group approached the largest of the hotels, the boys melted away into the darkness momentarily leaving him alone in the road until one of them re-emerged and grabbed Raphael by the arm pulling him with them.

The two young women seemed to know exactly what to do. From where he stood below the terrace Raphael could see them climb the marble front steps of the hotel, the larger girl stopping before a plate glass window to check her appearance in the reflection; she hitched her short skirt a little higher and adjusted her top while beside her the other girl studied her teeth for signs of lipstick. Satisfied with what they saw they stepped towards the doors which were opened by an overweight security guard standing inside. His stomach bulged heavily over the belt of his uniform trousers as he leaned forward to admit them – maybe Raphael was mistaken, but he appeared to know the girls and to be expecting them. Raphael still didn't know what they were doing here, but all this hiding in the bushes made it feel furtive and illegal. He felt trapped; he didn't want to take part in something bad, something his mother and father would not have approved of. Yet where could he run to?

The girls turned left in the glass-fronted lobby and moved into the bar which could clearly be seen through picture windows. It was darker in there but they were now seated by the window and occasionally it was possible to see them as they leaned closer in conversation. As far as he could see, there were few people inside and it appeared that nobody spoke to them; it was hard to tell from their position in the bushes lining the front terrace.

A trickle of guests arrived for dinner but nobody seemed interested in using the bar. After half an hour a taxi deposited a party of three foreigners with suitcases and they went to the front desk where they were soon lost from view. More than twenty minutes later two guys emerged onto the terrace. Both wore military uniforms with light coloured shirts and camouflaged trousers over combat boots. Raphael didn't know the uniforms, but the others with him seemed to and there was a whispered debate between the four guys beside him. Raphael could just hear snatches of it going this way and that. "We've been here for an hour... These are the only marks. Where are the girls? We can't stay here all bloody night, we've got nothing... This won't work... Where are the girls? We're five, well four." Someone gestured at the guy with the frail leg, and another cast a doubtful look at Raphael. The discussion clearly didn't involve him and he stayed quiet, but by now he had a very bad feeling about what was planned.

The taller of the two soldiers offered his friend a cigarette and the men were suddenly visible and seemed very close as they shared a light, cupping hands around the lighter to shelter the flame from the evening breeze. The smell of smoke reached Raphael who stood concealed from them only five metres away, and he wondered what it would be like to try a cigarette. He couldn't understand their language but he was close enough to hear their conversation, especially now that his partners in the bushes beside him had fallen silent. Even knowing where to look he could hardly make out their shapes in the darkness, but he could see them clearly when they drew on their cigarettes.

On the terrace above the concealed group a story was being told and there was shared laughter with some relaxed conversation as they stared up at the sky. If the men had stared down into the darkness a metre below the railing, it might all have ended differently.

The noise from the bar grew louder as a door opened and the girls came onto the terrace. There was a brief muttered word of warning from one of the smokers, and the other said something from the side of his mouth in reply before they both laughed scornfully.

Raphael still hadn't been told the plan but now it all seemed so obvious to him. One girl asked for a light and the prettier of the two kept a little distance by sitting on the low rail that ran around the decking. One of the men lit the girl's cigarette and she thanked them before joining her friend a couple of paces away. As the men watched, the seated girl slowly drew a cigarette from her bag and held it up towards them. The one with the lighter hesitated before taking a few steps towards where she sat on the rail. She seemed unable to get a light and turned her body sideways against the breeze, manoeuvring the soldier even closer to the edge. As he leaned forward again, a strong arm pulled him by the belt over the balcony and there was the flash of a knife being raised before he even hit the ground. The speed with which the attack began even surprised Raphael.

The soldier's friend was startled but not slow to react and must have seen the knife as he yelled a warning that certainly would have been heard within the hotel. He didn't wait any longer but vaulted the rail beside the two girls and quickly went down amid flailing arms and boots. He was on his feet again in an instant and Raphael could see that he was positioned close to the immobile body of his friend. The guy with the crutch was crouched over the body on the ground and was expertly emptying his pockets and removing his watch and rings. The standing soldier was in what seemed to Raphael to be a fighting stance, his legs slightly apart for balance, left arm extended almost horizontally and his right fist raised to his chest. He stepped forward and with a strong kick straight to the chest he made the thief fall backwards away from his friend. Snake came out of the darkness holding his gleaming stiletto knife and the soldier swivelled to meet the new threat while yelling again. This time he was not calling for help, he was shouting in visceral anger at what they had done to his companion. A second figure loomed from the shadows behind him and the soldier must have heard the man's approach for he anticipated the second strike, catching his attacker in the throat with a backward chop of his forearm. The man went down and Raphael could hear him making odd, gargling noises. Now there was a shout from the far end of the terrace above them and two civilians began to run towards the fight that had now spilled out of the shadowed bushes and onto the floodlit lawn.

First one of Snake's men broke away and ran then he was followed by the others, the man on the crutch managing to hop away at startling speed. When Raphael looked back, there was no sign of the two girls who had started it all. He was on the point of running too when someone punched him twice in the back in quick succession. When he turned, all he could see was Snake running away; he had no idea who had hit him, the others were all in front. The blows hadn't been hard but for some reason when he started to run after them Raphael's knees felt weak and his eyes wouldn't focus so that he managed only two paces. He was still wondering why he could feel something wet on the back of his legs when a flying tackle hit him from behind and knocked all the wind out of him. That was much more painful than the blows he'd received. The tackler's momentum had carried him past Raphael and when they both sat up Raphael's head spun and he found he was gasping for breath. Oddly, the white man who had tackled him seemed to have oil all over his shirt and face.

Then strong arms pinned Raphael to the ground and he lay looking up at the night sky. What had been a warm evening breeze suddenly felt icy cold and he was shivering uncontrollably. He wanted to ask the man who knelt on top of him if he would please have a look at his back because there was something wrong, but even before the man punched him twice in the face Raphael's tongue was refusing to co-operate and anyway he couldn't think of the words. All around him there was shouting, then torches shone blindingly in his eyes and someone kicked him hard in the stomach.

Raphael just wanted to tell them something but for the life of him he couldn't think what it was; he knew there was one word he had to tell them that was more important than any other. What was it? Yes, just listen please. It's Keisha.

Why could no one hear him saying 'Keisha'?

Chapter 25
Goma, North Kivu, DRC
Two Days Ago

Gahiji seethed with frustration. With Louis Businga dead he now found himself taking orders from the Major's father. Nobody asked him, everyone just assumed he was now working for the boss's father, giving him orders that were easy to say but bloody impossible to fulfil. Find Falkus, identify his accomplices, capture them, report back. Sure. Easy as that. They didn't pay him enough to take this shit.

With a backhanded flick he swept a coffee cup off the filing cabinet and watched it smash against the far wall. It broke with an irritatingly unsatisfying tinkle and a trickle of old coffee ran down the wall behind his desk where it met a damp patch heading upwards. He slammed the office door shut for good measure, but if anyone at the Ministry of Mines in Goma heard him they were smart enough not to come and investigate.

Gahiji looked around him, it certainly wasn't like the tatty army office at the barracks, he'd shared a desk there but never used it. There had been no paint on the walls and many of the windows had been broken or unglazed. He was a soldier, an outdoors man, but now he needed space and quiet in which to do some thinking and this was as good a place as any. His new boss had arranged it and the Ministry had even supplied him with a shared secretary and a new mobile so that Businga could reach him. The furniture was basic; a wooden table for a desk, two plastic chairs, a damp-stained and fly-spotted picture of the President, a laminated sheet of Fire Instructions and a scratched steel filing cabinet with lockable drawers but no key. Oh, and now a cracked cup on the floor.

He stood in front of the open window, hands on hips and breathed deeply, drawing in the humid air and trying to take control of himself and the situation. It had been bad enough working for Businga Junior, with his violent mood swings and vicious reactions to his staff. One minute he would be acting like your best friend, the next he was eyeing you without any feelings whatsoever. Now, in a subtle, more insidious way it was just as bad working for Louis' father. There were all the same expectations of round the clock duties, zero respect and still no meaningful support where he needed it in the field. He breathed out slowly, to that extent it was just like the Army.

It seemed that Businga Senior was like all men of his rank, expecting everything done his way, wanting results yesterday, only this time either he couldn't give them the tools for the job or he'd decided not to. He was forever playing the Big Man, but Gahiji was beginning to wonder what power the guy actually wielded. The boss had been clear enough about one thing; this man Falkus knew too much about the Businga family's involvement in smuggling, and in something else political although he wouldn't say what. Yet when they'd had the chance to kill him the Busingas hadn't done it. In fact, the Old Man had told his son to free the guy. No one would say why, and you didn't cross-question someone like the General. None of it made any sense to him anymore; at least with the Major you knew he was a spoiled jerk and you knew why he was doing shit.

The only information he'd been given by General Businga was that the Old Man had indeed told Louis to release Falkus, but that was before he had the full facts, before the blue hats had ambushed and killed his only son. It was now obvious to Businga that they had been acting on information Falkus had given them, it was obvious from the way he had fled straight to them. Equally obviously the General couldn't bring himself to admit that he'd made a mistake, but it was clearly weighing on his mind. In the past few hours he'd changed his mind again. "You can forget what I told Louis before," said the General, "I want Falkus dead and screw the consequences. Falkus betrayed Louis to MONUSCO. Even if they're the ones who killed him, the payback starts with Falkus. All you have to do is find him."

Gahiji and his man had looked at one another, knowing the scale of the task. "Can you give me any more men, sir? Everyone I have is being used, we're thinly stretched and I don't want him to slip through the net."

Businga sat stock still and studied Gahiji "I was told by Louis that you're a resourceful man, Gahiji. Maybe he was wrong, maybe he couldn't see through you. I'm not interested in you building your little empire here, I've already given you people and resources, just get on and use them. You hear me?"

Gahiji paused for a moment too long. Businga was a lot older but he was a big guy, physically powerful and still fit enough to pose a threat. He came out of his desk chair fast and it was so unexpected that he was in Gahiji's face before the younger man could react. The General leaned forward and the heat of his breath blew over Gahiji's face. It took an effort of will not to take the older man down. Had he done so, he would have had to finish him there and then or he'd have perished as a consequence.

"I don't hear you," said Businga.

"Yes. Sir." He spoke each word distinctly. It wasn't exactly disrespectful, but it was clear that he wasn't intimidated by the man's physical presence.

The General stared at Gahiji eyeball to eyeball from a few centimetres. He had shown his willingness to beat down the young officer and he would do whatever it took to bring some control back into his life. He turned and moved back towards his seat, talking over his shoulder as he did so.

"I expect you think this is mostly about revenge," he said. "It's not. Well, not entirely. It's about protecting our reputation and the Businga name. No one should think they can cross us and win, I don't care where they come from." He seemed to include the younger man, as though his reputation was at risk too. *It was a crude attempt to get him onside,* thought Gahiji.

"Of course, it will help when the only witness directly linking this family to some local politics disappears." Businga was assuming the man was already dead, and he had avoided describing the secret discussions with Hutu rebels to his junior; these two junior ranks would not have understood the bigger political picture that Louis, for all his faults had seen, the chance to unseat the President and his fellow parasites.

It meant that Falkus' information was still dynamite. After all these years, Moise Businga knew he could fall from power all too quickly; he could lose everything he'd worked so hard for if the photos fell into the wrong hands. If necessary Businga would follow his own earlier advice to his son and deny any knowledge of Louis' dealings with Didier Toko and the FDLR. These were enemies of Businga's own government and he couldn't afford to have his loyalty to the government questioned – there was too much at stake, financially and politically.

Hours later after he'd been dismissed from the meeting, Gahiji was still thinking it through. Instead of silencing Falkus, the Major had locked him up and then stupidly allowed him to escape. And now, when he was out there somewhere and probably telling everything to the UN or MI6 and God-knows-who-else, the General had changed his mind and decided he wanted Falkus finished after all. *It was bloody mad,* thought Gahiji, *but he had known better than to ask for an explanation.*

He daren't fail, that much he knew. So, what more could he do? He'd placed a couple of people on the nearest border crossings to Rwanda, he was paying someone to watch Departures from Goma airport and had even told the ferry captains there was a big tip for them if they found a spy leaving southbound for Bukavu. He didn't have enough people to watch the roads, but driving was a long slow way out. Although he reckoned he'd covered all the main exit routes, he knew that Falkus had escaped from imprisonment in the Major's warehouse and had then got away from the watcher on the border. He was obviously highly skilled; they were going to need a lot of luck.

The ex-soldier continued to stare out of the window. *Put yourself in the enemy's shoes,* he thought. What would he do in James Falkus' position? Find somewhere to lay up, check his weapons, count his assets, and plan his withdrawal. The next step was to find where he was staying; everyone knew the UN had moved out on manoeuvres, the charity would probably be too nervous to hide a wanted man, so he was either staying with a friend or in a hotel. He'd try them all himself one at a time, starting now.

******

He had involved Jessica in this and if he left now she could be at real risk. Axel didn't seem a bullshitter, so if he stayed James knew he might never get out at all. Dammit, why wasn't she answering her phone? Where was she? What he really wanted was to tell her the things he should have told her at lunch, instead they'd wasted time talking about other people. James sat on the hotel terrace and tried to think things through.

Axel had a lot of experience out here and clearly wasn't the kind of guy to panic. He had good contacts, and if he said it was time to leave then maybe he should listen. He didn't want to go, he had a feeling things were just starting to improve for him.

Lost in his thoughts James didn't hear anyone approaching until there was a tap on his shoulder that made him jump. "What does a girl have to do to get a dance round here?"

"Jessica. Thank God, I've been trying to reach you." He stood and held her hand. It was one of the first times they had touched, if you didn't count the time he had dumped her on the ground in the pouring rain or nearly stood on her in the refugee camp. He noticed once again how slender her fingers were and how her skin contrasted with his.

"I had my phone off while I was interviewing one of your rescuers. I hear they may give you a speeding ticket for the way you drove the push-back tractor. That's what it's called apparently – something else I've learned today." She was grinning at him and the light in her eyes sparkled. "It's a wreck, so full of bullet holes they could use it for a colander."

"Hey, I didn't shoot it I just drove it." He hadn't let go of her hand and she didn't make him. "Do you want a drink?"

"You don't need to ask. What are you having?"

"Well, I was about to get horribly drunk starting with this bottle of red. But this evening just took a distinct turn for the better." He smiled at her and she moved to sit down beside him. He let go of her hand and ordered another glass from the barman. Aside from him, they had the place to themselves.

"I went to look for you at the compound, but all I found was Serge," he said. "That was a bit of a let-down, I can tell you."

"I can imagine." A glass arrived and the barman poured some wine for Jessica. When he had gone, James raised his glass towards her in a toast.

"Here's to wine, long lunches and beautiful evenings," he said and as they touched glasses his fingers brushed hers.

"I got your text after my meeting. Thank you, it was sweet. I'm sorry I wasn't there when you called in your cab, I'm probably too late for dinner."

"No matter, you're here now and I couldn't be more pleased. We can ask about food in a second."

Some jazz was playing softly, then the mood music suddenly changed and James caught sight of the barman's smile as Jessica clapped her hands. "I love this; it's Summertime, Will Smith. Dance with me. Please?"

He stood up, and this time when he reached for her hand he didn't let go. As they began to dance, the volume rose, the barman melted away and the open air dance floor was theirs alone.

Will Smith was singing, *It's like the summer's a natural aphrodisiac,* and James pulled Jessica close to him ignoring the pain in his broken hand he raised his right and twirled her gently beneath his arm before returning her to him. She smiled at his skill and this time he held her tight, ceroc dancing with her and wishing the song would never end.

Mr Smith sang on ... *There's an air of love and of happiness*, and when the music faded away they stood together in the silence not taking their eyes from one another. Neither spoke and he leaned down to kiss her before the album played *Just Crusin'*. Food was forgotten as they danced, they talked and she stayed.

******

It was almost midday and they were standing together on his balcony overlooking the grey-blue waters of the lake when Jessica suddenly asked, "What are your worst traits? Just so that I know."

"Wow! Big question. How long have you got?" She pushed him away playfully but he pulled her back to him.

"I want to know a bit more about you," she insisted. "And what I'm getting into here?"

"A whole mess o' trouble, lady," he joked, mimicking her New York accent.

"I'm serious," she said.

"The honest answer is I've no idea either. One thing I do know is I'm so glad you came here. But I told you last night about the guys Axel says are looking for me. I don't want you to get hurt by being with me, so if you want to leave now I'll understand. Like I said, this isn't your problem."

"You don't get rid of me that easy, buster."

He stopped and looked into her eyes, searching for answers just as she was.

"OK," he said, "The low down; I'm almost thirty, I don't know where I live, I don't have a job, I've stuffed up two careers, apparently I don't always take things as seriously as I should, and my hair's all floppy." She started to respond but he held up a hand. "On the flipside, I can hold my drink, I make a mean spaghetti carbonara, I'm told I take nice pictures, and I can jig a bit."

"I'll say," she giggled.

"I meant dancing. You're shameless. Damn I like that." He studied her face for clues. "So, how about you? Who is Jessica?"

"Oh, I don't know. I can't seem to stay in one place for more than a few months, I'm glued to my work, but I don't much like doing what I'm told. I have a huge cut down the middle of my top lip, some people say I have a short fuse – but hell," she smiled up at him, "they're history. Oh, and I have a totally dysfunctional family – but then so do you – perhaps they made me headstrong, and ha, if you think your hair's a problem you don't know squat."

"And the good stuff?" he asked.

"That's easy, I paint pictures with my stories, I like French wine and English accents, otherwise I'm quite low maintenance, and I love carbonara and all things Italian. Will that do?"

He didn't reply, he just leaned forward and kissed her hard until she responded.

******

"Who were you calling?" James paused, wishing he hadn't spoken. "Sorry, none of my business."

It was nearly four in the afternoon and after a cab ride to collect and pack her things, their taxi was inching ever closer to the border crossing into Rwanda at Petite Barrière. Jessica looked worried and she was biting her lower lip as she thought about something.

He tried again. "What is it? Have you forgotten something?"

"Not exactly." She breathed a huge sigh, and looked down. She couldn't look at him as she spoke. "James, I don't think I can come. I have to go back."

James told the driver to pull over. "Why? I don't get this, what is it? I thought you were cool with this, you know, with us."

"I am, it's not that." She looked up at him with an agony of indecision in her eyes. "I've been calling Kanyaruchinya camp every few days to find out if there's any news of Raphael, I think I told you about him. His father was shot, his little sister is alone in an orphanage near Walikale, his mother and the rest of their family have vanished and I said I'd try to help find them. But he's drawn a blank with the UNHCR at the camp, and so have I with my own checking."

"Seriously, I don't get it. What more can you do, Jessica? The UN are geared up to deal with this kind of thing, you're not," James argued.

"I know, I know. I just feel I haven't tried hard enough and Raphael's been counting on someone, anyone to help him. He has no one else to ask. Now my friends at the camp are saying no one has heard from him in days."

"What can you do?"

"I can find him. I can go with him, help him, and maybe get through the red tape for him. And for Keisha. I told them I would try and I owe them that much at least." She was staring up at him with tears now filling her eyes, imploring him to understand.

James had to look away and stare out of the window; the cars behind slowly began to overtake them and creep towards the border barely fifty metres away. All around them people went about their ordinary business while the two of them wrestled with the rest of their lives. Just ahead of them a drinks vendor stood on the baked red earth serving a glass to a customer in the shade of a dusty red umbrella. James turned back to her.

"Please understand. I have to do this, James. I have to go back. I made him a promise, and no one else in his life has kept their promises for years. Just let me out here." She began to cry and turned away so that he would not see her.

"I've only just found you, Jessica and I'm sure as hell not going to say goodbye to you now. But there have been some heavy duty people coming after me and that could mean they'll try to get at anyone who's with me. If we don't leave now ..." he left the sentence hanging.

She was crying. "I can't James, I want to come with you but I can't do it. Not yet, anyway."

The taxi driver looked in his mirror and gestured to the border. James shook his head and made a wheeling motion with his hand. "Faire demi-tour" he said, and the cab driver muttered something unintelligible but probably not complimentary before swinging his car around in front of the minibus behind. There was a protesting horn and the drivers exchanged shouts. No one noticed the man under the umbrella peel away from the drinks cart and pull out his phone.

"James, what are you doing? You can't ..."

"I'm doing what I should have done before, keeping a close eye on you. If you want to do this, Jessica then let's do it together. I mean, what's the worst that can happen?"

Book 3

Kill not the moth nor butterfly,
For the Last Judgement draweth nigh.

William Blake, 1757 - 1827

Chapter 26
Goma, North Kivu, DRC
Two Days Ago

As soon as they were back in Goma, Jessica had gone to search for Raphael, heading north to see her friends and contacts at Kanyaruchinya camp. Wrapped up in her thoughts of travelling with James she felt ashamed that she had almost walked away from unfinished business with Raphael. For a while she had forgotten him, and when she realised it her euphoria evaporated. She couldn't leave until she knew if his search had been successful.

When James said that he would wait for her, Jessica was amazed, especially after what he'd been told by his father about the threat against him. In fact, she was struggling to take everything in at the moment, so much had been happening in her life; first she would talk to Raphael, and she just hoped that he would understand she had genuinely tried to find his family.

James had stayed in the city to check their travel options. There was no sign of Ashok when she reached the camp and her frustration began to grow. The Admissions team at the camp was operating at full stretch and understandably she was the lowest priority, so she had to wait for two hours before eventually finding someone with enough time to answer her questions. Jessica stood and waited as patiently as she could to speak to the dark-haired woman in her thirties who was in charge. The woman was obviously tired and harassed, her manner was curt – there were more deserving people to deal with. "I understand you are looking for someone in particular. My name's Carina, what do you want?"

Jessica stood up. "Yes, I'm looking for a boy called Raphael who arrived here recently."

"Who are you? Is this official?" the woman demanded. "We don't give out information on people who come here. These are vulnerable people, and their details are private. Surely you understand this."

Jessica changed tack, knowing she needed to be careful not to reveal that Ashok had already helped her. If this woman couldn't or wouldn't help them, she'd need to speak to Ashok after all, assuming he was still in Goma. "No, it's not official, it's personal. Raphael is a friend, and so is his sister Keisha." Jessica had few cards to play here, and she needed to use them carefully. "I met them a while back at an orphanage in Walikale, and they asked me to help find their mother, brother and sister. When no one could find them, Raphael decided to come here himself to see if his family had reached safety. He asked for my help, and because he and his sister were so young and alone I agreed. I just need to tell him that although I haven't found them I will keep looking."

Carina was clearly exhausted but Jessica could see that she was weighing the fact that this young woman in front of her already knew the boy. The rules were clear but it wasn't as though she was making an introduction, Jessica was evidently a friend whom the boy had turned to and she had been waiting here a long time. It would be easier just to get rid of her, so she asked for Raphael's details again and typed them into the system.

"Oh," was all she said at first.

"What is it?"

There was a long pause while Carina read whatever was on the screen. "Listen, I shouldn't be telling you this, but I have some bad news. I'm afraid your friend is dead."

"No! That can't be right. I saw him only recently. He's young and fit, he made it here on his own, and he was safe here."

"I'm sorry but it's true. The body hasn't been claimed but he has been identified."

"I don't believe you. There must be some mistake. He's only sixteen; he's very strong, very resilient."

Carina bristled at the doubt being cast on their work; the information was detailed and clear. "I can only tell you what it says here. We don't say it lightly and we check and double-check so that we don't get that kind of thing wrong. Listen, I'm sorry to break it to you like this, and I probably shouldn't have told you anything but I thought it was better that you knew rather than carry on your search for him when we know where he is."

"Can you at least tell me what happened? How do you know it's him? What's happened to Keisha?" Thoughts were tumbling through Jessica's head.

"We have no record of Keisha ever reaching the camp, she's not here so I can't say. All I know is it says that the police reported finding his body in the city a few days ago after an assault and robbery at a hotel. He had been involved in an attack on two soldiers; there was a fight of some kind. Apparently, when his body was taken to the hospital morgue they found a UN refugee registration card in the boy's ... in er, Raphael's pocket. The photo and details matched him exactly. I'm sorry to bring you such bad news. Now I have other people I must attend to, I suggest you ask at the police station or the hospital. I'll give you the address for both but I can't help you any further, that's all I know."

Carina laid a consoling hand on Jessica's shoulder, who never even registered her touch, and then moved on to a group of new arrivals. Jessica sat slumped, all the fight knocked out of her.

It was all too much to take in. Jessica stayed where she was, shocked and unmoving and a long time afterwards she continued to sit and stare dry-eyed into space. She had heard so often before about the human costs of the fighting here, but this time the conflict had reached out and struck her deeply.

Much later she thought back to the way she had witnessed Raphael and Keisha's isolation at the orphanage from their family and only then did she begin to cry. They were huge wracking sobs at the injustice of Raphael's life and death, and she felt a rage swelling inside her, with an intensity that surprised her and left her knotted inside.

When she had met Marc and Marianne, Jessica had listened to their view that the children's mother was probably dead. Then she had learned of Raphael's understandable indignation, and wondered how they could assume something so awful and so final when there was no proof at all. The boy had decided he would continue looking and Jessica knew that in his shoes she too would have continued the search for their mother and the twins.

At first she had been shocked at the bare details of what had happened, all she knew was that Raphael was accused of taking part in a robbery at a hotel. From what she knew of him that seemed so unlikely. Then her thoughts turned to Keisha and she was upset again at what this would mean for the little girl now completely alone in the world after her entire family had died or disappeared one by one. On top of all that, Jessica couldn't escape her own feelings of guilt. She had tried to help but she wondered if she had only made things worse by dangling in front of Raphael the possibility that his remaining family might have found their way to Goma. As she looked back on her interest in him, Jessica knew also that it lay partly in his story. It wasn't as if she'd hurried away to write the tragedy of his life story, nothing so crude; but she knew that his experience encapsulated the conflict here. Although she hadn't written about him now, she knew she would have done so later. And however much she consoled herself with the thought that Raphael's life and now his death were relevant experiences for her time in DRC, part of her felt that she had been using his pain and loss. Her rational, professional self could justify what she had done, but not her emotional self. A measure of guilt clung to her like a stubborn stain and she knew instinctively that it would not go quickly or easily.

Above all else, she felt a surge of anger at this senseless loss of life. There were people to blame for that, people in power in Congo and outside; Government ministers for their inability or unwillingness – she couldn't be sure how much of each – to end the fighting here and find a peace that lasted. She was sickened by the UN in New York which had turned a blind eye to the fighting for so many

397

years. Worse still were those just looking to enrich themselves from Congo's wealth without putting anything back, people like James's father, Axel Terberg. His type only ever brought suffering to the people here; he may not have created the conditions here but he'd exploited them, done nothing to end them and continued to profit from them.

Jessica had a mental picture of Raphael lying cold and unclaimed in a hospital morgue. It was unlikely that body would stay in Goma's morgue for long, she'd heard at Kanyaruchinya that the recent fighting meant there were more bodies than the morgue could cope with. The overflow would be stored for as long as possible awaiting collection and family funerals. She couldn't stand the thought of Raphael being kept there. And if no family members collected his body, she knew that it would soon have to be buried.

It was highly unlikely Keisha would know yet about her brother's death; how could the Audoussets have found out? They probably wouldn't even know for sure where Raphael had gone, and Jessica wondered if he had told them he was following her to Goma. If he had, they would surely blame her for his death every bit as much as she blamed herself. Christ, what had she done? He might still be alive if it hadn't been for her interfering. Jessica could no longer convince herself that it had all been done out of altruism, she had to acknowledge that a worse motive lurked behind it, she had been determined to write a news story that would get her noticed as a foreign correspondent and would literally put her on the map. It had always been in the back of her mind, even if she hadn't faced it so clearly before.

Now she had to get a message to the Audoussets and through them to Keisha but they were so remote that a message could only be radioed through to Walikale. After that there was no telling how reliably a message would travel up the valley to the mission, and this wasn't the kind of news she felt comfortable breaking like that.

Of course, she could easily have dodged the responsibility and no one at Taweza Road Orphanage and School would have been any the wiser. She herself would have known though, and Jessica was many things but she was not a coward. She already felt guilty for not doing more to help Raphael find his family and for getting involved when she had promised Marianne she would not. She wasn't going to make it worse by not getting the awful news to Keisha.

Jessica took a deep breath; she was probably the only person who knew where the young body in the morgue had come from, who this unclaimed teenager was, or any of the details of his life. She breathed a heavy sigh, she would have to go to Walikale and deal with this herself – however unpalatable it might be.

******

He had been behind the curve on just about everything that had happened to him since he set foot in Africa, and James did not enjoy being the pawn in other people's chess game. There were things he wanted to achieve, starting with finding out more about Raphael's death. Jessica had her hands full getting the message about his death to the orphanage, and he knew it was eating her up not knowing what had happened so he would make himself useful finding out whatever he could.

He had also weighed up Axel's earlier warning about the Busingas, a warning that he had so far ignored. It wasn't that James didn't believe his blood father, in fact he was sure the threat was real and Axel had been well-intentioned – although Jessica was altogether more sceptical about him. James hadn't cut and run because he was tired of being pushed around. It had happened ever since he got here and it was time he made his own plans.

The first of these was to help Jessica find some answers. He figured that the sooner she found out what she wanted here, the sooner they could leave, together. So how, he wondered, would he learn about Raphael's final days? Jessica had traced the boy's final movements as far as the camp. The next place he was known to have gone was the hotel where he had died in a knife fight. James still had the name, so he caught a cab from his own hotel and headed towards Goma's port district. He didn't have a clear idea of how he'd play it, he would just have to wing it.

When he pushed open the hotel's heavy glass doors and stepped into the air-conditioned relief inside he began to see why it was popular with ex-pats and military. To his right were two long dark wood counters, one with several Reception points but only one staff member and one nearby for the Concierge. The hotel lobby was anodyne in style but the bar to his left was cavernous, dimly lit, and modern; he could imagine it being much busier late at night. The cab driver had said it had a reputation for rowdiness and hookers, and it was said to be popular with soldiers and NGO workers. A chalkboard sign at the entrance promised a Happy Hour and Karaoke later.

James turned to survey the lobby. There was one staff member sitting behind the reception filing her nails. She didn't look up and he wasn't sure if she had even noticed his arrival. In any case it was the doorman he was looking for. He wandered over to the Concierge desk. There was no sign of anyone, no bell and no sounds of activity behind the scenes, so he stepped behind the desk and walked into the rear office. There was a torn leatherette sofa against one wall, a desk piled high with undelivered packages and newspaper all over the floor. On the sofa lay a man face down and immobile; he was so still that James fleetingly wondered if this was another body. Then there was a snort and a fart before the man turned his head the other way and settled again.

James spoke loudly. "Get up!"

One eye opened and tried to swivel at an impossible angle to take him in. Then, possibly seeing that James was not officialdom, the eye closed. "Va te faire foutre," he swore through the corner of his mouth that wasn't immersed in leatherette.

James kicked the man's foot. "I'm here about the boy that was killed."

The man mumbled some more in French that James was only just able to follow. "I've told the cops everything I know. Ten times. You're no cop, so you can ..."

"I know, you said. So you won't be wanting this then. He twirled a $20 bill between his fingers."

At the rustle of crisp paper the same eye opened and this time it stayed open. "Waddyawant?"

Well, that was some small progress, thought James. "What I want is for you to sit up and look at me."

A debate moved sluggishly behind the visible eye, and with a sigh as heavy as the man himself, the sleeper pushed himself upright. He had a cloud of ill-kempt hair, his shirt was far enough undone and untucked that you could see a once-white vest beneath. A thin brown belt encircled him, unequal to the task of grasping his large midriff.

"I've got a few questions for you. If you want this note, I need to believe your replies. If I don't believe them, you won't see me or it again."

The man rubbed his face slowly, spreading the saliva that had dribbled as he slept more evenly over the left side of his face. Either he hadn't shaved for days or he needed to stand closer to the razor. The hand continued its perusal of his face and swept slowly upwards temporarily forcing his hair back, only for the hair to return to its unruly condition.

"Who are you?"

"I'm the man with $20 and if I like what I hear, I'm the man with $40."

"Wotissit?"

"There was a boy killed here the other night. Were you here?"

"Of course. I'm always here, I live here."

"Were you on duty?"

"No. Well, yes."

"What the hell does that mean?"

"First I wasn't, then I was. When the girls came."

"Which girls?" James asked.

"Like I told the police, I don't know their names. They come here some nights. A fat one and a pretty one."

James looked down at the man's figure and added self-awareness to his long list of missing attributes. "Est-ce qu'elles étaient des prostituées? Were they hookers?"

"Of course! They arrived just after I came on duty."

"What time was that?"

"Why all the questions? Who are you?"

"If you want to ask me questions, you'll have to give me twenty bucks. Otherwise, just give me answers." It seemed no coincidence to James that the women arrived at the hotel just after he came on duty. They were probably paying him a cut to keep the number of hookers down, and more to get two room keys. James grimaced at the thought of staying here.

"What time did you come on duty that night?"

"About nine. A bit after," said the doorman and James had no trouble in picturing him being late.

"Was anything different that night?"

"Listen, how do I know you're going to pay me for all these questions?"

James looked at him for a moment, then he tore the twenty dollar bill in half and gave the man half. "You don't, but now it's useless to us both and you're half way to getting the rest of it."

The man grumbled but held onto his half of the bill.

"What was the first thing that happened, the first sign of trouble?"

The man gave a lazy shrug and exhaled contemptuously. "There were shouts and men were running along the terrace. The girls were outside, they'd been talking to some soldiers. Foreigners. Like I say, there were shouts then two other guys ran to help. One of the soldiers had fallen off the balcony and a fight was going on. Then we found him."

"Found who? The boy?" The doorman just nodded.

"Had you seen him before?"

A shake of the head. "Jamais."

"Was he alive when you reached him?"

Another shrug. "I guess."

James curled his fist around his half of the note, showing he was unhappy at the doorman's lack of co-operation. "Alive or dead?"

The man on the sofa had his eyes fixed on the half-a-note. "He was alive. But he wasn't saying anything, well not much. It was very faint, and no one could understand him. He kept repeating one word over and over. Maybe it was a name, but who knows?"

"Who else was with him? Who did you see?"

"No one. That was it. Now do I get my twenty bucks?"

"Have you had trouble like this at the hotel before?"

This time the doorman wouldn't look directly at him. "Not really."

"Either you have or you haven't. Which is it?"

"There's been the odd fight, particularly when the soldiers come. But nothing like this."

James looked at his torn twenty note. "You're gonna need some tape," and he flicked the second half to the doorman. It landed on the sofa and the man snatched it up.

"I may be back," said James.

"And I may be here," said the doorman.

"What's your name if I need to talk for another twenty?"

There was a pause while he weighed the benefits of telling James. Eventually he offered one word, "Eric," and with that he slid back down to lie stretched out on the sofa. Anyone who needed their bags carrying this afternoon would be out of luck.

******

James's next stop was the largest of Goma's four hospitals. There were patients and families talking or waiting in the lobby for who knew what? He made his way through the throng but could see no reception desk. In the absence of relevant signage a young man responded to his questions by taking James by the arm and leading him through the hospital's passages. He wasn't sure what he had expected but the building was clean and well lit through large windows. A thick coat of gloss cream paint stretched along each corridor and into every ward from floor to head height, topped by a neatly painted thin band of red. Nurses and doctors in white coats moved purposefully and the place had an air of calm efficiency.

Without help, however, he might never have found the morgue among the many rambling concrete buildings at the back of the hospital. At every junction the youth would guide James by the elbow and lead on, until a few minutes later they were at the door to the morgue. A rapid-fire conversation with the attendant then ensued, but it was in a local language that James could not follow. The attendant stood up and offered a handshake to James.

"How can I help you?"

"Ah, you speak English. Excellent."

"Yes, I am studying to be a Pharmacist. I learn English in the nights."

"I'm looking for someone who was brought here recently, a young man of fifteen or sixteen."

"Is he your family? We have no white men here."

"No, no. I work for a charity." It seemed the quickest way to cut through any red tape. James pulled out his wallet and showed the ID card they had not asked him to return. "A young man who did some work for us went missing and we understand he was injured and died at a hotel. Would he have been brought here?"

"That depends. What is his name?"

"We just knew him as Raphael. He was sixteen, and about this tall." James indicated his chin height. He may have had a UN identity card."

"One moment," and the young man began to flick through a folder on the desk in front of him. "There are many here. Too many." His finger ran down the pages working backwards through the ring file, stopping now and again to check an entry. Eventually he paused, his index finger hovering over a listing. "Do you want to see him?"

There was no pre-amble, but James had thought about this on the way. He had half expected that they would be unable to trace the boy, and he had gone as much in the hope of confirming Raphael's death as in finding the whereabouts of his body. He had got this far and it would look suspicious if he came all this way and then was disinterested in seeing Raphael. "Yes," he said.

"We do not have a place private. Come with me," said the attendant and James followed him down a corridor lit only through glass doors at the far end. The light became much brighter as they approached and suddenly they were out in a car park. Only it wasn't cars that filled the nearest spaces, it was shipping containers. From four refrigerated containers electricity cables ran in colourful snakes across the ground. There was a steady hum from the cooling units and the afternoon sun shone brightly on the smooth-sided boxes.

"This way, please."

All it had taken to reach this point was a glimpse of an out of date identity card, and James briefly wondered how his life had taken him from a secure job in Boston to a hospital deep in Africa where he was trying to confirm the identity of a body for his girlfriend. Oh, and trying not to get caught by some thugs who may or may not still be chasing him.

Adding to the surreal situation, the containers gave the car park the feeling of a port, but here he was at the back of a hospital surrounded by dead bodies. *Let's get this over with*, he thought. The attendant checked the container number and mimed putting a hand over his mouth. He pulled up his own mask but it could have had little effect. The smell struck him like a punch in the throat and James began to cough. The sickly sweet stench was enough to overwhelm the chemical smell of antiseptic. The man opened just one container door and they were confronted by adjustable shelving of the kind that might be seen in any warehouse. The shelving was arranged in three rows with the bodies lying end on to the doorway. The attendant beckoned James forward and reluctantly he stepped into the dark interior. There were no lights and they were reliant on the young man's flashlight. Fortunately, his organisational skills were such that he was able to lead James straight to a shelf in the middle rank where a grey body bag lay.

By now James had the tail of his shirt over his nose in a futile attempt to keep the smell at bay. James gestured to the bag on his back. "I need to show my colleagues that it is Raphael, they knew him much better than I did, so I just need a photo." He half-expected an argument but the young man shrugged. Clearly, this request was not the strangest he had heard.

"Can you open the bag for me?" He didn't trust himself to do it, and the gag reflex was strong within him.

The man stepped forward and unzipped it, peeling back the plastic so that James could see more clearly. He had seen one of Jessica's photos of Raphael with his sister, but now it was impossible for him to say with certainty that this was the same boy. The keen-eyed look in the earlier photo had been taken into the shade and now the black skin had turned an awful grey. The boy's eyes were closed and for all the world he looked as though he was asleep. It was a broad face with high cheekbones and a strong chin. There were no discernable marks to help identify him or to indicate how he had died, and James drew the line at asking to see his wound. He levelled his camera and took a few profile photos in the half-darkness, the flash working automatically. James checked the screen; there was a flare of light on the otherwise dull skin and for a moment he struggled to get a workable image. Finally, satisfied with his grim handiwork, and feeling more awkward than he had ever felt before at his intrusion into the boy's temporary resting place he stepped out of the container eager to be away from the smell and this ghastly scene.

"Thank you. On behalf of all his friends, thank you for letting me check that it is him," said James.

The young man inclined his head to one side. "It is sad," he said. "He was very young. This death happen too much."

He raised a hand and James reiterated his thanks before turning away and leaving as quickly as decently possible. Only Jessica would be able to identify the boy for sure, and he knew this could be very upsetting.

******

He waited until she had settled in the taxi and then James had to ask. "How was it?"

Jessica grunted and stared straight ahead as they drove back from the airport through Goma's suburbs to his hotel. James thought better of pressing her but in a few minutes she stirred and turned to him. Tears filled her eyes and she wiped them away hurriedly with the back of her hand. "You know sometimes you build fears up in your mind before you confront them and then things turn out better? Well, it wasn't like that."

James said nothing. She was not in a mood to be consoled and just looked straight ahead or out of the side window. The sun was dropping quickly and soon it would be too dark to make out her expression, but for now the agony was writ large across her face. He wanted to make her worries and self-loathing go away but this would take a long time and for now she wouldn't let him try, so instead he dealt with the taxi driver. When they reached his room, he gave her a towel, suggested the hottest shower the system could offer and went in search of strong drink for them both.

He ordered a beer for himself in the bar to give her some space and allow himself some thinking time, and after thirty minutes he headed back to the room clutching a fistful of miniatures for which the barman had stung him an extortionate price in dollars. They were probably knock-offs from the hotel minibars – certainly his own fridge was broken and empty – but the expensive armful of small bottles would be good value if they helped Jessica start to unwind and begin to deal with the last two days.

When he returned to the room, she was sitting on the bed wrapped in a towel. There was light from the bathroom and it was all he needed to open the first few bottles. He didn't ask her if she wanted it, just handed her the largest brandy she'd ever seen and told her to down it. For once she did as she was told.

"You asked me earlier how it was …"

"You don't have to talk about it."

She ignored that, now needing to share her thoughts. "It was hellish." She took a breath that sounded like a gasp. "The Audoussets blame me for everything. They said I had lured Raphael away to get a good story. I explained it wasn't like that. They wouldn't let me near Keisha, no surprise; said I'd already damaged her enough. In fact, they wouldn't let me in the building. At least I'd had the sense to keep the taxibike I went up on, I always knew I wouldn't be staying long, but it was long enough for them to tell me what a miserably selfish human being I am."

"Come on, you don't believe that any more than I do. You were trying to help him find his family, for Heaven's sake. How bad can that be?"

"You didn't hear them. They laid into me for being a liar – I had told them I wouldn't interfere and I did, so they got that much right. They said I was using him to boost my career, and maybe there's some truth in that too."

"Bollocks! You can't beat yourself up about this, Jessica. You tried to help both children and it didn't work out – not for Raphael when he came to Goma, not for you, not for the aid agencies, not for anyone. It's harsh but it's the kind of shitty thing that happens in a war. We all wish there'd been a happy ending for both of them; this isn't Hollywood, life's just not like that."

She didn't look remotely convinced and he had the sense to know it would take her a very long time to forgive herself, if she ever did. He thought better of trying to offer her advice and shut up for a while, instead he poured another drink and told her to get into bed. James sat in the only chair as she pulled the sheet protectively around herself and stared at the ceiling. There was silence between them but now it seemed more peaceful, and when he looked at her again Jessica's eyes were closed and her breathing even.

James finished his drink and thought about everything that she had told him of an astonishing young man who had worked so courageously to put the pieces of his family back together again. There must be plenty about Raphael that only his sister would ever know; somehow the boy had brought Keisha to safety and ensured that there were people around her who would look after her.

Then he looked at the woman sleeping in his bed and silently wished that one day she might be kinder to herself for trying to help them.

******

She woke him in the middle of the night when she gently lifted his good arm and pulled it around her. He stirred. "Sorry," Jessica whispered, "I didn't mean to wake you. I felt safer knowing you were there."

He mumbled something and pulled her close to him. Her warmth felt good and she smelled of shampoo.

"I know one thing, for sure," she said.

"What's that?" he said sleepily.

"I want to nail the bastards who did this to Raphael, to both of them. I mean the people who want to keep this conflict going and the ones who still profit from it. People like your father, James, your blood father." She was whispering the words in the darkness but there was venom in her tone. "I can never make amends to Keisha, I know that, but now I've got the news to Taweza there is something else I can do."

He was more awake now and looked at his phone, it was after three and pitch black outside. "What's your plan?"

"See that those sick bastards responsible for his death and for all the misery that led to it are exposed. I may not be able to bring them to justice, but I can let the world know what they did, what they do. That's one way I *can* help. And perhaps I can make it harder for them to do business here."

"I understand. Just remember you're not a police force and this isn't New York. I don't know much about it, but if it's as lucrative as you say then these people will have a lot of protection." She stiffened, guessing that he was not going to support her, but he carried on. "We may be related but you know I'm no fan of Axel Terberg or the government here. All I'm saying is some of these people have got a lot to lose and, as I found out, when they feel threatened they try to silence you. I'm not trying to scare you, I just want to be honest with you, tell you how I see it." He fell silent. Either she wasn't listening, or he was beginning to see how stubborn she could be.

"Anyway, he may be a shit in business, but at least Axel warned me to get out of Goma and forty-eight hours later we're still here. Like I said, I don't think he's a bull-shitter so if he's right we've outstayed our welcome. And I know what happens when you get on the wrong side of some people here so I'm happy to go right now. If the border was open this minute, I'd cross it tonight but it doesn't open till six in the morning. I plan to be at the Rwandan border at six and to get the hell out of here. Are you coming this time?"

It sounded harsher than he had meant, and he hoped that in the darkness she could hear that he was smiling. There was nothing he could do to make her leave with him.

"That's the problem," she said and he groaned inwardly. "If you're crossing to Rwanda, I can't go with you, I have things I need to find out in Kinshasa. I need to interview the leadership there, the President if I can get to him. Find out what he knows and what he's doing to end the fighting. If I leave now, they may not let me back in again. I'm serious about exposing these people, and I've always been taught to follow the money. In DRC the money either drives over the border into Rwanda in truckloads of minerals or I believe the money will be with the power brokers in Kinshasa. While I've got the chance that's where I've got to go."

"If he walked in now, I'd happily kill him for what he and his side-kicks are doing to people here. And he's only part of the supply chain. From what I've learned there's tons of conflict minerals being smuggled out illegally and winding up in Europe. The UN and national governments seem to know who's behind it but nothing happens to them. They're not arrested, or imprisoned, even though they're flouting national laws in Europe and the US, as well breaking UN sanctions.

"I want to know how big this trade is, and shine a light on it. See if I can close them down. I want Terberg and his people to go down for a long time for what he's done. I don't care who they are, or how they're connected. They have to pay the price for the way they're raping this country."

She was silent for a long time before adding, "It's not that I don't want to come with you James, I do. You gotta understand I have to do this. I'm gonna go west to see who's pulling the strings in the capital – after what you've been through I'll understand if you're headed the other way. I don't know how long this will take me, but we could always meet up afterwards."

He said nothing for a while. A future reunion sounded very uncertain, and not for the first time James felt himself torn in different directions. His head was telling him to get the hell out of here, by the shortest route. Axel had been very specific, they'd be looking out for him in Kinshasa.

He'd always had a reckless streak. Now James was sure he must be mad, too, but he had one idea that might help them. He kissed her neck, "You don't make things easy, do you?"

It was still dark when they checked out of the hotel and, after a search, the hotel driver was pulled sleepily from his bed and met them in his minivan by the front door.

Early in the afternoon a dusty white car pulled up at the same hotel and the driver went into Reception. He had done this many times already and showed little urgency, he was getting fed up with his boss just sitting in the front smoking. Less than a minute later, however, he sprinted out and Gahiji began to sit up straight in the front seat.

"It's them, boss, they were here!" Gahiji disliked looking at his new recruit but this time he made an exception. He had asked for more help and this was what the general had foisted on him. The man was long of limb and short of teeth. Although there was no single offending feature, the mouth was almost impossibly wide and his face had a dishevelled look as though Le Bon Dieu had been called away while assembling his countenance. The result was undeniably ugly, which was annoying and distracting when trying to listen to his reports.

Gahiji dragged his thoughts away from the dental wreckage confronting him, and back to what had been said. "So, they've checked out?"

"Yes, sir. Left this morning. But I know where they've gone. The hotel's driver took them to the airport. No one knows where they were headed after that but we've found 'em."

"Shut up and drive. We haven't got them yet, but we are closing in on the bastards. And when I do find them they're going to wish they'd never bloody heard of the Congo."

Of all people, it was the night porter doubling as hotel receptionist who had helped them on their way. Long before his colleagues arrived for the day shift, Lambert had begun to prove helpful. Of course, it was too late or early to buy a ticket, but the porter knew someone who could help him if James could pay in cash. He did. In that case, Lambert would see what he could do, make a few calls, and wake someone up. So while Jessica slept James had tipped Lambert well to get the help of whatever protocol was available at Goma airport. Goma being Goma there wasn't much call for protocols – or perhaps Lambert didn't know one. Either way, it was still dark when a scooter arrived from someone called Jeffery, leading James and Jessica's driver to an office at the side of the airport where they met the man himself. Jeffery smiled and stroked his moustache as he brought them the bad news that there were no passenger flights today. James' heart sank. In fact, there were no scheduled flights this week. Ambiguously, however, Jeffery said he would see what he could do. It was one of those African ambiguities; was there a flight or wasn't there? Sometimes it depended on how much you wanted one.

James spun Jeffery a story of how his girlfriend was sick, and they needed to get a plane back to Kinshasa as soon as possible. The man smiled and nodded but there was no knowing if any of it made a difference. With no flights out they were left sitting at the airport, contemplating going back to the hotel. Neither of them spoke much. He had deliberately ignored Axel's warning, and being in the airport reminded him forcibly of what he had escaped so recently nearby. If Axel was right, every day's delay made it more likely that they would be discovered by the men who had been holding him.

Jeffery's irrepressible good humour and seemingly unfounded optimism was wearing thin on the couple and they had been on the point of returning to the hotel when news came that there might be a flight after all. There was an air cargo route being operated for the UN by a local company with a take-off scheduled at lunchtime. Jeffery was making enquiries to see if there were any seats available, and within an hour he confirmed that his friends at Compagnie Congolaise d'Aviation would be pleased to transport them. There were no direct flights to Kinshasa but a cargo plane with eight seats would be able to fly them first to Lodja, roughly halfway to Kinshasa, and then take them onwards the next day to the capital. Jeffery had agreed a price on their behalf; most assuredly they would not get it cheaper, he said. Neither of them was in the mood for haggling which seemed to disappoint their travel agent, they just wanted out.

Around ten in the morning the pair were driven in a delivery van to one of the cargo sheds. On an internal flight like this there were no formalities, and the men at Passport Control were unaware of their existence. So Gahiji's man had nothing to report when his boss arrived at the airport after lunch, two hours after the flight to Lodja had taken off.

Gahiji had imagined that having men on the ground at the airport would now make it easy to catch them. He had been just a few hours behind the spies at the hotel; if it was true they were heading to the airport he knew that days went by without any passenger flights. The man in the terminal had been told to watch out for a young couple, one white one black, trying to fly out of Goma, but Gahiji's excitement began to slip when he reported back that no one matching their description had come through. Either the night porter had been lying in which case he would pay dearly for it, or the spies were taking another route out of Goma. Yet again Gahiji thought through all the road, sea and air alternatives, wondering if he had overlooked an escape route. He could not allow the spies to get away. General Businga's future was riding on their capture and he would be merciless to anyone who failed him.

Gahiji had already called the general to ask for more manpower from the Police or Military Intelligence, or even the President's own Garde Républicaine to catch these spies. The conversation had not gone well, relations had been bad before but now the two men had hit a new low point in their dealings. Businga had called him every name under the sun, saying he was lazy and incompetent, before he eventually calmed down enough to say that the spies were being helped by someone in the security services and until they knew how far the corruption had spread there would be no more assistance. So, no, he would not be permitted to call in outside help without the general's specific prior approval.

When the call had ended, Gahiji had sat down for a smoke and wondered why this manhunt was being led by General Businga. Everyone knew he had the ear of the President, and there were many stories of his bravery as a soldier. For all he knew, they might even be true. But why the hell was the Chief of Staff in the Ministry of Mines, a retired general, in charge of catching spies? It was clear there was a lot at stake for Businga, and Gahiji guessed there was a lot he wasn't being told, and that made him cautious. He couldn't tell if the general was more concerned about what the spies might be carrying, what they knew or who they were going to meet. As far as he could see, he was the only one doing any investigating and this could only make him vulnerable if Businga ever chose to deny his own role in this whole debacle. Gahiji wasn't bothered about the law, he could deal with policemen and lawyers all day, just as long as he had some protection at a political level if the shit hit the fan.

******

As he waited, James wondered again what the hell he was doing here. He'd been warned yesterday by his blood father, a man who knew Congo better than any outsider he could think of, that a heavy hitter held him personally responsible for his son's death. The man had access to government resources and Lord only knew what criminal back-up. There was said to be a high price on James's head. He'd already been kidnapped once, tortured for information he didn't have, and held in a makeshift prison barely half a mile from where was now standing. He'd escaped, evaded recapture through the UN's intervention, and now their main force had left town. If James got into trouble again, there would be no one to save his sorry pink skin this time, he knew that. Axel had gone, the UN forces had much greater concerns than his safety, and neither the police nor the army could be trusted. He was sure that even the charity he'd worked for would now wash their hands of him, he was a risk to their entire future here.

All told, James couldn't leave Goma soon enough.

Chapter 27
N'djili Airport, Kinshasa, DRC
Two Days Ago

The targets had been lucky once but Gahiji was wise to it now. Somehow James Falkus and Jessica Tsiba had managed to stay one step ahead of him in Goma. He had been forced to spread his men thinly by trying to watch all exits and they had lost precious time searching the hotels and guest houses. With hindsight, Gahiji knew he should have put more people on the airport but it was pointless to dwell on that now. General Businga had been calling him several times a day for the last week, demanding updates and threatening painful consequences for Gahiji and his men if they failed him – but whatever the consequences for him personally the former army officer knew that the price of failure for the general would be far more spectacular. He was a powerful man and he usually got what he wanted, it would be safer to keep it that way.

Gahiji himself had initiated the last call and in it he had made a few more demands of his own. He had laid down clearly that it was lack of manpower – manpower he had specifically requested and been denied – that enabled Falkus and the journalist to escape to Lodja. That had gone down badly with the General who wasn't used to people answering him back, but Gahiji knew from experience with the son that craven submission was more likely to lead to disaster than planning and initiative. If he was to save his position, even his skin – and that was certainly in the balance now – he would have to get the people he needed and deploy them effectively. He would deal with the Goma end of things first and then follow the targets' trail to Kinshasa – if that was indeed where they were going. It was up to the general to handle the Kinshasa end, at least until Gahiji could get there. If the general couldn't get people on the ground in Lodja quickly enough, and that looked unlikely, then Gahiji stressed to his boss that an experienced and discreet welcoming committee in Kinshasa would be the obvious alternative.

So it was that six middle-aged men in civilian clothes arrived at N'djili Airport and took up a position hanging around outside, smoking and talking in the late morning heat. The former members of Businga's regiment had been told little in their briefing; they understood they were there at the orders of the Ministry of Transport to support the airport police. It seemed strange to them that the airport police knew nothing about them, and had even tried to enforce N'djili's strict airport regulations preventing people waiting for friends and family in the Arrivals Hall or anywhere near the door. A young policeman had told them to leave the hall and keep away from the doors, whereupon he found himself surrounded by six large and unintimidated men who told him to piss off home to Mama. Any thoughts the policeman may have had about taking the matter further vanished when two of the smartly dressed men suddenly drew handguns with practised ease and advised him that they were here from the government and that he should keep on walking. "While you still can," volunteered a third man and there were guffaws of laughter from the group. The young policeman was no fool, and he'd always felt that the No Loitering rule was pointless in an airport anyway, so he continued his patrol until he could safely disappear for a smoke and a reviving coffee. To be honest, he could have done with something stronger.

A few minutes later the group's leader sent three men round to the Cargo Gate to watch for passenger arrivals, where within ten minutes they too ran into trouble with the gate police officer for standing on the grass, another strict rule at the airport. If they hadn't all been wearing matching Ray Bans, the gatekeeper might have read in their eyes that they were in no mood to be messed around. As it was, a few harsh words were exchanged and one of them punched the policeman in the kidneys to confirm that they had no intention of obeying such a pitiable regulation. Frankly, they said, this wasn't the kind of police co-operation they'd been expecting, but privately they put it down to the higher-ups not telling the cops on the beat that the General's A-Team had been re-assembled to catch two spies. It made them feel important that only the most senior airport police were authorised to know they were here – after all, weren't these things always dealt with on a need-to-know basis?

Their former NCO had clear instructions. Watch for the arrival around midday of a plane in the green and white livery of Compagnie Congolaise D'Aviation. There would be only one plane like it, a twin-engined plane arriving from Lodja in Sankuru District. Two foreigners would be on it, and they were to be arrested immediately, with whatever force was necessary. Further instructions would follow as soon as they had been detained.

******

By two o'clock in the afternoon the men watching the Cargo gate were hot, hungry, thirsty and irritable. There had been little traffic coming out and they had become so bored that they were searching vehicles going in, just for something to do. Woe betide any foreign spies they apprehended now, they said, they might just take matters into their own hands for a bit before handing over what was left to their former general.

At the same time Gahiji was sitting in a military plane heading to N'djili and wondering why he had heard nothing from General Businga before he left. He knew Businga would have called if his men had picked up the couple; he would have to ring the boss as soon as they landed to find out what was happening.

The drone of the twin propellers in the Congo Air Force's only serviceable Antonov 26 was enough to send Gahiji to sleep, and he was glad of the battered headphones he had been handed by one of the crew as he boarded. They were broken and no use for communicating but they still did a good job of noise reduction. He had been running around for days in pursuit of these bastards and he was physically and mentally exhausted; like all soldiers he knew that sleep and food were commodities you took where you could get, so at the earliest opportunity he had closed his eyes and slept. He came awake fast though when the co-pilot tapped his shoulder.

"We'll be in N'dolo in around thirty minutes," he shouted over the engine noise. The sound-proofing in the Russian-made workhorse was not what you'd associate with passenger travel, but then it didn't often carry passengers. The crew had known instantly when they were diverted from normal duties that this passenger had some heavyweight friends in high places. "It's almost fourteen-thirty," said the co-pilot. "I've been told to say there'll be a car and driver waiting on the apron for you."

Gahiji nodded in acknowledgement and was just closing his eyes again when the truth hit him. He sat bolt upright, unsnapped his safety belt and strode after the pilot, grabbing the startled flyer's shoulder and spinning him around. "We're landing at N'dolo, the military field, right?"

The pilot looked at him as though he was soft in the head. "Yeah ...," he began.

"And cargo traffic, charter flights for Kinshasa, where do they land?"

"The same. N'dolo."

"Ah, shit! I've got a bad feeling about this." He thought for a second before continuing. "OK, I need you to call the ground in Kinshasa. Now, right now. Get hold of someone there you trust, and tell them to call this number," and he handed over the General's business card he had been carrying, that gave his private line and mobile number. "They can explain why they are calling and remind him, ever so politely, that most charter flights land at N'dolo. Our friends cannot be met at N'djili. Have you got that?"

For a second the co-pilot studied Businga's business card with a mixture of awe and distaste. "Sure, charter flights to N'dolo. Friends can't be met at N'djili. Anything else?"

"No, that's it. Well, what the hell are you staring at? Make the bleeding call."

The man pulled himself upright and snapped out a crisp salute before hurrying back to the cockpit.

"Jesus," said Gahiji to no one in particular, "why do I have to think of everything?" And he sat down in a dangerously brooding mood.

******

At about the same time, the twin-engined Fokker 50 of Compagnie Congolese D'Aviation was taxiing in to its base at N'dolo airport. The charter airport was less-frequented than the international airfield at N'djili and the two Russian pilots neither saw nor expected much activity on the apron. Someone in orange high viz was waiting to guide them in to their stand, and behind him stood a fireman who must have been sweltering in his yellow helmet and heavy black jacket. Over to their right a soldier leaned against a passenger van that was painted in olive-drab. The pilots were both ex-forces and exchanged a joke about the trouble he was going to be in for failing to park his van in the shade. Some officer was going to have a very hot ride into Kinshasa.

"Don't forget we've got passengers of our own to let off," said the captain. The first officer heaved a sigh and levered himself out of his seat. The couple in the back had gathered their belongings and were making their way forward.

"Was OK flight for you?" asked the Russian. Like most pilots in the region he spoke reasonably good English. "Hold on, I let you off. You have someone meet you?"

The white guy muttered something that sounded very like, "I hope not."

Then the woman spoke, "Do you know where we can get a taxi?"

The Russian exhaled slowly. "Not easy here. Not airport for many passengers. You ask in office -- if they open." He pushed back the door and a blast of hot, humid air took their breath away. "Over there," he pointed to the aircraft's port side, "office there."

The couple thanked him and walked down the steps. After the refreshingly cool air during the flight, the heat on the concrete apron hit them like a blast from an open oven. It was momentarily disorientating and then they hoisted up their backpacks and headed towards the office door, only to find that it was locked. There was no sign of life inside and nobody came to answer their repeated knocks and shouts. James wandered around both sides of the building but it was backed by a massive, locked hangar with no side doors and this looked to be the best way in. There was a concrete balcony above them that provided some shade, and when they stepped back it appeared other offices led off the balcony but the building and the apron were deserted now that the aircraft had landed.

An army van was parked a hundred metres away but there was no one in it. James tried and failed to get a signal on his mobile. There was nothing for it but to sit down and wait for someone to open the office, then maybe they could call a taxi.

When he next looked up, he found Jessica staring at him. There wasn't much warmth in it. She held his gaze and for a moment neither of them said anything until he broke the silence. "What is it?"

She shook her head for a moment, looked down and then lifted her eyes again. "I don't get you."

"How d'you mean?"

"Doesn't any of this reach you? I mean doesn't any of this actually touch you, upset you?"

He shrugged, unable to put into a few words what had been happening to him, to both of them for days and weeks.

"James, you've found a father after thirty years, more or less, and it seems like you've lost him again – all in a few days. You've been kidnapped, tortured and shot at. I've witnessed the death of a group of miners, nearly been raped, watched a boy die in the dirt in front of me. I've met the sweetest kids, tried to help them and failed them badly. Now one of them is lying dead in Goma, too, with no one to collect his body and a little sister who has just lost everything even if she doesn't know it yet. You know all of this, too, and you just sit there with that faraway expression, like you're waiting for a bus."

"I am. Kind of."

"Dammit, don't piss me about. Why do you Brits always try to turn everything into a goddam joke? What is this, the classic British reserve? Is it some half-assed coping mechanism? Is this the stiff upper lip we read about? Cos if it is, man it really sucks! You're an OK guy but sometimes reality seems to be rushing past and you don't even notice it. I don't get it, why is that? You're not self-obsessed, you're not lacking in empathy, and you clearly have feelings. Is it a guy thing? A British thing? What's the matter with you? Tell me. I wanna know."

The pause that followed was so long it seemed he wasn't going to reply. James didn't look at her for a while; he leaned back against the wall, breathed deep and stared across the airport apron. "You seem to think that everyone should react in the way you do."

"And how is that?"

"Emotional. Dramatic. Making snap decisions, like going up to the mine when you were told not to by someone who should know, like helping those two kids – again when you were told not to."

"There's nothing wrong with that, at least I react, at least I'm in touch with my feelings."

"Maybe that's an American thing, a girl thing." She sucked in a breath but he continued, "Anyway, what makes you think I'm not in touch with mine?"

"So you think I shouldn't have helped those kids, I should have just left them. I shouldn't have gone to Bisie mine to find out who's running it, how it is and what they're doing to people there."

"I didn't say that, did I? But sometimes there's more than one way of reacting to events. In each case you've chosen one response, don't imagine it's automatically better than the alternatives. You said it yourself, you haven't helped Raphael or Keisha, one's dead and the other's now totally alone. Not your fault, of course, but you haven't helped. You couldn't help the people at the mine; they'll still be there in a year's time however well you write about it."

"You don't know that."

James ignored her. "No, I don't wear my heart on my sleeve – is that such a bad thing? You do, and that's one of the things I like about you. Don't beat me up for doing things differently."

"I'm not, James. I'm just trying to understand you. You don't think much of the power of the pen then? Or is it just my pen?"

"For God's sake, don't be so defensive. That's not like you. I've already told you you're a good writer, and you know you are. But you asked me to justify my reactions to everything that's been going on, and I'm saying there's more than one way of dealing with what we're facing. Besides, I never met Raphael, I never met Keisha. And I didn't see what you saw in Bisie so my outlook on this whole bloody mess is bound to be different from yours." He fell silent again and put on the shades that had been resting on his head before staring again at the planes parked across the apron.

Jessica couldn't leave it at that. "What's the matter with you, why can't you get fucking angry? I sure am. Don't you wanna get mad? Throw something? Beat up the bad guys?"

"Shit, Jessica, this isn't some movie. It's not that easy, where the hero roars into town in his Aston Martin, hunting them down, one by one. What do you think this is? No, let me tell you what this is, this is raw politics. Not the nice kind where people turn out to vote in the village hall. It's the kind where people all over the world pull their kids in off the street and lock the doors. The kind where people – good people – get hurt and worse, and where the only people who do well out of it are the people you really don't want governing the place. The bullies, the vicious, the greedy, the venal…" He tailed off.

She stared at him for a moment. "So there is some anger in you, after all."

"No shit, Sherlock. Course, there's anger in me. But I won't waste it where there's nothing to use it on. Maybe I am cold about it, it's my training. As a child, I couldn't do a damn thing about the bad things that happened to me and my brother. And my dad. I couldn't stop my parents fighting and separating, believe me I tried. I couldn't do a bloody thing about my mother never being there, not caring about us when she was, about her taking my father for a fool – which he wasn't. I was just a kid, and children were seen and not heard. Nobody asked my opinion about what was happening, the rows, the acid remarks that gnawed away at our family, the way Neil and I didn't seem to matter much. That made me angry, angry like you've no idea. But there was damn all I could do about it. So I channelled my anger into things I could influence."

"Like what?" asked Jessica.

He said nothing. She was about to ask again, when he shifted and spoke. "Bullies for one thing. There were two at school, I can picture them now. In hindsight they weren't much but they knew the ropes, knew the rules, and I was a new kid. Small, too, doesn't seem likely now, does it? It was the usual stuff: round-the-clock intimidation, a bit of low-grade violence, damage to my things, and some theft for good measure. I don't know why they did it or why they chose me, except I was at a boarding school miles from home and alone 'cos my big brother Neil was at another school. There was nothing to stop them, certainly the staff were too stupid to notice or to care and the seniors probably thought it was character building. Finally, one day I'd had enough. There was only one of them in my dormitory and I'd never really fought back so he was taken by surprise. He'd been having a go at me the day before, then it all started again in the morning and I couldn't face another day of it. He walked past my bed and was giving me grief again.

"In those days some schools still taught boxing and I'd listened hard to the ex-Army instructor telling us how to punch so we didn't break our hands. I knew, too, that if I hit him in the face it would show and he'd end up getting the teachers' sympathy. So I caught him with a right hook to the solar plexus, top of the stomach just as he turned towards me. I wasn't strong but he kind of walked into it which added to the impact. It was the only time I had ever punched anyone outside the ring. Anyway, he went down like a sack of potatoes. He was only winded but it left him gasping for what seemed like ages and everyone was in shock. I was the kid who never fought back; he was the one who didn't have to fight much because everyone was scared of him. It took him so long to get up I thought I'd killed him. Mind you, the punch felt good. Really good." James smiled at the recollection. "Well, that was the last day I was bullied by either of them and for a while people walked around me in case I was going to hit them too, at least until they saw I hadn't suddenly become an axe murderer. It sounds a bit prosaic now but it taught me to channel my anger, to use it when I have something to use it on."

They had been teetering on the edge of a full-blown row, tiredness prodding them towards a bad outcome. Jessica had felt James was bottling up his emotions but now she had glimpsed more of the man beneath. OK, most of the time she had no idea what he was thinking and that bugged the hell out of her. *But maybe,* she thought, *they would connect better if he could let go a bit more often.* She knew it was typical of her; she always worried away at problems like a terrier, confronting them full on whatever the size, never letting them go even when it would be better to do so. As a child, she had tried to grapple with problems alone and wrestle them into submission and she guessed that would never change. She may have been sporty but Jessica had always been a lousy team player, which was OK when there was no one else to rely on – in her line of work that was most of the time. It was not so good when the problems were as huge and intractable as the ones crowding in on them now.

This difference between them was affecting her, and deep down she feared it made them incompatible. They were just too different. It was an itch she wanted to keep on scratching, but this time she was deflected by their other problems.

"You say there's more than one way of dealing with what we're facing. What the hell are we facing?"

"Good question," said James. In the exasperating silence that followed Jessica was close again to losing her temper with him, but then he spoke. "I didn't just come here to learn to be a photographer; I came out here to see if there was anything more I could find out about my father, my natural father. I sure as hell wasn't expecting to find him, I know now I wasn't ready for it. And I wasn't ready for him to be up to his oxters in conflict minerals."

"Oxters? What are you talking about?"

"It's an old Scots expression. Armpits, it means armpits."

"Well, in the circumstances can we stick to English as that's something we do have in common?" It came out harsher than she meant, but too bad.

"We're facing a former general who's well connected in the Government and thinks I'm a threat because I took some photos of his now-dead son meeting a rebel group. And as a government adviser I guess the photos could be dangerous for him."

"Are you a threat to him?"

"No," he said forcibly. "At least, I wasn't before. But now that his son's imprisoned me, now that Businga's sent his men to try and kill me, now that the father seems to have taken up where the son left off, I'd be happy to become a threat."

"You don't mean that."

"As it happens, I do. Like I said, I won't waste my anger where there's no focus for it. But Businga …, well he's my focus."

"If the general wasn't in the photos, why is he chasing you? I mean, us?"

"I'm guessing that if the news got out it would damage the family's reputation so badly he'd lose his position in the government, his power and money, or all three."

Jessica shook her head. "That's not how they roll here. You don't just get demoted, slapped on the wrist and sent home early from school. You cross the

President and it's Goodnight Vienna. Which is why the general's been keen to shut you up and destroy the evidence. The way he sees it, it's him or us."

"True. He'll keep trying to stop us getting out of the country. He still wants to kill us."

"Which brings us back to the present. Where are we going and how are we gonna get there?"

They were still sitting there after thirty minutes when two dusty motor bikes pulled up beside them. "No luck with taxis." It was a statement of fact from the Russian pilot more than a question.

"We can't even find a phone, and I can't get a mobile signal here," James shrugged.

"You want a lift? We take you to Kin. Or you sit here a long time." He grinned at Jessica; it was obvious who he was offering to carry.

She stood up. "Sure. Can you get us to the ferry port?"

"No problem. You in a hurry? Traffic is always bad," and he slid his flight bag around to make room for her so that it rested on the trail bike's tank.

Jessica swung her own pack onto her back and turned to look at James, who was already swinging a leg over the second dirty Yamaha. "No big rush." James noticed a wink from the pilot to his friend as Jessica put one arm around his waist to steady herself. James double-tapped the co-pilot's shoulder to show that he was ready and there was a rasp as both the big single cylinder engines were revved and his bike drew alongside the first.

It may have been the noise of the bikes that brought him out of the shade. The army driver scratched his groin and watched them idly as he ambled back to his vehicle.

The riders glanced at one another, nodded to indicate they were ready and the bikes revved loudly again before pulling away down the access road, the engine noise reverberating as they passed between the aircraft hangars. If anyone was on duty at the gate, they never showed their faces and the four of them swept around the barrier and out of the main gate into the dense afternoon traffic.

As the sound of the Yamahas died away, the army driver could hear a continuous squawk from the radio in his van. His languid response met with a volley of abuse from someone at the other end demanding to know what the hell he had been doing. It wasn't the usual controller, in fact it didn't sound like it was coming from the despatch office at all. He could hear a persistent droning noise in the background that made it hard to catch everything that was said. Could he see two foreigners, a white man and a black woman anywhere nearby? They were dangerous criminals and he was now under new orders to get some police help on the base and detain them. Now, could he see anyone who matched their description?

The driver's confusion at this unexpected order began to give way to a feeling of excitement. Criminals? Dangerous criminals? What the hell was this about? And who was this giving him orders anyway?

He began to suspect he was on the end of a practical joke. A smile spread across his face. "Who is this?" he asked. "Is this Control?"

"I am Major Gahiji of the Republican Guard. And don't you ever question me again, soldier or you'll be shining boots for the next five years. Got that? Now tell me what you can see. Over."

"There's no one here," he said, and there it might have ended peacefully if a disarmingly honest streak in him hadn't led him to add, "Not now. Over." The squawk of static punctuated the call.

"What d'you mean 'not now'? Were they there before? Over."

"Erm, I don't know if it was them exactly, but a white man and a black woman were here but they just left. Over."

"Tell me exactly what you saw. And it's 'Sir' when you're addressing a senior officer. Don't they fucking train you in the army these days? Over."

The driver stood bolt upright as if to salute the angry, disembodied voice. Though why the officer was angry with him was one of a growing number of mysteries. "Sir. Yes, sir. Over."

"What did you see, soldier? Over."

"Well, at first there was no one around, I was just waiting for my passengers …," he began.

"That's us you idiot. What happened? Over."

If you shut up, I'll tell you, the driver thought. But what he said was, "A plane landed. It was the wrong kind; I knew it wasn't yours, sir. Two passengers got out followed by two pilots. I guess the passengers fit the description you gave. Sir. Well, they tried to get into one of the offices but it was locked. In the end they sat down. I went to take a … to relieve myself. When I came back, they were getting onto two bikes. Over."

"Bikes? Over."

"Motorbikes. Big ones, driven by the pilots, sir. Over."

"Jeez. That's them. Get back in your car and go after them. Now. That's an order. Do it now." The droning noise in the background made the officer hard to hear over the static. "What's your name, soldier? Over."

"Ghonda, sir. Augustin Ghonda. Over." He climbed back into his army van and started the engine.

"Well, Ghonda. As an officer in the Republican Guard, this is a national emergency and I'm ordering you to do whatever it takes to catch up with them and arrest them all. Including the bike riders, but above all I want their passengers. Whatever it takes! Got that? Over."

"Yes sir," he grinned and swung his vehicle around with a satisfying squeal of tyres. He was just a private in the army, this kind of shit didn't happen to soldiers like him, it only happened in the movies. And he certainly wasn't ordered to drive fast. "Thank you, sir! Over."

Ten miles from the airport and at fifteen hundred metres a momentarily puzzled former major, two years ago retired from the elite Republican Guard, the best-equipped soldiers in the entire republic, looked quizzical as these words came through on the flight deck. He smiled at the evident excitement in the young man's voice. "I'll be a few kilometres behind you, Ghonda. But I'm coming and I'm coming with back-up. Right now, this is all down to you. Are you armed? Over."

"No, sir. Over." He sensed the disappointment in the soldier's reply.

"Then find a cop who is and get after them. I'm counting on you, soldier. Over."

"I'm on my way, sir. Over." In the background Gahiji was sure he heard the squeal of tyres. Maybe this wasn't all finished just yet.

******

The green van screeched to a halt at the airfield gatehouse. Ghonda knew he had only moments in which to find someone and persuade them to do what he told them. He pulled the peak of his cap down, pushed the shades that had been sitting on his dashboard onto his face and strode through the door emulating the swagger of his own officers. Two blue-uniformed policemen were lounging in chairs that were tipped back into a restful pose where neither could be seen from the road.

"You and you. Attention." He kicked the leg of the nearest chair and it went over backwards taking its occupant crashing down with it amid oaths and expletives. He certainly had their attention. "You two are in deep shit. You've just slept at your posts while two criminals drove out of the gate on motorbikes, and you didn't even see them. Did you?"

"No, sir," the younger one spoke nervously. "I mean, yes I heard them shout to each other, they were going south on Lumumba. There's been an accident northbound."

"Good, that's the first useful thing you've done. Well there's an army force coming after them," he declined to elaborate, mainly because he had no idea what that force might be. "If you don't want to be on traffic duty for the rest of your lives, you have one chance to set things right. You," and he gestured at the older of the two, "Put the barrier down behind us as we leave and start doing your bloody job checking the vehicles coming in and out. There will be a Major Gahiji of the Republican Guard landing here in a few minutes. By that time I want you to have found him a new car and a driver. I have to go after the criminals, and I'm taking you with me," and he pointed unwaveringly at the younger man. Ghonda was beginning to think that one day he'd make a bloody brilliant officer.

He looked both policemen up and down, before turning his gaze to the younger man. "Is that your gun?"

The bewildered policeman looked at the sidearm lying unattended in its holster on the desktop and he nodded, too startled to speak. Neither of the gate officers had thought to ask Augustin Ghonda who the hell he was. It was clear to them that he was used to being obeyed. "Bring it, and any spare ammunition you have."

He turned to the older man, "Do you have a gun?" The man shook his head, still dumbstruck at this unexpected interruption to their late afternoon nap. *Damn*, thought Ghonda. "Never mind. Find a car for the major and get it out to the apron. You've got less than ten minutes before he lands, then get on the gate like I told you. Maybe he will let you off with just a warning. You, follow me," and without waiting for an answer he strode out to his minivan. He wished it was a jeep, they were cool, and this was a heap of crap. He'd also have liked to have his own gun, but since he was doing the driving the gun had better stay with the policeman, at least for now.

Ghonda was both pleased and amazed to see that his sixty second *tour de force* in the gatehouse had worked. The younger cop ran out after him, fumbling to get his gun belt on before jumping into the front passenger seat. Ghonda retained the initiative, "You are in charge of the radio until we catch up with them. The major will call soon with further instructions." At least, that was his fervent hope because from here on the soldier was winging it entirely. He gunned the engine with bravado and swung the van out into the dense traffic. Ghonda barely had time to register the sound of protesting horns and harsh braking behind and beside him as he created a space for himself in the nearside lane and switched on his hazard warnings and headlights.

He had always wanted to do this. In his imagination he had had expected it to be with a Colonel or General in the back, needing to get to an urgent meeting. He had never imagined that he and his van might be called upon by the Republican Guard to assist in a national emergency. Well, they would not let the major down.

The policeman next to him pulled a face at Ghonda's driving as he thrust his way out into the faster lane through a gap that wasn't there. Then he reached behind him and put his safety belt on, gripping hold of the handle set into the roof as they pushed, bustled and bullied their way through the rush hour traffic, with Ghonda blaring his horn even more than the surrounding vehicles. He could have done with a flashing light on the roof and those two-tone sirens, but you couldn't have everything.

******

Ahead of them, the bikes had made modest progress by avoiding the static traffic and heading briefly out of town until they picked up the dual carriageway of Boulevard Sendwe. There they turned right and found that the gridlock was every bit as bad. The riders were in no particular hurry and one of them was enjoying the tight grip of a good-looking woman who was leaning close to counteract the weight of her backpack. Whenever he accelerated hard, she clung on tighter; he smiled to himself, it was just the same with Russian girls. Behind them the second bike was burdened by two large men and a larger backpack. With a higher centre of gravity the rider of the second bike had lost some of his usual manoeuvrability but this was still the best way to slice through Kin's notorious traffic and they were all enjoying their superiority over other road users.

They were running the usual gauntlet of traffic travelling the wrong way down the road margins, and they were often forced to keep to the surrounding traffic's speed, only occasionally cutting through between slow-moving trucks. A taxi driver pulled out of the inside lane in front of them – it was probably a deliberate attempt to restrict their speed to the same as his, but with local taxis it was safer to assume they never used their mirrors. The taxi driver may not even have been aware of them. After a delay they were able to wriggle past him, riders and drivers exchanging views on their respective road skills and parentage.

There was a hold-up ahead and traffic had come to a standstill. The left side of a truck could be seen over the car roofs ahead, it had overturned whether though poor loading or a collision was impossible to tell from this distance. After a few minutes without progress the Russians managed to work their bikes out of the static lines and back onto the edge of the road. Here, on the dirt space in front of concrete shops and houses, a more anarchic two-way traffic of scooters, bicycles, pedestrians and the occasional four-wheeler made its way in and out of Kinshasa's suburbs.

The bike riders needed to keep their wits about them. Scores of pedestrians threaded their way through potholes up to thirty centimetres deep, around stinking puddles, seemingly oblivious to the risks they ran in crossing the road. There were choke points where the buildings came right up to the road and here the motorcycles lost their advantage again. The forecourt of an office building jutted out across the dirt and the riders were forced to rejoin the traffic as it inched forwards. The bikes had pulled up side by side, and the riders chatted to one another in Russian.

There was noise all around them but one dogged driver behind could be heard and then seen carving his way through the logjam more effectively than anyone around him. The pilot glanced in his wing mirror; the top of a green van was visible above the cars. Unable to make progress on the road it had joined those forcing their way along the roadside until it drew level with them. The driver was in army uniform and beside him was an excitable young man in a dark uniform who was gesticulating wildly. Instead of pushing ahead the pair had come to a standstill on the roadside, leaving their hazard lights on. The passenger was the first to jump from the van and he started to dodge through the traffic directly towards the two motorcycles. He was wearing dark blue fatigues with a peaked cap and it was now easier to see that he was an armed policeman. He was shouting something, probably in Lingala and waving a gun in the air.

James was closest to him and the first to react. He slammed a hand down onto the shoulder of the rider in front of him. "Go, dammit go! Now. He's after us!" To give him his due the Russian co-pilot responded quickly, he revved the engine hard, dumped the clutch and the bike's front wheel rose off the ground momentarily making James cling on harder. The rider pushed through a gap that a second ago he'd considered a shade too narrow, but with an armed man running at him their options had changed. He squeezed between two vehicles, his hips and elbows knocking car wing mirrors askew and his knees scraping down the flanks of a taxi and a private car. They trailed shouts of anger from the drivers as the bike rider bullied his way through. First one car was passed and then another; James looked back and saw their pursuers veer to their right as they tried to keep pace with the bikes by running along the other side of a line of cars.

James swung around to see the other rider deftly twist his bike to right and left as he followed in their route. He was skilled and his bike was carrying less weight so he made short work of catching up with them, but all of them were casting nervous glances back. Looking ahead he could see their path was blocked by the back of an open topped lorry. People who were standing in the rear of the truck were now craning to get a view of the disturbance behind. The bikes' path ahead and to the left away from their pursuers was blocked, so there was nothing for it but to swing right and now the policeman had a clear view of them beside the line of cars. First one bike pulled out into view and then the second carrying the pilot and Jessica. As he looked back, James saw the policeman level his gun and nothing happened.

In his excitement he had left the gun on safety. For a split second he stared at it then realising his mistake snapped the safety off and took aim again. There was a popping sound as the first shot was fired, then there were screams from the occupants of the truck as they realised what was happening and ducked low behind the tailboard for shelter. Fleetingly, James heard a ludicrously small sound behind them that didn't resemble any shots he had ever heard in the movies. Then the wind rush and the roar of the bikes obscured any further sound. Ahead of them a gaggle of birds flapped their way up from a roadside tree. The bikes were momentarily free of the standing traffic but now in a clear line of fire from the policeman who fired three more shots in quick succession. Beside them the rear window of a white van turned opaque as it smashed into crazed fragments and a dark circle appeared at its heart.

Conscious of how exposed the rear bike was, the pilot swung his machine further to the right and headed straight for the middle of a group of umbrellas beneath which people were sitting at white plastic tables enjoying a cold drink on their way home. The noise of two motorbikes approaching at full throttle was enough to make them scatter and the bikes roared through the gap then up an incline before dashing along the pavement in front of a parade of shops.

Behind them they could still hear shouts but when James looked back he couldn't see their pursuers. There was no way that the policeman and soldier could get their van through the same gaps and on foot they were already out of sight. The Russian co-pilot glanced back and shouted over his shoulder. "What the hell? Who are they?"

James wasn't sure how to answer that in a few words, so he gestured forwards repeatedly telling the rider to join the other bike. It was a couple of minutes with no further sign of pursuit before either rider felt calm enough to pull over, but when they did James and Jessica were caught in a storm of questions in broken English.

The co-pilot was telling James to get off the damn bike; the pilot was demanding to know from Jessica what the hell was going on. She was trying to explain when James bellowed at them all to shut up. He had heard something new that worried him, and then they all heard it. From up ahead came the rising tones of sirens, several of them, and it seemed too much of a coincidence to assume that it had nothing to do with what had just happened.

From their relatively high and exposed position in front of a long, low office block they saw something approaching that made James's blood run cold. This was no police car. A camouflage-painted armoured vehicle followed by two Jeeps were racing down the road from central Kinshasa where the bikes had been heading a moment before. They were still a long way off, but he could make out a tall aerial on top of the armoured car swinging wildly, and a man in sunglasses, green uniform and a dark red beret could be seen in the hatch. A flag flew in the vehicle's slipstream and in front of the soldier a heavy machine gun nosed towards the sky, like a hunting dog searching for a scent on the wind. The jeeps were painted in the same camouflage green and James could make out two or three figures in each of the open vehicles. He had no idea how many might be in the armoured car.

Any observational advantage from James's position was fleeting. The jeeps were still some way off, negotiating traffic that was growing heavier on their side now that they were close to the centre of Kinshasa. The bikes and riders were, however, in line of sight from the road, and it took only a few more seconds before the man in the turret began banging on the roof in front of him and yelling instructions to his driver. He was pointing to the pilots and passengers on the bikes who sat engines running, and as he did so he began to swing the machine gun towards them.

There was no time to debate it. Shots had already been fired at them without warning, either they could stop and argue it out with gun-toting soldiers who seemed way too trigger-happy, or they could use their agility to try to escape the closing net. James shouted, "Go! Go!" to the Russians and seeing the gun turning towards them they took immediate evasive action again, the pilot peeled away to the left side of the parking area while his colleague went right, making it impossible for the gunner to hit them both.

Staying and talking clearly held no appeal. There seemed to be a silent understanding between the pilots about the response to such a threat, and James began to wonder if these two were calling on previous military experience. The sudden revs came as a rasp, like the sound of tearing rags, as first one and then the second Yamaha blasted away from their rest point, each describing an arc before reuniting at a bottleneck where a ramp ran at right angles as it returned them to the main road.

The riders had to brake hard when they reached the traffic. Here at road level they couldn't see the oncoming military, equally the soldiers were unable to see them and had not yet drawn level on the other carriageway. To their right the road was still blocked with near-stationary cars and vans. Turning left would only take them straight back towards the first pursuers, it would also mean working against the press of traffic.

The pilot looked left and right, rapidly gauging his dwindling options, then he squeezed his way forward through a line of vehicles on the side road and onto the three-lane Boulevard Sendwe. This close to the city centre the traffic was frequently at a standstill. Somewhere between them and the airport the driver of a heavy truck had finally grown tired of waiting in the heat and, as Kin's truck drivers have been known to do, he had crossed the central reservation and was making his way north at a steady pace along the southbound side of the main road. Drivers on that side were forced to pull over to avoid him; using his horn more than his brakes, the trucker trumpeted his approach as he passed the static bikes. He was doing no more than fifty kilometres an hour, but he was raising a trail of dust from the road works that had been ongoing here for months. The evening light was fading but in it the pilot saw his chance. He pulled up the light scarf that hung around his neck and suddenly Jessica saw why it was needed. With the scarf to protect his nose, and his shades jabbed tighter onto his face he swung his bike out behind the truck. In seconds both bikes had closed the gap behind the truck and using it as cover they slid into the narrow space between the lumbering vehicle and the central markers.

Jessica tucked her nose down into her shirt in an effort to escape the choking dust kicked up by the lorry. She could easily have reached out to touch the truck it was so close; although she was used to riding pillion on a boyfriend's bike in New York this was different. There she had revelled in her parents' disapproval and had enjoyed the freedom of wide open roads. The closest she ever came to other vehicles had been in roaring through slow-moving delivery trucks on the classic Norton. Here she was squeezed onto an uncomfortably short saddle, hanging onto the rider for all she was worth and trying not to be swept over the back by the weight of her backpack whenever they accelerated.

Instead of escaping the heavy traffic they were now sticking as close to it as possible, hugging the truck's side to escape attention. Suddenly she could hear the sirens nearby, but although she searched all around the jeeps and armoured car were still invisible. If she couldn't see them, she just hoped that they couldn't see her. Worryingly, it was obvious that the truck driver had not seen them either – he kept straying closer to the central divide, sometimes it was just road markings but occasionally a raised concrete kerb appeared that would certainly flip them off the bike if they clipped it and might throw them under the truck's rear wheels.

Out of the gloom barely twenty metres ahead Jessica made out a huddle of pedestrians who had stopped on a pedestrian crossing as soon as they saw the truck approaching on the wrong side of the road. Two men among them decided to chance a suicidally small gap in the traffic and sprinted across the road. Horns blared but no one made much effort to slow down. Two schoolgirls hesitated as they thought about following the men. They clung to one another looking for their chance to cross, only to pull one another back hurriedly as they saw the bikes sandwiched between the lorry and stationary traffic.

The riders swept past them all with only a hand's breadth to spare and the frightened squeals of the girls who were nearest could be heard for a moment over the grinding of the truck's engine and the clash of gears

On the bike behind, James could see the gap beside the truck open and shut alarmingly close to the lead bike. It was hard to know which was of more concern, the chance of the bikes going under the truck's giant wheels or the prospect of them all being spotted by the oncoming soldiers. In the shadow of the truck and occasionally shrouded in pale brown dust, the first bike was sometimes invisible to James, even though on the second bike he was only metres behind. If James had trouble seeing it, then he hoped it would be impossible for the soldiers. The second rider must have shared James's concern for he moved closer into the gap behind the truck trying to remain hidden. Then they heard the change of tone as the sirens passed them and they continued down the road to the Martyrs' Stadium. A few seconds later, the sound of the sirens changed again as the jeeps and armoured car swung in towards the raised office fronts that the bikes had just vacated.

A wall of cars and multi-coloured minivans now filled the road on both sides, sometimes stopping unpredictably in the road to disgorge commuters. The truck was making slower progress now as they approached the city centre and a few cars took advantage of its passage by following in its wake. So far they had managed to obscure the bikes from view but it might not be long before someone recognised their description and the pursuit started again.

There was a constant risk of being squeezed under the truck's wheels, but if they pulled ahead of it into clear air the bikes would have no protection from oncoming traffic. If they resumed the city-bound side of the road, their progress would be even slower, so they continued to look for a balance between being crushed and being seen. The riders pulled level and the Russians shouted questions and instructions to each other. James couldn't understand a word but it didn't take a genius to work out that they were likely to be unceremoniously dumped.

The road was slightly narrower now, and where it was being resurfaced the central reservation had given way to slab after slab of rough concrete set vertically into the ground. These were punctuated by occasional gaps making them look like grey and broken teeth in a dusty mouth.

Everywhere people were squeezing out of minibuses and hurrying home. The traffic was gridlocked and drivers leaned on their horns as though this might suddenly clear their path. Where before the occasional pavements had held few people, here they were thick with pedestrians at this hour.

Then as quickly as they were in traffic, it began to thin again and the bikes were able to return to their own side of the road. Overtaking the truck that had shielded them they quickly picked up speed, weaving between cars and vans, and swopping lanes to ensure they outpaced their pursuers. For a couple of kilometres they tore through the light traffic, dodging pedestrians who stepped out in front of them and only slowing when traffic from side roads crossed their path.

Then without warning the leading bike titled violently as the co-pilot saw a gap in the traffic and a gateway at the roadside. As he and James flashed past, there was just time to read the sign saying Parc de Boeck and beside it another showing Kinshasa Zoo & Botanical Gardens, then they were into a haven of peaceful shrubbery, magnificent overhanging palms, and well-laid lawns. He expected a shout from a gatekeeper but none came and with Jessica and the pilot close behind them they swung left and right before riding deeper into the gardens, where they were now entirely hidden from the road.

The daylight was fading quickly behind cloud-filled skies, but neither rider bothered to put his lights on, the less they attracted attention to themselves the better. They skimmed past some animal cages, expecting to see a zookeeper but no one emerged and eventually they pulled up beside a timber-clad Welcome Centre painted a vivid green. It was closed and there was no one to ask them their business there. The Russians stopped their bikes under the trees, switched off the engines and studied one another's passengers.

James climbed off and Jessica followed suit as the riders put down the bike stands and got off to stretch their legs. For a second all that could be heard was the ticking of two cooling engines. The pilot was the first to break the silence. "Fuck.

Me. Sideways! What … in … hell was all that?" he said. "Who are you?" Evidently there had been enough time for him to rediscover some colloquial English. He pulled a clean rag out of his pocket and pushing back his shades, wiped his eyes. "Start talking, or I bloody shoot you myself."

"It's a long story," said James.

The pilot gestured to the empty space around them. "I think we got a time, now. This will be good story or else …," he left the threat hanging.

So first James, and then Jessica began to explain where and why they had come here, as they tried to wipe the thick coating of dust from their faces. It was in their eyes, and they pulled dirty clothes from their bags to wipe it away. James' mouth was lined with grit and he tried to spit it out but his throat was dry. Even though they had had their scarves pulled up the Russians were suffering too, until one of them noticed a tap at the corner of the building. Here they were able to wash the dust from their faces, to rinse their scarves and T-shirts and begin cleaning themselves again, this time with more success. Jessica appeared to have aged thirty years in the last hour, the dust was so ingrained that her black hair was now pale grey but she was unaware and it seemed a poor time to mention it.

James was more concerned with keeping the Russians onside. They could not afford to have them reveal their whereabouts and for now he was trying not to think too far ahead – the chances of escaping this mess were looking more remote with every hour. He looked again at the Russians. He didn't know their names and not unreasonably they wanted to know what they had stumbled in to. They had been forced to choose sides between gun-wielding and near-hysterical officials and two passengers who were no more to them than names on a flight manifest.

It was understandable that the Russians would be pissed off at being put in a situation where their instinctive flight from armed pursuers now put them on the wrong side of the law. James was expecting a grilling and for five minutes that's exactly what they got, but the more they explained the more the men's reaction surprised them. As the couple told their story, the Russians begin to laugh.

"Was the best ride we had here. Best anywhere this year!" said the pilot, and he began to laugh again. He raised an eyebrow at his friend.

The man grinned back at him. "Sure thing," he said. "I wanted testing my bike, but no chance. Till now."

"But we almost got you killed! Or at least arrested," said Jessica.

"No way!" said the pilot indignantly. "It takes more than shitty Panhard to catch me."

"Panhard?" said Jessica.

"Armoured car," he said jerking his thumb over his shoulder dismissively. "French shit."

"How did you know what it was?" said Jessica.

"We see them all over. In army, Russian army. They everywhere, Bosnia, Angola, Burkina. Panhard is fast, but what they do in the city? Machine gun the traffic?" They both laughed.

"Man, give me a bike every time. We too fast for the cops and the army," and he made a gesture with his hand like a fish darting upstream.

"So where you going now?" asked the co-pilot. "You in shit, right?"

"Thank you," said James. "Yes, we in shit as you say. We know they're looking for us only now they don't seem too worried about hiding it. Was that the army or police?"

"No man. Worse," he drew a thumb across his throat in an internationally recognised gesture. "They Republican Guard. Not like normal army here. They shit."

The pilot nodded. "They have more equipment. Some better soldiers. And the President he pay them himself … they loyal. Hey, you make big enemies here!" Somewhere during this description he had stopped smiling, in fact they all had.

"What do we do, James?" asked Jessica, and it was the first time he'd ever seen her look scared. "We can't go to a hotel. I don't know anyone here to stay with."

"No hotel, 'cos we not taking you," said the co-pilot. He'd obviously weighed the risks.

James was scratching his head, partly for the dust and partly to get his brain in gear. "I'm not sure. I need to think this through. What I really need, what we all need is a drink. My mouth tastes like a wrestler's … it's very dry."

At least he'd made her smile, if only for a moment.

"We not take you to hotel. Too dangerous if they are looking for you. Nearly dark. You stay here, my friends," said the pilot. "We get drinks and food, leave in gate. OK?" This last was directed to his friend who nodded his agreement. "Police," he paused and spat in the dirt, "they searching two bikes, so we quiet. After that," and he shrugged his shoulders theatrically, "you alone."

It was more than they had a right to expect. "Thanks," said Jessica.

James nodded and extended a hand to the co-pilot, the man's grip was like a python. "I don't know your name."

"No. You don't," said the pilot. "That's one good thing," and he laughed. "No worries. Was funny," he added and swung a leg back over his dusty bike. James couldn't help thinking they had different definitions of funny. The pilot pointed to the outside tap. "Wash. Not drink. We back later, drink by gate."

The engines both fired and the peace of the park was shattered. James was sure they must be attracting attention but still no one came and the animals remained quiet. The Russians turned their bikes; the pilot raised a hand in farewell and with their lights off the pair rode slowly back towards the gate, looking to left and right for any threat. There were no nasty surprises and the bikes pulled out onto Avenue

Kasa-Vubu and turned right into the city. The last James saw was a glimmer through the trees as they switched their lights on and accelerated up the main road.

Their options had narrowed dramatically. All he could think to do was ask for advice. The Russians were gone and the only other person James could think of who knew his way round Kinshasa and who could be relied on not to give them away was thousands of miles away. It went against the grain to ask him – after all, the man had expressly told him to get out of Goma days ago and not to go via Kinshasa. He wouldn't mention it to Jessica, but they had ridden their luck quite literally as far as it would go. James switched his phone on and breathed a sigh of relief as he saw he had charge and a strong signal.

******

A little over four thousand miles to the north a screen alert was flagged on a second-floor monitor at General Communications Headquarters in Cheltenham, the British government's eyes and ears on the world. These days GCHQ was busier than it had ever been. Its access to the Echelon global network of ten satellite dishes had been set up at RAF Menwith Hill in northern England in the early 1970s to monitor the Soviet threat. Forty years later it had outlasted the Soviet bloc and was still paying dividends globally. Echelon might not have the all the capabilities of US listening posts in Maryland and Hawaii, but its ability to monitor civilian voice and data traffic anywhere in the world continued to make it extremely valuable. With James using a US network's SIM card, GCHQ was also a deniable arm's length tool for America's NSA Signals Intelligence, enabling them to sidestep Congress and *US Signals Intelligence Directive 18* restricting the monitoring of American citizens and US mobile networks.

Within GCHQ the phone's identifying code was software-verified in microseconds and the alert automatically escalated to Global Access Operations division across the Atlantic in Fort Meade, Maryland. The only human interaction was a report filed by a civilian officer at GCHQ whose job was to inform her line manager at the Ministry of Defence in London of all intercepts. She enjoyed her role as a civilian cog in a secret military machine. To any outside observer her job was to audit Menwith's value to the Americans; happily for Carol no one had told her this made her an accounts clerk.

The handset belonging to James Falkus, a UK citizen, was one of thousands on a Watch list at any one time and there had been little activity on it for weeks. The US network confirmed his phone's code as soon as it was activated but still there were limits to what GCHQ could learn from it. Falkus was not a priority target and the contents of his message to a device in Antwerp could not be obtained by Echelon or by the NSA's probes in Verizon's network. That required higher authority and special measures, measures of which few in the Agency were even aware, however an SMS sent to a CIA asset's phone immediately gave it higher priority. The source of the text message was automatically triangulated to a location in Kinshasa and flagged to NSA.

******

Two hours later the pair were hungrier and thirstier than ever. They had climbed over the low fence into the zoo grounds and from where they were hiding they twice heard sirens. Through the trees of the Botanical Gardens they had seen two unmarked black SUVs with flashing blue lights in their windshields speeding by in the darkness. Their first warning had come close to midnight when a police car crept along the avenue, the sound of disembodied voices squawking on its radio reached them through its open windows. It turned into the Zoological Park and drove slowly down the main road towards them. Jessica was the first to hear its approach and she pulled James with her as they ran in a crouch to hide behind the Visitor Centre. If the policemen saw them, it would all be over, they were exhausted, knew little of the city and had no clear escape route in the darkness.

The car had stopped less than twenty metres away and then the doors opened. One of the policemen climbed out and noisily took a leak against the wall. The couple had held tightly to one another hoping that nothing would give away their presence, until finally the two men finished their smoke, climbed back in the car and drove slowly away. They both let out the breaths they had been holding, and that was the moment James decided to drop his pride and ask for help as soon as he could.

Worryingly, there had been no sound of returning motorcycles and he wondered if they had simply decided against returning, or if they had tried and found the security in the area too strong to get through unnoticed. The Russians must have known that two bikes ridden by two white guys would be a key part of the search, and this was not their problem. James just hoped that there was no more sinister motive for their non-appearance. It was possible the pilots could have reported the couple hiding in the zoo, but if that was the case surely they would already have been picked up. No, they were safely hidden for now but the problems ahead of them were mounting.

His thirst was strong and James was eyeing the door of the Visitor Centre wondering whether there would be bottled drinks inside. In the end he could wait no longer and picking up a rock from the gardens he smashed the flimsy lock on the back door and crunched his way through broken glass looking for bottled drinks inside, relieved that there was no alarm. He found some bottles of soda but there was no food and, tossing some money onto the counter for the sickly sweet soft drinks and the damaged door, he went back to Jessica. He was starting to run low on cash, but right now that was the least of his worries.

They pulled together two picnic tables which kept them off the ground and gave them a long platform on which to stretch out, but it was unyielding and they both fidgeted restlessly for a long time. Neither of them had expected to sleep but in the end exhaustion had caught up with them. The night time temperature remained warm but they curled up close anyway. In the darkness they could hear occasional grunts and movements from the nearby animal enclosures. Although the idea of spending the night in a zoo had unsettled Jessica it was the day's wild events that made it hard to rest, on top of which there had been endless interruptions from insects. As he lay still in the darkness, James was trying unsuccessfully to think how to get out of this situation.

When her breathing settled into a rhythm, he texted Axel. He hadn't discussed it with Jessica; her views on Axel were clear and though he understood them, even shared a few, right now he was ashamed to admit that he urgently needed the man's help. Message sent, he switched his phone off for a couple of hours to save battery while he slept; if Axel was still in Europe it could be hours before he even received it.

It felt like only minutes later when musical tones awoke James, but the sky was already bright. "Jessica, it's your phone."

She did not reply and he shook her shoulder but as he did so he realised the sound was coming from further away. He looked at his own phone but he remembered switching it off before. It seemed to him that his snatched sleep had come just before waking, leaving him unusually groggy. His befuddled brain was struggling to grasp their surroundings and to place this persistent noise. He switched on his phone and shook Jessica again, this time she stirred.

He couldn't recommend spending a night on a table in the middle of a city zoo, but that wasn't important, he knew instinctively that something was different. He could hear the animals calling as cage doors were opened and closed nearby; the daily routine was beginning around them and then there was that sound again. Congolese music drifted in on the air and from the way it constantly stopped and restarted it wasn't a recording.

"Jessica, wake up. We need to move, we can't stay here." He watched her rub the last road dust from her eyes and try hard to get her bearings.

"Wossa noise?"

"I don't know, maybe we'll find out as we go." He swung his bag onto one shoulder and went back to the tap to splash water on his face. It woke him up and it made him more aware how hungry he was. James stretched stiff back muscles and ran a hand through his hair. It was still dusty and he was unshaven, but the top priority was to find a way out of Kinshasa.

Jessica followed him along the track from the Centre through rough cut lawns. In their path lay a low white and grey concrete building fronted by black iron bars. As they walked along its front a chimpanzee over a metre tall bounded to the bars and pushed a hand through begging for food. Jessica stopped by the railing to look in, she could only shrug her shoulders and the chimp stepped back before startling her with several glorious spins, its arms held aloft and hands clasped together. At some point it had been taught to earn food by turning like a ballerina, and now that he looked harder James saw small plastic bags in the cage and lying just outside it that may once have had held the chimpanzee's rewards. The cage was barred in the ceiling at about three metres high and the only concession to the animal's exercise was an old car tyre that lay on the bare grey concrete floor. The chimpanzee appeared to be alone and James could just make out its sleeping quarters in darkness behind. There was clapping coming from another chimp in the neighbouring cage and it pushed its arm through the bars in supplication. If they had already been fed, there was no evidence of it, or of the keeper.

The couple pressed on and the path wound through the trees small cages housing the bird collection were set back from it at intervals. They walked quickly past a crocodile lying motionless close to the mesh of its cage, only its eyes moved. They had chosen a route away from the road towards the river, and soon they caught sight of a group of men and boys under a tree. One old guy sat tapping rhythmically on a bottle, the bass line and lead were coming from two middle-aged men playing home-made acoustic guitars, while a teenager stood and plucked on the single string of an instrument made from a large metal can and an articulating arm of wood. James had never seen or heard anything like it; the boy's musicianship was extraordinary as he bent the notes, playing with total concentration. Through it all, two middle-aged men sang alternate verses in plaintive tones before everyone came in with the chorus. Behind the players small boys scampered and played in the grass, occasionally breaking off to join a teenage girl as she danced slowly with her eyes closed.

The music was reminiscent of a rumba, overlaid with a blues-like lilt of loss. Far from detracting from the sound quality, the poverty of homemade instruments added an appealing vulnerability to the ensemble. There was no hesitancy in the playing, the songs flowed with passion and it was easy to see the enjoyment the men found in jamming together. Jessica and James stood a few metres from them transfixed by what they were hearing. All the men were on tricycles built from motorcycle parts or bicycles and handcarts. On the cycles the pedals had been inverted and were now set at hand height for their paraplegic owners. Others were ingeniously customised using the front of a motorbike, a comfortable seat and an engine mounted over the rear wheels. All of them had room between the handlebars and the seat in which to play their instruments. The band was rehearsing songs that James had no way of understanding – one sad and haunting, the next uplifting and energetic, but always mesmeric. It was easy to see why the children wanted to dance.

Jessica grabbed a camera out of her bag and mimed to them that she would like to take photos. The grey-haired bandleader smiled and nodded towards an open guitar case as the music continued. Photography meant a tip; she paid and filmed while James glanced nervously at his watch. It was a surreal wake-up call but the sooner they were out of here the better, they had to get moving to the port. As the song ended, the musicians began to pack away their instruments and he realised they must have begun practising long before he awoke. They stowed their instruments in the tricycles and one or two smiled at the couple, others ignored them. The musicians had sung in what he assumed was Lingala, but in French they told Jessica they practised here because it was quiet and private in the morning. Normally they played in one of the nightclubs, or in the street for tips.

Where were they going now? Breakfast, of course. Why so many questions? Was she another journalist? Yes? Well, if she wanted an interview she would have to pay them. But if she just wanted breakfast come along. Immediately, each of the children took a position behind the wheelchairs, sometimes two or three to a trike, and began to push the musicians away.

James tried not to think about his hunger, amid the talk of breakfast. The police and army were searching for them, th`at was the reality. He had some Congolese Francs, and Jessica still had dollars. They could use credit cards in some places, but their dirty clothes would attract attention anywhere smart, and wouldn't the authorities be able to trace them if they used their phones too long? Lying low in a hotel was out of the question; they needed to move fast. The Russians had been an unexpected bonus yesterday and in their exhaustion they had forgotten to check if the men had returned with drinks – neither of them had heard anyone. Now they were on their own. It was no use wishing they'd taken another route out of the country, what was done was done. He hadn't told Jessica that he had tried to contact Axel last night, but it was immaterial now, there had been no reply and James knew they must make their own choices using the resources they had.

He called her again and Jessica packed her camera and came over. She appeared as tired as he felt, and seemed to be trying not to look concerned. "OK, any ideas?" she asked.

He wanted to sound positive but he needed to be honest. "It's tricky. We knew there were risks in trying to get into Rwanda, and Kin's international connections seemed like the best option. But the airport authorities must know we're here now, which means the police will too. We can't get out unnoticed through either N'djili or N'dolo airports. Staying here doesn't answer anything, and any minute now someone will discover that door has been forced and we'll stick out like a sore thumb. There are no external rail connections as far as I know, the Angolan border is only a hundred miles from here but the roads aren't worth a damn. Besides we haven't got a vehicle. I reckon that leaves one way out and it's staring us in the face. The ferry port on the Congo River, and it can't be more than ten blocks north of here. If we can get on the ferry, we can be across the border into Brazzaville in half an hour. Different city, different country, no one's looking for us there. And we can get a flight to anywhere as long as we can buy tickets and use our credit cards. The trouble is, if we know that so will Businga and his people. There's bound to be a welcoming party waiting for us at the ferry, and they'll spot a tall white guy like me in a moment."

"Wouldn't it be better if we crossed at night?" asked Jessica.

"No, they only run by day, I remember looking into it from a tourist angle before I came out here." They both fell silent. "That's not much of a choice, is it?" He paused then said, "What if we could get to the port tonight, could we get on board in the dark?"

"Look at your hand, can you climb a rope with that?" she asked. He grimaced and she had her answer.

"In that case, there's nothing for it but to split up," he said. The reluctance in his voice was obvious.

"Why?" said Jessica and there was something in her eyes he hadn't seen before. Was it fear?

"Listen they're not looking for a black woman, they're looking for a tall, white guy or a couple. I'm sure you could slip through unnoticed. Particularly if you were dressed in something more local."

Jessica bristled momentarily, "There are plenty of women in jeans here."

"Jeez, I'm not looking for an argument about what you're wearing; I'm just saying there are more women in traditional long skirts than in jeans."

There was a long silence before she said, "I don't want to split up. How would you get out?"

"I suppose I could look for the British Embassy and throw myself on their mercy. God knows where it is though, and I don't know what they do with political refugees. I'm a British citizen and passport holder; that must count for something."

"But even if they took you in, you could be stuck there for ages."

"It's got to be better than a Kinshasa prison."

"Or we go to the authorities here," she said. James looked astonished. "No hear me out. This guy, Businga. He isn't the whole Government; he's just one corrupt man. He doesn't control everything they do; don't just assume they're all corrupt because he is."

"I don't assume anything like it. But I've already seen how far his tentacles reach. He's more than just well connected; he's the decision-maker in several key departments. We know he's mixed up in organised crime in the East; I've even been kidnapped by his son, for Chrissake. And he's a recently retired General – according to Axel he has the total loyalty of his former soldiers, they'll do anything for him. He obviously has at least part of the police force in his pocket because we saw them searching for us last night. Hell, yesterday they were shooting at us in broad daylight. If we turn up at a Police station, who do you think will hear about it first? Our embassies or General Businga with a finger in every pie? No, we can't do that."

She was obviously frustrated at their situation, just as he was, only now she was growing angry but she didn't contest what he said. "We don't have long to decide, someone's going to find us here soon."

"Well, now seems as good a time as any to make a confession," he said and hoped that his smile would dispel any anger.

Jessica's brow wrinkled. "What kind of confession?" She did not look like she would be easily appeased.

"I texted Axel last night."

A look of amazement creased her face. "You did what?"

"You heard. I asked for advice, which seems a bit rich as I ignored the last advice he gave. I just felt completely demoralised."

"Damn, James. I don't believe it. He's just like all the other reptiles in this conflict trade, he and his type got us into this business in the first place. Have you forgotten that Raphael died because of the conflict funded by his work and others like him? It's 'cos of these people that Keisha's orphaned. Why the hell did you do that?" Jessica was now seething with anger.

"For the simple reason that I could see no other option, and neither of us have come up with anything else this morning, have we? No one else I can call knows this place like him. He's also been in tight fixes himself. So if anyone has the mental resources and experience to help us then maybe he does."

She shook her head in amazement. "I guess it's true what they say, blood really is thicker than water. You know how much I despise that man, I loathe him. He is everything that's wrong with foreign involvement in Congo. And when we get out of here I *will* expose him, I've told you that too. Father or no father. Despite all that, he's the one person you turned to for advice. I'm just realising I don't know you so well." She stood still in the dappled shade, just staring at him.

"Shit, if you have a better idea, Jessica, then I'm all ears. Fire away. Let's find another way out…"

"I don't have an answer, I just know that if he's the solution we're really screwed. And if he's the person you turn to in a fix, I don't want to be with you."

"OK. If that's how you want it, I can't stop you. You might as well go, you'll stand a much better chance getting past the authorities without a big white guy standing next to you. Just for the record though, with both the local law *and* a crime boss with military connections looking for us, I'd say 'screwed' pretty well sums us up, wouldn't you?"

That was when they heard the sound of squeaking wheels behind them. A zookeeper was approaching through the trees pulling a handcart laden with food for the animals. He hadn't seen them yet but they couldn't wait any longer. They had been on the point of leaving by different routes but for now they grabbed their bags and hurried away.

Chapter 28
Marché Central, Kinshasa, DRC
Two Days Ago

Edouard Gahiji had found not one but two cars waiting for him at N'dolo Airport. An airport police car had been arranged by Ghonda before he sped off after the spies. He made a mental note to check out the youngster; he was just a driver yet when thrown into the firing line he'd reacted well. Seemed he had presence of mind, guts too. Could be useful.

The other car was less welcome. A couple of over-weight, over-age goons in civvies were waiting for him in a Land Cruiser and told him to get in, the general wanted to see him. Gahiji wasn't unduly concerned, if he was facing trouble with Businga it wouldn't come yet, the man still needed his skills. All the same, he'd need to tread carefully. The screw-ups of recent days had all been down to the general or his men, but he'd have to walk a tightrope to avoid taking the blame while not rubbing the general's nose in his own failings. Big noises like him didn't take it well if their authority was questioned.

Edouard Gahiji had held some 'insurance', a little protection from Businga Junior. Breaking into Falkus' base at the charity weeks ago had given him the memory card containing photos of Louis Businga's meeting with the Rwandans and the rebels. He would have been a fool to hand it over to the major without copying it first. Clear evidence of treason by Businga's son would have led most people to conclude the general was involved as well.

If General Businga's bid for power was successful, Gahiji might be thought to know too much. It was too soon to worry about that now but he would need to find some new protection against a one-way trip down the river.

He hesitated but knew that refusing to get in would make him look guilty – and he wasn't. He had little choice but to comply. The driver soon turned north onto Avenue du 24 Novembre and they passed no more than a five iron from the Golf de Kinshasa, playground of the capital's wealthy and powerful. He'd always wanted to play but first he needed the time. And the money. The driver and muscle exchanged no words and paid little attention to Gahiji behind them. The road curved westward following a bend in the Congo River until it became the Boulevard Colonel Tshatshi.

Gahiji was determined not to appear nervous although he had no idea where he was being taken and neither of the intellectuals in the front were going to tell him. They headed deeper into a wealthy neighbourhood he knew little, except that this was the route to Colonel Tshatshi Military Camp in Ngaliema. It not only housed the Republican Guard, it was home to the Defence Department, the central command of the Chiefs of Staff, and the headquarters of Military Intelligence. Yet, ironically, the one person you could be sure not to find here was the army's Commander-in-Chief, President Joseph Kabila. It was barely ten years since his father had been shot dead in his office there. Although the assassination had been blamed by loyalists on a single rogue bodyguard, all twenty of Kabila's bodyguards had been arrested and rumours still circulated that the killing had been organised by squabbling generals. Since the coalition government and all four vice presidents were drawn from former rebel groups it remained a convincing theory. True or not, Kabila had never again trusted his own generals to protect him and General Businga's increasingly open revolt against Kabila's regime showed his fears had been well grounded. President Kabila had relied instead on a parallel government of two hundred friends and family, backed by his Republican Guard in another part of Kinshasa.

Until a few months ago General Dr Businga had been commander of the 8th Military Region on the Rwandan border. The BBC had reported he was profiting from illegal mining and the evidence against him was stacking up all around; UN investigators were said to have fat files on him but no action had been taken against him and now his men were vying with the army and police for control of the capital. Gahiji had heard the rumours that old man Businga had personally killed a soldier with his bare hands and supervised the torture of others in Goma's military detention centre. He was even said to have ordered the killing of seventy-five civilians and local militia fighters captured by his 85th Brigade at the army-run Bisie mine.

The general denied it but Gahiji had become close enough to his inner circle to believe there was no smoke without fire. It was hard to keep secrets around here, and maybe the general was happy with his reputation. A Belgian journalist had been found drowned in the Congo River after reporting that Businga was behind a smuggling network ferrying arms and ammunition across the river from the neighbouring capital, Congo Brazzaville. Gahiji knew that the trade was brazen; arms shipments had been landed from speedboats at Businga's private house on the banks of the river then driven through Kinshasa and flown to the east of the country. What made it even worse was that Businga's men had sold the arms to the rebels fighting his own men. That was when relations between the president and his ambitious general had reached the point of no return.

Although the general said he had retired from the army, everyone knew he had been relieved of command by a president eager to separate the man from his power base of soldiers. Well, after the last few days it was clear to Gahiji that the president's strategy had failed. Every move that Businga made was being enforced by ex-soldiers from the 85th Brigade.

Despite this, the general was running out of options. With the president and the UN making life more difficult for him, Businga and his clan would have to make their bid for power or quit the country. At the very least, there was evidence out there that connected him through his son with a conspiracy to smuggle tin, tantalum, tungsten and gold out of the Congo, and evidence against him pointed to his corruption in public office; extortion, murder, kidnapping, the list went on. Businga's power now rivalled the president. His semi-independent role at the Ministry of Mines was a lucrative post, and the best way of preventing investigation by any successor was not to give it up.

If Businga was going to stage a coup, would he see Gahiji as an asset or a loose end to be chopped off? The general had other bright, ambitious young men who would obey his orders without questions. It was more likely he was viewed as someone whose loyalty could not be counted on; he wasn't from the right clan, and he was capable of dangerously independent thoughts and actions. Gahiji began to wonder if a tumbled exit from the car might be his best course of action, then he noted the locked doors. The co-driver was sitting at an angle that showed a readiness to use the gun holstered beneath his armpit. There would be a bullet in his back before he could force the door and escape. No, he would have to wait to see what Businga had in mind for him.

The Land Cruiser turned off the Avenue and drove briefly along a dusty, potholed road before pulling up outside a brightly lit office block. Its venetian blinds were all closed but the place was buzzing with activity. Then he was being ordered out of the vehicle with the passenger's gun now drawn and levelled at him. Any respect that his rank and regiment afforded him had clearly evaporated.

Maybe he had miscalculated his future usefulness to the general or the man's anger at the way matters had been handled. The mistakes and the failures of all concerned to find the spies had not been of Gahiji's making, but try telling that to a cornered snake like Businga.

Sandwiched between the driver who led the way and the armed passenger, Gahiji went inside and followed as uniformed soldiers of the 85th waved them through the throng of people. Two men were shouting on phones and others were studying computer screens. Fans swung back and forth in a feeble attempt to disturb the limpid air. The tension in the room was palpable, the activity was hurried and Gahiji could see anxiety in the faces around him. The place reeked of sweat, bad food, cigarette smoke and fear.

His small group made its way to a concrete staircase at the back and began to climb to the floor above, passing through an open door into a long room with a desk at the far end. Seated at the desk, head bowed and reading through some papers was General Dr Moise Businga. A cigar burned in the ashtray by his hand. He did not look up.

Two men armed with elderly Kalashnikov assault rifles were guarding the door and a bodyguard was placed between the general and the window. Another two men, both white, sat on a sofa to one side of Businga's desk; they were engrossed in reading something on a clipboard. The double doors closed behind him and Gahiji realised too late the scale of his miscalculation. The only other occupant was a man he didn't recognise who stood three paces from the desk facing the general. Gahiji was prodded forward by the guard to stand before the desk.

There were a couple of chairs but otherwise little furniture in the large room except for a brown-stained green canvas tarpaulin that covered the floor in place of a carpet. He stood on it and it was only then that he noticed the man beside him had his wrists bound and was silently crying, his shoulders heaving with stifled sobs.

It was a few minutes before anyone spoke to him. "You've let me down," was all Businga said. After an initial glance when Gahiji arrived he hadn't looked up from his paperwork. Now he had spoken in English – perhaps for the benefit of his white guests.

The man beside him looked across at Gahiji, obviously sure the remark wasn't directed at him. "I wanted those two spies found and stopped in Goma. You failed. I gave you photos, even their location, and I gave you men. I wanted them arrested or terminated there, you did neither. Then you should have caught them here in Kinshasa, but you failed again. I have no use for people who fail me." He stopped and said no more. Gradually Businga raised his gaze. It was a malevolent look, and his steely calm made it more so.

Gahiji knew that showing fear would confirm him as a victim. The general had laid the events out as he saw it and there was nothing to be gained from holding back. "I didn't need the photos, I had my own. The location was old, out of date, they had gone before we even received it." Only part of that was true but a small exaggeration might make the case more clearly. "Perhaps your people didn't tell you the full story but they sent me just two men to cover an entire city – I asked for eight. And then they placed the cordon at this end around the wrong airport – something that I discovered, not your staff." His key concession was that he hadn't blamed Businga personally. He was angry and in a tight corner but Gahiji was too smart for that. All the same, he had probably just sealed his own fate but he wasn't going to his grave without telling the arsehole in front of him how his coup attempt had been ballsed up. Coup? Huh! It didn't begin to deserve the description. And Businga called himself a general, for chrissakes.

The general in question continued to gaze steadily at the intelligence officer in front of him. No one had spoken to him that way in years and he was intrigued. Surely the young man was smart enough to know what he was facing.

Meanwhile, the guards remained impassive, as if they had heard nothing. The two white men were less circumspect, both looking from Gahiji to Businga in turn wondering how Businga would react to this loss of face.

The general leaned back and puffed on his cigar. A cloud of smoke wreathed him and he idly waved it aside. "I can't make you out," said Businga at last. "You know what happens to people who fail me."

There was no good reply to that comment so Gahiji kept silent. The silence lengthened as Businga studied him and then he looked briefly at the man next to him. He didn't acknowledge his other guests at all and they stayed quiet.

"Where are Tsiba and Falkus now, in your view?"

Gahiji spoke up with a strength he did not feel. "I need to question the soldiers I sent to track them. They are still in the city, I'm sure of that. They have no support network here. His employer, the charity, has publicly distanced itself from him. Our immigration records show that he has only spent one night in Kin up to yesterday, so he has no friends here to call on. We know less about her, but we will find out. The noose is tightening on them." There was absolute conviction in his voice.

Another contemplative silence and Gahiji looked at the white men seated to one side of Businga; they were being given free access to his operations so they were closely involved. Were they the money men, or intelligence officers? There was an edge, a hardness to them that spoke more of security services than bankers or embassy officials. French, British, American? Maybe France's DGSE, the Direction Générale de la Sécurité Extérieure or Britain's MI6, but if their uniform chino trousers and sports shirts were anything to go by they were more likely Americans. CIA? NSA? Department of Defense? Impossible to say on this evidence.

"Of course, if your friends can help ..." he looked meaningfully at the white men seated on Businga's right. He ploughed on, "If they can help track credit card payments, we could find them by sunrise. We need an ACH feed."

Businga looked momentarily puzzled, then turned to his two associates. The older one spoke up, "ACH. Automated Clearing House. It's where most credit and debit card payments are processed. We're already working on it," he added glancing at Gahiji.

American accent. *So the clothes had given them away*, he thought. CIA? Maybe.

"If you're working on it, why don't we have the results yet?" Gahiji was subtly allying himself with the general, and shifting responsibility.

"Guess it takes time, son. Even for the largest agencies." The agent glared back at him. "Either that or they haven't used their cards. Maybe they're just smarter than you."

Touché. Largest agency? Almost certainly CIA, especially operating outside the US.

Gahiji turned his attention back to Businga who looked him up and down before asking, "How do you know this business? Automated Clearing House?"

"It's a process, sir, not a single business. I spent a year covering financial fraud at Military Intelligence. We had to track people diverting funds from the Army, and some from the Air Force."

Businga said nothing at first, just shifted in his seat. "Interesting. That could be useful. No?" He glanced at one of the men by his desk who nodded almost imperceptibly.

"We are making progress ..." he looked down, "Gahiji." *He doesn't even know my name. He's ready to give the order to finish me, and the fucker knows nothing about me. I'll make him remember me,* thought Gahiji. *One way or another.* He bit his lip, it seemed he was safe for now.

"I don't want to fight a war of attrition. That will take too long and turn the people against us before we're even in power. As you've been travelling, you may not have heard, the president has confirmed that he will illegally stand for a third term in office. He's crazy if he thinks I will allow this. I've succeeded in blocking the fuel imports at Muanda on the Atlantic; there are already fuel and other shortages in Kinshasa's markets. This will stir up resentment against the government, and I can accelerate the overthrow of Kabila's illegal regime. The last time this happened, the army walked over a thousand kilometres from Goma to Kinshasa. We will move much faster, with lightning strikes on places like Katanga, Kabila's home province. I have many more men now arriving in Kinshasa. Soon the people here will help me to liberate them."

Gahiji said nothing but thought how little evidence there was on the ground of Businga's men being marshalled in large numbers, and how unlikely it was that the Kinois citizens would lift a finger to help an elected dictator be replaced by an unelected one. It made him think how much Businga was misjudging the population.

"Meanwhile, I think you have a job to finish, and so do I." He nodded at the guards behind him. Out of the corner of his eye Gahiji saw one of them step forward, angle a pistol down to the top of his neighbour's head and before the man could react he pulled the trigger twice. As the bullets struck him, two sprays of blood blew from his nose and mouth towards the general. None of it reached him, but the general's desk lamp showed a film of light droplets still falling to the tarpaulin. The victim had collapsed face down so close to him that the man's right arm lay across Gahiji's shoes. Thick, dark red blood began to pool on the tarpaulin beneath the man's head and then slowly spread outwards.

It had been clinical, quick, the work of a practised assassin. Businga had simply gone back to the paperwork on his desk as though nothing had happened, and the white men sat motionless and unreacting. One might have wondered if any of them had seen anything at all. Gahiji found himself hoping he was dismissed before the blood and tissue reached his boots. Funny the things that came to mind in moments of danger. Well, that confirmed the reason for the brown stains on the tarpaulin.

"Find those spies, Gahiji. There's a large detachment of men waiting for you downstairs. Use them well," Businga tapped the ash off his cigar on to the floor, and drew hard on it. "Bring them to me alive by this time tomorrow; I want to find out what they know. Do it or I'll be looking for all three of you. Go on, get out."

Gahiji gave a salute the man hadn't earned, turned crisply and marched from the room. His legs felt like water but he was damned if he would let any of them see they'd rattled him. Gahiji had no idea who the poor sod was who lay on the floor or what he'd done, or not done. All he knew was that he'd been lucky to walk out.

He made his way down the stairs, pushing through the throng of armed men and civilians before he strode off into the night. Then somewhere in the darkness he stopped and bending over double at the roadside he wretched and wretched until he felt a small amount of bile strike his boots. He had hardly eaten anything today, but even that didn't stop his stomach heaving at the narrowness of his escape.

Not for the first time Edouard Gahiji wondered what the hell he was doing, working for people who would kill him as soon as look at him. The enemy didn't even know he existed and hadn't targeted him but he was one mistake from his own boss putting a bullet through his head. He hated that bastard; it was all fucking back to front.

******

The pair had little choice. They walked in silence through the park, heading north towards the port. James put on his only shirt to hide his white arms and pulled his floppy hat down as low as it would go. With Jessica's scarf around his neck the casual eye might not detect him – but it wasn't the casual eye he was worried about.

They slowed as they reached the edge of the park, looked up and down the streets but they were clear of any police, and trying not to attract attention they strolled away from the shelter of the Zoo Gardens, and the curious contrasts of its hideously bored animals in bare metal cages, its concrete block buildings, tall trees, lush palms and quiet lawns. On the street they were hit by Kinshasa's bustle and felt immediately exposed. They walked the pavement until they reached a bookshop on Avenue Du Commerce that just was opening and here they quickly slipped inside. At this time of day they were the only customers but when their arguing in hushed whispers grew louder they began to attract the shopkeeper's attention. One thing they didn't want was to be too noticeable, the discussion was getting them nowhere and they knew they couldn't stay here long. It was as they stepped out of the door that James felt the silent phone buzz in his pocket. He stopped in the street as Jessica walked on unaware. The message was short and simple. *Extra Plus, Av Equateur. 12.00.* James wasn't sure what it meant and neither he nor his phone recognised the long number beginning +32, he had little doubt though that it was from Axel.

"Do you know an international dial code that starts 32?"

"No, why?"

"Doesn't matter really, I just had a message, and I'm sure it's from him, Axel Terberg. It's a bit cryptic." He showed her the message.

"Not really. Extra Plus is a chain of supermarkets. Maybe there's one on Avenue de l'Equateur, it runs through Gombe. It can't be far, hold on." She strode back into the bookshop and after a moment he followed. It was cool and dark inside where he found Jessica reading a Kinshasa street map with the sales assistant. She turned as he approached, "This lady tells me there's an Extra Plus market not far from here," she said. "And it's on Avenue de l'Equateur." He handed over a note to buy the map and they continued to study it.

They moved away from the desk for some privacy. "It's not far," he said.

"But I don't know what's waiting for us there at 12.00 hours, do you? Look it's only four or five blocks from here, and we've got to kill some time. It seems crazy not to head for the port when it's only ten blocks from here. If we can slip onto the ferry, we'll be in Brazzaville lunchtime." She looked imploringly at him. "I just wanna get going."

"Me, too, but that way we could walk straight into them. If you were looking for us, wouldn't you be covering the ferry? Show me the map again," and they spread it out on top of piles of French books all with a religious theme on one of the bookshop's tables. They were still the only people to have come in, and now that they had stopped arguing the store assistant paid them little attention. "Look, here. Why don't we go south a few blocks, there's a huge market? I doubt they'll be looking for us there, and even if they are they couldn't cover it all – it runs a long way. And we'll just look like any other tourists if we're walking slowly round, plus we can get some breakfast. I'm starving."

It may have been the thought of breakfast that persuaded Jessica. In any event, she nodded in agreement and started for the door. Two loud horns outside and then a third made her lift her eyes to the window and she saw a white windowless panel van pull up in front of the bookstore, followed rapidly by another. There had been other vehicles parked along the busy Avenue Du Commerce, but none here until now and suddenly she noticed two men in the cab of the first vehicle. They were heavily muscled, wearing sunglasses, the driver was white, the passenger black. As she looked, the passenger climbed from the cab and thrust what looked like a handgun into the waistband at his back. She couldn't identify them but she needed no further encouragement; turning she grabbed James's sleeve. With Jessica ahead of him she knew he could not have seen the vans blocking the morning traffic and causing the protesting horns that had alerted her. Still less would he have noticed the armed men in the cab. They had only seconds to spare and no time to explain; pulling his arm she ran past the startled bookstore keeper, through the back of her shop and into a long dark passage with an entrance picked out in sunlight at the end.

As she tugged him by the arm and they sprinted down the alley, James shouted, "What is it? What have you seen?"

"Nothing good. Run!"

They burst out of the alleyway into the blinding sunlight. There were piles of empty plastic boxes stacked neatly by the end of the alley and picking one up she hurled it into the darkened back door hoping to create a distraction before she swung right and sprinted away down the lane that served all the shops along the avenue. They reached the end of the lane with James right beside her. As they turned the corner, he heard shouting from behind and risked a quick glance over his shoulder. A shopkeeper was emerging from the doorway holding the box that Jessica had thrown in, he looked puzzled and unhappy. At the same moment two guys barrelled out of the bookshop alleyway and one had drawn his sidearm. He was white, the second one black; they looked fit and strong but they were taken aback by the anger of an indignant shopkeeper demanding to know who had come into his premises. After a moment's pause they rushed past him into the darkened shop, assuming the couple were ahead of them, and James spun around and raced after Jessica.

She was five paces ahead of him and heading south again towards the street. As they approached it, she put her hand up to slow him and together they stopped as they reached the pavement. He whispered, "Your trick worked, they've run on but they may double back soon." It might only have bought them a few moments.

She poked her head quickly around the corner and pulled back. Then she took a longer look down towards the front of the bookshop. "Two more goons, one black, one white, so probably not locals. And they're armed."

"Yeah, I just saw. We've got to move," he said glancing back. The alley was still empty.

"I think there are more people by the vans but come on," she said and raced into the road. Save for the quick reactions of a car driver approaching from the left it would have been the end of Jessica. The front of his car struck her a glancing blow but by now she was already halfway across the four lanes and weaving through the moving traffic, lucky not even to be limping. They headed along the main road towards the nearest corner before turning south at the next junction. There was a shout behind them from the driver who had climbed from his car, he was questioning her sanity and then James' too as he pushed through the vehicles that Jessica had halted. Then came more shouts behind them and the sound of running feet slapping the hot tarmac.

Side by side James and Jessica fled down the street and as they did so, market traders' stalls began to appear on their right. The couple were heading straight into the vast Marché Central, but with their pursuers close behind they dodged right to get out of their line of sight and continued sprinting the length of the street. The market stalls' blue and white striped awnings provided some screening from their pursuers, but the commotion they caused as they ran might give them away. At this time of the morning the market was still busy and Jessica was forced to swerve and weave her way through shoppers idly walking alone or in small groups. James was only a few paces behind, following in the path she cleared. He was sweating and breathing hard from Kinshasa's heat and humidity. Where Jessica slipped through gaps and was gone before anyone could complain, a couple of strides behind her James found indignation being heaped on him as shoppers overcame their surprise at Jessica and found their voice for James. They were carving a path that a blind man could have followed.

Intermittently, James thought he could catch the stamp of feet behind him as a runner in heavy boots began to gain on him, he cast a backward glance and caught a glimpse of a guy in combat trousers and a black T-shirt barely thirty paces behind him. Unencumbered by a large camera bag, the man was closing on him and further behind James thought he might have seen a white guy running too. There could have been more but he didn't stop to find out.

James pushed past a young couple selling rugs from their stall. She was sitting on a stool laughing with the shoe seller next door while her partner stood and called to passers-by. Unaware of James' approach he stepped back into the path and James caught a flash of a check grey and white shirt before he inadvertently knocked the man down. James scrambled to his feet murmuring an apology but all the time looking back. His closest pursuer had been held up by a party of women admiring a stall filled with bolts of cloth. James jumped up, the man grabbed at his wrist but he broke free and ran on.

Carved wooden masks hung in fearsome rows beneath a corrugated iron roof. Their thin slit eyes and pinched mouths matched his own. The din of pumping music here added to his disorientation and the varied masks all seemed to be staring at him, plain ones decked with straw hair, others with checked or zigzag skins. Sensing trouble the next trader flicked a cotton cover over his stall's carved ivory but James sped past oblivious. He dodged through stallholders offering wooden spears, masks, rugs, and skins, then they were into the food market with immaculate piles of eggs in cardboard trays, vegetables, herbs and pulses, and stacks of colourful fruits.

After a hundred metres a new market road opened to the left and the road they were on continued straight ahead. James had no idea if she knew where she was going but Jessica swung left, tracking alongside the dirt road that bordered the central market.

He made a decision but there was no time to tell her and James let her run on as he turned back. He couldn't see their pursuers but he heard shouts behind and then he heard running feet. A single pair, heavy boots from the sound of it. Hopefully one man. He stepped back into an open doorway he had just passed, from here he could see through a window to his left as anyone approached, it wasn't much but it should give him just a few seconds warning. He dropped his bag and tried to slow his breathing, fortunately he was in good physical shape, far better than when he'd arrived in Congo. There was a flash of movement and his pursuer came running through, his right arm raised and holding a pistol.

James crouched and ran, timing the impact to perfection he hit the guy low and hard in a perfect rugby tackle, wrapping both arms around the man's legs so that the pair of them went crashing down in the roadway, the gunman striking his head on the ground. James had surprise on his side and was swiftly up on his knees while the man beneath him groaned and reacting to the impact by slowly bringing his outstretched gun hand towards his body. With a swinging backhand blow James knocked the pistol from the man's grasp. The plaster cast on his hand protected him from most of the impact but it hurt like hell. The gunman's grip on the trigger had remained tight, and as the gun flew from his hand a single shot went off into the air missing James by less than a metre. The gun bounced once and slithered across the dirt-filled roadway into a pile of discarded boxes.

The man was clearly winded and struggling to regain his breath while James was balanced and kneeling above him. James swung a right hook into the man's face. It connected solidly with his nose, and he felt it break as the gunman's head snapped back before he lay still. James breathed deeply, that had gone better than he had expected but time was short and he scrambled to his feet.

Looking down at the unconscious man, he could see blood flowing from his nose but what he noticed most was that his pursuer was Hispanic, not black as he'd first thought from a hurried glance. He had the lean, powerful build of a middle weight boxer and sported the tattoos of an army veteran on his arms and neck. In his late twenties, he was dressed in jungle camouflage combat trousers, black T-shirt and olive green army boots; over the T-shirt he wore a lightweight webbing vest and on it a radio was linked to an earpiece coiling down his neck. This had been dislodged from his ear by the impact and James pulled the cable straight so that he could listen – he was taken aback by what he heard. "Six Alpha, Six Alpha.

D'you copy? Repeat, do … you … copy?" The voice was growing insistent, yet what struck him was the unmistakably American accent.

"What the fuck?" breathed James. "Now we've got bloody Yanks after us. What the hell do they want?" First it was Businga's people in Goma, then the Kinshasa police and the Republican Guard here; now the frigging Americans wanted a piece of him. Without planning anything he pressed the transmit button on the man's vest, "Six Alpha, Six Alpha, sure I copy." He had lived long enough in the States to pass a short test.

"No shit, Six Alpha. Left us hanging there. Location and Sit rep. Where are they?"

James swallowed hard, his mouth feeling dry again. "Got the guy. West entrance, Central Market. Give me back-up." They were at the north entrance; anything he could do now might draw them off Jessica.

"Radio protocol, Six Alpha. Target Foxtrot? Say again, d'you have Target Foxtrot? West entrance?"

"Affirmative," was all he would risk or he'd give himself away.

"We have your GPS. Give me a SitRep …" Shit, of course they would have a satellite lock on the man's location. Still, maybe he had sewn some confusion, enough to draw some of their pursuers away. James dropped the earpiece and stood up. If they had satellite positioning, they could have a satellite video feed too. That made him pause and he picked up his cap that had come off in the struggle, and pulled it on tight. He might just have delayed their back-up team for a minute, if he said any more he'd blow it. Frankly, James was amazed he'd got away with as much as he had. Whether they believed him for long was another matter; they'd certainly be sending a support team in to assist with what they thought was his capture – they must be based somewhere nearby. Time to find Jessica.

He looked up to see ten or more pairs of eyes watching him with mingled astonishment and suspicion. Those at the front of the crowd stood back and were excitedly telling those behind what they had just missed. Throughout it all, James couldn't understand why he still felt so calm, perhaps it was adrenaline.

He stepped away from his still unconscious tracker; he'd seen enough concussions in rugby to know the guy would be probably come round any moment. He couldn't stay here, he'd lost contact with Jessica and now a crowd had gathered and people were pointing to the gunman and firing questions at him. They obviously wanted to know who he was, who had been shooting and why he had laid out another foreigner – James wasn't sure if they'd seen the gun but the fella on the ground was wearing military garb so maybe they could draw their own conclusions about him.

One market customer was on his phone excitedly calling the police. A trader took hold of James' shirt sleeve and was rattling questions at him but he shrugged the man off and turned away. That was when he saw the gun lying among the boxes on the other side of the street. He wasn't going to leave it for the soldier to find and use when he woke up; he strode over, picked it up, checked the Safety was on, and walked back across the road with it. He probably should have hidden it, for suddenly the crowd were fearful of him and pushed to be out of his way. He ignored the frightened stares that traders young and old now gave him; to them he was now the gunman. There were so many people now that he had to push his way through the crowd to be able to pick up his camera bag from the shadows of the doorway where he had waited. People were still staring at him and some were asking him questions as he stuffed the gun into his bag but he ignored them and turned out of the doorway setting off at a jog after Jessica. God alone knew how far she might have gone before she noticed he was no longer behind her; she certainly hadn't doubled back here yet. Where the hell was she?

His mind was spinning as he ran on in search of her. Events in his life seemed to have spiralled far beyond his control in the last few days. James was a practical man and he liked to know what to do next – today had started out with the pair of them arguing before matters were taken out of their hands it and they had had to run together. Over the last few weeks there had been a horrible logic to it all, he had unwittingly taken photos of government officials meeting rebels for secret talks. It now seemed likely the two sides were aiming to carve up Congo for themselves, perhaps controlling the mineral-rich east of the country – that much he'd learned from Jessica's meeting with the man from the British Embassy; he was a spy if ever there was one. Now these secret negotiations with an enemy state had been blown by his photographs, and the danger and value in them was simply confirmed when he was kidnapped by Louis Businga.

He knew now that to the Congolese government the talks were treason, inevitably the people in the photos or their next of kin still wanted them silenced – he had seen too much. The stakes had already been high enough for him to be kidnapped and interrogated to find out who he was working for, and whatever the negotiations were about the whole affair had cost Louis Businga his life.

Thoughts had been tumbling through his head as he ran, and now he was as confused as ever. There were too many sides to this. He couldn't understand why the Americans were involved. It made no sense to him; it was a jigsaw puzzle still missing some vital pieces.

He ran on, his boots slapping the ground and the sound echoing around the buildings and the blue and white tarpaulins covering the market stalls. Somewhere further back the paved road had given way to hard-packed grey dirt, and the occasional traffic of vans and scooters had petered out. Here old ladies sat in the sun at the edge of the narrow roadway selling tomatoes, onions, peppers and potatoes, all piled neatly beside them on tarpaulins or cotton throws. To his right diagonal lanes ran in parallel lines towards a series of vast roofs supported on tall concrete columns. They were sheltering traders and customers from the sun and rain and this seemed to be the focal point of the market. He could clearly see two large free-standing roofs but there may have been more beyond, it was impossible to tell, just as it was impossible to see which route Jessica had taken. He had already passed two broad lanes and now seemed to be reaching one end of the market. He stopped and then he heard it. Over the normal buzz of people going about their daily business he heard a swelling roar that sounded like an argument, at that moment it meant only one thing to him.

******

Jessica had only fleeting snapshots of her surroundings as fear drove her deeper and deeper into the enormous market. The roadway was narrow but passable among the shoppers who walked slowly in the heat looking for bargains, stepping carefully among the scattered debris of the market. A man was forlornly holding out fresh fish to be examined, and everywhere vendors were shouting their offers while she blew through a host of unfamiliar scents. They had been running for several minutes, dodging from lane to lane, and she had led the way along narrow paths occasionally finding her way blocked by customers and traders. The market seemed to go on and on, at any moment she felt they must emerge on the other side but still it continued. This area was filled with electrical goods, and stallholders playing loud music vied with each other to attract Kin's famously musical populace.

Jessica had been running for a few minutes when she came to a crossing of two lanes. She halted and glanced back hurriedly to see where James was behind her. It was then she realised she hadn't heard his footsteps for a while. There was no sign of him and a sense of panic and isolation rose in her. She waited but couldn't see him or hear the reassuring sound of his approach. Then she looked to her right and the blood seemed to halt in her veins. A white man with dark glasses stepped nonchalantly from behind a market booth and, planting his feet wide, levelled a large handgun at her torso. He stood square on to her, holding the gun two-handed. It was just as she'd seen in the movies, only this time the muzzle was pointing unwaveringly at her chest.

Her next move wasn't wise or premeditated, but fear can do funny things to you. It ignited something in Jessica and she spun around and sprinted the way she had been heading. A practised marksman, he was the only one in the pursuit with experience of the Agency's Special Activities Division. He had a clear line on her over the lowered sights of his pistol, and it would have been easy enough to bring her down with one of the Springfield's seven rounds. He also knew that a single .45 round would likely finish her; and he had clear orders only to fire in self-defence. The agent swore at her refusal to stop.

He knew Target Tango was a US citizen and not even their primary target. Frankly, she didn't look much of a threat but appearances could be deceptive – he'd learned in Iraq to be wary of innocents, old men, women and children who turned out to be suicide bombers. Threats could come in all shapes and sizes. The agent swore again, holstered his weapon and raced after her.

She was tired but fear made Jessica run hard again, weaving in and out of the stalls, yet within fifty paces he had closed the gap and was able to drag her to the ground. Together they fell, his arms wrapped around her neck. There was no protection as her head hit the ground, with their combined mass. A scream was crushed out of her as he ensured that his two hundred pound bodyweight landed on top, and although her arms flailed as she fell he held on to her with a ferocious grip ensuring that she couldn't take off again. Their momentum tumbled them onwards into a table laden with butchered meat that was now thrown into the road. Live green and yellow turtles as big as a man's head slid off the table and rolled along the ground, butchered haunches of goat were pitched into the dust.

There was a shout of anger from the man behind the stall and when the agent looked up he saw the butcher had started towards him with a meat cleaver. The CIA man moved with speed and agility as he slid off Jessica who lay immobile. As he came to his feet, the gun filled his hand and was pointed once again at Jessica, but seeing the greater threat was coming straight at him from the butcher's sharpened steel he raised the pistol and barked an order. The butcher may not have understood the English instruction to back off but the gesture was clear enough. A squawk came from the radio hooked to his vest, and he pressed a button fixed high on the webbing that encased his torso. His voice came out as a strangulated shout, betraying the pressure he felt, "Nine Alpha, Nine Alpha. D'you copy? D'you copy? Immediate Assistance. I need immediate assistance." Jessica's eyes opened, her eyes flicked left and right as she sought to get her bearings. Then slowly she began trying to raise herself beneath him. He'd lost her once, he wasn't going to let that happen again. He swung his gun down, the pistol grip striking her across the back of the head. "Lie still, lady. Arms and legs spread wide." It was a pointless instruction, she was unconscious again, unmoving and with her face down in the dirt beneath him, her backpack somehow still in place. The crowd roared its anger at his treatment of her.

Again, the man barked into the radio, "Target Tango detained. Locals hostile. Gimme Alpha Eight and Six? Get a team in here. Fucking fast."

"Nine Alpha, copy that," came a calm, reassuring voice.

"Fucking A," he breathed. The soldier quickly glanced behind him but if he was expecting help from that direction none was visible, and now people were shouting at this foreigner waving a gun in their market, angered at the sight of a white man pistol-whipping a black girl. A group of teenage boys began to taunt him and two feinted threateningly towards him from either side. He flicked his aim

453

from one to the other and then back to the butcher who was gesticulating at all his damaged and dirt-covered meat. Clearly, he wanted to know who was going to recompense him.

There was an unintelligible sound from the radio clipped to his vest, and the agent managed to pull a large, metal-reinforced black plastic tie from the cargo pocket of his combats. "Easy bud," he said to the butcher, but the man still held a firm grip on his blooded cleaver and was now backed by a growing crowd of men, women and boys loudly demanding to know who this man was. The butcher showed no inclination to put down his carving knife and now there were more men closing on the prone figure and the gunman, some pushing into the circle to get a closer look and yelling their anger at what they saw.

The gunman knelt beside Jessica; he had deftly looped a tie over both her wrists before tugging it tight with his left hand. Her eyes were closed, she offered no resistance and her attacker managed one-handed to bind her wrists tightly while barely taking his eyes from the butcher's blade before him. He checked the others in the crowd to left and right and pressed the radio transmit button again. As he did so, a heavy piece of wood struck the American on the back of the head and a gasp went up from the crowd as the camouflage-clad figure toppled forward to land heavily on his face.

James put down the wooden pole, stepped over the man's still frame and walked into the circle of people surrounding Jessica. When he checked, he found she was breathing and had a pulse but she was unconscious. The crowd's nervousness told him to leave the gun he had acquired untouched in the top of his backpack. He took the precaution of removing the soldier's weapon, leaving his radio on the ground. The butcher stepped forward to pick the radio up, it might give him some recompense for his lost earnings. James gestured to Jessica's bound wrists and to the butcher's knife. Without a word the man leaned forward and slit the reinforced plastic bonds, at which there was a loud cheer from the crowd.

Thinking about it later, James assumed he was able to walk away from the tense scene carrying Jessica because of the care he showed for her. It was that or the feeling that their enemy's enemy was their friend. As he lifted her, Jessica's head sagged against his shoulder and one hand rested on his chest. Her eyes had closed and although they opened again briefly she was unable to focus – perhaps she knew who had picked her up, perhaps not. The crowd's hostility had been silenced by the heavy blow that ended the CIA's arrest attempt. With Jessica in his arms James stepped forward and the people parted in front of him. There were ululating cries behind him as he walked away leaving the officer on the ground. He neither knew nor cared what happened to the man, but he assumed the support team would be on site soon. It was time for the couple to vanish again.

He could not have been more conspicuous if he'd tried. A tall white guy with a blue-plastered hand carrying a semi-conscious black woman through the market to the Avenue Ruakadingi. There were several taxis waiting there and the driver of the first opened the rear door briskly for him, chattering his concern for Jessica. James tried to sit her on the rear bench seat, but she slid sideways and collapsed across its length. The driver looked at him in surprise when he asked to be taken to Extra Plus on the Avenue de l'Equateur instead of the hospital or a hotel.

******

They were driven slowly and carefully along the south side of the Zoo Park and Botanical Gardens. It seemed a lifetime ago that they had arrived there by motorbike, but it was only the night before and suddenly a wave of exhaustion and stomach cramps reminded James that they had eaten nothing since and drunk far too little. In the dramas of the previous hours he had managed not to dwell on his hunger but now he realised he'd never felt so thirsty or ravenous. It couldn't be helping Jessica's recovery either. When they pulled up in front of the supermarket James overpaid the driver with the last of his Francs and told him to wait with Jessica a little longer while he went inside. He emerged a few minutes later with the pharmacist, assorted wound dressings plus bottles of water, fruit, biscuits, and bags of biltong. She might not manage the dried meat straight away but when he lifted her up in the rear seat and held some water for her to drink her eyes opened more steadily and she began to take it in sips. Then it spilled from her mouth and she started to cough violently. He leaned her forwards in the hope of clearing her airway, waited a few minutes and then he began again more slowly. The speed of her recovery was impressive and within minutes Jessica was able to swallow pieces of banana and more water. He drank thirstily beside her and wolfed down some food while the taxi driver watched their recovery before asking him where they would like to go. The man looked baffled when James explained that they would stay here then, taking Jessica by the hand, he helped her to stand and led her inside to the Pharmacy. He needed to check her head wound. He could feel two large lumps on the back of her skull; she was talking a little now but she wasn't strong enough to discuss it in detail so he had to make up a story for the pharmacist.

It was as they sat on plastic chairs waiting to be served that James had the sense they were being watched. He was exhausted and knew he had little fight left in him, and Jessica could barely take a step. Maybe this was where it would end. When he looked behind him, there was no one there, if there ever had been. The last person in the queue ahead of them had been served and James stepped forward to explain Jessica's injury as best he could. The mere fact that he, not Jessica, was describing what had happened to her added to the pharmacist's concern. He sat her down and gently examined her skull before exhaling slowly. "Bien sûr, she must see a doctor. Head injuries can be, what do you say, unpredictable."

"There is no time, we must catch a ferry to Brazzaville as soon as possible," said James.

"Impossible, she cannot go to Brazzaville today," insisted the pharmacist.

James hesitated. He wasn't keen to discuss his plans with anyone but the thought was already out there. "It's important that we go."

The man shrugged eloquently. "This is mad, the ferry is very ... ah, en Anglais? Difficile. Stress. Il y a beaucoup de monde, too much people. She need a doctor in Kinshasa before she can travel; Elle s'est cassé la tête.It is dangerous to travel, she have damaged the head. Look, she cannot to concentrate, her eyes they are not focus. She must see a doctor, immédiatement."

The pharmacist was growing in his certainty that Jessica's head injury was serious enough to require more qualified medical attention.

"It's complicated," said James. "We have a plane to catch from Brazzaville and we don't have long."

The pharmacist threw up his hands. "Mais non, she must not fly unless her condition improves. She need a hospital, an X-ray."

"Then help me get her to one," said James. "Is there a good hospital here?"

The pharmacist scrutinised James more closely this time, having given most of his attention to Jessica. "Of course we have hospital here," he said indignantly. He paused again, "but the best is in Brazzaville, a new one built by the Chinese, there's new equipment and good doctors."

"OK, we'll go there." James could see that Jessica needed to be examined, and he hadn't told the pharmacist she had brought up some food soon after the taxi had gone. He couldn't share his real concerns about what would be waiting for them at the ferry terminal, and he was so tired he was struggling to think straight. He needed to get her away out of the city and out of the country, but she wouldn't be able to travel discreetly. As things stood, it was odds-on that they'd be found by the men searching for them. He had run out of solutions but this wasn't the place to discuss it.

The pharmacist raised an eyebrow and gave James a long, appraising look that said there must be more to this story, but as the patient was conscious and could talk – albeit feebly – he agreed to give her first aid and send Jessica on her way. James met his gaze until the pharmacist shook his head and turned away. Slowly, almost reluctantly the pharmacist applied a padded dressing for the swelling and fixed it in place with a bandage wrapped carefully around her head. James felt awkward paying for her care with cash from Jessica's wallet but he was the only one who knew it was hers. The man insisted she would need to see a doctor as soon as they landed on the river's north bank, and he recommended that they make for the new hospital in Brazzaville where they would get the best care in the city. James assured him that this was his plan too and, after a few minutes sitting and recovering during which Jessica began to ask questions about what had happened and where they were headed, he helped her to her feet and they made their way slowly to the exit.

They were still in the air-conditioned relief from the madness facing them outside when a hand was placed on James' shoulder. He turned to see a man in his early forties, dressed in smartly tailored trousers, business shirt and tie. "Excuse me," said the man. "Who is your father?"

He was blocking their path in the doorway, and then James noticed another two men standing behind him. His heart began to pound and he glanced left and right but they were hemmed in.

"What did you say?" asked James.

"I asked who is your father?"

"Who are you?"

"My name is Sebastien Luaba. It is a simple question."

James was so tired he was almost out on his feet, but even in this state it seemed obvious that there must be a connection to the anonymous text he had received earlier. This was the right place, *Extra Plus, Av Equateur. 12.00.* He bit back the natural answer, John Falkus. It was Axel he had texted yesterday in desperation for guidance, then last night this location and time had popped up.

"My father is …," he found himself hesitating, "… my father is Axel Terberg."

The man grasped him by the arm, "OK. Get in the car. Now."

James had a strange feeling he had just passed an exam; and there was a sense of urgency as Luaba held onto him and led the way outside. The other two men stepped forward and James now saw that both were armed, one carried a stubby looking revolver barely concealed beneath a jacket slung over his arm, while the other had a pistol thrust into his waistband. James didn't think they were being arrested, but it wasn't clear what was happening.

Luaba's men each took an arm and guided Jessica out of the supermarket, but she seemed to be having trouble balancing and they were almost carrying her. The door of a people carrier slid open and they lifted her into one of the rear seats where she lay slumped against a window, her eyes shut and her breathing shallow.

Then the door closed behind them and they swung out into the traffic on Avenue De L'Equateur and sped away eastwards, bypassing the ferry port.

"Where are we going?" James asked. Nobody responded. "I said, where are we going?"

"I heard," said Luaba without turning from his front seat, and he went back to contemplating whatever was occupying his mind. James studied the man. Luaba was probably in his early forties, his hair was receding and close cropped. He wore thick lenses in heavy, black-framed spectacles that gave him an owlish, thoughtful expression. He was clean shaven and his lusterless dark skin spoke of too many hours spent indoors, possibly in a desk job. Unlike his companions he was not muscular, but he was almost as tall as James and his stillness suggested a confidence in his team's abilities.

"You ask too many questions, particularly for someone whose ass we've just saved. Sit back and enjoy the air con, we'll be there in a minute and then you can talk. If not, I'll simply drop you at the next street corner and leave you to the wolf pack." He went back to his thoughts, punctuated by occasional bursts of high speed discussion in Lingala with his men. One in the second row of seats was receiving frequent texts and calls, and occasionally he leaned forward to brief Luaba.

James' heart had been racing since he felt the hand on his shoulder and the adrenaline was helping him to think more clearly than this morning. It seemed this guy and his team had been sent by Axel, but to do what? And what was in it for Luaba? James had no idea where they were going, what was coming, or who they answered to and his questions were no nearer being answered. He'd seen more guns in the last forty-eight hours than he'd seen before in a lifetime. He turned to look at Jessica who still lay slumped against the window; her eyes were closed. He checked her breathing which was slow and steady, then he put a hand on hers to see if she was awake but there was no response.

James tried to gauge their location and get his bearings. They had passed the Léon Hotel going east before heading north towards the Congo River. They drove through a huge square overlooked by an ugly concrete block roughly fifteen stories tall; at the far end of the square he could make out railway sidings and then they turned and passed a cathedral and several modern banks. They must be close to the port, warehouses lined both sides of the road now and most of the yards had shipping containers stacked three high. Then just as quickly there were trees softening the streets again and he caught glimpses of immaculate lawns and driveways behind high fences. It was all new to James but these seemed to be some of Kinshasa's more exclusive addresses.

The vehicle pulled into a drive and stopped at the gate. Somewhere dogs began to bark as a crisply uniformed Congolese guard came out of a smoked glass gatehouse and exchanged a few words with the driver through the open window. He shouldered a stubby little rifle as ducked his head to check the vehicle's occupants before going back to the gatehouse and opening the solid steel gates. The driver nosed the car forward impatiently as the gates swung back and they drove quickly around the side of the long low villa, the smooth asphalt giving way to a paved ramp leading down a steep slope into an underground car park. Steel roller doors descended behind them even before they came to a halt, and when the van was opened the warm outside air invaded their cool cocoon so that Jessica groaned gently and stirred. "Where are we?" she asked. "Who are these people?"

"I dunno. Think we're about to find out, but they don't seem hostile." He refrained from sharing that they weren't friendly either, she only needed so much information.

The men who had accompanied Luaba now gestured impatiently for them to get out of the people carrier, and then followed a few paces behind them through a steel door with Jessica leaning heavily on James. Security here was evidently tight around the perimeter and, while no guns had been drawn, James was acutely aware that his hosts were heavily armed. They all passed along a featureless underground corridor before entering a large, dimly lit room filled with IT equipment and the hum of powerful air-conditioning.

"Sit down and put your bags on the table," said Luaba. "Either you have bad timing or you keep bad company. Before you leave here, I aim to find out which." James was about to say something when their host held up a hand to silence him. "You have interrupted a difficult day and we've only lifted you for two reasons; because an old friend asked me to, and because you may have critical information. If you co-operate with us, we will escort you safely out of the DRC. If you do not, then no old friendship will protect you, nor would Axel expect it. Is that clear?"

James looked down at Jessica to see if she had taken this in. She seemed to have rallied well and was leaning less heavily on him. He said yes and she slowly nodded her assent. The couple put their bags on the tables and before they could react these had been taken by Luaba's men who ignored their protests. James stepped forward to prevent them and one of the men taking their bags simply raised a handgun and pointed it casually at James' midriff which made him stop.

"You asked who I am and where we were going. My name is Major Sebastien Luaba; I am a senior investigating officer in President Kabila's government. I need your passwords. I'm sure you will co-operate when I tell you that you have information about a man, a former government minister and army officer who has begun a coup d'état against the elected government."

"Hey, I'm just an NGO photographer and she's a journalist, we know nothing about a coup d'état," said James.

"And those are your first mistakes, Mr Falkus, and I trust your last. Sadly, every untruth you utter makes me question every truth more closely. Do not assume that because this is a small and poor country that we are stupid or ill-informed. You are no longer an NGO photographer because they fired you, Ms Tsiba may be a journalist but she's here on a tourist visa. Two lies already and we have hardly started. We know that you were kidnapped by General Businga's son because you took some highly compromising photographs of his betrayal of this country and illegal dealings with a rebel force and a hostile foreign power. We know that you managed to escape and still have those photographs. We want them. In exchange, we will give you certain information that may be of particular interest to you, Ms Tsiba."

Jessica said nothing but held his gaze.

Now the passwords please. I assure you this is a mere convenience, you could withhold them and it would then be a race to see whether we could extract them

459

from you by force faster than my Chinese colleagues here can access your hard drives. Either way it will hurt a lot, and we will ultimately have what we need. I'm just trying to save us some time and you a great deal of pain. He looked from one to the other. "As you have said little since we collected you from the supermarket, Ms Tsiba I want you to tell me that you have understood the seriousness of what I've just told you. As the future of this government is at stake and we have very little time, we will do whatever it takes to protect our country – do you understand?"

"Yes," said James. He looked at Jessica who now looked more alert than he had seen her for hours.

"What information are you offering me, Major?" said Jessica.

Luaba breathed the sigh of a man whose patience was being tested. "You are not in a position to negotiate, Ms Tsiba. Neither of you are. What we will give you depends on your co-operation right now. If you allow us to share your data – and we will return everything to you – then I assure you that the information we give you will not disappoint. In fact, it could help your career. On that, I'm afraid, you will simply have to take my word. In any case, we will not share anything with you if you fail to co-operate now. I know about the principles of independence that you journalists hold so dear, and for the record we can agree that you have stated your unwillingness to be a patsy – isn't that the Americanism? Now you need to mix your principles with intelligence and see that we will have this data, one way or another."

A young Congolese stood in the shadows, with a pen poised while a team of Chinese and Congolese software engineers began work on the two laptops on the far side of the large room. They had their backs to the couple seated at the table and were fully occupied. People came and went through two other doors and there was an air of tension and sustained activity.

James spoke first. "I have nothing to hide. As long as you leave my data undisturbed on there, I can tell you my password is LisaH987. How long will this take?" Nobody answered him. The young man scribbled it down and turned to Jessica. For the first time since they had arrived she looked at James for a long time. She put a hand on his knee beneath the table, he guessed it was an acknowledgement of the personal significance of his password.

Then she turned back to Luaba. "Looks like you have us every which ways. Here," and she beckoned to the young man with the pad, "this'll be quicker if I write it down for you."

One of the guards stepped forward and emptied both bags, removing the pistol that James had acquired and stuffed in the top of his belongings. Then holding a handheld scanner he beckoned James to stand. He ran the device slowly over James and then Jessica with no result before sweeping over their bags, and as he reached the top of Jessica's backpack there was a shrill squawk. He moved the sensor back and forth and the noise returned. All eyes were on her bag. His practiced search found nothing on the bag's exterior, but as soon as he ran his fingers inside the upper lip of the top compartment he found an obstruction and turned the compartment inside out. A grey plastic device, the size of a small memory stick, was fixed to the roof of the pocket with a strong adhesive.

The guard looked up at Luaba. "It's OK, any transmissions in here will be blocked. We've seen these before, they're trackers not microphones. American-made. The Russians and British have something similar. Our Chinese friends here think they're crap, they have one half the size. We will leave it there, perhaps the CIA will believe that we haven't spoken, that you simply hid in the home of a Chinese mobile network CEO. Personally I doubt it, but it doesn't matter much."

"How long? Who knows, Mr Falkus. That depends what we find on your systems. We have a secure room for you, I'm afraid it may not be very comfortable but it's clean and safer for you than being on the streets. I just hope you like Chinese takeaway." He grinned at his own wit.

To the guards he said, "Take them downstairs, give them blankets," and to Jessica, "You wouldn't believe how cold it gets down there." With that he walked out.

Guns had suddenly appeared in the hands of their two minders and the couple were escorted down a flight of stairs to a level below the garage. The corridor was damp, poorly lit and smelled as though it was used for chemical storage. It may have been the smell that finally proved too much for her but Jessica dropped to her knees and vomited a thin puddle of bile on the floor. The guards were momentarily suspicious but it became clear this was not an elaborate distraction and they pulled her to her feet, urging the couple at gunpoint into a small concrete room with a lockable steel door. It was roughly three metres by four, dimly lit with no window and a single mattress on the floor. When the door closed behind them, it was locked so they sat down and waited; James hoped to be fed, but Jessica needed rest.

Chapter 29

Chinese Mobile Network Operator, Kinshasa, DRC
Yesterday

The food that arrived was cold, congealed and greasy, but James bolted it all the same. He couldn't get Jessica to eat anything which only increased his concern; at least she was conscious again and sipping bottled water. Their argument had been forgotten for two or three hours afterwards as the pair slept curled together for warmth in the cold cellar. Later, through a fog of sleep he heard the door open and tried to focus; he felt sick with exhaustion and knew Jessica must feel worse with her head wound. The pair were kicked in the legs by two new guards to wake them and then pushed back upstairs.

Here they found their laptops running on the bench in front of them. They were immediately made to sit at a nearby desk. "You have been giving the Americans a window on everything you do for weeks," said Luaba.

"Bullshit," said James. "I'm careful what I let into my system."

"Oh? Like she was with her backpack?" Luaba snorted contemptuously at the pair of them. "Anyway, it was Jessica I was talking to. It doesn't matter how they got in there, they're in." Turning back to James he added, "We haven't found anything on yours yet but don't get too smug, we're still looking."

Luaba regarded her dismissively, "They've had total access to your contacts, emails, photos, videos, chats, all your articles and data." There was a look of astonishment on Jessica's face but she said nothing. "Well, now we're the ones managing your system remotely. Of course, it's easy enough to do and now we can control what they see. They'll realise they're being spoon-fed eventually, but it may fool them for a day or two. You'll be leaving tonight so it doesn't matter."

Instinctively, James looked around to see if there was still daylight but there were no windows. He guessed it must be late afternoon, but with no watch or phone he couldn't be sure. It wasn't clear if Luaba meant they'd be leaving the building, leaving Kinshasa, or leaving DRC, but every question he asked seemed to grant the man more authority so he bit his lip.

"If you're interested, there was a Trojan on your system, a virus imported a key logger to track every keystroke you made. It's a tried and tested NSA design, so it seems the Americans wanted to know what you were doing. What we didn't know until now, Ms Tsiba, is why. Why were the Americans interested in you? It's not because of the poor company you keep," he looked at James and the half smile never reached his eyes. "Do you want to tell James the reason?"

James couldn't be sure whether it was an act, but Jessica looked puzzled and when she spoke it was slow and some of her words were slurred. "I'm a freelance, a journo for hire. I write and film about foreign affairs. Did you say it was the National Security Agency?"

He nodded. "Shall we talk about what you're writing?"

Jessica put her head in her hands and stared at the floor. There was a long silence, then without looking up she said, "You mean about Axel Terberg? That's no secret, I despise the man. He may be James' blood father but I've always said I'm going to expose his trade in conflict minerals here, and globally. We have different views on the man, but that's none of your business. Besides, I'd have thought you'd approve of what I'm planning to expose; Terberg's not helping this country any."

"You still don't get it, do you? Either of you." Sebastien Luaba shook his head slowly in surprise. "You say you've been investigating him, Jessica but you haven't worked it out and you've talked to him, James, I guess at length. And you haven't sussed it either."

"Sussed what?"

"Axel isn't working for himself. He never has been, he's a frontman the Americans are using. We don't have all the background yet, perhaps he's just a cut-out."

"A cut-out?"

"Someone to do their work while giving them deniability. If the CIA or NSA want something done in DRC, sometimes it suits them to get someone else to do it for them so that they can sustain the illusion that they have clean hands. It's nothing to do with them," said Luaba. "We've had suspicions about his motivations here for a while – he didn't fit the mould, the type of mineral buyer we're used to seeing here. They may vary in nationality and attitude but they all have one thing in common – they're traders. Axel, well he's more of a collector, he likes a deal sure but talk to him about precious stones and his eyes light up. Conflict minerals don't excite or motivate him. He has money but he doesn't live lavishly. He never seemed credible as a mineral trader."

"Oh, spare me the cant. He's a white trader; does that make you think he's innocent?"

"I'll put that nonsense down to your blow to the head, Miss Tsiba. I'm a black man in a black country that's been more damaged by whites than any other country in Africa. And somehow you think I have a lingering belief in the beneficence of white men? Do you want to rethink that crock of shit?"

"Anyway, our hunches were confirmed by security contacts in Beijing. They've been watching him on and off for months although he goes off-radar completely from time to time – in itself a cause for suspicion."

She leaned back on the sofa and closed her eyes before speaking in a whisper. "Can we do this later? My head's banging."

Sebastien Luaba indicated Jessica's laptop to one of the engineers waiting nearby, who leaned over and opened several folders before turning it around for James to view. "He's pulling up everything in her system with the keyword 'Axel'," Luaba explained. "There's plenty there. Files, folders, photos, a timeline, mini-biography, known associates including you, she's mapping the man's life. And there's the draft of a series of articles – her exposé."

James was surprised at how much research she'd already done but he refused to give Luaba any satisfaction. "Like Jessica said, she told me already. Anyway, what's it to you?"

"I just thought you should know what you're dealing with, what kind of man your father is," Luaba appeared nonchalant. "Both good and bad."

"You can drop the public-spirited act. That's between us," said James. He paused before adding, "I have got a question for you though." Luaba turned back to him. "Why did you rescue us? Was it because of Axel?"

Luaba said nothing for a moment, then he seemed to choose his words carefully. "He and I go back a long way. He asked if I could help, I was intrigued – and surprised – when he told me of your relationship."

"Not half as surprised as he was," said James laconically.

Luaba continued, "No, that wasn't the only reason; let's just say you were small pieces in the jigsaw, finding you has helped us see the bigger picture."

"What is the big picture?" James demanded but Luaba simply stared at him in silence. "I have a right to know if people are trying to kill me for it."

Luaba gave an icy smile. "You're only half correct. You have no rights here, none whatsoever. But they *are* trying to kill you and if you do what we tell you then maybe both of you will live to tell your grandchildren about it. If you don't, then your death here is certain. The people coming after you are serious, with a rich country to win if they can silence you and everything to lose if they don't. Stand in their way and they will crush you. And what's more, Mr Falkus so will we. Which puts you in a bind, doesn't it? Can you trust them, when they've already imprisoned and damaged you once?" He nodded at James's hand. "I guess you know the answer to that. Or should you throw your lot in with us? We've detained you both – but we've fed you, explained some things and so far no one's taken the pliers to you, have they? I know which side I'd choose."

James tried to focus on something other than pliers. "You mentioned finding spyware on Jessica's laptop, and you didn't say anything about removing it."

Luaba grinned but his response was partial. "Very good, Mr Falkus. You have some of your father's perspicacity. We've left the spyware in place."

"Why?"

"And then you disappoint me again. I should have thought that was obvious."

"Humour me."

"Perhaps you're both good actors, anyway you convinced us this was no 'cover', the Trojan was a genuine plant to tell the Americans where you were, Jessica, what you were doing and what you had found."

"Unfortunately, Jessica's mobile phone also carries Smurf spyware they've hidden on your phone to control it remotely. James, your phone was clean – perhaps you haven't had it long or they weren't interested in you. Slightly humiliating to be upstaged like that by your girlfriend I'd say, but we'll leave that aside. In some ways, it's much more telling than the spyware on your PC. This is newer stuff, more sophisticated, which tells me they see her as a significant national security threat. Is she interested in anything that directly affects the Americans, or just Axel? Or are they one and the same?" They both looked at Jessica who had fallen asleep on the sofa.

Luaba continued. "She's made no secret of her focus on him – on the contrary, she wants to draw the world's attention to his conflict mineral trades. Wake her up." He nodded to where Jessica lay motionless.

"Give her a break. She's exhausted, she hasn't eaten or slept for days, we've been on the run and now she's had a blow on the head."

"Wake her, or I will."

James leaned over Jessica and gently shook her shoulder. Her eyes opened but she lay still, unable to focus on him. When she spoke, it was so quiet he had to lean close to hear, but her words were jumbled and made no sense. Then her eyes rolled back in her head and she passed out. "Shit, she needs a doctor, she's getting worse."

"She is not a priority. Doctors don't do house calls when there's fighting, and non-essential embassy staff are now being relocated. They're catching buses to the airport. So don't expect any help there. Of course, they may be back in a week or two but you don't have time to find out, do you?"

"Who's doing the fighting?"

"Am I supposed to believe you don't know?"

"All I know is that we've been chased halfway across Africa by a politician hood with a grudge against me, or us. His son's been shot dead by the UN and I understand he holds me responsible. If Jessica knows why she's being targeted, she hasn't told me. You said the spyware told you she's being watched by the Americans, not by General Businga."

Luaba studied James for a long time in silence before murmuring, "You are utterly out of your depth, aren't you?"

James said nothing.

"As far as recent events in your life are concerned, Businga and the Americans are one and the same, Uncle Sam will know Businga's after you. He does damn all without their OK," said Luaba. "The US tried to tell us how to run our affairs by paying us to have new elections, and when that didn't help Businga they backed his attempt to overthrow our president, our elected president, Joseph Kabila."

"Yes, I read about your elections, and your President's dynastic ambitions."

"You can sneer, Mr Falkus, but we've built a country in a lot less time than you took to make yours. And we've learned the hard way we can't rely on Europeans or Americans, so we'll find our successes and make our mistakes our way."

If there was a time to debate the issue, this sure as hell wasn't it, James just wanted to get Jessica out of here. But Luaba wasn't easily deflected. "Businga's not the only one with powerful friends, as you can see. The difference is our backers are in the ascendant, in twenty years' time the Chinese will be the undisputed global superpower. And we'll be their most important ally in Africa, selling those vital minerals and metals in exchange for building a new infrastructure of roads, dams and railways to replace the wreckage the West left behind. So you can see, our Chinese friends are only too happy for Jessica to expose Axel's work for the Americans."

"What proof do you have that he's working for the Yanks?"

"I don't need to prove it to you, Mr Falkus. But if you need convincing have you asked yourself how Axel is often well informed and well connected? Who do you think greases palms for him here and abroad? That takes a big network and huge resources, wouldn't you think?"

"I don't understand. We know he's trading in illegal conflict minerals, you've confirmed it, and yet he's working for the American authorities. But it's illegal there, too."

"Very much so since the Dodd-Frank Act. The US government will prosecute anyone found importing conflict minerals into the States. Only he's not importing into the States, he's very careful about that and so are his handlers. He may or may not be one of the bastards doing it, but he's their bastard. What is it the Americans call it? He's their skin in the game. This is the business you've stumbled into, and you may find it easier to get in than get out. You're starting to see, not everyone here in Kin is what they seem. What did he tell you he did for a living?"

James didn't answer. It was bad enough that his blood father was dealing in blood minerals, it seemed he was – well, what else could you call it? – a spy for the Americans. "Who exactly does he work for? I mean is he with the CIA or something?"

"Does it matter? Take my word, Uncle Sam picks up the tab for everything, and has done ever since Axel suddenly turned up here a few years ago. He said he had been in Zambia, but he was vague about what he'd been doing there."

"I thought spies operated in secret, somewhere in the shadows."

"They're not much bloody use if they don't mix, if they don't get out there."

James studied Luaba more carefully. "I guess you're no civil servant either."

Luaba held his stare.

James tried a different tack. "Why are you telling me all this?"

"To open your eyes to what your father really is, and I want you to tell Jessica since," he nodded at the recumbent journalist, "I can't tell her myself. So you can let her know that she's on the right track with Axel."

"You want to use her to expose him, clean up your shit for you."

"Inelegantly put, James, but close enough. We're all using one another – you used Axel to call for help. He used me to bail you out. Call it *quid pro quo*. You scratch my back, etc."

"For chrissakes, spare me the cod philosophy. You do it because it suits you, and because Jessica and I may be valuable if we undermine Axel and the Americans in DRC. I get that, it saves you a job if we neutralise a CIA agent – assuming he's with the CIA, and you're not denying it. And now your Chinese friends have given Jessica new ammunition to do it."

Luaba rubbed his chin pensively. "In a way it's a shame," he said, "I liked Axel, but he's backed the wrong side. America is yesterday's power. Soon there'll only be one, and we will be its vital economic partner. You can't imagine how good that sounds to us. We've never called the shots anywhere, not even at home. There's always been someone telling us what to do. Belgians, Americans, even the UN."

It was becoming too much for James. "You're bloody naïve if you think the Chinese will be any different."

"They're different already. For the first time, we have a customer for our materials and a business partner who doesn't tell us how to run our politics. I guess, they remember clearly what it's like to be ruled by uninvited house guests like you." There was venom in Luaba's reply and James began to see the anger beneath his cultivated exterior. "In the West you have no idea what that feels like. You British have invaded most countries at some time – you don't have the imagination to see that there could be another kind of relationship, that it's not always Master-Servant." He spat out the last words.

"The Americans back Businga, saying our president has been bought by the Chinese. And why? Because they're scared their mineral supplies will be shut down, their influence eliminated and Businga is the last good card left in their hand. They conveniently forget we deal with companies everywhere. It's true the Chinese are expanding aggressively here, we've signed some exclusive mineral extraction deals with them for cobalt, tin and tantalum, and they've set up joint ventures with Congolese firms.

"If we let him, Businga would just sell it all to the Americans for a fat Swiss account and US protection to keep him in power. So, the State Department can't let Jessica report what they're doing. It's not just a vicious local squabble, it's a pivotal moment in Africa."

James backtracked. "What did you call that program earlier? Smurf?"

Luaba looked at him long and hard, still assessing James. Perhaps he could be useful. "Yes. Like the Belgian cartoon characters. It would take a software engineer to find them. But let's just say it's annoying to find these programs on your screen. Smurf tools were developed at the NSA in Maryland, then used by GCHQ in Britain. Given the NSA's interest in Jessica, it's more likely to have come from them. They just send an encrypted text message to your phone, it's received but it's never displayed. As soon as it's received, they can access and control your device in ways you'll never know."

"One tool is Nosey Smurf, it lets them listen to conversations or whatever's going on around the phone, even when it's switched off. I'm guessing that could be embarrassing for you both – it was found on Jessica's phone." James didn't rise to the bait. "There's Dreamy Smurf that turns your phone on and off remotely. There's Paranoid Smurf that makes it hard, although not impossible, for users to see that their phone has been hacked. That was in there, too."

"There was one surprise though; they hadn't put Tracker Smurf on her phone. Not sure why," said Luaba. "That does what it says, locates you with greater accuracy than normal apps can manage with cell tower triangulation where network signals are weak. It would have been useful for the Americans to find her in some areas here but if there's no signal at all then ...," he spread his hands and shrugged. "As I say, it wasn't there and our guys had a good look. Maybe NSA had trouble delivering it to her phone, maybe they were interrupted. Who knows?"

"Again, we've left the Smurf tools on there," he continued. "The quickest way of alerting them that we're onto them would be removing them. We've monitored what they're doing. We'll just have to see if they believe Jessica has zero cellphone coverage again today."

Luaba nodded towards Jessica. "How's she doing? We've copied both hard drives, so we have all her photos and other data, we're analysing it now. Normally, I'd say don't leave town in case we want to talk to you again. This is different, you need to leave Kin now or you never will."

After a moment Luaba said, "There's one other thing you can tell her when she wakes up."

"She's not fucking resting, you know! She's passed out. I told you she needs a doctor."

"I can't help you there. Tell her, we haven't just taken things, we've given her new material – highly sensitive material that may finally give her some perspective on what's happening here. If she's going to be any good as a foreign correspondent, she's got to keep an eye on the big picture and she'll need good sources. I told the engineers to load some of our own data on General Businga. The American's protégé has very dirty hands indeed. We could have given her details of his war crimes during the Congolese Wars, or his unlawful arrests and mass killings, his torture of innocent men and women. But we're not fools; most people in Europe and America don't even know there's been a regional war here, never mind two. Nor do they give a shit that five million people have been killed in the fighting over the last decade. They don't care that the Peace Accord never stopped the fighting. Oddly, what may interest them is the scale of his recent corruption and embezzlement in office; sadly that's how the world works. It has to be news, otherwise its history. And the world ignores history. Let's just say that this time we're taking a lesson from the Americans. Didn't they finally imprison Al Capone for non-payment of taxes? I guess we all use whatever tools we can. He's our Capone, only worse, and we want him finished or put away. This bastard is so dangerous and ambitious he'll start a civil war without blinking if it'll bring him to power.

"We've given Jessica copies of some of Businga's bank statements proving payments were made from Rwanda to a Belgian account in his wife's name. The payments were made every time an arms shipment went through his distribution network from Kinshasa to Goma. Of course, we can't yet prove these payments were for arms, but it would be hard for a minister in the DRC to explain why he's receiving huge regular payments from an enemy country like Rwanda. It's only a few years since Rwanda invaded the Congo, and the payments align perfectly with the arms shipments we know about. The sums rose and fell in line with the size of the arms shipments. We interrogated a cargo handler at Goma airport who confirmed the size and date of the last ten movements. Arms into Goma, tin and tantalum out. And he profits from both."

"When you can talk to Jessica, tell her we can share more with her but we'll have to use secure email communication."

"I thought there was no such thing. Can't the CIA or NSA hack any email?"

"Not if it's never sent."

James frowned. "I don't get you."

"Messages are most vulnerable when they're sent. She'll be secure if she avoids her own laptop or phone, and internet cafés which are vulnerable to low-grade hacking. The security services will be logging all her key strokes. So she'll need to buy a cheap 'burner' laptop or prepaid smartphone, a device they don't know about. She must only use it for data, never for voice calls – her vocal patterns can be traced. This is the email address for her, memorise it and don't write any of this down. Don't let her write it either. This email address will also be her user name, her password will be Raphael911 – she should be able to remember that. When she logs in, she'll find some files in the Drafts folder. If she keeps them in Drafts, they'll stay secure; she must delete them as soon as she's read them. She can ask us questions in the same way, just draft an email and leave it there – we'll pick it up and any reply will be left there. The information will stay secure as long as she doesn't disclose those login details or send any of the Draft emails. And tell her, don't forget to delete. Have you got that?"

James nodded.

"OK, repeat the instructions back to me." James repeated them without error. "You haven't said what's going to be in there."

"I haven't, have I?" Luaba studied James again. Whatever he was considering, James appeared to have passed the test.

"As I said, we don't just want Jessica writing about Axel. It sounds as though nothing will stop her doing that. If she's going to be credible as a foreign correspondent, though she needs to cover more than one angle of the situation here. So we're giving her exclusive access – and when she reads it she'll understand what I mean by exclusive – access to incriminating data on the former General Businga and his associates including his private emails. None of us know how the next few days will play out, but if he's still alive she will have enough material for several scoops on his financial affairs worldwide. We've decrypted his coded instructions on recent local and offshore bank transfers. When it's ready, she will be sent more details of his bank accounts in Switzerland and the Cayman Islands – bank names and sort codes, account names and numbers, transactions and dates, payers and payees, everything financially speaking."

"How the hell did you get all that?" breathed James.

"Let's just say, it all depends who you know. The Swiss are so much more co-operative these days, especially when they want something in return."

"What do they want?" asked James.

"James, don't be obtuse. You're a smart guy, look around you. We've discussed who holds economic power these days, China. And what are Switzerland and Cayman famed for? Banks. They want to protect their position as banking supremoes, so the Swiss and others need full access to China's money markets. Believe me, if China asks for it they can have details of any account they want, details that it suits the Chinese to share with us. And in turn we expect Jessica to share select details with the world. So even if Businga survives, he will be finished politically and financially. Foutu. Penniless, wherever he hides."

James just shook his head. He was amazed how easily private information could be accessed, information that Businga had gone to great lengths to keep secret.

Luaba continued, "You're both more use to us outside the Congo so we're going to get you out of here now. There's one condition."

"Oh? What's that?"

"To show us your appreciation we want you to get closer to your father. Find Axel and keep us informed."

"You want me to spy on him!" James snorted derisively. "And if I refuse?"

"You won't; you're far too fond of Jessica – it would be terrible to think of anything happening to her."

"You need her, too. Why would you harm her?"

"We'd prefer not to, but there are always other ways of publishing this information."

******

It was always feast or famine with Businga, though mainly famine, thought Gahiji. He had been deprived of support at various times when he needed it, now here at the port there were so many reinforcements he was tripping over them.

Long after the last ferry crossing of the day the quayside was still the usual chaotic scene of activity. Police, customs officers and those affecting to help them mingled with the milling crowd just adding to the confusion. The sky blue ferry stood silent, a few bright lights burned high above the main deck, some cars had already been driven aboard and parked for the night. The occupants mingled with foot passengers and a queue of traders were wheeling bicycles, trolleys and pallet carriers onboard piled high with boxes and sacks. A pile of clothing had spilled across the boarding ramp and an argument broke out as three men struggled to reload it.

People were coming and going on foot, many of them carrying large hessian-wrapped bundles of goods on their heads or backs to sell in Brazzaville. A plain clothes official stepped forward at the gate demanding their papers but his bluster evaporated when he saw the unmarked SUV's heavily armed occupants. The papers forgotten, he hurriedly pushed aside the traders queuing to board, slapping those too slow to react and shouting at any out of reach. As he bullied his way through the throng to clear a path for the car, a team of helpers gathered and the spilled load was dragged out of the way. A few other officious types shouldered aside men and women who had been in the queue for hours and repeatedly beckoned their vehicle to follow. They clearly imagined Gahiji's party wanted to board so there was further confusion when the vehicle turned away from the ramp and nosed its way through the crowd to the quayside. A few hopeful passengers sleeping on the dockside were woken and roughly forced to move, others eating their supper stood up to make way for the vehicle. Indignant protests were silenced when Gahiji ordered two of his men with stubby assault rifles out of the car to escort the vehicle through.

He had finally gained the back-up he needed and he wasn't going to send them away again. For now he stood down some of the men and they wandered away to sleep in the bus that had brought them.

Gahiji still had twenty well-armed and trained men at his disposal and a working chain of command, so the ferry was cordoned off in minutes as they began checking the identities of those who had already boarded. The policemen who had been in the area all day were dismissed. One looked dazed by the arrival of so many armed men while the other hung around to see what was going to happen.

Gahiji set two armed men on the boarding ramp, three more on deck to check the ship and two more among the waiting passengers. This still left another with him as a runner in case their fragile radio communications went down. He could call on a mixed bag of fifteen assault rifles, an array of handguns, and there was even a rocket propelled grenade launcher in the SUV, though he hadn't asked for it. *Bloody feast or famine*, thought Gahiji for the third time.

The men began methodically to wake and search the travellers waiting for the first crossing at six the next morning. Everyone on deck was scrutinised, those that had been searched were herded forward to an area now cordoned off with crush barriers and old oil drums found on the jetty. Despite the tension in the city there was a steady stream of new arrivals at the ferry; they were corralled then checked for arms and their identity. Under the command of a tough and wiry little NCO, the incoming team had arrived fully briefed on who they were looking for. Gahiji was impressed and might have been tempted to leave them but his reputation and his life were hanging by a thread. No one working for Businga could afford a screw-up.

A couple of gendarmes had driven on to the dock a few hours before and still hung around chatting with the customs officials, but seeing the changed atmosphere since Gahiji and his men arrived they climbed back into their car and made themselves scarce. If they were loyal to the government, they had the sense not to show it.

The new watch soon found a rhythm to its duties and the soldiers settled to wait, knowing that if the spies hadn't fled by plane this must be their escape route.

******

"If I've got this right, you're blackmailing me to betray my blood father so that my ex-girlfriend can put him in prison." He might as well let Luaba know that he and Jessica were no longer an item. Luaba merely raised an eyebrow.

"Crudely put, but those are the essentials. Oh, and one other thing; be quick about it. Our information is that Dr Businga believes it was Axel who betrayed his

472

boy Louis to MONUSCO." James' heart began racing involuntarily at the mention of the man who had tortured him. Reminding himself that the man was dead did little to calm James' pulse rate. "Well, Businga has sent someone – we don't know who – after Axel and you. All we know is he's Congolese, well trained and is said to see a job through. He could be on the way to Europe by now, where Axel was last sighted. The Americans probably won't be happy when they find out their candidate for the Presidency here has a Kill Order on one of their own agents."

"Why are you telling me all this? I thought spies were supposed to be tight-lipped."

"Spies? I'm just a civil servant. I worked in the Ministry of Mines close to Businga until I was moved. But it's all to the same purpose, protecting and developing my country."

James shook his head in disbelief. "You say we should get after Axel, but you're holding us prisoners here. When are you going to release us?"

"If I let you walk out, even if she could," he nodded towards Jessica, "where would you go? You'd be picked up by Businga's men within the hour. Where were you heading when I found you?"

James was silent.

"That's what I thought. You don't have a clue. I could give you an armed escort but we can't guarantee your safety at the airport so I'd have to send a disproportionate number of men to protect you. We have other priorities." He looked them up and down. "I have a better idea."

"Well, unless you have a doctor here, you'd better make it quick. Jessica's not well enough for a long journey, I need to get her to a hospital."

Luaba smoothed a hand over his head as he thought things through. Eventually he looked up, "Don't take her to hospital here, it'll take too long. Your presence and her US passport will spark too many questions, and Businga may have friends there, too. You're better off getting her to Brazzaville." He jerked a thumb towards the river.

"We can't go that way," said James "they'll be expecting us at the ferry terminal."

"Which is why you won't be going there. If we can get hold of them there's still an alternative."

"What's that?"

"You might be able cross tonight in the dark, using the Rich Man's Ferry."

"The what?"

"There's an unofficial crossing upriver using power boats. They take people or goods that can't wait for the normal ferry or who don't want to be seen, which is why it's expensive."

"Smugglers then."

"Why do you British have to label everything? For someone trying to get out of here quickly and quietly you seem very judgmental," he sighed. "Do you have cash? I'll take care of the ferrymen so you won't need cash here, but you'll need it when you land the other side and to pay for the hospital in Brazz."

"We have some francs and dollars. And credit cards."

"Congolese francs won't help, use the dollars. You don't want to be traced so don't use the cards. I'll make a few calls now, get ready to leave immediately. She obviously can't carry her kit so you'll have to carry that as well as her. I'll come with you and we'll have an escort," said Luaba, "I need to see if the city is calm anyway – I'm getting very mixed reports," and with that he waved James away dismissively.

James looked at Jessica. Her breathing was shallow but steady, and although it was hard to tell in this light her skin looked unusually pale. She hadn't moved or made a sound since he'd last checked her. He pulled back her eyelids; her pupils were different sizes which seemed odd. He would have to carry her to the car and then to the boat, somehow he would have to manage their things too. There was nothing for it but to throw out anything they didn't need. He jettisoned all their clothes, saving only his fleece to cover her during the crossing. He would do without. Luaba's IT people had copied everything on their laptops already so it was easy enough to replace them with a single portable hard drive. He didn't fancy the insurance battle to replace their expensive cameras so he wrapped these in the fleece and put them in his backpack, pocketing all their memory cards.

There was a renewed buzz of activity in the room with Chinese and Congolese staff coming and going. When the word came to go, he put on the backpack and knelt down, scooped her up and holding Jessica to his chest he carried her to the underground car park where a battered Peugeot and a Jeep were waiting. She didn't even stir, her head fell against his neck as he carried her to what he hoped was the last leg of their Congolese journey.

******

Ten minutes later James and Jessica were travelling in the back of a car, following a road that ran upstream beside the River Congo. He couldn't get his bearings, but somewhere in the lush, well-appointed suburbs of Gombe, they turned right and began to circle south and east away from the port and its scattered industrial zones. They moved among high metal fences, with only occasional lights beyond showing stacks of rusting shipping containers. Somewhere out there in the darkness the muddy wide waters of one of Africa's largest rivers pushed and jostled past them to the sea.

Then a strong smell reached them through the car's open windows. An acrid stab of smoke blew in, it was strong, pungent and drifting so thickly that James guessed tyres were burning nearby. He couldn't see flames but the wind was billowing curtains of smoke across the road that slowed their progress. As they rounded a corner, he could see flames rising from lines of car tyres directly in their path, vehicles were being forced to slow as they weaved through. Were these the remnants of earlier rioting, or the build up to the coup attempt Luaba had predicted? The tyres were spewing endless pipes of black smoke into the Kinshasa sky, the breeze stirring it before it came together in a canopy above them. James looked up as they passed more street lights and could dimly see a dark cloud hanging above the city. The streets were deserted, the few cars they met sped on their way, some without lights.

A babble of tense conversation broke out in the front. The driver was gesticulating to left and right, perhaps fearful that these chicanes were an ambush, but Luaba slammed his fist on the dashboard, shouted something James didn't understand and jabbed a finger straight ahead. The driver had slowed to negotiate the obstacles but when Luaba pulled a handgun he put his foot down again. It wasn't clear if the gun was in readiness for an attack or simply to stiffen the driver's resolve.

James sat sideways on the bench seat and looked down at the worryingly still form beside him. The rear window was missing from the Peugeot saloon making it easier to look behind but his view was blocked by the protective vehicle that followed, a huge green Toyota pick-up with a heavy machine gun pintle-mounted behind the cab. Its presence was not reassuring. Behind the headlights he could just make out the uniformed gunner who swung the barrel to left and right as if sniffing out trouble on the night air. The roads remained eerily quiet.

Luaba had little time. He needed to get these two off his hands and into the boat, then he could head back to the Ministry and see what was happening across the city. They could have skirted south of Golf de Kinshasa but Luaba figured he just needed to avoid the port so he ordered the driver to turn east along Boulevard Du 30 Juin. That would carry them safely east at least three blocks south of the port.

There was so little traffic that the two vehicles barely slowed as they swung left at the wide junction, the Peugeot took the corner fast enough for its tyres to squeal. The pick-up behind had to slow a little to negotiate the turn but was soon revving its engine to catch up.

******

Across the street the two men had been watching the crossroads for hours from their car parked among abandoned vehicles outside the Ministry of Sport. Little had gone by, the number of pedestrians here – never high at this hour – was now zero. So, when two vehicles they didn't recognise came through at speed, the second one a 'Technical' carrying a manned heavy machine gun, they were on the phone immediately to Gahiji's NCO.

Within moments men were running across the nearby ferry port to their vehicles clutching AK-47s and finishing food as they went. Less than thirty seconds after that call came in the first SUV was forcing its way out of the ferry terminal scattering travellers, hawkers, and immigration officials as it revved hard along the service road. Within a minute another two vehicles were bouncing after it, swinging left out of the gate and tearing down the port road towards the Boulevard where Luaba had been spotted.

By now the car radios were alive with excited calls for support and when Gahiji in the second SUV turned left onto the Boulevard he calculated they must be less than a minute behind their quarry. Gahiji cursed his driver for a coward and urged him to speeds neither of them had ever managed before in Kinshasa's traffic; as they closed in on Luaba's route at the enormous Central Station roundabout he could see the Toyota they were trying to intercept as it exited the far side of the junction. The first of the pursuing SUVs was in between.

Edouard Gahiji was on the radio, he wanted maximum support and he knew where to find it. He needed eyes and there was only one way of catching up with them. He called Businga's direct line. "Sir, we have them on the run ahead of us."

The general didn't need to ask who he was talking about. "Good, bring them to me. Alive, remember."

"Yes sir. For that we need some help from your friends." He left a pause.

"What kind of help?"

"They're in faster vehicles than ours and supported by a pick-up with a big, er … sound system." It was force of habit to assume this wasn't a secure line. "If our friends use their eyes in the sky, we can make sure we don't lose them. A UAV could reach us from their base in a few minutes. We just need eyes and ears, that's all. No intervention."

"We've already arranged a Welcome Party to meet them. Isn't that enough?"

"Possibly, but I don't want them to give us the slip by finding another route out. Can they get a drone there, sir? Every second counts, will you ask?"

Businga knew he might be refused and replied carefully to avoid losing face. "We have your GPS coordinates. I will see what's available," and he rang off.

He was soon back on the phone. "They have a drone up already; it's being diverted, and will be over you in ninety seconds. They'll call you direct with an audio feed to advise what they see. I'm on my way, I'll be listening too. You end this now, or else. You hear me?" The threat had been voiced. It was capture them or be killed for failing, couldn't be much clearer.

******

Jessica lay totally still across the car's rear seat and it made her look small and vulnerable. The wind rushed in through the missing rear window and stirred a few loose curls of hair at her temple. Despite the draught there was a sheen of sweat across her face and her breathing was becoming more laboured. Then suddenly her head began to move violently, jerking backwards every few seconds. "Jessica, wake up. Speak to me!" James was shouting to be heard over the roar of the engine and the windrush. Then her whole body went rigid, her lips curled, her breath began to come in shallow gasps, and her legs and arms extended uncontrollably.

Luaba turned quickly. "What's happening?"

"I don't know. She wasn't moving at all before, now she seems ... I don't know, it's like she's having a fit. I have to get her to hospital."

Sebastien Luaba looked up at James but something caught his attention as he glanced over James shoulder; behind the protective Toyota he had a glimpse of two large black vehicles racing after them. Although two men were leaning out of the windows and pointing guns towards them, there was a surreal element to it, as he could hear nothing from the vehicles behind. He pushed James's head down and yelled a warning to the driver, then swung back to focus on the road ahead.

There was now a line of vehicles snaking around the junction and one by one they roared away down the broad, straight road from the Central Station towards the river. Luaba was looking for a particular left turn, not fully made-up but a route that would give them a direct run to the beaches and jetties of the rich Kinois.

Any attempt to pass through the area unnoticed had gone to hell, it was now an all-out race. As the sluggish Congo River reached Kinshasa, it began to sweep faster around to the left, and resume its westward journey to the Atlantic. On the inside of the bend the flow of water deposited so much sand that small islands and sandbars were constantly building up, shifting and reforming; it was here that a fortunate few found their playgrounds, running their speedboats out from the shore to picnic on sandy islands. In more settled times it was here that the ex-pat community barbecued racks of ribs and played cricket or softball on the beach.

It was this riverscape that Luaba and his driver were searching for. James darted a look behind them and now he could hear the crack and whine of small arms fire over the noise of the elderly Peugeot. The two pursuing SUVs were matching their speed in the darkness, their lights illuminating the Toyota, its gunner and the saloon car in front. The Toyota's gun had been swung around to meet the threat, and the gunner loosed a series of split-second ranging shots, before he began to hose the SUVs with staccato rips of automatic fire. It would have taken moments to end the pursuit from a stable firing point but the gunner's aim was thrown off by the swerving vehicle beneath him and he let go of the firing switch to yell at the driver to run straight. Then they were through the last of the big bends and the Toyota driver grinned as the Peugeot they were protecting began to pull away from them down the long straight road. The first Jeep was closing the gap a metre at a time, two of its passengers firing semi-automatics from the side windows at the gunner who faced them on the pick-up ahead. If he was unnerved at their gunfire, he didn't show it.

Briefly the SUVs had managed to close the gap undetected, but now the advantage of surprise was lost. The rear gunner had a heavier weapon on a superior platform, and the nearest Jeep's occupants didn't stand a chance. His next burst of gunfire smashed their windscreen, blew a ragged hole in the driver's chest and fatally struck the man behind him. Broken glass flew around inside the vehicle which careered across the central reservation to the opposite dual carriageway. It struck the wall of a container depot a glancing blow and rolled over twice before coming to a halt. Nothing happened for a few seconds and then there was a thunderous explosion as the fuel tank ignited.

******

Almost as soon as Gahiji ended the call his phone rang and an American voice said, "Sir, this is Liaison at 732 Ops Group, Creech, Nevada." There was a pause, "Creech, patching you through now." Then he could hear a crackle, the echo of a mic picking up an open room and suddenly the audio cleared so well that, even over the noise of his own vehicle, he could hear individual voices.

There was some brief static before another man's voice came on. "Predator over target. Two target vehicles heading bearing one-one-eight, speed six zero mph. Two vehicles are a four door sedan and a pick-up. Correction, three vehicles; third vehicle an SUV. Pick-up's a double cab, flat-bed with pintle-mount medium machine gun. Rear gunner appears to be solo. Eyeballing another pursuit vehicle, an SUV, it's been disabled one click further back. It's in flames, occupants immobile. Three more vehicles appear to be in pursuit, but falling behind."

"What's up ahead?" asked an older voice. "Show me terrain. And I need their predicted route. Get Analytics on this."

The younger voice again. "Copy that. Analytics says seventy percent probability they're headed for a river resort, to the east. Three clicks out. Few other destination options at this stage."

"How many in the lead two vehicles? Anyone we recognise?"

"Both unknown, sir," said a woman's voice, "as we weren't overhead at embarkation. No clear view yet."

"Tell me when you have something. I want facial recognition."

"The car's speed and suspension travel suggest three occupants, maybe four. The pick-up appears to have three – gunner, driver and passenger, sir. No IDs so far."

"Sir, we have one figure lying prone on the sedan's back seat. Immobile. We think four, repeat four, occupants in the car. No fire returned from the car yet. It's pulling away from the pick-up."

******

"I get it," said Gahiji's driver, "they're taking the smuggling route." He knew it well from transporting rich businessmen and his politician boss whenever they wanted to cross the river to Brazzaville quickly and discreetly.

There was no point in closing the gap again; Gahiji knew they would meet exactly the same fate as the first SUV. The second SUV had dropped back and the gunner in the Toyota kept it that way with short bursts of suppressive fire. Gahiji picked up his radio and began arranging a new rendezvous for them. Sure enough, two minutes later as they approached the eastern perimeter of N'dolo Airport two armoured cars travelling at speed broke out of the scrub cover to their right. Businga had mustered his forces at the airport, and these were exactly the vehicles Gahiji had requested – this time Businga had come through with the goods. The broken promises and endless waits for personnel in Goma were temporarily forgotten as the two Panhards surged up the incline and bounced roughly as they turned sharp right onto the road, ahead of the remaining SUV. Their huge aerials swung wildly, the tyres leaving curved streaks of black on the asphalt, and the exhausts belching noise and smoke as the engines hit maximum revs. Gahiji had spent time, too much time, in vehicles like this and knew well what the crew would be experiencing. The lack of suspension would bounce them around like peas in a drum, throwing them into the cockpit's hard edges, the noise would be deafening and would worsen as they gave chase. And firing their armaments would make the heat, noise and fumes even worse. No, he was happy to be back where he was.

The Panhards' reputation for speed compared to other armoured cars was well deserved and they immediately began to close the gap on the lumbering Toyota weighed down by what looked like a 12.7mm gun. Gahiji's driver tucked in their SUV behind the scout cars for protection from the pick-up's machine gun fire and slipstreamed them as they took up the pursuit.

When the armoured scout cars had crested the road and turned away from him, Gahiji had had a close-up view of both Panhards. The first of the vehicles was equipped with a long, thin autocannon probably twice the size of the Toyota's armament, while the other boasted a short stubby muzzle, some kind of mortar. *At last*, thought Gahiji, *they had something to match the machine gun*. Right on cue, the Toyota's rear-facing gun began firing at them but it was no surprise that the shots from a speeding flatbed struck the road harmlessly around them or carried over their heads.

With his initial range advantage and little chance of being hit by an AK-47 fired from a moving car window, the pick-up's rear gunner had been enjoying a turkey shoot. Now, suddenly the odds had swung heavily against him and he began to bang on the cab roof, yelling at the driver to hightail it. Whether the driver was slow to respond or the Toyota was already at maximum speed the pursuers would never know; either way the outcome was the same.

Driving in a staggered formation, the scout cars were both able to bring their barrels to bear but the crews knew their best chance was to stop and fire. The lead vehicle braked hard amid squealing tyres and the second came to a sudden halt beside it. Gahiji saw the autocannon swing a few degrees left, coming to bear on the departing pick-up. Inside the Panhard, as the driver held the vehicle steady, Gahiji could picture the gunner loading a clip of three shells. Within seconds they heard the first 30mm round being fired from the French-built armament. There was no visible impact so it must have carried over the Toyota, but Gahiji's men had front row seats for the two rapid fire strikes that followed as the first Panhard found its range. The second shell hit the Toyota's rear axle and the technical's gunner was thrown high in the air as the left rear wheel was ripped away. The vehicle began to tilt sideways, just as the cannon's third shell passed through the Toyota's cab and into the engine bay. It must have severed the fuel line for the resulting explosion shredded the pick-up like so much tin foil, lighting the night sky as brightly as any flare. Then pieces of the Toyota started to land on the road and in the verge ahead of them.

Gahiji's driver was slack-jawed at what he had seen and braked hard to avoid hitting the grizzly debris of men and machine. The chasing vehicles had all halted and Gahiji shouted into the radio for them to continue. "The spies are ahead, keep going. Over."

Not to be left out, the second Panhard was opening up with its mortar, but it was not designed for direct fire at anything over a few hundred metres and the shells fell short then far beyond their target. One by one the armoured cars gave chase again and Gahiji's two remaining SUVs followed.

Then a familiar voice came on the channel. "This is the General. Where are they, Gahiji? Over."

He didn't pause, "We believe they're making for one of the private beaches, probably at the new city development, sir. We've just destroyed the pick-up that was protecting them and we're closing on them. Over."

"I'm on my way. You know what to do. Out."

******

In the Peugeot James was trying to check on Jessica when the first mortar shell fell between them and where the Toyota had been. Her convulsions were subsiding but she looked frailer than ever, and for her sake he wished that they were anywhere but here.

"Look, on the left," yelled Luaba to his driver and without hesitation the man swung the elderly saloon car across the dual carriageway and down a road marked Cité du Fleuve. They nearly missed the turning, and Luaba knew he was lucky to have spotted it in the darkness. As they flashed past, they could just make out a billboard advertising the elegant homes being built in River City, and pictures showing the idyllic lifestyle on offer if you made your next home here – providing it was finished and you weren't being chased by armoured cars, James thought grimly.

The Peugeot's tyres squealed as they struggled to grip, understeer forcing the vehicle into a wide, carving turn that took them to the brink of the road. If they'd seen the turning even a second later, they would have missed it or rolled the car as they slid off the asphalt. The driver hung onto the bucking wheel and the car skimmed past the high pavement, missing it by centimetres before swinging back towards the middle, its rear end fishtailing as he fought to regain control. This part of the road had only just been finished and was unlit; there were kerbstones and drainage pipes stacked at intervals along the way, ready for installation. The road ran straight ahead in the darkness for half a kilometre towards the river, but their lights were too feeble to offer any reassurance. Fear gave them speed and the elderly Peugeot accelerated gamely, momentarily outrunning the pursuing pack.

The leading Panhard driver saw the car's rear lights as it veered off the main road and braked hard, knowing that the armoured car would never be able to match its speed in a turn. Inevitably, the pursuers lost further ground here but having made the turn their target was clearly visible several hundred metres ahead. There was no time to stop, so they fired at will on the move, the heavy vehicles bouncing hard and shaking the occupants like peas in a tin can. It was painful, it was hot, and the turret was filled with acrid fumes that the extractors did little to relieve. In the car, James could feel Jessica lying beside him but he could see little of her either from their own lights or the dancing illumination of the vehicles behind. One thing was clear though, the armoured cars were still following. He watched the car's speedo needle climb again; eighty kilometres an hour, ninety – then Luaba gave the order to kill their lights. The driver glanced sideways at his boss in horror to check he was serious. "Do it now!" yelled the officer, and suddenly they were plunged into darkness. Luaba had seen the security lights that surrounded the building site ahead and ordered his man to follow a straight line towards them. Maybe he had taken this road before, or maybe he figured that service roads to the riverside would be straight, either way it was a high risk strategy. Inevitably the driver began to slow slightly and Luaba roared at him to keep going. "If they catch us, we're dead anyway. Go!"

It was the roundabout that almost killed them. James was straining to look over their shoulders and see which way the road went when the heavy clouds above them began to part and the dust-pale route ahead was temporarily bathed in moonlight. Less than fifty metres ahead the road began a gentle right turn right onto a roundabout, but something was wrong. James was the first to see it; the road was unfinished, the tarmac stopped and beyond it was broken ground and discarded building materials.

"A gauche! A gauche!" he shouted and leaned over the driver's shoulder in an attempt to swing the wheel to the left just as Luaba and the driver spotted the hazard ahead. The car swerved violently left, James felt Jessica slide headfirst away from him into a crumpled heap by the passenger door. They left the road, bounced repeatedly, testing the Peugeot's robust suspension to its limits and then they lost control. It felt like slow motion as the car started to skid sideways, the driver doing his utmost to turn the wheel in the direction of travel, but as the rear of the car slewed around to the right it struck an oil drum marking the edge of the site and their slide was arrested. The rear spun back and the car came to an abrupt halt where it stalled. The driver turned the key frantically and the long-suffering Peugeot coughed as it came to life again, but as he engaged first and pulled away they could feel that one of the rear tyres had been wrecked or ripped away. The car was running on her rims on one rear wheel although the driven front wheels seemed intact. Acceleration was agonisingly slow and they could see sparks flying behind them but somehow the car was getting on the move once more.

That was the moment when their pursuers began to open up with machine gun fire – they had no hope of accuracy but were spraying the road with bursts of gunfire. One gunner was disciplined and squeezed the trigger for a second at a time, but in his excitement the leading gunner forgot his training and fired long bursts until the inevitable happened and his gun jammed. By now, not only had the gap closed between hunter and hunted, but the car was leaving a trail of sparks. A mortar round overshot them and exploded with a flash on the far side of the roundabout. They were saved by a narrowing of the service road which placed the mortar-equipped armoured car ahead, thereby blocking fire from the more accurate Panhard.

The loss of a tyre had forced the Peugeot driver to take a straight line wherever he could, so the car exited the roundabout and turned slowly left as they followed a brand new empty section of dual carriageway on the wrong side. The tortured grinding noise reverberated through the back of the car as they laboured loudly along the quayside. Large vacant apartment blocks could just be seen in the darkness on their right and a tributary to the Congo River lay opposite, then they began to pass a few boats at moorings to their left. As the road turned sharply right, Luaba jabbed a finger repeatedly towards the first turning they approached. "This way, this way! They should be here," and he started to search for lights or signs of a waiting boat.

Two men waited nervously under a solitary security light, and they discarded their cigarettes as the damaged Peugeot came into view. They stared in amazement at the speed it was doing on three wheels and the shower of sparks from a red-hot wheel rim. For the last few minutes they had heard a growing storm of noise from the approaching vehicles and had seen flashes of light on the horizon as explosions shook the port road.

As the protesting car ground to a halt nearby, they watched the doors fly open and three men leap out, before a white guy pulled the unconscious form of a woman from the rear and slung her over his shoulder beside a kitbag. The boatmen were unarmed and utterly unprepared for Luaba's appearance with a semi-automatic pistol. He shouted at them to tell him where the boat was and when they hesitated he lifted the Uzi, firing a short burst into the sky; the noise echoed around them and they instinctively ducked down before raising their hands. "Where's the boat?" Luaba shouted again and this time they eagerly pointed to a sleek black and white vessel shaped like a paper dart that was moored below and behind them in the shadows. Luaba seemed to be on the point of instructing them to slip the mooring lines when there was the shriek of a mortar shell tearing over their heads and exploding as it hit a building on the jetty. Machine gun fire followed it, puncturing and flattening a No Parking sign beside them. Everyone ducked for cover except James. Carrying the inert form of Jessica he was crouching as low as he could and he was already racing for the boat when the shooting restarted. The driver and Luaba ran after him while the boat crew, sensibly deciding that this was not their battle, legged it into the darkness. The boat was tied up less than fifty metres away on a darkened jetty that lay below them -- James felt every step as he ran holding Jessica over one shoulder in a fireman's lift with their bag over the other. He was gasping for breath as he ran, trying all the time to keep her out of the line of fire. Sebastien Luaba was fitter than he looked for he quickly overtook them and ran to untie the lines. James hoped that there were keys and fuel in the boat – if not it was game over. The Peugeot driver, however, was older and slower; he managed a dogged but flat-footed jog and only reached the boat as Luaba pressed the starter button. Twin diesels rumbled into life, the riding lights came on, only to be doused quickly by Luaba as James laid Jessica's inert figure on the plush white upholstery of the rear bench. Mercifully, the boat was facing downriver and ready to carry them out of this small tributary. His eyes adjusting to the darkness, James could make out sandbars barely a hundred metres away as Luaba swung the craft away from the jetty and a surge of power lifted the boat's nose. Their driver had stepped onto the flat bow and when he looked back into the darkness he was just in time to see the first three vehicles come to a halt above and behind them. Men had jumped out of the leading SUV and their AK-47s resumed fire spraying bullets wildly into the night, then the autocannon on the second armoured car fired a burst that hit the water somewhere out of sight. The position of the Panhards high on the quay above them favoured the boat and its passengers, the gunner could not depress the mortar barrel far enough to hit them. It may have been the smoke and fumes in the turret from the earlier cannon fire, for although it continued firing the aim was wild. If its searchlight had picked them up quickly, the gunner would surely have finished them, but he failed to locate the boat for vital seconds. With every moment the powerboat was putting more distance between the escaping group and their pursuers, until first one and then the other searchlight found them. By now, however, the boat was at the limits of even magnified visibility in the Panhards and when the heavy armaments came to bear the boat had rounded the first bend in the river.

Luaba kept the throttle wide open to make sure of their escape, and peered into the gloom trying to avoid running aground on one of the sand bars. The Peugeot driver seemed less at home on a boat and took a few unsteady steps in search of a seat. If he had fallen, he would have lived, but speculative fire from the only functioning machine gun reached him in the gathering darkness, striking him in the chest and flinging him overboard into the inky waters. James ran to the side to grab him, but he was gone and invisible and Luaba didn't stop for him, instead swinging the boat around another sand bar and into the darkness at the heart of the river.

******

At Creech Air Force base in Nevada the Predator commander was kept informed by his team and Gahiji was able to listen in. "Sir, we still have infra-red lock on the three targets in the boat. They're headed out into the river, appear to be making for Congo Brazzaville. Still a few miles. We aren't armed for engagement and now on reserve flying time, but we can relay their co-ordinates to the team on the ground for another two minutes. Request instruction, sir."

"Stay on the targets for as long as you can," came the command. "Relay changes of speed or bearing to ground forces. Otherwise, give me thirty second updates."

******

It was too dangerous to use running lights and there were no river buoys here. With the engines now at full throttle Luaba had to yell at James to get in the bow and shout if he saw any obstacles. The fitful moonlight revealed little of anything to the younger man but in what must have been one of the fastest craft on the river they were now able to sprint into the darkness. Their speed was both terrifying and exhilarating as they weaved a path down the shallow channel. The darkness was simultaneously their shield and another danger – in the boat they could still hear sporadic fire coming from the quayside but it was wildly speculative and seemed to be landing off to port. They pressed on until a near miss with a reedbed lining the edge of an island forced them to switch the lights on again. There was no sudden burst of gunfire, they had somehow negotiated two bends in the river and ridden their luck. Here they were able to use the cabin-mounted spotlight to see how far they had come and they swung into the open water, turning the boat downstream. Only then could James quit his bow watch and cautiously tread back to the bench seat where Jessica lay.

He found a torch in a locker which was enough to show Jessica's inert figure. It looked for all the world as though she was asleep, but when he searched her wrist for a pulse it was weak and the rocking of the boat made it difficult to detect. Eventually he located a pulse in her neck. Jessica felt icy cold, so he covered her body with a towel they found and he sat with her, talking to her about anything he could think of and telling her that she was safe now – even though he didn't feel it. The noise of the engines was so loud he wondered if she could hear anything, but a warm familiar hand on hers could do no harm.

******

Gahiji knew Businga would be listening but he had no options left. Everything depended on the drone. "I need a view. Does the drone still have contact with the targets?"

Immediately there was an American voice on the line. "Creech Liaison here, sir. Copy that. We have contact, but need to refuel." There were several clicks, then silence and Gahiji wondered if the connection was broken but just as quickly the liaison officer was back. "UAV contact with target boat still live, sir. Bearing two-nine-zero degrees, speed twenty-nine knots. Three passengers aboard; two males, one female. Female appears injured. No radio or cellular communications in or out."

"Thank God," Gahiji mumbled and then hoped Businga had not heard on the conference call. "Do you carry Hellfires?"

"Negative, sir. This is an RQ-1 reconnaissance vehicle." Gahiji knew little about the CIA's unmanned aerial fleet, but he had hoped it might have been an armed multi-role drone. He was out of luck, in every sense.

"Sir, are you still there?" It was liaison at the US Air Force base in Creech.

"I'm here."

"Do you have any instructions, sir? We have to disengage. We're standing off one click north; target approaching Congo Brazzaville border. Two more minutes on station, sir, then we return to base. No other UAV assets airborne or available in theatre."

"Roger that," said an older voice. He sounded weary or resigned to failure. This had started purely as a training exercise; they had taken off with a restricted fuel load which was now almost spent and more importantly they had no armaments. Creech's commander was weighing his options.

Gahiji had seen an ops room like this before and could picture the green and grey images from live infrared feeds flickering on screens as the drone showed the spies' escape. Alongside the real-time video images, other computer dashboards would be displaying fuel reserves, elapsed flight time, remaining time on station, time to base, and all the critical data that enabled them to control the drones from thousands of miles away.

"Maintain surveillance." Gahiji had not spoken, it was Businga who had given the order as he and Creech Command still hesitated. Then Businga added to the young officer, "Await my arrival, Gahiji."

"Sir," was all Gahiji replied. He left the call open, but his thoughts were elsewhere. The Panhards and their crews were of no use to him now. He ordered them to move out and began to send away the Jeep, the crews loading up. The men were angry, sullen and frustrated that their chase had ended in failure, and he had to repeat his orders to one or two, returning them to the main port to await instructions. The SUV led the cars back, then the Panhard crews remounted their vehicles and, with ill-disguised swearing, they swung around and roared away into the night. As the rumble of their engines receded, he detected the smoother sound of an approaching limousine.

Thirty seconds later a single set of headlights could be seen coming down the quayside road. The lights swung and bounced occasionally as the large car negotiated the unfinished roadway. The route to these luxury apartments would show some mortar scars when daylight came, the cause of which would be a mystery to the workmen arriving tomorrow.

Gahiji knew what was coming and felt utterly calm at the prospect. He had tried his best, in fact he had come damn close to catching them – but there were no prizes for close, close would not be good enough. The general was used to getting his own way, especially in matters this important.

Yet when the large black Mercedes pulled up at the quayside the area was deserted. The car stood for a moment, lights on and engine running with the windows up. Eventually, Businga's curiosity got the better of him and he ordered his driver out of the car to report what he saw. The door stayed open for a quick exit and, with the headlights illuminating the jetty ahead, the driver walked towards the water pulling a handgun from his zip jacket as he went. He was unhurried; dealing with his boss's problems seemed to be a routine task.

Time passed and the general's aide did not return. In the darkness it was just possible to make out the rear door opening and the silhouette of a large figure emerging from the Mercedes' air-conditioned comfort. A courtesy lamp in the bottom of the door threw a small circle of light onto the ground, showing a well-polished black shoe touch the ground as he stood and closed the door.

General Dr Businga never heard his young officer approach from the rear of the car so he had no time to react when a gun was pressed to the back of his head. "Raise your hands," said Edouard Gahiji, then with a sneer adding, "sir."

Businga began slowly to raise his hands, the cuff of his military uniform sliding down to reveal an immaculate Rolex Oyster. He began to turn around and speak, but Gahiji had no wish to hear his pleas or explanations. Without warning he shot the General in the back of the leg -- he didn't want it to be too quick. The shot rang around the waterfront but was eclipsed by Businga's squeal of agony. He fell forward, and lay fumbling at his hip trying to release a side-arm from its holster, but he was lying on it and it was partially covered by his belly. The next shot hit the older man's right arm leaving him incapacitated and moaning. Gahiji was under no illusions – if Businga had caught him this would have been the least he could have expected. His death would have been slow and agonising. To avoid a gunshot that would betray his position, Gahiji had knocked out the driver with a brick to the head as the man stepped onto the jetty, then he had circled back and waited for Businga to emerge from the limousine. The old man had not expected him to come from the empty buildings behind. Gahiji offered no self-justification, nor did he allow his commander the chance to plead for his life, he simply raised his gun to point at the old man's torso and fired.

The sound of the gunshot reached him a split second before it should have done, his mind raced to process the anomaly as he heard another shot. Two shots fired in quick succession appeared almost as one, yet one was much higher calibre than his sidearm and his instinct for self-preservation took over. A longer burst of automatic gunfire tore around him, assaulting his ear drums, and spraying glass as it punctured the windscreen. Another shot struck the car a glancing blow and whined away into the night. Gahiji had ducked into a crouch just as a bullet hit the ground in front of him spitting grit into his eyes and mouth. He was exposed on three sides, and guessed from the ricochets that the firing was coming from in front – perhaps he hadn't hit the chauffeur hard enough. He didn't wait for another shot, diving headlong through the open door into the driver's seat.

With the engine still running, Gahiji was able to push the gear selector into reverse and stamp on the accelerator. The rear wheels spun on the loose surface before biting into the dirt and launching the powerful car backwards amid a volley of gravel. He had the momentum to execute a clumsy J-turn and spun the car away from the scene. More shots overtook it but the car didn't slow. The Mercedes' engine had purred as it arrived, now it roared as he sped away kicking up a screen of dust and gravel before regaining the tarmac access road and swinging out onto the main highway heading north to the riverport.

When the shooting stopped and the dust began to settle, the chauffeur's voice called out repeatedly in the darkness for Dr Businga, but there was no reply.

In the limousine, Gahiji ducked down to see below the bullet holes and cursed violently as he drove. He hated politicians, even dead ones like this were still dangerous. General Dr Businga's piano-playing days were over, he would torture and kill no more, and his son was buried but the man had scores of influential allies. They could make a point of punishing those they held responsible; Gahiji knew he would have to leave Kinshasa for a very long time.

******

For safety from any pursuers and in search of the deepest water, Luaba immediately began to cross the Congo River. It was only then they saw bright lights of a boat off their port bow – whoever it was they were closing fast from Kinshasa. Luaba yelled to James to hang on and the young man braced himself, keeping a tight grip on Jessica's arm so that she wasn't thrown around. The breeze made the water choppy but the boat was ideal for conditions like this. As Sebastien Luaba opened the twin throttles, she surged forward, gaining speed rapidly. The pair watched to see what effect it would have on the approaching boat. Sure enough, it began turning to port to intercept them. Luaba pushed the throttles as far forward as they would go and prayed that they had enough fuel to reach their destination.

At this point in the river's journey the international border between the Democratic Republic of Congo in the south and its northern neighbour, the Republic of Congo followed the river hugging the north shore. Soon, however, they would reach the point where the border ran out to the river's mid-point. They were now in a straight race to the border but their pursuers were at least as fast as them and wouldn't bother about jurisdictions if they caught them.

The men could clearly see Brazzaville's street lights on the far shore; at some point in the last two minutes they had crossed the border from DRC but still they raced on. The moon was curtained again by heavy cloud, they were being overhauled from Kinshasa by an even quicker boat, and it was clear they would be stopped before they reached Brazzaville.

Sandbanks and shoals were still a constant threat, if they hit one or an unlit marker buoy at this speed it would be over for the three of them without a shot being fired. James had moved forward as a lookout, turning their boat's spotlight back and forth to search for danger – there was no longer any point in hiding their presence. They were only a little offshore when the pursuit boat drew level with them. It slackened speed slightly and held station beside them, standing off by thirty metres so that it was hard to identify the vessel in the darkness.

James had expected a challenge and to be ordered to heave to, cutting their engines, but the larger boat now matched their speed and came in closer. He had no idea how fast the two craft were going but he could tell from their own engine note that the twin diesels had no more to give. Would the soldiers shoot now, so far into foreign waters? If they did, there would be no way to shield Jessica. Luaba at the helm had reached the same conclusion; they had no option but to run at top speed for the harbour on the north bank.

Brazzaville's port buildings were clearly identifiable now, but James's eyes were fixed on the vessel beside them and he braced himself for the inevitable machine gun fire that would blow their boat to tiny pieces beneath them. He found himself offering a fleeting prayer that when the end came it would be quick from a bullet.

Amid the spray from the bouncing bow James could clearly make out the shape of the much larger inshore patrol vessel that had caught them, its green and red lights shining atop a short mast from which radio and radar antennas sprouted. As their courses converged more closely, the lights on the faster vessel showed armed men mustered on the foredeck. Each had a semi-automatic rifle and there was a machine gunner on the starboard side whose gun was trained on them. Then James noticed the flag painted on the wheelhouse; it wasn't the DRC's pale blue, it was unmistakably the diagonal green, gold and red of the Republic of Congo.

"Luaba, look. It's not DRC's, it's Congolese," he shouted. A flood of relief swept through him as he suddenly realised this was an escort not a firing squad; his blood felt like water and the strength drained from his legs so quickly that he had to sit down. His words were being whipped from his mouth, and almost certainly weren't heard by Luaba but he must have seen the same thing for he began to ease back the throttle and the bow of their powerboat sank slightly as they slowed. The patrol vessel matched their speed and, as they entered the harbour, a line was thrown to James and sign language from a sailor on the rear deck instructed him to tie off at the bow. The sailor drew a line across his throat telling them to kill their engine, and within a minute they were being towed into a secluded naval berth where an ambulance, numerous cars and military jeeps were waiting, their blue lights flashing.

Looking over the towline James could make out braided epaulettes on the shoulders of an officer, presumably the vessel's captain, while beside him stood a tall, heavily-built white man studying James closely.

As they came to rest, a booming voice on the tannoy called to them in French, "Stop your engine now and stay where you are. You are all under arrest. You have illegally entered the Republic of Congo. Prepare to be boarded by Congo Marines."

Searchlights were trained on them and in the glare James could at last see Jessica clearly. He stood up and walked slowly astern which set off a series of warning shouts from the police on deck, and somewhere above him he could hear running feet but he didn't even look up. As he walked back, he put his hands up to allay their fears, ignoring the policeman who fired warning shots in the air – James was not to be deterred. When he reached the cockpit, he pointed down to Jessica's recumbent form in case they hadn't noticed her.

He was holding her and still asking for a doctor a few minutes later when heavily armed marines and the border police cautiously stepped aboard, guns at the ready. Jessica's pulse was weak and she was semi-conscious now, moaning in discomfort. For a few minutes her cries grew louder and louder, and James tried desperately to soothe her.

He was exhausted and his mind kept wandering until he found a paramedic kneeling beside her and calling to his colleagues for help. Something had changed, and at first he wasn't sure what. The man couldn't find a pulse, he tried her neck, then her wrist. Nothing. The medic laid her out flat on her back with her chin tilted upward to open her airway; no longer concerned to keep her in the recovery position he began repeatedly to compress her chest, then held her nose and blew into her mouth. James saw her chest rise and fall before the man repeated the process rhythmically again and again, each time Jessica breathed out but it seemed her heart had not restarted. The medic called for silence and he leaned forward to listen, then held his hand close to her nose to feel for a breath. There was none. James could hear himself loudly urging her to breathe. He could see Sebastien Luaba watching the scene a few feet away and James was calling for him to get help, to run and find doctors but the Congolese official didn't move. Not a muscle.

After several minutes the paramedic was growing tired and James took over. The exhausted man slumped backwards on his heels and caught his breath. Three minutes later the roles were reversed again. Then, as James moved to take his place once more, Sebastien Luaba stepped forward and held him gently but firmly by the arm. James swung a fist to free himself and continue, Luaba saw it coming and the punch only half connected. Now he was joined by one of the policemen who gripped James's collar and ordered them both to be calm.

Calm. How could he feel calm? There was no time for calm. She was dying before his eyes and he wouldn't let this happen. He had lost someone precious before, this could not be happening again. He wanted to prevent it but the more James struggled the more they held him back – and then something broke within him and he felt waves of exhaustion and despair smothering him like an impossibly heavy blanket. The men didn't know it but at that moment they could have released him and he would have done no more to save her. He could only look at this beautiful person as she slipped beyond his reach. She was there, but she was not; the true Jessica had gone. He couldn't feel her infectious laughter, he couldn't picture her broad smile, he wanted to hold her, smell her hair, see the lights dancing in her dark eyes and tell her that it was all OK, would always be OK. But he couldn't. The one thing he couldn't do was lie to her.

Chapter 30
Brazzaville, Republic of Congo
Today

Bromhead stirred the coffee and handed a cup to James. "Go on, drink it. You can't have had anything for hours." Above them a ceiling fan squeaked intermittently as it tried and failed to stir the room's stale air.

James looked at the drink but didn't touch it, so Bromhead placed it on the hospital table between them.

"Like I said, I just want to talk."

A long pause. "So, talk."

"Do you know who we are? Who I work for?"

"Jeez, you told me last night. Commercial Attaché, you're his assistant. Does that ever fool anyone, do people ever buy that shit? Just get yourself a badge that says SPY."

"OK, that makes things a little easier," said Bromhead ignoring James's outburst. "We can cut to the chase. I never told you the organisation I work for."

James wasn't interested. He was sitting with his elbows on his knees and his head bowed under the weight of his thoughts, oblivious to the discomfort of his plastic chair, or their austere surroundings in an office by the Waiting Room. Once again he stared unseeingly at the bubbling grey paint around the door and watched as the morning sunlight from a high window crept across the wall, highlighting occasional blemishes in the plaster.

He had stayed in the hospital all night. The nursing staff had been extraordinary, bringing him drinks, sitting with him and letting him talk – in fact, encouraging him to talk about Jessica. One had placed a small blanket over his shoulders as he slept briefly on a line of chairs in the Waiting Room, and when a doctor woke him in the early hours before going off shift it was just to see if James had any questions. Jessica was long past help, the doctor's concern was now for those she left behind.

James had done what he could using her passport and New York driving licence to help fill in the blanks in their records. The truth was she had died long before she reached Brazzaville Hospital, they had simply recorded and formalised it and now her body lay in the hospital mortuary. All Jessica's warmth and vitality, the energy, grit and determination she had shown were gone. It wasn't that James didn't know what to do next, he simply didn't care.

He realised that Bromhead was talking again. "… Here I have to wear several hats, but I don't work directly for the embassy. I'm with SIS, the Secret Intelligence Service. I guess you'd call it MI6. My reports feed into other British services and a few foreign ones."

"Why are you telling me this? She's dead and I don't know anything about this."

"That last bit's not strictly true, is it?"

James sighed heavily. "Listen, I've hardly slept for days. My girlfriend's just been killed, I've been chased from Goma to Kinshasa, and now across the border to Brazzaville by some government nutjob with a vendetta against me. He thinks I killed his son, when in fact his son imprisoned and tortured me. I've been imprisoned again by the government in Kinshasa, with a lot of help from their Chinese friends. I've found and lost my natural father – and all in a matter of days. And now you fuckers want a piece of me!"

Bromhead said nothing for a moment. "What are you going to do now?"

"What do you care?"

"It's my job. You're a British citizen, who entered Brazzaville in a hurry, being chased by people who are trying to overthrow the recognised government in Kinshasa. That made you of interest to us and it's our job to ensure that, now you're safe, you stay safe. So it seems a reasonable question; what are you going to do now?"

"I'm going to look for a bed. Then I'm going to sleep for days."

"Then what?"

"I haven't got that far."

"How did you feel about Jessica's work?"

James gave a heavy sigh. He'd heard all this before, and he could think of nothing to add.

"It's not just about the conflict minerals now," said Bromhead. "There's been a major new oil discovery just across the border from DRC in Uganda. And if it's in Uganda in the quantities we hear, then the local geology suggests you can probably add oil reserves to all the other resources in the region. In fact, we believe the discovery was a trigger for General Businga and his son launching their coup attempt."

"You said 'attempt'. Has it failed?"

"Looks like it. BBC World Service echoes what we're hearing from our assets on the ground. We're also getting unconfirmed rumours from the French and

Belgians that Businga was killed in crossfire last night. The Americans are still trying to confirm it, because they can't reach him either."

"So, back to my question. Did you agree with what Jessica was doing?"

"You mean in exposing Axel?"

Bromhead nodded.

"No, not really. In any case, I know more about Axel's motivation now from Luaba, y'know the guy in the boat with us. Seems Axel was being coerced by the Yanks into spying on the illegal trade in conflict minerals. They used him to set a trap for the Chinese, but instead their own protégé walked into it. I don't believe Axel was doing it willingly, but I could be wrong. I still don't know him well enough to say if he's a complete shit or misunderstood."

"Doesn't that bother you, that you don't know him well enough. I mean, if he's innocent like you say, wouldn't you want to know your father better?"

"He's not my father. My father was Jonathan Falkus. Axel's just some relative, and a distant one. No more than that."

"So if he's in danger, it doesn't matter? It's of no concern to you?"

James Falkus shook his head. "The person I care about most is lying dead in this hospital. And the rest of my family and friends are either at home in Britain or in the States."

There was silence. Bromhead pushed his empty coffee cup around in circles. The habit was getting on James's nerves. Neither of them moved to go and thirty seconds went by.

"What kind of danger?"

"Pardon?" said Bromhead.

"I said, what kind of danger?"

"I thought you weren't interested."

James shrugged. He was losing patience with the man. "Ah, you know what? Go on; keep your little secret if it means that much to you."

The older man idly twisted his watch around on his wrist, then did it again before speaking. "Turns out it wasn't just Jessica following him. In fact, she was the least of his worries." Bromhead had set the bait, and James had bitten but he still wasn't hooked.

"I can't say much more without clearance. Just that he had a Chinese team on his tail."

"Here? I mean, in DRC?"

"Yeah. In fact, there was one man, an army officer on secondment to China's Politburo – a rising star in the Communist Party – who we were most concerned about. Well, the Americans were and we were helping them. Whoever the officer was he was well supported technologically but seemed to be working alone."

"So, the danger has passed?"

"Not at all, it's simply changed location. Moved to a new theatre."

"Does Axel know?"

"Of course. That's why he had to leave quickly."

"Why? What happened?"

"I can't say. Just that he seems to have stumbled into the middle of an international power play." For a man who couldn't say, Bromhead seemed to be sharing a lot, but James knew he was being played.

"What, in Kinshasa?"

"I bet he wishes it was just in Kin. Unfortunately, your blood father seems to have found a walk-on role in a major power struggle, in Beijing."

James slowly raised his head to be sure he'd heard that right. He stared across the table at Derek Bromhead, looking at him as if for the first time. The ceiling fan continued to squeak intermittently and he could hear patients in the room outside being called for their appointments. Life's daily routines were going on without him. Without Jessica. Without Axel. Without Raphael. The list was way too long.

James exhaled, and rubbed his eyes. "Go on then, tell me what you can."

EPILOGUE

Taweza Road Mission, Walikale, DRC, and London, UK

One Month Later

"They're here," said Marianne.

"Who are?" Marc Audousset's mind was elsewhere as he poured himself a coffee.

"Who do you think? The people from the programme."

"Ah, yes. Well, I'd better go and welcome them. Can you make a fresh pot, darling?"

Marianne rolled her eyes at his division of labour and went to put more water on to boil. Five minutes later she joined their guests in the relative cool of the sitting room.

The two visitors rose to their feet as she entered. Gilles Lefanu, a tall, bespectacled Swiss man with a bookish air was accompanied by Dunia Matala, from whom he contrasted in several ways. Matala was a short, solidly-built researcher at the Ministry of Mines from whom there shone an engaging smile.

With coffees and formalities exchanged, the four sat and resumed their conversation. "Gilles was just saying that he's seen more of the mines are back in the hands of artisan miners since he was last here," said Mark, "and some of the armed groups have pulled back."

The Swiss interjected a note of caution, "Indeed, but it is patchy and it has not improved the working conditions. There is still no government control in many areas, a vacuum of power really." *There was a stiffness about the man*, thought Marc, *and he seemed oblivious to any embarrassment his words might be causing his Congolese companion.*

"We're working hard to establish control," said Matala hurriedly, "but we estimate there are five thousand mines just in North and South Kivu. There must be tens of thousands of miners working in them. Maybe more, it's hard to say as the numbers are rising again since the West's import embargo was lifted. We just don't have the manpower to inspect all the mines, not on a regular basis."

495

Lefanu nodded in agreement. "There is still a big task ahead of us, but we are doing all we can."

"What does your organisation do?" Marianne asked.

"It's an initiative by some of the tin makers; we're working to ensure conflict-free minerals from the mines can be tracked right through the supply chain, all the way to the end customer. Some of the big manufacturers of laptops, mobile phones, and games consoles are on board, along with the biggest smelters. That way manufacturers can be sure they're working with materials that haven't come from forced or child labour."

"That's all fine now, but where were you guys five or ten years ago?" Marc demanded. "This problem has been going on for decades – and it's still going on – right across the east of the country."

"We're well aware of that, sir," Lefanu replied. "But to do our job effectively, we need peace in the region. We need to be able to visit and revisit mines and traders at any time. Otherwise, one week we can certify a mine as conflict-free and approve its output, only for it to be overrun by armed groups and change hands the next. You may have heard the army's had support from three thousand soldiers in the UN's intervention brigade. It's a slightly more positive situation for us to work in."

"So, do we thank the UN and the army for any improvements?" Marianne asked testily.

If Gilles noticed the acid tone, he ignored it. "Maybe. Along with tighter laws in America and Europe. Both overdue, but don't quote me." A resigned smile played on his lips.

"Gilles is right," Matala hesitated, weighing his words carefully. "Our corporate backers don't want to deal in this misery and its products, but in the past it was impossible for them to know which tin or coltan came from unsafe sources."

"Unsafe?" Marc snorted noisily. "That's one way of putting it."

Gilles did not respond to his host's interruption. "The minerals have changed hands many times by the time they reach the smelter. In the past it's always been impossible to know where they started. A German university is working on technology to identify the source of these minerals. Right now though, coltan could have come from Canada, Brazil, even Australia. Or it could have come from a child digging in a mine a few kilometres from here, it could have been washed and sieved by a pregnant woman, and carried from the mine by a young man working at gunpoint."

"All of them are paid a pittance," Dunia Matala acknowledged, "if they are paid at all."

"So, at least our backers are doing something to identify and promote the good sources. It's not perfect, and sometimes people fraudulently bag and tag cassiterite and coltan dug from these conflict areas. We know that, but every day we are making it a little harder for them. The supply chain used to be opaque, now some clean routes are easier to follow. There are electronics makers that buy only from cooperative-owned mines they have proved are safe; all we can do is try to extend that. The good news is that smelters in Germany, India and Malaysia are now some of our biggest supporters. I wish I could say the same for all of India and China."

"We don't mean to denigrate your efforts, gentlemen." It was uncharacteristic of Marc to backtrack on anything, and Marianne watched him with interest. "But we still see horrific effects of the fighting every day. We take in traumatised children who have been forced to fight and to commit atrocities, we treat women and girls who have been gang-raped by the militias, the rebels, or the army. Some have been held captive for months, even years. These groups all want to profit from the mines here, and it's not just the rebels. We just heard about a private Franco-Chinese company that has been handing out AK-47 rifles and money to armed groups just to get access to local gold deposits; the gold was then sold to companies in Dubai. You see, too many people are still taking advantage of what's happening here."

"Mr Matala," Marianne addressed the government official directly, "if you manage to stop the fighters' access to these mines will they run out of money? Will the fighting stop too?"

Dunia Matala's default smile faded and he pondered his reply, "I'm afraid not, Mrs Audousset."

"Please, call me Marianne."

Matala inclined his head in acknowledgement. "Conflict minerals are a large part of their revenues, but they make money in other ways like robbery and extortion and some money they are just given by outsiders. You saw how the fighting continued even after the M23 rebels were thrown out of Congo. The rebels just slipped back over the border into Rwanda and Uganda. You just have to ask yourself, who is paying for them to live there, after all they don't have jobs. Where do they get their arms and supplies? We think it's obvious. If our neighbours wanted the groups locked up or dispersed, then their governments could have arranged it long ago. Instead, rebels seem to be free to cross over into DRC to fight the army and the UN. It's a long border and very hard to police."

"You mentioned the embargo on Congo's minerals. Is that over?"

"Well, it was never an official embargo, Marianne. But when America and Europe passed tougher laws forcing companies to show where their minerals came from, it was easier – at least to begin with – for those companies to buy elsewhere. So, some mines closed and mining families went hungry again. Other traders just sold the minerals to smelters, mostly in China, who didn't care about being on the approved list, because they sold the tin and tantalum to firms not registered with the American authorities. And, of course, the traders here had no negotiating power

– where else were they going to sell it? – so the price fell to a third of what it was before."

"But everyone wants a new phone or laptop, don't they? So, with demand for coltan and tin still high, and recycling unable to supply enough, eventually the miners have begun digging again in unsupervised mines. They have no safety equipment or help available – no-one to call on if the mine floods or collapses. They are working long, long hours, sometimes deep underground. Even little kids, Marianne. In some places the kids sleep down there." He shook his head in disbelief. "We have to stop it. And for that we need reliable, independent eyes and ears on the ground, to alert us if things change in the area. We don't want you to compromise what you are doing, just to share any concerns."

The couple exchanged glances, and Marc nodded to their guests. "We've seen this, too. Tell us what you want."

******

The call from an unknown number woke James at one in the morning. A rich baritone said, "I have been playing again, at last. Mozart's Piano Concerto No.23. Very sad, very fitting." Then silence.

"Who is this?" said James.

There was a long silence, and James wondered if the caller had made a mistake and rung off. Then, sounding far away, it came again, "I've been playing for the first time since Louis died, playing long into the night and thinking what to do to you." James didn't recognise the voice, but mention of the name Louis brought it all back in a rush. "You probably thought I was dead, but now I can tell you know who I am!"

"I reckon I can guess."

"You see, I'm very much alive. You eluded me once, Mr Falkus. It won't happen again." There was a long pause and James was wide awake now. "Usually I find solace in my playing, it lifts me … but this time not so much. You have robbed me of that, too. So, I will settle this very soon."

"Mr Businga," James enjoyed circumventing his military and academic titles. "The threats might have worked on me once, months ago in Kin. But not here and not now. They have no effect. I see you for what you are." There was no answer, and he continued. "You're just a thief. Nothing more."

"You are a small man, aren't you, Falkus? One of the little people with no vision, no ambition, no idea of leadership and what it can achieve for so many people. I am the future here."

"Huh! If I'm so insignificant, why did you find my number in the night and call me thousands of miles away? Lame, Businga, pretty lame," said James dismissively. "Your son died 'cos he was greedy, vicious and stupid; I was just the catalyst. If he hadn't been in such a hurry to get rich with other people's belongings, he might be with you now, but I guess the apple never falls far from the tree. So yes, I know you, Businga."

"Then you know what I do to people who cross me."

"Save your breath, my fear of you died with my girlfriend. While I've got you, I should tell you I've written an article about you. Can you tell me on the record how, on a general's salary, you were able to buy an island in the middle of Lake Kivu and build a villa overlooking the Congo River in Kinshasa?"

There was an echoing silence as the line went dead.

"I'll just say 'No Comment', shall I?"

The End

Author's Note

No one in this story, no organisation or company is based upon an actual person, organisation or real business. The characters and outfits described here are the work of my imagination and nothing more. It should also be noted that there are many people and companies, within and without the Democratic Republic of Congo, dealing daily in tin, tantalum, tungsten, gold, diamonds, cobalt and the many riches that the country holds and doing so honourably and responsibly in every respect. This story is not about them.

This is simply a novel and lacks the academic rigour of many in-depth research or charity reports, or the fearless documentaries and articles on the topics discussed. If you have a few minutes, you may be surprised at what can be found online, from CIA country and industry analysis to video reports of children mining underground. The natural wealth of the Great Lakes Region is not the root cause of the fighting in DRC but for some it is a reason to continue. As Global Witness points out, the US and 12 African countries have laws requiring companies to source minerals ethically (although the US Congress may soon repeal the Dodd-Frank Act). The EU has only agreed to regulate raw minerals not imports of consumer goods like mobile phones, cars, and laptops. Europeans still have little indication if the products they are buying fund war.

It is perhaps inevitable in a book that has taken years to produce, that the political and economic backdrop to the story has evolved. It is disturbing though, that so little has changed in DRC in that time. As long as fighting continues in the Kivus, for as long as Congo's leaders are more focused on their own undemocratic positions than protecting their people, and all the time that her neighbours and outside powers use political instability as an excuse to interfere in Congo's affairs and economy, then this book may have some relevance.

The actions of the many and varied non-governmental organisations and agencies in-country, from the UN downwards in scale, will continue to be debated and scrutinised – and rightly so. This is not the place for that debate, but spare a thought for the bravery and selfless commitment of so many aid workers, peace-keepers and volunteers of all kinds who continue to help the people of Congo. Many have given their time and sweat, some have given their health and their lives to end the fighting and establish a peace where peace has been the scarcest resource of all for decades.

Anyone interested in learning more about the Congo's colonial and post-colonial history should consider reading books such as *In the Footsteps of Mr Kurtz*, a compelling study of Mobutu by Michela Wrong, *Congo Journey* by Redmond O'Hanlon, and *The Poisonwood Bible*, by Barbara Kingsolver. More recently, take a moment to see the work in DRC of non-profit organisations such as Global Witness and Human Rights Watch, as well as charities small and large ranging from War Child to Oxfam. If you can spare something for a contribution, I urge you to do so. Your purchase of this book has enabled a donation from each sale to be given by the author to War Child (www.warchild.org).

I am grateful to Mamadou Bady Baldé of Extractive Industries Transparency Initiative (https://eiti.org) for interrupting his travels in Africa to answer esoteric questions on DRC's mining. Thanks, too, to iTSCi, (ITRI Tin Supply Initiative – www.itri.co.uk) who showed how compliant companies are providing miners in 1,400 mines with safer, more secure and well-paid work in DRC and Rwanda. You will also find more information at: Global e-Sustainability Initiative (www.gesi.org).

J. J. Cowan
July 2017